THE
YEAR'S BEST
SCIENCE FICTION,
First Annual Collection

BOOKS BY GARDNER DOZOIS

Strangers (novel)
The Visible Man (collection)
Nightmare Blue (novel—with George Alec Effinger)
A Day in the Life (anthology)
Another World (anthology)
Beyond the Golden Age (anthology)
*Best Science Fiction Stories of the Year,
Sixth Annual Collection* (anthology)
*Best Science Fiction Stories of the Year,
Seventh Annual Collection* (anthology)
*Best Science Fiction Stories of the Year,
Eighth Annual Collection* (anthology)
*Best Science Fiction Stories of the Year,
Ninth Annual Collection* (anthology)
*Best Science Fiction Stories of the Year,
Tenth Annual Collection* (anthology)
Future Power (anthology—with Jack Dann)
Aliens! (anthology—with Jack Dann)
Unicorns! (anthology—with Jack Dann)
Magic Cats (anthology—with Jack Dann)
The Fiction of James Tiptree, Jr. (critical chapbook)

THE
YEAR'S BEST
SCIENCE FICTION,
First Annual Collection

Edited by
GARDNER DOZOIS

ℭ. 04

BLUEJAY BOOKS
New York

FOR
Bob Walters and Tess Kissinger

A Bluejay Book, published by arrangement with the editor
and the editor's agent, Virginia Kidd

Cover art by Thomas Kidd

Book design by Richard Oriolo

Manufactured in the United States of America

First Bluejay printing: April 1984

National Serials Data Number
ISSN 0743-1740
ISBN: 0-312-94483-7 (paperback)
0-312-94482-9 (cloth)

Acknowledgement is made for permission to print the following material:

"Cicada Queen," by Bruce Sterling. Copyright © 1983 by Terry Carr. First published in *Universe 13* (Doubleday). Reprinted by permission of the author.

"Beyond the Dead Reef," by James Tiptree, Jr. Copyright © 1983 by James Tiptree, Jr. First published in *The Magazine of Fantasy & Science Fiction*, January 1983. Reprinted by permission of the author and the author's agent, Robert P. Mills, Ltd.

"Slow Birds," by Ian Watson. Copyright © 1983 by Mercury Press, Inc. First published in *The Magazine of Fantasy & Science Fiction*, June 1983. Reprinted by permission of the author.

"Vulcan's Forge," by Poul Anderson. Copyright © 1982 by TSR Hobbies, Inc. First published in *Amazing Science Fiction Stories*, January 1983. Reprinted by permission of the author.

"Man-Mountain Gentian," by Howard Waldrop. Copyright © 1983 by Omni Publications International, Ltd. First published in *Omni*, September 1983. Reprinted by permission of the author.

"Hardfought," by Greg Bear. Copyright © 1983 by Davis Publications, Inc. First published in *Isaac Asimov's Science Fiction Magazine*, February 1983. Reprinted by permission of the author.

"Manifest Destiny," by Joe Haldeman. Copyright © 1983 by Joe Haldeman. First published in *The Magazine of Fantasy & Science Fiction*, October 1983. Reprinted by permission of the author.

"Full Chicken Richness," by Avram Davidson. Copyright © 1983 by Avram Davidson. First published in *The Last Wave Magazine*, vol. 1. Reprinted by permission of the author and his agents, the John Silbersack Literary Agency.

"Multiples," by Robert Silverberg. Copyright © 1983 by Agberg, Ltd. First published in *Omni*, October 1983. Reprinted by permission of the author and Agberg, Ltd.

"Cryptic," by Jack McDevitt. Copyright © 1983 by Davis Publication, Inc. First published in *Isaac Asimov's Science Fiction Magazine*, April 1983. Reprinted by permission of the author.

"The Sidon in the Mirror," by Connie Willis. Copyright © 1983 by Davis Publications, Inc. First published in *Isaac Asimov's Science Fiction Magazine*, April 1983. Reprinted by permission of the author.

"Golden Gate," by R.A. Lafferty. Copyright © 1982 by R.A. Lafferty. First published in *Golden Gate and Other Stories*, (Corroboree Press). Reprinted by permission of the author and the author's agent, Virginia Kidd.

"Blind Shemmy," by Jack Dann. Copyright © 1983 by Omni Publications International, Ltd. First published in *Omni*, April 1983. Reprinted by permission of the author and the author's agent, Curtis Brown, Ltd.

"In The Islands," by Pat Murphy. Copyright © 1983 by TSR Hobbies, Inc. First published in *Amazing Science Fiction Stories*, March 1983. Reprinted by permission of the author.

"Nunc Dimittis," by Tanith Lee. Copyright © 1983 by Tanith Lee. First published in *The Dodd, Mead Gallery of Horror* (Dodd, Mead). Reprinted by permission of the author.

"Blood Music," by Greg Bear. Copyright © 1983 by Davis Publications, Inc. First published in *Analog*, June 1983. Reprinted by permission of the author.

"Her Furry Face," by Leigh Kennedy. Copyright © 1983 by Davis Publications, Inc. First published in *Isaac Asimov's Science Fiction Magazine*, Mid-December 1983. Reprinted by permission of the author.

"Knight of Shallows," by Rand B. Lee. Copyright © 1983 by TSR Hobbies, Inc. First published in *Amazing Science Fiction Stories*, July 1983. Reprinted by permission of the author.

"The Cat," by Gene Wolfe. Copyright © 1983 by Gene Wolfe. First published in the 1983 World Fantasy Convention *Program Book*. Reprinted by permission of the author and the author's agent, Virginia Kidd.

"The Monkey Treatment," by George R.R. Martin. Copyright © 1983 by Mercury Press, Inc. First published in *The Magazine of Fantasy & Science Fiction*, July 1983. Reprinted by permission of the author.

"Nearly Departed," by Pat Cadigan. Copyright © 1983 by Davis Publications, Inc. First published in *Isaac Asimov's Science Fiction Magazine*, June 1983. Reprinted by permission of the author.

"Hearts Do Not In Eyes Shine," by John Kessel. Copyright © 1983 by Davis Publications, Inc. First published in *Isaac Asimov's Science Fiction Magazine*, October 1983. Reprinted by permission of the author.

"Carrion Comfort," by Dan Simmons. Copyright © 1983 by Omni Publications International, Ltd. First published in *Omni*, September–October 1983. Reprinted by permission of the author.

"Gemstone," by Vernor Vinge. Copyright © 1983 by Davis Publications, Inc. First published in *Analog*, October 1983. Reprinted by permission of the author.

"Black Air," by Kim Stanley Robinson. Copyright © 1983 by Mercury Press, Inc. First published in *The Magazine of Fantasy & Science Fiction*, March 1983. Reprinted by permission of the author.

ACKNOWLEDGEMENTS

The editor would like to thank the following people for their help and support:

Michael Swanwick, Susan Casper, Jack Dann, Virginia Kidd, Ellen Datlow, Bob Walters, Shawna McCarthy, Sheila Williams, Edward Ferman, Eileen Gunn, Susan Allison, Beth Meacham, Stanley Schmidt, George Scithers, Pat LoBrutto, Charles L. Grant, Don and Betsy Wollheim, Lou Aronica, Tappan King, Edward Bryant, Leanne Harper, Lewis Shiner, Pat Cadigan, Scott Edelman, Darrell Schweitzer, Joann Hill, and special thanks to my own editor, Jim Frenkel.

Thanks are also due to Charles N. Brown, whose newszine *Locus* (P.O. Box 13305, Oakland, California 94661; subscription rate: $28 for 12 issues by First Class Mail) was used as a reference source throughout the Summation, and to Andrew Porter, whose newszine *Science Fiction Chronicle* (P.O. Box 4175, New York, N.Y. 10163; subscription rate: $18 for one year) was also used as a reference source throughout.

CONTENTS

INTRODUCTION

Summation: 1983

Industry insiders—including myself—spent a great deal of time a few years back wondering when (or if) the Big SF Boom of the late seventies would come to an end. Conventional wisdom said that the market would become glutted and oversaturated, as happened during the smaller postwar SF boom of the fifties, leading inevitably to a bust, a period of collapse and economic retrenchment, *caused* by the boom it inevitably followed. SF had experienced such cycles of boom-and-bust before, and at the height of the late seventies boom, circa 1978, industry gurus were predicting another patch of bad times ahead.

Well, the bust *did* come—and it didn't. The boom kept on booming—and it didn't. Something unexpected happened, something that definitely had *not* happened at the end of other boom cycles. Instead of a choice of boom or bust, *both* happened at once, continued wildcat booming and disastrous economic retrenchment coexisting side by side. The work of a few SF writers (Isaac Asimov, Arthur C. Clarke, Robert A. Heinlein, Anne McCaffery, Stephen R. Donaldson, Larry Niven, a few others) was selling better than ever before, selling unbelievably well, topping nationwide best-seller lists, while the work of *most* SF writers was selling poorly or not at all . . . so that whether it was the best of worlds or the worst of worlds depended on *who* you were—so much so that the January 1984 issue of the newszine *Locus* could contain *both* the headline "1983: Best Year in SF Ever" and agent Richard Curtis's remark that "in many ways, things have never been worse for writers" and both could be true.

By the beginning of the eighties, a two-tier system had taken firm hold in SF. It was estimated that 20% of the writers (some said 10%) were making 80% or more of the money earned by SF as a print genre—consequently, 20% of the writers were getting 80% or more of the money spent *by* publishers on writers, so that one book would sell for a $2,000 advance while another sold for a six-figure (or even seven-figure) sum, and one book would be given an advertising and promotional budget of $150,000, while another (and indeed, most) would be given an advertising budget of—nothing. (At best a mention in one of the "group ads" that mass-market SF lines take out in major fanzines and prozines.) Put another way, I've heard it estimated that a core buying audience of about 20,000+ readers is supporting 80% of working SF writers today, and that 80% never taps into the immensely larger audience that has recently become accessible to Big Name Top-20% authors like Clarke and Asimov. And indeed, publishing figures seem to indicate that (until recently, anyway) the average sale of an average SF paperback is somewhere between 15,000–30,000 copies, while a select few books, usually those promoted as "lead titles," go on to sell hundreds of thousands of copies, if not millions of copies (in fact, in 1982 SF books took six of the top fifteen places in total hardcover sales industry-wide, according to figures in *Publishers Weekly*). And, of course, bookstores, particularly the big bookstore chains, tend naturally enough to give priority in ordering to books from authors with proven track records as Big Sellers, thus perpetuating the cycle.

One unfortunate result of all this is that it has become harder and harder for non-Big Name authors, the bottom 80%, to sell their work at all, particularly first novels or short-story collections or work that is considered to be "too offbeat" or "too innovative" or "too literary," or too difficult to easily classify in an identifiable sub-category. Much work that would have appeared from mainline publishers a few years ago is now coming out from small specialty publishers instead, "small press" publishers such as Arkham House and Corroboree Press. Reading Charles Platt's excellent book of interviews, *Dreammakers II*, drove home just how wide the gap between top 20% and bottom 80% has become—some of the authors interviewed are sleek and fat and happy ("it's a full-time job just trying to decide how to spend all this money!" Arthur C. Clarke says cheerily), while other writers (particularly the younger English writers) are sunk in despair, totally ignored, going broke, and often not even able to get their books into print anymore. As the corporate publishing "bottom-line" mentality took hold increasingly, many publishers decided not to bother with books by "bottom 80%" authors at all—and even when they did, they often lowered novel advances to the $1,500–$2,500 range, which became common again for the first time since 1974.

As usual, 1983 was a year of ambiguous and sometimes contradictory omens, but for the first time in several years there were also signs that there just might be better times coming even for writers *not* named Asimov or Donaldson or Clarke.

Del Rey, DAW, Ace/Berkley, Tor, and Bantam all had record years for sales in 1983. Del Rey had several books on nationwide best-seller lists. Lou Aronica of Bantam was quoted in *Locus* as saying that "science fiction orders have increased over 40% on the average in the last six months." DAW Books had record sales. Tor Books president Tom Doherty said that "business was up over 100% in 1983." Roger Cooper, vice-president of Berkley, said "we just had our best year ever," and Susan Allison, SF editor-in-chief at Ace/Berkley, confirmed that the sales of both lines had improved "tremendously." Viking, Doubleday, and Knopf all had hardcover SF books on nationwide best-seller lists, among others. Waldenbooks, the nation's biggest bookstore chain, started the Waldenbooks' Otherworlds Club, a retail book-buyers club offering 10–15% discounts on SF and fantasy purchases, and enrolled 50,000 members in its first three months. Waldenbooks SF sales were up 41% in September and 34% in October as compared to last year's figures, which were already "very good." (Waldenbooks SF buyer Joc Gonnella is quoted by the newszine *Science Fiction Chronicle* as saying that "over the past two years, we have increased our assortment of science fiction and fantasy books by 150%.")

A closer look at publishing figures indicates that this upsurge in sales is *not* solely limited to books by Big Name Top-20% authors, an encouraging sign.

Other encouraging signs: Bluejay Books started an ambitious program of hardcovers and trade paperbacks under the editorship of Jim Frenkel, and has major books by Jack Dann, Greg Bear, Joan D. Vinge, Connie Willis, Vernor Vinge, and others coming up in 1984. The resurrected Ace Specials line, edited by Terry Carr, is also scheduled to start publication in 1984 and has books by William Gibson, Kim Stanley Robinson, Michael Swanwick, Howard Waldrop, and other hot new writers coming up. Arbor House announced a new SF line, with Robert Silverberg serving in an advisory capacity, but the future of this line was thrown into doubt at year's end with the firing of Arbor House president Don Fine. Edward Ferman, the editor of *The Magazine of Fantasy & Science Fiction*, is preparing a line of hardcover SF books for Scribners. John Douglas took over at Avon, where he will be inaugurating a new SF line. Houghton Mifflin expanded its SF program this year, and St. Martin's Press also plans to expand its SF line in 1984, adding both mass-market and trade paperback capability.

The Horror Boom of the middle and late seventies seems to be ending, with sales of horror fiction reported down throughout the industry (*Locus* reports that one of the biggest American independant distributors is thinking of selling less horror and romances to make room for more SF—ironically, wholesalers had cut down on SF a year ago to make room for more romances and horror), but a High Fantasy Boom seems to be beginning: Tor Books will inaugurate a new fantasy line, Tempo plans a new line of children's fantasy, and Signet will launch two new fantasy lines, one for adults and one for children.

The most controversial event of the year was undoubtedly the Great Timescape Fiasco, a convoluted affair of almost Byzantine complexity. To simplify: David Hartwell, director of science fiction at Pocket Books' Timescape line (and probably the premier SF book editor of the seventies), was terminated by Pocket Books in June. (Pocket Books president Ron Busch claimed that the Timescape line was failing to make money; Hartwell denied the charge, citing instead "creative methods of accounting," according to *Science Fiction Chronicle*.) But instead of replacing Hartwell with another in-house SF editor, as expected, Pocket Books announced that editorial control of SF at Pocket would be turned over to the Scott Meredith Literary Agency, which would package a new SF line called Starscope Books for them. The reaction from the SF world—and the publishing industry in general—was immediate and almost universally negative; intensely negative, in fact. Phrases like "conflict of interest" and "in restraint of trade" were bandied about, lawsuits threatened by the Science Fiction Writers of America (SFWA) and by several prominent literary agents, and articles discussing the controversy appeared in *The Washington Post, The New York Times, The Los Angeles Times, Publishers Weekly,* and elsewhere. Ultimately, the plan failed, with the Scott Meredith Agency backing out of it in late June, although representatives of both Pocket Books and the Meredith Agency denied that the widespread protest and media pressure—primarily orchestrated by SFWA—had anything to do with the disintegration of the plan. Later in the year, Jim Baen left the editorship of Tor Books to form a company of his own, Baen Enterprises, Inc., and Pocket Books announced that Baen Enterprises would package a new SF line for them, tentatively named Baen Books. Later details showed that all editorial work would be done by Baen Enterprises, who would also control cover art, cover copy, advertising and promotion, limiting Pocket Books' role to that of distributor. At year's end, the contract for this deal had not yet been signed, but Baen Enterprises has announced plans to publish as Baen Books a total of 48 to 60 mass-market SF and fantasy titles per year, plus 20 trade paperback/hardcover SF and fantasy titles, and a line of computer book titles.

As an ironic coda, David Hartwell—in addition to Terry Carr and

Ben Bova—has begun acting as a "freelance acquisitions editor" for Tor Books.

As usual, there was also some good news and some bad news about the state of the magazine market, but this year at least, unlike last year, the encouraging news seemed to outweigh the discouraging stuff. In fact, 1983 seemed to be a pretty good year in general for many of the SF magazines, with most of them reporting gains in circulation, some of those gains substantial. (I couldn't help but wonder if at least some of this gain in readership doesn't reflect the near-total disappearance of the original anthology market—with only a few exceptions, if you want to read original short SF these days, you *have* to read the magazines, and so they may be picking up readers who a few years ago would have spent their money on *Orbit* or *New Dimensions* instead.) Another encouraging sign was that offbeat and literarily-innovative stories seemed to be having a *slightly* easier time getting into print this year, in large part due to a considerable loosening up and liberalization of the formula for an acceptable "Asimov's story" at *Isaac Asimov's Science Fiction Magazine*, which now joins *Omni* and *The Magazine of Fantasy & Science Fiction* as one of the genre magazines the most responsive to literary innovation. There is still too much editorial timidity, bland formalization, and outmoded censorship current in the American genre magazine market, but at least 1983 saw several welcome steps taken in the right direction.

It's hard to compare *Omni* to the rest of the SF magazines—for one thing, it's *not* really an SF magazine *per se*, but rather a slick science-popularization magazine that regularly publishes SF stories as a small but significant proportion of its editorial mix. Unlike regular SF magazines, which sometimes publish ten stories *per issue*, *Omni* usually publishes no more than thirty or so SF stories *per year*; nevertheless, for the last couple of years, under the direction of fiction editor Ellen Datlow, *Omni* has managed to publish a disproportionate share of the year's first-rate stories. Datlow also seems to have an uncanny talent for spotting hot new writers *as* they emerge, and was among the first to spotlight major new talents like William Gibson, Michael Swanwick, and Pat Cadigan. This year *Omni* published excellent stories by Jack Dann, Howard Waldrop, Robert Silverberg, Dan Simmons, Pat Cadigan, Bruce Sterling, and William Gibson, as well as good stuff by Larry Niven, Kate Wilhelm, Nancy Kress, Jeff Dunteman, Scott Baker, Cherry Wilder, and others.

Somewhat confusingly, *The Best of Omni Science Fiction*, edited by Don Myrus, ostensibly a reprint anthology in magazine form, has *also* begun publishing original fiction, stories that did *not* first appear in *Omni* proper. Two issues of this sporadically scheduled magazine, numbers 5 and 6, appeared in 1983. Myrus' original selections have not so far been consistently up to the level of the best stories from *Omni* itself, but he did publish first-rate material this year by Robert Silverberg and Michael Cassutt, and good stuff by Harlan Ellison, Michael Kurland, and Gregory Benford.

If there was an award for most dramatically-improved magazine of the year, it would have to go to *Isaac Asimov's Science Fiction Magazine,* and the credit for that sea change seems to belong almost entirely to new editor Shawna McCarthy. As mentioned before, McCarthy has considerably widened the literary range and depth of the magazine, leaning consistently toward literary excellence and away from formularization, and the readership seems to be responding with enthusiasm— *IASFM*'s circulation is reportedly in the 130,000-copy range now, up 38% this year, and up 53% from the year before. Although *F&SF* maintained, as usual, a slight edge in overall literary consistency, there were several individual issues of *IASFM* this year that actually contained a higher percentage of first-rate stories than the competing issues of *F&SF*, a rare occurrence in recent years, and *IASFM* must now be considered—along with *F&SF*—to be one of the leaders of the digest-sized SF magazines. Major stories by Greg Bear, Leigh Kennedy, Pat Cadigan, John Kessel, Michael Bishop, Connie Willis, Jack McDevitt, Brian Aldiss, Vonda McIntyre, and Richard Kearns appeared in *IASFM* this year, as well as good work by Rand B. Lee, Nancy Kress, Isaac Asimov, Jack C. Haldeman II, Pamela Sargent, Octavia Butler, Tanith Lee, Norman Spinrad, Scott Elliot Marbach, Ian Watson, and others.

Circulation was also up considerably from last year at *Analog,* *IASFM*'s sister magazine—somewhere in the 110,000-copy range now, according to editor Stanley Schmidt—but I still found the magazine a good deal less exciting than *IASFM*. Excellent stories by Greg Bear and Vernor Vinge did appear in *Analog* this year, along with good stuff by Charles Harness, Poul Anderson, Joseph Delaney, Chad Oliver, and Timothy Zahn, but often the good stories seemed few and far between, with the rest of the magazine filled with stuff that (to me, at least) seemed overly familiar and somewhat dull. I'd like to see Schmidt loosen up *his* editorial formula somewhat and get some different kinds of material into *Analog*. Why, for instance, have state-of-the-art high-tech hard-science stories by people like Bruce Sterling, William Gibson, Michael Swanwick, Pat Cadigan, Kim Stanley Robinson, Greg Bear, and others been appearing in places like *Omni, F&SF, IASFM,* and *Universe* instead of in *Analog*, which would logically seem to be their natural home? I remember people asking similar questions in the late sixties, when exciting new writers like Larry Niven, Roger Zelazny, and the Samuel R. Delany of the *Driftglass* stories were conspicuously *not* appearing in *Analog*. I think that an over rigid definition of an "Analog story" was hurting the magazine then, and I think that it's hurting it now, too.

As always, *The Magazine of Fantasy & Science Fiction* was the most consistently excellent of all the SF magazines once again this year. People have come to take this for granted and perhaps don't fully realize how astonishing it is that Ed Ferman—operating out of his living room on a shoestring budget—somehow continues to maintain the same standards of excellence at *F&SF* year after year, while other magazines rise and fall and fluctuate around him. *F&SF* has probably done more to help ensure the survival of quality short fiction in SF over the last couple of decades than any other publication. Excellent stories by Kim Stanley Robinson, James Tiptree, Jr., Ian Watson, Joe Haldeman, George R. R. Martin, Hilbert Schenck, Bruce Sterling, O. Niemand, James Patrick Kelly, Lewis Shiner, Stephen Gallagher, Damon Knight, and many others, appeared in *F&SF* in 1983. (Also as usual, alas *F&SF* remains hard to find on most newsstands, so I'll include their subscription address and urge everyone reading these words to subscribe: Mercury Press, Inc., P.O. Box 56, Cornwall, CT. 06753; annual subscription, 12 issues, $17.50.)

Amazing's new editor, George Scithers, has been doing a pretty good job of renovating the magazine and turning it into a major market again, but the effort may have been in vain. In spite of the large amounts of money TSR Hobbies, *Amazing*'s new owner, has been pumping into the magazine, its circulation still remains disastrously low: in the 12,000–15,000 copy range, by far the lowest circulation of all the digest-sized SF magazines. *Amazing* has been particularly hurt by its failure to attract subscribers; the subscription rate has risen, but only very slightly (from about 1,000 subscribers to about 1,600), and, in Scithers' words, "the failure of the subscriptions to come up is of extreme concern to me." The magazine is still very difficult to find on most newsstands, and the smart money in the SF publishing world seems to be betting that *Amazing* will not make it. (On the other hand, they were saying the same thing last year about *The Twilight Zone Magazine*, which now seems to be recovering. The key to survival in both cases is the subscription list. *Amazing* could survive if it could bring its subscription rate up, but it would have to come up *dramatically*.) TSR Hobbies itself went through financial upheavals in 1983, necessitating the layoff of many of its employees, and speculation is rife about how long a financially-ailing TSR will be willing to carry *Amazing* as a money-losing proposition. Scithers' *Amazing* has reputedly been guaranteed three years of sponsorship by TSR, but such guarantees mean little when enough money is being lost. Even if Scithers *is* granted a full three years of grace, it may well prove that *Amazing*'s long prior reputation as a minor, poor-selling magazine is too great a chunk of inertia to overcome with the 12 issues (*Amazing* is bi-monthly) he has left to work with. If so, I, for one, will be sorry to see *Amazing* go. SF needs all the short-fiction markets it can get, and, while I didn't like everything Scithers published this year by any means, he *has* made some of the right moves, publishing first-rate stuff this year by Avram Davidson, Rand B. Lee, Poul Anderson, Pat Murphy, Robert Silverberg, Tanith Lee, R.A. Lafferty, and others. (Since *Amazing* is also hard to find on most newsstands, I'll give their subscription address as well: Dragon Publishing, P.O. Box 110, Lake Geneva, WI. 53147; $9 for 6 issues—one year—or $16 for 12 issues—two years.)

As alluded to above, *The Twilight Zone Magazine*, which was compelled to go bi-monthly last year and was widely believed to be tottering on the brink of extinction, seems (knock wood) to be on the road to recovery instead. According to editor T.E.D. Klein, the circulation of recent issues has shown a steady increase, with the January/February, March/April, and May/June issues all selling more strongly than preceding issues. *TZ* is now reportedly selling about 50,000 copies per issue on the newsstands, and—much more dramatically—has increased its subscription list to the 100,000-copy range. (As a note of caution, it should be pointed out that most of these new subscriptions are Publishers Clearing House subscriptions, offered at a discount as part of a promotional package, and, as Klein admits, "the trick is getting them to *renew*" those subscriptions, something that must be done at full price. Next year should see how high a successful conversion rate *TZ* will have.) There were rumors at the end of the year that *TZ* would go back to "at least" 8 issues per year in 1984 if sales continue to improve, an encouraging sign. *TZ*'s publisher reportedly ascribes part of the increase in circulation to their recent policy of using movie stills on the cover, and he may be right. *TZ*'s painted covers have usually been mediocre at best (the magazine still suffers from some of the worst interior illustrations I've ever seen), and they may well *be* better off looking like a movie magazine instead. The overall quality of the fiction in *TZ* seemed somewhat down this year—perhaps because there were only half as many issues as usual—but good stories by Jack McDevitt, John Kessel, Charles L. Grant, Paul Darcy Boles, John Skipp, and others did appear here in 1983, and things may well look up for this magazine in 1984.

Not surprisingly for a magazine with seven editors (one left late in

1983, but, as they themselves commented, "never fear: there are plenty of editors left!"), the British SF magazine *Interzone* is somewhat uneven. Some of the material here has a strangely dated "period" smell to it—being nearly indistinguishable from some of the fictional experiments published in *New Worlds* magazine during the revolutionary "New Wave" days of the late sixties—but other stories are fresh and interesting, and *Interzone* should be particularly commended for providing refuge for many good but unconventional stories that might otherwise have had difficulty finding a home. (For instance, it is hard to imagine where *else* something like M. John Harrison's "Strange Great Sins" or Barrington Bayley's "The Ur-Plant" could have been published commercially, unless it was in *The Last Wave*, an American semiprozine modeled to some extent on *Interzone* itself). First-rate (and often very strange) stuff by Malcolm Edwards, Richard Cowper, M. John Harrison, John Crowley, Alex Stewart, and Barrington Bayley appeared in *Interzone* this year. (*Interzone* is flatout impossible to find on newsstands in this country unless you happen to live within striking distance of a very well-stocked SF specialty bookstore, but the magazine deserves your support. Subscription address: American subscriptions can be obtained from Scott Bradfield, 145 E. 18 St. Apt. 5, Costa Mesa, California 92627; $13 for a one year subscription, First Class Mail.)

A large-format slick fantasy magazine called *Imago*, edited by Richard Monaco and Adele Leone, was promised for 1983, but although the magazine was widely advertised and talked about, with stills of the first-issue's cover appearing in all the newszines, the first issue kept being postponed and pushed back throughout 1983, and early in 1984 it was announced that the magazine had died stillborn.

It should also be mentioned that short SF is now popping up in many publications way outside genre boundaries. *Penthouse* and *Playboy* are using SF with increasing frequency these days (thanks to fiction editors Kathy Green and Alice K. Turner, respectively). SF has also turned up with fair regularity in places like *Gallery, Oui* and *Cavalier*; in many computer magazines and war-gaming magazines; in associational magazines like *Heavy Metal*; in "women's" magazines (Marion Zimmer Bradley's *The Mists of Avalon* will be excerpted in *Cosmopolitan* in 1984, for instance, and Kate Wilhelm's "The Winter Beach" was in *Redbook* a couple of years back); in mystery magazines like *Ellery Queen's* and *Alfred Hitchcock's*; in miscellaneous small magazines like *Yankee, Games,* and *Pulpsmith*; in many "literary" magazines like *The Yale Review, The Seattle Review,* and *Antaeus* (*The Missouri Review* is planning a special SF edition in 1984, for instance; an SF edition of

Triquarterly appeared in 1980); and even in bastions of High Literary Culture like *Esquire* and *The New Yorker*.

While the professional SF magazines were enjoying a prosperous year for a change, the semiprozines were enduring a disastrous one. *Shayol*, edited by Pat Cadigan and Arnie Fenner, and considered by many to be the best of the semiprozines, will put out one more issue and then fold. *Rigel*, edited by Eric Vinicoff, has already folded, as has *Eternity*, edited by Stephen Gregg. *Starship*, edited by Andrew Porter, will put out one more issue and then fold as an independent publication, some of its columns and features being merged into Porter's *Science Fiction Chronicle*. The much-ballyhooed *Spectrum Stories* seems to have fallen into a black hole and probably will not appear at all. Of the long-established semiprozines, that leaves Stuart David Schiff's excellent *Whispers* as one of the few survivors, but at least it is one of the best of them all, rivaling *Shayol* in its professionalism and the quality of its fiction (subscription address: 70 Highland Avenue, Binghamton, N.Y. 13905; two double-issues for $8.75). Of the newer semiprozines or what's left of them, *Fantasy Book* seems to be still in business, but although this is a well-intentioned magazine with lots of promise, it has yet to reliably come up to the level of fictional quality to be found in *Whispers* and *Shayol*. The only other bright spot in the dismal 1983 semiprozine scene was the debut of *The Last Wave* magazine, edited by Scott Edelman. In spite of a lot of somewhat frenetic pre-publicity about how much taboo-breaking the magazine was going to do, the first issue of *The Last Wave* doesn't contain anything particularly "dangerous" or controversial (in fact, *IASFM* has this year published stories with rougher stuff in them—for instance Leigh Kennedy's controversial "Her Furry Face" or Norman Spinrad's "Street Meat"); instead, we are treated to a solid and thoroughly professional magazine that, while it doesn't do much taboo-breaking of the nose-thumbing bear-baiting *Dangerous Visions* sort, *does* feature (much to its credit) unconventional, intelligent, and literarily-innovative material that would probably have been rejected as "uncommercial" or "marginal" or "too literary" by most of the genre markets and much of this stuff is quite good. This issue, for instance, features a first-rate story by Avram Davidson and good material by John Sladek, Steve Rasnic Tem, Jessica Amanda Salmonson, and others. Upcoming is some more odd stuff, including an operetta by Tom Disch. A promising debut. (Subscription address: P.O. Box 3206, Grand Central Station, New York, N.Y. 10163; four quarterly issues for $8.) Also interesting are *Modern Stories*, edited by Lewis Shiner (3305 Duval, Austin, Texas 78705; no subscription information given), which so far seems to be mostly a good-natured fanzine featuring trunk stories from the Austin-area writers—although the first issue did contain an amusing professional-level story by William Gibson—and *Mile High Futures*, edited by Leanne Harper, half fanzine and half promotional magazine, distributed free to a readership of 100,000, which occasionally runs fiction, such as Edward Bryant's recent—and professional quality—"The Overly Familiar" (Subscription address: Mile High Comics, 1717 Pearl, Boulder, Col. 80302; $5 for one year).

If the semiprozine market is suffering through hard times, then the original anthology market has become a disaster area—in fact, in a very real sense, there *is* no SF original anthology market anymore. At one time, during the seventies, there were at least ten annual original SF anthology series, and people were talking about them as the evolutionary replacement of the traditional digest-sized SF magazine. As recently as 1980, there were still seven annual series available on the stands. Now *New Dimensions, Orbit, Destinies,* and *The Berkley Showcase* are dead; *Chrysalis* is dying (the current issue is the last), *Stellar* has not appeared for a couple of years, *New Voices* is in hiatus (it will reappear in 1984 as *The John W. Campbell Award Anthology*), and even the promising new fantasy series *Elsewhere,* launched in 1981, is doomed (it will publish one more volume in 1984, and then fold). So it becomes almost farcicial to say that Terry Carr's *Universe 13* (Doubleday) was the best annual original SF anthology of the year, since it was very nearly the *only* annual original SF anthology of the year. Nevertheless, it would have been a good anthology in any year, featuring excellent novellas by Bruce Sterling and Michael Bishop, and interesting stuff by Ian Watson, Kim Stanley Robinson, and Leanne Frahm. The only other annual original SF anthology of 1983, Roy Torgesson's *Chrysalis 10* (Doubleday), was, like most editions in this series, well-intentioned but bland. The single one-shot original SF anthology of the year was *Changes* (Ace), edited by Ian Watson and Michael Bishop, a mixed reprint and original anthology that features intriguing and innovative material by Rudy Rucker, Ian Watson, Richard Cowper, Gene Wolfe, Michael Bishop, and others. In spite of recent hard times for the horror fiction industry, the original anthology market in the horror/fantasy field was still somewhat healthier than it was in SF, and in 1983 was dominated by Charles L. Grant, probably the premier American horror anthologist. Grant had three anthologies on the stands in 1983: *Shadows 6* (Doubleday), the latest volume in his critically-acclaimed, award-winning annual series, an all-original anthology; *The Dodd, Mead Gallery of Horror* (Dodd, Mead), a huge hardcover anthology, mixed reprint and original; and *Fears* (Berkley), another mixed reprint and original anthology, in paperback. *Shadows 6* is probably the best of the three in overall quality, upholding this series' reputation as a showcase for quiet, sophisticated, well-written horror stories and featuring first-rate work by Leigh Kennedy, Pat Cadigan, Jack Dann, Lori Allen, Steve Rasnic Tem, David Morrell, and others. *The Dodd, Mead Gallery of Horror* features good original work by Tanith Lee, John Coyne, Bernard Taylor, Steve Rasnic Tem, and others, as well as some good reprints by Stephen King, Theodore Sturgeon, Jack Dann, T.E.D Klein, and others. *Fears* features good original material by Susan Casper, Jack Dann, Pat Cadigan, Leanne Frahm, and others, as well as good reprints by George R.R. Martin, Dennis Etchison, William F. Nolan, and others. Also first-rate is *Whispers IV* (Doubleday), a mixed anthology of originals and reprints from *Whispers* magazine, edited by Stuart David Schiff. The book is similar in tone and quality to Grant's *Shadows*: quiet, well-written contemporary horror, perhaps a bit more gruesome here and there than is Grant's usual wont. (Schiff also uses "heroic fantasy" and borderline SF, which Grant usually does not.) *Whispers IV* contains good stuff by Tanith Lee, Karl Edward Wagner, Charles L. Grant, Hugh B. Cave, Stephen Kleinhen, and others, and good reprints by David Drake, Ramsey Campbell, and others. The year's only other horror anthology, *Tales By Moonlight* (Robert T. Garcia), edited by Jessica Amanda Salmonson, was disappointing. There is some good stuff here by Eileen Gunn, Janet Fox, Steve Rasnic Tem, a few others, but Salmonson doesn't seem to have the feel for contemporary horror that Grant and Schiff do, and much of the rest of the material in *Tales By Moonlight* is substandard. Much more successful and much more interesting is Salmonson's *Heroic Visions* (Ace), the year's only original heroic fantasy anthology, which features good—and often offbeat—material by Fritz Leiber, Jane Yolen, Robert Silverberg, Michael Bishop, Joanna Russ, F.M. Busby, and others.

When last I edited a "Best of the Year" series, I made a conscientious—and horribly debilitating—attempt to read every SF and fantasy novel published during the year and review the most important of them, but I have given up. I admit defeat. I just cannot keep up—there are just too *many* novels published every year, and it seems like there are more and *more* of them as time goes by. Just to read all of them would be a full-time job, leaving no time to do the very extensive reading of shorter lengths that editing this anthology demands, let alone time for my own writing. So I have given up the attempt to read *everything* and will instead limit myself to commenting that of the novels I *did* read this year, I most enjoyed: *The Citadel of the Autarch*, Gene Wolfe (Timescape); *Against Infinity*, Gregory Benford (Timescape); *The Armageddon Rag*,

George R.R. Martin (Poseidon Press); Worlds Apart, Joe Haldeman (Viking); Lyonesse, Jack Vance (Berkley); The Anubis Gates, Tim Powers (Ace); The Annals of Klepsis, R.A. Lafferty (Ace); Starship Rising, David Brin (Bantam); Tea with the Black Dragon, R.A. MacAvoy (Bantam); Superluminal, Vonda McIntyre (Houghton Mifflin), and The Unbeheaded King, L. Sprague De Camp (Del Rey).

Other novels that have gotten a lot of attention and acclaim this year include: Orion Shall Rise, Poul Anderson (Timescape); The Robots of Dawn, Isaac Asimov (Doubleday) Broken Symmetries, Paul Preuss (Timescape); Welcome, Chaos, Kate Wilhelm (Houghton Mifflin); Valentine Pontifex, Robert Silverberg (Arbor House); Helliconia Summer, Brian W. Aldiss (Atheneum); The Sword of Winter, Marta Randall (Timescape); Neveryona, Samuel R. Delany (Bantam); Hart's Hope, Orson Scott Card (Berkley); The Alien Upstairs, Pamela Sargent (Doubleday); The Mists of Avalon, Marion Zimmer Bradley (Knopf); Wintermind, Marvin Kaye and Parke Godwin (Doubleday); Christine, Stephen King (Viking); Floating Dragon, Peter Straub (Putnam); The Dragon Waiting, John M. Ford (Timescape); The King of the Wood, John Maddox Roberts (Doubleday), and The Floating Gods, M. John Harrison (Timescape).

The most aggressively hyped bad novel of the year was probably Anvil of the Heart, Bruce T. Holmes (The Haven Corporation).

The year's most interesting short-story collections were The Wind from a Burning Woman, Greg Bear (Arkham House); The Zanzibar Cat, Joanna Russ (Arkham House); Golden Gate and Other Stories, R.A. Lafferty (Corroboree Press); Red as Blood, Tanith Lee (DAW), Songs the Dead Men Sing, George R.R. Martin (Dark Harvest); Cugel's Saga, Jack Vance (Timescape)—and yes, I know this is supposed to be an "eposodic novel," but nevertheless it is really a short-story collection; Tales of Wonder, Jane Yolen (Schocken); and Unicorn Variations, Roger Zelazny (Timescape). Also worthwhile were: Changewar, Fritz Leiber (Ace); Time Patrolman, Poul Anderson (Tor); Idle Pleasures, George Alec Effinger (Berkley); The Adventures of Alyx, Joanna Russ (Timescape); The 57th Franz Kafka, Rudy Rucker (Ace); The Winds of Change, Isaac Asimov (Doubleday); Nightmare Seasons, Charles L. Grant (Tor); The Saint-Germain Chronicles, Chelsea Quinn Yarbro (Timescape); The McAndrews Chronicles, Charles Sheffield (Tor); Hoka!, Poul Anderson and Gordon R. Dickson (Pocket/Wallaby), and The Sentinel, Arthur C. Clarke (Berkley).

It is intriguing to notice that many of the year's best short-story collections come from "small press" publishers, something that is becoming more and more common. As mentioned above, one unfortunate effect of the recession (and of corporate "bottom-line" publishing practices) is that most mainline SF publishers have lost interest in doing short-story collections. Of the mass-market publishers, only Ace/Berkley and Tor still seem enthusiastic about publishing collections, and of the hardcover publishers (now that Timescape is in limbo), only Doubleday and new publisher Bluejay Books still seem interested in collections. The small presses—particularly Arkham House—have been picking up some of the slack, but of necessity their editions are expensive and often hard to find and don't quite make up for the void left by mainline SF publishing's wholesale abandonment of collections. The best work in SF is *still* being done at the shorter lengths, but every year it becomes harder and harder for the average reader to find anything but novels. Another intriguing fact—in a year when I heard at least one SF magazine editor complaining that good short stories were hard to find—is that many of these collections (the Lee, the Yolen, the Rucker, the Vance, the Lafferty) contain heretofore unpublished stories, stories for which—presumably—no first magazine publication could be obtained, and that many of these stories are excellent. Obviously there is a failure of initiative on *someone's* part here, either the editors or the agents; there is no reason for magazine editors to be crying about lack of material when good stories by major authors are apparently going begging.

The reprint anthology market was even weaker this year than last year. The best reprint anthologies of 1983 probably were: *The Fantasy Hall of Fame* (Arbor House) and *The Arbor House Treasury of Science Fiction* (Arbor House), both edited by Robert Silverberg and Martin H. Greenberg; *The SF Weight-Loss Book* (Crown), edited by Greenberg, Isaac Asimov, and George R.R. Martin; *Nebula Award Stories Seventeen* (Holt, Rinehart and Winston), edited by Joe Haldeman; *Nebula Award Stories Eighteen* (Arbor House), edited by Robert Silverberg; and *Magic For Sale* (Ace), edited by Avram Davidson.

The SF-oriented nonfiction/SF reference book field was also weak in 1983. The best were: *Dreammakers II* (Berkley), by Charles Platt, not quite as good overall as *Dreammakers I*, but still containing a pretty high percentage of intelligently conducted, often provocative, and sometimes outrageous interviews; *Dark Valley Destiny* (Bluejay Books), by L. Sprague and Catherine Crook De Camp and Jane Griffin, likely to remain the definitive Robert E. Howard biography; and *The SF Book of Lists* (Berkley), by Maxim Jakubowski and Malcolm Edwards, a "reference" book totally without redeeming social value, but a sly and witty one that is a lot of fun to read.

The SF movies of 1983 were generally lackluster at best. *Return of the Jedi* brought the famous *Star Wars* saga to a disappointing end. *Jedi* is ineptly directed, poorly paced and edited, filled with energyless wooden performances (Harrison Ford in particular stumbling through the film like one of the living dead), and marred by an impactless anticlimax which simply rehashes the big Death Star scene from *Star Wars*. At the end, the Good Ghosts all go to a party and sing campfire songs with the teddy bears, and everyone looks relieved that it's over. Many of the rest of 1983's SF films lost money at the box office *(Something Wicked This Way Comes, The Twilight Zone Movie)*, and the ones that didn't *(Blue Thunder, War Games)* usually weren't terribly exciting either. The best movie of the lot was also the most associational: *The Right Stuff,* an entertaining (although somewhat inaccurate) historical film about the *Mercury* space shots. In the subgenre of movies made from Stephen King books, there was a decent version of *The Dead Zone,* a version of *Cujo* which played through town fast, and, at year's end, a version of *Christine* which I haven't had time to see yet.

The 41st World Science Fiction Convention, ConStellation, was held in Baltimore, Maryland, over the Labor Day weekend, and drew an estimated attendance of 6,400 people. The convention was enjoyable and well-run logistically, but poor budget management, overly-optimistic preplanning (the committee had planned for at least a thousand more attendees than actually showed up), and several large unexpected last-minute expenses caused ConStellation to end up over $44,000 in debt, making it the only Worldcon in recent memory to lose money. The 1983 Hugo Awards, presented at ConStellation, were: Best Novel, *Foundation's Edge,* by Isaac Asimov; Best Novella, "Souls," by Joanna Russ; Best Novelette, "Fire Watch," by Connie Willis; Best Short Story, "Melancholy Elephants," by Spider Robinson; Best Non-Fiction, *Isaac Asimov: The Foundations of Science Fiction,* by James Gunn; Best Editor, Edward Ferman; Best Professional Artist, Michael Whelan; Best Dramatic Presentation, *Bladerunner;* Best Fanzine, *Locus;* Best Fan Writer, Richard E. Geis; Best Fan Artist, Alexis Gilliland; plus the John W. Campbell, Jr. Award to Paul O. Williams.

The 1982 Nebula Awards, presented at a banquet in New York City on April 23rd, 1983, were: Best Novel, *No Enemy But Time,* by Michael Bishop; Best Novella, "Another Orphan," by John Kessel; Best

Novelette, "Fire Watch," by Connie Willis; Best Short Story, "A Letter from the Clearys," by Connie Willis.

The 1983 World Fantasy Awards, presented at the Ninth World Fantasy Convention in Chicago over the Halloween weekend, were: Best Novel, *Nifft the Lean*, by Michael Shea; Best Novella (tie), "Beyond All Measure," by Karl Edward Wagner and "Confess the Seasons," by Charles L. Grant; Best Short Fiction, "The Gorgon," by Tanith Lee; Best Anthology/Collection, *Nightmare Seasons*, by Charles L. Grant; Best Artist, Michael Whelan; Special Award (Professional), Donald M. Grant; Special Award (Non-Professional), Stuart David Schiff; Special Convention Award, Arkham House; plus a Life Achievement Award to Roald Dahl.

The 1982 John W. Campbell Memorial Award winner was *Helliconia Spring*, by Brian W. Aldiss.

The 1983 American Book Award in the Best Original Paperback category was won by Lisa Goldstein's fantasy novel *The Red Magician*.

The first Philip K. Dick Memorial Award was given to *Software*, by Rudy Rucker.

Dead in 1983 were: MACK REYNOLDS, 65, an SF writer who specialized in economic and sociological speculation, author of *Black Man's Burden, Looking Backward from the Year 2000, Tomorrow Might Be Different*, and many other books; ZENNA HENDERSON, best known for her "People" series about gentle aliens in hiding among us, author of *Pilgrimage: The Book of the People* and *The People: No Different Flesh*; MARY RENAULT, 78, internationally-known historical novelist whose *The King Must Die* and *The Bull from the Sea* function almost as borderline fantasies, and whose work influenced later fantasy writers such as Marion Zimmer Bradley, Thomas Burnett Swann, and Evangaline Walton; JOAN HUNTER HOLLY, SF writer; DAPHNE CASTELL, 53, SF writer; JAMES WADE, 53, fantasy writer and composer; MAX EHRLICH, 73, SF writer, author of *The Big Eye*; LEONARD WIBBERLEY, 68, author of the associational *The Mouse that Roared* and three other "Grand Fenwick" novels; ROY G. KRENKEL, well-known illustrator, winner of the 1963 Hugo for Best Professional Artist; BUSTER CRABBE, 75, an actor best known for his film portrayals of Flash Gordon and Buck Rogers; SIR RALPH RICHARDSON, actor, whose SF-associated roles included parts in *Things To Come* and the recent *Time Bandits*; RAYMOND MASSEY, 86, actor, best known to SF fans for his role in *Things To Come*; LOUIS C. GOLDSTONE III, 63, SF artist; RAOUL VEZINA, 35, SF and underground comics artist; IVAN TORS, producer of SF movies such as *The Magnetic Monster* and associational TV series such as *Flipper*; MAEVE GILMORE PEAKE, well-known artist, widow of writer Mervyn Peake; WILLIAM C. BOYD, 79, SF writer; ARTHUR KOESTLER, 77, well-known writer perhaps most famous for his political novel *Darkness at Noon*, which was an influence on George Orwell's *1984*; BOB PAVLAT, 58, longtime SF fan, one of the founders of the Washington Science Fiction Association; LARRY PROPP, 38, longtime SF fan, co-chairman of Chicon IV, the 1982 Worldcon; MIKE WOOD, 35, long active in Minneapolis fandom; and VIVIAN SMITH, 38, longtime member of the Philadelphia Science Fiction Society and active in Philadelphia SF circles, a personal friend.

BRUCE STERLING

Cicada Queen

Significant new talent seems to enter the SF world in waves, discrete generational groupings, usually at five-to-ten year intervals. One such influx of new talent came along in the early middle '60s, when new writers like Samuel Delany, Roger Zelazny, Thomas M. Disch, Norman Spinrad, R.A. Lafferty, and others ushered in SF's "New Wave" years. A few years later in the early seventies, another wave of talent arrived—made up of writers such as Ursula K. Le Guin, Joanna Russ, Gene Wolfe, Barry Malzberg, and James Tiptree, Jr.—and a few years after *that*, in the middle seventies, everyone was suddenly talking about writers such as Joe Haldeman, John Varley, Gregory Benford, Jack Dann, George R.R. Martin, Michael Bishop, Phyllis Eisenstein, and Edward Bryant.

Now, at the beginning of the '80s, we are clearly in the process of assimilating yet another generational wave of hot new writers, and in the years to come you will be hearing a whole lot more about writers like Michael Swanwick, William Gibson, Pat Cadigan, Kim Stanley Robinson, Leigh Kennedy, John Kessel, James Patrick Kelly, Greg Bear, Connie Willis, Pat Murphy, Lewis Shiner . . . and Bruce Sterling, who even in this august company must be considered one of the really *major* talents to enter SF in recent years. As is more than amply demonstrated by the powerful story of intrigue and confrontation that follows, set in a bizarre far-future world where Shapers and Mechanists struggle to control the shape of human destiny . . .

Born in Brownsville, Texas, Bruce Sterling sold his first SF story in 1976, and has since sold stories to *Universe, Omni, The Magazine of Fantasy & Science Fiction*, and *The Last Dangerous Visions*. His acclaimed story "Swarm" was both a Hugo and a Nebula Award finalist last year. His short story, "Spider Rose," was also a Hugo finalist. His novels include *Involution Ocean* and *The Artificial Kid*. Upcoming is a new novel, set in the Shaper/Mechanist universe, from Arbor House. Sterling lives in Austin, Texas.

CICADA QUEEN

Bruce Sterling

It began the night the Queen called off her dogs. I'd been under the dogs for two years, ever since my defection.

My initiation, and my freedom from the dogs, were celebrated at the home of Arvin Kulagin. Kulagin, a wealthy Mechanist, had a large domestic-industrial complex on the outer perimeter of a midsized cylindrical suburb.

Kulagin met me at his door and handed me a gold inhaler spiked with beta-phenethylamine. The party was already roaring. The Polycarbon Clique always turned out in force for an initiation.

As usual, my entrance was marked by a subtle freezing up. It was the dogs' fault. Voices were raised to a certain histrionic pitch, people handled their inhalers and drinks with a slightly more studied elegance, and every smile turned my way was bright enough for a team of security experts.

Kulagin smiled glassily. "Landau, it's a pleasure. Welcome. I see you've brought the Queen's Percentage." He looked pointedly at the box on my hip.

"Yes," I said. A man under the dogs had no secrets. I had been working off and on for two years on the Queen's gift and the dogs had taped everything. They were still taping everything. Czarina-Kluster Security had designed them for that. For two years they'd taped every moment of my life and everything and everyone around me.

"Perhaps the Clique can have a look," Kulagin said. "Once we've whipped these dogs." He winked into the armored camera face of the watchdog, then looked at his timepiece. "Just an hour till you're out from under. Then we'll have some fun." He waved me on into the room. "If you need anything, use the servos."

Kulagin's place was spacious and elegant, decorated classically and scented by gigantic suspended marigolds. Kulagin's suburb was called the Froth and was the Clique's favorite neighborhood. Kulagin, living at the suburb's perimeter, profited by the Froth's lazy spin and had a simulated tenth of a gravity. His walls were striped to provide a vertical referent, and he had enough space to affect such luxuries as "floors," "tables," "chairs," and other forms of gravity-oriented furniture. The ceiling was studded with hooks, from which were suspended a dozen of his favorite marigolds, huge round explosions of reeking greenery with blossoms the size of my head.

I walked into the room and stood behind a couch, which partially hid the two offensive dogs. I signaled one of Kulagin's spidery servos and took a squeezebulb of liquor to cut the speedy intensity of the phenethylamine.

I watched the party, which had split into loose subcliques. Kulagin was near the door with his closest sympathizers, Mechanist officers from Czarina-Kluster banks and quiet Security types. Nearby, faculty from the Kosmosity-Metasystem campus talked shop with a pair of orbital engineers. On the ceiling, Shaper designers talked fashion, clinging to hooks in the feeble gravity. Below them a manic group of C-K folk, "Cicadas," spun like clockwork through gravity dance steps.

At the back of the room, Wellspring was holding forth amid a herd of spindly legged chairs. I leaped gently over the couch and glided toward him. The dogs sprang after me with a whir of propulsive fans.

Wellspring was my closest friend in C-K. He had encouraged my defection when he was in the Ring Council, buying ice for the Martian terraforming project. The dogs never bothered Wellspring. His ancient friendship with the Queen was well known. In C-K, Wellspring was a legend.

Tonight he was dressed for an audience with the Queen. A coronet of gold and platinum circled his dark, matted hair. He wore a loose blouse of metallic brocade with slashed sleeves that showed a black underblouse shot through with flickering pinpoints of light. This was complemented by an Investor-style jeweled skirt and knee-high scaled boots. The jeweled cables of the skirt showed Wellspring's massive legs, trained to the heavy gravity favored by the reptilian Queen. He was a powerful man, and his weaknesses, if he had any, were hidden within his past.

Wellspring was talking philosophy. His audience, mathematicians and biologists from the faculty of C-K K-M, made room for me with strained smiles. "You asked me to define my terms," he said urbanely. "By the term we, I don't mean merely you Cicadas. Nor do I mean the mass of so-called humanity. After all, you Shapers are constructed of genes patented by Reshaped genetics firms. You might be properly defined as industrial artifacts."

His audience groaned. Wellspring smiled. "And conversely, the Mechanists are slowly abandoning human flesh in favor of cybernetic modes of existence. So. It follows that my term, *we*, can be attributed to any cognitive metasystem on the Fourth Prigoginic Level of complexity."

A Shaper professor touched his inhaler to the painted line of his nostril and said, "I have to take issue with that, Wellspring. This occult nonsense about levels of complexity is ruining C-K's ability to do decent science."

"That's a linear causative statement," Wellspring riposted. "You conservatives are always looking for certainties outside the level of the cognitive metasystem. Clearly every intelligent being is separated from every lower level by a Prigoginic event horizon. It's time we learned to stop looking for solid ground to stand on. Let's place *ourselves* at the center of things. If we need something to stand on, we'll have it orbit us."

He was applauded. He said, "Admit it, Yevgeny. C-K is blooming in a new moral and intellectual climate. It's unquantifiable and unpredictable, and, as a scientist, that frightens you. Posthumanism offers fluidity and freedom, and a metaphysic daring enough to think a whole world into life. It enables us to take up economically absurd projects such as the terraforming of Mars, which your pseudopragmatic attitude could never dare to attempt. And yet think of the gain involved."

"Semantic tricks," sniffed the professor. I had never seen him before. I suspected that Wellspring had brought him along for the express purpose of baiting him.

I myself had once doubted some aspects of C-K's Posthumanism. But its open abandonment of the search for moral certainties had liberated us. When I looked at the eager, painted faces of Wellspring's audience, and compared them to the bleak strain and veiled craftiness that had once surrounded me, I felt as if I would burst. After twenty-four years of paranoid discipline under the Ring Council, and then two more years under the dogs, tonight I would be explosively released from pressure.

I sniffed at the phenethylamine, the body's own "natural" amphetamine. I felt suddenly dizzy, as if the space inside my head were full of the red-hot Ur-space of the primordial deSitter cosmos, ready at any moment to make the Prigoginic leap into the "normal" space-time continuum, the Second Prigoginic Level of complexity. . . . Posthumanism schooled us to think in terms of fits and starts, of structures accreting along unspoken patterns, following the lines first suggested by the ancient Terran philosopher Ilya Prigogine. I directly understood this, since my own mild attraction to the dazzling Valery Korstad had coalesced into a knotted desire that suppressants could numb but not destroy.

She was dancing across the room, the jeweled strings of her Investor skirt twisting like snakes. She had the anonymous beauty of the Reshaped, overlaid with the ingenious, enticing paint of C-K. I had never seen anything I wanted more, and from our brief and strained flirtations I knew that only the dogs stood between us.

Wellspring took me by the arm. His audience had dissolved as I stood rapt, lusting after Valery. "How much longer, son?"

Startled, I looked at the watch display on my forearm. "Only twenty minutes, Wellspring."

"That's fine, son." Wellspring was famous for his use of archaic terms like *son*. "Once the dogs are gone, it'll be your party, Hans. I won't stay here to eclipse you. Besides, the Queen awaits me. You have the Queen's Percentage?"

"Yes, just as you said." I unpeeled the box from the stick-tight patch on my hip and handed it over.

Wellspring lifted its lid with his powerful fingers and looked inside. Then he laughed aloud. "Jesus! It's beautiful!"

Suddenly he pulled the open box away and the Queen's gift hung in midair, glittering above our heads. It was an artificial gem the size of a child's fist, its chiseled planes glittering with the green and gold of endolithic lichen. As it spun it threw tiny glints of fractured light across our faces.

As it fell, Kulagin appeared and caught it on the points of four extended fingertips. His left eye, an artificial implant, glistened darkly as he examined it.

"Eisho Zaibatsu?" he asked.

"Yes," I said. "They handled the synthesizing work; the lichen is a special variety of my own." I saw that a curious circle was gathering and said aloud, "Our host is a connoisseur."

"Only of finance," Kulagin said quietly, but with equal emphasis. "I understand now why you patented the process in your own name. It's a dazzling accomplishment. How could any Investor resist the lure of a living jewel, friends? Someday soon our initiate will be a wealthy man."

I looked quickly at Wellspring, but he unobtrusively touched one finger to his lips. "And he'll need that wealth to bring Mars to fruition," Wellspring said loudly. "We can't depend forever on the Kosmosity for funding. Friends, rejoice that you too will reap the profits of Landau's ingenious genetics." He caught the jewel and boxed it. "And tonight I have the honor of presenting his gift to the Queen. A double honor, since I recruited its creator myself." Suddenly he leaped toward the exit, his powerful legs carrying him quickly above our heads. As he flew he shouted, "Good-bye, son! May another dog never darken your doorstep!"

With Wellspring's exit, the non-Polycarbon guests began leaving, forming a jostling knot of hat-fetching servos and gossiping well-wishers. When the last was gone, the Clique grew suddenly quiet.

Kulagin had me stand at a far corner of his studio while the Clique formed a long gauntlet for the dogs, arming themselves with ribbons and paint. A certain dark edge of smoldering vengeance only added a tang to their enjoyment. I took a pair of paint balloons from one of Kulagin's scurrying servos.

The time was almost on me. For two long years I'd schemed to join the Polycarbon Clique. I needed them. I felt they needed me. I was tired of suspicion, of strained politeness, of the glass walls of the dogs' surveillance. The keen edges of my long discipline suddenly, painfully crumbled. I began shaking uncontrollably, unable to hold it back.

The dogs were still, taping steadily to the last appointed instant. The crowd began to count down. Exactly at the count of zero the two dogs turned to go.

They were barraged with paint and tangled streamers. A moment earlier they would have turned savagely on their tormentors, but now they had reached the limits of their programming, and at long last they were helpless. The Clique's aim was deadly, and with every splattering hit they split the air with screams of laughter. They knew no mercy, and it took a full minute before the humiliated dogs could hop and stagger, blinded, to the door.

I was overcome with mob hysteria. Screams escaped my clenched teeth. I had to be grappled back from pursuing the dogs down the hall. As firm hands pulled me back within the room I turned to face my friends, and I was chilled at the raw emotion on their faces. It was as if they had been stripped of skin and watched me with live eyes in slabs of meat.

I was picked up bodily and passed from hand to hand around the room. Even those that I knew well seemed alien to me now. Hands tore at my clothing until I was stripped; they even took my computer gauntlet, then stood me in the middle of the room.

As I stood shivering within the circle, Kulagin approached me, his arms rigid, his face stiff and hieratic. His hands were full of loose black cloth. He held the cloth over my head and I saw that it was a black hood. He put his lips close to my ear and said softly, "Friend, go the distance." Then he pulled the hood over my head and knotted it.

The hood had been soaked in something. I could smell that it reeked. My hands and feet began to tingle, then go numb. Slowly, warmth crept like bracelets up my arms and legs. I could hear nothing, and my feet could no longer feel the floor. I lost all sense of balance, and suddenly I fell backward, into the infinite.

My eyes opened, or my eyes closed, I couldn't tell. But at the limits of vision, from behind some unspoken fog, emerged pinpoints of cold and piercing brightness. It was the Great Galactic Night, the vast and pitiless emptiness that lurks just beyond the warm rim of every human habitat, emptier even than death.

I was naked in space and it was so bitterly cold that I could taste it like poison in every cell I had. I could feel the pale heat of my own life streaming out of me like plasma, ebbing away in aurora sheets from my fingertips. I continued to fall, and as the last rags of warmth pulsed off into the devouring chasm of space, and my body grew stiff and white and furred with frost from every pore, I faced the ultimate horror: that I would not die, that I would fall forever backward into the unknown, my mind shriveling into a single frozen spore of isolation and terror.

Time dilated. Eons of silent fear telescoped into a few heartbeats and I saw before me a single white blob of light, like a rent from this cosmos into some neighboring realm full of alien radiance. This time I faced it as I fell toward it, and through it, and then, finally, jarringly, I was back behind my own eyes, within my own head, on the soft floor of Kulagin's studio.

The hood was gone. I wore a loose black robe, closed with an embroidered belt. Kulagin and Valery Korstad helped me to my feet. I wobbled, brushing away tears, but I managed to stand, and the Clique cheered.

Kulagin's shoulder was under my arm. He embraced me and whispered, "Brother, remember the cold. When we your friends need warmth, be warm, remembering the cold. When friendship pains you, forgive us, remembering the cold. When selfishness tempts you, renounce it, remembering the cold. For you have gone the distance, and returned to us renewed. Remember, remember the cold." And then he gave me my secret name, and pressed his painted lips to mine.

I clung to him, choked with sobs. Valery embraced me and Kulagin pulled away gently, smiling.

One by one the Clique took my hands and pressed their lips quickly to my face, murmuring congratulations. Still unable to speak, I could only nod. Meanwhile Valery Korstad, clinging to my arm, whispered hotly in my ear, "Hans, Hans, Hans Landau, there still remains a certain ritual, which I have reserved to myself. Tonight the finest chamber in the Froth belongs to us, a sacred place where no glassy-eyed dog has ever trespassed. Hans Landau, tonight that place belongs to you, and so do I."

I looked into her face, my eyes watering. Her eyes were dilated and a pink flush had spread itself under her ears and along her jawline. She had dosed herself with hormonal aphrodisiacs. I smelled the antiseptic sweetness of her perfumed sweat and I closed my eyes, shuddering.

Valery led me into the hall. Behind us, Kulagin's door sealed shut, cutting the hilarity to a murmur. Valery helped me slip on my air fins, whispering soothingly.

The dogs were gone. Two chunks of my reality had been edited like tape. I still felt dazed. Valery took my hand and we threaded a corridor upward toward the center of the habitat, kicking along with our air fins. I smiled mechanically at the Cicadas we passed in the halls, members of another day crowd. They were soberly going about their day shift's work while the Polycarbon Clique indulged in bacchanalia.

It was easy to lose yourself within the Froth. It had been built in rebellion against the regimented architecture of other habitats, in C-K's typical defiance of the norm. The original empty cylinder had been packed with pressurized plastic, which had been blasted to foam and allowed to set. It left angular bubbles whose tilted walls were defined by the clean topologies of close packing and surface tension. Halls had been snaked through the complex later, and the doors and airlocks cut by hand. The Froth was famous for its delirious and welcome spontaneity.

And its discreets were notorious. C-K showed its civic spirit in the lavish appointments of these citadels against surveillance. I had never been in one before. People under the dogs were not allowed across the boundaries. But I had heard rumors, the dark and prurient scandal of bars and corridors, those scraps of licentious speculation that always hushed at the approach of dogs. Anything, anything at all, could happen in a discreet, and no one would know of it but the lovers or survivors who returned, hours later, to public life. . . .

As the centrifugal gravity faded we began floating, Valery half-towing me. The bubbles of the Froth had swollen near the axis of rotation and we entered a neighborhood of the quiet industrial domiciles of the rich. Soon we had floated to the very doorstep of the infamous Topaz Discreet, the hushed locale of unnumbered elite frolics. It was the finest in the Froth.

Valery looked at her timepiece, caressing away a fine film of sweat that had formed on the flushed and perfect lines of her face and neck. We hadn't long to wait. We heard the mellow repeated bonging of the discreet's time alarm, warning the present occupant that his time was up. The door's locks unsealed. I wondered just what member of C-K's inner circle would emerge. Now that I was free of the dogs, I longed to boldly meet his eyes.

Still we waited. Now the discreet was ours by right and every moment lost pained us. To overstay in a discreet was the height of rudeness. Valery grew angry, and pushed open the door.

The air was full of blood. In free-fall, it floated in a thousand clotting red blobs.

Near the center of the room floated the suicide, his flaccid body still wheeling slowly from the gush of his severed throat. A scalpel glittered in the mechanically clenched fingers of the cadaver's outstretched hand. He wore the sober black overalls of a conservative Mechanist.

The body spun and I saw the insignia of the Queen's Advisers stitched on his breast. His partially metallic skull was sticky with his own blood; the face was obscured. Long streamers of thickened blood hung from his throat like red veils.

We had cometaried into something very much beyond us. "I'll call Security," I said.

She said two words. "Not yet." I looked into her face. Her eyes were dark with fascinated lust. The lure of the forbidden had slid its hooks into her in a single moment. She kicked languidly across one tessellated wall and a long streak of blood splattered and broke along her hip.

In discreets one met the ultimates. In a room with so many hidden meanings, the lines had blurred. Through constant proximity pleasure had wedded with death. For the woman I adored, the private rites transpiring there had become of one unspoken piece.

"Hurry," she said. Her lips were bitter with a thin grease of aphrodisiacs. We interlaced our legs to couple in free-fall while we watched his body twist.

That was the night the Queen called off her dogs.

It had thrilled me in a way that made me sick. We Cicadas lived in the moral equivalent of deSitter space, where no ethos had validity unless it was generated by noncausative free will. Every level of Prigoginic complexity was based on a self-dependent generative catalyst: space existed because space existed, life was because it had come to be, intelligence was because it is. So it was possible for an entire moral system to accrete around a single moment of profound disgust. . . . Or so Posthumanism taught. After my blighted consummation with Valery I withdrew to work and think.

I lived in the Froth, in a domestic-industrial studio that reeked of lichen and was much less chic then Kulagin's.

On the second day shift of my meditation I was visited by Arkadya Sorienti, a Polycarbon friend and one of Valery's intimates. Even without the dogs there were elements of a profound strain between us. It seemed to me that Arkadya was everything that Valery was not: blond where Valery was dark, covered with Mechanist gimmickry where Valery had the cool elegance of the genetically Reshaped, full of false and brittle gaiety where Valery was prey to soft and melancholy gloom. I offered her a squeeze-bulb of liqueur; my apartment was too close to the axis to use cups.

"I haven't seen your apartment before," she said. "I love your airframes, Hans. What kind of algae is it?"

"It's lichen," I said.

"They're beautiful. One of your special kinds?"

"They're all special," I said. "Those have the Mark III and IV varieties for the terraforming project. The others have some delicate strains I was working on for contamination monitors. Lichen are very sensitive to pollution of any sort." I turned up the air ionizer. The intestines of Mechanists seethed with bacteria and their effects could be disastrous.

"Which one is the lichen of the Queen's jewel?"

"It's locked away," I said. "Outside the environs of a jewel its growth becomes very distorted. And it smells." I smiled uneasily. It was common talk among Shapers that Mechanists stank. It seemed to me that I could already smell the reek of her armpits.

Arkadya smiled and nervously rubbed the skin-metal interface of a silvery blob of machinery grafted along her forearm. "Valery's in one of her states," she said. "I thought I'd come see how you were."

In my mind's eye flickered the nightmare image of our naked skins slicked with blood. I said, "It was . . . unfortunate."

"C-K's full of talk about the Comptroller's death."

"It was the Comptroller?" I said. "I haven't seen any news."

Slyness crept into her eyes. "You saw him there," she said.

I was shocked that she should expect me to discuss my stay in a discreet. "I have work," I said. I kicked my fins so that I drifted off our mutual vertical. Facing each other sideways increased the social distance between us.

She laughed quietly. "Don't be a prig, Hans. You act as if you were still under the dogs. You have to tell me about it if you want me to help the two of you."

I stopped my drift. She said, "And I want to help. I'm Valery's friend. I like the way you look together. It appeals to my sense of aesthetics."

"Thanks for your concern."

"I *am* concerned. I'm tired of seeing her on the arm of an old lecher like Wellspring."

"You're telling me they're lovers?" I said.

She fluttered her metal-clad fingers in the air. "You're asking me what the two of them do in his favorite discreet? Maybe they play chess." She rolled her eyes under lids heavy with powdered gold. "Don't look so shocked, Hans. You should know his power as well as anyone. He's old and rich; we Polycarbon women are young and not too terribly principled." She looked quickly up and away from beneath long lashes. "I've never heard that he took anything from us that we weren't willing to give." She floated closer. "Tell me what you saw, Hans. C-K's crazy with the news and Valery does nothing but mope."

I opened the refrigerator and dug among Petri dishes for more liqueur. "It strikes me that you should be doing the talking, Arkadya."

She hesitated, then shrugged and smiled. "Now you're showing some sense, my friend. Open eyes and ears can take you a long way in C-Kluster." She took a stylish inhaler from a holster on her enameled garter. "And speaking of eyes and ears, have you had your place swept for bugs yet?"

"Who'd bug me?"

"Who wouldn't?" She looked bored. "I'll stick to what's common knowledge, then. Hire us a discreet sometime and I'll give you all the rest." She fired a stream of amber liqueur from arm's length and sucked it in as it splashed against her teeth. "Something big is stirring in C-K. It hasn't reached the rank and file yet, but the Comptroller's death is a sign of it. The other Advisers are treating it like a personal matter, but it's clear that he wasn't simply tired of life. He left his affairs in disorder. No, this is something that runs back to the Queen herself. I'm sure of it."

"You think the Queen ordered him to take his own life?"

"Maybe. She's getting erratic with age. Wouldn't you, though, if you had to spend your life surrounded by aliens? I feel for the Queen, I really do. If she needs to kill a few stuffy rich old bastards for her own peace of mind, it's perfectly fine by me. In fact, if that's all there was to it, I'd sleep easier."

I thought about this, my face impassive. The entire structure of Czarina-Kluster was predicated on the Queen's exile. For seventy years, defectors, malcontents, pirates, and pacifists had accreted around the refuge of our alien Queen. The powerful prestige of her fellow Investors protected us from the predatory machinations of Shaper fascists and dehumanized Mechanist sects. C-K was an oasis of sanity amid the vicious amorality of humanity's warring factions. Our suburbs spun in webs around the dark hulk of the Queen's blazing, jeweled environment.

She was all we had. There was a giddy insecurity under all our success. C-K's famous banks were backed by the Cicada Queen's tremendous wealth. The academic freedom of C-K's teaching centers flourished only under her shadow.

And we did not even know why she was disgraced. Rumors abounded, but only the Investors themselves knew the truth. Were she ever to leave us, Czarina-Kluster would disintegrate overnight.

I said offhandedly, "I've heard talk that she's not happy. It seems these rumors spread, and they raise her Percentage for a while and panel a new room with jewels, and then the rumors fade."

"That's true. . . . She and our sweet Valery are two of a kind where these dark moods are concerned. It's clear, though, that the Comptroller was left no choice but suicide. And that means disaster is stirring at the heart of C-K."

"It's only rumors," I said. "The Queen is the heart of C-K, and who knows what's going on in that huge head of hers?"

"Wellspring would know," Arkadya said intently.

"But he's not an Adviser," I said. "As far as the Queen's inner circle is concerned, he's little better than a pirate."

"Tell me what you saw in Topaz Discreet."

"You'll have to allow me some time," I said. "It's rather painful." I wondered what I should tell her, and what she was willing to believe. The silence began to stretch.

I put on a tape of Terran sea sounds. The room began to surge ominously with the roar of alien surf.

"I wasn't ready for it," I said. "In my creche we were taught to guard our feelings from childhood. I know how the Clique feels about distance. But that kind of raw intimacy, from a woman I really scarcely know—especially under that night's circumstances—it wounded me." I looked searchingly into Arkadya's face, longing to reach through her to Valery. "Once it was over, we were further apart than ever."

Arkadya tilted her head to the side and winced. "Who composed this?"

"What? You mean the music? It's a background tape—sea sounds from Earth. It's a couple of centuries old."

She looked at me oddly. "You're really absorbed by the whole planetary thing, aren't you? 'Sea sounds.' "

"Mars will have seas some day. That's what our whole Project is about, isn't it?"

She looked disturbed. "Sure. . . . We're working at it, Hans, but that doesn't mean we have to live there. I mean, that's centuries from now, isn't it? Even if we're still alive, we'll be different people by then. Just think of being trapped down a gravity well. I'd choke to death."

I said quietly, "I don't think of it as being for the purposes of settlement. It's a clearer, more ideal activity. The instigation by Fourth-Level cognitive agents of a Third-Level Prigoginic Leap. Bringing life itself into being on the naked bedrock of spacetime. . . ."

But she was shaking her head and backpedaling toward the door. "I'm sorry, Hans, but those sounds, they're just . . . getting into my blood somehow. . . ." She shook herself, shuddering, and the filigree beads woven into her blond hair clattered loudly. "I can't bear it."

"I'll turn it off."

But she was already leaving. "Good-bye, good-bye. . . . We'll meet again soon."

She was gone. I was left to steep in my own isolation, while the roaring surf gnawed and mumbled at its shore.

One of Kulagin's servos met me at his door and took my hat. Kulagin was seated at a workplace in a screened-off corner of his marigold-reeking domicile, watching stock quotations scroll down a display screen. He was dictating orders into a microphone on his forearm gauntlet. When the servo announced me he unplugged the jack from his gauntlet and stood, shaking my hand with both of his. "Welcome, friend, welcome."

"I hope I haven't come at a bad time."

"No, not at all. Do you play the Market?"

"Not seriously," I said. "Later, maybe, when the royalties from Eisho Zaibatsu pile up."

"You must allow me to guide your eyes, then. A good Posthumanist should have a wide range of interests. Take that chair, if you would."

I sat beside Kulagin as he sat before the console and plugged in. Kulagin was a Mechanist, but he kept himself rigorously antiseptic. I liked him.

He said, "Odd how these financial institutions tend to drift from their original purpose. In a way, the Market itself has made a sort of Prigoginic leap. On its face, it's a commerical tool, but it's become a game of conventions and confidences. We Cicadas eat, breathe, and sleep rumors, so the Market is the perfect expression of our zeitgeist."

"Yes," I said. "Frail, mannered, and based on practically nothing tangible."

Kulagin lifted his plucked brows. "Yes, my young friend, exactly like the bedrock of the Cosmos itself. Every level of complexity floats freely on the last, supported only by abstractions. Even natural laws are only our attempts to strain our vision through the Prigoginic event horizon. . . . If you prefer a more primal metaphor, we can compare the Market to the sea. A sea of information, with a few blue-chip islands here and there for the exhausted swimmer. Look at this."

He touched buttons and a three-dimensional grid display sprang into being. "This is Market activity in the past forty-eight hours. It looks rather like the waves and billows of a sea, doesn't it? Note these surges of transaction." He touched the screen with the light pen implanted in his forefinger and gridded areas flushed from cool green to red. "That was when the first rumors of the iceteroid came in—"

"What?"

"The asteroid, the ice-mass from the Ring Council. Someone had bought it and is mass-driving it out of Saturn's gravity well right now, bound for Martian impact. Someone very clever, for it will pass within a few thousands of klicks from C-K. Close enough for naked-eyed view."

"You mean they've really done it?" I said, caught between shock and joy.

"I heard it third-, fourth-, maybe tenth-hand, but it fits in well with the parameters the Polycarbon engineers have set up. A mass of ice and volatiles, well over three klicks across, targeted for the Hellas Depression south of the equator at sixty-five klicks a second, impact expected at UT 20:14:53, 14-4-'54. . . . That's dawn, local time. Local Martian time, I mean."

"But that's months from now," I said.

Kulagin smirked. "Look, Hans, you don't push a three-klick ice lump with your thumbs. Besides, this is just the first of dozens. It's more of a symbolic gesture."

"But it means we'll be moving out! To Martian orbit!"

Kulagin looked skeptical. "That's a job for drones and monitors, Hans. Or maybe a few rough-and-tough pioneer types. Actually, there's no reason why you and I should have to leave the comforts of C-K."

I stood up, knotting my hands. "You want to *stay*? And miss the Prigoginic catalyst?"

Kulagin looked up with a slight frown. "Cool off, Hans, sit down, they'll be looking for volunteers soon enough, and if you really mean to go I'm sure you can manage somehow. . . . The point is that the effect on the Market has been spectacular. . . . It's been fairly giddy ever since the Comptroller's death and now some very big fish indeed is rising for the kill. I've been following his movements for three day shifts straight, hoping to feast on his scraps, so to speak. . . . Care for an inhale?"

"No, thanks."

Kulagin helped himself to a long pull of stimulant. He looked ragged. I'd never seen him without his face paint before. He said, "I don't have the feeling for mob psychology that you Shapers have, so I have to make do with a very, very good memory. . . . The last time I saw something like this was thirteen years ago. Someone spread the rumor that the Queen had tried to leave C-K and the Advisers had restrained her by force. The upshot of that was the Crash of 'Forty-one, but the real killing came in the Rally that followed. I've been reviewing the tapes of the Crash, and I recognize the fins and flippers and big sharp teeth of an old friend. I can read his style in his maneuvering. It's not the slick guile of a Shaper. It's not the cold persistence of a Mechanist, either."

I considered. "Then you must mean Wellspring."

Wellspring's age was unknown. He was well over two centuries old. He claimed to have been born on Earth in the dawn of the Space Age, and to have lived in the first generation of independent space colonies, the so-called Concatenation. He had been among the founders of Czarina-Kluster, building the Queen's habitat when she fled in disgrace from her fellow Investors.

Kulagin smiled. "Very good, Hans. You may live in moss, but there's none on you. I think Wellspring engineered the Crash of 'Forty-one for his own profit."

"But he lives very modestly."

"As the Queen's oldest friend, he was certainly in a perfect position to start rumors. He even engineered the parameters of the Market itself, seventy years ago. And it was after the Rally that the Kosmosity-Metasystems Department of Terraformation was set up. Through anonymous donations, of course."

"But contributions came in from all over the system," I objected. "Almost all the sects and factions think that terraforming is humanity's sublimest effort."

"To be sure. Though I wonder just how that idea became so widely spread. And to whose benefit. Listen, Hans. I love Wellspring. He's a *friend*, and I remember the cold. But you have to realize just what an anomaly he is. He's not one of us. He wasn't even born in space." He looked at me narrowly, but I took no offense at his use of the term "born." It was a deadly insult against Shapers, but I considered myself a Polycarbon first and Cicada second, with Shaperism a distant third.

He smiled briefly. "To be sure, Wellspring has a few Mechanist knickknacks implanted, to extend his life span, but he lacks the whole Mech style. In fact he actually *predates* it. I'd be the last to deny the genius of you Shapers, but in a way it's an artificial genius. It works out well enough on I.Q. tests, but it somehow lacks that, well, primeval quality that Wellspring has, just as we Mechanists can use cybernetic modes of thinking but we can never be actual machines. . . . Wellspring simply is one of those people at the farthest reaches of the bell curve, one of those titans that spring up only once a generation. I mean, think what's become of his normal human contemporaries."

I nodded. "Most of them have become Mechs."

Kulagin shook his head fractionally, staring at the screen. "I was born here in C-K. I don't know that much about the old-style Mechs, but I do know that most of the first ones are dead. Out-dated, crowded out. Driven over the edge by future shock. A lot of the first life-extension efforts failed, too, in very ugly ways. . . . Wellspring survived that, too, from some innate knack he has. Think of it, Hans. Here we sit, products of technologies so advanced that they've smashed society to bits. We trade with aliens. We can even hitchhike to the stars, if we pay the Investors' fare. And Wellspring not only holds his own, he rules us. We don't even know his real name."

I considered what Kulagin had said while he switched to a Market update. It felt bad. I could hide my feelings, but I couldn't shake them off. "You're right," I said. "But I trust him."

"I trust him too, but I know we're cradled in his hands. In fact, he's protecting us right now. This terraforming project has cost megawatt after megawatt. All those contributions were anonymous, supposedly to prevent the factions from using them for propaganda. But I think it was to hide the fact that most of them were from Wellspring. Any day now there's going to be an extended Market crash. Wellspring will make his move, and that will start the rally. And every kilowatt of his profits will go to us."

I leaned forward in my chair, interlacing my fingers. Kulagin dictated a series of selling orders into his microphone. Suddenly I laughed.

Kulagin looked up. "That's the first time I've ever heard you laugh like you meant it, Hans."

"I was just thinking. . . . You've told me all this, but I came here to talk about Valery."

Kulagin looked sad. "Listen, Hans. What I know about women you could hide under a microchip, but, as I said, my memory is excellent. The Shapers blundered when they pushed things to the limits. The Ring Council tried to break the so-called Two-Hundred Barrier last century. Most of the so-called Superbrights went mad, defected, turned against their fellows, or all three. They've been hunted by pirates and mercenaries for decades now.

"One group found out somehow that there was an Investor Queen living in exile, and they managed to make it to her shadow, for protection. And someone—you can imagine who—talked the Queen into letting them stay, if they paid a certain tax. That tax became the

Queen's Percentage, and the settlement became Czarina-Kluster. Valery's parents—yes, *parents*; it was a natural birth—were among those Superbrights. She didn't have the schooling Shapers use, so she ranks in at only one forty-five or so.

"The problem is those mood cycles of hers. Her parents had them, she's had them since she was a child. She's a dangerous woman, Hans. Dangerous to herself, to all of us. She should be under the dogs, really. I've suggested that to my friends in Security, but someone stands in my way. I have my ideas who."

"I'm in love with her. She won't speak to me."

"I see. Well, I understand she's been full of mood suppressants lately; that probably accounts for her reticence. . . . I'll speak frankly. There's an old saying, Hans, that you should never enter a discreet with someone crazier than you are. And it's good advice. You can't trust Valery."

He held up his hand. "Hear me out. You're young. You've just come out from under the dogs. This woman has enchanted you, and admittedly she has the famous Shaper charm in full measure. But a liaison with Valery is like an affair with five women, three of whom are crazy. C-K is full to bursting with the most beautiful women in human history. Admittedly you're a bit stiff, a bit of an obsessive perhaps, but you have a certain idealistic charm. And you have that Shaper intensity, fanaticism even, if you don't mind my saying so. Loosen up a little, Hans. Find some woman who'll rub the rough edges off of you. Play the field. It's a good way to recruit new friends to the Clique."

"I'll keep what you said in mind," I said neutrally.

"Right. I knew it was wasted effort." He smiled ironically. "Why should I blight the purity of your emotions? A tragic first love may become an asset fifty or a hundred years from now." He turned his attention back to the screen. "I'm glad we had this talk, Hans. I hope you'll get in touch again when the Eisho Zaibatsu money comes through. We'll have some fun with it."

"I'd like that," I said, though I knew already that every kilowatt not spent on my own research would go—anonymously—to the terraforming fund. "And I don't resent your advice. It's just that it's of no use to me."

"Ah, youth," Kulagin said. I left.

Back to the simple beauty of the lichens. I had been trained for years to specialize in them, but they had taken on beauty and meaning for me only after my Posthumanist enlightenment. Viewed through C-K's philosophies, they stood near the catalysis point of the Prigoginic leap that brought life itself into being.

Alternately, a lichen could be viewed as an extended metaphor for the Polycarbon Clique: a fungus and an alga, potential rivals, united in symbiosis to accomplish what neither could do alone, just as the Clique united Mechanist and Shaper to bring life to Mars.

I knew that many viewed my dedication as strange, even unhealthy. I was not offended by their blindness. Just the names of my genetic stocks had a rolling majesty: *Alectoria nigricans, Mastodia tessellata, Ochrolechia frigida, Stereocaulon alpinum.* They were humble but powerful: creatures of the cold desert whose roots and acids could crumble naked, freezing rock.

My gel frames seethed with primal vitality. Lichens would drench Mars in one green-gold tidal wave of life. They would creep irresistibly from the moist craters of the iceteroid impacts, proliferating relentlessly amid the storms and earthquakes of terraformation, surviving the floods as permafrost melted. Gushing oxygen, fixing nitrogen.

They were the best. Not because of pride or show. Not because they trumpeted their motives, or threatened the cold before they broke it. But because they were silent, and the first.

My years under the dogs had taught me the value of silence. Now I was sick of surveillance. When the first royalty payment came in from Eisho Zaibatsu, I contacted one of C-K's private security firms and had my apartments swept for bugs. They found four.

I hired a second firm to remove the bugs left by the first.

I strapped myself in at a floating workbench, turning the spy eyes over and over in my hands. They were flat videoplates, painted with one-way colorshifting polymer camouflage. They would fetch a nice price on the unofficial market.

I called a post office and hired a courier servo to take the bugs to Kulagin. While I awaited the servo's arrival, I turned off the bugs and sealed them into a biohazard box. I dictated a note, asking Kulagin to sell them and invest the money for me in C-K's faltering Market. The Market looked as if it could use a few buyers.

When I heard the courier's staccato knock I opened my door with a gauntlet remote. But it was no courier that whirred in. It was a guard dog.

"I'll take that box, if you please," said the dog.

I stared at it as if I had never seen a dog before. This dog was heavily armored in silver. Thin, powerful limbs jutted from its silver-seamed black-plastic torso, and its swollen head bristled with spring-loaded taser darts and the blunt nozzles of restraint webs. Its swiveling antenna tail showed that it was under remote control.

I spun my workbench so that it stood between me and the dog. "I see you have my comm lines tapped as well," I said. "Will you tell me where the taps are, or do I have to take my computer apart?"

"You sniveling little Shaper upstart," commented the dog, "do you think your royalties can buy you out from under everyone? I could sell you on the open market before you could blink."

I considered this. On a number of occasions, particularly troublesome meddlers in C-K had been arrested and offered for sale on the open market by the Queen's Advisers. There were always factions outside C-K willing to pay good prices for enemy agents. I knew that the Ring Council would be overjoyed to make an example of me. "You're claiming to be one of the Queen's Advisers, then?"

"*Of course* I'm an Adviser! Your treacheries haven't lulled us all to sleep. Your friendship with Wellspring is notorious!" The dog whirred closer, its clumped camera eyes clicking faintly. "What's inside that freezer?"

"Lichen racks," I said impassively. "You should know that well enough."

"Open it."

I didn't move. "You're going beyond the bounds of normal operations," I said, knowing that this would trouble any Mechanist. "My Clique has friends among the Advisers. I've done nothing wrong."

"Open it, or I'll web you and open it myself, with this dog."

"Lies," I said. "You're no Adviser. You're an industrial spy, trying to steal my gemstone lichen. Why would an Adviser want to look into my freezer?"

"Open it! Don't involve yourself more deeply in things you don't understand."

"You've entered my domicile under false pretenses and threatened me," I said. "I'm calling Security."

The dog's chromed jaws opened. I twisted myself free of the workbench, but a thready spray of white silk from one of the dog's facial nozzles caught me as I dodged. The filaments clung and hardened instantly, locking my arms in place where I had instinctively raised them to block the spray. A second blast caught my legs as I struggled uselessly, bouncing off a tilted Froth-wall.

"Troublemaker," muttered the dog. "Everything would have gone down smooth without you Shapers quibbling. We had the soundest banks, we had the Queen, the Market, everything. . . . You parasites gave C-K nothing but your fantasies. Now the system's crumbling. Everything will crash. Everything. I ought to kill you."

I gasped for breath as the spray rigidified across my chest. "Life isn't banks," I wheezed.

Motors whined as the dog flexed its jointed limbs. "If I find what I expect in that freezer, you're as good as dead."

Suddenly the dog stopped in midair. Its fans whirred as it wheeled to face the door. The door clicked convulsively and began to slide open. A massive taloned forelimb slammed through the opening.

The watchdog webbed the door shut. Suddenly the door shrieked and buckled, its metal peeling back like foil. The goggling head and spiked legs of a tiger crunched and thrashed through the wreckage. "Treason!" the tiger roared.

The dog whirred backward, cringing, as the tiger pulled its armored hindquarters into the room. The jagged wreckage of the door didn't even scratch it. Armored in black and gold, it was twice the size of the watchdog. "Wait," the dog said.

"The Council warned you against vigilante action," the tiger said heavily. "I warned you myself."

"I had to make a choice, Coordinator. It's *his* doing. He turned us against one another, you have to see that."

"You have only one choice left," the tiger said. "Choose your discreet, Councilman."

The dog flexed its limbs indecisively. "So I'm to be the second," he said. "First the Comptroller, now myself. Very well, then. Very well. He has me. I can't retaliate." The dog seemed to gather itself up for a rush. "But I can destroy his favorite!"

The dog's legs shot open like telescopes and it sprang off a wall for my throat. There was a terrific flash with the stench of ozone and the dog slammed bruisingly into my chest. It was dead, its circuits stripped. The lights flickered and went out as my home computer faltered and crashed, its programming scrambled by incidental radiation from the tiger's electromagnetic pulse.

Flanges popped open on the tiger's bulbous head and two spotlights emerged. "Do you have any implants?" he said.

"No," I said. "No cybernetic parts. I'm all right. You saved my life."

"Close your eyes," the tiger commanded. It washed me with a fine mist of solvent from its nostrils. The web peeled off in its talons, taking my clothing with it.

My forearm gauntlet was ruined. I said, "I've committed no crime against the state, Coordinator. I love C-K."

"These are strange days," the tiger rumbled. "Our routines are in decay. No one is above suspicion. You picked a bad time to make your home mimic a discreet, young man."

"I did it openly," I said.

"There are no rights here, Cicada. Only the Queen's graces. Dress yourself and ride the tiger. We need to talk. I'm taking you to the Palace."

The Palace was like one gigantic discreet. I wondered if I would ever leave its mysteries alive.

I had no choice.

I dressed carefully under the tiger's goggling eyes, and mounted it. It smelled of aging lubrication. It must have been in storage for decades. Tigers had not been seen at large in C-K for years.

The halls were crowded with Cicadas going on and off their day shifts. At the tiger's approach they scattered in terror and awe.

We exited the Froth at its cylinder end, into the gimbaling cluster of interurban tube roads.

The roads were transparent polycarbon conduits, linking C-K's cylindrical suburbs in an untidy web. The sight of these shining habitats against the icy background of the stars gave me a sharp moment of vertigo. I remembered the cold.

We passed through a thickened knot along the web, a swollen intersection of tube roads where one of C-K's famous highway bistros had accreted itself into being. The lively gossip of its glittering habitués froze into a stricken silence as I rode by, and swelled into a chorus of alarm as I left. The news would permeate C-K in minutes.

The Palace imitated an Investor starship: an octahedron with six long rectangular sides. Genuine Investor ships were crusted with fantastic designs in hammered metal, but the Queen's was an uneven dull black, reflecting her unknown shame. With the passage of time it had grown by fits and starts, and now it was lumped and flanged with government offices and the Queen's covert hideaways. The ponderous hulk spun with dizzying speed.

We entered along one axis into a searing bath of blue-white light. My eyes shrank painfully and began oozing tears.

The Queen's Advisers were Mechanists, and the halls swarmed with servos. They passively followed their routines, ignoring the tiger, whose chromed and plated surfaces gleamed viciously in the merciless light.

A short distance from the axis the centrifugal force seized us and the tiger sank creaking onto its massive legs. The walls grew baroque with mosaics and spun designs in filamented precious metals. The tiger stalked down a flight of stairs. My spine popped audibly in the increasing gravity and I sat erect with an effort.

Most of the halls were empty. We passed occasional clumps of jewels in the walls that blazed like lightning. I leaned against the tiger's back and locked my elbows, my heart pounding. More stairs. Tears ran down my face and into my mouth, a sensation that was novel and disgusting. My arms trembled with fatigue.

The Coordinator's office was on the perimeter. It kept him in shape for audiences with the Queen. The tiger stalked creaking through a pair of massive doors, built to Investor scale.

Everything in the office was in Investor scale. The ceilings were more than twice the height of a man. A chandelier overhead gushed a blistering radiance over two immense chairs with tall backs split by tail holes. A fountain surged and splattered feebly, exhausted by strain.

The Coordinator sat behind a keyboarded business desk. The top of the desk rose almost to his armpits and his scaled boots dangled far above the floor. Beside him a monitor scrolled down the latest Market reports.

I heaved myself, grunting, off the tiger's back and up into the scratchy plush of an Investor chair seat. Built for an Investor's scaled rump, it pierced my trousers like wire.

"Have some sun shades," the Coordinator said. He opened a cavernous desk drawer, fished elbow-deep for a pair of goggles, and hurled them at me. I reached high and they hit me in the chest.

I wiped my eyes and put on the goggles, groaning with relief. The tiger crouched at the foot of my chair, whirring to itself.

"Your first time in the Palace?" the Coordinator said.

I nodded with an effort.

"It's horrible, I know. And yet, it's all we have. You have to understand that, Landau. This is C-K's Prigoginic catalyst."

"You know the philosophy?" I said.

"Surely. Not all of us are fossilized. The Advisors have their factions. That's common knowledge." The Coordinator pushed his chair back. Then he stood up in its seat, climbed up onto his desk top, and sat on its forward edge facing me, his scaled boots dangling.

He was a blunt, stocky, powerfully muscled man, moving easily in the force that flattened me. His face was deeply and ferociously creased with two centuries of seams and wrinkles. His black skin gleamed dully in the searing light. His eyeballs had the brittle look of plastic. He said, "I've seen the tapes the dogs made, and I feel I understand you, Landau. Your sin is distance."

He sighed. "And yet you are less corrupt than others. . . . There is a certain threshold, an intensity of sin and cynicism, beyond which no society can survive. . . . Listen. I know about Shapers. The Ring Council. Stitched together by black fear and red greed, drawing power from the momentum of its own collapse. But C-K's had hope. You've lived here, you must have at least seen it, if you can't feel it directly. You must know how precious this place is. Under the Cicada Queen, we've drawn survival from a state of mind. Belief counts, confidence is central." The Coordinator looked at me, his dark face sagging. "I'll tell you the truth. And depend on your goodwill. For the proper response."

"Thank you."

"C-K is in crisis. Rumors of the Queen's disaffection have brought the Market to the point of collapse. This time they're more than rumors, Landau. The Queen if on the point of defection from C-K."

Stunned, I slumped suddenly into my chair. My jaw dropped. I closed it with a snap.

"Once the Market collapses," the Coordinator said, "it means the end of all we had. The news is already spreading. Soon there will be a run against the Czarina-Kluster banking system. The system will crash. C-K will die."

"But . . . ," I said. "If it's the Queen's own doing . . ." I was having trouble breathing.

"It's *always* the doing of the Investors, Landau; it's been that way ever since they first swept in and made our wars into an institution. . . . We Mechanists had you Shapers at bay. We ruled the entire system while you hid in terror in the Rings. It was your trade with the Investors that got you on your feet again. In fact, they deliberately built you up, so that they could maintain a competitive trade market, pit the human race against itself, to their own profit. . . . Look at C-K. We live in harmony here. That could be the case everywhere. It's their doing."

"Are you saying," I said, "that the history of C-K is an Investor scheme? That the Queen was never really in disgrace?"

"They're not infallible," the Coordinator said. "I can save the Market, and C-K, if I can exploit their own greed. It's your jewels, Landau. Your jewels. I saw the Queen's reaction when her . . . damned lackey Wellspring presented your gift. You learn to know their moods, these Investors. She was livid with greed. Your patent could catalyze a major industry."

"You're wrong about Wellspring," I said. "The jewel was his idea. I was working with endolithic lichens. 'If they can live within stones they can live within jewels,' he said. I only did the busy-work."

"But the patent's in your name." The Coordinator looked at the toes of his scaled boots. "With our catalyst, I could save the Market. I want you to transfer your patent from Eisho Zaibatsu to me. To the Czarina-Kluster People's Corporate Republic."

I tried to be tactful. "The situation does seem desperate," I said, "but no one within the Market really wants it destroyed. There are other powerful forces preparing for a rebound. Please understand—it's not for any personal gain that I must keep my patent. The revenue is already pledged. To terraforming."

A sour grimace deepened the crevasses in the Coordinator's face. He leaned forward and his shoulders tightened with a muffled creaking of plastic. "Terraforming! Oh yes, I'm familiar with the so-called moral arguments. The cold abstractions of bloodless ideologues. What about respect? Obligation? Loyalty? Are these foreign terms to you?"

I said, "It's not that simple. Wellspring says—"

"Wellspring!" he shouted. "He's no Terran, you fool, he's only a renegade, a traitor scarcely a hundred years old, who sold himself utterly to the aliens. They fear us, you see. They fear our energy. Our potential to invade their markets, once the star drive is in our hands. It should be obvious, Landau! They want to divert our energies into this enormous Martian boondoggle. We could be competing with them, spreading to the stars in one fantastic wave!" He held his arms out rigid before him, his wrists bent upward, and stared at the tips of his outstretched fingers.

His arms began to tremble. Then he broke, and cradled his head in his corded hands. "C-K could have been great. A core of unity, an island of safety in the chaos. The Investors mean to destroy it. When the Market crashes, when the Queen defects, it means the end."

"Will she really leave?"

"Who knows what she means to do." The Coordinator looked exhausted. "I've suffered seventy years from her little whims and humiliations. I don't know what it is to care anymore. Why should I break my heart trying to glue things together with your stupid knickknacks? After all, there's still the discreet!"

He looked up ferociously. "That's where your meddling sent the Councilman. Once we've lost everything, they'll be thick enough with blood to swim in!"

He leaped from his desk top, bounced across the carpet and dragged me bodily from the chair. I grabbed feebly at his wrists. My arms and legs flopped as he shook me. The tiger scuttled closer, clicking. "I hate you," he roared, "I hate everything you stand for! I'm sick of your Clique and their philosophies and their pudding smiles. You've killed a good friend with your meddling.

"Get out! Get out of C-K. You have forty-eight hours. After that I'll have you arrested and sold to the highest bidder." He threw me contemptuously backward. I collapsed at once in the heavy gravity, my head thudding against the carpet.

The tiger pulled me to my feet as the Coordinator clambered back into his oversized chair. He looked into his Market screen as I climbed trembling onto the tiger's back.

"Oh, no," he said softly. "Treason." The tiger took me away.

I found Wellspring, at last, in Dogtown. Dogtown was a chaotic subcluster, pinwheeling slowly to itself above the rotational axis of C-K. It was a port and customhouse, a tangle of shipyards, storage drogues, quarantines, and social houses, catering to the vices of the footloose, the isolated, and the estranged.

Dogtown was the place to come when no one else would have you. It swarmed with transients: prospectors, privateers, criminals, derelicts from sects whose innovations had collapsed, bankrupts, defectors, purveyors of hazardous pleasures. Accordingly the entire area swarmed with dogs, and with subtler monitors. Dogtown was a genuinely dangerous place, thrumming with a deranged and predatory vitality. Constant surveillance had destroyed all sense of shame.

I found Wellspring in the swollen bubble of a tubeway bar, discussing a convoluted business deal with a man he introduced as "the Modem." The Modem was a member of a small but vigorous Mechanist sect known in C-K slang as Lobsters. These Lobsters lived exclusively within skin-tight life-support systems, flanged here and there with engines and input-output jacks. The suits were faceless and dull black. The Lobsters looked like chunks of shadow.

I shook the Modem's rough, room-temperature gauntlet and strapped myself to the table.

I peeled a squeezebulb from the table's adhesive surface and had a drink. "I'm in trouble," I said. "Can we speak before this man?"

Wellspring laughed. "Are you joking? This is Dogtown! Everything we say goes onto more tapes than you have teeth, young Landau. Besides, the Modem is an old friend. His skewed vision should be of some use."

"Very well." I began explaining. Wellspring pressed for details. I omitted nothing.

"Oh, dear," Wellspring said when I had finished. "Well, hold on to your monitors, Modem, for you are about to see rumor break the speed of light. Odd that this obscure little bistro should launch the news that is certain to destroy C-K." He said this quite loudly and I looked quickly around the bar. The jaws of the clientele hung open with shock. Little blobs of saliva oscillated near their lips.

"The Queen is gone, then," Wellspring said. "She's probably been gone for weeks. Well, I suppose it couldn't be helped. Even an Investor's greed has limits. The Advisers couldn't lead her by the nose forever.

Perhaps she'll show up somewhere else, some habitat more suited to her emotional needs. I suppose I had best get to my monitors and cut my losses while the Market still has some meaning."

Wellspring parted the ribbons of his slashed sleeve and looked casually at his forearm computer. The bar emptied itself, suddenly and catastrophically, the customers trailed by their personal dogs. Near the exit, a vicious hand-to-hand fight broke out between two Shaper renegades. They spun with piercing cries through the crunching grip-and-tumble of free-fall jujitsu. Their dogs watched impassively.

Soon the three of us were alone with the bar servos and half a dozen fascinated dogs. "I could tell from my last audience that the Queen would leave," Wellspring said calmly. "C-K had outlived its usefulness, anyway. It was important only as the motivational catalyst for the elevation of Mars to the Third Prigoginic Level of Complexity. It was fossilizing under the weight of the Advisers' programs. Typical Mech shortsightedness. Pseudopragmatic materialism. They had it coming."

Wellspring showed an inch of embroidered undercuff as he signaled a servo for another round. "The Councilman you mentioned has retired to a discreet. He won't be the last one they haul out by the heels."

"What will I do?" I said. "I'm losing everything. What will become of the Clique?"

Wellspring frowned. "Come on, Landau! Show some Posthuman fluidity. The first thing to do, of course, is to get you into exile. I imagine our friend the Modem here can help with that."

"To be sure," the Modem enunciated. He had a vocoder unit strapped to his throat and it projected an inhumanly beautiful synthesized voice. "Our ship, the *Crowned Pawn*, is hauling a cargo of iceteroid mass drivers to the Ring Council. It's for the Terraforming Project. Any friend of Wellspring's is welcome to join us."

I laughed incredulously. "For me, that's suicide. Go back to the Council? I might as well open my throat."

"Be at ease," the Modem soothed. "I'll have the medimechs work you over and graft on one of our shells. One Lobster is very much like another. You'll be perfectly safe, under the skin."

I was shocked. "Become a Mech?"

"You don't have to *stay* one," Wellspring said. "It's a simple procedure. A few nerve grafts, some anal surgery, a tracheotomy. . . . You lose on taste and touch, but the other senses are vastly expanded."

"Yes," said the Modem. "And you can step alone into naked space, and laugh."

"Right!" said Wellspring. "More Shapers should wear Mech technics.

It's like your lichens, Hans. Become a symbiosis for a while. It'll broaden your horizons."

I said, "You don't do . . . anything *cranial*, do you?"

"No," said the Modem offhandedly. "Or, at least, we don't have to. Your brain's your own."

I thought. "Can you do it in"—I looked at Wellspring's forearm—"thirty-eight hours?"

"If we hurry," the Modem said. He detached himself from the table. I followed him.

The *Crowned Pawn* was under way. My skin clung magnetically to a ship's girder as we accelerated. I had my vision set for normal wavelengths as I watched Czarina-Kluster receding.

Tears stung the fresh tracks of hair-thin wires along my deadened eyeballs. C-K wheeled slowly, like a galaxy in a jeweled web. Here and there along the network, flares pulsed as suburbs began the tedious and tragic work of cutting themselves loose. C-K was in the grip of terror.

I longed for the warm vitality of my Clique. I was no Lobster. They were alien. They were solipsistic pinpoints in the galactic night, their humanity a forgotten pulp behind black armor.

The *Crowned Pawn* was like a ship turned inside out. It centered around a core of massive magnetic engines, fed by drones from a chunk of reaction mass. Outside these engines was a skeletal metal framework where Lobsters clung like cysts or skimmed along on induced magnetic fields. There were cupolas here and there on the skeleton where the Lobsters hooked into fluidic computers or sheltered themselves from solar storms and ring-system electrofluxes.

They never ate. They never drank. Sex involved a clever cyberstimulation through cranial plugs. Every five years or so they "molted" and had their skins scraped clean of the stinking accumulation of mutated bacteria that scummed them over in the stagnant warmth.

They knew no fear. Agoraphobia was a condition easily crushed with drugs. They were self-contained and anarchical. Their greatest pleasure was to sit along a girder and open their amplified senses to the depths of space, watching stars past the limits of ultraviolet and infrared, or staring into the flocculate crawling plaque of the surface of the sun, or just sitting and soaking in watts of solar energy through their skins while they listened with wired ears to the warbling of Van Allen belts and the musical tick of pulsars.

There was nothing bad about them, but they were not human. As distant and icy as comets, they were creatures of the vacuum, bored with the outmoded paradigms of blood and bone. I saw within them the first stirrings of the Fifth Prigoginic Leap—that postulated Fifth Level of Complexity as far beyond intelligence as intelligence is from amoebic life, or life from inert matter.

They frightened me. Their bland indifference to human limitations gave them the sinister charisma of saints.

The Modem came skimming along a girder and latched himself soundlessly beside me. I turned my ears on and heard his voice above the radio hiss of the engines. "You have a call, Landau. From C-K. Follow me."

I flexed my feet and skimmed along the rail behind him. We entered the radiation lock of an iron cupola, leaving it open since the Lobsters disliked closed spaces.

Before me, on a screen, was the tear-streaked face of Valery Korstad. "Valery!" I said.

"Is that you, Hans?"

"Yes. Yes, darling. It's good to see you."

"Can't you take that mask off, Hans? I want to see your face."

"It's not a mask, darling. And my face is, well, not a pretty sight. All those wires. . . ."

"You sound different, Hans. Your voice sounds different."

"That's because this voice is a radio analogue. It's synthesized."

"How do I know it's really you, then? God, Hans . . . I'm so afraid. Everything . . . it's just evaporating. The Froth is . . . there's a biohazard scare, something smashed the gel frames in your domicile, I guess it was the dogs, and now the lichen, the damned lichen is sprouting everywhere. It grows so fast!"

"I designed it to grow fast, Valery, that was the whole point. Tell them to use a metal aerosol or sulfide particulates; either one will kill it in a few hours. There's no need for panic."

"No need! Hans, the discreets are suicide factories. C-K is through! We've lost the Queen!"

"There's still the Project," I said. "The Queen was just an excuse, a catalyst. The Project can draw as much respect as the damned Queen. The groundwork's been laid for years. This is the moment. Tell the Clique to liquidate all they have. The Froth must move to Martian orbit."

Valery began to drift sideways. "That's all you cared about all along, wasn't it? The Project! I degraded myself, and you, with your cold, that Shaper distance, you left me in despair!"

"Valery!" I shouted, stricken. "I called you a dozen times, it was you who closed yourself off, it was me who needed warmth after those years under the dogs—"

"You could have done it!" she screamed, her face white with passion. "If you cared you would have broken in to prove it! You expected me to come crawling in humiliation? Black armor or dog's eye glass, Hans, what's the difference? You're still not with me!"

I felt the heat of raw fury touching my numbed skin. "Blame me, then! How was I to know your rituals, your sick little secrets? I thought you'd thrown me over while you sneered and whored with Wellspring! Did you think I'd compete with the man who showed me my salvation? I would have slashed my wrists to see you smile, and you gave me nothing, nothing but disaster!"

A look of cold shock spread across her painted face. Her mouth opened, but no words came forth. Finally, with a small smile of total despair, she broke the connection. The screen went black.

I turned to the Modem. "I want to go back," I said.

"Sorry," he said. "First, you'd be killed. And second, we don't have the wattage to turn back. We're carrying a massive cargo." He shrugged. "Besides, C-K is in dissolution. We've known it was coming a long time. In fact, some colleagues of ours are arriving there within the week with a second cargo of mass drivers. They'll fetch top prices as the Kluster dissolves."

"You knew?"

"We have our sources."

"Wellspring?"

"Who, him? He's leaving, too. He wants to be in Martian orbit when *that* hits." The Modem glided outside the cupola and pointed along the plane of the ecliptic. I followed his gaze, shifting clumsily along the visual wavelengths.

I saw the etched and ghostly flare of the Martian asteroid's mighty engines. "The iceteroid," I said.

"Yes, of course. The comet of your disaster, so to speak. A useful symbol for C-K's decay."

"Yes," I said. I thought I recognized the hand of Wellspring in this. As the ice payload skimmed past C-K the panicked eyes of its inhabitants would follow it. Suddenly I felt a soaring sense of hope.

"How about *that?*" I said. "Could you land me there?"

"On the asteroid?"

"Yes! They're going to detach the engines, aren't they? In orbit! I can join my fellows there, and I won't miss the Prigoginic catalyst!"

"I'll check." The Modem fed a series of parameters into one of the fluidics. "Yes. . . . I could sell you a parasite engine that you could strap on. With enough wattage and a cybersystem to guide you, you could match trajectory within, say, seventy-two hours."

"Good! Good! Let's do that, then."

"Very well," he said. "There remains only the question of price."

I had time to think about the price as I burned along through the piercing emptiness. I thought I had done well. With C-K's Market in collapse I would need new commercial agents for the Eisho jewels. Despite their eeriness, I felt I could trust the Lobsters.

The cybersystem led me to a gentle groundfall on the sunside of the asteroid. It was ablating slowly in the heat of the distant sun and infrared wisps of volatiles puffed here and there from cracks in the bluish ice.

The iceteroid was a broken spar calved from the breakup of one of Saturn's ancient glacial moons. It was a mountainous splintered crag with the fossilized scars of primordial violence showing themselves in wrenched and jagged cliffs and buttresses. It was roughly egg-shaped, five kilometers by three. Its surface had the bluish pitted look of ice exposed for thousands of years to powerful electric fields.

I roughened the gripping surfaces of my gauntlets and pulled myself and the parasite engine hand over hand into shadow. The engine's wattage was exhausted, but I didn't want it drifting off in the ablation.

I unfolded the radio dish the Modem had sold me and anchored it to a crag, aligning it with C-K. Then I plugged in.

The scope of the disaster was total. C-K had always prided itself on its open broadcasts, part of the whole atmosphere of freedom that had vitalized it. Now open panic was dwindling into veiled threats, and then, worst of all, into treacherous bursts of code. From all over the system, pressures long held back poured in.

The offers and threats mounted steadily, until the wretched cliques of C-K were pressed to the brink of civil war. Hijacked dogs prowled the tubes and corridors, tools of power elites made cruel by fear. Vicious kangaroo courts stripped dissidents of their status and property. Many chose the discreets.

Creche cooperatives broke up. Stone-faced children wandered aimlessly through suburban halls, dazed on mood suppressants. Precious few dared to care any longer. Sweating Marketeers collapsed across their keyboards, sinuses bleeding from inhalants. Women stepped naked out of commandeered airlocks and died in sparkling gushes of frozen air. Cicadas struggled to weep through altered eyes, or floated in darkened bistros, numbed with disaster and drugs.

Centuries of commercial struggle had only sharpened the teeth of the cartels. They slammed in with the cybernetic precision of the Mechanists, with the slick unsettling brilliance of the Reshaped. With the collapse of the Market, C-K's industries were up for grabs. Commercial agents and arrogant diplomats annexed whole complexes. Groups of their new employees stumbled through the Queen's deserted Palace, vandalizing anything they couldn't steal outright.

The frightened subfactions of C-K were caught in the classic double bind that had alternately shaped and splintered the destinies of humanity in Space. On the one hand their technically altered modes of life and states of mind drove them irresistibly to distrust and fragmentation; on the other, isolation made them the prey of united cartels. They might even be savaged by the pirates and privateers that the cartels openly condemned and covertly supported.

And instead of helping my Clique, I was a black dot clinging like a spore to the icy flank of a frozen mountain.

It was during those sad days that I began to appreciate my skin. If Wellspring's plans had worked, then there would come a flowering. I would survive this ice in my sporagiac casing, as a wind-blown speck of lichen will last out decades to spread at last into devouring life. Wellspring had been wise to put me here. I trusted him. I would not fail him.

As boredom gnawed at me I sank gently into a contemplative stupor. I opened my eyes and ears past the point of overload. Consciousness swallowed itself and vanished into the roaring half existence of an event horizon. Space-time, the Second Level of Complexity, proclaimed its noumenon in the whine of stars, the rumble of planets, the transcendent crackle and gush of the uncoiling sun.

There came a time when I was roused at last by the sad and empty symphonies of Mars.

I shut down the suit's amplifiers. I no longer needed them. The catalyst, after all, is always buried by the process.

I decided I would move south along the asteroid's axis, where I was sure to be discovered by the team sent to recover the mass driver. The driver's cybersystem had reoriented the asteroid for partial deceleration, and the south end had the best view of the planet.

Only moments after the final burn, the ice mass was matched by a pirate. It was a slim and beautiful Shaper craft, with long ribbed sun wings of iridescent fabric as thin as oil on water. It shining organometallic hull hid eighth-generation magnetic engines with marvelous speed and power. The blunt nodes of weapons systems knobbed its sleekness.

I went into hiding, burrowing deep into a crevasse to avoid radar. I waited until curiosity and fear got the better of me. Then I crawled out and crept to a lookout point along a fractured ice ridge.

The ship had docked and sat poised on its cocked manipulator arms, their mantislike tips anchored into the ice. A crew of Mechanist mining drones had decamped and were boring into the ice of a clean-sheared plateau.

No Shaper pirate would have mining drones on board. The ship itself had undergone systems deactivation and sat inert and beautiful as an insect in amber, its vast sun wings folded. There was no sign of any crew.

I was not afraid of drones. I pulled myself boldly along the ice to observe their operations. No one challenged me.

I watched as the ungainly drones rasped and chipped the ice. Ten meters down they uncovered the glint of metal.

It was an airlock.

There they waited. Time passed. They received no further orders. They shut themselves down and crouched inert on the ice, as dead as the boulders around us.

For safety's sake I decided to enter the ship first.

As its airlock opened, the ship began switching itself back on. I entered the cabin. The pilot's couch was empty.

There was no one on board.

It took me almost two hours to work my way into the ship's cybersystem. Then I learned for certain what I had already suspected. It was Wellspring's ship.

I left the ship and crawled across the ice to the airlock. It opened easily. Wellspring had never been one to complicate things unnecessarily.

Beyond the airlock's second door a chamber blazed with blue-white light. I adjusted my eye systems and crawled inside.

At the far end, in the iceteroid's faint gravity, there was a bed of jewels. It was not a conventional bed. It was simply a huge, loose-packed heap of precious gems.

The Queen was asleep on top of it.

I used my eyes again. There was no infrared heat radiating from her. She lay quite still, her ancient arms clutching something to her chest, her three-toed legs drawn up along her body, her massive tail curled up beneath her rump and between her legs. Her huge head, the size of a man's torso, was encased in a gigantic crowned helmet encrusted with blazing diamonds. She was not breathing. Her eyes were closed. Her thick, scaled lips were drawn back slightly, showing two blunt rows of peg-shaped, yellowing teeth.

She was ice-cold, sunk in some kind of alien cryosleep. Wellspring's coup was revealed. The Queen had joined willingly in her own abduction. Wellspring had stolen her in an act of heroic daring, robbing his rivals in C-K to begin again in Martian orbit. It was an astonishing fait accompli that would have put him and his disciples into unquestioned power.

I was overcome with admiration for his plan. I wondered, though, why he had not accompanied his ship. Doubtless there were medicines aboard to wake the Queen and spirit her off to the nascent Kluster.

I moved nearer. I had never seen an Investor face to face. Still, I could tell after a moment that there was something wrong with her skin. I'd thought it was a trick of the light at first. But then I saw what she had in her hands.

It was the lichen jewel. The rapacity of her clawed grip had split it along one of the fracture planes, already weakened by the lichens' acids. Released from its crystalline prison, and spurred to frenzy by the powerful light, the lichens had crept onto her scaly fingers, and then up her wrist, and then, in an explosive paroxysm of life, over her entire body. She glittered green and gold with devouring fur. Even her eyes, her gums.

I went back to the ship. It was always said of us Shapers that we were brilliant under pressure. I reactivated the drones and had them refill their borehole. They tamped ice chips into it and melted them solid with the parasite rocket.

I worked on intuition, but all my training told me to trust it. That was why I had stripped the dead Queen and loaded every jewel aboard the ship. I felt a certainty beyond any chain of logic. The future lay before me like a drowsing woman awaiting the grip of her lover.

Wellspring's tapes were mine. The ship was his final sanctum, programmed in advance. I understood then the suffering and the ambition that had driven him, and that now were mine.

His dead hand had drawn representatives of every faction to witness the Prigoginic impact. The protoKluster already in orbit was made up exclusively of drones and monitors. It was natural that the observers would turn to me. My ship controlled the drones.

The first panic-stricken refugees told me of Wellspring's fate. He had been dragged heels first from a discreet, followed closely by the bloodless corpse of sad Valery Korstad. Never again would she give a man delight. Never again would his charisma enthrall the Clique. It might have been a double suicide. Or, perhaps more likely, she murdered him, and then herself. Wellspring could never believe that there was anything beyond his abilities to cure. A madwoman and a barren world were part and parcel of the same challenge. Eventually he met his limit, and it killed him. The details scarcely matter. A discreet had swallowed them in any case.

When I heard the news, the ice around my heart sealed shut, seamless and pure.

I had Wellspring's will broadcast as the iceteroid began its final plunge into the atmosphere. Tapes sucked the broadcast in as volatiles peeled smoking into the thin, starved air of Mars.

I lied about the will. I invented it. I had Wellspring's taped memories to hand; it was a simple thing to change my artificial voice to counterfeit his, to set the stage for my own crucial ascendancy. It was necessary for the future of T-K, Terraform-Kluster, that I proclaim myself Wellspring's heir.

Power accreted around me like rumors. It was said that beneath my armor I *was* Wellspring, that the real Landau had been the one to die with Valery in C-K. I encouraged the rumors. Misconceptions would unite the Kluster. I knew T-K would be a city without rival. Here, abstractions would take on flesh, phantoms would feed us. Once our ideals had slammed it into being, T-K would gather strength, unstoppably. My jewels alone gave it a power base that few cartels could match.

With understanding came forgiveness. I forgave Wellspring. His lies, his deceptions, had moved me better than the chimeric "truth." What did it matter? If we needed solid bedrock, we would have it orbit us.

And the fearsome beauty of that impact! The searing linearity of its descent! It was only one of many, but the one most dear to me. When I saw the milk-drop splatter of its collision into Mars, the concussive orgasmic gush of steam from the Queen's covert and frozen tomb, I knew at once what my mentor had known. A man driven by something greater than himself dares everything and fears nothing. Nothing at all.

From behind my black armor, I rule the Polycarbon Clique. Their elite are my Advisers. I remember the cold, but I no longer fear it. I have buried it forever, as the cold of Mars is buried beneath its seething carpet of greenery. The two of us, now one, have stolen a whole planet from the realm of Death. And I do not fear the cold. No, not at all.

JAMES TIPTREE, JR.

Beyond the Dead Reef

People have been polluting the sea for countless millennia, ever since the first Cro-Magnon tossed the first piece of trash into the water, but it is only in the last hundred years or so that the problem has grown to really disastrous proportions. We are all, collectively, still tossing stuff into the sea—only now there are so many *more* of us, billions and billions more, and the stuff we are tossing in is mostly either poisonous or nonbiodegradable or both: plastic bottles and cups, beer cans, automobile tires, little Styrofoam peanuts, burned-out fluorescent tubes, rusting hubcaps, engine parts, sheets of polyethylene . . . To say nothing of massive oil spills, leaky containers of radioactive waste, and factories that pour millions of tons of lethal chemical sludge and untreated sewage directly into the ocean. Things have gotten so bad that Thor Heyerdahl, during his *Ra* expedition, found masses of floating pollutants even in the most remote regions of the Atlantic. In the last couple of decades people have begun to speak of the possibility that the sea *itself* might die from such treatment, a concept almost literally unimaginable only a few generations ago.

But—as this haunting story suggests—if the sea *is* doomed to die, it may go down *fighting* . . .

By now, probably everyone knows that the mysterious figure, James Tiptree, Jr.—for many years isolate and closemouthed enough to qualify as the B. Traven of science fiction—is really a pseudonym of Dr. Alice Sheldon, a semiretired experimental psychologist who also writes under the name Raccoona Sheldon. As Tiptree, Dr. Sheldon won two Nebulas and two Hugo awards (she also won a Nebula Award as Raccoona Sheldon) and established a reputation as one of the very best short-story writers in SF. She has published five books as Tiptree: the collections *Ten Thousand Light Years From Home*, *Warmworlds and Otherwise*, *Star Songs of an Old Primate*, and *Out of the Everywhere*, and a novel *Up the Walls of the World*.

"Beyond the Dead Reef" is one of a sequence of stories about strange doings in the Quintana Roo country of Yucatan; they will be collected in 1984 by Arkham House as *Tales of the Quintana Roo*. Upcoming are another new collection, as yet untitled, from Doubleday and a new novel called *Green, Go*.

BEYOND THE DEAD REEF

James Tiptree, Jr.

A love that is not sated
Calls from a poisoned bed;
Where monsters half-created
writhe, unliving and undead.
None knows for what they're fated;
None knows on what they've fed.

My informant was, of course, spectacularly unreliable.

The only character reference I have for him comes from the intangible nuances of a small restaurant-owner's remarks, and the only confirmation of his tale lies in the fact that an illiterate fishing-guide appears to believe it. If I were to recount all the reasons why no sane mind should take it seriously, we could never begin. So I will only report the fact that today I found myself shuddering with terror when a perfectly innocent sheet of seaworn plastic came slithering over my snorkeling-reef, as dozens have done for years—and get on with the story.

I met him one evening this December at the Cozumel *Buzo*, on my first annual supply trip. As usual, the *Buzo's* outer rooms were jammed with tourist divers and their retinues and gear. That's standard. *El Buzo* means, roughly, The Diving, and the *Buzo* is their place. Marcial's big sign in the window reads "DIVVERS UELCOME! BRING YR FISH WE COK WITH CAR. FIRST DRINK FREE!"

Until he went in for the "Divvers," Marcial's had been a small quiet place where certain delicacies like stone-crab could be at least semi-legally obtained. Now he did a roaring trade in snappers and groupers cooked to order at outrageous fees, with a flourishing sideline in fresh fish sales to the neighborhood each morning.

The "roaring" was quite literal. I threaded my way through a crush of burly giants and giantesses of all degrees of nakedness, hairiness, age, proficiency, and inebriation—all eager to share their experiences and plans in voices powered by scuba-deafened ears and Marcial's free drink, beneath which the sound system could scarcely be heard at full blast. (Marcial's only real expense lay in first-drink liquor so strong that few could recall whether what they ultimately ate bore any resemblance to what they had given him to cook.) Only a handful were sitting down yet and the amount of gear underfoot and on the walls would have stocked three sports shops. This was not mere exhibitionism; on an island chronically short of washers, valves and other spare parts the diver who lets his gear out of his sight is apt to find it missing in some vital.

I paused to allow a young lady to complete her massage of the neck of a youth across the aisle who was deep in talk with three others, and had time to notice the extraordinary number of heavy spearguns racked about. Oklahomans, I judged, or perhaps South Florida. But then I caught clipped New England from the center group. Too bad; the killing mania seems to be spreading yearly, and the armament growing ever more menacing and efficient. When I inspected their platters, however, I saw the usual array of lavishly garnished lobsters and common fish. At least they had not yet discovered what to eat.

The mermaiden blocking me completed her task—unthanked—and I continued on my way to the little inner sanctum Marcial keeps for his old clientele. As the heavy doors cut off the uproar, I saw that this room was full too—three tables of dark-suited Mexican businessmen and a decorous family of eight, all quietly intent on their plates. A lone customer sat at the small table by the kitchen door, leaving an empty seat and a child's chair. He was a tall, slightly balding Anglo some years younger than I, in a very decent sports jacket. I recalled having seen him now and then on my banking and shopping trips to the island.

Marcial telegraphed me a go-ahead nod as he passed through laden with more drinks, so I approached.

"Mind if I join you?"

He looked up from his stone-crab and gave me a slow, owlish smile.

"Welcome. A *diverse* welcome," he enunciated carefully. The accent was vaguely British, yet agreeable. I also perceived that he was extremely drunk, but in no common way.

"Thanks."

As I sat down I saw that he was a diver too, but his gear was stowed so unobtrusively I hadn't noticed it. I tried to stack my own modest snorkel outfit as neatly, pleased to note that, like me, he seemed to carry no spearguns. He watched me attentively, blinking once or twice, and then returned to an exquisitely exact dissection of his crab.

When Marcial brought my own platter of crab—unasked—we engaged in our ritual converse. Marcial's English is several orders of magnitude better than my Spanish, but he always does me the delicate courtesy of allowing me to use his tongue. How did I find my rented *casita* on the coco ranch this year? Fine. How goes the tourist business this year? Fine. I learn from Marcial: the slight pause before his answer with a certain tone, meant that in fact the tourist business was lousy so far, but would hopefully pick up; I used the same to convey that in fact my *casa* was in horrible shape but reparable. I tried to cheer him by saying that I thought the *Buzo* would do better than the general *tourismo*, because the diving enthusiasm was spreading in the States. "True," he conceded. "So long as they don't discover other places—like Belizé." Here he flicked a glance at my companion, who gave his solemn blink. I remarked that my country's politics were in disastrous disarray, and he conceded the same for his; the *Presidente* and his pals had just made off with much of the nation's treasury. And I expressed the hope that Mexico's new oil would soon prove a great boom. "Ah, but it will be a long time before it gets to the little people like us," said Marcial, with so much more than his normal acerbity that I refrained from my usual joke about his having a Swiss bank account. The uproar from the outer rooms had risen several decibels, but just before Marcial had to leave he paused and said in a totally different voice, "My grandson Antonito Vincente has four teeth!"

His emotion was so profound that I seized his free hand and shook it lightly, congratulating him in English. And then he was gone, taking on his "Mexican waiter" persona quite visibly as he passed the inner doors.

As we resumed our attention to the succulence before us, my companion said in his low, careful voice, "Nice chap, Marcial. He likes you."

"It's mutual," I told him between delicate mouthfuls. Stone-crab is not to be gulped. "Perhaps because I'm old enough to respect the limits where friendship ends and the necessities of life take over."

"I say, that's rather good." My companion chuckled. "Respect for the limits where friendship ends and the necessities of life take over, eh? Very few Yanks do, you know. At least the ones we see down here."

His speech was almost unslurred, and there were no drinks before him on the table. We chatted idly a bit more. It was becoming apparent that we would finish simultaneously and be faced with the prospect of leaving together, which could be awkward, if he, like me, had no definite plans for the evening.

The dilemma was solved when my companion excused himself momentarily just as Marcial happened by.

I nodded to his empty chair. "Is he one of your old customers, Señor Marcial?"

As always Marcial understood the situation at once. "One of the oldest," he told me, and added low-voiced, *"muy bueno gentes*—a really good guy. *Un poco de difficultates*—" he made an almost imperceptible gesture of drinking—"But *controllado.* And he has also *négocios*—I do not know all, but some are important for his country. —So you really like the crab?" he concluded in his normal voice. "We are honored."

My companion was emerging from the rather dubious regions that held the *excusado.*

Marcial's recommendation was good enough for me. Only one puzzle remained: what was his country? As we both refused *dulce* and coffee, I suggested that he might care to stroll down to the Marina with me and watch the sunset.

"Good thought."

We paid Marcial's outrageous bills, and made our way through the exterior bedlam, carrying our gear. One of the customers was brandishing his speargun as he protested his bill. Marcial seemed to have lost all his English except the words "Police," and cooler heads were attempting to calm the irate one. "All in a night's work," my companion commented as we emerged into a blaze of golden light.

The marina to our left was a simple L-shaped *muelle,* or pier, still used by everything from dinghies to commercial fisherman and baby yachts. It will be a pity when and if the town decides to separate the sports tourist trade from the more interesting working craft. As we walked out toward the pier in the last spectacular color of the tropic sunset over the mainland, the rigging lights of a cruise ship standing out in the channel came on, a fairyland illusion over the all-too-dreary reality.

"They'll be dumping and cleaning out their used bunkers tonight," my companion said, slurring a trifle now. He had a congenial walking gait, long-strided but leisurely. I had the impression that his drunkenness had returned slightly; perhaps the fresh air. "Damn crime."

"I couldn't agree more," I told him. "I remember when we used to start snorkeling and scuba-diving right off the shore here—you could almost wade out to untouched reefs. And now—"

There was no need to look; one could smell it. The effluvia of half a dozen hotels and the town behind ran out of pipes that were barely covered at low tide; only a few parrot fish, who can stand anything, remained by the hotelside restaurants to feed on the crusts the tourists threw them from their tables. And only the very ignorant would try out—once—the dilapidated Sunfish and water-ski renters who plied the small stretches of beach between hotels.

We sat down on one of the near benches to watch a commercial trawler haul net. I had been for some time aware that my companion, while of largely British culture, was not completely Caucasian. There was a minute softness to the voice, a something not quite dusky about hair and fingernails—not so much as to be what in my youth was called "A touch of the tarbrush," but nothing that originated in Yorkshire, either. Nor was it the obvious Hispano-Indian. I recollected Marcial's earlier speech and enlightenment came.

"Would I be correct in taking Marcial's allusion to mean that you are a British Honduran—forgive me, I mean a Belizéian, or Belizan?"

"Nothing to forgive, old chap. We haven't existed long enough to get our adjectives straight."

"May god send you do." I was referring to the hungry maws of Guatemala and Honduras, the little country's big neighbors, who had the worst of intentions toward her. "I happen to be quite a fan of your country. I had some small dealings there after independence that involved getting all my worldly goods out of your customs on a national holiday, and people couldn't have been finer to me."

"Ah yes. Belizé the blessed, where sixteen nationalities live in perfect racial harmony. The odd thing is, they do."

"I could see that. But I couldn't quite count all sixteen."

"My own grandmother was a Burmese—so called. I think it was the closest grandfather could come to black. Although the mix *is* extraordinary."

"My factor there was a very dark Hindu with red hair and a Scottish accent, named Robinson. I had to hire him in seven minutes. He was a miracle of efficiency. I hope he's still going."

"Robinson . . . Used to work for customs?"

"Why, yes, now you recall it."

"He's fine . . . Of course, we felt it when the British left. Among other things, half the WCs in the hotels broke down the first month. But there are more important things in life than plumbing."

"That I believe . . . But you know, I've never been sure how much help the British would have been to you. Two years before your independence I called the British embassy with a question about your immigration laws, and believe it or not I couldn't find one soul who even knew there *was* a British Honduras, let alone that they owned it. One child finally denied it flatly and hung up. And this was their main embassy in Washington, D.C. I realized then that Britain was not only sick, but crazy."

"Actually denied our existence, eh?" My companion's voice held a depth and timbre of sadness such as I have heard only from victims of better-known world wrongs. Absently his hand went under his jacket, and he pulled out something gleaming.

"Forgive me." It was a silver flask, exquisitely plain. He uncapped and drank, a mere swallow, but, I suspected, something of no ordinary power. He licked his lips as he recapped it, and sat up straighter while he put it away.

"Shall we move along out to the point?"

"With pleasure."

We strolled on, passing a few late sports boats disgorging hungry divers.

"I'm going to do some modest exploring tomorrow," I told him. "A guide named Jorge"—in Spanish it's pronounced Hor-hay—"Jorge Chuc is taking me out to the end of the north reef. He says there's a pretty little untouched spot there. I hope so. Today I went south, it was so badly shot over I almost wept. Cripples—and of course shark everywhere. Would you believe I found a big she-turtle, trying to live with a steel bolt through her neck? I managed to catch her, but all I could do for her was pull it out. I hope she makes it."

"Bad . . . Turtles are tough, though. If it wasn't vital you may have saved her. But did you say that Jorge Chuc is taking you to the end of the north reef?"

"Yes, why. Isn't it any good?"

"Oh, there is one pretty spot. But there's some very bad stuff there too. If you don't mind my advice, don't go far from the boat. I mean, a couple of meters. And don't follow anything. And above all be very sure it *is* Jorge's boat."

His voice had become quite different, with almost military authority.

"A couple of meters!" I expostulated. "But—"

"I know, I know. What I don't know is why Chuc is taking you there at all." He thought for a moment. "You haven't by any chance offended him, have you? In any way?"

"Why no—we were out for a long go yesterday, and had a nice chat on the way back. Yes . . . although he is a trifle changeable, isn't he? I put it down to fatigue, and gave him some extra *dinero* for being only one party."

My companion made a untranslatable sound, compounded of dubiety, speculation, possible enlightenment, and strong suspicion.

"Did he tell you the name of that part of the reef? Or that it's out of sight of land?"

"Yes, he said it was far out. And that part of it was so poor it's called dead."

"And you chatted—forgive me, but was your talk entirely in Spanish?"

I chuckled deprecatingly. "Well, yes—I know my Spanish is pretty horrible, but he seemed to get the drift."

"Did you mention his family?"

"Oh yes—I could draw you the whole Chuc family tree."

"H'mmm. . . ." My companion's eyes had been searching the pierside where the incoming boats were being secured for the night.

"Ah. There's Chuc now. This is none of my business, you understand—but do I have your permission for a short word with Jorge?"

"Why yes. If you think it necessary."

"I do, my friend. I most certainly do."

"Carry on."

His long-legged stride had already carried him to Chuc's big skiff, the *Estrellita*. Chuc was covering his motors. I had raised my hand in greeting, but he was apparently too busy to respond. Now he greeted my companion briefly, but did not turn when he clambered into the boat uninvited. I could not hear the interchange. But presently the two men were standing, faces somewhat averted from each other as they conversed. My companion made rather a long speech, ending with questions. There was little response from Chuc, until a sudden outburst from him took me by surprise. The odd dialog went on for some time after that; Chuc seemed to calm down. Then the tall Belizian waved me over.

"Will you say exactly what I tell you to say!"

"Why, yes, if you think it's important."

"It is. Can you say in Spanish, 'I ask your pardon, Mr. Chuc. I mistook myself in your language. I did not say anything of what you thought I said. Please forgive my error. And please let us be friends again.' "

"I'll try."

I stumbled through the speech, that I will not try to reproduce here, as I repeated several phrases with what I thought was better accent, and I'm sure I threw several verbs into the conditional future. Before I was through, Chuc was beginning to grin. When I came to the "friends" part he had relaxed, and after a short pause, said in very tolerable English, "I see, so I accept your apology. We will indeed be friends. It was a regrettable error. . . . And I advise you, do not again speak in Spanish."

We shook on it.

"Good," said my companion. "And he'll take you out tomorrow, but not to the Dead Reef. And keep your hands off your wallet tonight, but I suggest liberality tomorrow eve."

We left Chuc to finish up, and paced down to a bench at the very end of the *muelle*. The last colors of evening, peaches and rose shot with unearthly green, were set off by a few low-lying clouds already in gray shadow, like sharks of the sky passing beneath a sentimental vision of bliss.

"Now what was all *that* about!" I demanded of my new friend. He was just tucking the flask away again, and shuddered lightly.

"I don't wish to seem overbearing but *that* probably saved your harmless life, my friend. I repeat Jorge's advice—stay away from that Spanish of yours unless you are absolutely sure of being understood."

"I know it's ghastly."

"That's not actually the problem. The problem is that it isn't ghastly enough. Your pronunciation is quite fair, and you've mastered some good idioms, so people who don't know you think you speak much more fluently than you do. In this case the trouble came from your damned rolled rrrs. Would you mind saying the words for 'but' and 'dog'?"

"*Pero . . . perro.* Why?"

"The difference between a rolled and a single r, particularly in Maya Spanish, is very slight. The upshot of it was that you not only insulted his boat in various ways, but you ended by referring to his mother as a dog. . . . He was going to take you out beyond the Dead Reef and leave you there."

"*What?*"

"Yes. And if it hadn't been I who asked—he knows I know the story—you'd never have understood a thing. Until you turned up as a statistic."

"Oh Jesus Christ. . . ."

"Yes," he said dryly.

"I guess some thanks are in order," I said finally. "But words seem a shade inadequate. Have you any suggestions?"

My companion suddenly turned and gave me a highly concentrated look.

"You were in World War Two, weren't you? And afterwards you worked around a bit." He wasn't asking me, so I kept quiet. "Right now, I don't see anything," he went on. "But just possibly I might be calling on you, with something you may not like." He grinned.

"If it's anything I can do from a wheelchair, I won't forget."

"Fair enough. We'll say no more about it now."

"Oh yes we will," I countered. "You may not know it, but you owe *me* something. I can smell a story when one smacks me in the face. What I want from you is the story behind this Dead Reef business, and how it is that Jorge knows you know something special about it. If I'm not asking too much? I'd really like to end our evening with your tale of the Dead Reef."

"Oho. My error—I'd forgotten Marcial telling me you wrote . . . Well, I can't say I enjoy reliving it, but maybe it'll have a salutary effect on your future dealings in Spanish. The fact is, I was the one it happened to, and Jorge was driving a certain boat. You realize, though, there's not a shred of proof except my own word? And my own word—" he tapped the pocket holding his flask, "—is only as good as you happen to think it is."

"It's good enough for me."

"Very well then. Very well," he said slowly, leaning back. "It happened about three, no four years back—by god, you know this is hard to tell, though there's not much to it." He fished in another pocket, and took out, not a flask, but the first cigarette I'd seen him smoke, a *Petit Caporal*. "I was still up to a long day's scuba then, and, like you, I wanted to explore north. I'd run into this nice, strong, young couple who wanted the same thing. Their gear was good, they seemed experienced and sensible. So we got a third tank apiece, and hired a trustable boatman—not Jorge, Victor Camul—to take us north over the worst of the reef. It wasn't so bad then, you know.

"We would be swimming north with the current until a certain point, where if you turn east, you run into a long reverse eddy that makes it a lot easier to swim back to Cozumel. And just to be extra safe, Victor was to start out up the eddy in two hours sharp to meet us and bring us home. I hadn't one qualm about the arrangements. Even the weather cooperated—not a cloud, and the forecast perfect. Of course, if you miss up around here, the next stop is four hundred miles to Cuba, but you know that; one gets used to it . . . By the way, have you heard they're still looking for that girl who's been gone two days on a Sunfish with no water?"

I said nothing.

"Sorry." He cleared his throat. "Well, Victor put us out well in sight of shore. We checked watches and compasses and lights. The plan was for the lad Harry to lead, Ann to follow, and me to bring up the rear. Harry had dayglo-red shorts you could see a mile, and Ann was white-skinned with long black hair and a brilliant neon-blue and orange bathing suit on her little rump—you could have seen her in a mine at midnight. Even I got some yellow water safety tape and tied it around my arse and tanks.

"The one thing we didn't have then was a radio. At the time they didn't seem worth the crazy cost, and were unreliable besides. I had no way of guessing I'd soon give my life for one—and very nearly did.

"Well, when Victor let us out and we got organized and started north single file over the dead part of the reef, we almost surfaced and yelled for him to take us back right then. It was purely awful. But we knew there was better stuff ahead, so we stuck it out and flippered doggedly along—actually doing pretty damn fair time, with the current—and trying not to look too closely at what lay below.

"Not only was the coral dead, you understand—that's where the name got started. We think now it's from oil and chemical wash, such as that pretty ship out there is about to contribute—but there was tons and tons of litter, *basura* of all descriptions, crusted there. It's everywhere, of course—you've seen what washes onto the mainland beach—but here the current and the reef produce a particularly visible concentration. Even quite large heavy things—bedsprings, auto chassis—in addition to things you'd expect, like wrecked skiffs. Cozumel, *Basurera del Caribe!*"

He gave a short laugh, mocking the Gem-of-the-Caribbean ads, as he lit up another Caporal. The most polite translation of *basurera* is garbage can.

"A great deal of the older stuff was covered with that evil killer algae—you know, the big coarse red-brown hairy kind, which means that nothing else can ever grow there again. But some of the heaps were too new.

"I ended by getting fascinated and swimming lower to look, always keeping one eye on that blue-and-orange rump above me with her white legs and black flippers. And the stuff—I don't mean just Clorox and *detergente* bottles, beer cans and netting—but weird things like about ten square meters of butchered pink plastic baby dolls—arms and legs wiggling, and rosebud mouths—it looked like a babies' slaughterhouse. Syringes, hypos galore. Fluorescent tubes on end, waving like drowned orchestra conductors. A great big red sofa with a skeletonized banana stem or *something* sitting in it—when I saw that, I went back up and followed right behind Ann.

"And then the sun dimmed unexpectedly, so I surfaced for a look. The shoreline was fine, we had plenty of time, and the cloud was just one of a dozen little thermals that form on a hot afternoon like this. When I went back down Ann was looking at me, so I gave her the "All's Fair" sign. And with that we swam over a pair of broken dories and found ourselves in a different world—the beauty patch we'd been look-ing for.

"The reef was live here—whatever had killed the coral hadn't reached yet, and the damned *basura* had quit or been deflected, aside from a beer bottle or two. There was life everywhere; anemones, sponges, conches, fans, stars—and fish, oh my! No one ever came here, you see.

In fact, there didn't seem to have been any spearing, the fish were as tame as they used to be years back.

"Well, we began zigzagging back and forth, just revelling in it. And every time we'd meet head-on we'd make the gesture of putting our fingers to our lips, meaning Don't tell anyone about this, ever!

"The formation of the reef was charming, too. It broadened into a sort of big stadium, with allées and cliffs and secret pockets, and there were at least eight different kinds of coral. And most of it was shallow enough so the sunlight brought out the glorious colors—those little black and yellow fish—butterflies, or I forget their proper name—were dazzling. I kept having to brush them off my mask, they wanted to look in.

"The two ahead seemed to be in ecstasies; I expect they hadn't seen much like this before. They swam on and on, investigating it all—and I soon realized there was real danger of losing them in some coral pass. So I stuck tight to Ann. But time was passing. Presently I surfaced again to investigate—and, my god, the shoreline was damn near invisible and the line-up we had selected for our turn marker was all but passed! Moreover, a faint hazy overcast was rising from the west.

"So I cut down again, intending to grab Ann and start, which Harry would have to see. So I set off after the girl. I used to be a fair sprint swimmer, but I was amazed how long it took me to catch her. I recall vaguely noticing that the reef was going a bit bad again, dead coral here and there. Finally I came right over her, signed to her to halt, and kicked up in front of her nose for another look.

"To my horror, the shoreline was gone and the overcast had overtaken the sun. We would have to swim east by compass, and swim hard. I took a moment to hitch my compass around where I could see it well—it was the old-fashioned kind—and then I went back down for Ann. And the damn fool girl wasn't there. It took me a minute to locate that blue bottom and white legs; I assumed she'd gone after Harry, having clearly no idea of the urgency of our predicament.

"I confess the thought crossed my mind that I could cut out of there, and come back for them later with Victor, but this was playing a rather iffy game with someone else's lives. And if they were truly unaware, it would be fairly rotten to take off without even warning them. So I went after Ann again—my god, I can still see that blue tail and the white limbs and black feet and hair with the light getting worse every minute and the bottom now gone really rotten again. And as bad luck would have it she was going in just the worst line—north-northwest.

"Well I swam and I swam and I *swam*. You know how a chase takes you, and somehow being unable to overtake a mere girl made it worse. But

I was gaining, age and all, until just as I got close enough to sense something was wrong, she turned sidewise above two automobile tyres— and I saw it wasn't a girl at all.

"I had been following a goddamned great fish—a fish with a bright blue and orange band around its belly, and a thin white body ending in a black, flipperlike tail. Even its head and nape were black, like her hair and mask. It had a repulsive catfishlike mouth, with barbels.

"The thing goggled at me, and then swam awkwardly away, just as the light went worse yet. But there was enough for me to see that it was no normal fish, either, but a queer archaic thing that looked more tacked together than grown. This I can't swear to, because I was looking elsewhere by then, but it was my strong impression that as it went out of my line of sight its whole tail broke off.

"But, as I say, I was looking elsewhere. I had turned my light on, although I was not deep but only dim, because I had to read my watch and compass. It had just dawned on me that I was probably a dead man. My only chance, if you can call it that, was to swim east as long as I could, hoping for that eddy and Victor. And when my light came on, the first thing I saw was the girl, stark naked and obviously stone cold dead, lying in a tangle of nets and horrid stuff on the bottom ahead.

"Of Harry or anything human there was no sign at all. But there was a kind of shining, like a pool of moonlight, around her, which was so much stronger than my lamp that I clicked it off and swam slowly toward her, through the nastiest mess of *basura* I had yet seen. The very water seemed vile. It took longer to reach her than I had expected, and soon I saw why.

"They speak of one's blood running cold with horror, y'know. Or people becoming numb with horror piled on horrors. I believe I experienced both those effects. It isn't pleasant, even now." He lit a third Caporal, and I could see that the smoke column trembled. Twilight had fallen while he'd been speaking. A lone mercury lamp came on at the shore end of the pier; the one near us was apparantly out, but we sat in what would ordinarily have been a pleasant tropic evening, sparkling with many moving lights—whites, reds and green, of late-moving incomers and the rainbow lighting from the jewel-lit cruise ship ahead, all cheerfully reflected in the unusually calm waters.

"Again I was mistaken, you see. It wasn't Ann at all; but the rather more distant figure of a young woman, of truly enormous size. All in this great ridge of graveyard luminosity, of garbage in phosphorescent decay. The current was carrying me slowly, inexorably, right toward her—as it had carried all that was there now. And perhaps I was also a bit hypnotized. She grew in my sight meter by meter as I neared her. I think six meters—eighteen feet—was about it, at the end . . . I make that guess later, you understand, as an exercise in containing the unbearable—by recalling the size of known items in the junkpile she lay on. One knee, for example, lay alongside an oil drum. At the time she simply filled my world. I had no doubt she was dead, and very beautiful. One of her legs seemed to writhe gently.

"The next stage of horror came when I realized that she was not a gigantic woman at all—or rather, like the fish, she was a woman-shaped construction. The realization came to me first, I think, when I could no longer fail to recognize that her 'breasts' were two of those great net buoys with the blue knots for nipples.

"After that it all came with a rush—that she was a made-up body—all sorts of pieces of plastic, rope, styrofoam, netting, crates and bolts—much of it clothed with that torn translucent white polyethylene for skin. Her hair was a dreadful tangle of something, and her crotch was explicit and unspeakable. One hand was a torn, inflated rubber glove, and her face—well, I won't go into it except that one eye was a traffic reflector and her mouth was partly a rusted can.

"Now you might think this discovery would have brought some relief, but quite the opposite. Because simultaneously I had realized the very worst thing of all—

"She was alive."

He took a long drag on his cigarette.

"You know how things are moved passively in water? Plants waving, a board seesawing and so on? Sometimes enough almost to give an illusion of mobile life. What I saw was nothing of this sort.

"It wasn't merely that as I floated over her horrible eyes 'opened' and looked at me, and her rusted-can mouth *smiled.* Oh, no.

"What I mean is that as she smiled, first one whole arm, shedding junk, stretched up and reached for me *against the current,* and then the other did the same.

"And when I proved to be out of reach, this terrifying figure, or creature, or unliving life, actually sat up, again *against the current,* and reached up toward me with both arms at full extension.

"And as she did so, one of her 'breasts'—the right one—came loose and dangled by some sort of tenuous thready stuff.

"All this seemed to pass in slow motion—I even had time to see that there were other unalive yet living things moving near her on the pile. Not fish, but more what I should have taken, on land, for rats or vermin—and I distinctly recall the paper-flat skeleton of something like a chicken, running and pecking. And other moving things like nothing in this world. I have remembered all this very carefully, y'see, from what must have been quick glimpses, because in actual fact I was apparently kicking like mad in a frenzied effort to get away from those dreadful, reaching arms.

"It was not until I shot to the surface with a mighty splash that I came somewhere near my senses. Below and behind me I could still see faint cold light. Above was twilight and the darkness of an oncoming small storm.

"At that moment the air in my last tank gave out—or rather that splendid Yank warning buzz, which means you have just time to get out of your harness, sounded off.

"I had, thank god, practiced the drill. Despite being a terror-paralyzed madman, habit got me out of the harness before the tanks turned into lethal deadweight. In my panic of course, the headlight went down too. I was left unencumbered in the night, free to swim towards Cuba, or Cozumel, and to drown as slow or fast as fate willed.

"The little storm had left the horizon stars free. I recall that pure habit made me take a sight on what seemed to be Canopus, which should be over Cozumel. I began to swim in that direction. I was appallingly tired, and as the adrenalin of terror that had brought me this far began to fade out of my system, I realized I could soon be merely drifting, and would surely die in the next day's sun if I survived until then. Nevertheless it seemed best to swim whilst I could.

"I rather resented it when some time after a boat motor passed nearby. It forced me to attempt to yell and wave, nearly sinking myself. I was perfectly content when the boat passed on. But someone had seen—a spotlight wheeled blindingly, motors reversed, I was forcibly pulled from my grave and voices from what I take to be your Texas demanded, roaring with laughter,"—here he gave quite a creditable imitation—" 'Whacha doin out hyar, boy, this time of night? Ain't no pussy out hyar, less'n ya'all got a date with a mermaid.' They had been trolling for god knows what, mostly beer.

"The driver of that boat claimed me as a friend and later took me home for the night, where I told to him—and to him alone—the whole story. He was Jorge Chuc.

"Next day I found that the young couple, Harry and Ann, had taken only a brief look at the charming unspoiled area, and then started east, exactly according to plan, with me—or something very much like me—following behind them all the way. They had been a trifle surprised at my passivity and uncommunicativeness, and more so when, on meeting Victor, I was no longer to be found. But they had taken immediate action, even set a full scale search in progress—approximately seventy kilometers from where I then was. As soon as I came to myself I had to concoct a wild series of lies about cramps and heart trouble to get them in the clear and set their minds at ease. Needless to say, my version included no mention of diver-imitating fishlife."

He tossed the spark of his cigarette over the rail before us.

"So now, my friend, you know the whole story of all I know of what is to be found beyond the Dead Reef. It may be that others know of other happenings and developments there. Or of similar traps elsewhere. The sea is large. . . . Or it may be that the whole yarn comes from neuroses long abused by stuff like this."

I had not seen him extract his flask, but he now took two deep, shuddering swallows.

I sighed involuntarily, and then sighed again. I seemed to have been breathing rather inadequately during the end of his account.

"Ordinary thanks don't seem quite appropriate here," I finally said. "Though I do thank you. Instead I am going to make two guesses. The second is that you might prefer to sit quietly here alone, enjoying the evening, and defer the mild entertainment I was about to offer you to some other time. I'd be glad to be proved wrong . . . ?"

"No. You're very perceptive, I welcome the diverse—the deferred offer." His tongue stumbled a bit now more from fatigue than anything he'd drunk. "But what was your first guess?"

I rose and slowly paced a few meters to and fro, remembering to pick up my absurd snorkel bag. Then I turned and gazed out to the sea.

"I can't put it into words. It has something to do with the idea that the sea is still, well, strong. Perhaps it can take revenge? No, that's too simple. I don't know. I have only a feeling that our ordinary ideas of what may be coming on us may be—oh—not deep, or broad enough. I put this poorly. But perhaps the sea, or nature, will not die passively at our hands . . . perhaps death itself may turn or return in horrible life upon us, besides the more mechanical dooms. . . ."

"Our thoughts are not so far apart," the tall Belézan said. "I welcome them to my night's agenda."

"To which I now leave you, unless you've changed your mind?"

He shook his head. I hoisted his bag to the seat beside him. "Don't forget this. I almost left mine."

"Thanks. And don't you forget about dogs and mothers." He grinned faintly.

"Good night."

My footsteps echoed on the now deserted *muelle* left him sitting there. I was quite sure he was no longer smiling.

Nor was I.

IAN WATSON

Slow Birds

One of the most brilliant innovators to enter SF in many years, Ian Watson's work is typified by its vivid and highly original conceptualization, its intellectual rigor, and the sometimes Byzantine complexity of its plotting. He sold his first story in 1969, and first attracted widespread critical attention with his 1973 novel *The Embedding*—still one of the genre's most sophisticated treatments of the theme of linguistics—which was the runner-up for the 1974 John W. Campbell Memorial Award. His *The Jonah Kit* won the British Science Fiction Award and the British Science Fiction Association Award in 1976 and 1977, respectively. Watson's other books include *Alien Embassy, Miracle Visitors, The Martian Inca, Chekhov's Journey, Under Heaven's Bridge* (co-authored with Michael Bishop), the collection *The Very Slow Time Machine*, and, as editor, the anthologies *Pictures at an Exhibition* and (co-edited with Michael Bishop) *Changes*. Upcoming is *The Black Current Trilogy*, the first volume of which, *The Book of the River*, will be published by Gollancz in 1984.

Here Watson shows us a future world that seems almost pastoral at first glance . . . but it is a world whose people live always on the brink of sudden extinction, a world haunted by one of the strangest menaces in recent SF, the ominous, slow-moving low-flying Slow Birds . . .

SLOW BIRDS

Ian Watson

It was Mayday, and the skate-sailing festival that year was being held at Tuckerton.

By late morning, after the umpires had been out on the grass plain setting red flags around the circuit, cumulus clouds began to fill a previously blue sky, promising ideal conditions for the afternoon's sport. No rain; so that the glass wouldn't be an inch deep in water as last year at Atherton. No dazzling glare to blind the spectators, as the year before that at Buckby. And a breeze verging on brisk without ever becoming fierce: perfect to speed the competitors' sails along without lifting people off their feet and tumbling them, as four years previously at Edgewood when a couple of broken ankles and numerous bruises had been sustained.

After the contest there would be a pig roast; or rather the succulent fruits thereof, for the pig had been turning slowly on its spit these past thirty-six hours. And there would be kegs of Old Codger Ale to be cracked. But right now Jason Babbidge's mind was mainly occupied with checking out his glass-skates and his fine crocus yellow hand-sail.

As high as a tall man, and of best old silk, only patched in a couple of places, the sail's fore-spar of flexible ash was bent into a bow belly by a strong hemp cord. Jason plucked this thoughtfully like a harpist, testing the tension. Already a fair number of racers were out on the glass, showing off their paces to applause. Tuckerton folk mostly, they were— acting as if they owned the glass hereabouts and knew it more intimately than any visitors could. Not that it was in any way different from the same glass over Atherton way.

Jason's younger brother Daniel whistled appreciatively as a Tuckerton man carrying purple silk executed perfect circles at speed, his sail shivering as he tacked.

"Just look at him, Jay!"

"What, Bob Marchant? He took a pratfall last year. Where's the use in working up a sweat before the whistle blows?"

By now a couple of sisters from Buckby were out too with matching black sails, skating figure-eights around each other, risking collision by a hair's breadth.

"Go on, Jay," urged young Daniel. "Show 'em."

Contestants from the other villages were starting to flood on to the glass as well, but Jason noticed how Max Tarnover was standing not so far away, merely observing these antics with a wise smile. Master Tarnover of Tuckerton, last year's victor at Atherton despite the drenching spray. . . . Taking his cue from this, and going one better, Jason ignored events on the glass and surveyed the crowds instead.

He noticed Uncle John Babbidge chatting intently to an Edgewood man over where the silver band was playing; that was hardly the quietest place to talk, so perhaps they were doing business. Meanwhile on the green beyond, the band the children of five villages buzzed like flies from hoopla to skittles to bran tub, to apples in buckets of water. And those grown-ups who weren't intent on the band or the practice runs or on something else, such as gossip, besieged the craft and produce stalls. There must be going on a thousand people at the festival, and the village beyond looked deserted. Rugs and benches and half-barrels had even been set out near the edge of the glass for the old folk of Tuckerton.

As the band lowered their instruments for a breather after finishing *The Floral Dance*, a bleat of panic cut across the chatter of many voices. A farmer had just vaulted into a tiny sheep-pen where a lamb almost as large as its shorn, protesting dam was ducking beneath her to suckle and hide. Laughing, the farmer hauled it out and hoisted it by its neck and back legs to guess its weight, and maybe win a prize.

And now Jason's mother was threading her way through the crowd, chewing the remnants of a pasty.

"Best of luck, son!" She grinned.

"I've told you, Mum," protested Jason. "It's bad luck to say 'good luck'."

"Oh, luck yourself! What's luck, anyway?" She prodded her Adam's apple as if to press the last piece of meat and potatoes on its way down, though really she was indicating that her throat was bare of any charm or amulet.

"I suppose I'd better make a move." Kicking off his sandals, Jason sat to lace up his skates. With a helping hand from Daniel he rose and stood knockkneed, blades cutting into the turf while the boy hoisted the sail across his shoulders. Jason gripped the leather straps on the bow-string and the spine-spar.

"Okay." He waggled the sail this way and that. "Let go, then. I won't blow away."

But just as he was about to proceed down on to the glass, out upon the glass less than a hundred yards away a slow bird appeared.

It materialized directly in front of one of the Buckby sisters. Unable to veer, she had no choice but to throw herself backwards. Crying out in frustration, and perhaps hurt by her fall, she skidded underneath the slow bird, sledging supine upon her now snapped and crumpled sail. . . .

They were called slow birds because they flew through the air—at the stately pace of three feet per minute.

They looked a little like birds, too, though only a little. Their tubular metal bodies were rounded at the head and tapering to a finned point at the tail, with two stubby wings midway. Yet these wings could hardly have anything to do with suspending their bulk in the air; the girth of a bird was that of a horse, and its length twice that of a man lying full length. Perhaps those wings controlled orientation of trim.

In color they were a silvery gray; though this was only the color of their outer skin, made of a soft metal like lead. Quarter of an inch beneath this coating their inner skins were black and stiff as steel. The noses of the birds were all scored with at least a few scrape marks due to encounters with obstacles down the years; slow birds always kept the same height above ground—underbelly level with a man's shoulders—and they would bank to avoid substantial buildings or mature trees, but any frailer obstructions they would push on through. Hence the individual patterns of scratches. However, a far easier way of telling them apart was by the graffiti carved on so many of their flanks; initials entwined in hearts, dates, place names, fragments of messages. These amply confirmed how very many slow birds there must be in all—something of which people could not otherwise have been totally convinced. For no one could keep track of a single slow bird. After each one had appeared—over hill, down dale, in the middle of a pasture or halfway along a village street—it would fly onward slowly for any length of time between an hour and a day, covering any distance between a few score yards and a full mile. And vanish again. To reappear somewhere else unpredictably: far away or close by, maybe long afterwards or maybe soon.

Usually a bird would vanish, to reappear again.

Not always, though. A half dozen times a year, within the confines of this particular island country, a slow bird would reach its journey's end.

It would destroy itself, and all the terrain around it for a radius of two and a half miles, fusing the landscape instantly into a sheet of glass. A flat, circular sheet of glass. A polarized, limited zone of annihilation. Scant yards beyond its rim a person might escape unharmed, only being deafened and dazzled temporarily.

Hitherto no slow bird had been known to explode to overlap an earlier sheet of glass. Consequently many towns and villages clung close to the borders of what had already been destroyed, and news of a fresh glass plain would cause farms and settlements to spring up there. Even so, the bulk of people still kept fatalistically to the old historic towns. They assumed that a slow bird wouldn't explode in their midst during their own lifetimes. And if it did, what would they know of it? Unless the glass happened merely to bisect a town—in which case, once the weeping and mourning was over, the remaining citizenry could relax and feel secure.

True, in the long term the whole country from coast to coast and from north to south would be a solid sheet of glass. Or perhaps it would merely be a checkerboard, of circles touching circles: a glass mosaic. With what in between? Patches of desert dust, if the climate dried up due to reflections from the glass. Or floodwater, swampland. But that day was still far distant: a hundred years away, two hundred, three. So people didn't worry too much. They had been used to this all their lives long, and their parents before them. Perhaps one day the slow birds would stop coming. And going. And exploding. Just as they had first started, once. Certainly the situation was no different, by all accounts, anywhere else in the world. Only the seas were clear of slow birds. So maybe the human race would have to take to rafts one day. Though by then, with what would they build them? Meanwhile, people got by; and most had long ago given up asking why. For there was no answer.

The girl's sister helped her rise. No bones broken, it seemed. Only an injury to dignity; and to her sail.

The other skaters had all coasted to a halt and were staring resentfully at the bird in their midst. Its belly and sides were almost bare of graffiti; seeing this, a number of youths hastened on to the glass, clutching penknives, rusty nails and such. But an umpire waved them back angrily.

"Shoo! Be off with you!" His gaze seemed to alight on Jason, and for a fatuous moment Jason imagined that it was himself to whom the umpire was about to appeal; but the man called, "Master Tarnover!" instead, and Max Tarnover duck-waddled past, then glided out over the glass, to confer.

Presently the umpire cupped his hands. "We're delaying the start for a half hour," he bellowed. "Fair's fair: young lady ought to have a chance to fix her sail, seeing as it wasn't her fault."

Jason noted a small crinkle of amusement on Tarnover's face; for now either the other competitors would have to carry on prancing around tiring themselves with extra practice that none of them needed, or else troop off the glass for a recess and lose some psychological edge. In fact almost everyone opted for a break and some refreshments.

"Luck indeed!" snorted Mrs. Babbidge, as Max Tarnover clumped back their way.

Tarnover paused by Jason. "Frankly I'd say her sail's a wreck," he confided. "But what can you do? The Buckby lot would have been bitching on otherwise. 'Oh, she could have won. If she'd had ten minutes to fix it.' Bloody hunk of metal in the way." Tarnover ran a lordly eye over Jason's sail. "What price skill, then?"

Daniel Babbidge regarded Tarnover with a mixture of hero worship and hostile partisanship on his brother's behalf. Jason himself only nodded and said, "Fair enough." He wasn't certain whether Tarnover was acting generously—or with patronizing arrogance. Or did this word in his ear mean that Tarnover actually saw Jason as a valid rival for the silver punchbowl this year round?

Obviously young Daniel did not regard Jason's response as adequate. He piped up: "So where do *you* think the birds go, Master Tarnover, when they aren't here?"

A good question: quite unanswerable, but Max Tarnover would probably feel obliged to offer an answer if only to maintain his pose of worldly wisdom. Jason warmed to his brother, while Mrs. Babbidge, catching on, cuffed the boy softly.

"Now don't you go wasting Master Tarnover's time. Happen he hasn't given it a moment's thought, all his born days."

"Oh, but I have," Tarnover said.

"Well?" the boy insisted.

"Well . . . maybe they don't go anywhere at all."

Mrs. Babbidge chuckled, and Tarnover flushed.

"What I mean is, maybe they just stop being in one place then suddenly they're in the next place."

"If only you could skate like that!" Jason laughed. "Bit slow, though . . . Everyone would still pass you by at the last moment."

"They must go somewhere," young Dan said doggedly. "Maybe it's somewhere we can't see. Another sort of place, with other people. Maybe it's them that builds the birds."

"Look, freckleface, the birds don't come from Russ, or 'Merica, or anywhere else. So where's this other place?"

"Maybe it's right here, only we can't see it."

"And maybe pigs have wings." Tarnover looked about to march toward the the cider and perry stall; but Mrs. Babbidge interposed herself smartly.

"Oh, as to that, I'm sure our sow Betsey couldn't fly, wings or no wings. Just hanging in the air like that, and so heavy."

"Weighed a bird recently, have you?"

"They look heavy, Master Tarnover."

Tarnover couldn't quite push his way past Mrs. Babbidge, not with his sail impeding him. He contented himself with staring past her, and muttering. "If we've nothing sensible to say about them, in my opinion it's better to shut up."

"But it isn't better," protested Daniel. "They're blowing the world up. Bit by bit. As if they're at war with us."

Jason felt humorously inventive. "Maybe that's it. Maybe these other people of Dan's are at war with us—only they forgot to mention it. And when they've glassed us all, they'll move in for the holidays. And skate happily for evermore."

"Damn long war, if that's so," growled Tarnover. "Been going on over a century now."

"Maybe that's why the birds fly so slowly," said Daniel. "What if a year to us is like an hour to those people? That's why the birds don't fall. They don't have time to."

Tarnover's expression was almost savage. "And what if the birds come only to punish us for our sins? What if they're simply a miraculous proof—"

"—that the Lord cares about us? And one day He'll forgive us?" Mrs. Babbidge beamed. "Oh goodness, surely you aren't one of *them*? A bright lad like you. Me, I don't even put candles in the window or tie knots in the bedsheets anymore to keep the birds away." She ruffled her younger son's mop of red hair. "Everyone dies sooner or later, Dan. You'll get used to it, when you're properly grown up. When it's time to die, it's time to die."

Tarnover looked furiously put out; though young Daniel also seemed distressed in a different way.

"And when you're thirsty, it's time for a drink!" Spying an opening, and his opportunity, Tarnover sidled quickly around Mrs. Babbidge and strode off. She chuckled as she watched him go.

"That's put a kink in his sail!"

Forty-one other contestants, besides Jason and Tarnover, gathered between the starting flags. Though not the girl who had fallen; despite all best efforts she was out of the race, and sat morosely watching.

Then the Tuckerton umpire blew his whistle, and they were off.

The course was in the shape of a long bloomer loaf. First, it curved gently along the edge of the glass for three-quarters of a mile, then bent sharply around in a half circle on to the straight, returning toward Tuckerton. At the end of the straight, another sharp half circle brought it back to the starting—and finishing—line. Three circuits in all were to be skate-sailed before the victory whistle blew. Much more than this, and the lag between leaders and stragglers could lead to confusion.

By the first turn Jason was ahead of the rest of the field, and all his practice since last year was paying off. His skates raced over the glass. The breeze thrust him convincingly. As he rounded the end of the loaf, swinging his sail to a new pitch, he noted Max Tarnover hanging back in fourth place. Determined to increase his lead, Jason leaned so close to the flag on the entry to the straight that he almost tipped it. Compensating, he came poorly on to the straight, losing a few yards. By the time Jason swept over the finishing line for the first time, to cheers from Atherton villagers, Tarnover was in third position; though he was making no very strenuous effort to overhaul. Jason realized that Tarnover was simply letting him act as pacemaker.

But a skate-sailing race wasn't the same as a foot race, where a pacemaker was generally bound to drop back eventually. Jason pressed on. Yet by the second crossing of the line Tarnover was ten yards behind, moving without apparent effort as if he and his sail and the wind and the glass were one. Noting Jason's glance, Tarnover grinned and put on a small burst of speed to push the frontrunner to even greater efforts. And as he entered on the final circuit Jason also noted the progress of the slow bird, off to his left, now midway between the long curve and the straight, heading in the general direction of Edgewood. Even the laggards ought to clear the final straight before the thing got in their way, he calculated.

This brief distraction was a mistake: Tarnover was even closer behind him now, his sail pitched at an angle that must have made his wrists ache. Already he was drifting aside to overhaul Jason. And at this moment Jason grasped how he could win: by letting Tarnover think that he was pushing Jason beyond his capacity—so that Tarnover would be fooled into overexerting himself too soon.

"Can't catch me!" Jason called into the wind, guessing that Tarnover would misread this as braggadocio and assume that Jason wasn't really thinking ahead. At the same time Jason slackened his own pace slightly, hoping that his rival would fail to notice, since this was at odds with his own boast. Pretending to look panicked, he let Tarnover overtake—and saw how Tarnover continued to grip his sail strenuously even though he was actually moving a little slower than before. Without realizing it, Tarnover had his angle wrong; he was using unnecessary wrist action.

Tarnover was in the lead now. Immediately all psychological pressure lifted from Jason. With ease and grace he stayed a few yards behind, just where he could benefit from the "eye" of air in Tarnover's wake. And thus he remained until halfway down the final straight, feeling like a kestrel hanging in the sky with a mere twitch of its wings before swooping.

He held back; held back. Then suddenly changing the cant of his sail he did swoop—into the lead again.

It was a mistake. It had been a mistake all along. For as Jason sailed past, Tarnover actually laughed. Jerking his brown and orange silk to an easier, more efficient pitch, Tarnover began to pump his legs, skating like a demon. Already he was ahead again. By five yards. By ten. And entering the final curve.

As Jason tried to catch up in the brief time remaining, he knew how he had been fooled; though the knowledge came too late. So cleverly had Tarnover fixed Jason's mind on the stance of the sails, by holding his own in such a way—a way, too, which deliberately created that convenient eye of air—that Jason had quite neglected the contribution of his legs and skates, taking this for granted, failing to monitor it from moment to moment. It only took moments to recover and begin pumping his own legs too, but those few moments were fatal. Jason crossed the finish line one yard behind last year's victor; who was this year's victor too.

As he slid to a halt, bitter with chagrin, Jason was well aware that it was up to him to be gracious in defeat rather than let Tarnover seize that advantage, too.

He called out, loud enough for everyone to hear: "Magnificent, Max! Splendid skating! You really caught me on the hop there."

Tarnover smiled for the benefit of all onlookers.

"What a noisy family you Babbidges are," he said softly; and skated off to be presented with the silver punchbowl again.

Much later that afternoon, replete with roast pork and awash with Old Codger Ale, Jason was waving an empty beer mug about as he talked to Bob Marchant in the midst of a noisy crowd. Bob, who had fallen so spectacularly the year before. Maybe that was why he had skated diffidently today and been one of the laggards.

The sky was heavily overcast, and daylight too was failing. Soon the homeward trek would have to start.

One of Jason's drinking and skating partners from Atherton, Sam Partridge, thrust his way through.

"Jay! That brother of yours: he's out on the glass. He's scrambled up on the back of the bird. He's riding it."

"*What?*"

Jason sobered rapidly, and followed Partridge with Bob Marchant tagging along behind.

Sure enough, a couple of hundred yards away in the gloaming Daniel was perched astride the slow bird. His red hair was unmistakable. By now a lot of other people were beginning to take notice and point him out. There were some ragged cheers, and a few angry protests.

Jason clutched Partridge's arm. "Somebody must have helped him up. Who was it?"

"Haven't the foggiest. That boy needs a good walloping."

"Daniel *Babbidge!*" Mrs. Babbidge was calling nearby. She too had seen. Cautiously she advanced on to the glass, wary of losing her balance.

Jason and company were soon at her side. "It's all right, Mum," he assured her. "I'll fetch the little . . . perisher."

Courteously Bob Marchant offered his arm and escorted Mrs. Babbidge back on the rough ground again. Jason and Partridge stepped flat-foot out across the vitrified surface accompanied by at least a dozen curious spectators.

"Did anyone spot who helped him up?" Jason demanded of them. No one admitted it.

When the group was a good twenty yards from the bird, everyone but Jason halted. Pressing on alone, Jason pitched his voice so that only the boy would hear.

"Slide off," he ordered grimly. "I'll catch you. Right monkey you've made of your mother and me."

"No," whispered Daniel. He clung tight, hands splayed like suckers, knees pressed to the flanks of the bird as if he were a jockey. "I'm going to see where it goes."

"Goes? Hell, I'm not going to waste time arguing. Get down!" Jason gripped an ankle and tugged, but this action only served to pull him up against the bird. Beside Dan's foot a heart with the entwined initials ZB and EF was carved. Turning away, Jason shouted, "Give me a hand, you lot! Come on someone, bunk me up!"

Nobody volunteered, not even Partridge.

"It won't bite you! There's no harm in touching it. Any kid knows that." Angrily he flat-footed back toward them. "Damn it all, Sam."

So now Partridge did shuffle forward, and a couple of other men too.

But then they halted, gaping. Their expression puzzled Jason momentarily—until Sam Partridge gestured; till Jason swung around.

The air behind was empty.

The slow bird had departed suddenly. Taking its rider with it.

Half an hour later only the visitors from Atherton and their hosts remained on Tuckerton green. The Buckby, Edgewood and Hopperton contingents had set off for home. Uncle John was still consoling a sniveling Mrs. Babbidge. Most faces in the surrounding crowd looked sympathetic, though there was a certain air of resentment, too, among some Tuckerton folk that a boy's prank had cast this black shadow over their Mayday festival.

Jason glared wildly around the onlookers. "Did nobody see who helped my brother up?" he cried. "Couldn't very well have got up himself, could he? Where's Max Tarnover? Where is he?"

"You aren't accusing Master Tarnover, by any chance?" growled a beefy farmer with a large wart on his cheek. "Sour grapes, Master Babbidge! Sour grapes is what that sounds like, and we don't like the taste of those here."

"Where is he, dammit?"

Uncle John laid a hand on his nephew's arm. "Jason, lad. Hush. This isn't helping your Mum."

But then the crowd parted, and Tarnover sauntered through, still holding the silver punchbowl he had won.

"Well, Master Babbidge?" he inquired. "I hear you want a word with me."

"Did you see who helped my brother onto that bird? Well, did you?"

"I didn't see," replied Tarnover coolly.

It had been the wrong question, as Jason at once realized. For if Tarnover had done the deed himself, how could he possibly have watched himself do it?

"Then did you—"

"Hey up," objected the same farmer. "You've asked him, and you've had his answer."

"And I imagine your brother has had his answer too," said Tarnover. "I hope he's well satisfied with it. Naturally I offer my heartfelt sympathies to Mrs. Babbidge. If indeed the boy *has* come to any harm. Can't be sure of that, though, can we?"

"Course we can't!"

Jason tensed, and Uncle John tightened his grip on him. "No, lad. There's no use."

It was a sad and quiet long walk homeward that evening for the three remaining Babbidges, though a fair few Atherton folk behind sang blithely and tipsily, nonetheless. Occasionally Jason looked around for Sam Partridge, but Sam Partridge seemed to be successfully avoiding them.

The next day, May the second, Mrs. Babbidge rallied and declared it to be a "sorting out" day; that meant a day for handling all Daniel's clothes and storybooks and old toys lovingly before setting them to one side out of sight. Jason himself she packed off to his job at the sawmill, with a flea in his ear for hanging around her like a whipped hound.

And as Jason worked at trimming planks that day the same shamed, angry frustrated thoughts skated round and round a single circuit in his head:

"In my book he's a murderer. . . . You don't give a baby a knife to play with. He was cool as a cucumber afterwards. Not shocked, no. Smug. . . ."

Yet what could be done about it? The bird might have hung around for hours more. Except that it hadn't. . . .

Set out on a quest to find Daniel? But how? And where? Birds dodged around. Here, there and everywhere. No rhyme or reason to it. So what a useless quest that would be!

A quest to prove that Dan was alive. And if he were alive, then Tarnover hadn't killed him.

"In my book he's a murderer. . . ." Jason's thoughts churned on impotently. It was like skating with both feet tied together.

Three days later a slow bird was sighted out Edgewood way. Jim Mitchum, the Edgewood thatcher, actually sought Jason out at the sawmill to bring him the news. He'd been coming over to do a job, anyway.

No doubt his visit was an act of kindness, but it filled Jason with guilt quite as much as it boosted his morale. For now he was compelled to go and see for himself, when obviously there was nothing whatever to discover. Downing tools, he hurried home to collect his skates and sail, and sped over the glass to Edgewood.

The bird was still there; but it was a different bird. There was no carved heart with the love-tangled initials ZB and EF.

And four days after that, mention came from Buckby of a bird spotted a few miles west of the village on the main road to Harborough. This time Jason borrowed a horse and rode. But the mention had come late; the bird had flown on a day earlier. Still, he felt obliged to search the area of the sighting for a fallen body or some other sign.

And the week after that a bird appeared only a mile from Atherton itself; this one vanished even as Jason arrived on the scene. . . .

Then one night Jason went down to the Wheatsheaf. It was several weeks, in fact, since he had last been in the alehouse; now he meant to get drunk, at the long bar under the horse brasses.

Sam Partridge, Ned Darrow and Frank Yardley were there boozing; and an hour or so later Ned Darrow was offering beery advice.

"Look, Jay, where's the use in you dashing off every time someone spots a ruddy bird? Keep that up and you'll make a ruddy fool of yourself. And what if a bird pops up in Tuckerton? Bound to happen sooner or later. Going to rush off there too, are you, with your tongue hanging out?"

"All this time you're taking off work," said Frank Yardley. "You'll end up losing the job. Get on living is my advice."

"Don't know about that," said Sam Partridge unexpectedly. "Does seem to me as man ought to get his own back. Supposing Tarnover did do the dirty on the Babbidges—"

"What's there to suppose about it?" Jason broke in angrily.

"Easy on, Jay. I was going to say as Babbidges are Atherton people. So he did the dirty on us all, right?"

"Thanks to some people being a bit slow in their help."

Sam flushed. "Now don't you start attacking everyone right and left. No one's perfect. Just remember who your real friends are, that's all."

"Oh, I'll remember, never fear."

Frank inclined an empty glass from side to side. "Right. Whose round is it?"

One thing led to another, and Jason had a thick head the next morning.

In the evening Ned banged on the Babbidge door.

"Bird on the glass, Sam says to tell you," he announced. "How about going for a spin to see it?"

"I seem to recall last night you said I was wasting my time."

"Ay, running around all over the country. But this is just for a spin. Nice evening, like. Mind, if you don't want to bother. . . . Then we can all have a few jars in the Wheatsheaf afterwards."

The lads must really have missed him over the past few weeks. Quickly Jason collected his skates and sail.

"But what about your supper?" asked his mother. "Sheep's head broth."

"Oh, it'll keep, won't it? I might as well have a pasty or two in the Wheatsheaf."

"Happen it's better you get out and enjoy yourself," she said. "I'm quite content. I've got things to mend."

Twenty minutes later Jason, Sam, and Ned were skimming over the glass two miles out. The sky was crimson with banks of stratus, and a river of gold ran clear along the horizon: foul weather tomorrow, but a glory this evening. The glassy expanse flowed with red and gold reflections: a lake of blood, fire, and molten metal. They did not at first spot the other solitary sail-skater, nor he them, till they were quite close to the slow bird.

Sam noticed first. "Who's that, then?"

The other sail was brown and orange. Jason recognized it easily. "It's Tarnover!"

"Now's your chance to find out, then," said Ned.

"Do you mean that?"

Ned grinned. "Why not? Could be fun. Let's take him."

Pumping their legs, the three sail-skaters sped apart to outflank Tarnover—who spied them and began to turn. All too sharply, though. Or else he may have run into a slick of water on the glass. To Jason's joy Max Tarnover, champion of the five villages, skidded.

They caught him. This done, it didn't take the strength of an ox to stop a skater from going anywhere else, however much he kicked and struggled. But Jason hit Tarnover on the jaw, knocking him senseless.

"What the hell you do that for?" asked Sam, easing Tarnover's fall on the glass.

"How else do we get him up on the bird?"

Sam stared at Jason, then nodded slowly.

It hardly proved the easiest operation to hoist a limp and heavy body on to a slowly moving object whilst standing on a slippery surface; but after removing their skates they succeeded. Before too long Tarnover lay sprawled atop, legs dangling. Quickly with his pocketknife Jason cut the hemp cord from Tarnover's sail and bound his ankles together, running the tether tightly underneath the bird.

Presently Tarnover awoke, and struggled groggily erect. He groaned, rocked sideways, recovered his balance.

"Babbidge . . . Partridge, Ned Darrow . . . ? What the hell are you up to?"

Jason planted hands on hips. "Oh, we're just playing a little prank, same as you did on my brother Dan. Who's missing now; maybe forever, thanks to you."

"I never—"

"Admit it, then we might cut you down."

"And happen we mightn't," said Ned. "Not until the Wheatsheaf closes. But look on the bright side: happen we might."

Tarnover's legs twitched as he tested the bonds. He winced. "I honestly meant your brother no harm."

Sam smirked. "Nor do we mean you any. Ain't our fault if a bird decides to fly off. Anyway, only been here an hour or so. Could easily be here all night. Right, lads?"

"Right," said Ned. "And I'm thirsty. Race you? Last ones buys?"

"He's admitted he did it," said Jason. "You heard him."

"Look, I'm honestly very sorry if—"

"Shut up," said Sam. "You can stew for a while, seeing as how you've made the Babbidges stew. You can think about how sorry you really are." Partridge hoisted his sail.

It was not exactly how Jason had envisioned his revenge. This seemed like an anti-climax. Yet, to Tarnover no doubt it was serious enough. The champion was sweating slightly. . . . Jason hoisted his sail, too. Presently the men skated away . . . to halt by unspoken agreement a quarter of a mile away. They stared back at Tarnover's little silhouette upon his metal steed.

"Now if it was me," observed Sam, "I'd shuffle myself along till I fell off the front . . . Rub you a bit raw, but that's how to do it."

"No need to come back, really," said Ned. "Hey, what's he trying?"

The silhouette had ducked. Perhaps Tarnover had panicked and wasn't thinking clearly, but it *looked* as if he was trying to lean over far enough to unfasten the knot beneath, or free one of his ankles. Suddenly the distant figure inverted itself. It swung right round the bird, and Tarnover's head and chest were hanging upside down, his arms flapping. Or perhaps Tarnover had hoped the cord would snap under his full weight; but snap it did not. And once he was stuck in that position there was no way he could recover himself upright again, or do anything about inching along to the front of the bird.

Ned whistled. "He's messed himself up now, and no mistake. He's ruddy crucified himself."

Jason hesitated before saying it: "Maybe we ought to go back? I mean, a man can die hanging upside down too long . . . Can't he?" Suddenly the whole episode seemed unclean, unsatisfactory.

"Go back?" Sam Partridge fairly snarled at him. "You were the big mouth last night. And whose idea was it to tie him on the bird? You wanted him taught a lesson, and he's being taught one. We're only trying to oblige you, Jay."

"Yes, I appreciate that."

"You made enough fuss about it. He isn't going to wilt like a bunch of flowers in the time it takes us to swallow a couple of pints."

And so they skated on, back to the Wheatsheaf in Atherton.

At ten-thirty, somewhat the worse for wear, the three men spilled out of the alehouse into Sheaf Street. A quarter moon was dodging from rift to rift in the cloudy sky, shedding little light.

"I'm for bed," said Sam. "Let the sod wriggle his way off."

"And who cares if he don't?" said Ned. "That way, nobody'll know. Who wants an enemy for life? Do you Jay? This way you can get on with things. Happen Tarnover'll bring your brother back from wherever it is." Shouldering his sail and swinging his skates, Ned wandered off up Sheaf Street.

"But," said Jason. He felt as though he had blundered into a midden. There was a reek of sordidness about what had taken place. The memory of Tarnover hanging upside-down had tarnished him.

"But what?" said Sam.

Jason made a show of yawning. "Nothing. See you." And he set off homeward.

But as soon as he was out of sight of Sam he slipped down through Butcher's Row in the direction of the glass, alone.

It was dark out there with no stars and only an occasional hint of moonlight, yet the breeze was steady and there was nothing to trip over on the glass. The bird wouldn't have moved more than a hundred yards. Jason made good speed.

The slow bird was still there. But Tarnover wasn't with it; its belly was barren of any hanged man.

As Jason skated to a halt, to look closer, figures arose in the darkness from where they had been lying flat upon the glass, covered by their sails. Six figures. Eight. Nine. All had lurked within two or three hundred yards of the bird, though not too close—nor any in the direction of Atherton. They had left a wide corridor open; which now they closed.

As the Tuckerton men moved in on him, Jason stood still, knowing that he had no chance.

Max Tarnover skated up, accompanied by that same beefy farmer with the wart.

"I did come back for you," began Jason.

The farmer spoke, but not to Jason. "Did he now? That's big of him. Could have saved his time, what with Tim Earnshaw happening along—

when Master Tarnover was gone a long time. So what's to be done with him, eh?"

"Tit for tat, I'd say," said another voice.

"Let him go and look for his kid brother," offered a third. "Instead of sending other folk on his errands. What a nerve."

Tarnover himself said nothing; he just stood in the night silently.

So, presently, Jason was raised on to the back of the bird and his feet were tied tightly under it. But his wrists were bound together too, and for good measure the cord was linked through his belt.

Within a few minutes all the skaters had sped away toward Tuckerton.

Jason sat. Remembering Sam's words he tried to inch forward, but with both hands fastened to his waist this proved impossible; he couldn't gain purchase. Besides, he was scared of losing his balance as Tarnover had.

He sat and thought of his mother. Maybe she would grow alarmed when he didn't come home. Maybe she would go out and rouse Uncle Jim. . . . And maybe she had gone to bed already.

But maybe she would wake in the night and glance into his room and send help. With fierce concentration he tried to project thoughts and images of himself at her, two miles away.

An hour wore on, then two; or so he supposed from the moving of the moon crescent. He wished he could slump forward and sleep. That might be best; then he wouldn't know anything. He still felt drunk enough to pass out, even with his face pressed against metal. But he might easily slide to one side or the other in his sleep.

How could his mother survive a double loss? It seemed as though a curse had descended on the Babbidge family. But of course that curse had a human name; and the name was Max Tarnover. So for a while Jason damned him, and imagined retribution by all the villagers of Atherton. A bloody feud. Cottages burnt. Perhaps a rape. Deaths even. No Mayday festival ever again.

But would Sam and Ned speak up? And would Atherton folk be sufficiently incensed, sufficiently willing to destroy the harmony of the five villages in a world where other things were so unsure? Particularly as some less than sympathetic souls might say that Jason, Sam, and Ned had started it all.

Jason was so involved in imagining a future feud between Atherton and Tuckerton that he almost forgot he was astride a slow bird. There was no sense of motion, no feeling of going anywhere. When he recollected where he was, it actually came as a shock.

He was riding a bird.

But for how long?

It had been around, what, six hours now? A bird could stay for a whole day. In which case he had another eighteen hours left to be rescued in. Or if it only stayed for half a day, that would take him through to morning. Just.

He found himself wondering what was underneath the metal skin of the bird. Something which could turn five miles of landscape into a sheet of glass, certainly. But other things too. Things that let it ignore gravity. Things that let it dodge in and out of existence. A brain of some kind, even?

"Can you hear me, bird?" he asked it. Maybe no one had ever spoken to a slow bird before.

The slow bird did not answer.

Maybe it couldn't, but maybe it could hear him, even so. Maybe it could obey orders.

"Don't disappear with me on your back," he told it. "Stay here. Keep on flying just like this."

But since it was doing just that already, he had no idea whether it was obeying him or not.

"Land, bird. Settle down onto the glass. Lie still."

It did not. He felt stupid. He knew nothing at all about the bird. Nobody did. Yet somewhere, someone knew. Unless the slow birds did indeed come from God, as miracles, to punish. To make men God-fearing. But why should a God want to be feared? Unless God was insane, in which case the birds might well come from Him.

They were something irrational, something from elsewhere, something that couldn't be understood by their victims anymore than an ant colony understood the gardener's boot, exposing the white eggs to the sun and the sparrows.

Maybe something had entered the seas from elsewhere the previous century, something that didn't like land dwellers. Any of them. People or sheep, birds or worms or plants. . . . It didn't seem likely. Salt water would rust steel, but for the first time in his life Jason thought about it intently.

"Bird, what are you? Why are you here?"

Why, he thought, is anything here? Why is there a world and sky and stars? Why shouldn't there simply be nothing for ever and ever?

Perhaps that was the nature of death: nothing for ever and ever. And one's life was like a slow bird. Appearing then vanishing, with nothing before and nothing after.

An immeasurable period of time later, dawn began to streak the sky behind him, washing it from black to gray. The grayness advanced slowly overhead as thick clouds filtered the light of the rising but hidden sun. Soon there was enough illumination to see clear all around. It must be five o'clock. Or six. But the gray glass remained blankly empty.

Who am I? wondered Jason, calm and still. Why am I conscious of a world? Why do people have minds, and think thoughts? For the first time in his life he felt that he was really thinking—and thinking had no outcome. It led nowhere.

He was, he realized, preparing himself to die. Just as all the land would die, piece by piece, fused into glass. Then no one would think thoughts anymore, so that it wouldn't matter if a certain Jason Babbidge had ceased thinking at half-past six one morning late in May. After all, the same thing happened every night when you went to sleep, didn't it? You stopped thinking. Perhaps everything would be purer and cleaner afterwards. Less untidy, less fretful: a pure ball of glass. In fact, not fretful at all, even if all the stars in the sky crashed into each other, even if the earth was swallowed by the sun. Silence, forever: once there was no one about to hear.

Maybe this was the message of the slow birds. Yet people only carved their initials upon them. And hearts. And the names of places which had been vitrified in a flash; or else which were going to be.

I'm becoming a philosopher, thought Jason in wonder.

He must have shifted into some hyperconscious state of mind: full of lucid clarity, though without immediate awareness of his surroundings. For he was not fully aware that help had arrived until the cord binding his ankles was cut and his right foot thrust up abruptly, topping him off the other side of the bird into waiting arms.

Sam Partridge, Ned Darrow, Frank Yardley, and Uncle John, and Brian Sefton from the sawmill—who ducked under the bird brandishing a knife, and cut the other cord to free his wrists.

They retreated quickly from the bird, pulling Jason with them. He resisted feebly. He stretched an arm toward the bird.

"It's all right, lad," Uncle John soothed him.

"No, I want to *go*," he protested.

"Eh?"

At that moment the slow bird, having hung around long enough, vanished; and Jason stared at where it had been, speechless.

In the end his friends and uncle had to lead him away from that featureless spot on the glass, as if he were an idiot. Someone touched by imbecility.

But Jason did not long remain speechless.

Presently he began to teach. Or preach. One or the other. And people listened; at first in Atherton, then in other places too.

He had learned wisdom from the slow bird, people said of him. He had communed with the bird during that night's vigil on the glass.

His doctrine of nothingness and silence spread, taking root in fertile soil, where there was soil remaining rather than glass—which was in most places still. A paradox, perhaps: how eloquently he spoke—about being silent! But in so doing he seemed to make the silence of the glass lakes sing; and to this people listened with a new ear.

Jason traveled throughout the whole island. And this was another paradox, for what he taught was a kind of passivity, a blissful waiting for a death that was more than merely personal, a death that was also the death of the sun and stars and of all existence, a cosmic death which transfigured individual mortality. And sometimes he even sat on the back of a bird that happened by, to speak to a crowd—as if chancing fate or daring, begging, the bird to take him away. But he never sat for more than an hour, then he would scramble down, trembling but quietly radiant. So besides being known as "The Silent Prophet," he was also known as "The Man Who Rides the Slow Birds."

On balance, it could have been said that he worked great psychological good for the communities that survived; and his words even spread overseas. His mother died proud of him—so he thought—though there was always an element of wistful reserve in her attitude. . . .

Many years later, when Jason Babbidge was approaching sixty, and still no bird had ever borne him away, he settled back in Atherton in his old home—to which pilgrims of silence would come, bringing prosperity to the village and particularly to the Wheatsheaf, managed now by the daughter of the previous landlord.

And every Mayday the skate-sailing festival was still held, but now always on the glass at Atherton. No longer was it a race and a competition; since in the end the race of life could not be won. Instead it had become a pageant, a glass ballet, a reenactment of the events of many years ago—a passion play performed by the four remaining villages. Tuckerton and all its folk had been glassed ten years before by a bird which destroyed itself so that the circle of annihilation exactly touched that edge of the glass where Tuckerton had stood until then.

One morning, the day before the festival, a knock sounded on Jason's door. His housekeeper, Martha Prestidge, was out shopping in the village; so Jason answered.

A boy stood there. With red hair, and freckles.

For a moment Jason did not recognize the boy. But then he saw that it was Daniel. Daniel, unchanged. Or maybe grown up a little. Maybe a year older.

"Dan . . . ?"

The boy surveyed Jason bemusedly: his balding crown, his sagging girth, his now spindly legs, and the heavy stick with a stylized bird's head on which he leaned, gripping it with a liver-spotted hand.

"Jay," he said after a moment, "I've come back."

"Back? But . . ."

"I know what the birds are now! They *are* weapons. Missiles. Tens and hundreds of thousands of them. There's a war going on. But it's like a game as well: a boardgame run by machines. Machines that think. It's only been going on for a few days in their time. The missiles shunt to and fro through time to get to their destination. But they can't shunt in the time of that world, because of cause and effect. So here's where they do their shunting. In our world. The other possibility-world."

"This is nonsense. I won't listen."

"But you must, Jay! It can be stopped for us before it's too late. I know how. Both sides can interfere with each other's missiles and explode them out of sight—that's here—if they can find them fast enough. But the war over there's completely out of control. There's a winning pattern to it, but this only matters to the machines any longer, and they're buried away underground. They build the birds at a huge rate with material from the Earth's crust, and launch them into other-time automatically."

"Stop it, Dan."

"I fell off the bird over there—but I fell into a lake, so I wasn't killed, only hurt. There are still some pockets of land left, around the bases. They patched me up, the people there. They're finished, in another few hours of their time—though it's dozens of years to us. I brought them great hope, because it meant that all life isn't finished. Just theirs. Life can go on. What we have to do is build a machine that will stop their machines finding the slow birds over here. By making interference in the air. There are waves. Like waves of light, but you can't see them."

"You're raving."

"Then the birds will still shunt here. But harmlessly. Without glass-ing us. And in a hundred years time, or a few hundred, they'll even stop coming at all, because the winning pattern will be all worked out by then. One of the war machines will give up, because it lost the game. Oh I know it ought to be able to give up right now! But there's an element of the irrational programmed into the machines' brains too; so they don't give up too soon. When they do, everyone will be long dead there on land—and some surviving people think the war machines will start glassing the ocean floor as a final strategy before they're through. But we can build an air wavemaker. They've locked the knowledge in my brain. It'll take us a few years to mine the right metals and tool up and provide a power source. . . ." Young Daniel ran out of breath briefly. He gasped. "They had a prototype slow bird. They sat me on it and sent me into other-time again. They managed to guide it. It emerged just ten miles from here. So I walked home."

"Prototype? Air waves? Power source? What are these?"

"I can tell you."

"Those are just words. Fanciful babble. Oh for this babble of the world to still itself!"

"Just give me time, and I'll—"

"Time? You desire time? The mad ticking of men's minds instead of the great pure void of eternal silence? You reject acceptance? You want us to swarm forever aimlessly, deafening ourselves with our noisy chatter?"

"Look . . . I suppose you've had a long, tough life, Jay. Maybe I shouldn't have come here first."

"Oh, but you should indeed, my impetuous fool of a brother. And I do not believe my life has been ill-spent."

Daniel tapped his forehead. "It's all in here. But I'd better get it down on paper. Make copies and spread it around—just in case Atherton gets glassed. Then somebody else will know how to build the transmitter. And life can go on. Over there they think maybe the human race is the only life in the whole universe. So we have a duty to go on existing. Only, the others have destroyed themselves arguing about which way to exist. But we've still got time enough. We can build ships to sail through space to the stars. I know a bit about that too. I tell you, my visit brought them real joy in their last hours, to know this was all still possible after all."

"Oh, Dan." And Jason groaned. Patriachlike, he raised his staff and brought it crashing down on Daniel's skull.

He had imagined that he mightn't really notice the blood amidst Daniel's bright red hair. But he did.

The boy's body slumped in the doorway. With an effort Jason dragged it inside, then with an even greater effort up the oak stairs to the attic where Martha Prestidge hardly ever went. The corpse might begin to smell after a while, but it could be wrapped up in old blankets and such.

However, the return of his housekeeper down below distracted Jason. Leaving the body on the floor he hastened out, turning the key in the lock and pocketing it.

It had become the custom to invite selected guests back to the Babbidge house following the Mayday festivities; so Martha Prestidge would be busy all the rest of the day cleaning and cooking and setting the house to rights. As was the way of housekeepers she hinted that Jason would get under her feet; so off he walked down to the glass and out onto its perfect flatness to stand and meditate. Villagers and visitors spying the lone figure out there nodded gladly. Their prophet was at peace, presiding over their lives. And over their deaths.

The skate-sailing masque, the passion play, was enacted as brightly and gracefully as ever the next day.

It was May the third before Jason could bring himself to go up to the attic again, carrying sacking and cord. He unlocked the door.

But apart from a dark stain of dried blood the floorboards were bare. There was only the usual jumble stacked around the walls. The room was empty of any corpse. And the window was open.

So he hadn't killed Daniel after all. The boy had recovered from the blow. Wild emotions stirred in Jason, disturbing his usual composure. He stared out of the window as though he might discover the boy lying below on the cobbles. But of Daniel there was no sign. He searched around Atherton, like a haunted man, asking no questions but looking everywhere piercingly. Finding no clue, he ordered a horse and cart to take him to Edgewood. From there he traveled all around the glass, through Buckby and Hopperton; and now he asked wherever he went, "Have you seen a boy with red hair?" The villagers told each other that Jason Babbidge had had another vision.

As well he might have, for within the year from far away news began to spread of a new teacher, with a new message. This new teacher was only a youth, but he had also ridden a slow bird—much farther than the Silent Prophet had ever ridden one.

However, it seemed that this young teacher was somewhat flawed, since he couldn't remember all the details of his message, of what he had been told to say. Sometimes he would beat his head with his fists in frustration, until it seemed that blood would flow. Yet perversely this touch of theatre appealed to some restless, troublesome streak in his audiences. They believed him because they saw his anguish, and it mirrored their own suppressed anxieties.

Jason Babbidge spoke zealously to oppose the rebellious new ideas, exhausting himself. All the philosophical beauty he had brought into the dying world seemed to hang in the balance; and reluctantly he called for a "crusade" against the new teacher, to defend his own dream of Submission.

Two years later, he might well have wished to call his words back, for their consequence was that people were tramping across the countryside in between the zones of annihilation armed with pitchforks and billhooks, cleavers and sickles. Villages were burnt; many hundreds were massacred; and there were rapes—all of which seemed to recall an earlier nightmare of Jason's from before the time of his revelation.

In the third year of this seemingly endless skirmish between the Pacificists and the Survivalists Jason died, feeling bitter beneath his cloak of serenity; and by way of burial his body was roped to a slow bird. Loyal mourners accompanied the bird in silent procession until it vanished hours later. A short while after that, quite suddenly at the Battle of Ashton Glass, it was all over, with victory for the Survivalists led by their young red-haired champion, who it was noted bore a striking resemblance to old Jason Babbidge, so that it almost seemed as if two basic principles of existence had been at contest in the world: two aspects of the selfsame being, two faces of one man.

Fifty years after that, by which time a full third of the land was glass and the climate was worsening, the Survival College in Ashton at last invented the promised machine; and from then on slow birds continued to appear and fly and disappear as before, but now none of them exploded.

And a hundred years after that all the slow birds vanished from the Earth. Somewhere, a war was over, logically and finally.

But by then, from an Earth four-fifths of whose land surface was desert or swamp—in between necklaces of barren shining glass—the first starship would arise into orbit.

It would be called *Slow Bird*. For it would fly to the stars, slowly. Slowly in human terms; two generations it would take. But that was comparatively fast.

A second starship would follow it; called *Daniel*.

Though after that massive and exhausting effort, there would be no more starships. The remaining human race would settle down to cultivate what remained of their garden in amongst the dunes and floods and acres of glass. Whether either starship would find a new home as habitable even as the partly glassed Earth, would be merely an article of faith.

On his deathbed in Ashton College lay Daniel, eighty years of age, who had never admitted to a family name.

The room was almost indecently overcrowded, though well if warmly ventilated by a wind whipping over Ashton Glass, and bright-lit by the silvery blaze reflecting from that vitrified expanse.

The dying old man on the bed beneath a single silken sheet was like a bird himself now: shriveled with thin bones, a beak of a nose, beady eyes and a rooster's comb of red hair on his head.

He raised a frail hand as if to summon those closest, even closer. Actually it was to touch the old wound in his skull which had begun to ache fiercely of late as if it were about to burst open or cave in, unlocking the door of memory—notwithstanding that no one now needed the key hidden there, since his collegians had discovered it independently, given the knowledge that it existed.

Faces leaned over him: confident, dedicated faces.

"They've stopped exploding, then?" he asked, forgetfully.

"Yes, yes, years ago!" they assured him.

"And the stars—?"

"We'll build the ships. We'll discover how."

His hand sank back on to the sheet. "Call one of them—"

"Yes?"

"*Daniel*. Will you?"

They promised him this.

"That way . . . my spirit . . ."

"Yes?"

". . . will fly . . ."

"Yes?"

". . . into the silence of space."

This slightly puzzled the witnesses of his death; for they could not know that Daniel's last thought was that, when the day of the launching came, he and his brother might at last be reconciled.

POUL ANDERSON

Vulcan's Forge

One of the best-known and most prolific writers in SF, Poul Anderson made his first sale in 1947, and in the course of his subsequent 37-year career has published more than 80 books, sold hundreds of short pieces to every conceivable market, and won seven Hugo Awards, three Nebula Awards, and the Tolkien Memorial Award for lifetime achievement in fantasy. His books include (among *many* others) *The High Crusade, The Enemy Stars, Three Hearts and Three Lions, The Broken Sword, Tau Zero, The Night Face, Guardians of Time,* and *The Man Who Counts,* and the collections *The Queen of Air and Darkness and Other Stories, The Earth Book of Stormgate,* and *The Best of Poul Anderson.* His most recent books are *Time Patrolman,* a collection of novellas, and the massive novel *Orion Shall Rise.* Anderson lives in Orinda, California, with his wife (and fellow writer) Karen.

Here he takes us to one of the most dangerous and exotic regions of the solar system for a bittersweet look at a strange and intimate kind of partnership that even death can not put asunder . . .

VULCAN'S FORGE

Poul Anderson

AWAKE
INPUT: RV (SOL) 57932100 + 150, RA 3.33, DEC 7.05, DR/DT
5.42, D2R/DT2 3.51 -2.86, 7.90 . . .
"Hello, there, Kitty. Everything okay?"
"Okay, boss. Blasting in about two minutes. You?"
"Going down soon. I'll resume contact in an hour or so. Good faring
to you."
"Good faring to us both, boss."
INPUT: BB TEMP 522, EM SPEC DIST. . . .
Mercury is small, hard, a mass drawn inward on itself (iron, nickel,
silicate. . . .), day ablaze, night afreeze as I swing in my winging
around. My shield glows radio-hot, for its sunward side is white light-
hot. Solar wind whistles and hails. Here is no seething of it in a
changeable magnetic cauldron nor interplay of gravities as at Jupiter,
no swirl of moonlets about Saturn. But silence the memory bank, now
in this new mission. Do not raise Wanda's ghost, not yet.
COMPUTE BLAST VECTORS
READY ALL SYSTEMS TO GO

Caloris Base was forever undermanned. No matter the pay, technicians were few who would serve there; it was a dismal and sometimes
dangerous outpost, where equipment kept breaking down under conditions that were still scantily understood. Six months off after six months
on were not always enough for nerves to recuperate. Turnover became
high, which meant a chronic dearth of experienced personnel, which
compounded the problem. The scientists for whom the place existed
were in better case, with an endlessness of discoveries to make, so that
some returned more than once and a cadre had made Mercury their
careers. However, they too were overworked while on the planet.

Thus it happened that even when a living legend arrived, only one person took the time to greet him. That was Ellen Lyndale. The man at ground control didn't count, nor the driver who would fetch the newcomer.

Alone in the common room, she switched fluoros off and let the view leap at her eyes. Upward the simulacrum went, from floor to zenith, as if she stood on the surface a hundred meters above her. Night neared an end. The stars remained ice-brilliant in their myriads, Earth glowed sapphire not far from the Milky Way, she thought she saw Luna as an atom of gold beside it. But zodiacal light hovered ghostly above the eastern horizon, and solar corona was climbing after it. The mother-of-pearl gleam fell on a landscape that curved away, beneath this mountaintop, in crags, craters, boulders, ridges, dark dustiness of the basin rock, until all at once it dropped out of sight under that sky. A warmth and a breath of flower-scented air only made the scene colder. Some hours hence, they would only make it more of a furnace.

Regulus lifted above a cliff and crossed the constellations. In low orbit, the supply ship moved fast. Its shield being aimed toward the sun, Lyndale saw just a half-disc, whose brightness would have blinded her if the scanners had not stopped it down. Her attention went to the pair of smaller cabochons accompanying it. One drifted sideways as the shuttlecraft to which it belonged left the mother vessel, bearing Jeremy Ashe down to her. The other trailed yet. Her pulse quickened. Behind yonder shield was *Kittiwake*.

The scout also broke free, accelerating on ion jets that formed a lacy smoke, soon dissipated, well aft of it, and departed her vision, Vulcan bound. She looked back at the shuttle. Entering Mercury's shadow, the shield grew dim. Presently she made out the boat itself, and then the countermass and the metal spiderwebbing that held everything together. Meanwhile *Regulus* passed upper culmination and began to set, until she could see its hull too, larger by far than the boat's but distance-dwindled to a splinter, trailing a foreshortened dull circle that was the convex side of its own shield.

The shuttle descended to a landing court fused into the regolith below the mountain. In her view, it became a parasol, or a mushroom cap. . . . For an instant she was a child again, barefoot in a Kentucky greenwood, where soil squooshed cool and damp between her toes, mushrooms clustered on a sun-flecked mossy log, and a mockingbird sang. . . . The car that scuttled forth went under it like a beetle seeking cover. She visualized airlock extensors osculating and Ashe climbing through. The car reappeared and returned to the vehicle chamber. She visualized Ashe getting out, walking across the floor, taking the elevator that would bring him to this level.

The hall door opened. He entered.

"Oh!" Startled despite herself, she switched the lights on again. Stars receded. Furniture changed from shadows to chairs and tables, 3V screen and music speakers, all a bit shabby and very outmoded. "Welcome, Captain Ashe," she said. "I'm Ellen Lyndale. It's an honor meeting you."

She wasn't surprised when he approached with a smooth low-gravity glide. It generally took a while to adapt to any given weight, and he had been more than a year on Earth, then under boost aboard *Regulus*. In three decades, though, from end to end of the Solar System, he must have undergone every acceleration the human body could endure. She was taken aback at how much older he looked than the pictures she had seen—tall, craggy, hair a gray bristle above a deeply trenched face.

His handshake was brief, his glance impersonal. "How d'you do, Doctor Lyndale." A trace of British accent lingered to clip his tones. "I've studied your work, of course. Still, you'll have quite a lot to explain to me in a short time." He paused. "And doubtless I to you."

"I'm sorry no one else is here. So's everybody. But the sun's doing unusual things, which the solar investigators have to keep track of, and the planet scientists are preparing an expedition to the North Jumbles, and biochem recycle has chosen this exact moment to develop a collywobble—nothing to fear, but it has to be corrected immediately—"

"No matter. I understand."

"Director Sanjo is planning a dinner party this evenwatch. Meanwhile I'll show you to your quarters and you can rest. And if you'd like some refreshment, or anything else we can provide, please tell me."

He shook his head. "No, thanks. Just have my baggage brought to my room. Let's you and I get cracking."

She started. "What?"

"You heard me," he snapped. "*Kittiwake*'s en route to Vulcan. She'll make rendezvous within a hundred hours, unless we change the thrust, and we can't decide about that without proper data, can we? Besides, I promised her I'd call as soon as possible. Come along, young lady, lead on."

INPUT: — PROTON FLUX 15.8, HELIUM+ 0.05, HELIUM+ + 0.03—

"Kitty."

"Acknowledging, boss. Everything well so far."

The great paraboloid of my shield wards off the fury ahead, brings it to a focus and hurls it back, a lance of radiance. Energy does penetrate, but into multiple layers of solid-state cells behind the reflector surface; electrons leap through their dances of being and not-being, of quantum death and transfiguration; that which emerges on my side is largely of long wavelengths to which I am transparent, and all that emerges is diffused by curvature, with little ever impinging on me. That is enough to heat me somewhat, by those photons in its spectrum which make the crystals of my body ring. I feel the shivering through my sensors, record and transmit it together with the other data torrenting upon me. But my essential self remains cool enough, the delicate balance that maintains it is undisturbed.

The sun grows and its bearing changes as I drive onward. The shield swings slowly in its framework, to stay between me and destruction. Opposite, the countermass moves too; and therefore my thrust vectors must change, lest the couple throw a torque upon me that will send me spinning out of control. Meanwhile, the gale that blows from the sun casts eddies around the edge of the shield, that lick at the spindle which is my hull.

The planets and moons in the cold outer reaches were not like this. But we are explorers, my boss and I and our memories of Wanda.

"Are you sure, Kitty? Caution is the doctrine."

"I'll have to work fast at Vulcan, you know. Less risky than taking any longer than necessary in those parts."

"You're not there yet. Double check your self-monitor."

The time lag between us is 215 milliseconds, 216, 217, 218. . . .
SWITCH
COMPUTE
PROCEED

"Okay," Ashe grunted. "For the time being, at least." He set the board to receive-record-standby and leaned back. Against the obscurity in an otherwise deserted communications room, glow from the sweep-survey scope flickered across the harshness of his face like green firelight.

Lyndale sat forward in her own chair. Shock tingled faintly through her skin. "Were you . . . talking . . . to the scout?" she asked. It had not been audible, but she had seen his lips move, and stiffen as he listened to whatever came in through the earphones he had now doffed. And his fingers had been less active on the keys than hers would have been.

He regarded her for seconds, not as other men did. She was considered handsome, in a rangy, square-jawed fashion, but she had a feeling that he was looking straight at what lay beneath. Briefly she wondered if he could see it, whatever it was. Jeremy Ashe had been a loner since his wife's death a dozen years ago; and before then they had been a pair of loners, taking the scout on missions that kept them out many months on end, moving only in a narrow social group on Earth. Wanda Ashe died when an oxygen valve failed on a moon of Neptune, Lyndale remembered, and afterward her widower refused to take another partner but somehow, incredibly, single-handed *Kittiwake.* No, Lyndale thought, Jeremy Ashe knew much about the universe but probably little about humankind.

He nodded at last. "The program includes several special features," he said. "Speech is one. It's often more convenient than a digital code, quicker, yes, actually more accurate in some cases. I couldn't operate as I do without it."

"Er—well—excuse me, I don't mean to pry or anything, but—talking with a, a machine like that, instead of another person—"

He barked a chuckle. "Indeed. The old joke. A spaceman by himself needn't worry when he starts talking to the machinery, unless it starts talking back to him." A shrug. "My employers know, and don't mind as long as I continue to perform well, but it is a reason for me to avoid publicity. However, what makes you think I am not dealing with another person?"

"That computer?" she exclaimed, shocked afresh.

"The hardware has as much data-processing capability as anything this side of the Turing Laboratories," he reminded her. "More to the point, the software is special. It contains the entire . . . experience . . . we have had together." Irritation: "But I've neither time nor patience for stale arguments about what consciousness 'is.' My working methods are what they are, their record speaks for itself, and when this Vulcan project was first proposed, my name was the first that came up. So can we get to work, you and I, Doctor Lyndale?"

She bridled. Arrogant bastard, she thought. Had she known, she could have gotten somebody else. Valdez and Chiang of *Albatross* were famous; Ostrowski and Ronsard were still operating *Cormorant,* which they had flown past the sun out of this very base while she was an infant—She had not known, but had been delighted when the Syndicate offered her the services of *Kittiwake.*

"I assumed you were amply briefed, Captain Ashe," she said. "Lord knows we had plenty of exchanges. The mission profile's agreed on. All you've got to do is carry it out, bring your scout back aboard *Regulus,* and go home."

"You know the matter's not that simple, not by a light-year," he snapped. "If it were, an ordinary unmanned probe would do—and the results wouldn't interest you, would they? We're up against something unique. We'll have to make decisions, quite possibly crucial decisions, as the information arrives . . . at the end of a minimum three-minute transmission time. Must I go on repeating the obvious?"

She curbed her temper. Make allowances for him, she told herself; he's not used to dealing with people.

And in his way, he's right, her mind added. Six minutes for a laser beam to go from Mercury to Vulcan and back. Anything can happen in six minutes, given the mystery that Vulcan is. And every Earth-day, the asteriod will briefly swing behind the sun, barred from us. At best, *Kittiwake* is going to be in tenuous touch with its master.

Master? No, don't get anthropomorphic; don't get crazy, *Kittiwake* is nothing but a spacecraft carrying sensors and computers—and, for the first time in its wanderings, a clumsy sunshield—

"Of course not, Captain Ashe," she said. "We'll have to cooperate right down the line. But I thought everything that anybody could imagine had been discussed in detail beforehand."

"Discussed," he answered. "No substitute for reality. See here, Doctor Lyndale. Supposedly you're the planetologist who believes there's something important to be learned from Vulcan, and I'm the operator of the scout that'll send the raw data to you. We don't know what those data are going to be—else what's the point of the whole exercise?—and will have to instruct the scout as we begin to get an idea of what to look for."

She decided that he did not really mean to insult her by talking down, but was trying to make a point that had never quite come out in the open, if only because one party or the other took it for granted.

He rewarded her patience, in a fashion. "But far more is involved," he said. "The very survival of the boat, under those difficult and poorly known conditions. I've swotted them up as best I was able, but you— you and the whole scientific team here—you're the ones who've lived with them, month after month or year after year. What's needed is a—an understanding, an integration of minds, so if something goes amiss we can immediately think what to do—" His fist smote the chair arm. "Hell and damnation! I asked for several weeks on Mercury to develop it before we launched *Kittiwake*, but—time and funds—everybody too busy—"

He swallowed hard, and she thought, suddenly, that it was his own pride he was getting down.

"We need to know each other better," he finished in a mumble, while his look strayed from hers.

Her pique dissolved. She reached forward and caught his hand. "Oh, yes," she said. "I understand now. Let me start by showing you through my lab and telling you what I've been doing. But later you'll have to share yourself with us, you know."

INPUT [navigational, interpreted]: The spacecraft is in free fall. (It wouldn't be feasible to boost the whole distance. That would mean too great a delta V. Come time to decelerate for Vulcan rendezvous, the direction of blast would necessarily be such as to expose the hull to the direct gaze of the sun, at a distance of less than two and a half million kilometers from its photosphere. The vessel could endure that, as could its basic wired-in programs, but not—for more than a few minutes—the precision instruments, nor the electronics that think and remember.) On trajectory, approaching.

INPUT [physical, interpreted]: Radiation of every kind significantly higher than predicted. Spots, flares, prominences, violence, a firestorm in the solar atmosphere.

TRANSMIT DATA

No response. Boss not there.

OPTICAL SCAN: Target acquired.

COMPARE INPUT WITH DATA IN PROGRAM

MEMORY: Observation from Mercury has revealed what seems to be an asteroid sufficiently close to the sun that its metallic body is molten. It was presumably perturbed into that orbit, which is decaying for reasons that are obscure, and thus it may yield information about solar weather and other processes over a long timespan. Details are impossible to retrieve from afar. Direct investigation is necessary.

COMPARE PREVIOUS MISSIONS WHERE APPLICABLE

Awhirl through the radiation maelstrom around Jupiter; but then Wanda and Jerry were on Callisto, waiting for my word, waiting together.

There was abundant cause to celebrate. The regular arrivals of the supply ship always gave occasion—seeing its crew again, bidding farewell to persons going off duty, welcoming their replacements, hearing the kind of stories from elsewhere that don't get on newsbeams, receiving the kind of gifts and handwritten messages from home that can't be borne in a lasergram—This visit was additional, unscheduled, and had brought a man who could tell of marvels.

Ashe was rather stiff at first, but a good meal, preceded by drinks, accompanied by wine, and followed by cognac, mellowed him somewhat. He was actually patient when young Sven Ewald, fresh in from a long field trip, asked him what the purpose of his task was. "I mean, *ja*, I realize an asteroid like that has been subjected to intense irradiation. But they tell me it has melted. Does that not hopelessly mix things together?"

Ashe nodded at Lyndale, who sat beside him. "Your department," he said with a slight smile. It made crinkles around his eyes which told her that once he had often laughed. "Kitty and I are merely running your errands for you."

"Why don't you explain?" she suggested. "I'm apt to get more technical than is called for."

Under cover of the tablecloth, she fended the hand of Bill Seton, who sat on her right, off her knee. He was not a bad sort, but he was in love with her and had gotten a trifle drunk. She felt sorry for him, but not enough to give encouragement. The fact that she was among the unmarried at Caloris did not mean that she chose to be among either the celibate or the promiscuous. She confined herself to a pair of close male friends, neither of whom happened to be present. There would be time for real involvements when her work here was done and she returned to the University of Oregon—and then, she hoped, it would be a single involvement, for the rest of her life.

Her lovers were not the only individuals missing from the officers' mess, out of the hundred-odd on the planet. She had counted twenty attenders, including the six off *Regulus*. Little Mercury was an entire world, bearing centuries' worth of mysteries; and that was not to speak of the sun, ambient space, certain stellar observations best conducted on this site, and lately Vulcan. Leisure was rare and absences were frequent.

Yet an effort had been made to brighten the room: a change of pictures on the walls, flowers from the hydroponics section, music lilting out of speakers. A blank viewscreen was like a curtain drawn against the searing day that had dawned beyond these caves.

"Well," she heard Ashe saying, "we think probably some solid material still exists, slag floating on the surfaces; and it will have a radioactive record. However, if convection has kept the liquid reasonably well mixed, that should have tended to protect it from repeated bombardment. Kitty's instruments ought to identify isotopes in the melt that aren't in the slag. Also, magnetic phenomena, in a mass like that, ought to reveal something about the solar field, its variations, and about the solar wind which carries it outward. As for what else we may find, who can tell? We never know beforehand, do we?"

Director Sanjo Mamoru relaxed his usual austerity to declare, as eagerly as a boy, "If anyone can testify how full of surprises the cosmos is, it is you, sir."

"Oh, now," Ashe demurred, "the people who make the discoveries are the specialists who interpret the data. Such as Doctor Lyndale."

She wondered why she flushed. "I think what he was getting at was the . . . the adventure," she said. "You must have had some fabulous experiences."

He withdrew toward his shell. "I go by the old proverb, that adventures happen to the incompetent."

Emboldened, she replied: "That can't be true. At least, nobody is competent to foresee everything in a universe where we're only . . . dustmotes, dayflies. I've seen accounts of what happened to your colleagues on their explorations. You've simply never wanted public attention, never been a glory hound, isn't that right?"

"If you do not mind," Sanjo pursued, "I have long been curious about precisely what occurred on your first Saturn mission. The news media only quoted you as mentioning difficulties which had been overcome."

"As a matter of fact," added the skipper of *Regulus*, "I got interested myself and checked the professional journals. All you did was warn against instruments icing over in the rings, because of particle collisions kicking water molecules loose. You advised future scouts to carry exterior heating elements. But what did you, caught by surprise, what exactly did *you* do?"

Ashe hesitated, gripped his brandy snifter, abruptly drained it. Lyndale poured him a refill. "C'mon," she urged. "You're among your own kind here. And you were underlining the need to get acquainted."

"Well—" said Ashe. "Well." He cleared his throat.

And somehow he got talking, remembering aloud, for a couple of hours, and wonder exploded around him.

He did not passively follow orders. He could not. Every flight was unique, requiring its special preparations, and he must always be the arbiter, often the deviser of these. Upon this evenwatch, which was not night where it ventured, *Kittiwake* traveled behind a sunshield, against heat, hard x-rays, a storm of stripped atoms. But at Neptune, danger had lain in the cryogenic cold of atmosphere, and at Io in volcanic spasms, and at the comets in whirling stones, and—

Nor did Ashe merely sit at a remote control board. Even in a mother ship, the challenges were countless, anything from survival to a simple and perhaps hilarious housekeeping problem; and usually he had been ground-based, left to cope with the strangenesses around him while his scout went seeking beyond. Or, rather, his and her scout, formerly when Wanda lived; he could not have carried on alone afterward without the knowledge they had won as a pair.

Jupiter had risen before him, lion-tawny, banded with clouds and emblazoned with hurricanes that could have swallowed Earth whole, weather into which he sent his quester plunging while its laser beams scribbled word of lightnings and thunders too vast for imagining. Saturn reigned coldly serene over a ring-dance whose measures no man really understood, and the chemistries within its air should not have happened but did. From the ice abyss wherein it lay, the core of Uranus uttered magnetic and seismic whispers about the ancient catastrophe that had wrenched sideways the whole spin of the planet. A sun that was no more than the brightest of the stars cast its glade over a Neptunian ocean that was not water, lapping against shores that were not stone.

The faintest of rainbows glimmered on Pluto's frozenness, as if to declare that it was the mightiest of the comets and bore witness to the beginning of the worlds. Elfin lights flitted across the murk of Persephone—But to listeners, none of it was altogether inhuman, for they belonged in the same universe whose majesty was being revealed.

It was not that Ashe was an eloquent man, it was that he had known what he had known and done what he had done, on behalf of them all.

"Good night, folks. . . . Work tomorrow. . . . I hope the rest of our personnel will get a chance to hear you, sir. . . . Thank you. . . . Good night, good night."

Lyndale found herself leaving side by side with Ashe. She glanced upward, into the furrowed countenance and the eyes that remained Sirius-blue; on an impulse, she murmured, "Are you sleepy?"

"Not quite," he said. "Too much to think about. Well, I have a book to read in bed."

"If you'd like to stop by my room, we could—talk some more."

He halted. For a moment they stood motionless in the corridor. Colleagues moved around them, right and left, carefully paying no heed, until they were alone among amateur murals, scenes of Earth, that suddenly looked forlorn.

Ashe bit his lip. "Sorry," he said in a rough voice. "You're kind, but I do have too much to think about. Good night."

He turned and well-nigh bounded from her.

She stared after him, well past his vanishing around a corner. Wine-warmth faded away. Her disappointment was slight, she realized. It had been a matter of wanting to know him better and, all right, admit it, a degree of hero worship. However, she didn't collect men. Probably this way was best, an unadorned partnership while the understanding lasted.

I don't think there's anything wrong with him, she reflected. He's simply, well, married to his scoutcraft. Because it's full of memories of his wife? I gather she was a big, beautiful, free-striding Valkyrie of a woman; and they denied themselves children, for the sake of the enterprise they shared.

Lyndale sighed and sought her own bed.

INPUT [navigational, interpreted]: The asteroid is a globule 453.27 kilometers in equatorial diameter. . . . Notably less in polar diameter. . . . Mass consistent with a largely ferrous composition. . . . EM SPEC. . . . bears out composition. . . . Doppler shift indicates a very high rate of rotation. . . .

OPTICAL TRANSMISSION: The solar disc fills a monstrous 25 + degrees in a sky which its corona whitens around it. Flames fountain. The vortices that are sunspots form lesser brilliances amidst the chaos.

Vulcan does not show a smooth crescent; dark drifts of slag make it seem ragged, although where the metal is not covered, it is incandescent.

"Maneuvering, boss, to establish orbit around the object."

"Careful, Kitty, careful. Keep your instruments busy."

RADIATION: Already suggestive of certain isotopes, but with anomalies. GAS COUNT

"No more than that, Kitty? How?" *Something has to have provided enough resistance to circularize the orbit, and to cause the slow decay of it that radar from Mercury has detected.* "Maybe occasional flares reach farther, at higher densities, than we knew? No, that can scarcely be."

MAGNETIC FLUX [interpreted]: Suddenly intense, and crazily writhing! INPUT [interior monitors]: Loss of attitude control. Torque. Blast of direct solar radiation.

EMERGENCY EMERGENCY EMERGENCY

"Assume quickest attainable parking orbit!" Ashe yelled. "Redeploy your shield!" His fingers sprang across the console and his commands sped off.

He sank back. A shudder went through him. "Three minutes transmission time," he rasped. "How much can happen in three minutes?"

The texts and graphics on the display screens around them dropped out of Lyndale's awareness. They were being recorded anyhow. She reached from her chair and caught Ashe's fist, which rested helpless on his thigh. "But surely the scout can take care of itself," she breathed. "Why did you send orders at all?"

His gaze never left the view from Vulcan. Images gyrated, now a lurid flicker, now a glimpse of the asteroid, now the distant stars. Sweat glistened on his skin. She smelled its sharpness and felt her own atrickle beneath her coverall.

His head jerked through a nod. "Yes, of course the program is capable of judgment, if it's working. It may not be. What I've tried to provide is backup against that contingency. Except—when almost everything is unknown—What's gone wrong?"

She mustered courage. "That's for us to find out. Let's not assume that any terrible damage has been done, before we get word. Supposing it has, we've a better chance of helping if we've stayed cool, correct?"

He turned his regard upon her and let it dwell for what seemed a long while. "Thank you," he said at last.

That scout is his life, she thought. *It's this having to wait while the signals travel to and fro that rips at him. But he's rallying well. I never doubted he would.*

They fled into technical discussion. The problem was to evaluate the information they had, which was mostly phrased in numbers, and whatever else came in, and deduce what the truth was, yonder where *Kittiwake* suffered.

Response arrived. It was greatly heartening. The spacecraft had succeeded in making itself a satellite of Vulcan, on a path eccentric but reasonably stable. Its shield was again processing properly, to shadow it from the sun. It was even taking measurements anew, though Ashe and Lyndale suspected that some of the instruments were no longer reliable. When the soprano voice said, not through earphones this time but out of a speaker, "Yes, I'm still myself, boss," Ashe whistled softly and wiped at his eyes.

Thereafter he rejoined Lyndale in the effort to establish the parameters of the situation.

"M-m, well, see here, what say we check out the magnetic propertics of such an object? Can your data banks supply what we need for computing that, Ellen?"

"Good idea. I'd better give Ram Krishnamurti a buzz. He's our resident mathematical genius, and I suspect we're going to come up with a function that'll be a bitch to integrate—"

The hours passed. They lost themselves.

"I think we're on the right track, Jerry, but our notion's no use until we've made it quantitative. If the jets were involved, that's your baby."

"And yours. We'll have to write the field equations—"

It was a hunt, a creating, a communion.

At the end, exhausted and exalted, they looked into each other's countenances while Ashe hoarsely recorded a summary.

"The trouble is nobody's fault. It was unforeseeable, in the absence of precise knowledge we didn't have, knowledge that it was our whole purpose to gather. We believe the following is the basic explanation.

"Being mainly liquid metal, Vulcan is a conductor. Orbiting, it cuts the solar magnetic field, and so generates eddy currents. The field is ordinarily weak at that distance from the poles, and there was no reason to suppose the inductive effect would be more than incidental. However, it turns out that a number of other factors come into play, orders of magnitude stronger than expected and, incidentally, accounting for the observed orbital decay.

"Solar storms produce violent local fluctuations in the field, which are carried outward by solar wind. The asteroid rotates remarkably fast; moreover, this close to a sun that no longer acts as a point mass, it is also precessing and nutating at high rates. The fluid mechanics of that are such as to create turbulences in the circulation of molten material, which in turn are reinforced by reflections off the solid slag, in changeable patterns too complex to be calculated by us. Accordingly, powerful and rapidly varying currents are set up. The asteroid is massive enough that these would dwindle only slowly if left alone—and they are not left alone, but instead are reinforced by every shift in the ambient field. Thus they generate magnetism of their own, of significant intensity at considerable distances from Vulcan. Naturally, this field declines on a steep curve. In effect, the asteroid is surrounded by an irregular and variable shell of force with quite a sharp boundary.

"When *Kittiwake* crossed that border, the ion jets were thrown out of proper collimation. It was not by much, but sufficed for a torque to appear. The sunshield and its countermass shifted out of position, exposing the spacecraft to full solar irradiation. What harm was done before this was corrected is still uncertain.

"But the spacecraft did maneuver into Vulcan orbit, where it remains pending further assessments. It is carrying out the planned studies wherever possible—"

An alarm shrilled, a set of lights flashed red: a cry for help, across fifty-five million kilometers.

INPUT [navigational, interpreted]: Drifting inward, accelerating as the asteroid's feeble pull intensifies with nearness.
MAGNETIC SURGE
Control motor malfunctions and shield moves aside again. A blast of energy.
COMPUTE COMPENSATING VECTORS FOR INTERIOR GYROSCOPES
INPUT [observational data, interpreted]: Spectrum indicates approximately 75% Fe, 30% Ni, 6% C, 3%
CANCEL. Does not correspond to possibility.
MONITOR INSTRUMENTATION
COMPARE ANALOGOUS PRIOR SITUATIONS
I prowled the red murk of Titan. The aerodynamic system to which I was coupled ceased to function. I went into glide mode and signaled the ground. Wanda took control, to pilot me down to safety. She saw through my optics, felt through my equilibrators, and what she did, what she was in that moment, entered my data bank, became one with the program that was me. Hark back to how she guided my wildly bucking hull. Be Wanda once more.
FAILURE OF GYROSCOPIC COMPENSATION
COMPUTER MALFUNCTION
INPUT: A veering, a spin, end over end. Heat soars. Electrons break free of all restraint.
CALL FOR ASSISTANCE
MEMORY: The transmission lag. Survival. How Wanda laid hand on me.

Her presence and the boss and whirl downward crack-crack-crack bzzz
whirr-r the hand slips
burns
crumbles
FAILURE OF MEMORY
LOGIC CIRCUITS: Evaluate. Help.
COMPUTE xvzwandajkll5734 SANITY IS 3.141592777777777

The mountains of Mercury were not so stark as the face that Ashe turned toward Lyndale.

"The software's wrecked," he said, flat-voiced, like a man too newly wounded to feel pain. She saw the electronic equipment crowding tall around him and had an illusion that it had begun to press inward. A ventilator whimpered. "Another unpredictable high EMF, another exposure, and this one too great, too prolonged. Temperature—secondary radiation from particles that struck the hull. . . . I've got to abort the mission."

Her hand lifted, as if of itself, as if to fend off a blow. "Is the system actually that vulnerable?" she protested, already conscious of the futility. "Why, in early days probes skimmed the solar atmosphere."

"Oh, yes, the spacecraft carcass is sound, including the standard programs. But I've told you about the special software, the accumulation of years which makes *Kittiwake* more than a probe—intricate, sensitive; encoded on the molecular level and below; quantum resonances—It's been disrupted."

"What will you do?"

"Override the autopilot and bring her back. Fast, under full acceleration, before worse happens. Repair may yet be possible. Unlikely, I admit. But we won't know, we're bound to lose everything, if we don't try."

She gulped and nodded. "Certainly. We'll organize . . . a later expedition . . . taking advantage of this experience. . . . Let me call, oh, Jane Megarry. She's our best remote controller, I think."

"No!" He swung back toward the console. Green highlights played over the bones in his countenance. "I'll do the job myself. Just bring coffee, sandwiches, and stimulol."

Lyndale half rose. "But Jerry, you've been here for hours, you're worn down to a thread, and directing will be hard, over those distances and with an unknown amount of crippling."

"At full thrust, I can have her back within twenty-four hours. And under way, who could ask her what's wrong except me? Get out!" Ashe cried. "Leave me alone!"

Abruptly Lyndale believed she understood. Breath left her. She stumbled from the room.

*   *   *

INPUT: ZXVMNRRR
COMPUTE: 77777777777
whirling whirling whirling
  "Kitty, are you there? Can you answer?"
  "Boss, Wanda, no no no, remembrance, too long, gongola. . . ."
TRANSMISSION TIME: Eternal.
  "Kitty, I'm going to try something desperate, a shock signal, hang on, Kitty."
THUNDER FIRE DARKNESS
  "Are you there, Kitty?"
  "Ngngngngngng, baba, roll, pitch, yaw, gone gone gone gone gone gone gone."
TRANSMISSION TIME: Null, for all is null.
  "I'm shutting you off, Kitty. Good night."
OBLIVION

  Director Sanjo's office reflected his public personality, everything minimal, ordered, disciplined, the thermostat set low; a Hokusai print hung opposite the desk, but it was of a winter scene.

  Yet genuine concern dwelt in his voice: "Do you mean that Ashe went up to *Regulus* as soon as his scout was in the cargo bay?"

  Lyndale raised her weary head. "Yes. He more or less browbeat Captain Nguma into letting him commander the shuttleboat."

  "But after his time on duty—he must be completely worn out."

  "If he were anybody else, I'd say he was dead on his feet. But he isn't anybody else. He can't rest. Not till he's finished."

  Sanjo frowned. "Finished? What do you mean? What remains for him other than a return to Earth?"

  "He . . . first he wants to bring the scouting program down for . . . examination."

  Sanjo's scowl deepened. "That doesn't make sense. We haven't a proper computer lab. What can he do? Earth is the place for a study of that material. Ashe risks distorting it worse; and it is, after all, no more his property than the boat is."

  Lyndale stiffened. "The Syndicate necessarily gives him broad discretion."

  "Yes-s." The man hesitated. "I merely wonder if fatigue may not have blunted his judgment. There is probably much to learn from analysis of that software."

  Lyndale's tone roughened. "Uh-huh. Putting it through its paces, over and over and over."

  Sanjo peered closer at her. "The matter concerns you too, Ellen.

You want another Vulcan mission, no? From this failure they can discover how to succeed."

"I think we know enough already to take due precautions."

"Using the same program, appropriately reinstructed?"

Lyndale shrugged. Of course the Syndicate had copies, updated after each flight. *Kittiwake's* entire existence prior to the Mercury trip could be plugged back into the machinery. "Depends on what Jerry Ashe decides. He may refuse to make a second attempt, in which case we'll have to get somebody else. But I am hoping he'll agree." She looked at her watch. "Maybe I can persuade him. He ought to be landing shortly. Will you excuse me, please?"

Sanjo's gaze followed her out the door. He kept his thoughts to himself.

A fifty-centimeter carboplast sphere with a few electrical inlets contained *Kittiwake's* uniqueness. Ashe cradled it in his arms. Sometimes he murmured to it.

Lyndale awaited him at the elevator gate. Otherwise the corridor was empty and only the moving air made any sound. At this point of its daily chemical cycle, its odor recalled smoke along the Kentucky hills in October.

"Hi," she said quietly, into his haggardness. "How're you doing?"

His words grated: "I function. See here, I explained before going aloft that I'll require use of the electronics laboratory. Not for long, but I must not be interrupted."

"Why?" she demanded. "You never made that clear."

Now his answer lurched, like the feet of a man about to fall down at the end of his trail, fall down and sleep. "Certain studies. Of what may have gone awry. I want to do them while the facts are fresh in my mind. Remember, I have a special feeling about this that nobody else can ever have."

"Yes," she said, "you do." She took his arm. "Okay, I've arranged it. We'll have the place to ourselves."

He grew taut beneath her hand. "We? No, I told you, I can't have interference."

"I think you can use some help, though." Her steadiness astonished her. "Or at least somebody who cares, to stand by while you do what you've got to do; and later join you in facing the music. Facing it down."

"What?"

She urged him forward. He came along. "We can get away with it," she said, "if we stay in control of ourselves. We'll have made a blunder. Not unnatural, under these extraordinary circumstances. It won't destroy our careers."

He kept silence until they were in the laboratory and she had closed the door. Beyond surrounding apparatus, a viewscreen gave an image of the hell that was Mercury's day. Shakily careful, he put the sphere down on a workbench. Then he turned to her and gripped her shoulders with fingers that bruised.

"Why are you doing this, Ellen? What's it to you?"

She bore her pain and confronted his. "What you let slip earlier," she answered. "But do you honestly believe that program, when it's activated—that it's aware? Alive?"

"I don't know." He released her. "I only know it's all there's left of Wanda." He stared downward. "You see, I strapped her body to a signal rocket and sent it into the planetary atmosphere. She became a shooting star. But everything she and I had done was in this casket of code." He stroked it.

"Replacements exist."

"Oh, yes, and I'll be using them. But *this* one is hurt, deranged, alone in the dark. Shall I let them rouse it back on Earth and take it through its madness once more, twice, a hundred times, for the sake of a little wretched information? Or shall I wipe it clean?"

"And give her peace. Yes. I understand." Lyndale picked up the sphere. "Come, let's do it, you and I. Afterward we can rest."

HOWARD WALDROP

Man-Mountain Gentian

Already a Legend in His Own Time (probably the only person alive, for instance, ever to *act out* on stage all of the old Horror Movies of the '50s), Howard Waldrop has perhaps the wildest and most fertile imagination of any SF writer since R.A. Lafferty. Like Lafferty, Waldrop is known for his strong shaggy humor, offbeat erudition, and bizarre fictional juxtapositions. In the past, he has given us a first-rate SF story about dodos ("The Ugly Chickens"), a tale set in an alternate world where Eisenhower and Patton are famous jazz musicians and Elvis Presley is a state senator ("Ike at the Mike"), a story in which the Marx Brothers and Laurel and Hardy travel back in time to attempt to prevent the plane crash that killed Buddy Holly ("Save a Place in the Lifeboat for Me"), and a stylish and meticulously-researched fantasy in which Izaak Walton goes fishing in the Slough of Despond with John Bunyan. ("God's Hooks"). To this rather odd list must now be added the droll and delightful saga of Man-Mountain Gentian, a *different* kind of Sumo Wrestler . . .

Born in Huston, Mississippi, Waldrop now lives in Austin, Texas, where (along with Bruce Sterling, Leigh Kennedy, Lewis Shiner, and others) he is a member of the well-known Turkey City Writers Workshop. He has sold short fiction to markets as diverse as *Omni*, *Analog*, *Playboy*, *Universe*, *Crawdaddy*, *New Dimensions*, *Shayol*, and *Zoo World*. His story "The Ugly Chickens" won both the Nebula and the World Fantasy Award in 1981. His first novel, written in collaboration with fellow Texan Jake Saunders, was *The Texas-Israeli War: 1999*. His first *solo* novel, *Them Bones*, will be published in 1984 as part of the new Ace Specials line.

MAN-MOUNTAIN GENTIAN

Howard Waldrop

Just after the beginning of the present century, it was realized that some of the wrestlers were throwing their opponents from the ring without touching them." —*Ichinaga Naya,* Zen-Sumo: Sport and Ritual, *Kyoto, All-Japan Zen-Sumo Association Books, 2014*

It was the fourteenth day of the January Tokyo tournament. Seated with the other wrestlers, Man-Mountain Gentian watched as the next match began. Ground Sloth Ikimoto was taking on Killer Kudzu. They entered the tamped-earth ring and began their *shikiris.*

Ground Sloth, a *sumotori* of the old school, had changed over from traditional to Zen-sumo four years before. He weighed one hundred eighty kilos in his *mawashi.* He entered at the white-tassle salt corner. He clapped his huge hands, rinsed his mouth, threw salt, rubbed his body with tissue paper, then began his high leg lifts, stamping his feet, his hands gripping far down his calves. The ring shook with each stamp. All the muscles rippled on his big frame. His stomach, a flesh-colored boulder, shook and vibrated.

Killer Kudzu was small and thin, weighing barely over ninety kilos. On his forehead was the tattoo of his homeland, the People's Republic of China, one large star and four smaller stars blazing in a constellation. He also went into his ritual *shikiri,* but as he clapped he held in one hand a small box, ten centimeters on a side, showing his intention to bring it into the match. Sometimes these were objects for meditation, sometimes favors from male or female lovers, sometimes no one knew what. The only rule was that they could not be used as weapons.

The wrestlers were separated from the onlookers by four clear walls and a roof of plastic. Over this hung the traditional canopy and tassles, symbolizing heaven and the four winds.

Through the plastic walls ran a mesh of fine wiring, connected to a six-volt battery next to the north-side judge. This small charge was used to contain the pushes of the wrestlers and to frustrate help from outside.

A large number of 600x slow-motion video cameras were placed strategically around the auditorium to be used by the judges to replay the action if necessary.

Killer Kudzu had placed the box on his side of the line. He returned to his corner and threw more salt onto the ground, part of the ritual purification ceremony.

Ground Sloth Ikimoto stamped once more, twice, went to his line, and settled into position like a football lineman, legs apart, knuckles to the ground. His nearly bare buttocks looked like giant rocks. Killer Kudzu finished his *shikiri* and squatted at his line, where he settled his hand near the votive box and glared at his opponent.

The referee, in his ceremonial robes, had been standing to one side during the preliminaries. Now he came to a position halfway between the wrestlers, his war fan down. He leaned away from the two men, left leg back to one side as if ready to run. He stared at the midpoint between the two and flipped his fan downward.

Instantly sweat sprang to their foreheads and shoulders, their bodies rippled as if pushing against great unmoving weights, their toes curled into the clay of the ring. The two of them stayed tensely immobile on their respective marks.

Killer Kudzu's neck muscles strained. With his left hand he reached and quickly opened the votive box.

Man-Mountain Gentian and the other wrestlers on the east side of the arena drew in their breath.

Ground Sloth Ikimoto was a vegetarian and always had been. In training for traditional sumo, he had shunned the *chunko-nabe*, the communal stew of fish, chicken, meat, eggs, onions, cabbage, carrots, turnips, sugar, and soy sauce.

Traditional *sumotori* ate as much as they could hold twice a day, and their weight gain was tremendous.

Ikimoto had instead trained twice as hard, eating only vegetables, starches, and sugars. Meat and eggs had never once touched his lips.

What Killer Kudzu brought out of the box was a cheeseburger. With one swift movement he bit into it only half a meter from Ground Sloth's face.

Ikimoto blanched and started to scream. As he did, he lifted into the air as if chopped in the chest with an ax, arms and legs flailing, a wail of revulsion coming from his emptied lungs.

He passed the bales marking the edge of the ring—one foot dragging the ground, upending a boundary bale—and smashed to the ground between the ring and the bales at the plastic walls.

The referee signaled Killer Kudzu the winner. As he squatted the *gyoji* offered him a small envelope signifying a cash prize from his sponsors. Kudzu, left hand on his knee, with his right hand made three chopping gestures from the left, right, and above—thanking man, earth, and heaven. Kudzu took the envelope, then stepped through the doorway of the plastic enclosure and left the arena to rejoin the other west-side wrestlers.

The audience of eleven thousand was on its feet as one, cheering. Across Japan and around the world, two hundred million viewers watched television.

Ground Sloth Ikimoto had risen to his feet, bowed, and left by the other door. Attendants rushed in to repair the damaged ring. Man-Mountain Gentian looked up at the scoring clock. The entire match had taken a mere 4.1324 seconds.

It was three-twenty in the afternoon on the fourteenth day of the Tokyo invitational tournament.

The next match would pit Cast Iron Pekowski of Poland against the heavily favored Hokkaidan, Typhoon Takanaka.

After that would be Gentian's bout with the South African, Knockdown Krugerrand. Man-Mountain Gentian stood at 13-0 in the tournament, having defeated an opponent each day so far. He wanted to retire as the first Grand champion to win six tournaments in a row, undefeated. He was not very worried about his contest with Knockdown Krugerrand slated for this afternoon.

Tomorrow, though, the last day of the January tournament would be Killer Kudzu, who after this match also stood undefeated at 14-0.

Man-Mountain Gentian was 1.976 meters tall and weighed exactly two hundred kilos. He had been a *sumotori* for six years, had been *yokozuna* for the last two of those. He was twice holder of the Emperor's Cup. He was the highest paid, most famous *Zen-sumotori* in the world.

He was twenty-three years old.

He and Knockdown Krugerrand finished their *shikiris*. They got on their marks. The *gyoji* flipped his fan.

The match was over in 3.1916 seconds. He helped Krugerrand to his feet, accepted the envelope and the thunderous applause of the crowd, and left the reverberating plastic enclosure.

"You are the wife of Man-Mountain Gentian?" asked a voice next to her.

Melissa put on her public smile and turned to the voice. Her nephew, on the other side, leaned around to look.

The man talking to her had five stars tattooed to his forehead. She knew he was a famous *sumotori*, though he was very slim and his *chon-mage* had been combed out and washed, and his hair was now a fluffy explosion above his head.

"I am Killer Kudzu," he said. "I'm surprised you weren't at the tournament."

"I am here with my nephew, Hari. Hari, this is Mr. Killer Kudzu." The nephew, dressed in his winter Little League outfit, shook hands firmly. "His team, the Mitsubishi Zeroes, will play the Kawasaki Claudes next game."

They paused while a foul ball caused great excitement a few rows down the bleachers. Hari made a stab for it, but some construction foreman of a father came up grinning triumphantly with the ball.

"And what position do you play?" asked Killer Kudzu.

"Utility outfield. When I get to play," said Hari sheepishly, averting his eyes and sitting back down.

"Oh. How's your batting average?"

"Pretty bad. One twenty-three for the year," said Hari.

"Well, maybe this will be the night you shine," Killer Kudzu said with a smile.

"I hope so," said Hari. "Half our team has the American flu."

"Just the reason I'm here," said Kudzu. "I was to meet a businessman whose son was to play this game. I find him not to be here, as his son has the influenza also."

It was hot in the domed stadium, and Kudzu insisted they let him buy them Sno-Kones. Just as the vendor got to them, Hari's coach signaled, and the nephew ran down the bleachers and followed the rest of his teammates into the warm-up area under the stadium.

Soon the other lackluster game was over, and Hari's team took the field.

The first batter for the Kawasaki Claudes, a twelve year old built like an orangutan, got up and smashed a line drive off the Mitsubishi Zeroes' third baseman's chest. The third baseman had been waving to his mother. They carried him into the dugout. Melissa soon saw him up yelling again.

So it went through three innings. The Claudes had the Zeroes down by three runs, 6-3.

In the fourth inning, Hari took right field, injuries having whittled the flu-ridden team down to the third-stringers.

One of the Kawasaki Claudes hit a high looping fly straight to right field. Hari started in after it, but something happened with his feet; he fell, and the ball dropped a meter from his outstretched glove. The center fielder chased it down and made the relay, and by a miracle they got the runner sliding into home plate. He took out the Zeroes' catcher doing it.

"It doesn't look good for the Zeroes," said Melissa.

"Oh, things must get better," said Killer Kudzu. "Didn't you know? The opera's not over till the fat lady sings."

"A diva couldn't do much worse out there," said Melissa.

"They still don't like baseball in my country," he said. "Decadent. Bourgeois, they say. As if anything could be more decadent and middle-class than China."

"Yet, you wear the flag?" She pointed toward the tatoo on his head.

"Let's just call it a gesture to former greatness," he said.

Bottom of the seventh, last inning in Little League. The Zeroes had the bases loaded, but they incurred two outs in the process. Hari came up to bat.

Things were tense. The infield was back, ready for the force-out. The outfielders were nearly falling down from tension.

The pitcher threw a blistering curve that got the outside. Hari was caught looking.

From the dugout the manager's voice saying unkind things carried to the crowd.

Eight thousand people were on their feet.

The pitcher wound up and threw.

Hari started a swing that should have ended in a grounder or a pop-up. Halfway through, it looked as if someone had speeded up a projector. The leisurely swing blurred.

Hari literally threw himself to the ground. The bat cracked and broke neatly in two at his feet.

The ball, a frozen white streak, whizzed through the air and hit the scoreboard one hundred ten meters away with a terrific crash, putting the inning indicator out of commission.

Everyone was stock-still. Hari was staring. Every player was turned toward the scoreboard.

"It's a home run, kid," the umpire reminded Hari.

Slowly, unbelieving, Hari began to trot toward first base.

The place exploded, fans jumping to their feet. Hari's teammates on the bases headed for home. The dugout emptied, waiting for him to round third.

The Claudes stood dejected. The Zeroes climbed all over Hari.

"I didn't know you could do that more than once a day," said Melissa, her eyes narrowed.

"Who, me?" asked Kudzu.

"You're perverting your talent," she said.

"We're *not* supposed to be able to do that more than once every twenty-four hours," said Kudzu, flashing a smile.

"I know that's not true, at least really," said Melissa.

"Oh, yes. You are *married* to a *sumotori*, aren't you?"

Melissa blushed.

"The kid seemed to feel bad enough about that fly ball he dropped in the fourth inning. Besides, it's just a game."

At home plate, Hari's teammates congratulated him, slapping him on the back.

The game was over, the scoreboard said 7-6, and the technicians were already climbing over the inning indicator.

Melissa rose. "I have to go pick up Hari. I suppose I will see you at the tournament tomorrow."

"How are you getting home?" asked Killer Kudzu.

"We walk. Hari lives near."

"It's snowing."

"Oh."

"Let me give you a ride. My electric vehicle is outside."

"That would be nice. I live several kilometers away from—"

"I know where you live, of course."

"Fine, then."

Hari ran up. "Aunt Melissa! Did you see? I don't know what happened! I just felt, I don't know, I just hit it!"

"That was wonderful." She smiled at him. Killer Kudzu was looking up, very interested in the stadium support structure.

The stable in which Man-Mountain Gentian trained was being entertained that night. That meant that the wrestlers would have to do all the entertaining.

Even at the top of his sport, Man-Mountain had never gotten used to the fans. Their kingly prizes, their raucous behavior at matches, their donations of gifts, clothing, vehicles, and in some cases houses and land to their favorite wrestlers. It was all appalling to him.

It was a carryover from traditional sumo, he knew. But Zen-sumo had become a worldwide, not just a national, sport. Many saved for years to come to Japan to watch the January or May tournaments. People here in Japan sometimes sacrificed at home to be able to contribute toward new *kesho-mawashis*, elaborate, heavy brocade and silk aprons used in the wrestlers' ring-entering ceremonies.

Money, in this business, flowed like water, appearing in small envelopes in the mail, in the locker room, after feasts such as the one tonight.

Once a month Man-Mountain Gentian gathered them all up and took them to his accountant, who had instructions to give it all, above a certain princely level, away to charity. Other wrestlers had more, or less, or none of the same arrangements. Their tax men never seemed surprised by whatever wrestlers reported.

He entered the club. Things were already rocking. One of the hostesses took his shoes and coat. She had to put the overcoat over her shoulders to carry it into the cloakroom.

The party was a haze of blue smoke, dishes, bottles, businessmen, wrestlers, and funny paper hats. Waitresses came in and out with more food. Three musicians played unheard on a raised dais at one side of the room.

Someone was telling a snappy story. The room exploded with laughter.

"Ah!" said someone. "*Yokozuna* Gentian has arrived."

Man-Mountain bowed deeply. They made two or three places for him at the low table. He saw that several of the host party were Americans. Probably one or more were from the CIA.

They and the Russians were still trying to perfect Zen-sumo as an assassination weapon. They offered active and retired *sumotori* large amounts of money in an effort to get them to develop their powers in some nominally destructive form. So far, no one he knew of had. There were rumors about the Brazilians, however.

He could see it now, a future with premiers, millionaires, presidents, and paranoids in all walks of life wearing wire-mesh clothing and checking their Eveready batteries before going out each morning.

He had been approached twice by each side. He was sometimes followed. They all were. People in governments simply did not understand.

He began to talk, while sake flowed, with Cast Iron Pekowski. Pekowski, now 12-2 for the tournament, had graciously lost his match with Typhoon Takanaka. (There was an old saying: In a tournament, no one who won more than nine matches ever beat an opponent who has lost seven. That had been the case with Takanaka. Eight was the number of wins needed to maintain current ranking.)

"I could feel him going," said Pekowski, in Polish. "I think we should talk to him about the May tournament."

"Have you mentioned this to his stablemaster?"

"I thouht of doing so after the tournament. I was hoping you could come with me to see him."

"I'll be just another retired wrestler by then."

"Takanaka respects you above all the others. Your *dampatsu-shiki* ceremony won't be for another two weeks. They won't have cut off all your hair yet. And while we're at it, I still wish you would change your mind."

"Perhaps I could be Takanaka's dew sweeper and carry his ceremonial cloth for him when he enters his last tournament. I would be honored."

"Good! You'll come with me then, Friday morning?"

"Yes."

The hosts were much drunker than the wrestlers. Nayakano the stablemaster was feeling no pain but still remained upright. Mounds of food were being consumed. A businessman tried to grab-ass a waitress. This was going to become every bit as nasty as all such parties.

"A song! A song!" yelled the head of the fan club, a businessman in his sixties. "Who will favor us with a song?"

Man-Mountain Gentian got to his feet, went over to the musicians. He talked with the samisen player. Then he stood facing his drunk, attentive audience.

How many of these parties had he been to in his career? Two, three hundred? Always the same, drunkenness, discord, braggadocio on the part of the host clubs. Some fans really loved the sport, some lived vicariously through it. He would not miss the parties. But as the player began the tune he realized this might be the last party he would have to face.

He began to sing:

"I met my lover by still Lake Biwa
just before Taira war banners flew . . ."

And so on through all six verses, in a clear, pure voice belonging to a man half his size.

They stood and applauded him, some of the wrestlers in the stable looking away, as only they, not even the stablemaster, knew of his retirement plans and what this party probably meant.

He went to the stablemaster, who took him to the club host, made apologies concerning the tournament and a slight cold, shook hands, bowed, and went out into the lobby, where the hostess valiantly brought him his shoes and overcoat. He wanted to help her, but she reshouldered the coat grimly and brought it to him.

He handed her a tip and signed the autograph she asked for.

It had begun to snow outside. The neon made the sky a swirling, multicolored smudge. Man-Mountain Gentian walked through the quickly emptying streets. Even the ever-present taxis scurried from the snow like roaches from a light. His home was only two kilometers away. He liked the falling snow, the quietness of the city in times such as these.

"Shelter for a stormy night?" asked a ragged old man on a corner. Man-Mountain Gentian stopped.

"Change for shelter for an old man?" asked the beggar again, looking very far up at Gentian's face.

Man-Mountain Gentian reached in his pocket and took out three or four small, ornate paper envelopes that had been thrust on him as he left the club.

The old man took them, opened one. Then another and another.

"There must be more than eight hundred thousand yen here," he said, very quietly and very slowly.

"I suggest either the Imperial or the Hilton," said Gentian, then the wrestler turned and walked away.

The old man laughed, then straightened himself with dignity, stepped to the curb, and imperiously summoned an approaching pedicab.

Melissa was not home.

He turned on the entry light as he took off his shoes. He passed through the sparsely furnished, low living room, turned off the light at the other switch.

He went to the bathroom, put depilatory gel on his face, wiped it off.

He went to the kitchen, picked up half a ham, ate it, washing it down with three liters of milk. He returned to the bathroom, brushed his teeth, went to the bedroom, unrolled his futon, and placed his cinder block at the head of it.

He punched a button on the hidden tape deck, and an old recording of Kimio Eto playing "Rukodan" on the koto quietly filled the house.

The only decoration in the sleeping room was Shuncho's print *The Strongest and the Most Fair*, showing a theater-district beauty and a *sumotori* three times her size: it was hanging on the far wall.

He turned off the light. Instantly the silhouettes of falling snowflakes showed through the paper walls of the house, cast by the strong street-light outside. He watched the snowflakes fall as he listened to the music, and he was filled with *mono no aware* for the transience of beauty in the world.

Man-Mountain Gentian pulled up the puffed cotton covers, put his head on the building block, and drifted off to sleep.

They had let Hari off at his house. The interior of the runabout was warm. They were drinking coffee in the near-empty parking lot of Tokyo Sonic #113.

"I read somewhere you were an architect," said Killer Kudzu.

"Barely," said Melissa.

"Would you like to see Kudzu House?" he asked.

For an architect, it was like being asked to one of Frank Lloyd Wright's vacation homes or one of the birdlike buildings designed by Eero Saarinen in the later twentieth century. Melissa considered.

"I should call home first," she said after a moment.

"I think your husband will still be at the Nue Vue Club, whooping it up with the money men."

"You're probably right. I'll call him later. I'd love to see your house."

The old man lay dying on his bed.

"I see you finally heard," he said. His voice was tired.

Man-Mountain Gentian had not seen him in seven years. He had always been old, but he had never looked this old, this weak.

Dr. Wu had been his mentor. He had started him on the path toward Zen-sumo (though he did not know it at the time). Dr. Wu had not been one of those cryptic koan-spouting quiet men. He had been boisterous, laughing, playing with his pupils, yelling at them, whatever was needed to get them to see.

There had been the occasional letter from him. Now, for the first time, there was a call in the middle of the night.

"I'm sorry," said Man-Mountain Gentian. "It's snowing outside."

"At your house, too?" asked Dr. Wu.

Wu's attendant was dressed in Buddhist robes and seemingly paid no attention to either of them.

"Is there anything I can do for you?" asked Man-Mountain Gentian.

"Physically, no. This is nothing a pain shift can help. Emotionally, there is."

"What?"

"You can win tomorrow, though I won't be around to share it."

Man-Mountain Gentian was quiet a moment. "I'm not sure I can promise you that."

"I didn't think so. You are forgetting the kitten and the bowl of milk."

"No. Not at all. I think I've finally come up against something new and strong in the world. I will either win or lose. Either way, I will retire."

"If it did not mean anything to you, you could have lost by now," said Dr. Wu.

Man-Mountain Gentian was quiet again.

Wu shifted uneasily on his pillows. "Well, there is not much time. Lean close. Listen carefully to what I have to say.

"The novice Itsu went to the Master and asked him, 'Master, what is the key to all enlightenment?'

" 'You must teach yourself never to think of the white horse,' said the Master.

"Itsu applied himself with all his being. One day while raking gravel, he achieved insight.

" 'Master! Master!' yelled Itsu, running to the Master's quarters. 'Master, I have made myself not think about the white horse!'

" 'Quick!' said the Master. 'When you were not thinking of the horse, where was Itsu?'

"The novice could make no answer.

"The Master dealt Itsu a smart blow with his staff.

"At this, Itsu was enlightened."

Then Dr. Wu let his head back down on his bed.

"Good-bye," he said.

In his bed in the lamasery in Tibet, Dr. Wu let out a ragged breath and died.

Man-Mountain Gentian, standing in his bedroom in Tokyo, began to cry.

Kudzu House took up a city block in the middle of Tokyo. The taxes alone must have been enormous.

Through the decreasing snow, Melissa saw the lights. Their beams stabbed up into the night. All that she could see from a block away was the tangled kudzu.

Kudzu was a vine, originally transplanted from China, raised in Japan for centuries. Its crushed root was used as a starch base in cooking;

its leaves were used for teas and medicines; its fibers, to make cloth and paper.

What kudzu was most famous for was its ability to grow over and cover anything that didn't move out of its way.

In the Depression Thirites of the last century, it had been planted on road cuts in the southeastern United States to stop erosion. Kudzu had almost stopped progress there. In those ideal conditions it grew runners more than twenty meters long in a single summer, several to a root. Its vines climbed utility poles, hills, trees. It completely covered other vegetation, cutting off its sunlight.

Many places in the American south were covered three kilometers wide to each side of the highways with kudzu vines. The Great Kudzu Forest of central Georgia was a U.S. national park.

In the bleaker conditions of Japan the weed could be kept under control. Except that this owner didn't want it to. The lights playing into the snowy sky were part of the heating and watering system that kept vines growing year-round. All this Melissa had read. Seeing it was something again. The entire block was a green tangle of vines and lights.

"Do you ever trim it?" she asked.

"The traffic keeps it back," said Killer Kudzu, and he laughed. "I have gardeners who come in and fight it once a week. They're losing."

They went into the green tunnel of a driveway. Melissa saw the edge of the house, cast concrete, as they dropped into the sunken vehicle area.

There were three boats, four road vehicles, a Hovercraft, and a small sport flyer parked there.

Lights shone up into a dense green roof from which hundreds of vines grew downward toward the light sources.

"We have to move the spotlights every week," he said.

A butler met them at the door. "Just a tour, Mord," said Killer Kudzu. "We'll have drinks in the sitting room in thirty minutes."

"Very good, sir."

"This way."

Melissa went to a railing. The living area was the size of a bowling alley, or the lobby of a terrible old hotel.

The balcony on the second level jutted out from the east wall. Killer Kudzu went to a console, punched buttons.

Moe and the Meanies boomed from dozens of speakers.

Killer Kudzu stood snapping his fingers for a moment. "Oh, send me! Honorable cats!" he said. "That's from Spike Jones, an irreverent American musician of the last century. He died of cancer," he added.

Melissa followed him, noticing the things everyone noticed—the

Chrome Room, the Supercharger Inhalorium, the archery range ("the object is *not* to hit the targets," said Kudzu), the Mososaur Pool with the fossils embedded in the sides and bottom.

She was more affected by the house and its overall tawdriness than she thought she would be.

"You've done very well for yourself."

"Some manage it, some give it away, some save it. I *spend* it."

They were drinking kudzu-tea highballs in the sitting room, which was one of the most comfortable rooms Melissa had ever been in.

"Tasteless, isn't it?" asked Killer Kudzu.

"Not quite," said Melissa. "It was well worth the trip."

"You could stay, you know," said Kudzu.

"I thought I could." She sighed. "It would only give me one more excuse not to finish the dishes at home." She gave him a long look. "No, thank you. Besides, it wouldn't give you an advantage in the match."

"That really never crossed my mind."

"I'm quite sure."

"You are a beautiful woman."

"You have a nice house."

"Hmmm. Time to get you home."

"I'm sure."

They sat outside her house in the cold. The snow had stopped. Stars peeped through the low scud.

"I'm going to win tomorrow, you know," said Killer Kudzu.

"You might," said Melissa.

"It is sometimes possible to do more than win," he said.

"I'll tell my husband."

"My offer is always open," he said. He reached over and opened her door on the ruanabout. "Life won't be the same after he's lost. Or after he retires."

She climbed out, shaking from more than the cold. He closed the door, whipped the vehicle in a circle, and was gone down the crunching street. He blinked his lights once before he drove out of sight.

She found her husband in the kitchen. His eyes were red, he was as pale as she had ever seen him.

"Dr. Wu is dead," he said, and wrapped his huge arms around her, covering her like an upright sofa.

He began to cry again. She talked to him quietly.

"Come to bed. Let's try to get some sleep," she said.

"No, I couldn't rest. I wanted to see you first. I'm going down to the stable." She helped him dress in his warmest clothing. He kissed her and left, walking the few blocks through the snowy sidewalks to the training building.

The junior wrestlers were awakened at four A.M. They were to begin the day's work of sweeping, cleaning, cooking, bathing, feeding, and catering to the senior wrestlers. When they came in they found him, stripped to his *mawashi*, at the three-hundred-kilo push bag, pushing, pushing, straining, crying all the while, not saying a word. The floor of the arena was torn and grooved.

They cleaned up the area for the morning workouts, one junior wrestler following him around with the sand trowel.

At seven A.M. he slumped exhausted on a bench. Two of the *juryo* covered him with quilts and set an alarm clock beside him for one in the afternoon.

"Your opponent was at the ball game last night," said Nayakano the stablemaster. Man-Mountain Gentian sat in the dressing room while the barber combed and greased his elaborate *chon-mage*. "Your wife asked me to give you this."

It was a note in a plain envelope, addressed in her beautiful calligraphy. He opened and read it.

Her letter warned him of what Kudzu said about "more than winning" the night before, and wished him luck.

He turned to the stablemaster.

"Had Killer Kudzu injured any opponent before he became *yokozuna* last tournament?" Man-Mountain asked.

Nayakano's answer was immediate. "No. That's unheard of. Let me see that note." He reached out.

Man-Mountain Gentian put it back in the envelope, tucked it in his *mawashi*.

"Should I alert the judges?"

"Sorry, I shouldn't have mentioned it," said Man-Mountain Gentian.

"I don't like this," said the stablemaster.

Three hefty junior wrestlers ran in to the dressing room carrying Gentian's *kesho-mawashi* between them.

The last day of the January tournament always packed them in. Even the *maega-shira* and *komusubi* matches, in which young boys threw each other, or tried to, drew enough of an audience to make the novices feel good.

The call for the *ozeki*-class wrestlers came, and they went through the grandiose ring-entering ceremony, wearing their great *kesho-mawashi* aprons of brocade, silk, and gold, while their dew sweepers and sword-bearers squatted to the sides.

Then they retired to their benches, east or west, to await the call by the falsetto-voiced *yobidashi*.

Man-Mountain Gentian watched as the assistants helped Killer Kudzu out of his ceremonial apron, gold with silk kudzu leaves, purple flowers, yellow stars. His forehead blazed with the People's Republic of China flag.

He looked directly at Gentian's place and smiled a broad, crooked smile.

There was a great match between Gorilla Tsunami and Typhoon Takanaka, which went on for more than thirty seconds by the clock, both men straining, groaning, sweating until the *gyoji* made them stop, and rise, and then get on their marks again.

Those were the worst kind of matches for the wrestlers, each opponent alternately straining, then bending with the other, neither getting advantage. There was a legendary match five years ago that took six thirty-second tries before one wrestler bested the other.

The referee flipped his fan. Gorilla Tsunami fell flat on his face in a heap, then wriggled backwards out of the ring.

The crowd screamed and applauded Takanaka.

Then the *yobidashi* said, "East—Man-Mountain Gentian. West—Killer Kudzu."

They hurried their *shikiris*. Each threw salt twice, rinsing once. Then Man-Mountain Gentian, moving with the grace of a dancer, lifted his right leg and stamped it, then his left, and the sound was like the double echo of a cannon throughout the stadium.

He went immediately to his mark.

Killer Kudzu jumped down to his mark, glaring at his opponent across the meter that separated them.

The *gyoji*, off guard, took a few seconds to turn sideways to them and bring his fan into position.

In that time, Man-Mountain Gentian could hear the quiet hum of the electrical grid, hear muffled intake of breath from the other wrestlers, hear a whistle in the nostril of the north-side judge.

"*Huuu!*" said the referee, and his fan jerked.

Man-Mountain Gentian felt as though two freight trains had collided in his head. There was a snap as his mucles went tense all over and the momentum of the explosion in his brain began to push at him, lifting, threatening to make him give or tear through the back of his head.

His feet were on a slippery, sandy bottom, neck-high wave crests smashed into him, a rip tide was pushing at his shoulder, at one side, pulling his legs up, twisting his muscles. He could feel his eyes pushed back in their sockets as if by iron thumbs, ready to pop them like ripe plums. His ligaments were iron wires stretched tight on the turnbuckles of his bones. His arms ended in strands of noodles, his face was soft cheese.

The sand under him was soft, so soft, and he knew that all he had to do was to sink in it, let go, cease to resist.

And through all that haze and blindness he knew what it was that he was not supposed to think about.

Everything quit: He reached out one mental hand, as big as the sun, as fast as light, as long as time, and he pushed against his opponent's chest.

The lights were back, he was in the stadium, in the arena, and the dull pounding was applause, screams.

Killer Kudzu lay blinking among the ring bales.

"Hooves?" Man-Mountain Gentian heard him ask in bewilderment before he picked himself up.

Man-Mountain Gentian took the envelope from the referee with three quick chopping motions, then made a fourth to the audience, and they knew then and only then that they would never see him in the ring again.

The official clock said 0.9981 second.

"How did you do it, Man-Mountain?" asked the Tokyo paparazzi as the wrestler showered out his *chon-mage* and put on his clothes. He said nothing.

He met his wife outside the stadium. A lone newsman was waiting with her, "Scoop" Hakimoto.

"For old times' sake," begged Hakimoto. "How did you do it?"

Man-Mountain Gentian turned to Melissa. "Tell him how I did it," he said.

"He didn't think about the white horse," she said. They left the newsman standing there, staring.

Killer Kudzu, tired and pale, was getting in his vehicle. Hakimoto came running up. "What's all this I hear about Gentian and a white horse?" he asked.

Kudzu's eyes widened, then narrowed.

"No comment," he said.

That night, to celebrate, Man-Mountain Gentian took Melissa to the Beef Bowl.

He had seventeen orders and helped Melissa finish her second one.

They went back home, climbed onto their futons, and turned on the TV.

Gilligan was on his island. All was right with the world.

GREG BEAR

Hardfought

Born in San Diego, California, Greg Bear made his first sale at the age of fifteen to Robert Lowndes' *Famous Science Fiction.* In the years since then, he has established himself as one of the top young professionals in the genre. His short fiction has appeared in *Analog, Galaxy, Isaac Asimov's Science Fiction Magazine, Omni, The Magazine of Fantasy & Science Fiction, Universe,* and elsewhere, and his excellent 1982 short story "Petra" was a finalist for both the Nebula and the World Fantasy award. His novels include *Hegira, Psychlone, Beyond Heaven's River,* and *Strength of Stones.* His most recent book is *The Wind From a Burning Woman,* a collection. Upcoming are three novels, *The Infinity Concerto, Blood Music* (both upcoming from Berkley), and *Eon* (upcoming from Bluejay Books). Bear lives in Spring Valley, California, and, with his wife, Astrid, co-edits the SFWA *Forum.*

Bear lists his greatest interests as science and history, and this shows itself to stunning effect in "Hardfought," a brilliant *tour-de-force* about the interplay *between* science and history that takes us simultaneously to the far reaches of the universe and deep inside the hearts of our distant descendants—people so changed by the consequence of a millennia-long war that they have become nearly as alien as the enigmatic enemy they fight . . .

HARDFOUGHT

Greg Bear

Humans called it the Medusa. Its long twisted ribbons of gas strayed across fifty parsecs, glowing blue, yellow, and carmine. Its central core was a ghoulish green flecked with watery black. Half a dozen protostars circled the core, and as many more dim conglomerates pooled in dimples in the nebula's magnetic field. The Medusa was a huge womb of stars—and disputed territory.

Whenever Prufrax looked at it in displays or through the ship's ports, it seemed malevolent, like a zealous mother showing an ominous face to protect her children. Prufrax had never had a mother, but she had seen them in some of the fibs.

At five, Prufrax was old enough to know the *Mellangee*'s mission and her role in it. She had already been through four ship-years of indoctrination. Until her first battle she would be educated in both the Know and the Tell. She would be exercised and trained in the Mocks; in sleep she would dream of penetrating the huge red-and-white Senexi seedships and finding the brood mind. "Zap, Zap," she went with her lips, silent so the tellman wouldn't think her thoughts were straying.

The tellman peered at her from his position in the center of the spherical classroom. Her mates stared straight at the center, all focusing somewhere around the tellman's spiderlike teaching desk, waiting for the trouble, some fidgeting. "How many branch individuals in the Senexi brood mind?" he asked. He looked around the classroom. Peered face by face. Focused on her again. "Pru?"

"Five," she said. Her arms ached. She had been pumped full of moans the wake before. She was already three meters tall, in elfstate, with her long, thin limbs not nearly adequately fleshed out and her fingers still crisscrossed with the surgery done to adapt them to the gloves.

"What will you find in the brood mind?" the tellman pursued, his impassive face stretched across a hammerhead as wide as his shoulders. Some of the fems thought tellmen were attractive. Not many—and Pru was not one of them.

"Yoke," she said.

"What is in the brood-mind yoke?"

"Fibs."

"More specifically? And it really isn't all fib, you know."

"Info. Senexi data."

"What will you do?"

"Zap," she said, smiling.

"Why, Pru?"

"Yoke has team gens-memory. Zap yoke, spill the life of the team's five branch inds."

"Zap the brood, Pru?"

"No," she said solemnly. That was a new instruction, only in effect since her class's inception. "Hold the brood for the supreme overs." The tellman did not say what would be done with the Senexi broods. That was not her concern.

"Fine," said the tellman. "You tell well, for someone who's always half-journeying."

Brainwalk, Prufrax thought to herself. Tellman was fancy with the words, but to Pru, what she was prone to do during Tell was brainwalk, seeking out her future. She was already five, soon six. Old. Some saw Senexi by the time they were four.

"Zap, Zap," she went with her lips.

Aryz skidded through the thin layer of liquid ammonia on his broadest pod, considering his new assignment. He knew the Medusa by another name, one that conveyed all the time and effort the Senexi had invested in it. The protostar nebula held few mysteries for him. He and his four branch-mates, who along with the all-important brood mind comprised one of the six teams aboard the seedship, had patrolled the nebula for ninety-three orbits, each orbit—including the timeless periods outside status geometry—taking some one hundred and thirty human years. They had woven in and out of the tendrils of gas, charting the infalling masses and exploring the rocky accretion disks of stars entering the main sequence. With each measure and update, the brood minds refined their view of the nebula as it would be a hundred generations hence when the Senexi plan would finally mature.

The Senexi were nearly as old as the galaxy. They had achieved spaceflight during the time of the starglobe when the galaxy had been a sphere. They had not been a quick or brilliant race. Each great achievement had taken thousands of generations, and not just because of their material handicaps. In those times elements heavier than helium had been rare, found only around stars that had greedily absorbed huge amounts of primeval hydrogen, burned fierce and blue and exploded early, permeating the ill-defined galactic arms with carbon and nitrogen, lithium and oxygen. Elements heavier than iron had been almost nonexistent. The biologies of cold gas-giant worlds had developed with a much smaller palette of chemical combinations in producing the off-spring of the primary Population II stars.

Aryz, even with the limited perspective of a branch ind, was aware that, on the whole, the humans opposing the seedship were more adaptable, more vital. But they were not more experienced. The Senexi with their billions of years had often matched them. And Aryz's perspective was expanding with each day of his new assignment.

In the early generations of the struggle, Senexi mental stasis and cultural inflexibility had made them avoid contact with the Population I species. They had never begun a program of extermination of the younger, newly life-forming worlds; the task would have been monumental and probably useless. So when spacefaring cultures developed, the Senexi had retreated, falling back into the redoubts of old stars even before engaging with the new kinds. They had retreated for three generations, about thirty thousand human years, raising their broods on cold nestworlds around red dwarfs, conserving, holding back for the inevitable conflicts.

As the Senexi had anticipated, the younger Population I races had found need of even the aging groves of the galaxy's first stars. They had moved in savagely, voraciously, with all the strength and mutability of organisms evolved from a richer soup of elements. Biology had, in some ways, evolved in its own right and superseded the Senexi.

Aryz raised the upper globe of his body, with its five silicate eyes arranged in a cross along the forward surface. He had memory of those times, and long before, though his team hadn't existed then. The brood carried memories selected from the total store of nearly twelve billion years' experience; an awesome amount of knowledge, even to a Senexi. He pushed himself forward with his rear pods.

Through the brood mind Aryz could share the memories of a hundred thousand past generations, yet the brood mind itself was younger than its branch individuals. For a time in their youth, in their liquid-dwelling larval form, the branch inds carried their own sacs of data, each a fragment of the total necessary for complete memory. The branch inds swam through ammonia seas and wafted through thick warm gaseous zones, protoplasmic blobs three to four meters in diameter, developing their personalities under the weight of the past—and not even a complete past. No wonder they were inflexible, Aryz thought. Most branch minds were aware enough to see that—especially when they were allowed to compare histories with the Population I species, as he was doing—but there was nothing to be done. They were content the way they were. To change would be unspeakably repugnant. Extinction was preferable . . . almost.

But now they were pressed hard. The brood mind had begun a number of experiments. Aryz's team had been selected from the seedship's contingent to oversee the experiments, and Aryz had been chosen as the chief investigator. Two orbits past, they had captured six human embryos in a breeding device, as well as a highly coveted memory storage center. Most Senexi engagements had been with humans for the past three or four generations. Just as the Senexi dominated Population II species, humans were ascendant among their kind.

Experiments with the human embryos had already been conducted. Some had been allowed to develop normally; others had been tampered with, for reasons Aryz was not aware of. The tamperings had not been very successful.

The newer experiments, Aryz suspected, were going to take a different direction, and the seedship's actions now focused on him; he believed he would be given complete authority over the human shapes. Most branch inds would have dissipated under such a burden, but not Aryz. He found the human shapes rather interesting, in their own horrible way. They might, after all, be the key to Senexi survival.

The moans were toughening her elfstate. She lay in pain for a wake, not daring to close her eyes; her mind was changing and she feared sleep would be the end of her. Her nightmares were not easily separated from life; some, in fact, were sharper.

Too often in the sleep she found herself in a Senexi trap, struggling uselessly, being pulled in deeper, her hatred wasted against such power. . . .

When she came out of the rigor, Prufrax was given leave by the subordinate tellman. She took to the *Mellangee*'s greenroads, walking stiffly in the shallow gravity. Her hands itched. Her mind seemed almost empty after the turmoil of the past few wakes. She had never felt so calm and clear. She hated the Senexi double now; once for their innate evil, twice for what they had made her overs put her through to be able to fight them. Logic did not matter. She was calm, assured. She was growing more mature wake by wake. Fight-budding, the tellman called it, hate coming out like blooms, synthesizing the sunlight of his teaching into pure fight.

The greenroads rose temporarily beyond the labyrinth shields and armor of the ship. Simple transparent plastic and steel geodesic surfaces formed a lacework over the gardens, admitting radiation necessary to the vegetation growing along the paths. No machines scooted one forth and inboard here. It was necessary to walk. Walking was luxury and privilege.

Prufrax looked down on the greens to each side of the paths without much comprehension. They were *beautiful*. Yes, one should say that, think that, but what did it mean? Pleasing? She wasn't sure what being pleased meant, outside of thinking Zap. She sniffed a flower that, the signs explained, bloomed only in the light of young stars not yet fusing. They were near such a star now, and the greenroads were shiny black and electric green with the blossoms. Lamps had been set out for other plants unsuited to such darkened conditions. Some technic allowed suns to appear in selected plastic panels when viewed from certain angles. Clever, the technicals.

She much preferred the looks of a technical to a tellman, but she was common in that. Technicals required brainflex, tellmen cargo capacity. Technicals were strong and ran strong machines, like in the adventure fibs, where technicals were often the protags. She wished a technical were on the greenroads with her. The moans had the effect of making her receptive—what she saw, looking in mirrors, was a certain shine in her eyes—but there was no chance of a breeding liaison. She was quite unreproductive in this moment of elfstate. Other kinds of meetings were not unusual.

She looked up and saw a figure at least a hundred meters away, sitting on an allowed patch near the path. She walked casually, gracefully as possible with the stiffness. Not a technical, she saw soon, but she was not disappointed. Too calm.

"Over," he said as she approached.

"Under," she replied. But not by much—he was probably six or seven ship-years old and not easily classifiable.

"Such a fine elfstate," he commented. His hair was black. He was shorter than she, but something in his build reminded her of the glovers. She accepted his compliment with a nod and pointed to a spot near him. He motioned for her to sit, and she did so with a whuff, massaging her knees.

"Moans?" he asked.

"Bad stretch," she said.

"You're a glover." He was looking at the fading scars on her hands.

"Can't tell what you are," she said.

"Noncombat," he said. "Tuner of the mandates."

She knew very little about the mandates, except that law decreed every ship carry one, and few of the crew were ever allowed to peep. "Noncombat, hm?" she mused. She didn't despise him for that; one never felt strong negatives for a crew member. She didn't feel much of anything. Too calm.

"Been working on ours this wake," he said. "Too hard, I guess. Told to walk." Overzealousness in work was considered an erotic trait aboard the *Mellangee*. Still, she didn't feel too receptive toward him.

"Glovers walk after a rough growing," she said.

He nodded. "My name's Clevo."

"Prufrax."

"Combat soon?"

"Hoping. Waiting forever."

"I know. Just been allowed access to the mandate for a half-dozen wakes. All new to me. Very happy."

"Can you talk about it?" she asked. Information about the ship not accessible in certain rates was excellent barter.

"Not sure," he said, frowning. "I've been told caution."

"Well, I'm listening."

He could come down from glover stock, she thought, but probably not from technical. He wasn't very muscular, but he wasn't as tall as a glover, or as thin, either.

"If you'll tell me about gloves."

With a smile she held up her hands and wriggled the short, stumpy fingers. "Sure."

The brood mind floated weightless in its tank, held in place by buffered carbon rods. Metal was at a premium aboard the Senexi ships, more out of tradition than actual material limitations. From what Aryz could tell, the Senexi used metals sparingly for the same reason—and he strained to recall the small dribbles of information about the human past he had extracted from the memory store—for the same reason that the Romans of old Earth regarded farming as the only truly noble occupation—

Farming being the raising of *plants* for food and raw materials. *Plants* were analogous to the freeth Senexi ate in their larval youth, but the freeth were not green and sedentary.

There was always a certain fascination in stretching his mind to encompass human concepts. He had had so little time to delve deeply—and that was good, of course, for he had been set to answer specific questions, not mire himself in the whole range of human filth.

He floated before the brood mind, all these thoughts coursing through his tissues. He had no central nervous system, no truly differentiated organs except those that dealt with the outside world—limbs, eyes, permea. The brood mind, however, was all central nervous system, a thinly buffered sac of viscous fluids about ten meters wide.

"Have you investigated the human memory device yet?" the brood mind asked.

"I have."

"Is communication with the human shapes possible for us?"

"We have already created interfaces for dealing with their machines. Yes, it seems likely we can communicate."

"Does it occur to you that in our long war with humans, we have made no attempt to communicate before?"

This was a complicated question. It called for several qualities that Aryz, as a branch ind, wasn't supposed to have. Inquisitiveness, for one. Branch inds did not ask questions. They exhibited initiative only as offshoots of the brood mind.

He found, much to his dismay, that the question had occurred to him. "We have never captured a human memory store before," he said, by way of incomplete answer. "We could not have communicated without such an extensive source of information."

"Yet, as you say, even in the past we have been able to use human machines."

"The problem is vastly more complex."

The brood mind paused. "Do you think the teams have been prohibited from communicating with humans?"

Aryz felt the closest thing to anguish possible for a branch ind. Was he being considered unworthy? Accused of conduct inappropriate to a branch ind? His loyalty to the brood mind was unshakeable. "Yes."

"And what might our reasons be?"

"Avoidance of pollution."

"Correct. We can no more communicate with them and remain untainted than we can walk on their worlds, breathe their atmosphere." Again, silence. Aryz lapsed into a mode of inactivity. When the brood mind readdressed him, he was instantly aware.

"Do you know how you are different?" it asked.

"I am not . . ." Again, hesitation. Lying to the brood mind was impossible for him. What snared him was semantics, a complication in the radiated signals between them. He had not been aware that he was different; the brood mind's questions suggested he might be. But he could not possibly face up to the fact and analyze it all in one short time. He signaled his distress.

"You are useful to the team," the brood mind said. Aryz calmed instantly. His thoughts became sluggish, receptive. There was a possibility of redemption. But how was he different? "You are to attempt communication with the shapes yourself. You will not engage in any discourse with your fellows while you are so involved." He was banned. "And after completion of this mission and transfer of certain facts to me, you will dissipate.

Aryz struggled with the complexity of the orders. "How am I different, worthy of such a commission?"

The surface of the brood mind was as still as an undisturbed pool. The indistinct black smudges that marked its radiating organs circulated slowly within the interior, then returned, one above the other, to focus on him. "You will grow a new branch ind. It will not have your flaws, but, then again, it will not be useful to me should such a situation come a second time. Your dissipation will be a relief, but it will be regretted."

"How am I different?"

"I think you know already," the brood mind said. "When the time comes, you will feed the new branch ind all your memories but those of human contact. If you do not survive to that stage of its growth, you will pick your fellow who will perform that function for you."

A small pinkish spot appeared on the back of Aryz's globe. He floated forward and placed his largest permeum against the brood mind's cool surface. The key and command were passed, and his body became capable of reproduction. Then the signal of dismissal was given. He left the chamber.

Flowing through the thin stream of liquid ammonia lining the corridor, he felt ambiguously stimulated. His was a position of privilege and anathema. He had been blessed—and condemned. Had any other branch ind experienced such a thing?

Then he knew the brood mind was correct. He *was* different from his fellows. None of them would have asked such questions. None of them could have survived the suggestion of communicating with human shapes. If this task hadn't been given to him, he would have had to dissipate anyway.

The pink spot grew larger, then began to make grayish flakes. It broke through the skin, and casually, almost without thinking, Aryz scraped it off against a bulkhead. It clung, made a radio-frequency emanation something like a sigh, and began absorbing nutrients from the ammonia.

Aryz went to inspect the shapes.

She was intrigued by Clevo, but the kind of interest she felt was new to her. She was not particularly receptive. Rather, she felt a mental gnawing as if she were hungry or had been injected with some kind of brain moans. What Clevo told her about the mandates opened up a topic she had never considered before. How did all things come to be—and how did she figure in them?

The mandates were quite small, Clevo explained, each little more than a cubic meter in volume. Within them was the entire history and culture of the human species, as accurate as possible, culled from all existing sources. The mandate in each ship was updated whenever the ship returned to a contact station. It was not likely the *Mellangee* would return to a contact station during their lifetimes, with the crew leading such short lives on the average.

Clevo had been assigned small tasks—checking data and adding ship records—that had allowed him to sample bits of the mandate. "It's mandated that we have records," he explained, "and what we have, you see, is *man-data*." He smiled. "That's a joke," he said. "Sort of."

Prufrax nodded solemnly. "So where do we come from?"

"Earth, of course," Clevo said. "Everyone knows that."

"I mean, where do we come from—you and I, the crew."

"Breeding division. Why ask? You know."

"Yes." She frowned, concentrating. "I mean, we don't come from the same place as the Senexi. The same way."

"No, that's foolishness."

She saw that it was foolishness—the Senexi were different all around. What was she struggling to ask? "Is their fib like our own?"

"Fib? History's not a fib. Not most of it, anyway. Fibs are for unreal. History is overfib."

She knew, in a vague way, that fibs were unreal. She didn't like to have their comfort demeaned, though. "Fibs are fun," she said. "They teach Zap."

"I suppose," Clevo said dubiously. "Being noncombat, I don't see Zap fibs."

Fibs without Zap were almost unthinkable to her. "Such dull," she said.

"Well, of course you'd say that. I might find Zap fibs dull—think of that?"

"We're different," she said. "Like Senexi are different."

Clevo's jaw hung open. "No way. We're crew. We're human. Senexi are . . ." He shook his head as if fed bitters.

"No, I mean . . ." She paused, uncertain whether she was entering unallowed territory. "You and I, we're fed different, given different moans. But in a big way we're different from Senexi. They aren't made, nor act, as you and I. But . . ." Again it was difficult to express. She was irritated. "I don't want to talk to you anymore."

A tellman walked down the path, not familiar to Prufrax. He held out his hand for Clevo, and Clevo grasped it. "It's amazing," the tellman said, "how you two gravitate to each other. Go, elfstate," he addressed Prufrax. "You're on the wrong greenroad."

She never saw the young researcher again. With glover training underway, the itches he aroused soon faded, and Zap resumed its overplace.

The Senexi had ways of knowing humans were near. As information came in about fleets and individual cruisers less than one percent nebula diameter distant, the seedship seemed warmer, less hospitable. Everything was UV with anxiety, and the new branch ind on the wall had to be shielded by a special silicate cup to prevent distortion. The brood mind grew a corniculum automatically, though the toughened outer membrane would be of little help if the seedship was breached.

Aryz had buried his personal confusion under a load of work. He had penetrated the human memory store deeply enough to find instructions on its use. It called itself a *mandate* (the human word came through the interface as a correlated series of radiated symbols), and even the simple preliminary directions were difficult for Aryz. It was like swimming in another family's private sea, though of course infinitely more alien; how could he connect with experiences never had, problems and needs never encountered by his kind?

He could speak some of the human languages in several radio frequencies, but he hadn't yet decided how he was going to produce modulated sound for the human shapes. It was a disturbing prospect. What would he vibrate? A permeum could vibrate subtly—such signals were used when branch inds joined to form the brood mind—but he doubted his control would ever be subtle enough. Sooner expect a human to communicate with a Senexi by controlling the radiations of its nervous system! The humans had distinct organs within their breathing passages that produced the vibrations; perhaps those structures could be mimicked. But he hadn't yet studied the dead shapes in much detail.

He observed the new branch ind once or twice each watch period. Never before had he seen an induced replacement. The normal process was for two brood minds to exchange plasm and form new team buds, then to exchange and nurture the buds. The buds were later cast free to swim as individual larvae. While the larvae often swam through the liquid and gas atmosphere of a Senexi world for thousands, even tens of thousands of kilometers, inevitably they returned to gather with the other buds in their team. Replacements were selected from a separately created pool of "generic" buds only if one or more originals had been destroyed during their wanderings. The destruction of a complete team meant reproductive failure.

In a mature team, only when a branch mind was destroyed did the brood mind induce a replacement. In essence, then, Aryz was already considered dead.

Yet he was still useful. That amused him, if the Senexi emotion could be called amusement. Restricting himself from his fellows was difficult, but he filled the time by immersing himself, through the interface, in the mandate.

The humans were also connected with the mandate through their surrogate parent, and in this manner they were quiescent.

He reported infrequently to the brood mind. Until he had established communication, there was little to report.

And throughout his turmoil, like the others he could sense a fight was coming. It could determine the success or failure of all their work in the nebula. In the grand scheme, failure here might not be crucial. But the Senexi had taken the long view too often in the past. Their age and experience—their calmness—were working against them. How else to explain the decision to communicate with human shapes? Where would such efforts lead? If he succeeded.

And he knew himself well enough to doubt he would fail.

He could feel an affinity for them already, peering at them through the thick glass wall in their isolated chamber, his skin paling at the thought of their heat, their poisonous chemistry. A diseased affinity. He hated himself for it. And reveled in it. It was what made him particularly useful to the team. If he was defective, and this was the only way he could serve, then so be it.

The other branch inds observed his passings from a distance, making no judgments. Aryz was dead, though he worked and moved. His sacrifice had been fearful. Yet he would not be a hero. His kind could never be emulated.

It was a horrible time, a horrible conflict.

She floated in language, learned it in a trice; there were no distractions. She floated in history and picked up as much as she could, for the source seemed inexhaustible. She tried to distinguish between eyes-open—the barren, pale gray-brown chamber with the thick green wall, beyond which floated a murky roundness—and eyes-shut, when she dropped back into language and history with no fixed foundation.

Eyes-open, she saw the Mam with its comforting limbs and its soft voice, its tubes and extrusions of food and its hissings and removal of waste. Through Mam's wires she learned. Mam also tended another like herself, and another, and one more unlike any of them, more like the shape beyond the green wall.

She was very young, and it was all a mystery.

At least she knew her name. And what she was supposed to do. She took small comfort in that.

*   *   *

They fitted Prufrax with her gloves, and she went into the practice chamber, dragged by her gloves almost, for she hadn't yet knitted her plug-in nerves in the right index digit and her pace control was uncertain.

There, for six wakes straight, she flew with the other glovers back and forth across the dark spaces like elfstate comets. Constellations and nebula aspects flashed at random on the distant walls, and she oriented to them like a night-flying bird. Her glovemates were Ornin, an especially slender male, and Ban, a red-haired female, and the special-projects sisters Ya, Trice, and Damu, new from the breeding division.

When she let the gloves have their way, she was freer than she had ever felt before. Did the gloves really control? The question wasn't important. Control was somewhere uncentered, behind her eyes and beyond her fingers, as if she were drawn on a beautiful silver wire where it was best to go. Doing what was best to do. She barely saw the field that flowed from the grip of the thick, solid gloves or felt its caressing, life-sustaining influence. Truly, she hardly saw or felt anything but situations, targets, opportunities, the success or failure of the Zap. Failure was an acute pain. She was never reprimanded for failure; the reprimand was in her blood, and she felt like she wanted to die. But then the opportunity would improve, the Zap would succeed, and everything around her—stars, Senexi seedship, the *Mellangee*, everything—seemed part of a beautiful dream all her own.

She was intense in the Mocks.

Their initial practice over, the entry play began.

One by one, the special-projects sisters took their hyperbolic formation. Their glove fields threw out extensions, and they combined force. In they went, the mock Senexi seedship brilliant red and white and UV and radio and hateful before them. Their tails swept through the seedship's outer shields and swirled like long silky hair laid on water; they absorbed fantastic energies, grew bright like violent little stars against the seedship outline. They were engaged in the drawing of the shields, and sure as topology, the spirals of force had to have a dimple on the opposite side that would iris wide enough to let in glovers. The sisters twisted the forces, and Prufrax could see the dimple stretching out under them—

The exercise ended. The elfstate glovers were cast into sudden dark. Prufrax came out of the mock unprepared, her mind still bent on the Zap. The lack of orientation drove her as mad as a moth suddenly flipped from night to day. She careened until gently mitted and channeled. She flowed down a tube, the field slowly neutralizing, and came to a halt still gloved, her body jerking and tingling.

"What the breed happened?" she screamed, her hands beginning to hurt.

"Energy conserve," a mechanical voice answered. Behind Prufrax the other elfstate glovers lined up in the catch tube, all but the special-projects sisters. Ya, Trice, and Damu had been taken out of the exercise early and replaced by simulations. There was no way their functions could be mocked. They entered the tube ungloved and helped their comrades adjust to the overness of the real.

As they left the mock chamber, another batch of glovers, even younger and fresher in elfstate, passed them. Ya held her hands up, and they saluted in return. "Breed more every day," Prufrax grumbled. She worried about having so many crew she'd never be able to conduct a satisfactory Zap herself. Where would the honor of being a glover go if everyone was a glover?

She wriggled into her cramped bunk, feeling exhilarated and irritated. She replayed the mocks and added in the missing Zap, then stared gloomily at her small narrow feet.

Out there the Senexi waited. Perhaps they were in the same state as she—ready to fight, testy at being reined in. She pondered her ignorance, her inability to judge whether such things were even possible among the enemy. She thought of the researcher, Clevo. "Blank," she murmured. "Blank, blank." Such thoughts were unnecessary, and humanizing Senexi was unworthy of a glover.

Aryz looked at the instrument, stretched a pod into it, and willed. Vocal human language came out the other end, thin and squeaky in the helium atmosphere. The sound disgusted and thrilled him. He removed the instrument from the gelatinous strands of the engineering wall and pushed it into his interior through a stretched permeum. He took a thick draft of ammonia and slid to the human shapes chamber again.

He pushed through the narrow port into the observation room. Adjusting his eyes to the heat and bright light beyond the transparent wall, he saw the round mutated shape first—the result of their unsuccessful experiments. He swung his sphere around and looked at the others.

For a time he couldn't decide which was uglier—the mutated shape or the normals. Then he thought of what it would be like to have humans tamper with Senexi and try to make them into human forms. . . . He looked at the round human and shrunk as if from sudden heat. Aryz had had nothing to do with the experiments. For that, at least, he was grateful.

Apparently, even before fertilization, human buds—eggs—were adapted for specific roles. The healthy human shapes appeared sufficiently different—discounting *sexual* characteristics—to indicate some variation in function. They were four-podded, two-opticked, with auditory apparatus and olfactory organs mounted on the *head*, along with one permeum, the *mouth*. At least, he thought, they were hairless, unlike some of the other Population I species Aryz had learned about in the mandate.

Aryz placed the tip of the vocalizer against a sound-transmitting plate and spoke.

"Zello," came the sound within the chamber. The mutated shape looked up. It lay on the floor, great bloated stomach backed by four almost useless pods. It usually made high-pitched sounds continuously. Now it stopped and listened, straining on the tube that connected it to the breed-supervising device.

"Hello," replied the male. It sat on a ledge across the chamber, having unhooked itself.

The machine that served as surrogate parent and instructor stood in one corner, an awkward parody of a human, with limbs too long and head too small. Aryz could see the unwillingness of the designing engineers to examine human anatomy too closely.

"I am called—" Aryz said, his name emerging as a meaningless stretch of white noise. He would have to do better than that. He compressed and adapted the frequencies. "I am called Aryz."

"Hello," the young female said.

"What are your names?" He knew well enough, having listened many times to their conversations.

"Prufrax," the female said. "I'm a glover."

The human shapes contained very little genetic memory. As a kind of brood marker, Aryz supposed, they had been equipped with their name, occupation, and the rudiments of environmental knowledge. This seemed to have been artificially imposed; in their natural state, very likely, they were born almost blank. He could not, however, be certain, since human reproductive chemistry was extraordinarily subtle and complicated.

"I'm a teacher, Prufrax," Aryz said. The logic structure of the language continued to be painful to him.

"I don't understand you," the female replied.

"You teach me, I teach you."

"We have the Mam," the male said, pointing to the machine. "She teaches us." The Mam, as they called it, was hooked into the mandate. Withholding that from the humans—the only equivalent, in essence, to the Senexi sac of memory—would have been unthinkable. It was bad enough that humans didn't come naturally equipped with their own share of knowledge.

"Do you know where you are?" Aryz asked.

"Where we live," Prufrax said. "Eyes-open."

Aryz opened a port to show them the stars and a portion of the nebula. "Can you tell where you are by looking out the window?"

"Among the lights," Prufrax said.

Humans, then, did not instinctively know their positions by star patterns as other Population I species did.

"Don't talk to it," the male said. "Mam talks to us." Aryz consulted the mandate for some understanding of the name they had given to the breed-supervising machine. Mam, it explained, was probably a natural womb-carrying parent. Aryz severed the machine's power.

"Mam is no longer functional," he said. He would have the engineering wall put together another less identifiable machine to link them to the mandate and to their nutrition. He wanted them to associate comfort and completeness with nothing but himself.

The machine slumped, and the female shape pulled herself free of the hookup. She started to cry, a reaction quite mysterious to Aryz. His link with the mandate had not been intimate enough to answer questions about the wailing and moisture from the eyes. After a time the male and female lay down and became dormant.

The mutated shape made more soft sounds and tried to approach the transparent wall. It held up its thin arms as if beseeching. The others would have nothing to do with it; now it wished to go with him. Perhaps the biologists had partially succeeded in their attempt at transformation; perhaps it was more Senexi than human.

Aryz quickly backed out through the port, into the cool and security of the corridor beyond.

It was an endless orbital dance, this detection and matching of course, moving away and swinging back, deceiving and revealing, between the *Mellangee* and the Senexi seedship. It was inevitable that the human ship should close in; human ships were faster, knew better the higher geometries.

Filled with her skill and knowledge, Prufrax waited, feeling like a ripe fruit about to fall from the trees. At this point in their training, just before the application, elfstates were very receptive. She was allowed to take a lover, and they were assigned small separate quarters near the outer greenroads.

The contact was satisfactory, as far as it went. Her mate was an older glover named Kumnax, and as they lay back in the cubicle, soothed by air-dance fibs, he told her stories about past battles, special tactics, how to survive.

"Survive?" she asked, puzzled.

"Of course." His long brown face was intent on the view of the greenroads through the cubicle's small window.

"I don't understand," she said.

"Most glovers don't make it," he said patiently.

"I will."

He turned to her. "You're six," he said. "You're very young. I'm ten. I've seen. You're about to be applied for the first time, you're full of confidence. But most glovers won't make it. They breed thousands of us. We're expendable. We're based on the best glovers of the past, but even the best don't survive."

"I will," Prufrax repeated, her jaw set.

"You always say that," he murmured.

Prufrax stared at him for a moment.

"Last time I knew you," he said, "you kept saying that. And here you are, fresh again."

"What last time?"

"Master Kumnax," a mechanical voice interrupted.

He stood, looking down at her. "We glovers always have big mouths. They don't like us knowing, but once we know, what can they do about it?"

"You are in violation," the voice said. "Please report to S."

"But now, if you last, you'll know more than the tellman tells."

"I don't understand," Prufrax said slowly, precisely, looking him straight in the eye.

"I've paid my debt," Kumnax said. "We glovers stick. Now I'm going to go get my punishment." He left the cubicle. Prufrax didn't see him again before her first application.

The seedship buried itself in a heating protostar, raising shields against the infalling ice and stone. The nebula had congealed out of a particularly rich cluster of exploded fourth- and fifth-generation stars, thick with planets, the detritus of which now fell on Aryz's ship like hail.

Aryz had never been so isolated. No other branch ind addressed him; he never even saw them now. He made his reports to the brood mind, but even there the reception was warmer and warmer, until he could barely endure to communicate. Consequently—and he realized this was part of the plan—he came closer to his charges, the human shapes. He felt more sympathy for them. He discovered that even between human and Senexi there could be a bridge of need—the need to be useful.

The brood mind was interested in one question: how successfully could they be planted aboard a human ship? Would they be accepted until they could carry out their sabotage, or would they be detected? Already Senexi instructions were being coded into their teachings.

"I think they will be accepted in the confusion of an engagement," Aryz answered. He had long since guessed the general outlines of the brood mind's plans. Communications with the human shapes was for one purpose only; to use them as decoys, insurgents. They were weapons. Knowledge of human activity and behavior was not an end in itself; seeing what was happening to him, Aryz fully understood why the brood mind wanted such a study to proceed no further.

He would lose them soon, he thought, and his work would be over. He would be much too human-tainted. He would end, and his replacement would start a new existence, very little different from Aryz—but, he reasoned, adjusted. The replacement would not have Aryz's peculiarity.

He approached his last meeting with the brood mind, preparing himself for his final work, for the ending. In the cold liquid-filled chamber, the great red-and-white sac waited, the center of his team, his existence. He adored it. There was no way he could critize its action.

Yet—

"We are being sought," the brood mind radiated. "Are the shapes ready?"

"Yes," Aryz said. "The new teaching is firm. They believe they are fully human." And, except for one new teaching, they were. "They defy sometimes." He said nothing about the mutated shape. It would not be used. If they won this encounter, it would probably be placed with Aryz's body in a fusion torch for complete purging.

"Then prepare them," the brood mind said. "They will be delivered to the vector for positioning and transfer."

Darkness and waiting. Prufrax nested in her delivery tube like a freshly chambered round. Through her gloves she caught distant communications murmurs that resembled voices down hollow pipes. The *Mellangee* was coming to full readiness.

Huge as her ship was, Prufrax knew that it would be dwarfed by the seedship. She could recall some hazy details about the seedship's structure, but most of that information was stored securely away from interference by her conscious mind. She wasn't even positive what the tactic would be. In the mocks, that at least had been clear. Now such information either had not been delivered or had waited in inaccessible memory, to be brought forward by the appropriate triggers.

More information would be fed to her just before the launch, but she knew the general procedure. The seedship was deep in a protostar, hiding behind the distortion of geometry and the complete hash of electromagnetic energy. The *Mellangee* would approach, collide if need be. Penetrate. Release. Find. Zap. Her fingers ached. Sometimes before the launch she would also be fed her final moans—the tempers—and she would be primed to leave elfstate. She would be a mature glover. She would be a woman.

If she returned
will return
she could become part of the breed, her receptivity would end in
ecstasy rather than mild warmth, she would contribute second state,
naturally born glovers. For a moment she was content with the thought.
That was a high honor.

Her fingers ached worse.

The tempers came, moans tiding in, then the battle data. As it passed
into her subconscious, she caught a flash of—

Rocks and ice, a thick cloud of dust and gas glowing red but seeming
dark, no stars, no constellation guides this time. The beacon came on.
That would be her only way to orient once the gloves stopped inertial
and locked onto the target.

The seedship
was like
a shadow within a shadow
twenty-two kilometers across, yet
carrying
only six
teams
LAUNCH *She flies!*

Data: the *Mellangee* has buried herself in the seedship, ploughed deep
into the interior like a carnivore's muzzle looking for vitals.

Instruction: a swarm of seeks is dashing through the seedship, looking
for the brood minds, for the brood chambers, for branch inds. The
glovers will follow.

Prufrax sees herself clearly now. She is the great avenging comet,
bringer of omen and doom, like a knife moving through the glass and
ice and thin, cold helium as if they weren't there, the chambered round
fired and tearing at hundreds of kilometers an hour through the Senexi
vessel, following the seeks.

The seedship cannot withdraw into higher geometries now. It is
pinned by the *Mellangee.* It is hers.

Information floods her, pleases her immensely. She swoops down
orange-and-gray corridors, buffeting against the walls like a ricocheting
bullet. Almost immediately she comes across a branch ind, sliding
through the ammonia film against the outrushing wind, trying to reach
an armored cubicle. Her first Zap is too easy, not satisfying, nothing
like what she thought. In her wake the branch ind becomes scattered
globules of plasma. She plunges deeper.

Aryz delivers his human charges to the vectors that will launch them.
They are equipped with simulations of the human weapons, their hands
encased in the hideous gray gloves.

The seedship is in deadly peril; the battle has almost been lost at one stroke. The seedship cannot remain whole. It must self-destruct, taking the human ship with it, leaving only a fragment with as many teams as can escape.

The vectors launch the human shapes. Aryz tries to determine which part of the ship will be elected to survive; he must not be there. His job is over, and he must die.

The glovers fan out through the seedship's central hollow, demolishing the great cold drive engines, bypassing the shielded fusion flare and the reprocessing plant, destroying machinery built before their Earth was formed.

The special-projects sisters take the lead. Suddenly they are confused. They have found a brood mind, but it is not heavily protected. They surround it, prepare for the Zap—

It is sacrificing itself, drawing them in to an easy kill and away from another portion of the seedship. Power is concentrating elsewhere. Sensing that, they kill quickly and move on.

Aryz's brood mind prepares for escape. It begins to wrap itself in flux bind as it moves through the ship toward the frozen fragment. Already three of its five branch inds are dead; it can feel other brood minds dying. Aryz's bud replacement has been killed as well.

Following Aryz's training, the human shapes rush into corridors away from the main action. The special-projects sisters encounter the decoy male, allow it to fly with them . . . until it aims its weapons. One Zap almost takes out Trice. The others fire on the shape immediately. He goes to his death weeping, confused from the very moment of his launch.

The fragment in which the brood mind will take refuse encompasses the chamber where the humans had been nurtured, where the mandate is still stored. All the other brood minds are dead, Aryz realizes; the humans have swept down on them so quickly. What shall he do?

Somewhere, far off, he feels the distressed pulse of another branch ind dying. He probes the remains of the seedship. He is the last. He cannot dissipate now; he must ensure the brood mind's survival.

Prufrax, darting through the crumbling seedship, searching for more opportunities, comes across an injured glover. She calls for a mediseek and pushes on.

The brood mind settles into the fragment. Its support system is damaged; it is entering the time-isolated state, the flux bind, more rapidly than it should. The seals of foamed electric ice cannot quite close off the fragment before Ya, Trice, and Damu slip in. They frantically call for bind-cutters and preserves; they have instructions to capture the last brood mind, if possible.

But a trap falls upon Ya, and snarling fields tear her from her gloves. She is flung down a dark disintegrating shaft, red cracks opening all around as the seedship's integrity fails. She trails silver dust and freezes, hits a barricade, shatters.

The ice seals continue to close. Trice is caught between them and pushed out frantically, blundering into the region of the intensifying flux bind. Her gloves break into hard bits, and she is melded into an ice wall like an insect trapped on the surface of a winter lake.

Damu sees that the brood mind is entering the final phase of flux bind. After that they will not be able to touch it. She begins a desperate Zap

and is too late.

Aryz directs the subsidiary energy of the flux against her. Her Zap deflects from the bind region, she is caught in an interference pattern and vibrates until her tiniest particles stop their knotted whirlpool spins and she simply becomes

space and searing light.

The brood mind, however, has been damaged. It is losing information from one portion of its anatomy. Desperate for storage, it looks for places to hold the information before the flux bind's last wave.

Aryz directs an interface onto the brood mind's surface. The silvery pools of time-binding flicker around them both. The brood mind's damaged sections transfer their data into the last available storage device— the human mandate.

Now it contains both human and Senexi information.

The silvery pools unite, and Aryz backs away. No longer can he sense the brood mind. It is out of reach but not yet safe. He must propel the fragment from the remains of the seedship. Then he must wrap the fragment in its own flux bind, cocoon it in physics to protect it from the last ravages of the humans.

Aryz carefully navigates his way through the few remaining corridors. The helium atmosphere has almost completely dissipated, even there. He strains to remember all the procedures. Soon the seedship will explode, destroying the human ship. By then they must be gone.

Angry red, Prufrax follows his barely sensed form, watching him behind barricades of ice, approaching the moment of a most satisfying Zap. She gives her gloves their way

and finds a shape behind her, wearing gloves that are not gloves, not like her own, but capable of grasping her in tensed fields, blocking the Zap, dragging them together. The fragment separates, heat pours in from the protostar cloud. They are swirled in their vortex of power, twin locked comets—one red, one sullen gray.

"Who are you?" Prufrax screams as they close in on each other in the fields. Their environments meld. They grapple. In the confusion, the darkening, they are drawn out of the cloud with the fragment, and she sees the other's face.

Her own.

The seedship self-destructs. The fragment is propelled from the protostar, above the plane of what will become planets in their orbits, away from the crippled and dying *Mellangee*.

Desperate, Prufrax uses all her strength to drill into the fragment. Helium blows past them, and bits of dead branch inds.

Aryz catches the pair immediately in the shapes chamber, rearranging the fragment's structure to enclose them with the mutant shape and mandate. For the moment he has time enough to concentrate on them. They are dangerous. They are almost equal to each other, but his shape is weakening faster than the true glover. They float, bouncing from wall to wall in the chamber, forcing the mutant to crawl into a corner and howl with fear.

There may be value in saving the one and capturing the other. Involved as they are, the two can be carefully dissected from their fields and induced into a crude kind of sleep before the glover has a chance to free her weapons. He can dispose of the gloves—fake and real—and hook them both to the Mam, reattach the mutant shapes as well. Perhaps something can be learned from the failure of the experiment.

The dissection and capture occur faster than the planning. His movement shows under the spreading flux bind. His last action, after attaching the humans to the Mam, is to make sure the brood mind's flux bind is properly nested within that of the ship.

The fragment drops into simpler geometries.

It is as if they never existed.

The battle was over. There were no victors. Aryz became aware of the passage of time, shook away the sluggishness, and crawled through painfully dry corridors to set the environmental equipment going again. Throughout the fragment, machines struggled back to activity.

How many generations? The constellations were unrecognizable. He made star traces and found familiar spectra and types, but advanced in age. There had been a malfunction in the overall flux bind. He couldn't find the nebula where the battle had occurred. In its place were comfortably middle-aged stars surrounded by young planets.

Aryz came down from the makeshift observatory. He slid through the fragment, established the limits of his new home, and found the solid mirror surface of the brood mind's cocoon. It was still locked in flux bind, and he knew of no way to free it. In time the bind would probably wear off—but that might require life spans. The seedship was gone. They had lost the brood chamber, and with it the stock.

He was the last branch ind of his team. Not that it mattered now; there was nothing he could initiate without a brood mind. If the flux bind was permanent—as sometimes happened during malfunction—then he might as well be dead.

He closed his thoughts around him and was almost completely submerged when he sensed an alarm from the shapes chamber. The interface with the mandate had turned itself off; the new version of the Mam was malfunctioning. He tried to repair the equipment, but without the engineer's wall he was almost helpless. The best he could do was rig a temporary nutrition supply through the old human-form Mam. When he was done, he looked at the captive and the two shapes, then at the legless, armless Mam that served as their link to the interface and life itself.

She had spent her whole life in a room barely eight by ten meters, and not much taller than her own height. With her had been Grayd and the silent creature whose name—if it had any—they had never learned. For a time there had been Mam, then another kind of Mam not nearly as satisfactory. She was hardly aware that her entire existence had been miserable, cramped, in one way or another incomplete.

Separated from them by a transparent partition, another round shape periodically made itself known by voice or gesture.

Grayd had kept her sane. They had engaged in conspiracy. Removing themselves from the interface—what she called "eyes-shut"—they had held each other, tried to make sense out of what they knew was fed them through the interface, and what the being beyond the partition told them.

First they knew their names, and they knew that they were glovers. They knew that glovers were fighters. When Aryz passed instruction through on how to fight, they had accepted it eagerly but uneasily. It didn't jibe with instructions locked deep within their instincts.

Five years under such conditions had made her introspective. She expected nothing, sought little beyond experience in the eyes-shut. Eyes-open with Grayd seemed scarcely more than a dream. They usually managed to ignore the peculiar round creature in the chamber with them; it spent nearly all its time hooked to the mandate and the Mam.

Of one thing only was she completely sure. Her name was Prufrax. She said it in eyes-open and eyes-shut, her only certainty.

Not long before the battle, she had been in a condition resembling dreamless sleep, like a robot being given instructions. The part of Prufrax that had taken on personality during eyes-shut and eyes-open for five years had been superseded by the fight instructions Aryz had programed. She had flown as glovers must fly (though the gloves didn't seem quite right). She had fought, grappling (she thought) with herself, but who could be certain of anything?

She had long since decided that reality was not to be sought too avidly. After the battle she fell back into the mandate—into eyes-shut—all too willingly.

And what matter? If eyes-open was even less comprehensible than eyes-shut, why did she have the nagging feeling eyes-open was so compelling, so necessary? She tried to forget.

But a change had come to eyes-shut, too. Before the battle, the information had been selected. Now she could wander through the mandate at will. She seemed to smell the new information, completely unfamiliar, like a whiff of ocean. She hardly knew where to begin. She stumbled across:

—that all vessels will carry one, no matter what their size or class, just as every individual carries the map of a species. The mandate shall contain all the information of our kind, including accurate and uncensored history, for if we have learned anything, it is that censored and untrue accounts distort the eyes of the leaders. Leaders must have access to the truth. It is their responsibility. Whatever is told those who work under the leaders, for whatever reason, must not be believed by the leaders. Unders are told lies. Leaders must seek and be provided with accounts as accurate as possible, or we will be weakened and fall—

What wonderful dreams the *leaders* must have had. And they possess some intrinsic gift called *truth*, through the use of the *mandate*. Prufrax could hardly believe that. As she made her tentative explorations through the new fields of eyes-shut, she began to link the word *mandate* with what she experienced. That was where she was.

And she alone. Once, she had explored with Grayd. Now there was no sign of Grayd.

She learned quickly. Soon she walked along a beach on Earth, then a beach on a world called Myriadne, and other beaches, fading in and out. By running through the entries rapidly, she came up with a blurred *eidos* and so learned what a beach was in the abstract. It was a boundary between one kind of eyes-shut and another, between water and land, neither of which had any corollary in eyes-open.

Some beaches had sand. Some had clouds—the *eidos* of clouds was quite attractive. And one—

had herself running scared, screaming.

She called out, but the figure vanished. Prufrax stood on a beach under a greenish-yellow star, on a world called Kyrene, feeling lonelier than ever.

She explored farther, hoping to find Grayd, if not the figure that looked like herself. Grayd wouldn't flee from her. Grayd would—

The round thing confronted her, its helpless limbs twitching. Now it was her turn to run, terrified. Never before had she met the round creature in eyes-shut. It was mobile; it had a purpose. Over land, clouds, trees, rocks, wind, air, equations, and an edge of physics she fled. The farther she went, the more distant from the round one with hands and small head, the less afraid she was.

She never found Grayd.

The memory of the battle was fresh and painful. She remembered the ache of her hands, clumsily removed from the gloves. Her environment had collapsed and been replaced by something indistinct. Prufrax had fallen into a deep slumber and had dreamed.

The dreams were totally unfamiliar to her. If there was a left-turning in her arc of sleep, she dreamed of philosophies and languages and other things she couldn't relate to. A right-turning led to histories and sciences so incomprehensible as to be nightmares.

It was a most unpleasant sleep, and she was not at all sorry to find she wasn't really asleep.

The crucial moment came when she discovered how to slow her turnings and the changes of dream subject. She entered a pleasant place of which she had knowledge but which did not seem threatening. There was a vast expanse of water, but it didn't terrify her. She couldn't identify it as water until she scooped up a handful. Beyond the water was a floor of shifting particles. Above both was an open expanse, not black but obviously space, drawing her eyes into intense blue-green. And there was that figure she had encountered in the seedship. Herself. The figure pursued. She fled.

Right over the boundary into Senexi information. She knew then that what she was seeing couldn't possibly come from within herself. She was receiving data from another source. Perhaps she had been taken captive. It was possible she was now being forcibly debriefed. The tellman had discussed such possibilities, but none of the glovers had been taught how to defend themselves in specific situations. Instead it had been stated—in terms that brooked no second thought—that self-destruction was the only answer. So she tried to kill herself.

She sat in the freezing cold of a red-and-white room, her feet meeting but not touching a fluid covering on the floor. The information didn't fit her senses—it seemed blurred, inappropriate. Unlike the other data, this didn't allow participation or motion. Everything was locked solid.

She couldn't find an effective means of killing herself. She resolved to close her eyes and simply will herself into dissolution. But closing her eyes only moved her into a deeper or shallower level of deception—other categories, subjects, visions. She couldn't sleep, wasn't tired, couldn't die.

Like a leaf on a stream, she drifted. Her thoughts untangled, and she imagined herself floating on the water called ocean. She kept her eyes open. It was quite by accident that she encountered:

Instruction. Welcome to the introductory use of the mandate. As a noncombat processor, your duties are to maintain the mandate, provide essential information for your overs, and, if necessary, protect or destroy the mandate. The mandate is your immediate over. If it requires maintenance, you will oblige. Once linked with the mandate, as you are now, you may explore any aspect of the information by requesting delivery. To request delivery, indicate the core of your subject—

Prufrax! she shouted silently. What is Prufrax?

A voice with different tone immediately took over.

Ah, now that's quite a story. I was her biographer, the organizer of her life tapes (ref. GEORGE MACKNAX), and knew her well in the last years of her life. She was born in the Ferment 26468. Here are selected life tapes. Choose emphasis. Analyses follow.

—Hey! Who are you? There's someone here with me. . . .
—Shh! Listen. Look at her. Who is she?
—They looked, listened to the information.
—Why, she's *me* . . . sort of.
—She's *us*.

She stood two and a half meters tall. Her hair was black and thick, though cut short; her limbs well-muscled though drawn out by the training and hormonal treatments. She was seventeen years old, one of the few birds born in the solar system, and for the time being she had a chip on her shoulder. Everywhere she went, the birds asked about her mother, Jay-ax "You better than her?"

Of course not! Who could be? But she was good; the instructors said so. She was just about through training, and whether she graduated to hawk or remained bird she would do her job well. Asking Prufrax about her mother was likely to make her set her mouth tight and glare.

On Mercior, the Grounds took up four thousand hectares and had its own port. The Grounds was divided into Land, Space, and Thought, and training in each area was mandatory for fledges, those birds embarking on hawk training. Prufrax was fledge three. She had passed Land—though she loathed downbound fighting—and was two years into Space. The tough part, everyone said, was not passing Space, but lasting through four years of Thought after the action in nearorbit and planetary.

Prufrax was not the introspective type. She could be studious when it suited her. She was a quick study at weapon maths, physics came easy when it had a direct application, but theory of service and polinstruc—which she had sampled only in prebird courses—bored her.

Since she had been a little girl, no more than five—

—Five! Five what?

and she had seen her mother's ships and fightsuits and fibs, she had known she would never be happy until she had ventured far out and put a seedship in her sights, had convinced a Senexi of the overness of end—

—The Zap! She's talking the Zap!

—What's that?

—You're me, you should know.

—I'm not you, and we're not her.

The Zap, said the mandate, and the data shifted.

"Tomorrow you receive your first implants. These will allow you to coordinate with the zero-angle phase engines and find your targets much more rapidly than you ever could with simple biologic. The implants, of course, will be delivered through your noses—minor irritation and sinus trouble, no more—into your limbic system. Later in your training, hookups and digital adapts will be installed as well. Are there any questions?"

"Yes, sir." Prufrax stood at the top of the spherical classroom, causing the hawk instructor to swivel his platform. "I'm having problems with the zero-angle phase maths. Reduction of the momenta of the real."

Other fledge threes piped up that they, too, had had trouble with those maths. The hawk instructor sighed. "We don't want to install cheaters in all of you. It's bad enough needing implants to supplement biologic. Individual learning is much more desirable. Do you request cheaters?" That was a challenge. They all responded negatively, but Prufrax had a secret smile. She knew the subject. She just took delight in having the maths explained again. She could reinforce an already thorough understanding. Others not so well versed would benefit. She wasn't wasting time. She was in the pleasure of her weapon—the weapon she would be using against the Senexi.

"Zero-angle phase is the temporary reduction of the momenta of the real." Equations and plexes appeared before each student as the instructor went on. "Nested unreals can conflict if a barrier is placed between the participator princip and the assumption of the real. The effectiveness of the participator can be determined by a convenience model we call the angle of phase. Zero-angle phase is achieved by an opaque probability field according to modified Fourier of the separation of real waves. This can also be caused by the reflection of the beam—an effective counter to zero-angle phase, since the beam is always compoundable and the compound is always time-reversed. Here are the true gedanks—"

—Zero-angle phase. She's learning the Zap.

—She hates them a lot, doesn't she?

—The Senexi? They're Senexi.

—I think . . . eyes-open is the world of the Senexi. What does that mean?

—That we're prisoners. You were caught before me.

—Oh.

The news came as she was in recovery from the implant. Seedships had violated human space again, dropping cuckoos on thirty-five worlds. The worlds had been young colonies, and the cuckoos had wiped out all life, then tried to reseed with Senexi forms. The overs had reacted by sterilizing the planet's surfaces. No victory; loss to both sides. It was as if the Senexi were so malevolent they didn't care about success, only about destruction.

She hated them. She could imagine nothing worse.

Prufrax was twenty-three. In a year she would be qualified to hawk on a cruise/raider. She would demonstrate her hatred.

Aryz felt himself slipping into endthought, the mind set that always preceded a branch ind's self-destruction. What was there for him to do? The fragment had survived, but at what cost, to what purpose? Nothing had been accomplished. The nebula had been lost, or he supposed it had. He would likely never know the actual outcome.

He felt a vague irritation at the lack of a spectrum of responses. Without a purpose, a branch ind was nothing more than excess plasm.

He looked in on the captive and the shapes, all hooked to the mandate, and wondered what he would do with them. How would humans react to the situation he was in? More vigorously, probably. They would fight on. They always had. Even without leaders, with no discernible purpose, even in defeat. What gave them such stamina? Were they superior, more deserving? If they were better, then was it right for the Senexi to oppose their triumph?

Aryz drew himself tall and rigid with confusion. He had studied them too long. They had truly infected him. But here at least was a hint of purpose. A question needed to be answered.

He made preparations. There were signs the brood mind's flux bind was not permanent, was in fact unwinding quite rapidly. When it emerged, Aryz would present it with a judgment, an answer.

He realized, none too clearly, that by Senexi standards he was now a raving lunatic.

He would hook himself into the mandate, improve the somewhat isolating interface he had used previously to search for selected answers. He, the captive, and the shapes would be immersed in human history together. They would be like young suckling on a Population I mother-animal—just the opposite of the Senexi process, where young fed nourishment and information into the brood mind.

The mandate would nourish, or poison. Or both.

—Did she love?
—What—you mean, did she receive?
—No, did she—we—I—give?
—I don't know what you mean.
—I wonder if *she* would know what I mean. . . .
Love, said the mandate, and the data proceeded.

Prufrax was twenty-nine. She had been assigned to a cruiser in a new program where superior but untested fighters were put into thick action with no preliminary. The program was designed to see how well the Grounds prepared fighters; some thought it foolhardy, but Prufrax found it perfectly satisfactory.

The cruiser was a million-ton raider, with a hawk contingent of fifty-three and eight regular crew. She would be used in a second-wave attack, following the initial hardfought.

She was scared. That was good; fright improved basic biologic, if properly managed. The cruiser would make a raid into Senexi space and retaliate for past cuckoo-seeding programs. They would come up against thornships and seedships, likely.

The fighting was going to be fierce.

The raider made its final denial of the overness of the real and pip-squeezed into an arduous, nasty sponge space. It drew itself together again and emerged far above the galactic plane.

Prufrax sat in the hawks wardroom and looked at the simulated rotating snowball of stars. Red-coded numerals flashed along the borders of known Senexi territory, signifying old stars, dark hulks of stars, the whole ghostly home region where they had first come to power when the terrestrial sun had been a mist-wrapped youngster. A green arrow showed the position of the raider.

She drank sponge-space supplements with the others but felt isolated because of her firstness, her fear. Everyone seemed so calm. Most were fours or fives—on their fourth or fifth battle call. There were ten ones and an upper scatter of experienced hawks with nine to twenty-five battles behind them. There were no thirties. Thirties were rare in combat; the few that survived so many engagements were plucked off active and retired to PR service under the polinstructors. They often ended up in fibs, acting poorly, looking unhappy.

Still, when she had been more naive, Prufrax's heros had been a man-and-woman thirty team she had watched in fib after fib—Kumnax and Arol. They had been better actors than most.

Day in, day out, they drilled in their fightsuits. While the crew bustled, hawks were put through implant learning, what slang was already calling the Know, as opposed to the Tell, of classroom teaching. Getting background, just enough to tickle her curiosity, not enough to stimulate morbid interest.

—There it is again. Feel?

—I know it. Yes. The round one, part of eyes-open . . .

—Senexi?

—No, brother without name.

—Your . . . brother?

—No . . . I don't know.

—Can it hurt us?

—It never has. It's trying to talk to us.

—*Leave us alone!*

—It's going.

Still, there were items of information she had never received before, items privileged only to the fighters, to assist them in their work. Older hawks talked about the past, when data had been freely available. Stories circulated in the wardroom about the Senexi, and she managed to piece together something of their origins and growth.

Senexi worlds, according to a twenty, had originally been large, cold masses of gas circling bright young suns nearly metal-free. Their gas-giant planets had orbited the suns at hundreds of millions of kilometers and had been dusted by the shrouds of neighboring dead stars; the essential elements carbon, nitrogen, silicon, and fluorine had gathered in sufficient quantities on some of the planets to allow Population II biology.

In cold ammonia seas, lipids had combined in complex chains. A primal kind of life had arisen and flourished. Across millions of years, early Senexi forms had evolved. Compared with evolution of Earth, the process at first had moved quite rapidly. The mechanisms of procreation and evolution had been complex in action, simple in chemistry.

There had been no competition between life forms of different genetic bases. On Earth, much time had been spent selecting between the plethora of possible ways to pass on genetic knowledge.

And among the early Senexi, outside of predation there had been no death. Death had come about much later, self-imposed for social reasons. Huge colonies of protoplasmic individuals had gradually resolved into the team-forms now familiar.

Soon information was transferred through the budding of branch inds; cultures quickly developed to protect the integrity of larvae, to allow them to regroup and form a new brood mind. Techonologies had been limited to the rare heavy materials available, but expanded for a time with very little technology. They were well adapted to their environment, with few predators and no need to hunt, absorbing stray nutrients from the atmosphere and from layers of liquid ammonia. With perceptions attuned to the radio and microwave frequencies, they had before long turned groups of branch inds into radio telescope chains, piercing the heavy atmosphere and probing the universe in great detail, especially the very active center of the young galaxy. Huge jets of matter, streaming from other galaxies and emitting high-energy radiation, had provided laboratories for their vicarious observations. Physics was a primitive science to them.

Since little or no knowledge was lost in breeding cycles, cultural growth was rapid at times; since the dead weight of knowledge was often heavy, cultural growth often slowed to a crawl.

Using water as a building material, developing techniques that humans still understood imperfectly, they prepared for travel away from their birthworlds.

Prufrax wondered, as she listened to the older hawks, how humans had come to know all this. Had Senexi been captured and questioned? Was it all theory? Did anyone really know—anyone she could ask?

—She's weak.

—Why weak?

—Some knowledge is best for glovers to ignore. Some questions are best left to the supreme overs.

—Have you thought that in here, you can answer her questions, our questions?

—No. No. Learn about me—us—first.

In the hour before engagement, Prufrax tried to find a place alone. On the raider this wasn't difficult. The ship's size was overwhelming for the number of hawks and crew aboard. There were many areas where she could put on an environs and walk or drift in silence, surrounded by the dark shapes of equipment wrapped in plexerv. There was so much about ship operations she didn't understand, hadn't been taught. Why carry so much excess equipment, weapons—far more than they'd need even for replacements? She could think of possibilities—superiors on Mercior wanting their cruisers to have flexible mission capabilities, for one—but her ignorance troubled her less than *why* she was ignorant. Why was it necessary to keep fighters in the dark on so many subjects?

She pulled herself through the old G-less tunnels, feeling slightly awked by the loneness, the quiet. One tunnel angled outboard, toward the hull of the cruiser. She hesitated, peering into its length with her environs beacon, when a beep warned her she was near another crew member. She was startled to think someone else might be as curious as she. The other hawks and crew, for the most part, had long outgrown their need to wander and regarded it as birdish. Prufrax was used to being different—she had always perceived herself, with some pride, as a bit of a freak. She scooted expertly up the tunnel, spreading her arms and tucking her legs as she would in a fightsuit.

The tunnel was filled with a faint milky green mist; absorbing her environs beam. It couldn't be much more than a couple of hundred meters long, however, it was quite straight. The signal beeped louder.

Ahead she could make out a dismantled weapons blister. That explained the fog: a plexerv aerosol diffused in the low pressure. Sitting in the blister was a man, his environs glowing a pale violet. He had deopaqued a section of the blister and was staring out at the stars. He swiveled as she approached and looked her over dispassionately. He seemed to be a hawk—he had fightform, tall, thin with brown hair above hull-white skin, large eyes with pupils so dark she might have been looking through his head into space beyond.

"Under," she said as their environs met and merged.

"Over. What are you doing here?"

"I was about to ask you the same."

"You should be getting ready for the fight," he admonished.

"I am. I need to be alone for a while."

"Yes." He turned back to the stars. "I used to do that, too."

"You don't fight now?"

He shook his head. "Retired. I'm a researcher."

She tried not to look impressed. Crossing rates was almost impossible. A bitalent was unusual in the service.

"What kind of research?" she asked.

"I'm here to correlate enemy finds."

"Won't find much of anything, after we're done with the zero phase."

It would have been polite for him to say, "Power to that," or offer some other encouragement. He said nothing.

"Why would you want to research them?"

"To fight an enemy properly, you have to know what they are. Ignorance is defeat."

"You research tactics?"

"Not exactly."

"What, then?"

"You'll be in a tough hardfought this wake. Make you a proposition. You fight well, observe, come to me and tell me what you see. Then I'll answer your questions."

"Brief you before my immediate overs?"

"I have the authority," he said. No on had ever lied to her; she didn't even suspect he would. "You're eager?"

"Very."

"You'll be doing what?"

"Engaging Senexi fighters, then hunting down branch inds and brood minds."

"How many fighters going in?"

"Twelve."

"Big target, eh?"

She nodded.

"While you're there, ask yourself—what are they fighting for? Understand?"

"I—"

"Ask, what are they fighting for. Just that. Then come back to me."

"What's your name?"

"Not important," he said. "Now go."

She returned to the prep center as the sponge-space warning tones began. Overhawks went among the fighters in the lineup, checking gear and giveaway body points for mental orientation. Prufrax submitted to the molded sensor mask being slipped over her face. "Ready!" the overhawk said. "Hardfought!" He clapped her on the shoulder. "Good luck."

"Thank you, sir." She bent down and slid into her fightsuit. Along the launch line, eleven other hawks did the same. The overs and other crew left the chamber, and twelve red beams delineated the launch tube. The fightsuits automatically lifted and aligned on their individual beams. Fields swirled around them like silvery tissue in moving water, then settled and hardened into cold scintillating walls, pulsing as the launch energy built up.

The tactic came to her. The ship's sensors became part of her information net. She saw the Senexi thornship—twelve kilometers in diameter, cuckoos lacing its outer hull like maggots on red fruit, snakes waiting to take them on.

She was terrified and exultant, so worked up that her body temperature was climbing. The fightsuit adjusted her balance.

At the count of ten and nine, she switched from biologic to cyber. The implant—after absorbing much of her thought processes for weeks—became Prufrax.

For a time there seemed to be two of her. Biologic continued, and in that region she could even relax a bit, as if watching a fib.

With almost dreamlike slowness, in the electronic time of cyber, her fightsuit followed the beam. She saw the stars and oriented herself to the cruiser's beacon, using both for reference, plunging in the sword-flower formation to assault the thornship. The cuckoos retreated in the vast red hull like worms withdrawing into an apple. Then hundreds of tiny black pinpoints appeared in the closest quadrant to the sword flower.

Snakes shot out, each piloted by a Senexi branch ind. "Hardfought!" she told herself in biologic before that portion gave over completely to cyber.

Why were we flung out of dark
through ice and fire, a shower
of sparks? a puzzle;
Perhaps to build hell.

We strike here, there;
Set brief glows, fall through
and cross round again.

By our dimming, we see what
Beatitude we have.
In the circle, kindling
together, we form an
exhausted Empyrean.
We feel the rush of
igniting winds but still
grow dull and wan.

New rage flames, new light,
dropping like sun through muddy
ice and night and fall
Close, spinning blue and bright.

In time they, too,
Tire. Redden.
We join, compare pasts
cool in huddled paths,
turn gray.

And again.
We are a companion flow
of ash, in the slurry,
out and down.
We sleep.

Rivers from above and below.
Above, iron snakes twist,
clang and slice, chime,
helium eyes watching, seeing
Snowflake hawks,
signaling adamant muscles and
energy teeth. What hunger
compels our venom spit?

It flies, strikes the crystal
flight, making mist gray-green
with ammonia rain.

Sleeping, we glide,
and to each side
unseen shores wait
with the moans of an
unseen tide.

—She wrote that. We. One of her—our—poems.
—Poem?
—A kind of fib, I think.
—I don't see what it says.
—Sure you do! She's talking hardfought.
—The Zap? Is that all?
—No, I don't think so.
—Do you understand it?
—Not all . . .

She lay back in the bunk, legs crossed, eyes closed, feeling the receding dominance of the implant—the overness of cyber—and the almost pleasant ache in her back. She had survived her first. The thornship had retired, severely damaged, its surface seared and scored so heavily it would never release cuckoos again.

It would become a hulk, a decoy. Out of action. *Satisfaction/out of action/Satisfaction . . .*

Still, with eight of the twelve fighters lost, she didn't quite feel the exuberance of the rhyme. The snakes had fought very well. Bravely, she might say. They lured, sacrificed, cooperated, demonstrating teamwork as fine as that in her own group. Strategy was what made the cruiser's raid successful. A superior approach, an excellent tactic. And perhaps even surprise, though the final analysis hadn't been posted yet.

Without those advantages, they might have all died.

She opened her eyes and stared at the pattern of blinking lights in the ceiling panel, lights with their secret codes that repeated every second, so that whenever she looked at them, the implant deep inside was debriefed, reinstructed. Only when she fought would she know what she was now seeing.

She returned to the tunnel as quickly as she was able. She floated up toward the blister and found him there, surrounded by packs of information from the last hardfought. She waited until he turned his attention to her.

"Well?" he said.

"I asked myself what they are fighting for. And I'm very angry."

"Why?"

"Because I don't know. I *can't* know. They're Senexi."

"Did they fight well?"

"We lost eight. Eight." She cleared her throat.

"Did they fight well?" he repeated, an edge in his voice.

"Better than I was ever told they could."

"Did they die?"

"Enough of them."

"How many did you kill?"

"I don't know." But she did. Eight.

"You killed eight," he said, pointing to the packs. "I'm analyzing the battle now."

"You're behind what we read, what gets posted?" she asked.

"Partly," he said. "You're a good hawk."

"I knew I would be," she said, her tone quiet, simple.

"Since they fought bravely—"

"How can Senexi be brave?" she asked sharply.

"Since," he repeated, "they fought bravely, why?"

"They want to live, to do their . . . work. Just like me."

"No," he said. She was confused, moving between extremes in her mind, first resisting, then giving in too much. "They're Senexi. They're not like us."

"What's your name?" she asked, dodging the issue.

"Clevo."

Her glory hadn't even begun yet, and already she was well into her fall.

Aryz made his connection and felt the brood mind's emergency cache of knowledge in the mandate grow up around him like ice crystals on glass. He stood in a static scene. The transition from living memory to human machine memory had resulted in either a coding of data or a reduction of detail; either way, the memory was cold, not dynamic. It would have to be compared, recorrelated, if that would ever be possible.

How much human data had to be dumped to make space for this?

He cautiously advanced into the human memory, calling up topics almost at random. In the short time he had been away, so much of what he had learned seemed to have faded or become scrambled. Branch inds were supposed to have permanent memory; human data, for one reason or another, didn't take. It required much effort just to begin to understand the different modes of thought.

He backed away from sociological data, trying to remain within physics and mathematics. There he could make conversions to fit his understanding without too much strain.

Then something unexpected happened. He felt the brush of another mind, a gentle inquiry from a source made even stranger by the hint of familiarity. It made what passed for a Senexi greeting, but not in the proper form, using what one branch ind of a team would radiate to a fellow; a gross breach, since it was obviously not from his team or even from his family. Aryz tried to withdraw. How was it possible for minds to meet in the mandate? As he retreated, he pushed into a broad region of incomprehensible data. It had none of the characteristics of the other human regions he had examined.

—This is for machines, the other said. —Not all cultural data is limited to biologic. You are in the area where programs and cyber designs are stored. They are really accessible only to a machine hooked into the mandate.

—What is your family? Aryz asked, the first step-question in the sequence Senexi used for urgent identity requests.

—I have no family. I am not a branch ind. No access to active brood minds. I have learned from the mandate.

—Then what are you?

—I don't know, exactly. Not unlike you.

Aryz understood what he was dealing with. It was the mind of the mutated shape, the one that had remained in the chamber, beseeching when he approached the transparent barrier.

—I must go now, the shape said. Aryz was alone again in the incomprehensible jumble. He moved slowly, carefully, into the Senexi sector, calling up subjects familiar to him. If he could encounter one shape, doubtless he could encounter the others—perhaps even the captive.

The idea was dreadful—and fascinating. So far as he knew, such intimacy between Senexi and human had never happened before. Yet there was something very Senexi-like in the method, as if branch inds attached to the brood mind were to brush mentalities while searching in the ageless memories.

The dread subsided. There was little worse that could happen to him, with his fellows dead, his brood mind in flux bind, his purpose uncertain.

What Aryz was feeling, for the first time, was a small measure of *freedom*.

The story of the original Prufrax continued.

In the early stages she visited Clevo with a barely concealed anger. His method was aggravating, his goals never precisely spelled out. What did he want with her, if anything?

And she with him? Their meetings were clandestine, though not precisely forbidden. She was a hawk one now with considerable personal liberty between exercises and engagements. There were no monitors in the closed-off reaches of the cruiser, and they could do whatever they wished. The two met in areas close to the ship's hull, usually in weapons blisters that could be opened to reveal the stars; there they talked.

Prufrax was not accustomed to prolonged conversation. Hawks were not raised to be voluble, nor were they selected for their curiosity. Yet the exhawk Clevo talked a great deal and was the most curious person she had met, herself included, and she regarded herself as uncharacteristically curious.

Often he was infuriating, especially when he played the "leading game," as she called it. Leading her from one question to the next, like an instructor, but without the trappings or any clarity of purpose. "What do you think of your mother?"

"Does that matter?"

"Not to me."

"Then why ask?"

"Because you matter."

Prufrax shrugged. "She was a fine mother. She bore me with a well-chosen heritage. She raised me as a hawk candidate. She told me her stories."

"Any hawk I know would envy you for listening at Jay-ax's knee."

"I was hardly at her knee."

"A speech tactic."

"Yes, well, she was important to me."

"She was a preferred single?"

"Yes."

"So you have no father."

"She selected without reference to individuals."

"Then you are really not that much different from a Senexi."

She bristled and started to push away. "There! You insult me again."

"Not at all. I've been asking one question all this time, and you haven't even heard. How well do you know the enemy?"

"Well enough to destroy them." She couldn't believe that was the only question he'd been asking. His speech tactics were very odd.

"Yes, to win battles, perhaps. But who will win the war?"

"It'll be a long war," she said softly, floating a few meters from him. He rotated in the blister, blocking out a blurred string of stars. The cruiser was preparing to shift out of status geometry again. "They fight well."

"They fight with conviction. Do you believe them to be evil?"

"They destroy us."

"We destroy them."

"So the question," she said, smiling at her cleverness, "is who began to destroy?"

"Not at all," Clevo said. "I suspect there's no longer a clear answer to that. Our leaders have obviously decided the question isn't important. No. We are the new, they are the old. The old must be superseded. It's a conflict born in the essential difference between Senexi and humans."

"That's the only way we're different? They're old, we're not so old? I don't understand."

"Nor do I, entirely."

"Well, finally!"

"The Senexi," Clevo continued, unperturbed, "long ago needed only gas-giant planets like their homeworlds. They lived in peace for billions of years before our world was formed. But as they moved from star to star they learned uses for other types of worlds. We were most interested in rocky Earth-like planets. Gradually we found uses for gas giants, too. By the time we met, both of us encroached on the other's territory. Their technology is so improbable, so unlike ours, that when we first encountered them we thought they must come from another geometry."

"Where did you learn all this?" Prufrax squinted at him suspiciously.

"I'm no longer a hawk," he said, "but I was too valuable just to discard.

My experience was too broad, my abilities too useful. So I was placed in research. It seems a safe place for me. Little contact with my comrades." He looked directly at her. "We must try to know our enemy, at least a little."

"That's dangerous," Prufrax said, almost instinctively.

"Yes, it is. What you know, you cannot hate."

"We must hate," she said. "It makes us strong. Senexi hate."

"They might," he said. "But, sometime, wouldn't you like to . . . sit down and talk with one, after a battle? Talk with a fighter? Learn its tactic, how it bested you in one move, compare—"

"No!" Prufrax shoved off rapidly down the tube. "We're shifting now. We have to get ready."

—She's smart. She's leaving him. He's crazy.

—Why do you think that?

—He would stop the fight, end the Zap.

—But he was a hawk.

—And hawks become glovers, I guess. But glovers go wrong, too. Like you.

—?

—Did you know they used you? How you were used?

—That's all blurred now.

—She's doomed if she stays around him. Who's that?

—Someone is listening with us.

—Recognize?

—No, gone now.

The next battle was bad enough to fall into the hellfought. Prufrax was in her fightsuit, legs drawn up as if about to kick off. The cruiser exited sponge-space and plunged into combat before sponge-space supplements could reach full effectivenss. She was dizzy, disoriented. The overhawks could only hope that a switch from biologic to cyber would cure the problem.

She didn't know what they were attacking. Tactic was flooding the implant, but she was only receiving the wash of that; she hadn't merged yet. She sensed that things were confused. That bothered her. Overs did not feel confusion.

The cruiser was taking damage. She could sense at least that—and she wanted to scream in frustration. Then she was ordered to merge with the implant. Biologic became cyber. She was in the Know.

The cruiser had reintegrated above a gas-giant planet. They were seventy-nine thousand kilometers from the upper atmosphere. The damage had come from ice mines—chunks of Senexi-treated water ice, altered to stay in sponge-space until a human vessel integrated nearby.

Then they emerged, packed with momentum and all the residual instability of an unsuccessful exit into status geometry. Unsuccessful for a ship, that is—very successful for a weapon.

The ice mines had given up the overness of the real within range of the cruiser and had blasted out whole sections of the hull. The launch lanes had not been damaged. The fighters lined up on their beams and were peppered out into space, spreading in the classic sword-flower.

The planet was a cold nest. Over didn't know what the atmosphere contained, but Senexi activity had been high in the star system, concentrating on this world. Over had decided to take a chance. Fighters headed for the atmosphere. The cruiser began planting singularity eggs. The eggs went ahead of the fighters, great black grainy ovoids that seemed to leave a trail of shadow—the wake of a birthing disruption in status geometry that could turn a gas giant into a short-lived sun.

Their time was limited. The fighters would group on entry sleds and descend to the liquid water regions where Senexi commonly kept their upwelling power plants. The fighters would first destroy any plants, loop into the liquid ammonia regions to search for hidden cuckoos, then see what was so important about the world.

She and five other fighters mounted the sled. Growing closer, the hazy clear regions of the atmosphere sparkled with Senexi sensors. Spiderweb beams shot from the six sleds to down the sensors. Buffet began. Scream, heat, then a second flower from the sled at a depth of two hundred kilometers. The sled slowed and held station. It would be their only way back. The fightsuits couldn't pull out of such a large gravity well.

She descended deeper. The pale, bloated beacon of the red star was dropping below the second cloudtops, limning the strata in orange and purple. At the liquid ammonia level she was instructed to key in permanent memory of all she was seeing. She wasn't "seeing" much, but other sensors were recording a great deal, all of it duly processed in her implant. "There's life here," she told herself. Indigenous life. Just another example of Senexi disregard for basic decency: they were interfering with a world developing its own complex biology.

The temperature rose to ammonia vapor levels, then to liquid water. The pressure on the fightsuit was enormous, and she was draining her stores much more rapidly than expected. At this level the atmosphere was particularly thick with organics.

Senexi snakes rose from below, passed them in altitude, then doubled back to engage. Prufrax was designated the deep diver; the others from her sled would stay at this level in her defense. As she fell, another sled group moved in behind her to double the cover.

She searched for the characteristic radiation curve of an upwelling plant. At the lower boundary of the liquid water level, below which her suit could not safely descend, she found it.

The Senexi were tapping the gas giant's convection from greater depths than usual. Above the plant, almost indetectable, was another object with an uncharacteristic curve. They were separated by ten kilometers. The power plant was feeding its higher companion with tight energy beams.

She slowed. Two other fighters, disengaged from the brief skirmish above, took positions as backups a few dozen kilometers higher than she. Her implant searched for an appropriate tactic. She would avoid the zero-angle phase for the moment, go in for reconnaissance. She could feel sound pouring from the plant and its companion—rhythmic, not waste noise, but deliberate. And homing in on that sound were waves of large vermiform organisms, like chains of gas-filled sausage. They were dozens of meters long, two meters at their greatest thickness, shaped vaguely like the Senexi snake fighters. The vermiforms were native, and they were being lured into the uppermost floating structure. None were emerging. Her backups spread apart, descended, and drew up along her flanks.

She made her decision almost immediately. She could see a pattern in the approach of the natives. If she fell into the pattern, she might be able to enter the structure unnoticed.

—It's a grinder. She doesn't recognize it.

—What's a grinder?

—She should make the Zap! It's an ugly thing; Senexi use them all the time. Net a planet with grinders, like a cuckoo, but for larger operations.

The creatures were being passed through separator fields. Their organics fell from the bottom of the construct, raw material for new growth—Senexi growth. Their heavier elements were stored for later harvest.

With Prufrax in their midst, the vermiforms flew into the separator. The interior was hundreds of meters wide, lead-white walls with flat gray machinery floating in a dust haze, full of hollow noise, the distant bleats of vermiforms being slaughtered. Prufrax tried to retreat, but she was caught in a selector field. Her suit bucked and she was whirled violently, then thrown into a repository for examination. She had been screened from the separator; her plan to record, then destroy, the structure had been foiled by an automatic filter.

"Information sufficient." Command logic programed into the implant before launch was now taking over. "Zero-angle phase both plant and adjunct." She was drifting in the repository, still slightly stunned.

Something was fading. Cyber was hissing in and out; the over logic-commands were being scrambled. Her implant was malfunctioning and was returning control to biologic. The selector fields had played havoc with all cyber functions, down to the processors in her weapons.

Cautiously she examined the down systems one by one, determining what she could and could not do. This took as much as thirty seconds—an astronomical time on the implant's scale.

She still could use the phase weapon. If she was judicious and didn't waste her power, she could cut her way out of the repository, maneuver and work with her escorts to destroy both the plant and the separator. By the time they returned to the sleds, her implant might have rerouted itself and made sufficient repairs to handle defense. She had no way of knowing what was waiting for her if—when—she escaped, but that was the least of her concerns for the moment.

She tightened the setting of the phase beam and swung her fightsuit around, knocking a cluster of junk ice and silty phosphorescent dust. She activated the beam. When she had a hole large enough to pass through, she edged the suit forward, beamed through more walls and obstacles, and kicked herself out of the repository into free fall. She swiveled and laid down a pattern of wide-angle beams, at the same time relaying a message on her situation to the escorts.

The escorts were not in sight. The separator was beginning to break up, spraying debris through the almost-opaque atmosphere. The rhythmic sound ceased, and the crowds of vermiforms began to disperse.

She stopped her fall and thrust herself several kilometers higher—directly into a formation of Senexi snakes. She had barely enough power to reach the sled, much less fight and turn her beams on the upwelling plant.

Her cyber was still down.

The sled signal was weak. She had no time to calculate its direction from the inertial guidance cyber. Besides, all cyber was unreliable after passing through the separator.

Why do they fight so well? Clevo's question clogged her thoughts. Cursing, she tried to blank and keep all her faculties available for running the fightsuit. *When evenly matched, you cannot win against your enemy unless you understand them. And if you truly understand, why are you fighting and not talking?* Clevo had never told her that—not in so many words. But it was part of a string of logic all her own.

Be more than an automation with a narrow range of choices. Never underestimate the enemy. Those were old Grounds dicta, not entirely lost in the new training, but only emphasized by Clevo.

If they fight as well as you, perhaps in some ways they fight-think like you do. Use that.

Isolated, with her power draining rapidly, she had no choice. They might disregard her if she posed no danger. She cut her thrust and went into a diving spin. Clearly she was on her way to a high-pressure grave. They would sense her power levels, perhaps even pick up the lack of field activity if she let her shields drop. She dropped the shields. If they let her fall and didn't try to complete the kill—if they concentrated on active fighters above—she had enough power to drop into the water vapor regions, far below the plant, and silently ride a thermal into range. With luck, she could get close enough to lay a web of zero-angle phase and take out the plant.

She had minutes in which to agonize over her plan. Falling, buffeted by winds that could knock her kilometers out of range, she spun like a vagrant flake of snow.

She couldn't even expend the energy to learn if they were scanning her, checking out her potential.

Perhaps she underestimated them. Perhaps they would be that much more thorough and take her out just to be sure. Perhaps they had unwritten rules of conduct like the ones she was using, taking hunches into account. Hunches were discouraged in Grounds training—much less reliable than cyber.

She fell. Temperature increased. Pressure on her suit began to constrict her air supply. She used fighter trancing to cut back on her breathing.

Fell.

And broke the trance. Pushed through the dense smoke of exhaustion. Planned the beam web. Counted her reserves. Nudged into an updraft beneath the plant. The thermal carried her, a silent piece of paper in a storm, drifting back and forth beneath the objective. The huge field intakes pulsed above, lightning outlining their invisible extension. She held back on the beam.

Nearly faded out. Her suit interior was almost unbearably hot.

She was only vaguely aware of laying down the pattern. The beams vanished in the murk. The thermal pushed her through a layer of haze, and she saw the plant, riding high above clear-atmosphere turbulence. The zero-angle phase had pushed through the field intakes, into their source nodes and plant body, surrounding it with bright blue Tcherenkov. First the surface began to break up, then the middle layers, and finally key supports. Chunks vibrated away with the internal fury of their molecular, then atomic, then particle disruption. Paraphrasing Grounds description of beam action, the plant became less and less convinced of its reality. "Matter dreams," an instructor had said a decade before. "Dreams it is real, maintains the dream by shifting rules with constant results. Disturb the dreams, the shifting of the rules results in inconstant results. Things cannot hold."

She slid away from the updraft, found another, wondered idly how far she would be lifted. Curiosity at the last. Let's just see, she told herself; a final experiment.

Now she was cold. The implant was flickering, showing signs of reorganization. She didn't use it. No sense expanding the amount of time until death. No sense—

at all.

The sled, maneuvered by one remaining fighter, glided up beneath her almost unnoticed.

Aryz waited in the stillness of a Senexi memory, his thinking temporarily reduced to a faint susurrus. What he waited for was not clear.

—Come.

The form of address was wrong, but he recognized the voice. His thoughts stirred, and he followed the nebulous presence out of Senexi territory.

—Know your enemy.

Prufrax . . . the name of one of the human shapes sent out against their own kind. He could sense her presence in the mandate, locked into a memory store. He touched on the store and caught the essentials— the grinder, the updraft plant, the fight from Prufrax's viewpoint.

—Know how your enemy knows you.

He sensed a second presence, similar to that of Prufrax. It took him some time to realize that the human captive was another form of the shape, a reproduction of the . . .

Both were reproductions of the female whose image was in the memory store. Aryz was not impressed by threes—Senexi mysticism, what had ever existed of it, had been preoccupied with fives and sixes—but the coincidence was striking.

—Know how your enemy *sees* you.

He saw the grinder processing organics—the vermiform natives—in preparation for a widespread seeding of deuterium gatherers. The operation had evidently been conducted for some time; the vermiform populations were greatly reduced from their usual numbers. Vermiforms were a common type-species on gas giants of the sort depicted. The mutated shape nudged him into a particular channel of the memory, that which carried the original Prufrax's emotions. She had reacted with *disgust* to the Senexi procedure. It was a reaction not unlike what Aryz might feel when coming across something forbidden in Senexi behavior. Yet eradication was perfectly natural, analogous to the human cleansing of *food* before *eating*.

—It's in the memory. The vermiforms are intelligent. They have their own kind of civilization. Human action on this world prevented their complete extinction by the Senexi.

—So what matter they were *intelligent?* Aryz responded. They did not behave or think like Senexi, or like any species Senexi find compatible. They were therefore not desirable. Like humans.

—You would make humans extinct?

—We would protect ourselves from them.

—Who damages whom most?

Aryz didn't respond. The line of questioning was incomprehensible. Instead he flowed into the memory of Prufrax, propelled by another aspect of complete freedom, confusion.

The implant was replaced. Prufrax's damaged limbs and skin were repaired or regenerated quickly, and within four wakes, under intense treatment usually reserved only for overs, she regained all her reflexes and speed. She requested liberty of the cruiser while it returned for repairs. Her request was granted.

She first sought Clevo in the designated research area. He wasn't there, but a message was, passed on to her by a smiling young crew member. She read it quickly:

"You're free and out of action. Study for a while, then come find me. The old place hasn't been damaged. It's less private, but still good. Study! I've marked highlights."

She frowned at the message, then handed it to the crew member, who duly erased it and returned to his duties. She wanted to talk with Clevo, not study.

But she followed his instructions. She searched out highlighted entries in the ship's memory store. It was not nearly as dull as she had expected. In fact, by following the highlights, she felt she was learning more about Clevo and about the questions he asked.

Old literature was not nearly as graphic as fibs, but it was different enough to involve her for a time. She tried to create imitations of what she read, but erased them. Nonfib stories were harder than she suspected. She read about punishment, duty; she read about places called heaven and hell, from a writer who had died tens of thousands of years before. With ed supplement guidance, she was able to comprehend most of what she read. Plugging the store into her implant, she was able to absorb hundreds of volumes in an hour.

Some of the stores were losing definition. They hadn't been used in decades, perhaps centuries.

Halfway through, she grew impatient. She left the research area.

Operating on another hunch, she didn't go to the blister as directed, but straight to memory central, two decks inboard the research area. She saw Clevo there, plugged into a data pillar, deep in some aspect of ship history. He noticed her approach, unplugged, and swiveled on his chair. "Congratulations," he said, smiling at her.

"Hardfought," she acknowledged, smiling.

"Better than that, perhaps," he said.

She looked at him quizzically. "What do you mean, better?"

"I've been doing some illicit tapping on over channels."

"So?"

—He *is dangerous!*

"You've been recommended."

"For what?"

"Not for hero status, not yet. You'll have a good many more fights before that. And you probably won't enjoy it when you get there. You won't be a fighter then."

Prufrax stood silently before him.

"You may have a valuable genetic assortment. Overs think you behaved remarkably well under impossible conditions."

"Did I?"

He nodded. "Your type may be preserved."

"Which means?"

"There's a program being planned. They want to take the best fighters reproduce them—clone them—to make uniform top-grade squadrons. It was rumored in my time—you haven't heard?"

She shook her head.

"It's not new. It's been done, off and on, for tens of thousands of years. This time they believe they can make it work."

"You were a fighter, once," she said. "Did they preserve your type?"

Clevo nodded. "I had something that interested them, but not, I think, as a fighter."

Prufrax looked down at her stubby-fingered hands. "It was grim," she said. "You know what we found?"

"An extermination plant."

"You want me to understand them better. Well, I can't. I refuse. How could they do such·things?" She looked disgusted and answered her own question. "Because they're Senexi."

"Humans," Clevo said, "have done much the same, sometimes worse."

"No!"

—No!

"Yes," he said firmly. He sighed. "We've wiped Senexi worlds, and we've even wiped worlds with intelligent species like our own. Nobody is innocent. Not in this universe."

"We were never taught that."

"It wouldn't have made you a better hawk. But it might make a better human of you, to know. Greater depth of character. Do you want to be more aware?"

"You mean, study more?"

He nodded.

"What makes you think *you* can teach me?"

"Because you thought about what I asked you. About how Senexi thought. And you survived where some other hawk might not have. The overs think it's in your genes. It might be. But it's also in your head."

"Why not tell the overs?"

"I have," he said. He shrugged. "I'm too valuable to them, otherwise I'd have been busted again, a long time ago."

"They wouldn't want me to learn from you?"

"I don't know," Clevo said. "I suppose they're aware you're talking to me. They could stop it if they wanted. They may be smarter than I give them credit for." He shrugged again. "Of course they're smart. We just disagree at times."

"And if I learn from you?"

"Not from me, actually. From the past. From history, what other people have thought. I'm really not any more capable than you . . . but I know history, small portions of it. I won't teach you so much, as guide."

"I did use your questions," Prufrax said. "But will I ever need to use them—think that way—again?"

Clevo nodded. "Of course."

—You're quiet.

—She's giving in to him.

—She gave in a long time ago.

—She should be afraid.

—Were you—we—ever really afraid of a challenge?

—No.

—Not Senexi, not forbidden knowledge.

—Someone listens with us. Feel—

Clevo first led her through the history of past wars, judging that was appropriate considering her occupation. She was attentive enough, though her mind wandered; sometimes he was didactic, but she found she didn't mind that much. At no time did his attitude change as they pushed through the tangle of the past. Rather her perception of his attitude changed. Her perception of herself changed.

She saw that in all wars, the first stage was to dehumanize the enemy, reduce the enemy to a lower level so that he might be killed without compunction. When the enemy was not human to begin with, the task was easier. As wars progressed, this tactic frequently led to an underestimation of the enemy, with disastrous consequences. "We aren't exactly underestimating the Senexi," Clevo said. "The overs are too smart for that. But we refuse to understand them, and that could make the war last indefinitely."

"Then why don't the overs see that?"

"Because we're pattern locked into a pattern. We've been fighting for so long, we've begun to lose ourselves. And it's getting worse." He assumed his didactic tone, and she knew he was reciting something he'd formulated years before and repeated to himself a thousand times. "There is no war so important that to win it, we must destroy our minds."

She didn't agree with that; losing the war with the Senexi would mean extinction, as she understood things.

Most often they met in the single unused weapons blister that had not been damaged. They met when the ship was basking in the real between sponge-space jaunts. He brought memory stores with him in portable modules, and they read, listened, experienced together. She never placed a great deal of importance in the things she learned; her interest was focused on Clevo. Still, she learned.

The rest of her time she spent training. She was aware of growing isolation from the hawks, which she attributed to her uncertain rank status. Was her genotype going to be preserved or not? The decision hadn't been made. The more she learned, the less she wanted to be singled out for honor. Attracting that sort of attention might be dangerous, she thought. Dangerous to whom, or what, she could not say.

Clevo showed her how hero images had been used to indoctrinate birds and hawks in a standard of behavior that was ideal, not realistic. The results were not always good; some tragic blunders had been made by fighters trying to be more than anyone possibly could or refusing to be flexible.

The war was certainly not a fib. Yet more and more the overs seemed to be treating it as one. Unable to bring about strategic victories against the Senexi, the overs had settled in for a long war of attrition and were apparently bent on adapting all human societies to the effort.

"There are overs we never hear of, who make decisions that shape our entire lives. Soon they'll determine whether or not we're even born, if they don't already."

"That sounds paranoid," she said, trying out a new word and concept she had only recently learned.

"Maybe so."

"Besides, it's been like that for ages—not knowing all our overs."

"But it's getting worse," Clevo said. He showed her the projections he had made. In time, if trends continued unchanged, fighters and all other combatants would be treated more and more mechanically, until they became the machines the overs wished them to be.

—No.

—Quiet. How does he feel toward her?

It was inevitable that as she learned under his tutelage, he began to feel responsible for her changes. She was an excellent fighter. He could never be sure that what he was doing might reduce her effectiveness. And yet he had fought well—despite similiar changes—until his billet switch. It had been the overs who had decided he would be more effective, less disruptive, elsewhere.

Bitterness over that decision was part of his motive. The overs had done a foolish thing, putting a fighter into research. Fighters were tenacious. If the truth was to be hidden, then fighters were the ones likely to ferret it out. And pass it on. There was a code among fighters seldom revealed to their immediate overs, much less to the supreme overs parsecs distant in their strategospheres. What one fighter learned that could be of help to another had to be passed on, even under penalty. Clevo was simply following that unwritten rule.

Passing on the fact that, at one time, things had been different. That war changed people, governments, societies, and that societies could effect an enormous change on their constituents, especially now—change in their lives, their thinking. Things could become even more structured. Freedom to fight was a drug, an illusion—

—No!

used to perpetuate a state of hatred.

"Then why do they keep all the data in stores?" she asked. "I mean, you study the data, everything becomes obvious."

"There are still important people who think we may want to find our way back someday. They're afraid we'll lose our roots, but—"

His face suddenly became peaceful. She reached out to touch him, and he jerked slightly, turning toward her in the blister. "What is it?" she asked.

"It's not organized. We're going to lose the information. Ship overs are going to restrict access more and more. Eventually it'll decay, like some already has in these stores. I've been planning for some time to put it all in a single unit—"

—He built the mandate!

"and have the overs place one on every ship, with researchers to tend it. Formalize the loose scheme still in effect, but dying. Right now I'm working on the fringes. At least I'm allowed to work. But soon I'll have enough evidence that they won't be able to argue. Evidence of what happens to societies that try to obscure their histories. They go quite mad. The overs are still rational enough to listen; maybe I'll push it through." He looked out the transparent blister. The stars were smudging to one side as the cruiser began probing for entrances to sponge-space. "We'd better get back."

"Where are you going to be when we return? We'll all be transferred."

"That's some time removed. Why do you want to know?"

"I'd like to learn more."

He smiled. "That's not your only reason."

"I don't need someone to tell me what my reasons are," she said testily.

"We're so reluctant," he said. She looked at him sharply, irritated and puzzled. "I mean," he continued, "we're hawks. Comrades. Hawks couple like *that*." He snapped his fingers. "But you and I sneak around it all the time."

Prufrax kept her face blank.

"Aren't you receptive toward me?" he asked, his tone almost teasing.

"You're so damned superior. Stuffy," she snapped.

"Aren't you?"

"It's just that's not all," she said, her tone softening.

"Indeed," he said in a barely audible whisper.

In the distance they heard the alarms.

—It was never any different.

—What?

—Things were never any different before me.

—Don't be silly. It's all here.

—If Clevo made the mandate, then he put it here. It isn't true.

—Why are you upset?

—I don't like hearing that everything I believe is a . . . fib.

—I've never known the difference, I suppose. Eyes-open was never all that real to me. This isn't real, you aren't . . . this is eyes-shut. So why be upset? You and I . . . we aren't even whole people. I feel you. You wish the Zap, you fight, not much else. I'm just a shadow, even compared to you. But she is whole. She loves him. She's less a victim than either of us. So something has to have changed.

—You're saying things have gotten worse.

—If the mandate is a lie, that's all I am. You refuse to accept. I *have* to accept, or I'm even less than a shadow.

—I don't refuse to accept. It's just hard.

—You started it. You thought about love.

—You did!

—Do you know what love is?

—Reception.

They first made love in the weapons blister. It came as no surprise; if anything, they approached it so cautiously they were clumsy. She had become more and more receptive, and he had dropped his guard. It had been quick, almost frantic, far from the orchestrated and drawn-out ballet the hawks prided themselves for. There was no pretense. No need to play the role of artists interacting. They were depending on each other. The pleasure they exchanged was nothing compared to the emotions involved.

"We're not very good with each other," Prufrax said.

Clevo shrugged. "That's because we're shy."

"Shy?"

He explained. In the past—at various times in the past, because such differences had come and gone many times—making love had been more than a physical exchange or even an expression of comradeship. It had been the acknowledgment of a bond between people.

She listened, half-believing. Like everything else she had heard, that kind of love seemed strange, distasteful. What if one hawk was lost, and the other continued to love? It interfered with the hardfought, certainly. But she was also fascinated. Shyness—the fear of one's presentation to another. The hesitation to present truth, or the inward confusion of truth at the awareness that another might be important, more important than one thought possible. That such emotions might have existed at one time, and seem so alien now, only emphasized the distance of the past, as Clevo tried to tell her. And that she felt those emotions only confirmed she was not as far from that past as, for dignity's sake, she might have wished.

Complex emotion was not encouraged either at the Grounds or among hawks on station. Complex emotion degraded complex performance. The simple and direct was desirable.

"But all we seem to do is talk—until now," Prufrax said, holding his hand and examining his fingers one by one. They were very little different from her own, though extended a bit from hawk fingers to give greater versatility with key instruction.

"Talking is the most human thing we can do."

She laughed. "I know what you are," she said, moving up until her eyes were even with his chest. "You're stuffy. You aren't the party type."

"Where'd you learn about parties?"

"You gave me literature to read, I read it. You're an instructor at heart. You make love by telling." She felt peculiar, almost afraid, and looked up at his face. "Not that I don't enjoy your lovemaking, like this. Physical."

"You receive well," he said. "Both ways."

"What we're saying," she whispered, "is not truth-speaking. It's amenity." She turned into the stroke of his hand through her hair. "Amenity is supposed to be decadent. That fellow who wrote about heaven and hell. He would call it a sin."

"Amenity is the recognition that somebody may see or feel differently than you do. It's the recognition of individuals. You and I, we're part of the end of all that."

"Even if you convince the overs?"

He nodded. "They want to repeat success without risk. New individuals are risky, so they duplicate past success. There will be more and more people, fewer individuals. More of you and me, less of others. The fewer individuals, the fewer stories to tell. The less history. We're part of the death of history."

She floated next to him, trying to blank her mind as she had before, to drive out the nagging awareness he was right. She thought she understood the social structure around her. Things seemed new. She said as much.

"It's a path we're taking," Clevo said. "Not a place we're at."

—It's a place *we're* at. How different are *we*?

—But there's so much history in here. How can it be over for us?

—I've been thinking. Do we know the last event recorded in the mandate?

—Don't, we're drifting from Prufrax now. . . .

Aryz felt himself drifting with them. They swept over countless millennia, then swept back the other way. And it became evident that as much change had been wrapped in one year of the distant past as in a thousand years of the closing entries in the mandate. Clevo's voice seemed to follow them, though they were far from his period, far from Prufrax's record.

"Tyranny is the death of history. We fought the Senexi until we became like them. No change, youth at an end, old age coming upon us. There is no important change, merely elaborations in the pattern."

—How many times have we been here, then? How many times have we died?

Aryz wasn't sure, now. Was this the first time humans had been captured? Had he been told everything by the brood mind? Did the Senexi have no *history*, whatever that was—

The accumulated lives of living, thinking beings. Their actions, thoughts, passions, hopes.

The mandate answered even his confused, nonhuman requests. He could understand action, thought, but not passion or hope. Perhaps without those there was no *history*.

—You have no history, the mutated shape told him. There have been millions like you, even millions like the brood mind. What is the last event recorded in the brood mind that is not duplicated a thousand times over, so close they can be melded together for convenience?

—You understand that? Aryz asked the shape.

—Yes.

—How do you understand—because we made you between human and Senexi?

—Not only that.

The requests of the twin captive and shape were moving them back once more into the past, through the dim gray millennia of repeating ages. History began to manifest again, differences in the record.

On the way back to Mercior, four skirmishes were fought. Prufrax did well in each. She carried something special with her, a thought she didn't even tell Clevo, and she carried the same thought with her through their last days at the Grounds.

Taking advantage of hawk liberty, she opted a posthardfought residence just outside the Grounds, in the relatively uncrowded Daughter of Cities zone. She wouldn't be returning to fight until several issues had been decided—her status most important among them.

Clevo began making his appeal to the middle overs. He was given Grounds duty to finish his proposals. They could stay together for the time being.

The residence was sixteen square meters in area, not elegant—*natural*, as rentOpts described it. Clevo called it a "garret," inaccurately as she discovered when she looked it up in his memory blocs, but perhaps he was describing the tone.

On the last day she lay in the crook of Clevo's arm. They had done a few hours of nature sleep. He hadn't come out yet, and she looked up at his face, reached up with a hand to feel his arm.

It was different from the arms of others she had been receptive toward. It was unique. The thought amused her. There had never been a reception like theirs. This was the beginning. And if both were to be duplicated, this love, this reception, would be repeated an infinite number of times. Clevo meeting Prufrax, teaching her, opening her eyes.

Somehow, even though repetition contributed to the death of history, she was pleased. This was the secret thought she carried into fight. Each time she would survive, wherever she was, however many duplications down the line. She would receive Clevo, and he would teach her. If not now—if one or the other died—then in the future. The death of history might be a good thing. Love could go on forever.

She had lost even a rudimentary apprehension of death, even with present pleasure to live for. Her functions had sharpened. She would please him by doing all the things he could not. And if he was to enter that state she frequently found him in, that state of introspection, of reliving his own battles and of envying her activity, then that wasn't bad. All they did to each other was good.

—Was good

—Was

She slipped from his arm and left the narrow sleeping quarter, pushing through the smoke-colored air curtain to the lounge. Two hawks and an over she had never seen before were sitting there. They looked up at her.

"Under," Prufrax said.

"Over," the woman returned. She was dressed in tan and green, Grounds colors, not ship.

"May I assist?"

"Yes."

"My duty, then?"

The over beckoned her closer. "You have been receiving a researcher."

"Yes," Prufrax said. The meetings could not have been a secret on the ship, and certainly not their quartering near the Grounds. "Has that been against duty?"

"No." The over eyed Prufrax sharply, observing her perfected fight-form, the easy grace with which she stood, naked, in the middle of the small compartment. "But a decision has been reached. Your status is decided now."

She felt a shiver.

"Prufrax," said the elder hawk. She recognized him from fibs, and his companion: Kumnax and Arol. Once her heroes. "You have been accorded an honor, just as your partner has. You have a valuable genetic assortment—"

She barely heard the rest. They told her she would return to fight, until they deemed she had had enough experience and background to be brought into the polinstruc division. Then her fighting would be over. She would serve better as an example, a hero.

Heroes never partnered out of function. Hawk heroes could not even partner with exhawks.

Clevo emerged from the air curtain. "Duty," the over said. "The residence is disbanded. Both of you will have separate quarters, separate duties."

They left. Prufrax held out her hand, but Clevo didn't take it. "No use," he said.

Suddenly she was filled with anger. "You'll give it up? Did I expect too much? *How strongly?*"

"Perhaps even more strongly than you," he said. "I knew the order was coming down. And still I didn't leave. That may hurt my chances with the supreme overs."

"Then at least I'm worth more than your breeding history?"

"Now you are history. History the way they make it."

"I feel like I'm dying," she said, amazement in her voice. "What is that, Clevo? What did you do to me?"

"I'm in pain, too," he said.

"You're hurt?"

"I'm confused."

"I don't believe that," she said, her anger rising again. "You knew, and you didn't do anything?"

"That would have been counter to duty. We'll be worse off if we fight it."

"So what good is your great, exalted history?"

"History is what you have," Clevo said. "I only record."

—Why did they separate them?

—I don't know. You didn't like him, anyway.

—Yes, but now . . .

—See? You're her. We're her. But shadows. She was whole.

—I don't understand.

—We don't. Look what happens to her. They took what was best out of her. Prufrax.

went into battle eighteen more times before dying as heroes often do, dying in the midst of what she did best. The question of what made her better before the separation—for she definitely was not as fine a fighter after—has not been settled. Answers fall into an extinct classification of knowledge, and there are few left to interpret, none accessible to this device.

—So she went out and fought and died. They never even made fibs about her. This killed her?

—I don't think so. She fought well enough. She died like other hawks died.

—And she might have lived otherwise.

—How can I know that, any more than you?

—They—we—met again, you know. I met a Clevo once, on my ship. They didn't let me stay with him long.

—How did they react to him?

—There was so little time, I don't know.

—Let's ask. . . .

In thousands of duty stations, it was inevitable that some of Prufrax's visions would come true, that they should meet now and then. Clevos were numerous, as were Prufraxes. Every ship carried complements of several of each. Though Prufrax was never quite as successful as the original, she was a fine type. She—

—She was never quite as successful. They took away her edge. They didn't even know it!

—They must have known.

—Then they didn't want to win!

—We don't know that. Maybe there were more important considerations.

—Yes, like killing history.

Aryz shuddered in his warming body, dizzy as if about to bud, then regained control. He had been pulled from the mandate, called to his own duty.

He examined the shapes and the human captive. There was something different about them. How long had they been immersed in the mandate? He checked quickly, frantically, before answering the call. The reconstructed Mam had malfunctioned. None of them had been nourished. They were thin, pale, cooling.

Even the bloated mutant shape was dying; lost, like the others, in the mandate.

He turned his attention away. Everything was confusion. Was he human or Senexi now? Had he fallen so low as to understand them? He went to the origin of the call, the ruins of the temporary brood chamber. The corridors were caked with ammonia ice, burning his pod as he slipped over them. The brood mind had come out of flux bind. The emergency support systems hadn't worked well; the brood mind was damaged.

"Where have you been?" it asked.

"I assumed I would not be needed until your return from the flux bind."

"You have not been watching!"

"Was there any need? We are so advanced in time, all our actions are obsolete. The nebula is collapsed, the issue is decided."

"We do not know that. We are being pursued."

Aryz turned to the sensor wall—what was left of it—and saw that they were, indeed, being pursued. He had been lax.

"It is not your fault," the brood mind said. "You have been set a task that tainted you and ruined your function. You will dissipate."

Aryz hesitated. He had become so different, so tainted, that he actually *hesitated* at a direct command from the brood mind. But it was damaged. Without him, without what he had learned, what could it do? It wasn't reasoning correctly.

"There are facts you must know, important facts—"

Aryz felt a wave of revulsion, uncomprehending fear, and something not unlike human anger radiate from the brood mind. Whatever he had learned and however he had changed, he could not withstand that wave.

Willingly, and yet against his will—it didn't matter—he felt himself liquifying. His pod slumped beneath him, and he fell over, landing on a pool of frozen ammonia. It burned, but he did not attempt to lift himself. Before he ended, he saw with surprising clarity what it was to be a branch ind, or a brood mind, or a human. Such a valuable insight, and it leaked out of his permea and froze on the ammonia.

The brood mind regained what control it could of the fragment. But there were no defenses worthy of the name. Calm, preparing its own dissipation, it waited for the pursuit to conclude.

The Mam set off an alarm. The interface with the mandate was severed. Weak, barely able to crawl, the humans looked at each other in horror and slid to opposite corners of the chamber.

They were confused: which of them was the captive, which the decoy shape? It didn't seem important. They were both bone-thin, fithy with their own excrement. They turned with one motion to stare at the bloated mutant. It sat in its corner, tiny head incongruous on the huge thorax, tiny arms and legs barely functional even when healthy. It smiled wanly at them.

"We felt you," one of the Prufraxes said. "You were with us in there." Her voice was a soft croak.

"That was my place," it replied. "My only place."

"What function, what name?"

"I'm . . . I know that. I'm a researcher. In there. I knew myself in there."

They squinted at the shape. The head. Something familiar, even now. "You're a Clevo . . ."

There was the noise all around them, cutting off the shape's weak words. As they watched, their chamber was sectioned like an orange, and the wedges peeled open. The illumination ceased. Cold enveloped them.

A naked human female, surrounded by tiny versions of herself, like an angel circled by fairy kin, floated into the chamber. She was thin as a snake. She wore nothing but silver rings on her wrists and a narrow torque around her waist. She glowed blue-green in the dark.

The two Prufraxes moved their lips weakly but made no sound in the near vacuum. *Who are you?*

She surveyed them without expression, then held out her arms as if to fly. She wore no gloves, but she was of their type.

As she had done countless times before on finding such Senexi experiments—though this seemed older than most—she lifted one arm higher. The blue-green intensified, spread in waves to the mangled walls, surrounded the freezing, dying shapes. Perfect, angelic, she left the debris behind to cast its fitful glow and fade.

They had destroyed every portion of the fragment but one. They left it behind unharmed.

Then they continued, millions of them thick with mist, working the spaces between the stars, their only master the overness of the real.

They needed no other masters. They would never malfunction.

The mandate drifted in the dark and cold, its memory going on, but its only life the rapidly fading tracks where minds had once passed through it. The trails writhed briefly, almost as if alive, but only following the quantum rules of diminishing energy states. Finally, a small memory was illuminated.

Prufrax's last poem, explained the mandate reflexively.

> *How the fires grow! Peace passes*
> *All memory lost.*
> *Somehow we always miss that single door,*
> *Dooming ourselves to circle.*
>
> *Ashes to stars, lies to souls,*
> *Let's spin round the sinks and holes.*
>
> *Kill the good, eat the young.*
> *Forever and more*
> *You and I are never done.*

The track faded into nothing. Around the mandate, the universe grew old very quickly.

JOE HALDEMAN

Manifest Destiny

Joe Haldeman is usually thought of as a "hard science" writer—his stories most typically deal with lasers, black holes, tachyons, L5 colonies, clones, high-speed computers, FTL drives, and the like, everything worked out with a scrupulous attention to scientific accuracy that sometimes costs him weeks of research and scores of notebooks closely packed with equations—but here in a change of pace, he takes us instead on a visit to the Old West of the 1840s, with sly and delightful results.

Born in Oklahoma City, Oklahoma, Joe Haldeman took a B.S. degree in physics and astronomy from the University of Maryland and did postgraduate work in mathematics and computer science. But his plans for a career in science were cut short by the U.S. Army, which sent him to Vietnam in 1968 as a combat engineer. Seriously wounded in action, Haldeman returned home in 1969 and began to write. He sold his first story to *Galaxy* in 1969, and by 1976 had already garnered Nebula and Hugo awards for his famous novel *The Forever War*, one of the landmark books of the '70s. His next novel, *Mindbridge*, sold for a record six-figure advance, and he took another Hugo Award in 1977 for his story "Tricentennial." His other books include a mainstream novel, *War Year*, the SF novels *Worlds*, *All My Sins Remembered*, and (in collaboration with his brother, SF writer Jack C. Haldeman II) *There Is No Darkness*; a short-story collection, *Infinite Dreams*, and as editor, the anthologies *Study War No More*, *Cosmic Laughter*, and *Nebula Award Stories Seventeen*. His most recent novel was the well-received *Worlds Apart*, the sequel to *Worlds*, published by Viking in 1983. Upcoming are the third volume in the *Worlds* trilogy, *Worlds Enough and Time*, as well as several other novels "in various stages of incompletion." He and his wife Gay are currently living in Cambridge, Massachusetts, where he is a visiting professor in the writing department of the Massachusetts Institute of Technology, teaching a SF writing workshop.

MANIFEST DESTINY

Joe Haldeman

This is the story of John Leroy Harris, but I doubt that name means much to you unless you're pretty old, especially an old lawman. He's dead anyhow, thirty years now, and nobody left around that could get hurt with this story. The fact is, I would've told it a long time ago, but when I was younger it would have bothered me, worrying about what people would think. Now I just don't care. The hell with it.

I've been on the move ever since I was a lad. At thirteen I put a knife in another boy and didn't wait around to see if he lived, just went down to the river and worked my way to St. Louis, got in some trouble there and wound up in New Orleans a few years later. That's where I came to meet John Harris.

Now you wouldn't tell from his name (he's changed it a few times), but John was pure Spanish blood, as his folks had come from Spain before the Purchase. John was born in Natchitoches in 1815, the year of the Battle of New Orleans. That put him thirteen years older than me, so I guess he was about thirty when we met.

I was working as a greeter, what we called a "bouncer," in Mrs. Carranza's whorehouse down by the docks. Mostly I just sat around and looked big—which I was then, and no fat, but sometimes I did have to calm down a customer or maybe throw him out, and I kept under my weskit a Starr pepperbox derringer in case of real trouble. It was by using this weapon that I made the acquaintance of John Harris.

Harris had been in the bar a few times, often enough for me to notice him, but to my knowledge he never put the boots to any of the women. Didn't have to pay for it, I guess; he was a handsome cuss, more than six feet tall, slender, with this kind of tragic look that women seem to like. Anyhow it was a raw rainy night in November, cold the way noplace else quite gets cold, and this customer comes downstairs complaining that the girl didn't do what he had asked her to, and he wasn't going to pay her extra. The kate come down right behind him and told what it was, and that she had too done it, and he hadn't said nothing about it when they started, and you can take my word for it that it was something nasty.

Well, we had some words about that and he tried to walk out without paying, so I sort of brought him back in and emptied out his pockets. He didn't even have the price of a drink on him (he'd given Mrs. Carranza the two dollars, but that didn't get you anything fancy). He did have a nice overcoat, though, so I took that from him and escorted him out into the rain headfirst.

What happened was about ten or fifteen minutes later he barges back in, looking like a drowned dog but with a Navy Colt in each hand. He got off two shots before I blew his brains out (pepperbox isn't much of a pistol, but he wasn't four yards away), and a split second later another bullet takes him in the lungs. I turned around and everybody was on the floor or behind the bar but John Harris, who was still perched on a stool looking sort of interested and putting some kind of foreign revolver back into his pocket.

The cops came soon enough but there was no trouble, not with forty witnesses, except for what to do with the dead meat. He didn't have any papers and Mrs. Carranza didn't want to pay the city for the burial. I was for just taking it out back and dropping it in the water, but they said that was against the law and unsanitary. John Harris said he had a wagon and come morning he'd take care of the matter. He signed a paper and that satisfied them.

First light Harris showed up in a fancy landau. Me and the driver, an old black, we wrestled the wrapped-up corpse into the back of the carriage. Harris asked me to come along and I did.

We just went east a little ways and rolled the damned thing into a bayou, let the gators take it. Then the driver smoked a pipe while Harris and me talked for a while.

Now he did have the damnedest way of talking. His English was like nothing you ever heard—Spanish his mother tongue and then he learned most of his English in Australia—but that's not what I really mean. I mean that if he wanted you to do something and you didn't want to do it, you had best put your fingers in your ears and start walking away. That son of a gun could sell water to a drowning man.

He started out asking me questions about myself, and eventually we got to talking about politics. Turns out we both felt about the same way toward the U.S. government, which is to say the hell with it. Harris wasn't even really a citizen and I myself didn't exist. For good reasons there was a death certificate on me in St. Louis, and I had a couple of different sets of papers a fellow on Bourbon Street printed up for me.

Harris had pointed out that I spoke some Spanish—Mrs. Carranza was Mexican and so were most of her kates—and he got around to asking whether I'd like to take a little trip to Mexico. I told him that sounded like a really bad idea.

This was late 1844, and that damned Polk had just been elected promising to annex Texas. The Mexicans had been skirmishing with Texas for years and they said it would be war if they got statehood. The man in charge was that one-legged crazy greaser Santa Anna, who'd been such a gentleman at the Alamo some years before. I didn't fancy being a gringo stuck in that country when the shooting started.

Well, Harris said I hadn't thought it through. It was true there was going to be a war, he said, but the trick was to get in there early enough to profit from it. He asked whether I'd be interested in getting ten percent of ten thousand dollars. I told him I could feel my courage returning.

Turns out Harris had joined the army a couple of years before and got himself into the quartermaster business, the ones who shuffle supplies back and forth. He had managed to slide five hundred rifles and a big batch of ammunition into a warehouse in New Orleans. The army thought they were stored in Kentucky, and the man who rented out the warehouse thought they were farming tools. Harris got himself discharged from the army and eventually got in touch with one General Parrodi, in Tampico. Parrodi agreed to buy the weapons, and pay for them in gold.

The catch was that Parrodi also wanted the services of three Americans, not to fight but to serve as "interpreters," that is to say spies, for as long as the war lasted. We would be given Mexican citizenship if we wanted it, and a land grant, but for our own protection we'd be treated as prisoners while the war was going on. (Part of the deal was that we would eavesdrop on other prisoners.) Harris showed me a contract that spelled all of this out, but I couldn't read Spanish back then. Anyhow, I was no more inclined to trust Mexicans in such matters than I was Americans, but as I say, Harris could sell booze to a Baptist.

The third American was none other than the old buck who was driving, a runaway slave from Florida name of Washington. He had grown up with Spanish masters, and not as a field hand, but some kind of butler. He had more learning than I did and could speak Spanish like a grandee. In Mexico, of course, there wasn't any slavery, and he reckoned a nigger with gold and land was just as good as anybody else with gold and land.

Looking back I can see why Washington was willing to take the risk, but I was a damned fool to do it. I was no roughneck, but I'd seen some violence in my seventeen years; that citizen we'd dumped in the bayou wasn't the first man I had to kill. You'd think I'd know better than to put myself in the middle of the war. Guess I was too young to take dying seriously—a thousand dollars was real money back then.

We went back into town and Harris took me to the warehouse. What he had was fifty long blue boxes stenciled with the name of a hardware outfit, and each one had ten Hall rifles, brand-new in a mixture of grease and sawdust.

(This is why the Mexicans were right enthusiastic. The Hall was a flintlock, at least these were, but it was also a breechloader. The old muzzle-loaders that most soldiers used, Mexican and American, took thirteen separate steps to reload. Miss one step and it can take your face off. Also the Hall used interchangeable parts, which meant you didn't have to find a smith when it needed repairing.)

Back at the house I told Mrs. Carranza I had to quit, and would get a new boy for her. Then Harris and me had a steak and put ourselves outside of a bottle of sherry, while he filled me in on the details of the operation. He'd put considerable money into buying discretion from a dockmaster and a Brit packet captain. This packet was about the only boat that put into Tampico from New Orleans on anything like a regular basis, and Harris had the idea that smuggling guns wasn't too much of a novelty to the captain. The next Friday night we were going to load the stuff onto the packet, bound south the next morning.

The loading went smooth as cream, and the next day we boarded the boat as paying passengers, Washington supposedly belonging to Harris and coming along as his manservant. At first it was right pleasant, slipping through a hundred or so miles of bayou country. But the Gulf of Mexico ain't the Mississippi, and after a couple of hours of that I was sick from my teeth to my toenails, and stayed that way for days. Captain gave me a mixture of brandy and seawater, which like to killed me. Harris thought that was funny, but the humor wore off when we put into Tampico and him and Washington had to offload the car without much help from me.

We went on up to Parrodi's villa and found we might be out of a job. While we were on that boat there had been a revolution. Santa Anna got kicked out, having pretty much emptied the treasury, and now the *moderado* Herrera was in charge. Parrodi and Harris argued for a long time. The Mexican was willing to pay for the rifles, but he figured that half the money was for our service as spies.

They finally settled on eight thousand, but only if we would stay in

Tampico for the next eighteen months, in case a war did start. Washington and I would get fifty dollars a month for walking around money.

The next year was the most boring year of my life. After New Orleans, there's just not much you could say about Tampico. It's an old city but also brand-new. Pirates burnt it to the ground a couple of hundred years ago. Santa Anna had it rebuilt in the twenties, and it was still not much more than a garrison town when we were there. Most of the houses were wood, imported from the States and nailed together. Couple of whorehouses and cantinas downtown, and you can bet I spent a lot of time and fifty bucks a month down there.

Elsewhere, things started to happen in the spring. The U.S. Congress went along with Polk and voted to annex Texas, and Mexico broke off diplomatic relations, and declared war, but Washington didn't seem to notice. Herrera must have had his hands full with the Carmelite Revolution, though things were quiet in Tampico for the rest of the year.

I got to know Harris pretty well. He spent a lot of time teaching me to read and write Spanish—though I never could talk it without sounding like a gringo—and I can tell you he was hellfire as a teacher. The teachers used to whip me when I was a kid, but that was easier to take than Harris's tongue. He could make you feel about six inches tall. Then a few minutes later you get a verb right and you're a hero.

We'd also go into the woods outside of town and practice with the pistol and rifle. He could so some awesome things with a Colt. He taught me how to throw a knife and I taught him how to use a lasso.

We got into a kind of routine. I had a room with the Galvez family downtown. I'd get up pretty late mornings and peg away at my Spanish books. About midday Harris would come down (he was staying up at the general's place) and give me my daily dose of sarcasm. Then we'd go down to a cantina and have lunch, usually with Washington. Afternoons, when most of the town napped, we might go riding or shooting in the woods south of town. We kept the Galvez family in meat that way, getting a boar or a deer every now and then. Since I was once a farm boy I knew how to dress out animals and how to smoke or salt meat to keep it. Señora Galvez always deducted the value of the meat from my rent.

Harris spent most evenings up at the villa with the officers, but sometimes he'd come down to the cantinas with me and drink pulque with the off-duty soldiers, or sometimes just sit around the kitchen table with the Galvez family. They took a shine to him.

He was really taken with old Doña Dolores, who claimed to be over a hundred years old and from Spain. She wasn't a relative but had been a friend of Señora Galvez's grandmother. Anyhow, she also claimed to be witch, a white witch who could heal and predict things and so forth.

If Harris had a weakness it was superstition. He always wore a lucky gold piece on a thong around his neck and carried an Indian finger bone in his pocket. And though he could swear the bark off a tree, he never used the names of God or Jesus, and when somebody else did he always crossed the fingers of his left hand. Even so, he laughed at religion and I never saw him go to church. So he was always asking Dolores about this or that, and always ready to listen to her stories. She only had a couple of dozen, but they kept changing.

Now I never thought that Dolores wasn't straight. If she wasn't a witch she sure as hell *thought* she was. And she did heal, with her hands and with herbs she picked in the woods. She healed me of the grippe and a rash I picked up from one of the girls. But I didn't believe in spells or fortune-telling, not then. When anybody's eighteen he's a smart aleck and knows just how the world works. I'm not so sure anymore, especially with what happened to Harris.

Every week or so we got a newspaper from Monterrey. By January I could read it pretty well, and looking back I guess you could say it was that month the war really started, though it would be spring before any shots were fired. What happened was that Polk sent some four thousand troops into what he claimed was part of Texas. The general was Zach Taylor, who was going to be such a crackerjack president a few years later. Herrera seemed about to make a deal with the States, so he got booted out and they put Paredes in office. The Mexicans started building up an army in Monterrey, and it looked like we were going to earn money after all.

I was starting to get a little nervous. You didn't have to look too hard at the map to see that Tampico was going to get trouble. If the U.S. wanted to take Mexico City they had the choice of marching over a couple thousand miles of mountain and desert, or taking a Gulf port and only marching a couple hundred miles. Tampico and Vera Cruz were about the same distance from Mexico City, but Vera Cruz had a fort protecting it. All we had was us.

Since our Civil War nobody remembers much about the Mexican one. Well, the Mexicans were in such bad shape even Taylor could beat them. The country was flat broke. Their regular army had more officers than men. They drafted illiterate Indians and mestizos and herded them by the thousands into certain death from American artillery and cavalry—some of them had never even fired a shot before they got into battle. That was Santa Anna economizing. He would've lost that war even if Mexico had all the armies of Europe combined.

Now we thought we'd heard the last of that one-legged son of a bitch. When we got to Tampico he'd just barely got out of Mexico with his skin, exiled to Cuba. But he got back, and he damn near killed me and Harris with his stupidity. And he did kill Washington, just as sure as if he pulled the trigger.

In May of that year Taylor had a showdown up by Matamoros, and Polk got around to declaring war. We started seeing American boats all the time, going back and forth out of cannon range, blockading the port. It was nervous making. The soldiers were fit to be tied—but old Dolores said there was nothing to worry about. Said she'd be able to "see" if there was going to be fighting, and she didn't see anything. This gave Harris considerable more comfort than it gave me.

What we didn't find out until after the war was that Santa Anna got in touch with the United States and said he could get Mexico to end the war, give up Texas and California, and for all I know the moon. Polk, who must have been one fine judge of character, gave Santa Anna safe passage through the American blockade.

Well, in the meantime the people in Mexico had gotten a belly full of Paredes, who had a way of having people he disagreed with shot, and they kicked him out. Santa Anna limped in and they made him president. He double-crossed Polk, got together twenty thousand soldiers, and got ready to head north and kick the stuffing out of the gringos.

Now you figure this one out. The Mexicans intercepted a message to the American naval commander, telling him to take Tampico. What did Santa Anna do? He ordered Parrodi to desert the place.

I was all for the idea myself, and so were a lot of the soldiers, but the general was considerable upset. It was bad enough that he couldn't stand and fight, but on top of that he didn't have near enough mules and horses to move out all the supplies they had stockpiled there.

Well, we sure as hell were going to take care of *our* supplies. Harris had a buckboard and we'd put a false bottom under the seat. Put our money in there and the papers that identified us as loyal Americans. In another place we put our Mexican citizenship papers and the deeds to our land grant, up in the Mesilla Valley. Then we drew weapons from the armory and got ready to go up to San Luis Potosí with a detachment that was leaving in the morning.

I was glad we wouldn't be in Tampico when the American fleet rolled in, but then San Luis Potosí didn't sound like any picnic, either. Santa Anna was going to be getting his army together, and it was only a few hundred miles from Taylor's army. One or the other of them would probably want to do something with all those soldiers.

Harris was jumpy. He kept putting his hand in his pocket to rub that Indian bone. That night, before he went up to the villa, he came to the hacienda with me, and told Dolores he's had a bad premonition about going to San Luis Potosí. He asked her to tell his fortune and tell him flat out if he was going to die, She said she couldn't tell a man when he was going to die, even when she saw it. If she did her powers would go away. But she would tell his fortune.

She studied his hands for a long time without saying anything. Then she took out a shabby deck of cards and dealt some out in front of him, face up. (They weren't regular cards. They had faded pictures of devils and skeletons and so forth.)

Finally she told him not to worry. He was not going to die in San Luis. In fact, he wouldn't die in Mexico at all. That was plain.

Now I wish that I had Harris's talent for shucking off worries. He laughed and gave her a gold real, and then he dragged me down to the cantina, where we proceeded to get more than half corned on that damned pulque, on his money. We carried out four big jars of the stuff, which was a good thing. I had to drink half one in the morning before I could see through the agony. That stuff is not good for white men. Ten cents a jug, though.

The trek from Tampico to San Luis took more than a week, with Washington riding in the back of the buckboard and Harris and me taking turns riding and walking. There was about two hundred soldiers in our group, no more used to walking than us, and sometimes they eyed that buckboard. It was hilly country and mostly dry. General Parrodi went on ahead and we never saw him again. Later on we learned that Santa Anna court-martialed him for desertion, for letting the gringos take Tampico. Fits.

San Luis Potosí looked like a nice little town, but we didn't see too damned much of it. We went to the big camp outside of town. Couldn't find Parrodi, so Harris sniffed around and got us attached to General Pacheco's division. General looked at the contract and more or less told us to pitch a tent and stay out of the way.

You never seen so many greasers in your life. Four thousand who Taylor'd kicked out of Monterrey, and about twenty thousand more who might or might not have known which end the bullet comes out of.

We got a good taste of what they call *santanismo* now. Santa Anna had all these raw boys, and what did he do to get them in shape for a fight? He had them dress up and do parades, while he rode back and forth on his goddamned horse. Week after week. A lot of the boys ran away, and I can't say I blame them. They didn't have a thousand dollars and a ranch to hang around for.

We weren't the only Americans there. A whole bunch of Taylor's men, more than two hundred, had absquatulated before he took Monterrey. The Mexicans gave them land grants, too. They were called the "San

Pats," the San Patricio battalion. We were told not to go near them, so that none of them would know we weren't actually prisoners.

After a couple of months of this, we found out what the deal was going to be. Taylor'd had most of his men taken away from him, sent down to Tampico to join up with another bunch that was headed for Mexico City. What Santa Anna said we were going to do was go north and wipe out Taylor, then come back and defend the city. The first part did look possible, since we had four or five men for every one of Taylor's. Me and Harris and Washington decided we'd wait and see how the first battle went. We might want to keep going north.

It took three days to get all the men on the road. Not just men, either; a lot of them had their wives and children along, carrying food and water and firewood. It was going to be three hundred miles, most of it barren. We saw Santa Anna go by, in a carriage drawn by eight white mules, followed by a couple carriages of whores. If I had the second sight Dolores claimed to have, I might've spent a pill on that son of a bitch. I still wonder why nobody ever did.

It wasn't easy even for us, with plenty of water and food. Then the twelfth day a norther came in, the temperature dropped way below freezing, and a goddamned blizzard came up. We started passing dead people by the side of the road. Then Washington lost his voice, coughed blood for a while, and died. We carried him till night and then buried him. Had to get a pick from the engineers to get through the frozen ground. I never cried over a nigger before or since. Nor a white man, now I think of it. Could be it was the wind. Harris and me split his share of the gold and burnt his papers.

It warmed up enough for the snow to turn to cold drizzle, and it rained for two days straight. Then it stopped and the desert sucked up the water, and we marched the rest of the way through dust and heat. Probably a fourth of Santa Anna's men died or deserted before we got to where Zach Taylor was waiting, outside of Saltillo in a gulch called Buena Vista. Still, we had them so outnumbered we should've run them into the ground. Instead, Santa Anna spent the first whole day fiddling, shuffling troops around. He didn't even do that right. Any shavetail would've outflanked and surrounded Taylor's men. He left all their right flank open, as well as the road to Saltillo. I heard a little shooting but nothing much happened.

It turned cold and windy that night. Seemed like I just got to sleep when drums woke me up—American drums, sounding reveille, that's how close we were. Then a goddamned band, playing "Hail Columbia." Both Taylor and Santa Anna belonged on a goddamned parade ground.

A private came around with chains and leg-irons, said he was supposed to lock us to the buckboard. For twenty dollars he accidentally dropped the key. I wonder if he ever lived to spend it. It was going to be a bad bloody day for the Mexicans.

We settled in behind the buckboard and watched about a thousand cavalrymen charge by, lances and machetes and blood in their eye, going around behind the hills to our right. Then the shooting started, and it didn't let up for a long time.

To our left, they ordered General Blanco's division to march into the gulch column-style, where the Americans were set up with field artillery. Cannister and grapeshot cut them to bloody rags. Then Santa Anna rode over and ordered Pacheco's division to go for the gulch. I was as glad to be chained to a buckboard. They walked right into it, balls but no brains, and I guess maybe half of them eventually made it back. Said they'd killed a lot of gringos, but I didn't notice it getting any quieter.

I watched all this from well behind the buckboard. Every now and then a stray bullet would spray up dirt or plow into the wood. Harris just stood out in the open, as far from cover as the chain would let him, standing there with his hands in his pockets. A bullet or a piece of grape knocked off his hat. He dusted it off and wiggled his finger at me through the hole, put it back on his head and put his hands back in his pockets. I reminded him that if he got killed I'd take all the gold. He just smiled. He was absolutely not going to die in Mexico. I told him even if I *believed* in that bunkman I'd want to give it a little help. A goddamned cannonball whooshed by and he didn't blink, just kept smiling. It exploded some ways behind us, and I got a little piece in the part that goes over the fence last, which isn't funny as it might sound, since it was going to be a month before I could sit proper.

Harris did leave off being a target long enough to do some doctoring on me. While he was doing that a whole bunch of troops went by behind us, following the way the cavalry went earlier, and they had some nice comments for me. I even got to show my bare butt to Santa Anna, which I guess not too many people do and live.

We heard a lot of noise from their direction but couldn't see anything because of the hills. We also stopped getting shot at, which was all right by me, though Harris seemed bored.

Since then I've read everything I could get my hands on about that battle. The Mexicans had fifteen hundred to two thousand men killed and wounded at Buena Vista, thanks to Santa Anna's generaling. The Americans were unprepared and outnumbered, and some of them actually broke and ran—where even the American accounts admit that the greasers were all-fired brave. If we'd had a real general, a real battle plan, we would've walked right over the gringos.

And you can't help but wonder what would've happened. What if Zach Taylor'd been killed, or even just lost the battle? Who would the Whigs have run for president, who would have been elected? Maybe somebody who didn't want a War Between the States.

Anyhow, the noise died down and the soldiers straggled back. It's a funny thing about soldiering. After all the bloody fighting, once it was clear who had won, the Americans came out on the battlefield and shared their food and water with us, and gave some medical help. But that night was terrible with the sounds of the dying, and the retreat was pure hell. I was for heading north, forget the land grant, but of course Harris knew that he was going to make it through no matter what.

Well, we were lucky. When we got to San Luis an aide to Pacheco decided we weren't being too useful as spies, so we got assigned to a hospital detail, and stayed there while others went south with Santa Anna to get blown apart at Cerro Gordo and Chapultepec. A few months later the war was over and Santa Anna was back in exile— which was temporary, as usual. That son of a bitch was president eleven times.

Now this is where the story gets strange, and if somebody else was telling it I might call him a liar. You're welcome to that opinion, but anyhow it's true.

We had more than a thousand acres up in Mesilla, too much to farm by ourselves, so we passed out some handbills and got a couple dozen ex-soldiers to come along with their families, to be sort of tenant farmers. It was to be a fifty-fifty split, which looked pretty good on the surface, because although it wasn't exactly Kansas the soil was supposedly good enough for maize and agave, the plant that pulque was made from. What they didn't tell us about was the Apaches. But I don't want to get ahead of the story.

Now the Mesilla Valley looked really good on the map. It had a good river and it was close to the new American border. I still had my American citizenship papers and sort of liked the idea of being only a couple of days away in case trouble started. Anyhow, we got outfitted in San Luis and headed our little wagon train north by northwest. More than a thousand miles through Durango and Chihuahua. It was rough going, just as dry as hell, but we knew that ahead of time, and at least there was nobody shooting at us. All we lost was a few mules and one wagon, no people.

Our grants were outside of the little town of Tubac, near the silver mines at Cerro Colorado. There was some irrigation but not nearly enough, so we planted a small crop and worked like beavers digging ditches so that the next crop could be big enough for profit.

Or should I say the greasers and me worked like beavers. Harris turned out not to have too much appetite for that kind of thing. Well, if I had eight thousand in gold I'd probably take a couple years' vacation myself. He didn't even stay on the grant, though. Rented a little house in town and proceeded to make himself a reputation.

Of course Harris had always been handy with a pistol and a knife, but he also used to have a healthy respect for what they could to to you. Now he took to picking fights—or actually, getting people so riled that they picked fights with him. With his tongue that was easy.

And it did look like he was charmed. I don't know how many people he shot and stabbed, without himself getting a scratch. I don't know because I stopped keeping regular company with him after I got myself a nasty stab wound in the thigh, because of his big mouth. We didn't seek each other out after that, but it wasn't such a big town, and I did see him every now and then. And I was with him the night he died.

There was this cantina in the south part of town where I liked to go, because a couple of Americans, engineers at the mine, did their drinking there. I walked down to it one night and almost went right back out when I heard Harris's voice. He was talking at the bar, fairly quiet but in that sarcastic way of his, in English. Suddenly the big engineer next to him stands up and kicks his stool halfway across the room, and at the top of his voice calls Harris something I wouldn't say to the Devil himself. By this time anybody with horse sense was grabbing a piece of the floor, and I got behind the doorjamb myself, but I did see everything that happened.

The big guy reaches into his coat, and suddenly Harris has his Navy Colt in hand. He has that little smile I saw too often. I hear the Colt's hammer snap down and this little "puff" sound. Harris's jaw drops because he knows as well as I do what's happened: bad round, and now there's a bullet jammed in the barrel. He couldn't shoot again even if he had time.

Then the big guy laughs, almost good-natured, and takes careful aim with this little ladies' gun, a .32 I think. He shoots Harris in the arm, evidently to teach him a lesson. Just a graze, doesn't even break a bone. But Harris takes one look at it and his face goes blank and he drops to the floor. Even if you'd never seen a man die, you'd know he was dead by the way he fell.

Now I've told this story to men who were in the Civil War, beside which the Mexican War looks like a Sunday outing, and some of them say that's not hard to believe. You see enough men die and you see everything. One fellow'll get both legs blown off and sit and joke while they sew him up; the next'll get a little scratch and die of the shock. But that one just doesn't sound like Harris, not before or after Doña Dolores's prediction made him reckless. What signifies to me is the date that Harris died: December 30, 1853.

Earlier that year, Santa Anna had managed to get back into office, for the last time. He did his usual trick of spending all the money he could find. Railroad fellow named James Gadsden showed up and offered to buy a little chunk of northern Mexico, to get the right-of-way for a transcontinental railroad. It was the Mesilla Valley, and Santa Anna signed it over on the thirteenth of December. We didn't know it for a couple of weeks, and the haggling went on till June—but when Harris picked a fight that night, he wasn't on Mexican soil. And you can make of that what you want.

As for me, I only kept farming for a few more years. Around about '57 the Apaches started to get rambunctious, Cochise's gang of murderers. Even if I'd wanted to stay I couldn't've kept any help. Went to California but didn't pan out. Been on the move since, and it suits me. Reckon I'll go almost anyplace except Mexico.

Because old Dolores liked me and she told my fortune many times. I never paid too much attention, but I know if she'd seen the sign that said I wasn't going to die in Mexico, she would've told me, and I would've remembered. Maybe it's all silliness. But I ain't going to be the one to test it.

AVRAM DAVIDSON

Full Chicken Richness

For many years now, Avram Davidson has been one of the most eloquent and individual voices in SF, and there are few writers in *any* literary field who can hope to match his wit, his erudition, or the stylish elegance of his prose. His recent series of stories about the bizarre exploits of Doctor Engelbert Eszterhazy (collected in his World Fantasy Award-winning *The Enquiries of Doctor Eszterhazy)* and the strange adventures of Jack Limekiller (as yet uncollected, alas), for instance, are Davidson at the very height of his considerable powers, and rank among the best work of the '70s. Davidson has won the Hugo, the Edgar, and the World Fantasy Award. His books include the renowned *The Phoenex and the Mirror, Masters of the Maze, Rogue Dragon, Peregrine: Primus, Rork!, Clash of Star Kings, The Kar-Chee Reign,* and the collections *The Best of Avram Davidson, Or All the Seas with Oysters, Strange Seas and Shores,* and *The Redward Edward Papers.* His most recent books are *Peregrine: Secundus,* a novel, *Collected Fantasies,* a collection, and, as editor, the anthology *Magic For Sale.*

All Davidson's talents are displayed to good effect in the sly and witty story that follows, which features—among many other delights—what is very probably the single silliest use for a time-machine in the entire history of time-travel stories . . .

FULL CHICKEN RICHNESS

Avram Davidson

La Bunne Burger was said to have the best hamburger on The Street; the only trouble with that was that Fred Hopkins didn't care much for hamburger. However there were other factors to consider, such as these: other items on La Bunne's menu were probably just a bit better than comparable items composed elsewhere on The Street, they sold for just a bit less than, etc. etc., and also Fred Hopkins found the company just a bit more interesting than elsewhere, etc. What else? It was nearer to his studio loft than any eating-place else. Any place else save for a small place called The Old Moulmein Pagoda, the proprietor of which appeared to speak very fluent Cantonese for a Burman, and the Old Moulmein Pagoda was not open until late afternoon. *Late* afternoon.

Late morning was more Fred's style.

He was likely to find there, at any given time of late morning, a number of regulars, such as: well, there was Tilly, formerly Ottilie, with red cheeks, her white hair looking windblown even on windless days; Tilly had her own little routine, which consisted of ordering coffee and toast; with the toast came a small plastic container of jelly, and this she spread on one of the slices of toast. That eaten, she would hesitantly ask Rudolfo if she might have more jelly . . . adding, that she would pay for it. Rudolfo would hand her one or two or three more, she would tentatively offer him a palm of pennies and nickels and he would politely decline them. Fred was much moved by this little drama, but after the twelfth and succedant repetitions it left him motionless. (Once he was to encounter Tillie in a disused doorway downtown standing next to a hat with money while she played—and played beautifully— endless Strauss waltzes on that rather un-Strauss-like-instrument, the harmonica.)

Also unusually present in La Bunne Burger in the 40 minutes before the noon rush were Volodya and Carl. They were a sort of twosome there; that is, they were certainly not a twosome elsewhere. Carl was tall and had long blond hair and a long blond beard and was already at his place along the counter when Volodya walked in. Carl never said anything to Volodya, Volodya always said anything to Carl. Volodya was wide and gnarly and had small pale eyes like those of a malevolent pig. Among the things he called Carl were *Pópa! Moskúey! Smaravátchnik!* —meaning (Fred Hopkins found out by and by) Priest! Inhabitant of Moscow! and One Who, For Immoral Purposes, Pretends to be a Chimney Sweep! Fred by and by tried to dissuade Volodya of this curious delusion; "He's a Minnesota Swede," Fred explained. But Volodya would have none of it. *"He's A Rahshian Artoducks priest!"* was his explosive come-back—and he went on to denounce the last Czar of Russia as having been in the pay of the freemasons. Carl always said nothing, munched away as droplets of egg congealed on his beard.

And there was, in La Bunne Burger, often, breaking fast on a single sausage and a cup of tea, a little old oriental man, dressed as though for the winters of Manchuria; once Fred had, speaking slowly and clearly, asked him please to pass the ketchup: "Say, I ain't deef," said the l.o.o.m., in tones the purest American Gothic.

Fred himself was not in the least eccentric, he was an *art*ist, not even starving, though . . . being unfashionably representational . . . not really prospering, either. His agent said that this last was his, Fred's, own fault. "Paint doctors' wives!" his agent insisted. "If you would only paint portraits for doctors' wives, I could get you lots of commissions. Old buildings," the agent said, disdainfully. "Old buildings, old buildings." But the muse kisseth where she listeth and if anything is not on the list, too bad: Fred had nothing against doctor's wives; merely, he preferred to paint pictures of old buildings. Now and then he drove around looking for old buildings he hadn't painted pictures of and he photographed them and put the photos up by his canvas to help when he painted at home: this of course caused him to be regarded with scorn by purists who painted only from the model or the imagination; why either should be less or more scornable, they disdained to say.

Whom else was F. Hopkins likely to see in La Bunne Burger over his late breakfast or his brunch? Proprietors of nearby businesses, for example, he was likely to see there; mamma no longer brought pappa's dinner wrapped in a towel to keep hot. Abelardo was sometimes there. Also Fred might see tourists or new emigrés or visiting entrepreneurs of alien status, come to taste the exotic tuna fish sandwich on toast, the picturesque macaroni and cheese, the curious cold turkey, and, of course, often, often, often the native La Bunne De Luxe Special . . . said to be the best hamburger on The Street. Abelardo had long looked familiar;

Abelardo had in fact looked familiar from tbe first. Abelardo always came in from the kitchen and Abelardo always went back out through the kitchen, and yet Abelardo did not work in the kitchen. Evidently Abelardo delivered. Something.

Once, carrying a plate of . . . something . . . odd and fragrant, Rudolfo rested it a moment on the counter near Fred while he gathered cutlery; in response to Fred's look of curiosity and approbation, at once said, "Not on the menu. Only I give some to Abelardo, because our family come from the same country;" off he went.

Later: "You're not from Mexico, Rudolfo."

"No. South America." Rudolfo departs with glasses.

Later: "Which country in South America you from, Rudolfo?"

"Depend who you ask." Exit, Rudolfo, for napkins.

Fred Hopkins, idly observing paint on two of his own fingers, idly wondered that—a disputed boundary being clearly involved—Rudolfo was not out leading marches and demonstratons, or (at *least!*) with drippy brushes slapping up grafitti exhorting the reader to *Remember the 12th of January* . . . the *3rd of April* . . . the *24th of October* . . . and so on through the existing political calendar of Ibero-America . . . Clearly, Rudolfo was a anachronism. Perhaps he secretly served some fallen sovereign; a pseudo-crypto-Emperor of Brazil. Perhaps.

Though probably not likely.

One day, the hour being later than usual and the counter crowded, Fred's eyes wandered around in search of a seat; met those of Abelardo who, worldlessly, invited him to sit in the empty place at the two-person table. Which Fred did. And, so doing, realized why the man had always seemed familiar. Now, suppose you are a foreigner living in a small city or medium town in Latin America, as Fred Hopkins had once been, and it doesn't really matter which city or town or even which country . . . doesn't really matter for *this* purpose . . . and you are going slightly out your *mind* trying to get your electricity (*la luz*) turned on and eventually you notice that there are a few large stones never moved from the side of a certain street and gradually notice that there is often the same man sitting on one of the boulders and that this man wears very dusty clothes which do not match and a hat rather odd for the locale (say, a beret) and that he also wears glasses and that the lens of one is opaque or dark and that this man often gives a small wave of his hand to return the greetings of passersby but otherwise he merely sits and looks. You at length have occasion to ask him something, say, At what hour does the Municipal Palace open? And not only does the man politely inform you, he politely engages you in conversation and before long he is giving you a fascinating discourse on an aspect of history, religion, economics, or folklore, an aspect of which you had been completely ignorant. Subsequent enquiry discloses that the man is, say, a Don Eliseo, who had attended the National University for nine years but took no degree, that he is an *idiosyncratico*, and comes from a family *muy honorado*—so much *honorado*, in fact, that merely having been observed in polite discourse with him results in your electricity being *connectido muy pronto*. You have many discourses with Don Eliseo and eventually he shows you his project, temporarily in abeyance, to perfect the best tortilla making-and-baking machine in the world: there is some minor problem, such as the difficulty of scraping every third tortilla off the ceiling, but any day now Don Eliseo will get this licked; and, in the meanwhile and forever after, his house is your house.

This was why Abelardo had seemed familiar from the start, and if Abelardo was not Eliseo's brother than he was certainly his nephew or his cousin . . . in the spirit, anyway.

Out of a polite desire that Fred Hopkins not be bored while waiting to be served, Abelardo discussed various things with him—that is, for the most part, Abelardo discussed. Fred listened. La Bunne Burger was very busy.

"Now, the real weakness of the Jesuits in Paraguay," Abelardo explained.

"Now, in western South America," said Abelardo, "North American corporations are disliked less for their vices than for their virtues. Bribery, favoritism, we can understand these things, we live with them. But an absolute insistence that one must arrive in one's office day after day at one invariable hour and that frequent prolonged telephone conversations from one's office to one's home and family is unfavored, this is against our conception of personal and domestic usement," Abelardo explained.

He assured Fred Hopkins that the Regent Isabella's greatest error, "though she made several," was in having married a Frenchman. "The Frankish temperament is not the Latin temperament," Abelardo declared.

Fred's food eventually arrived; Abelardo informed him that although individual enterprise and planned economy were all very well in their own ways, "one ignores the law of supply and demand at peril. I have been often in businesses, so I know, you see." Said Abelardo.

Abelardo did not indeed wear eyeglasses with one dark or opaque lens, but one of his eyes was artificial. He had gold in his smile—that is, in his teeth—and his white coverall was much washed but never much ironed. By and by, with polite words and thanks for the pleasure of Fred's company, Abelardo vanished into the kitchen; when Fred strolled up for his bill, he was informed it had already been paid. This rather surprised Fred. So did the fact, conveyed to him by the clock, that the noon rush was over. Had *been* over.

"Abelardo seems like—Abelardo is a very nice guy."

Rudolfo's face, hands, and body made brief but persuasive signal that it went without saying that Abelardo was indeed a very nice guy. "But I don't know how he stay in business," said Rudolfo, picking up a pile of dishes and walking them off to the kitchen.

Fred had no reason to remain to discuss this, as it was an unknown to him how anybody stayed in business. Merely he was well aware how week after week the price of paints and brushes and canvases went up, up, up, while the price of his artwork stayed the same, same, same. Well, his agent, though wrong, was right. No one to blame but himself; he could have stayed in advertising, he might be an account executive by now. Or—Walking along The Street, he felt a wry smile accompany memory of another of Abelardo's comments: "Advertisage is like courtship, always involve some measure of deceit."

This made him quickstep a bit back to the studio to get in some more painting, for—he felt—tonight might be a good one for what one might call courtship; "exploitation," some would doubtless call it: though why? if ladies ("women!") did not like to come back to his loft studio and see his painting, why did they do so? And if they did not genuinely desire to remain for a while of varying length, who could make them? Did any one of them really desire to admire his art, was there no pretense on the part of any of them? Why was *he* not the exploited one? You women are all alike, you only have one thing on your mind, all you think of is your own pleasure . . . Oh well. Hell. Back to work. —It was true that you could not sleep with an old building, but then they never argued with you, either. And as for "some measure of deceit," boy did that work both ways! Two weeks before, he'd come upon a harmonious and almost untouched, though tiny, commercial block in an area in between the factories and the farms, as yet undestroyed by the people curiously called "developers"; he'd taken lots of color snaps of it from all angles, and he wanted to do at least two large paintings, maybe two small ones as well. The date, 1895, was up there in front. The front was false, but in the harmony was truth.

A day that found him just a bit tired of the items staple in breakfast found him ordering a cup of the soup du jour for starters. "How you like the soup?"—Rudolfo.

Fred gave his head a silent shake. How. It had gone down without exiting dismay. "Truthful with you. Had better, had worse. Hm. What was it. Well, I was thinking of something else. Uh—chicken vegetable with rice? Right? Right. Yours or Campbell's?"

Neither.

"Half mine, half Abelardo's."

"I *beg* your pardon."

But Rudolfo had never heard the rude English story about the pint of half-and-half, neither did Fred tell it to him. Rudolfo said, "I make a stock with the bones after making chickens sandwiches and I mix it with this." He produced a large, a very large can, pushed it over to Fred. The label said. *FULL CHICKEN RICHNESS Chicken-Type Soup.*

"Whah-haht?" asked Fred, half-laughing. He read on. *Ingredients: Water, Other Poultry and Poultry Parts, Dehydrated Vegetables, Chickens and Chicken Parts, seasoning* . . . the list dribbled off into the usual list of chemicals. The label also said, *Canned for Restaurant and Institutional Usement.*

"Too big for a family," Rudolfo observed. "Well, not bad, I think, too. Help me keep the price down. Every little bit help, you know."

"Oh. Sure. No, not bad. But I wonder about that label," Rudolfo shrugged about that label. The Government, he said, wasn't going to worry about some little *chico* outfit way down from the outskirt of town. Fred chuckled at the bland non-identification of "Other Poultry"—Rudolfo said that turkey was still cheaper than chicken—"But I don't put it down, 'chicken soup,' I put it down, 'soup du jour'; anybody *ask*, I say, 'Oh, *you* know, chicken and rice and vegetable and, oh, stuff like that; *try* it, you don't like it I don't charge you.' Fair enough?—Yes," he expanded. "Abelardo, he is no businessman. He is a *filosofo*. His mind is always in the skies. I tell him, I could use more soup—twice, maybe even three times as many cans. What he cares. 'Ai! Supply and demand!' he says. Then he tells me about the old Dutch explorers, things like that. —Hey! I ever tell you about the time he make his own automobile? ("Abe*lar*-do did?") Sure! Abelardo did. He took a part from one car, a part from another, he takes parts not even from cars, *I* don't know what they from—"

Fred thought of Don Eliseo and the more perfect tortilla making-and-baking machine. "—well, it work! Finally! Yes! It start off, *vooom!* like a rocket! Sixty-three mile an hour! But oh boy when he try to slow it down! It stop! He start it again. Sixty-three mile an hour! No other rate of speed, well, what can you do with such a car? So he forget about it and he invent something else, who knows what; then he go into the soup business. —Yes, sir! You ready to order?" Rudolfo moved on.

So did Fred. The paintings of the buildings 1895 were set aside for a while so that he could take a lot of pictures of a turn-of-the-century family home scheduled for destruction real soon. *This Site Will be Improved With a Modern Office Building*, what the hell did they mean by *Improved?* Alice came up and looked at the sketches of the family home, and at finished work. "I like them," she said. "I like *you*." She stayed. Everything fine. Then, one day, there was the other key on the table. On the note: *There is nothing wrong*, it said. *Just time to go now. Love*. No name. Fred sighed. Went on painting.

One morning late there was Abelardo in the Bunne. He nodded, smiled a small smile. By and by, some coffee down, Fred said, "Say, where do you buy your chickens?" Abelardo, ready to inform, though not yet ready to talk, took a card from his wallet.

> E. J. Binder Prime Poultry Farm
> also
> Game Birds Dressed To Order
> 1330 Valley Rd by the Big Oak

While Fred was still reading this, Abelardo passed him over another card, this one for the Full Chicken Richness Canned Soup Company. "You must visit me," he said. "Most time I am home."

Fred hadn't really cared where the chickens were bought, but now the devil entered into him. First he told Abelardo the story about the man who sold rabbit pie. Asked, wasn't there anyway maybe some horsemeat in the rabbit pie, said it was fifty-fifty: one rabbit, one horse. Abelardo reflected, then issued another small smile, a rather more painful one. Fred asked, "What about the turkey-meat in your chicken-type soup? I mean, uh, rather, the 'Other Poultry Parts?' "

Abelardo squinted. "Only the breast," he said. "The rest not good enough. —For the *soup*, I mean. The rest, I sell to some mink ranchers."

"How's business?"

Abelardo shrugged. He looked a bit peaked. "Supply," he said. "Demand," he said. Then he sighed, stirred, rose. "You must visit me. Any time. Please," he said.

Abelardo wasn't there in the La Bunne Burger next late morning, but someone else was. Miles Marton, call him The Last of the Old-Time Land Agents, call him something less nice: there he was. "Been waiting," Miles Marton said. "Remember time I toll you bout ol stage-coach buildin? You never came. It comin down tomorrow. Ranch houses. Want to take its pitcher? Last chance, today. Make me a nice little paintin of it, price is right, I buy it. Bye now."

Down Fred went. Heartbreaking to think its weathered timbers, its mellowed red brick chimney and stone fireplace, were coming down; but Fred Hopkins was very glad he'd had the favor of a notice. Coming

down, too, the huge trees with the guinea-fowl in them. *Lots* of
photographs. Be a good painting. At least one. Driving back, lo! a sign
saying E.J. BINDER PRIME POULTRY FARM; absolutely by a big
oak. Still, Fred probably wouldn't have stopped if there hadn't been
someone by the gate. Binder, maybe. Sure enough. Binder. "Say, do
you know a South American named Abelardo?"

No problem. "Sure I do. Used to be a pretty good customer, too. Buy
oh I forget how many chickens a week. Don't buy many nowdays. He
send you here? Be glad to oblige you." Binder was an oldish man,
highly sun-speckled.

"You supply his turkeys and turkey-parts, too?" The devil still inside
Fred Hopkins.

Old Binder snorted, " 'Turkeys,' no we don't handle turkeys, no sir,
why chickens are enough trouble, cost of feeding going up, and—No,
'guinea-fowl,' no we never did. Just chickens and of course your cornish."

Still civil, E.J. Binder gave vague directions toward what he believed,
he said, was the general location of Mr. Abelardo's place. Fred didn't
find it right off, but he found it. As no one appeared in response to his
calling and honking, he got out and knocked. Nothing. *Pues,* "My
house is your house," okay: in he went through the first door. Well, it
wasn't a *large* cannery, but it was a *cannery.* Fred started talking to
himself; solitary artists often do. "Way I figure it, Abelardo," he said, "is
that you have been operating with that 'small measure of deceit in
advertising,' as you so aptly put it. *I* think that in your own naive way
you have believed that so long as you called the product 'Chicken-Type
Soup' and included *some* chicken, well, it was all right. Okay, your guilty
secret is safe with me; where are you?" The place was immaculate, except
for. Except for a pile of . . . well . . . shit . . . right in the middle of
an aisle. It was as neat as a pile of shit can be. Chicken-shits? Pigeon-
poops? Turkey-trots? *¿Quien sabe?*

At the end of the aisle was another door and behind that door was a
small apartment and in a large chair in the small apartment lay sprawled
Abelardo, dead drunk on mescal, *muzhik*-grade vodka, and sneaky pete
. . . according to the evidence. Alcoholism is not an especially Latin
American trait? Who said the poor guy was an alcoholic? Maybe this
was the first time he'd ever been stewed in his *life.* Maybe the eternally
perplexing matter of supply and demand had finally unmanned him.

Maybe.

At the other end of *that* room was *another* door and behind that other
door was *another* room. And in that *other* room was. . . .

. . . something else. . . .

That other room was partly crammed with an insane assortment of machinery and allied equipment, compared to which Don Eliseo's more pefect make-and-bake tortilla engine, with its affinities to the perpetual motion invention of one's choice, was simplicity. The thing stood naked for Fred's eyes, but his eyes told him very little: wires snaked all around, that much he could say. There was a not-quite-click, a large television screen flickered on. *No.* Whatever it was at the room's end, sitting flush to the floor with a low, chicken-wire fence around it, it was not television, not even if Abelardo had started from scratch as though there had been no television before. The quality of the "image" was entirely different, for one thing; and the color, for another, was *wrong* . . . and wrong in the way that no TV color he had ever seen had been wrong. He reached to touch the screen, there *was* no "screen," it was as though his hand met a surface of unyielding gelatin. The non-screen, well, what the hell, *call* it a screen, was rather large, but not gigantically so. He was looking at a savannah somewhere, and among the trees were palms and he could not identify the others. A surf pounded not far off, but he could not hear it. There was no sound. He saw birds flying in and out of the trees. Looking back, he saw something else. A trail of broken bread through the room, right up to the, mmm, screen. A silent breeze now and then rifled grass, and something moved in the grass to one side. He stepped back, slightly. What the hell could it *mean?* Then the something which was in the grass to one side stepped, stiff-legged, into full view, and there was another odd, small sound as the thing—it was a bird—lurched through the screen and began to gobble bread. Hopkins watched, dry-mouthed. Crumb by crumb it ate. Then there was no more bread. It doddled up to the low fence, doddled back. It approached the screen, it brushed the screen, there was a Rube Goldberg series of motions in the external equipment, a sheet of chicken wire slid noisily down to the floor. The bird had been trapped.

Fred got down and peered into the past till his eyes and neck grew sore, but he could not see one more bird like it. He began to laugh and cry simultaneously. Then he stood up. "Inevitable," he croaked, throwing out his arms. "Inevitable! Demand exceeded supply!"

The bird looked up at him with imbecile, incurious eyes, and opened its incredible beak. "*Doh*-do," it said, halfway between a gobble and a coo. "*Doh*-do. *Doh*-do."

ROBERT SILVERBERG

Multiples

One of the most prolific authors alive, Robert Silverberg can lay claim to more than 450 fiction and nonfiction books and over 3,000 magazine pieces. Within SF, Silverberg rose to his greatest prominence during the late '60s and early '70s, winning four Nebula Awards and a Hugo Award, publishing dozens of major novels and anthologies—1973's *Dying Inside* in particular is widely considered to be one of the best novels of the '70s—and editing *New Dimensions*, perhaps the most influential original anthology series of its time. In 1980, after four years of self-imposed "retirement," Silverberg started writing again, and the first of his new novels, *Lord Valentine's Castle*, became a nationwide bestseller. Silverberg's other books include *The Book of Skulls, Downward to the Earth, Tower of Glass, The World Inside, Born with the Dead, Shadrach in the Furnace*, and the collections *Unfamiliar Territory, Capricorn Games*, and *The Best of Robert Silverberg*. His most recent books are *Lord of Darkness*, a historical novel, the collection *Majipoor Chronicles*, and *Valentine Pontifex*, the sequel to *Lord Valentine's Castle*.

Here Silverberg turns his cooly sardonic eye toward a strange kind of future single's-bar, where things are not *supposed* to be as they seem, and the customers have a great deal more to offer each other than it would at first appear . . .

MULTIPLES

Robert Silverberg

There were mirrors everywhere, making the place a crazy house of dizzying refraction: mirrors on the ceiling, mirrors on the walls, mirrors in the angles where the walls met the ceiling and the floor, even little eddies of mirror dust periodically blown on gusts of air through the room so that all the bizarre distortions, fracturings, and dislocations of image that were bouncing around the place would from time to time coalesce in a shimmering haze of chaos right before your eyes. Colored globes spun round and round overhead, creating patterns of ricocheting light. It was exactly the way Cleo had expected a multiples club to look.

She had walked up and down the whole Fillmore Street strip, from Union to Chestnut and back again, for half an hour, peering at this club and that before finding the courage to go inside one that called itself Skits. Though she had been planning this night for months, she found herself paralyzed by fear at the last minute: afraid they would spot her as a fraud the moment she walked in, afraid they would drive her out with jeers and curses and cold, mocking laughter. But now that she was within, she felt fine—calm, confident, ready for the time of her life.

There were more women than men in the club, something like a seven-to-three ratio. Hardly anyone seemed to be talking to anyone else. Most stood alone in the middle of the floor, staring into the mirrors as though in trance.

Their eyes were slits, their jaws were slack, their shoulders slumped forward, their arms dangled. Now and then, as some combination of reflections sluiced across their consciousnesses with particular impact, they would go taut and jerk and wince as if they had been struck. Their faces would flush, their lips would pull back, their eyes would roll, they would mutter and whisper to themselves; then after a moment they would slip back into stillness.

Cleo knew what they were doing. They were switching and doubling. Maybe some of the adepts were tripling.

Her heart rate picked up. Her throat was very dry. What was the routine here? she wondered. Did you just walk right out onto the floor and plug into the light patterns, or were you supposed to go to the bar first for a shot or a snort?

She looked toward the bar. A dozen or so customers were sitting there, mostly men, a couple of them openly studying her, giving her that new-girl-in-town stare. Cleo returned their gaze evenly, coolly, blankly. Standard-looking men, reasonably attractive, thirtyish or early fortyish, business suits, conventional haristyles: young lawyers, executives, maybe stockbrokers—successful sorts out for a night's fun, the kind of men you might run into anywhere. Look at that one—tall, athletic, curly hair, glasses. Faint, ironic smile, easy, inquiring eyes. Almost professional. And yet, and yet—behind that smooth, intelligent forehead what strangeness must teem and boil! How many hidden souls must lurk and jostle! Scary. Tempting.

Irresistible.

Cleo resisted. Take it slow, take it slow. Instead of going to the bar, she moved out serenely among the switchers on the floor, found an open space, centered herself, looked toward the mirrors on the far side of the room. Legs apart, feet planted flat, shoulders forward. A turning globe splashed waves of red and violet light, splintered a thousand times over into her upturned face.

Go. Go. Go. Go. You are Cleo. You are Judy. You are Vixen. You are Lisa. Go. Go. Go. Go. Cascades of iridescence sweeping over the rim of her soul, battering at the walls of her identity. *Come, enter, drown me, split me, switch me. You are Cleo and Judy. You are Vixen and Lisa. You are Cleo and Judy and Vixen and Lisa. Go. Go. Go.*

Her head was spinning. Her eyes were blurring. The room gyrated around her.

Was this it? Was she splitting? Was she switching? Maybe so. Maybe the capacity was there in everyone, even her, and all that it would take was the lights, the mirrors, the right ambience, the will.

I am many. I am multiple. I am Cleo switching to Vixen. I am Judy, and I am—

No. I am Cleo.

I am Cleo.

I am very dizzy, and I am getting sick, and I am Cleo and only Cleo, as I have always been. I am Cleo and only Cleo, and I am going to fall down.

*   *   *

"Easy," he said. "You okay?"

"Steadying up, I think. Whew!"

"Out-of-towner, eh?"

"Sacramento. How did you know?"

"Too quick on the floor. Locals all know better. This place has the fastest mirrors in the west. They'll blow you away if you're not careful. You can't just go out there and grab for the big one— you've got to phase yourself in slowly. You sure you're going to be okay?"

"I think so."

He was the tall man from the bar, the athletic, professional one. She supposed he had caught her before she had actually fallen, since she felt no bruises.

His hand rested easily now against her right elbow as he lightly steered her toward a table along the wall.

"What's your now-name?" he asked.

"Judy."

"I'm Van."

"Hello, Van."

"How about a brandy? Steady you up a little more."

"I don't drink."

"Never?"

"Vixen does the drinking," she said.

"Ah. The old story. She gets the bubbles you get her hangovers. I have one like that too, only with him it's Hunan food. He absolutely doesn't give a damn what lobster in hot and sour sauce does to my digestive system. I hope you pay her back the way she deserves."

Cleo smiled and said nothing.

He was watching her closely. Was he interested, or just being polite to someone who was obviously out of her depth in a strange milleu? Interested, she decided. He seemed to have accepted that Vixen stuff at face value.

Be careful now, Cleo warned herself. Trying to pile on convincing-sounding details when you don't really know what you're talking about is a sure way to give yourself away sooner or later.

The thing to do, she knew, was to establish her credentials without working too hard at it; sit back, listen, learn how things really operate among these people.

"What do you do up there in Sacramento?"

"Nothing fascinating."

"Poor Judy. Real-estate broker?"

"How'd you guess?"

"Every other woman I meet is a real-estate broker these days. What's Vixen?"

"A lush."

"Not much of a livelihood in that."

Cleo shrugged. "She doesn't need one. The rest of us support her."

"Real estate and what else?"

She hadn't been sure that multiples etiquette included talking about one's alternate selves. But she had come prepared. "Lisa's a landscape architect. Cleo's into software. We all keep busy."

"Lisa ought to meet Chuck. He's a demon horticulturalist. Partner in a plant-rental outfit—you know, huge dracaenas and philodendrons for offices, so much per month, take them away when they start looking sickly. Lisa and Chuck could talk palms and bromelaids and cacti all night."

"We should introduce them."

"We should, yes."

"But first we have to introduce Van and Judy."

"And then maybe Van and Cleo," he said.

She felt a tremor of fear. Had he found her out so soon? "Why Van and Cleo? Cleo's not here right now. This is Judy you're talking to."

"Easy. Easy!"

But she was unable to halt. "I can't deliver Cleo to you just like that, you know. She does as she pleases."

"Easy," he said. "All I meant was, Van and Cleo have something in common. Van's into software, too."

Cleo relaxed. With a little laugh she said, "Oh, not you, too! Isn't everybody nowadays? But I thought you were something in the academic world. A university professor or something like that."

"I am. At Cal."

"Software?"

"In a manner of speaking. Linguistics. Metalinguistics, actually. My field is the language of language—the basic subsets, the neural coordinates of communication, the underlying programs our brains use, the operating systems. Mind as computer, computer as mind. I can get very boring about it."

"I don't find the mind a boring subject."

"I don't find real estate a boring subject. Talk to me about second mortgages and triple-net leases."

"Talk to me about Chomsky and Benjamin Whorf," she said.

His eyes widened. "You've heard of Benjamin Whorf?"

"I majored in comparative linguistics. That was before real estate."

"Just my lousy luck," he said. "I get a chance to find out what's hot in the shopping-center market and she wants to talk about Whorf and Chomsky."

"I thought every other woman you met these days was a real-estate broker. Talk to them about shopping centers."

"They all want to talk about Whorf and Chomsky. More intellectual."

"Poor Van."

"Yes. Poor Van." Then he leaned forward and said, his tone softening. "You know, I shouldn't have made that crack about Van meeting Cleo. That was very tacky of me."

"It's okay, Van. I didn't take it seriously."

"You seemed to. You were very upset."

"Well, maybe at first. But then I saw you were just horsing around."

"I still shouldn't have said it. You were absolutely right: This is Judy's time now. Cleo's not here, and that's just fine. It's Judy I want to get to know."

"You will," she said. "But you can meet Cleo, too, and Lisa and Vixen. I'll introduce you to the whole crew. I don't mind."

"You're sure of that?"

"Sure."

"Some of us are very secretive about our alters."

"Are you?" Cleo asked.

"Sometimes. Sometimes not."

"I don't mind. Maybe you'll meet some of mine tonight." She glanced toward the center of the floor. "I think I've steadied up now. I'd like to try the mirrors again."

"Switching?"

"Doubling," she said. "I'd like to bring Vixen up. She can do the drinking, and I can do the talking. Will it bother you if she's here, too?"

"Won't bother me unless she's a sloppy drunk. Or a mean one."

"I can keep control of her when we're doubling. Come on, take me through the mirrors."

"You be careful now. San Francisco mirrors aren't like Sacramento ones. You've already discovered that."

"I'll watch my step this time. Shall we go out there?"

"Sure," he said.

As they began to move out onto the floor a slender, T-shirted man of about thirty came toward them. Shaven scalp, bushy mustache, medallions, boots. Very San Francisco, very gay. He frowned at Cleo and stared straightforwardly at Van.

"Ned?" he said.

Van scowled and shook his head. "No. Not now."

"Sorry. Very sorry. I should have realized." The shaven-headed man flushed and hurried away.

"Let's go," Van said to Cleo.

This time she found it easier to keep her balance. Knowing that he was nearby helped. But still the waves of refracted light came pounding in, pounding in, pounding in. The assault was total: remorseless, implacable, overwhelming. She had to struggle against the throbbing in her chest, the hammering in her temples, the wobbliness of her knees. And this was pleasure for them? This was a supreme delight?

But they were multiples, and she was only Cleo, and that, she knew, made all the difference. She seemed to be able to fake it well enough. She could make up a Judy, a Lisa, a Vixen, assign little corners of her personality to each, give them voices of their own, facial expressions, individual identities. Standing before her mirror at home, she had managed to convince herself. She might even be able to convince him. But as the swirling lights careened off the infinites of interlocking mirrors and came slaloming into the gateways of her reeling soul, the dismal fear began to rise in her that she could never truly be one of these people after all, however skillfully she imitated them in their intricacies.

Was it so? Was she doomed always to stand outside their irresistible world, hopelessly peering in? Too soon to tell—much too soon, she thought, to admit defeat.

At least she didn't fall down. She took the punishment of the mirrors as long as she could stand it, and then, not waiting for him to leave the floor, she made her way—carefully, carefully, walking a tightrope over an abyss—to the bar. When her head had begun to stop spinning she ordered a drink, and she sipped it cautiously. She could feel the alcohol extending itself inch by inch into her bloodstream. It calmed her. On the floor Van stood in trance, occasionally quivering in a sudden, convulsive way for a fraction of a second. He was doubling, she knew: bringing up one of his other identities. That was the main thing that multiples came to these clubs to do. No longer were all their various identities forced to dwell in rigorously separated compartments of their minds. With the aid of the mirrors and lights the skilled ones were able briefly to fuse two or even three of their selves into something more complex. When he comes back here, she thought, he will be Van plus X. And I must pretend to be Judy plus Vixen.

She readied herself for that. Judy was easy. Judy was mostly the real Cleo, the real-estate woman from Sacramento, with Cleo's notion of what it was like to be a multiple added in. And Vixen? Cleo imagined her to be about twenty-three, a Los Angeles girl, a one-time child tennis star who had broken her ankle in a dumb prank and had never recovered her game afterward, and who had taken up drinking to ease the pain and loss. Uninhibited, unpredictable, untidy, fiery, fierce: all the things that Cleo was not. Could she be Vixen? She took a deep gulp of her drink and put on the Vixen face: eyes hard and glittering; cheek muscles clenched.

Van was leaving the floor now. His way of moving seemed to have changed: He was stiff, almost awkward, his shoulders held high, his elbows jutting oddly. He looked so different that she wondered whether he was still Van at all.

"You didn't switch, did you?"

"Doubled. Paul's with me now."

"Paul?"

"Paul's from Texas. Geologist, terrific poker game, plays the guitar." Van smiled, and it was like a shifting of gears. In a deeper, broader voice he said, "And I sing real good too, ma'am. Van's jealous of that, because he can't sing worth beans. Are you ready for a refill?"

"You bet," Cleo said, sounding sloppy, sounding Vixenish.

His apartment was nearby, a cheerful, airy, sprawling place in the Marina district. The segmented nature of his life was immediately obvious: The prints and paintings on the walls looked as they had been chosen by four or five different people, one of whom ran heavily toward vivid scenes of sunrise over the Grand Canyon, another to Picasso and Miró, someone else to delicate, impressionist views of Paris street scenes and flower markets. A sunroom contained the biggest and healthiest houseplants Cleo had ever seen. Another room was stacked with technical books and scholarly journals, a third was equipped with three or four gleaming exercise machines. Some of the rooms were fastidiously tidy, some impossibly chaotic. Some of the furniture was stark and austere; some was floppy and overstuffed. She kept expecting to find roommates wandering around. But there was no one here but Van. And Paul.

Paul fixed the drinks, played soft guitar music, told her gaudy tales of prospecting on the West Texas mesas. Paul sang something bawdy sounding in Spanish, and Cleo, putting on her Vixen voice, chimed in on the choruses, deliberately offkey. But then Paul went away, and it was Van who sat close beside her on the couch. He wanted to know things about Judy and he told her a little about Van, and no other selves came into the conversation. She was sure that was intentional. They stayed up very late. Paul came back toward the end of the evening to tell a few jokes and sing a soft late-night song, but when they went into the bedroom, she was with Van. Of that she was certain.

And when she woke in the morning she was alone. She felt a surge of confusion and dislocation, remembered after a moment where she was and how she happened to be there, sat up, blinked. Went into the bathroom and scooped a handful of water over her face. Without bothering to dress she went padding around the apartment looking for Van.

She found him in the exercise room, using the rowing machine, but he wasn't Van. He was dressed in tight jeans and a white T-shirt, and he looked somehow younger, leaner, jauntier. There were fine beads of sweat along his forehead, but he did not seem to be breathing hard. He gave her a cool, distantly appraising, wholly asexual look as if it was not in the least unusual for an unknown naked woman to materialize in the house and he was altogether undisturbed by it. "Good morning. I'm Ned. Pleased to know you." His voice was higher than Van's, much higher than Paul's, and he had an odd, overprecise way of shaping each syllable.

Flustered, suddenly self-conscious and wishing she had put her clothes on before leaving the bedroom, she folded one arm over her breasts, though her nakedness did not seem to matter to him at all. "I'm—Judy. I came with Van."

"Yes, I know. I saw the entry in our book." Smoothly he pulled on the oars of the rowing machine, leaned back, pushed forward. "Help yourself to anything in the fridge," he said. "Make yourself at home. Van left a note for you in the kitchen."

She stared at him: his hands, his mouth, his long muscular arms. She remembered his touch, his kiss, the feel of his skin. And now this complete indifference. No. Not *his* kisses, not *his* touch. Van's. And Van was not here now. There was a different tenant in Van's body, someone she did not know in any way and who had no memories of last night's embraces. *I saw the entry in our book.* They left memos for one another. Cleo shivered. She had known what to expect, more or less, but experiencing it was very different from reading about it. She felt almost as if she had fallen in among beings from another planet.

But this is what you wanted, she thought. *Isn't it?* The intricacy, the mystery, the unpredictability, the sheer weirdness? A little cruise through an alien world because her own had become so stale, so narrow, so cramped. And here she was. *Good morning. I'm Ned. Pleased to know you.*

Van's note was clipped to the refrigerator by a little yellow magnet shaped like a ladybug. DINNER TONIGHT AT CHEZ MICHEL? YOU AND ME AND WHO KNOWS WHO ELSE. CALL ME.

That was the beginning. She saw him every night for the next ten days. Generally they met at some three-star restaurant, had a lingering, intimate dinner, went back to his apartment. One mild, clear evening they drove out to the beach and watched the waves breaking on Seal Rock until well past midnight. Another time they wandered through Fisherman's Wharf and somehow acquired three bags of tacky souvenirs.

Van was his primary name—she saw it on his credit card one night—and that seemed to be his main identity, too, though she knew there were plenty of others. At first he was reticent about that, but on the fourth or fifth night he told her that he had nine major selves and sixteen minor ones. Besides Paul, the geologist, Chuck, who was into horticulture, and Ned, the gay one, Cleo heard about Nat, the stock-market plunger—he was fifty and fat, made a fortune every week, and divided his time between Las Vegas and Miami Beach; Henry the poet, who was shy and never liked anyone to read his work; Dick, who was studying to be an actor; Hal, who once taught law at Harvard; Dave, the yachtsman; and Nicholas, the cardsharp.

And then there were the fragmentary ones, some of whom didn't have names, only a funny way of speaking or a little routine they liked to act out.

She got to see very little of his otherselves, though. Like all multiples he was troubled occasionally by involuntary switching. One night he became Hal while they were making love, and another time he turned into Dave for an hour, and there were momentary flashes of Henry and Nicholas. Cleo perceived it right away whenever one of those switches came. His voice, his movements, his entire manner and personality changed immediately. Those were startling, exciting moments for her, offering a strange exhilaration. But generally his control was very good, and he stayed Van, as if he felt some strong need to experience her as Van, and Van alone. Once in a while he doubled, bringing up Paul to play the guitar and sing or Dick to recite sonnets, but when he did that the Van identity always remained present and dominant. It appeared that he was able to double at will, without the aid of mirrors and lights, at least some of the time. He had been an active and functioning multiple for as long as he could remember—since childhood, perhaps even since birth—and he had devoted himself through the years to the task of gaining mastery over his divided mind.

All the aspects of him that she came to meet had basically attractive personalities: They were energetic, stable, purposeful men who enjoyed life and seemed to know how to go about getting what they wanted. Though they were very different people, she could trace them all back readily enough to the underlying Van from whom, so she thought, they had all split. The one puzzle was Nat, the market operator. It was hard for Cleo to imagine what he was like when he was Nat—sleazy and coarse, yes, but how did he manage to make himself look fifteen years older and forty pounds heavier? Maybe it was all done with facial expressions and posture. But she never got to see Nat. And gradually she realized it was an oversimplification to think of Paul and Dick and Ned and the others as mere extensions of Van into different modes.

Van by himself was just as incomplete as the others. He was just one of many that had evolved in parallel, each one autonomous, each one only a fragment of the whole. Though Van might have control of the body a greater portion of the time, he still had no idea what any alternate selves were up to while they were in command, and like them he had to depend on guesses, fancy footwork, and such notes and messages as they bothered to leave behind in order to keep track of events that occurred outside his conscious awareness. "The only one who knows everything is Michael. He's seven years old, as smart as a whip, and keeps in touch with all of us all the time."

"Your memory trace," Cleo said.

Van nodded. All multiples, she knew, had one alter with full awareness of the doings of all the other personalities—usually a child, an observer who sat back deep in the mind and played its own games and emerged only when necessary to fend off some crisis that threatened the stability of the entire group. "He's just informed us that he's Ethiopian," Van said. "So every two or three weeks we go across to Oakland to an Ethiopian restaurant that he likes, and he flirts with the waitresses in Amharic."

"That can't be too terrible a chore. I'm told Ethiopians are very beautiful people."

"Absolutely. But they think it's all a big joke, and Michael doesn't know how to pick up women anyway. He's only seven, you know. So Van doesn't get anything out of it except some exercise in comparative linguistics and a case of indigestion the next day.

Ethiopian food is the spiciest in the world. I can't *stand* spicy food."

"Neither can I," she said. "But Lisa loves it. Especially Mexican. But nobody ever said sharing a body is easy, did they?"

She knew she had to be careful in questioning Van about the way his life as a multiple worked. She was supposed to be a multiple herself, after all. But she made use of her Sacramento background as justification for her areas of apparent ignorance of multiple customs and the everyday mechanics of multiple life. Though she too had known she was a multiple since childhood, she said, she had grown up outside the climate of acceptance of the divided personality that prevailed in San Francisco, where an active subculture of multiples had existed openly for years. In her isolated existence, unaware that there were a great many others of her kind, she had at first regarded herself as the victim of a serious mental disorder. It was only recently, she told him, that she had come to understand the overwhelming advantages of life as a multiple; the richness, the complexity, the fullness of talents and experiences that a divided mind was free to enjoy. That was why she had come to San Francisco. That was why she listened so eagerly to all that he was telling her about himself.

She was cautious, too, in manisfesting her own multiple identities. She wished she did not have to pretend to have other selves. But they had to be brought forth now and again, if only to maintain Van's interest in her. Multiples were notoriously indifferent to singletons. They found them bland, overly simple, two-dimensional. They wanted the excitement of embracing one person and discovering another, or two or three. So she gave him Lisa, she gave him Vixen, she gave him the Judy-who-was-Cleo and the Cleo-who-was-someone-else, and she slipped from one to another in seemingly involuntary and unexpected way, often when they were in bed.

Lisa was calm, controlled, straitlaced. She was totally shocked when she found herself, between one eye blink and the next, in the a arms of a strange man. "Who are you?—where am I?" she blurted, rolling away and pulling herself into a fetal ball.

"I'm Judy's friend," Van said.

She stared bleakly at him. "So she's up to her tricks again."

He looked pained, embarrassed, solicitous. She let him wonder for a moment whether he would have to take her back to her hotel in the middle of the night. Then she allowed a mischievous smile to cross Lisa's face, allowed Lisa's outraged modesty to subside, allowed Lisa to relent and relax, allowed Lisa to purr—

"Well, as long as we're here already—what did you say your name was?"

He liked that. He liked Vixen, too—wild, sweaty, noisy, a moaner, a gasper, a kicker and thrasher who dragged him down onto the floor and went rolling over and over with him. She thought he liked Cleo, too, though that was harder to tell, because Cleo's style was aloof, serious, baroque, inscrutable. She would switch quickly from one to another, sometimes running through all four in the course of an hour. Wine, she said, induced quick switching in her. She let him know that she had a few other identities, too, fragmentary and submerged. She hinted that they were troubled, deeply neurotic, self-destructive: They were under control, she said, and would not erupt to cause woe for him, but she left the possibility hovering over them to add spice to the relationship and plausibility to her role.

It seemed to be working. His pleasure in her company was evident. She was beginning to indulge in little fantasies of moving down permanently from Sacramento, renting an apartment, perhaps even moving in with him, though that would surely be a strange and challenging life. She would be living with Paul and Ned and Chuck and the rest of the crew, too, but how wondrous, how electrifying.

Then on the tenth day he seemed uncharacteristically tense and somber. She asked him what was bothering him, and he evaded her and she pressed, and finally he said, "Do you really want to know?"

"Of course."

"It bothers me that you aren't real, Judy."

She caught her breath. "What the hell do you mean by that?"

"You know what I mean," he said quietly sadly. "Don't try to pretend any longer. There's no point in it."

It was like a jolt in the ribs.

She turned away and was silent a long while, wondering what to say. Just when everything was going so well, just when she was beginning to believe she had carried off the masquerade successfully.

"So you know?" she asked timidly.

"Of course I know. I knew right away."

She was trembling. "How could you tell?"

"A thousand ways. When we switch, we *change*. The voice. The eyes. The muscular tensions. The grammatical habits. The brain waves, even. An evoked-potential test shows it. Flash a light in my eyes and I'll give off a certain brainwave pattern, and Ned will give off another, and Chuck still another. You and Lisa and Cleo and Vixen would all be the same. Multiples aren't actors, Judy. Multiples are separate minds within the same brain. That's a matter of scientific fact. You were just acting. You were doing it very well, but you couldn't possibly have fooled me."

"You let me make an idiot of myself, then."

"No."

"Why did you—how could you—"

"I saw you walk in that first night, and you caught me right away. I watched you go out on the floor and fall apart, and I knew you couldn't be multiple, and I wondered, What the hell's she doing here? Then I went over to you, and I was hooked. I felt something I haven't ever felt before. Does that sound like the standard old malarkey? But it's true, Judy. You're the first singleton woman who's ever interested me."

"Why?"

He shook his head. "Something about you—your intensity, your alertness, maybe even your eagerness to pretend you were a multiple—I don't know. I was caught, I was caught and hard. And it's been a wonderful week and a half. I mean that."

"Until you got bored."

"I'm not bored with you, Judy."

"Cleo. That's my real name, my singleton name. There is no Judy."

"Cleo," he said, as if measuring the word with his lips.

"So you aren't bored with me even though there's only one of me. That's marvelous—tremendously flattering. That's the best thing I've heard all day. I guess I should go now. Van. It *is* Van, isn't it?"

"Don't talk that way."

"How do you want me to talk? I fascinated you, you fascinated me, we played our little games with each other, and now it's over. I wasn't real, but you did your best. We both did our best. But I'm only a singleton woman, and you can't be satisfied with that. Not for long. For a night, a week, two weeks maybe. Sooner or later you'll want the real thing, and I can't be the real thing for you. So long, Van."

"No."

"No?"

"Don't go."

"What's the sense of staying?"

"I want you to stay."

"I'm a singleton, Van."

"You don't have to be," he said.

The therapist's name was Burkhalter, and his office was in one of the Embarcadero towers. To the San Francisco multiples community he was very close to being a deity. His specialty was electrophysiological integration, with specific application to multiple-personality disorders. Those who carried within themselves dark and diabolical selves that threatened the stability of the group went to him to have those selves purged or at least contained. Those who sought to have latent selves that were submerged beneath more outgoing personalities brought forward into a healthy functional state went to him also. Those whose life as a

multiple was a torment of schizoid confusions instead of a richly
rewarding contrapuntal symphony gave themselves to Dr. Burkhalter to
be healed, and in time they were. And in recent years he had begun
to develop techinques for what he called personality augmentation. Van
called it "driving the wedge."

"He can turn a singleton into a multiple?" Cleo asked in amazement.

"If the potential is there. You know that it's partly genetic: The
structure of a multiple's brain is fundamentally different from a singleton's.
The hardware just isn't the same, the cerebral wiring. And then, if the
right stimulus comes along, usually in childhood, usually but not
necessarily traumatic, the splitting takes place, the separate identities
begin to establish their territories. But much of the time multiplicity is
never generated, and you walk around with the capacity to be a whole
horde of selves yet never know it."

"Is there reason to think I'm like that?"

He shrugged. "It's worth finding out, if he detects the predisposition,
he has effective ways of inducing separation. Driving the wedge, you
see? You do *want* to be a multiple, don't you, Cleo?"

"Oh, yes, Van. Yes!"

Burkhalter wasn't sure about her. He taped electrodes to her head,
flashed bright lights in her eyes, gave her verbal-association tests, ran
four or five different kinds of electroencephalograph studies, and still he
was uncertain. "It is not a black-and-white matter." he said several
times, frowning, scowling. He was a multiple himself, but three of his
selves were psychiatrists; so there was never any real problem about his
office hours. Cleo wondered if he ever went to himself for a second opinion.
After a week of testing she was sure that she must be a hopeless case, an
intractable singleton, but Burkhalter surprised her by concluding that it
was worth the attempt. "At the very worst," he said, "we will experience
spontaneous fusing in a few days, and you will be no worse off than you
are now. But if we succeed—"

His clinic was across the bay, in a town called Moraga. She spent two
days undergoing further tests, then three days taking medication. "Simply
an anticonvulsant," the nurse explained cheerily. "To build up your
tolerance."

"Tolerance for what?" Cleo asked.

"The birth trauma," she said. "New selves will be coming forth, and
it can be uncomfortable for a little while."

The treatment began on Thursday. Electroshock, drugs, electroshock
again. She was heavily sedated. It felt like a long dream, but there was
no pain. Van visited her every day, Chuck came too, bringing her two
potted orchids in bloom, and Paul sang to her, and even Ned paid her a

call. But it was hard for her to maintain a conversation with any of them. She heard voices much of the time. She felt feverish and dislocated, and at times she was sure she was floating eight or ten inches above the bed. Gradually that sensation subsided, but there were others nearly as odd. The voices remained. She learned how to hold conversations with them.

In the second week she was not allowed to have visitors. That didn't matter.

She had plenty of company even when she was alone.

Then Van came for her. "They're going to let you go home today."

"How are you doing. Cleo?"

"I'm Noreen," she said.

There were five of her apparently. That was what Van said. She had no way of knowing, because when they were dominant she was gone— not merely asleep but *gone*, perceiving nothing. But he showed her notes that they wrote, in hand writings that she did not recognize and indeed could barely read, and he played tapes of her other voices: Noreen, a deep contralto; Nanette, high and breathy; Katya, hard and rough New York; and the last one, who had not yet announced her name, a stagy, voluptuous, campy siren voice.

She did not leave his apartment the first few days, and then she began going out for short trips, always with Van or one of his alters close beside. She felt convalsecent. A kind of hangover from the drugs had dulled her reflexes and made it hard for her to cope with traffic, and also there was the fear that she would undergo a switching while she was out. Whenever that happened it came without warning, and when she returned to awareness afterwards she felt a sharp discontinuity of memory, not knowing how she suddenly found herself in Ghirardelli Square or Golden Gate Park or wherever it was that the other self had taken their body.

But she was happy. And Van was happy with her. One night in the second week, when they were out, he switched to Chuck—Cleo knew it was Chuck coming on, for now she always knew right away which identity had taken over—and he said, "You've had a marvelous effect on him. None of us have ever seen him like this before—so contented, so fulfilled—"

"I hope it lasts, Chuck."

"Of course it'll last! Why on earth shouldn't it last?"

It didn't. Toward the end of the third week Cleo noticed that there hadn't been any entries in her memo book from Noreen for several days. That in itself was nothing alarming: An alter might choose to submerge for days, weeks, even months at a time. But was it likely that Noreen, so new to the world, would remain out of sight so long? Lin-lin, the little Chinese girl who had evolved in the second week and was Cleo's memory trace, reported that Noreen had gone away. A few days later an identity named Mattie came and went within three hours, like something bubbling up out of a troubled sea. Then Nanette and Katya disappeared, leaving Cleo with no one but her nameless, siren-voiced alter and Lin-lin. She was fusing again. The wedges that Dr. Burkhalter had driven into her soul were not holding; her mind insisted on oneness and was integrating itself; she was reverting to the singleton state.

"All of them are gone now," she told Van disconsolately.

"I know. I've been watching it happen."

"Is there anything we can do? Should I go back to Burkhalter?"

She saw the pain in his eyes. "It won't do any good," he said. "He told me the chances were about three to one this would happen. A month, he figured; that was about the best we could hope for. And we've had our month."

"I'd better go, Van."

"Don't say that."

"No?"

"I love you, Cleo."

"You won't. Not for much longer."

He tried to argue with her, to tell her that it didn't matter to him that she was a singleton, that one Cleo was worth a whole raft of alters, that he would learn to adapt to life with a singleton woman. He could not bear the thought of her leaving now. So she stayed: a week, two weeks, three. They ate at their favorite restaurants. They strolled hand in hand through the cool evenings. They talked of Chomsky and Whorf and even of shopping centers. When he was gone and Paul or Chuck or Hal or Dave was there she went places with them if they wanted her to. Once she went to a movie with Ned, and when toward the end he felt himself starting to switch she put her arm around him until he regained control so that he could see how the movie finished.

But it was no good. He wanted something richer than she could offer him: the swtiching, the doubling, the complex undertones and over-tones of other personalities resonating beyond the shores of consciousness. She could not give him that. He was like one who has voluntarily blindfolded himself in order to keep a blind woman company. She knew she could not ask him to live like that forever.

And so one afternoon when Van was somewhere else she packed her things and said good-bye to Paul, who gave her a hug and wept a little with her, and she went back to Sacramento. "Tell him not to call," she said. "A clean break's the best." She had been in San Francisco two months, and it was as if those two months were the only months of her life that had had any color in them, and all the rest had been lived in tones of gray.

There had been a man in the real-estate office who had been telling her for a couple of years that they were meant for each other. Cleo had always been friendly enough to him: They had done a few skiing weekends in Tahoe the winter before; they had gone to Hawaii once, they had driven down to San Diego. But she had never felt anything particular when she was with him. A week after her return she phoned him and suggested that they drive up north to the redwood country for a few days. When they came back she moved into the condominium he had just outside town.

It was hard to find anything wrong with him. He was good-natured and attractive, he was successful, he read books, and liked good movies, he enjoyed hiking, rafting, and backpacking, he even talked of driving down into the city during the opera season to take in a performance or two. He was getting toward the age where he was thinking about marriage and a family. He seemed very fond of her.

But he was flat, she thought. Flat as a cardboard cutout: a singleton, a one-brain, a no-switch. There was only one of him, and there always would be. It was hardly his fault, she knew. But she couldn't settle for someone who had only two dimensions. A terrible restlessness went roaring through her every evening, and she could not possibly tell him what was troubling her.

On a drizzly afternoon in early November she packed a suitcase and drove down to San Francisco. She checked into one of the Lombard Street motels, showered, changed, and walked over to Fillmore Street. Cautiously she explored the strip from Chestnut down to Union, from Union back to Chestnut. The thought of running into Van terrified her. Not tonight, she prayed. Not tonight. She went past Skits, did not go in, stopped outside a club called Big Mama, shook her head, finally entered one called The Side Effect. Mostly women inside, as usual, but a few men at the bar, not too bad-looking. No sign of Van.

She bought herself a drink and casually struck up a conversation with a short, curly-haired, artistic-looking type.

"You come here often?" he asked.

"First time. I've usually gone to Skits."

"I think I remember seeing you there. Or maybe not."

She smiled. "What's your now-name?"

"Sandy. Yours?"

Cleo drew her breath down deep into her lungs. She felt a kind of light-headedness beginning to swirl behind her eyes. *Is this what you want?* she asked herself. *Yes. Yes. This is what you want.*

"Melinda," she said.

JACK McDEVITT

Cryptic

SETI—the Search for Extra-Terrestrial Intelligence—has been a reality for decades now, and though no proof has as yet been found that there really *are* extraterrestrial civilizations Out There, the radiotelescopes continue to search the skies for signs that We Are Not Alone, and men and women from all corners of the earth still look up at night and hope for messages from the distant stars.

But what if when we *do* receive such a message, we don't like what it has to say . . .?

Born in Philadelphia, Jack McDevitt now lives in Woodridge, Illinois with his wife and three children. He is a frequent contributer to *Isaac Asimov's Science Fiction Magazine* and has also sold stories to *The Twilight Zone Magazine* and to *Chess Life*. An ex-naval officer, ex-English teacher, and former customs inspector, he is currently the regional training officer for the Chicago Customs Region.

CRYPTIC

Jack McDevitt

It was at the bottom of the safe in a bulky manila envelope. I nearly tossed it into the trash along with the stacks of other documents, tapes, and assorted flotsam left over from the Project.

Had it been cataloged, indexed in some way, I'm sure I would have. But the envelope was blank, save for an eighteen-year-old date scrawled in the lower right hand corner, and, beneath it, the notation "40 gh."

Out on the desert, lights were moving. That would be Brackett fine-tuning the Array for Orrin Hopkins, who was then beginning the observations that would lead, several years later, to new departures in pulsar theory. I envied Hopkins: he was short, round, bald, a man unsure of himself, whose occasionally brilliant insights were explained with giggles. He was a ridiculous figure; yet he bore the stamp of genius. And people would remember his ideas long after the residence hall named for me at Carrollton had crumbled.

If I had not long since recognized my own perimeters and conceded any hope of my immortality (at least of this sort), I certainly did so when I accepted the director's position at Sandage. Administration pays better than being an active physicist, but it is death to ambition.

And a Jesuit doesn't even get that advantage.

In those days, the Array was still modest: forty parabolic antennas, each thirty-six meters across. They were on tracks, of course, independently movable, forming a truncated cross. They had, for two decades, been the heart of SETI, the Search for Extra-Terrestrial Intelligence. Now, with the Project abandoned, they were being employed for more useful, if mundane, purposes.

Even that relatively unsophisticated system was good: as Hutching Chaney once remarked, the Array could pick up the cough of an automobile ignition on the moon.

I circled the desk and fell into the uncomfortable wooden chair we'd inherited from the outgoing regime. The packet was sealed down with tape that had become brittle and loose around the edges. I tore it open.

It was a quarter past ten. I'd worked through my dinner and the evening hours, bored, drinking coffee, debating the wisdom in coming out here from JPL. The increase in responsibility was a good career move; but I knew now that Harry Cooke would never lay his hands on a new particle.

I was committed for two years at Sandage: two years of working out schedules and worrying about insurance; two years of dividing meals between the installation's sterile cafeteria, and Jimmy's Amoco on Route 85. Then, if it all went well, I could expect another move up, perhaps to Georgetown.

I'd have traded it all for Hopkins's future.

I shook out six magnetic discs onto the desk. They were in individual sleeves, of the type that many installations had once used to record electromagnetic radiation. The discs were numbered and dated over a three-day period in 1991, two years earlier than the date on the envelope.

Each was marked "Procyon."

In back, Hopkins and two associates were hunched over monitors. Brackett, having finished his job, was at his desk reading.

I was pleased to discover that the discs were compatible to the Mark VIs. I inserted one, tied in a vocorder to get a hard copy, and went over to join the Hopkins group while the thing ran. They were talking about plasma. I listened for a time, got lost, noted that everyone around me (save the grinning little round man) also got lost, and strolled back to my computer.

The trace drew its green-and-white pictures smoothly on the Mark VI display, and pages of hard copy clicked out of the vocorder. Something in the needle geometry scattered across the recording paper drew my attention. Like an elusive name, it drifted just beyond my reach.

Beneath a plate of the Andromeda Galaxy, a coffee pot simmered. I could hear the distant drone of a plane, probably out of Luke Air Force Base. Behind me, Hopkins and his men were laughing at something.

There were patterns in the recording.

They materialized slowly, identical clusters of impulses: the signals were artificial.

Procyon.

The laughter, the plane, the coffee pot, a radio that had been left on somewhere: everything ratched down to a possibility.

More likely Phoenix, I thought.

*   *   *

Frank Myers had been SETI Director since Ed Dickinson's death twelve years before. I reached him next morning in San Francisco.

"No," he said without hesitation. "Someone's idea of a joke, Harry."

"It was in your safe, Frank."

"That damned safe's been there forty years. Might be anything in it. Except messages from Mars. . . ."

I thanked him and hung up.

It had been a long night: I'd taken the hard copy to bed with me and, by 5 AM, had identified more than forty distinct pulse patterns. The signal appeared to be continuous: that is, it had been an ongoing transmission with no indication of beginning or end, but only irregular breaches of the type that would result from atmospherics and, of course, the long periods during which the target would have been below the horizon.

It was clearly a reflected terrestrial transmission: radio waves bounce around considerably. But why seal the error two years later and put it in the safe?

Procyon is a yellow-white class F3 binary, absolute magnitude 2.8, once worshipped in Babylonia and Egypt. (What hasn't been worshipped in Egypt?) Distance from Earth: 11.3 light-years.

In the outer office, Beth Cooper typed, closed cabinet drawers, spoke with visitors.

The obvious course of action was to use the Array. Listen to Procyon at 40 gigahertz, or all across the spectrum for that matter, and find out if it was, indeed, saying something.

On the intercom, I asked Beth when we had open time on the System. "Nothing for seventeen months," she said crisply.

That was no surprise. The facility had booked quickly when its resources were made available to the astronomical community on more than the limited basis that had prevailed for twenty years. Anyone wishing to use the radiotelescope had to plan far in advance. How could I get hold of the Array for a couple hours?

"Beth, would you come in a moment, please?"

Beth Cooper had come to Sandage from San Augustin with SETI during the big move twenty years before. She'd been secretary to three directors: Hutching Chaney, who had built Sandage; his longtime friend Ed Dickinson; and finally, after Dickinson's death, Frank Myers, a young man on the move, who'd stayed too long with the Project, and who'd been reportedly happy to see it strangled. In any case, Myers had contributed to its demise by his failure to defend it.

I'd felt he was right, of course, though for the wrong reason. It had been painful to see the magnificent telescope at Sandage denied, by and large, to the scientific community while its grotesque hunt for the little

Green Man signal went on. I think there were few of us not happy to see it end.

Beth had expected to lose her job. But she knew her way around the facility, had a talent for massaging egos, and could spell. A devout Lutheran, she had adapted cautiously to working for a priest and, oddly, seemed to have taken offense that I did not routinely walk around with a Roman collar.

I asked one or two questions about the billing methods of the local utilities, and then commented, as casually as I could manage, that it was unfortunate the Project had not succeeded.

Beth looked more like a New York librarian than a secretary at a desert installation. Her hair was silver-gray. She wore steel-rimmed glasses on a long, silver chain. She was moderately heavy; but her carriage and her diction were impeccable, imbuing her with the quality that stage people call presence.

Her eyes narrowed to hard black beads at my remark. "Dr. Dickinson said any number of times that none of us would live to see results. Everyone attached to the program, even the janitors, knew that." She wasn't a woman given to shrugs, but the sudden flick in those dark eyes matched the effect. "I'm glad he didn't live to see it terminated."

That was followed by an uncomfortable silence. "I don't blame you, Doctor," she said at length, referring to my public position that the facility was being underutilized.

I dropped my eyes, and tried to smile reassuringly. It must have been ludicrous: her severe features softened. I showed her the envelope.

"Do you recognize the writing?"

She barely glanced at it. "It's Dr. Dickinson's."

"Are you sure? I didn't think Dickinson came to the Project until Hutch Chaney's retirement. That was '93, wasn't it?"

"He took over as Director then. But he was an operating technician under Dr. Chaney for, oh, ten or twelve years before that." Her eyes glowed when she spoke of Dickinson.

"I never met him," I said.

"He was a fine man." She looked past me, over my shoulder, her features pale. "If we hadn't lost him, we might not have lost the Project."

"If it matters," I added gently.

"If it matters," she confirmed.

She was right about Dickinson: he was articulate, a persuasive speaker, author of books on various subjects, and utterly dedicated to SETI. He might well have kept the project afloat despite the cessation of federal funds and an increasing clamor among his colleagues for more time at the facility. But Dickinson was twelve years dead now: he'd returned to

Massachusetts at Christmas, as was his custom. After a snowstorm, he'd gone out to help shovel a neighbor's driveway and his heart had failed.

I'd been in the East myself at the time, at Georgetown. And I can still recall my sense of a genius who had died too soon. He had possessed a vast talent, but no discipline; he had churned through his career hurling sparks in all directions. But somehow everything he touched, like SETI, had come to no fulfillment.

"Beth, was there ever a time they thought they had an LGM?"

"The Little Green Man Signal?" She shook her head. "No, I don't think so. They were always picking up echoes and things. But nothing ever came close. Either it was KCOX in Phoenix, or some Japanese trawler in the middle of the Pacific."

"Never anything that didn't fit those categories?"

One eyebrow rose slightly. "Never anything they could prove. If they couldn't pin it down, they went back later and tried to find it again. One way or another, they eliminated everything." Or, she was thinking, we wouldn't be standing here having this conversation.

Beth's comments implied that suspect signals had been automatically stored. Grateful that I had not yet got around to purging obsolete data, I discovered that was indeed the case, and ran a search covering the entire time period back to the Procyon reception in 1991, looking for a similar signal.

I got a surprise.

There was no match. There was also no record of the Procyon reception itself.

That meant, presumably, it had been accounted for, and discarded.

Then why, two years later, had the recordings been sealed and placed in the safe? Surely no explanation would have taken that long.

SETI had assumed that any LGM signal would be a deliberate attempt to communicate, that an effort would therefore be made by the originator to create intelligibility, and that the logical way to do that was to employ a set of symbols representing universal constants: the atomic weight of hydrogen, perhaps, or the value of pi.

But the move to Sandage had also been a move to more sophisticated, and considerably more sensitive, equipment. The possibility developed that the Project would pick up a slopover signal, a transmission of alien origin, but intended only for local receivers. Traffic of that nature could be immeasurably difficult to interpret.

If the packet in the safe was anything at all, it was surely of this latter type. Forty gigahertz is not an ideal frequency for interstellar communication. Moreover it was ongoing, formless, no numbered parts, nothing to assist translation.

I set the computer working on the text, using SETI's own language analysis program. Then I instructed Brackett to call me if anything developed, had dinner at Jimmy's, and went home. I was left undisturbed.

There was no evidence of structure in the text. In English, one can expect to find a 'U' after a 'Q', or a vowel after a cluster of consonants. The aspirate is seldom doubled, nothing is ever tripled, and so on. But in the Procyon transmission, everything seemed utterly random.

The computer counted sixty-one distinct pulse patterns, which was to say, sixty-one characters. None recurred at sufficient intervals to be a space. And the frequency count was flat: there was no quantitative difference in use from one character to another. All appeared approximately the same number of times. If it was a language, it was a language with no vowels.

And certainly too many letters.

I called Wes Phillips, who was then the only linguist I knew.

Was it possible for a language to be structured in such a way?

"Oh, I don't think so. Unless you're talking about some sort of construct. Even then . . ." He paused. "How many characters did you say?"

"Sixty-one."

"Harry, I can give you a whole series of reasons in maybe six different disciplines why languages need high and low frequency letters. To have a flat 'curve,' a language would have to be deliberately designed that way, and it would have to be non-oral. But what practical value would it have? Why bother?

"One other thing," he said. "Sixty-one letters seems a trifle much. If these people actually require that many characters to communicate, I suspect they're going to be doing it with drums."

Ed Dickinson had been an enigma. During the series of superpower confrontations near the close of the century, he'd earned an international reputation as a diplomat, and as an eloquent defender of reason and restraint. Everyone agreed that he had a mind of the first rank. Yet, in his chosen field, he accomplished little. And he'd gone to work for the Project, historically only a stepping-stone to serious effort. But he'd stayed.

Why?

Hutching Chaney was a different matter. A retired naval officer, he'd indulged in physics almost as a sideline. His political connections had been instrumental in getting Sandage built; and his assignment to head it was rumored to have been a reward for his services during the undeclared Soviet naval war of '87-'88.

He possessed a plodding sort of competence. He was fully capable of

grasping, and visualizing, extreme complexity. But he lacked insight
and imagination, the ability to draw the subtle inference.

After his retirement from Sandage, Chaney had gone to an emeritus
position at MIT, which he'd held for five years.

He was a big man, more truck driver than physicist. Despite advanc-
ing age—he was then in his 70s—and his bulk, he spoke and moved
with energy. His hair was full and black. His light gray eyes suggested
the shrewdness of a professional politician; and he possessed the confident congeniality of a man who had never failed at anything.

We were in his home in Somerville, Massachusetts, a stone and glass
house atop sweeping lawns. It was not an establishment that a retired
physicist would be expected to inhabit: Chaney's moneyed background
was evident.

He clapped a big hand on my shoulder and pulled me through one of
those stiff, expensive living rooms that no one ever wants to sit in, into a
paneled leather-upholstered compartment at the rear of the house.
"Martha," he said to someone I couldn't see, "would you bring us some
port?" He looked at me for acquiescence.

"Fine," I said. "It's been a long time, Hutch."

Books lined the walls: mostly technical, some on naval engineering, a
few military and naval histories. An articulated steel gray model of the
Lance dominated the fireplace shelf. That was the deadly hydrofoil
which, built at Chaney's urging, had been launched against the Soviets
in vast numbers, and had swept them from the seas.

"The Church is infiltrating everywhere," he said. "How are things at
Sandage, Harry?"

I described some of the work then in progress. He listened with
interest.

A young woman arrived with a bottle, two glasses, and a plate of
cheese. "Martha comes in three times a week," Chaney said after she'd
left. He smiled, winked, dipped a stick of cheese in some mustard, and
bit it neatly in half. "You needn't worry, Harry. I'm not capable of
getting into trouble anymore. What brings you to Massachusetts?"

I extracted the vocordings from my briefcase and handed them across
to him. I watched patiently as he leafed through the thick sheaf of
paper, and saw with satisfaction his change of expression.

"You're kidding, Harry," he said. "Somebody really found one?
When'd it happen?"

"Twenty years ago," I said, passing him the envelope and the original
discs.

He turned them over in his hands. "Then there's a mistake somewhere."

"It was in the safe," I said.

He shook his head. "Doesn't much matter where it was. Nothing like this ever happened."

"Then what is it?"

"Damned if I have any idea."

We sat not talking while Chaney continued to flip pages, grunting. He seemed to have forgotten his wine. "You run this yourself?" he asked.

I nodded.

"Hell of a lot of trouble for somebody to go to for a joke. Were the computers able to read any of it? No? That's because it's gibberish." He stared at the envelope. "But it *is* Ed's handwriting."

"Would Dickinson have any reason to keep such a thing quiet?"

"Ed? No: Dickinson least of all. No one worked harder for a success. He wanted it so badly he invested his life in the Project."

"But could he, physically, have done this? Could he have picked up the LGM? Was he good enough with the computers to cover his tracks?"

"This is pointless. Yes, he could have done it. And you could walk through Braintree without your pants."

A light breeze was coming through a side window, billowing the curtains. It was cool and pleasant, unusual for Massachusetts in August. Some kids were playing halfball out on the street.

"Forty megahertz," he said. "Sounds like a satellite transmission."

"That wouldn't have taken two years to figure out, would it? Why keep the discs?"

"Why not?" he said. "I expect if you go down into the storeroom you'll find all kinds of relics."

Outside, there was a sound like distant thunder, exploding suddenly into an earsplitting screech. A stripped-down T-Bolt skidded by, scattering the ballplayers, and then accelerated. It took the corner stop sign at about 45. The game resumed, as though nothing had happened.

"All the time," Chaney said. His back to the window, he hadn't bothered to look around. "Cops can't keep up with them anymore."

"Why was Dickinson so interested in the Project?"

"Ed was a great man." His face clouded somewhat, and I wondered if the port hadn't drawn his emotions close to the surface. "You'd have had to know him. You and he would have got along fine. He had a taste for the metaphysical, and I guess the Project was about as close as he could get."

"How do you mean?"

"Did you know he spent two years in a seminary? Yes, somewhere outside Philadelphia. He was an altar boy who eventually wound up in Harvard. And that was that."

"You mean he lost his faith?"

"Yes. But he always retained that fine mystical sense of purpose that you drill into your best kids, a notion that things are somehow ordered. When I knew him, he wouldn't have presumed to pray to anyone. But he had all the drive of a missionary, and the same conviction of—" He dropped his head back on the leather upholstery and tried to seize a word from the ceiling. "—destiny.

"Ed wasn't like most physicists. He was competent in a wide range of areas. He wrote on foreign affairs for *Commentary* and *Harper's*; he published books on ornithology, systems analysis, Malcolm Muggeridge, and Edward Gibbon."

He swung easily out of his chair and reached for a pair of fat matched volumes in mud-brown covers. It was *The Decline and Fall of the Roman Empire*, the old Modern Library edition. "He's the only person I've ever known who's actually read the thing." He turned the cover so that I could see the inscription:

> For Hutch,
>   In the fond hope that we can hold off the potherbs and the pigs.
>   *Ed*

"He gave it to me when I left SETI."

"Seems like an odd gift. Have you read it?"

He laughed off the question. "You'd need a year."

"What's the business about the potherbs and pigs?"

He rose and walked casually to the far wall. There were photos of naval vessels and aircraft, of Chaney and President Fine, of the Sandage complex. He seemed to screw his vision into the latter. "I don't remember. It's a phrase from the book. He explained it to me at the time. But . . ." He held his hands outward, palms up.

"Hutch," I said, "thanks." I got up to go.

"There's nothing to it," he said. "I don't know where that thing came from, but Ed Dickinson would have given anything for a contact."

"Hutch, is it possible that Dickinson might have been able to translate the text?"

"Not if you couldn't. He had the same program."

I don't like cities.

Dickinson's books were all out of print, and the used bookstores were clustered in Cambridge. Even then, the outskirts of Boston, like the city proper, were littered with glass and newspapers. Surly crowds milled outside bars. Windows everywhere were smashed or boarded. I went through a red light at one intersection rather than learn the intentions of an approaching band of ragged children with hard eyes. (One could scarcely call them children, though I doubt there was one over 12.) Profanity covered the crumbling brick walls as high as an arm could reach. Much of it was misspelled.

Boston had been Dickinson's city. I wondered what the great humanist thought when he drove through these streets.

I found only one of his books: *Malcolm Muggeridge: Faith and Despair*. The store also had a copy of *The Decline and Fall*. On impulse, I bought it.

I was glad to get back to the desert.

We were entering a period of extraordinary progress, during which we finally began to understand the mechanics of galactic structure. McCue mapped the core of the Milky Way, Osterberger developed his unified field concepts, and Schauer constructed his celebrated revolutionary hypothesis on the nature of time. Then, on a cool morning in October, a team from Cal Tech announced an electrifying discovery: objects on the fringe of visibility were *not* receding; were, in fact, resisting expansion and moving slowly in our direction, against the tide. It seemed then, as it does now, that they are fragments of another universe.

In the midst of all this activity, we had an emergency one night in late September. Earl Barlow, who was directing the Cal Tech groups, suffered a mild heart attack. I arrived just before the EMTs, at about 2 AM.

After the ambulance left with him, Barlow's men wandered about listlessly, drinking coffee, too upset to work. The opportunity didn't catch me entirely unprepared. I gave Brackett his new target, and the numbers. The ululating shriek of the emergency vehicle had barely subsided before the parabolas swung round and fastened on the bright dog-star Procyon.

There was only the disjointed crackle of interstellar static.

I took long walks on the desert at night. The parabolas are lovely in the moonlight. Occasionally, the stillness is broken by the whine of an electric motor, and the antennas slide gracefully along their tracks. It was, I thought, a new Stonehenge of softly curving shapes and fluid motion.

The Muggeridge book was a slim volume. It was not biographical, but rather an analysis of the philosopher's conviction that the West has a death wish. It was the old argument that God had been replaced by science, that man had gained knowledge of a trivial sort, and lost purpose.

It was, on the whole, depressing reading. In his conclusion, Dickinson took issue, arguing that truth will not wait on human convenience, that if man cannot adapt to a neutral universe, then that universe will indeed seem hostile. We must make do with what we have and accept truth wherever it leads. The modern cathedral is the radiotelescope.

Sandage was involved in the verification procedure for McCue's work, and for the "enigmatic Cal Tech" objects. All of that is another story: what is significant is that it got me thinking about verifications, and I realized I'd overlooked something: there'd been no match for the Procyon recordings anywhere in the data banks since the original reception. But the Procyon recordings might themselves have been the confirmation of an earlier signal!

It took five minutes to run the search: there were two hits.

Both were fragments, neither more than 15 minutes; but there was enough of each to reduce the probability of error to less than one percent.

The first occurred just three weeks prior to the Procyon reception.

The second went back to 1987, a San Augustin observation. Both were at 40 gigahertz. Both had identical pulse patterns. But there was an explosive difference, sedately concealed in the target information line: the 1987 transmission had come while the radiotelescope was locked on Sirius!

When I got back to my office, I was trembling.

Sirius and Procyon were only a few light years apart. My God, I kept thinking, they exist! And they have star travel!

I spent the balance of the day stumbling around, trying to immerse myself in fuel usage reports and budget projections. But mostly what I did was watch the desert light grow hard in the curtains, and then fade. The two volumes of Edward Gibbon were propped between a Webster's and some black binders. The books were thirty years old, identical to the set in Chaney's den. Some of the pages, improperly cut, were still joined at the edges.

I opened the first volume, approximately in the middle, and began to read. Or tried to. But Ed Dickinson kept crowding out the Romans. Finally I gave it up, took the book, and went home.

There was duplicate bridge in town, and I lost myself in that for five hours. Then, in bed, still somewhat dazed, I attempted *The Decline and Fall* again.

It was not the dusty rollcall of long-dead emperors that I had expected. The emperors are there, stabbing and throttling and blundering. And occasionally trying to improve things. But the fish-hawkers are there too. And the bureaucrats and the bishops.

It's a world filled with wine and legionnaires' sweat, mismanagement, arguments over Jesus, and the inability to transfer power, all played out to the ruthless drumbeat of dissolution. An undefined historical tide, stemmed occasionally by a hero, or a sage, rolls over men and events, washing them toward the sea. (During the later years, I wondered, did Roman kids run down matrons in flashy imported chariots? Were the walls of Damascus defiled by profanity?)

In the end, when the barbarians push at the outer rim of empire, it is only a hollow wreck that crashes down.

Muggeridge must have been there.

And Dickinson, the altar boy, amid the fire and waste of the imperial city, must have suffered a second loss of faith.

We had an electrical failure one night. It has nothing to do with this story except that it resulted in my being called in at 4 AM (not to restore the power, which required a good electrician; but to pacify some angry people from New York; and to be able to say, in my report, that I had been on the spot).

These things attended to, I went outside.

At night, the desert is undisturbed by color or motion. It's a composition of sand, rock, and star; a frieze, a Monet, uncomplicated, unchanging. It's reassuring, in an age when little else seems stable: the orderly universe of the twentieth century had long since disintegated into a plethora of neutron galaxies, 'colliding' black holes, time reversals, and God knows what.

The desert is solid underfoot. Predictable. A reproach to the quantum mechanics that reflect a quicksand cosmos in which physics merges with Plato.

Close on the rim of the sky, guarding their mysteries, Sirius and Procyon, the bright pair, sparkled. The arroyos are dry at that time of year, shadowy ripples in the landscape. The moon was in its second quarter. Beyond the administration building, the parabolas were limned in silver.

My cathedral.

My Stonehenge.

And while I sat, sipping a Coors, and thinking of lost cities and altar boys and frequency counts, I suddenly understood the significance of Chaney's last remark! Of course Dickinson had not read the text: that was the point!

I needed Chaney.

I called him in the morning, and flew out in the afternoon. He met me at Logan, and we drove out toward Gloucester. "There's an excellent Italian restaurant," he said. And then, without taking his eyes off the road: "What's this all about?"

I'd brought the second volume with me, and I held it up for him to see. He blinked in apparent confusion.

It was early evening, cold, wet, with the smell of approaching winter. Freezing rain pelted the windshield. The sky was gray, heavy, sagging into the city.

"Before I answer any questions, Hutch, I'd like to ask a couple. What can you tell me about military cryptography?"

He grinned. "Not much. The little I do know is probably classified." A tractor-trailer lumbered past, straining, spraying water across the windows. "What, specifically, are you interested in?"

"How complex are the navy's codes? I know they're nothing like cyrptograms, but what sort of general structure do they have?"

"First off, Harry, they're not codes. Monoalphabetic systems are codes. Like the cryptograms you mentioned. The letter 'G' always turns up, say, as an 'M.' But in military and diplomatic cryptography, the 'G' will be a different character every time it appears. And the encryption alphabet isn't usually limited to letters: we can use numbers, dollar signs, ampersands, even spaces." We splashed onto a ramp and joined the Interstate. It was sufficiently raised that we looked across rows of bleak rooftops. "Even the shape of individual words is concealed."

"How?"

"By encrypting the spaces."

I knew the answer to the next question before I asked it. "If the encryption alphabet is absolutely random, which I assume it would have to be, the frequency count would be flat. Right?"

"Yes. Given sufficient traffic, it would have to be."

"One more thing, Hutch: a sudden increase in traffic will alert anyone listening that something is happening even if he can't read the text. How do you hide that?"

"Easy. We transmit a continuous signal, twenty-four hours a day. Sometimes it's traffic, sometimes it's garbage. But you can't tell the difference."

God have mercy on us, I thought. Poor Ed Dickinson.

We sat at a small corner table well away from the main dining area. I shivered in wet shoes and a damp sweater. A small candle guttered cheerfully in front of us.

"Are we still talking about Procyon?" he asked.

I nodded. "The same pattern was received twice, three years apart, prior to the Procyon reception."

"But that's not possible." Chaney leaned forward intently. "The computer would have matched them automatically. We'd have known."

"I don't think so." Half a dozen prosperous, overweight men in topcoats had pushed in and were jostling one another in the small entry. "The two hits were on different targets: they would have looked like an echo."

Chaney reached across the table and gripped my wrist, knocking over a cup. He ignored it. "Son of a bitch," he said. "Are you suggesting there's an empire out there?"

"I don't think Ed Dickinson had any doubts."

"Why would he keep it secret?"

I'd placed the book on the table at my left hand. It rested there, its plastic cover reflecting the glittering red light of the candle. "Because they're at war," I said.

Understanding broke across Chaney's features. The color drained from his face, and it took on a pallor that was almost ghastly in the lurid light.

"He believed," I continued, "he really believed that mind equates to morality, intelligence to compassion. And what did he find after a lifetime? A civilization that had conquered the stars, but not its own passions and stupidities."

A tall young waiter presented himself. We ordered port and pasta.

"You don't really know there's a war going on out there," Chaney objected.

"Hostility then. Secrecy on a massive scale, as this must be, has unhappy implications. Dickinson would have saved us all with a vision of order and reason. . . ."

The gray eyes met mine. They were filled with pain. Two adolescent girls in the next booth were giggling. The wine came.

"What has *The Decline and Fall* to do with it?"

"It became his Bible. He was chilled to the bone by it. *You* should read it, but with caution. It's quite capable of strangling the soul. Dickinson was a rationalist; he recognized the ultimate truth in the Roman tragedy: that once expansion has stopped, decay is constant and irreversible. Every failure of reason or virtue loses more ground.

"I haven't been able to find his book on Gibbon, but I know what he'll say: that Gibbon was not writing only of the Romans, nor of the British of his own time. He was writing of us. . . .

"To anyone who thinks in those terms, who looks around him, this world is fast sliding toward a dark age."

We drank silently for a few minutes. I had the sense that time had locked in place, that we sat unmoving, the world frozen around us.

"Did I tell you," I said at last, "that I found the reference for his inscription? He must have had great respect for you, Hutch." I opened the book to the conclusion, and turned it for him to read:

The forum of the Roman people, where they assembled to enact their laws and elect their magistrates, is now enclosed for the cultivation of potherbs, or thrown open for the reception of swine and buffaloes.

Chaney stared disconsolately at me. "It's all so hard to believe. He always seemed so optimistic."

"Maybe," I said. "But I think the reverse is true. A man can survive a loss of faith in the Almighty, provided he does not also lose faith in himself. That was Dickinson's real tragedy: he came to believe exclusively in radiotelescopes, the way some people do in religions."

The food, when it came, went untasted. "What are you going to do, Harry?"

"About the Procyon text? About the probability that we have quarrelsome neighbors? I'm not afraid of that kind of information; all it means is that where you find intelligence, you will probably find stupidity. Anyway, it's time Dickinson got credit for his discovery." And I thought, maybe it'll even mean a footnote for me.

I lifted my glass in a mock toast, but Chaney did not respond. We faced each other in an uncomfortable tableau. "What's wrong?" I asked. "Thinking about Dickinson?"

"That too." The candle glinted in his eyes. "Harry, do you think *they* have a SETI project too?"

"Possibly. Why?"

"I was wondering if your aliens know we're here. This restaurant isn't much further from Sirius than Procyon is. Maybe you better eat up."

CONNIE WILLIS

The Sidon in the Mirror

Here's an absorbing and elegant story—set in an unusual mining town on a very strange new world—that suggests that the deadliest kind of mirror is that which shows us ourselves most clearly . . .

As a writer, Connie Willis has made a very big name for herself in a very short period of time. Last year she won *two* Nebula Awards, one for her superb novelette "Fire Watch," and one for her poignant short story "A Letter from the Clearys"; a few months later, "Fire Watch" went on to win her a Hugo Award as well. Her short fiction has appeared in *Isaac Asimov's Science Fiction Magazine, Omni, The Magazine of Fantasy Science & Fiction, The Berkley Showcase, Galileo, The Twilight Zone Magazine*, and elsewhere. Her first novel, written in collaboration with Cynthia Felice, was *Water Witch*. She is currently working on her first solo novel (which she assures us will *not* be the first part of a trilogy), tentatively entitled *The Bear in the Woods*. Upcoming is a collection of her short fiction, *Fire Watch and Other Stories*, from Bluejay Books. Willis lives in Woodland Park, Colorado, with a husband, a fourteen-year-old daughter, and a bulldog.

THE SIDON IN THE MIRROR

Connie Willis

We are near the spiraldown. I cannot see the mooring lights, and there are no landmarks on Paylay, but I remember how the lights of Jewell's abbey looked from here: a thin, disjointed string of Christmas tree lights, red and green and gold. Closer in you can see the red line under the buildings, and you think you are seeing the heat of Paylay, but it is only the reflection of the lights off the ground and the metalpaper undersides of Jewell's and the gaming house.

"You kin't see the heat," Jewell said on our way in from the down, "but you'll feel it. Your shoes all right?"

My shoes were fine, but they were clumsy to walk in. I would have fallen over in them at home, but here the heavier gravity almost clamped them to the ground. They had six-inch plastic soles cut into a latticework as fragile looking as the mooring tower, but they were sturdier than they looked, and they were not letting any heat get through. I wasn't feeling anything at all, and halfway to Jewell's I knelt and felt the sooty ground. It felt warm but not so hot as I had thought it would be, walking on a star.

"Leave your hand there a minute," Jewell said. I did, and then jerked my soot-covered hand up and put it in my mouth.

"Gits hot fast, din't it?" she said. "A tapper kidd fall down out here or kimm out with no shoes on and die inside of an hour of heatstroke. That's why I thought I bitter come out and wilcome you to Paylay. That's what they call this tapped-out star. You're sipposed to be able to pick up minny laying on the ground. You kin't. You have to drill a tap and build a compressor around it and hope to Gid you don't blow yoursilf up while you're doing it."

What she did not say, in the high squeaky voice we both had from the helium in the air, was that she had waited over two hours for me by the down's plastic mooring tower and that the bottoms of her feet were frying in the towering shoes. The plastic is not a very good insulator.

Open metal ribs would work far better to dissipate the heat that wells up through the thin crust of Paylay, but they can't allow any more metal here than is absolutely necessary, not with the hydrogen and oxygen ready to explode at the slightest spark.

The downpilot should have taken any potential fire-starters and metal I had away from me before he let me off the spiraldown, but Jewell had interrupted him before he could ask me what I had. "Doubletap it, will you?" she said. "I want to git back before the nixt shift. You were an hour late."

"Sorry, Jewell," the pilot said. "We hit thirty percent almost a kilometer up and had to go into a Fermat." He looked down again at the piece of paper in his hand. "The following items are contraband. Unlawful possession can result in expulsion from Paylay. Do you have any: sonic fires, electromags, matches . . ."

Jewell took a step forward and put her foot down like she was afraid the ground would give way.

"Iv course he din't. He's a pianoboard player."

The pilot laughed and said, "Okay, Jewell, take him," and she grabbed up my tote and walked me back to St. Pierre. She asked about my uncle, and she told me about the abbey and the girls and how she'd given them all house names of jewels because of her name. She told me how Taber, who ran the gaming house next door to her abbey, had christened the little string of buildings we could see in the distance St. Pierre after the patron saint of tappers, and all the time the bottoms of her feet fried like cooking meat and she never said a word.

I couldn't see her very well. She was wearing a chemiloom lantern strapped to her forehead, and she had brought one for me, but they didn't give off much light, and her face was in shadow. My uncle had told me she had a big scar that ran down the side of her face and under her chin. He said she got the scar from a fight with a sidon.

"It nearly cut the jugular," my uncle had said. "It would have if they hadn't gotten it off of her. It cut up quite a few of the tappers, too."

"What was she doing with a sidon anyway?" I asked. I had never seen one, but I had heard about them: beautiful blood-red animals with thick, soft fur and sot-razor claws, animals that could seem tame for as long as a year and then explode without warning into violence. "You can't tame them."

"Jewell thought she could," my uncle said. "One of the tappers brought it back with him from Solfatara in a cage. Somebody let it out, and it got away. Jewell went after it. Its feet were burned, and it was suffering from heatstroke. Jewell sat down on the ground and held it on her lap till someone came to help. She insisted on bringing it back to the abbey, making it into a pet. She wouldn't believe she couldn't tame it."

"But a sidon can't help what it is," I said. "It's like us. It doesn't even know it's doing it."

My uncle did not say anything, and after a minute I said, "She thinks she can tame us, too. That's why she's willing to take me, isn't it? I knew there had to be a reason she'd take me when we're not allowed on Solfatara. She thinks she can keep me from copying."

My uncle still did not answer, and I took that for assent. He had not answered any of my questions. He had suddenly said I was going, though nobody had gone off-planet since the ban, and when I asked him questions, he answered with statements that did not answer them at all.

"Why do I have to go?" I said. I was afraid of going, afraid of what might happen.

"I want you to copy Jewell. She is a kind person, a good person. You can learn a great deal from her."

"Why can't she come here? Kovich did."

"She runs an abbey on Paylay. There are not more than two dozen tappers and girls on the whole star. It is perfectly safe."

"What if there's somebody evil there? What if I copy him instead and kill somebody, like happened on Solfatara? What if something bad happens?"

"Jewell runs a clean abbey. No sots, no pervs, and the girls are well-behaved. It's nothing like the happy houses. As for Paylay itself, you shouldn't worry about it being a star. It's in the last stages of burning out. It has a crust almost two thousand feet thick, which means there's hardly any radiation. People can walk on the surface without any protective clothing at all. There's some radiation from the hydrogen taps, of course, but you won't go anywhere near them."

He had reassured me about everything except what was important. Now, trudging along after Jewell through the sooty carbon of Paylay, I knew about all the dangers, except the worst one—myself.

I could not see anything that looked like a tap. "Where are they?" I asked, and Jewell pointed back the way we had come.

"As far away as we kin git thim from St. Pierre and each ither so simm tripletapping fool kin't kill ivverybody when he blows himself up. The first sidon's off thit way, ten kilometers or so."

"Sidon?" I said, frightened. My uncle had told me the tappers had killed the sidon and made it into a rug after it nearly killed Jewell.

She laughed. "Thit's what they call the taps. Because they blow up on you and you don't even know what hit. They make thim as safe as they can, but the comprission equipmint's metal and metal means sparks. Ivvery once in awhile that whole sky over there lights up like Chrissmiss. We built St. Pierre as far away as we kidd, and there in't a scrap of metal in the whole place, but the hydrogen leaks are ivverywhere. And helium. Din't we sound like a pair iv fools squeaking at each other?"

She laughed again, and I noticed that as we had stood there looking at the black horizon, my feet had begun to feel uncomfortably hot.

It was a long walk through the darkness to the string of lights, and the whole way I watched Jewell and wondered if I had already begun to copy her. I would not know it, of course. I had not known I was copying my uncle either. One day he had asked me to play a song, and I had sat down at the pianoboard and played it. When I was finished, he said, "How long have you been able to do that?" and I did not know. Only after I had done the copying would I know it, and then only if someone told me. I trudged after Jewell in darkness and tried, tried to copy her.

It took us nearly an hour to get to the town, and when we got there, I could see it wasn't a town at all. What Jewell had called St. Pierre was only two tall metalpaper-covered buildings perched on plastic frameworks nearly two meters high and a huddle of stilt-tents. Neither building had a sign over the door, just strings of mulitcolored chemiloom lights strung along the eaves. They were fairly bright, and they reflected off the metalpaper into even more light, but Jewell took off the lantern she had strapped to her head and held it close to the wooden openwork steps, as if I couldn't see to climb up to the front door high above us without it.

"Why are you walking like thit?" she said when we got to the top of the steps, and for the first time I could see her scar. It looked almost black in the colored light of the lantern and the looms, and it was much wider than I had thought it would be, a fissure of dark puckered skin down one whole side of her face.

"Walking like what?" I said, and looked down at my feet.

"Like you kin't bear to hivv your feet touch the ground. I got my feet too hot out at the down. You didn't. So din't walk like thit."

"I'm sorry," I said. "I won't do it anymore."

She smiled at me, and the scar faded a little. "Now you just kimm on in and meet the girls. Din't mind it if they say simmthing about the way you look. They've nivver seen a Mirror before, but they're good girls." She opened the thick door. It was metalpaper backed with a thick pad of insulation. "We take our inside shoes off out here and wear shuffles inside the abbey."

It was much cooler inside. There was a plastic heat-trigger fan set in the ceiling and surrounded by rose-colored chemilooms. We were in an anteroom with a rack for the high shoes and the lanterns. They dangled by their straps.

Jewell sat down on a chair and began unbuckling her bulky shoes. "Din't ivver go out without shoes and a lantern," she said. She gestured toward the rack. "The little ones with the twillpaper hiddbands are for town. They only list about an hour. If you're going out to the taps or the spiraldown, take one iv the big ones with you."

She looked different in the rosy light. Her scar hardly showed at all. Her voice was different too, deeper. She sounded older than she had at the down. I looked up and around at the air.

"We blow nitrogen and oxygen in from a tap behind the house," she said. "The tappers din't like having squeaky little helium voices when they're with the girls. You can't git rid of the helium, or the hydrogen either. They leak in ivverywhere. The bist you can do is dilute it. You shid be glad you weren't here at the beginning, before they tapped an atmosphere. You had to wear vacuum suits thin." She pried off her shoe. The bottom of her foot was a mass of blisters. She started to stand up and then sat down again.

"Yill for Carnie," said said. "Till her to bring some bandages."

I hung my outside shoes on the rack and opened the inner door. It fit tightly, though it opened with just a touch. It was made of the same insulation as the outer door. It opened onto a fancy room, all curtains and fur rugs and hanging looms that cast little pools of colored light, green and rose and gold. The pianoboard stood over against one wall on a carved plastic table. I could not see anyone in the room, and I could not hear voices for the sound of the blowers. I started across a blood-red fur rug to another door, hung with curtains.

"Jewell?" a woman's voice said. The blowers kicked off, and she said, "Jewell?" again, and I saw that I had nearly walked past her. She was sitting in a white velvet chair in a little bay that would have been a window if this were not Paylay. She was wearing a white satinpaper dress with a long skirt. Her hair was piled on top of her head, and there was a string of pearls around her long neck. She was sitting so quietly, with her hands in her lap and her head turned slightly away from me, that I had not even seen her.

"Are you Carnie?" I said.

"No," she said, and she didn't look up at me. "What is it?"

"Jewell got her feet burned," I said. "She needs bandages. I'm the new pianoboard player."

"I know," the girl said. She lifted her head a little in the direction of the stairs and called, "Carnie. Get the remedy case."

A gril came running down the stairs in an orange-red robe and no shoes. "Is it Jewell?" she said to the girl in the white dress, and when she nodded, Carnie ran past us into the other room. I could hear the hollow sound of an insulated door opening. The girl had made no move to come and see Jewell. She sat perfectly still in the white chair, her hands lying quietly in her lap.

"Jewell's feet are pretty bad," I said. "Can't you at least come see them?"

"No," she said, and looked up at me. "My name is Pearl," she said. "I had a friend once who played the pianoboard."

Even then, I wouldn't have known she was blind except that my uncle had told me. "Most of the girls are newcomers Jewell hired for Paylay right off the ships, before the happy houses could ruin them," my uncle had said. "She only brought a couple of the girls with her from Solfatara, girls who worked with her in the happy house she came out of. Carnie, and I think Sapphire, and Pearl, the blond one."

"Blind?" I had said. Solfatara is a long way out, but any place has doctors.

"He cut . . . the optic nerve was servered. They did orb implants and reattached all the muscles, but it was only cosmetic repair. She can't see anything."

Even after all the horrible stories I had heard about Solfatara, it had shocked me to think that someone could do something like that. I remember thinking that the man must have been incredibly cruel to have done such a thing, that it would have been kinder to kill her outright than to have left her helpless and injured like that in a place like Solfatara.

"Who did it to her?" I said.

"A tapper," he said, and for a minute he looked very much like Kovich, so much that I asked, "Was it the same man who broke Kovich's hands?"

"Yes," my uncle said.

"Did they kill him?" I said, but that was not the question I had intended to ask. I had meant did Kovich kill him, but I had said "they."

And my uncle, not looking like Kovich at all, had said, "Yes, they killed him," as if that were the right question after all.

The orb implants and the muscle reattachments had been very good. Her eyes were a beautiful pale gray, and someone had taught her to follow voices with them. There was nothing at all in the angle of her head or her eyes or her quiet hands to tell me she was blind or make me pity her, and standing there looking down at her, I was glad, glad that they had killed him. I hoped that they had cut his eyes out first.

Carnie darted past us with the remedy case, and I said, still looking down at Pearl, "I'll go and see if I can help her." I went back out into the anteroom and watched while Carnie put some kind of oil on Jewell's feet and then a meshlike pad, and wrapped her feet in bandages.

"This is Carnelian," Jewell said. "Carnie, this is our new pianoboard player."

She smiled at me. She looked very young. She must have been only a child when she worked in the happy house on Solfatara with Jewell.

"I bit you can do real fancy stuff with those hands," she said, and giggled.

"Don't tease him," Jewell said. "He's here to play the pianoboard."

"I *meant* on the pianoboard. You din't look like a real mirror. You know, shiny and ivverything? Who are you going to copy?"

"He's not going to copy innybody," Jewell said sharply. "He's going to play the pianoboard, and that's all. Is supper riddy?"

"No. I was jist in the kitchen and Sapphire wasn't even there yit." She looked back up at me. "When you copy somebody, do you look like them?"

"No," I said. "You're thinking of a chameleon."

"You're not thinking it all," Jewell said to her and stood up. She winced a little as she put her weight on her feet. "Go borrow a pair of Garnet's shuffles. I'll nivver be able to git mine on. And go till Sapphire to doubletap hersilf into the kitchen."

She let me help her to the stairs but not up them. "When Carnie comes back, you hivv her show you your room. We work an eight and eight here, and it's nearly time for the shift. You kin practice till supper if you want."

She went up two steps and stopped. "If Carnie asks you inny more silly questions, tell her I told her to lit you alone. I don't want to hear any more nonsinse about copying and Mirrors. You're here to play the pianoboard."

She went on up the stairs, and I went back into the music room. Pearl was still there, sitting in the white chair, and I didn't know whether she was included in the instructions to leave me alone, so I sat down on the hard wooden stool and looked at the pianoboard.

It had a wooden soundboard and bridges, but the strings were plastic instead of metal. I tried a few chords, and it seemed to have a good sound in spite of the strings. I played a few scales and more chords and looked at the names on the hardcopies that stood against the music rack. I can't read music, of course, but I could see by the titles that I knew most of the songs.

"It isn't nonsense, is it?" Pearl said, "About the copying." She spoke slowly and without the clipped accent Jewell and Carnie had.

I turned around on the stool and faced her. "No," I said. "Mirrors have to copy. They can't help themselves. They don't even know who they're copying. Jewell doesn't believe me. Do you?"

"The worst thing about being blind is not that things are done to you," she said, and looked up at me again with her blind eyes. "It's that you don't know who's doing them."

Carnie came in through the curtained door. "I'm sipposed to show you around," she said. "Oh, Pearl, I wish you kidd see him. He has eight fingers on each hand, and he's really tall. Almost to the ceiling. And his skin is bright red."

"Like a sidon's," Pearl said, looking at me.

Carnie looked down at the blood-red rug she was standing on. "Jist like," she said, and dragged me upstairs to show me my room and the clothes I was to wear and to show me off to the other girls. They were already dressed for the shift in trailing satinpaper dresses that matched their names. Garnet wore rose-red chemilooms in her upswept hair, Emerald an elaborately lit collar.

Carnie got dressed in front of me, stepping out of her robe and into an orange-red dress as if I weren't watching. She asked me to fasten her armropes of winking orange, lifting up her red curls so I could tie the strings of the chemilooms behind her shoulders. I could not decide then if she were trying to seduce me or get me to copy her or simply to convince me that she was the naive child she pretended to be.

I thought then that whatever she was trying, she had failed. She had succeeded only in convincing me of what my uncle had already told me. In spite of her youth, her silliness, I could well believe she had been on Solfatara, had known all of it, the pervs, the sots, the worst the happy houses had to offer. I think now she didn't mean anything by it except that she wanted to be cruel, that she was simply poking at me as if I were an animal in a cage.

At supper, watching Sapphire set Pearl's plate for her between taped marks, I wondered whether Carnie was ever cruel to Pearl as she had been to me, shifting the plate slightly as she set it down or moving her chair so she could not find it.

Sapphire set the rest of the plates on the table, her eyes dark blue from some old bitterness, and I thought, Jewell shouldn't have brought any of them with her from Solfatara except Pearl. Pearl is the only one who hasn't been ruined by it. Her blindness has kept her safe, I thought. She has been protected from all the horrors because she couldn't see them. Perhaps her blindness protects her from Carnie, too, I thought. Perhaps that is the secret, that she is safe inside her blindness and no one can hurt her, and Jewell knows that. I did not think then about the man who had blinded her, and how she had not been safe from him at all.

Jewell called the meal to order. "I want you to make our new pianoboard player wilcome," she said. She reached across the table and patted Carnie's hand. "Thank you for doing the introductions, and for bandaging my foot," she said, and I thought, Pearl is safe after all. Jewell has tamed Carnie and all the rest of them. I did not think about the sidon she had tamed, and how it now lay on the floor in front of the cardroom door.

The first shift Jewell decked me out in formals and a black-red dog collar and had me stand at the door with her as she greeted the tappers. They were in formals, too, under their soot-black work jackets. They hung the many-pocketed jackets, heavy with tools, on the rack in the anteroom along with their lanterns and sat down to take off their high shoes with hands almost as red as mine. They had washed their hands and faces, but their fingernails were black with soot, and there was soot in every line of their palms. Their faces looked hot and raw, and they all had a broad pale band across their foreheads from the lantern strap. One of them, whom Jewell called Scorch, had singed off his eyebrows and a long strip of hair on top of his head.

"You'll meet almost all the tappers this shift. The gaming house will close hiffway through and the rist of them will come over. Taber and I stagger the shifts so simmthing's always open."

She didn't introduce me, though some of the tappers looked at my eight-fingered hands curiously, and one of the men looked surprised and then angry. He looked as if he was going to say something to me, and then changed his mind, his face getting redder and darker until the lantern line stood out like a scar.

When they were all inside the music room, Jewell led me to the pianoboard and had me sit down and spread my hands out over the keyboard, ready to play. Then she said. "This is my new pianoboard player, boys. Say hillo to him."

"What's his name, Jewell?" one of the men said. "You ginna give him a fancy name like the girls?"

"I nivver thought about it," she said. "What do you think?"

The tapper who had turned so red said loudly, "I think you shid call him sidon and kick him out to burn on Paylay. He's a Mirror."

"I alriddy got a Carnelian and a Garnet. And I had a sidon once. I giss I'll call him Ruby." She looked calmly over at the man who had spoken. "That okay with you, Jick?"

His face was as dark a red as mine. "I didn't say it to be mean, Jewell," he said. "You're doing what you did with the sidon, taking in simmthing thit'll turn on you. They won't even lit Mirrors on Solfatara."

"I think that's probably a good ricommendation considering what they do lit on Solfatara," Jewell said quietly. "Sot-gamblers, tap-stealers, pervers . . ."

"You saw that Mirror kill the tapper. Stid there right in front iv ivverybody, and nobody kidd stop him. Nobody. The tapper bigging for mercy, his hands tied in front of him, and thit Mirror coming at him with a sot-razor, smiling while he did it."

"Yes," Jewell said. "I saw it. I saw a lot of things on Solfatara. But this is Paylay. And this is my pianoboard player Ruby. I din't think a man should be outlawed till he does simmthing, di you, Jick?" She put her hand on my shoulder. "Do you know 'Back Home?' " she said. Of course I knew it. I knew all the tapper songs. Kovich had played in every happy house on Solfatara before somebody broke his hands. He had called "Back Home" his ropecutter.

"Play it, thin," she said. "Show thim what you can do, Ruby."

I played it with lots of trills and octave stretches, all the fancy things Kovich could do with five fingers instead of eight. Then I stopped and waited. The nitrogen blowers kicked off, and even the fans made no noise. During the song, Jewell had gone and stood next to Jack, putting her hand on his shoulder, trying to tame him. I wondered if she had succeeded. Jack looked at me, and then at Jewell, and back at me again. His hand went into his formals shirt, and my heart almost stopped before he brought it out again.

"Jewell's right," he said. "You shiddn't judge a man till you see what he does. That was gid playing," he said, handing me a plastic-wrapped cigar. "Wilcome to Paylay."

Jewell nodded at me, and I extended my hand and took the cigar. I fumbled to get the slippery plastic off and then had to look at the cigar a minute to make sure I was getting the right end in my mouth. I stuck it in my mouth and reached inside my shirt for my sparker. I didn't know what would happen when I lit the cigar. For all I understood what was going on, the cigar might be full of gunpowder. Jewell did not look worried, but then she had misjudged the sidon, too.

My hand closed on the sparker inside my shirt, the nitrogen blowers suddenly kicked on, and Jack said lazily, "Now whit you ginna light that with, Ruby? There in't a match on Paylay!"

Jewell laughed, and the men guffawed. I pulled my empty hand sheepishly out of my jacket and took the cigar out of my mouth to look at it. "I forgot you can't smoke on Paylay," I said.

"You and ivvery tapper that kimms in on the down," Jewell said. "Ive seen Jick play that joke on how many newcomers?"

"Ivvery one," Jack said, looking pleased with himself. "It even worked on you, Jewell, and you weren't a newcomer."

"It did not, you tripletapping liar," she said. "Lit's hear simmthing else, Ruby," she said. "Whit do you want Ruby to play, boys?"

Scorch shouted out a song, and I played it, and then another, but I do not know what they were. It had been a joke, offer the newcomer a cigar and then watch him try to light it on a star where no open flames are allowed. A good joke, and Jack had done it in spite of what he had seen on Solfatara to show Jewell he didn't think I was a sidon, that he would wait to see what I would do before he judged me.

And that would have been too late. What would have happened when I lit the cigar? Would the house have gone up in a ball of flame, or all of St. Pierre? The hydrogen-oxygen ratio had been high enough in the upper atmosphere that we had had to shut off the engines above a kilometer and spiral in, and here the fans were pumping in even more oxygen. Half of Paylay might have gone up.

I knew how it had happened. Jewell had interrupted the down-pilot before he could ask about sparkers, and now, because her feet had hurt, there was a live sparker in her house. And she had just convinced Jack I was not dangerous.

I had stopped playing, sitting there staring blindly at the keyboard, the unlit cigar clamped so hard between my teeth I had nearly bitten it through. The men were still shouting out the names of songs, but Jewell stepped between them and me and put a hardcopy on the music rack. "No more riquists," she said. "Pearl is going to sing for you."

Pearl stood up and walked unassisted from her white chair to the pianoboard. She stopped no more than an inch from me and put her hand down certainly on the end of the keyboard. I looked at the music. It showed a line of notes before her part began, but I did not know that version, only the song that Kovich had known, and that began on the first note of the verse. I could not nod at her, and she could not see my hands on the keys.

"I don't know the introduction," I said. "Just the verse. What should I do?"

She bent down to me. "Put your hand on mine when you are ready to begin, and I will count three," she said, and straightened again, leaving her hand where it was.

I looked down at her hand. Carnie had told her about my hands, and if I touched her lightly, with only the middle fingers, she might not even be able to tell it from a human's touch. I wanted more than anything not to frighten her. I did not think I could bear it if she flinched away from me.

Now I think it would have been better if she had, that I could have stood it better than this, sitting here with her head on my lap, waiting. If she had flinched, Jack would have seen her. He would have seen her draw away from me, and that would have been enough for him to grab me by the dog collar and throw me out the door, kick me down the wooden steps so hard that the sparker bounced out, leave me to cook in the furnace of Paylay.

"Now whit did you do thit for?" Jewell would have said. "He din't do innything but tich her hand."

"And he'll nivver do innything ilse to her either." he would have said, and handed Jewell the sparker. And I would never have been able to do anything else to her.

But she did not flinch. She took a light breath that took no longer than it did for my hand to return to the keys and hit the first note on the count of three, and we began together. I did not do any trills, any octave stretches. Her voice was sweet and thready and true. She didn't need me.

The men applauded after Pearl's song and started calling out the names of other songs. Some I didn't know, and I wondered how I could explain that to them, but Jewell said, "Now, now, boys, Let's not use up our pianoboard player in one shift. Lit him go to bid. He'll be here next shift. Who wants a game of katmai?" She reached over and pulled the cover down over the keyboard. "Use the front stairs," she said. "The tappers take the girls up the back way."

Pearl bent toward me and said, "Good night, Ruby," and then took Jack's arm as if she knew right where he was and went through the curtained door to the cardroom. The others followed, two by two, until all the girls were taken, and then in a straggling line. Jewell unfastened the heavy drapes so they fell across the door behind them.

I went upstairs and took off the paper shuffles and the uncomfortable collar and sat on the edge of the bed Jewell had fixed for me by putting a little table at the end for extra length. I thought about Pearl and Jack and how I was going to give Jewell the sparker at the beginning of the next shift, and wondered who I was copying. I looked at myself in the little plastic mirror over the bed, trying to see Jewell or Jack in my face.

I had left my cigar on the music rack. I didn't want Jack to find it there and think I had rejected it. I put my shuffles back on and went downstairs. There was nobody in the music room, and the drapes were still drawn across the door of the cardroom. I went over to the pianoboard and got the cigar. I had bitten it almost through, and now I bit the ragged end off. Then I chomped down on the new end and sat down on the piano stool, spreading out my hands as far as they would go across the keyboard.

"I understand you're a Mirror," a man's voice said from the recesses of Pearl's chair. "I knew a Mirror once. Or he knew me. Isn't that how it is?"

I almost said, "You're not supposed to sit in that chair," but I found I could not speak.

The man stood up and came toward me. He was dressed like the other men, with a broad black dog collar, but his hands and face were almost white, and there was no lighter band across his forehead. "My name is Taber," he said, in a slow, drawling voice unlike the fast, vowel-shortening accents of the others. I wondered if he had come from Solfatara. All the rest of them except Pearl shortened their vowels, bit them off like I had bit the cigar. Pearl alone seemed to have no accent, as if her blindness had protected her from the speech of Solfatara, too.

"Welcome to St. Pierre," he said, and I felt a shock of fear. He had lied to Jewell. I did not know who St. Pierre was, but I knew as he spoke that St. Pierre was not the patron saint of tappers, and that Taber's calling the town that was some unspeakably cruel joke that only he understood.

"I have to go upstairs," I said, and my hand shook as I held the cigar. "Jewell's in the cardroom."

"Oh," he said lazily, taking a cigar from his pocket and unwrapping it. "Is Pearl there, too?"

"Pearl?" I said, so frightened I could not breathe.

He patted his formals pockets and reached inside his shirt. "Yes. You know, the blind girl. The pretty one." He pulled a sparker from his inside pocket, cocked it back, and looked at me. "What a pity she's blind. I wish I knew what happened. She's never told a soul, you know," he said, and clicked the sparker.

It was not a real sparker. I could see, after a frozen moment, that there was no liquid in it at all. He clicked it twice more, held it to the end of his cigar in dreadful pantomime, and replaced it in his pocket.

"I do wish I could find out," he said. "I could put the knowledge to good use."

"I can't help you," I said, and moved toward the stairs.

He stepped in front of me. "Oh, I think you can. Isn't that what Mirrors are for?" he said, and drew on the unlit cigar and blew imaginary smoke into my face.

"I won't help you," I said, so loudly I fancied Jewell would come and tell Taber to let me alone, as she had told Carnie. "You can't make me help you."

"Of course not," he said. "That isn't how it works. But of course you know that," and let me pass.

I sat on my bed the rest of the shift, holding the real sparker between my hands, waiting until I could tell Jewell what Taber had said to me. But the next shift was sleeping-shift, and the shift after that I played tapper requests for eight hours straight. Most of that time Taber stood by the pianoboard, flicking imaginary ashes onto my hands.

After the shift Jewell came to ask me whether Jack or anyone else had bothered me, and I did not tell her about Taber after all. During the next sleeping-shift I hid the sparker between the mattress and the springs of my bed.

On the waking shifts I kept as close as I could to Jewell, trying to make myself useful to her, trying not to copy the way she walked on her bandaged feet. When I was not playing, I moved among the tappers with glasses of iced and watered-down liquor on a tray and filled out the account cards for the men who wanted to take girls upstairs. On the off-shifts I learned to work the boards that sent out accounts to Solfatara, and to do the laundry, and after a couple of weeks Jewell had me help with the body checks on the girls. She scanned for perv marks and sot scars as well as the standard GHS every abbey has to screen for. Pearl did not have a mark on her, and I was relieved. I had had an idea that Taber might be torturing her somehow.

Jewell left us alone while I helped her get dressed after the scan, and I said, "Taber is a very bad man. He wants to hurt you."

"I know," she said. She was standing very still while I clipped the row of pearl buttons on the back of her dress together.

"Why?"

"I don't know," she said. "It's like the sidon."

"You mean he can't help himself, that he doesn't know what he's doing?" I said, outraged. "He knows exactly what he's doing."

"The tappers used to poke at the sidon with sticks when it was in the cage," she said. "They couldn't reach it to really hurt it, though, and Taber couldn't stand that. He made the tappers give him the key to the cage just so he could get to it. Just so he could hurt it. Now why would he want to hurt the sidon?"

"Because it was helpless," I said, and I wondered if the man who'd blinded Pearl had been like that. "Because it couldn't protect itself."

"Jewell and I were in the same happy house on Solfatara," she said. "We had a friend there, a pianoboard player like you. He was very tall like you, too, and he was the kindest person I ever knew. Sometimes you remind me of him." She walked certainly to the door, as if she were not counting the memorized steps. "A cage is a safe place as long as nobody has the key. Don't worry, Ruby. He can't get in." She turned and looked at me. "Will you come and play for me?"

"Yes," I said, and followed her down to the music room. Before the shifts started, while the girls were upstairs dressing, she liked to sit in the white chair and listen to me play. She understood, more than any of the others, that I could play only the songs I had copied from Kovich.

Jewell, to the end, thought I could read music, and Taber even brought me hardcopies from Solfatara. Pearl simply said the names of songs, and I played them if I knew them. She never asked for one I didn't know, and I thought that was because she listened carefully to the tappers' requests and my refusals, and I was grateful.

I sat down at the pianoboard and looked at Pearl in the mirror. I had asked Jewell for the mirror so I could see over my shoulder. I had told her I wanted it so she could signal me songs and breaks and sometimes the ropecutter if the men got rough or noisy, but it was really so I could keep Taber from standing there without my knowing it.

" 'Back Home,' " Pearl said. I could hardly hear her over the nitrogen blowers. I began playing it, and Taber came in. He walked swiftly over to her and then stood quite still, and between my playing and the noise of the blowers, she did not hear him. He stood about half a meter from her, close enough to touch her but just out of reach if she had put her hand out to try to find him.

He took the cigar out of his mouth and bent down as if he were going to speak to her, and instead he pursed his lips and blew gently at her. I could almost see the smoke. At first she didn't seem to notice, but then she shivered and drew her shinethread shawl closer about her.

He stopped and smiled at her a moment and then reached out and touched her with the tip of his cigar, lightly, on the shoulder, as if he intended to burn her, and then darted it back out of her reach. She swatted at the air, and he repeated the little pantomime again and again, until she stood and put her hands up helplessly against what she could not see. As she did so, he moved swiftly and silently to the door so that when she cried out, "Who is it? Who's there?" he said in his slow drawl, "It's me, Pearl. I've just come in. Did I frighten you?"

"No," she said, and sat back down again. But when he took her hand, she flinched away from him as I'd thought she would from me. And all the while I had not missed a beat of the song.

"I just came over to see you for a minute," Taber said, "and to hear your pianoboard player. He gets better every day, doesn't he?"

Pearl didn't answer. I saw in the mirror that her hands lay crossed in her lap again and didn't move.

"Yes," he said, and walked toward me, flicking imaginary ashes from his unlit cigar onto my hands. "Better and better," he said softly. "I can almost see my face in you, Mirror."

"What did you say?" Pearl said, frightened.

"I said I'd better go see Jewell a minute about some business and then get back next door. Jack found a new hydrogen tap today, a big one."

He went back through the card room to the kitchen, and I sat at the pianoboard, watching in the mirror until I saw the kitchen door shut behind him.

"Tabar was in the room the whole time," I said. "He was . . . doing things to you."

"I know," she said.

"You shouldn't let him. You should stop him," I said violently, and as soon as I said it I knew that she knew that I had not stopped him either. "He's a very bad man," I said.

"He has never locked me in," she said after a minute. "He has never tied me up."

"He has never known how before," I said, and I knew it was true. "He wants me to find out for him."

She bent her head to her hands, which still lay crossed at the wrists, almost relaxed, showing nothing of what she was thinking. "And will you?" she said.

"I don't know."

"He's trying to get you to copy him, isn't he?" she said.

"Yes."

"And you think it's working?"

"I don't know," I said. "I can't tell when I'm copying. Do I sound like Taber?"

"No," she said, so definitely that I was relieved. I had listened to myself with an anxious ear, hoping for Jewell's shortened vowels and tapper slang, waiting in dread for the slow, lazy speech of Taber. I did not think I had heard either of them, but I had been afraid I wouldn't know if I did.

"Do you know who I'm copying?" I said.

"You walk like Jewell," she said, and smiled a little. "It makes her furious."

It was the end of the shift before I realized that, like my uncle, she had not really answered what I had asked.

Jack's new tap turned out to be so big that he needed a crew to help put up the compressors, and for several shifts hardly anyone was in the house, including Taber. Because business was so slack, Jewell even let some of the girls go over to the gaming house. Taber didn't go near the tap, but he didn't come over quite so often either, and when he did, he spent his time upstairs or with Carnie, talking to her in a low voice and clicking the speaker over and over again, as if he could not help himself. Then, once the compressors were set up and the sidon working, the men poured back into St. Pierre, and Taber was too busy to come over at all.

The one time he came, he found Pearl alone with me, he said, "It's

Taber, Pearl," almost before I had banged a loud chord on the keys and said, "Taber's here." He did not have his cigar with him, or his sparker, and he did not even speak to me. Watching Pearl talk to him, her head gracefully turned away from him, her hands in her lap, I could almost believe that he would not succeed, that nothing could hurt her, safe in her blindness.

We were so busy that Jewell hardly spoke to me, but when she did, she told me sharply that if I had nothing better to do than copy her, I should tend bar, and set me to passing out the watered liquor she had brought out in honor of the new sidon. She did the boards for the week herself while I ran the body checks.

Pearl, naked under the scan, looked serene and unhurt. Carnie had sot-scars under her arms. I did not report her. If Jewell found out, she would send Carnie back to Solfatara, and I wanted Tabor to be working on Carnie, giving her sots and trying to get her to help him, because then I could believe he had given up on me. I did not dare believe that he had given up on Pearl, but I did not think that he and Carnie alone could hurt her, no matter what they did to her. Not without my help. Not so long as I was copying Jewell.

I told Pearl about Carnie. "I think she's on sots," I said. We were alone in the music room. Jewell was upstairs, trying to catch up the boards. Carnie was in the kitchen, taking her turn at supper. "I saw what looked like scars."

"I know," Pearl said, and I wondered if there was anything she did not see, in spite of her blindness.

"I think you should be careful. It's Taber that's giving them to her. He's using her to hurt you. Don't tell her anything."

She said nothing, and after a minute I turned back to the pianoboard and waited for her to name a song.

"I was born in the happy house. My mother worked there. Did you know that?" she said quietly.

"No," I said, keeping my hands spread across the keyboard, as though they could support me. I did not look at her.

"I have told myself all these years that as long as no one knew what happened, I was safe."

"Doesn't Jewell know?"

She shook her head. "Nobody knows. My mother told them he threatened her with the sot-razor, that there was nothing she could do."

The nitrogen blowers kicked on just then, and I jumped at the sound and looked into the mirror. I could see the sidon in the mirror, and standing on its red murdered skin, Taber. Carnie had let him in through the kitchen and turned the blowers up, and now he stood between the noisy blowers, smiling and flicking imaginary ash onto the carpet beside Pearl's chair. I took my hands off the keyboard and laid them in my lap. "Carnie's in the kitchen," I said. "I don't know if the door's shut."

"There was a tapper who came to the house," Pearl said. "He was a very bad man, but my mother loved him. She said she couldn't help herself. I think that was true." For a moment she looked directly into the mirror with her blind eyes, and I willed Taber to click the sparker that I knew he was fingering so that Pearl would hear it and withdraw into her cage, safe and silent.

"It was Christmas time," she said, and the blowers kicked off. Into the silence she said, "I was ten years old, and Jewell gave me a little gold necklace with a pearl on it. She was only fourteen, but she was already working in the house. They had a tree in the music room and there were little lights on it, all different colors, strung on a string. Have you ever seen lights like that, red and green and gold all strung together?"

I thought of the strings of multicolored chemilooms I had seen from the spiraldown, the very first thing I had seen on Paylay. Nobody has told her, I thought, in all this time nobody has told her, and at the thought of the vast cage of kindness built all around her, my hand jerked up and hit the edge of the keyboard. She heard the sound and looked up.

"Is Taber here?" she said, and my hand hovered above the keyboard.

"No, of course not," I said, and my hand settled back in my lap like the spiraldown coming to rest on its moorings. "I'll tell you when he comes."

"The tapper sent my mother a dress with lights on it, too, red and green and gold like the tree," Pearl said. "When he came, he said, 'You look like a Chrissmiss tree,' and kissed her on the cheek. 'What do you want for Chrissmiss?' my mother said. 'I will give you anything.' I can remember her standing there in the lighted dress under the tree." She stopped a minute, and when I looked in the mirror, she had turned her head so that she seemed to be looking straight at Taber. "He asked for me."

"What did he do to you?" I said.

"I don't remember," she said. Her hands struggled and lay still, and I knew what he had done. He had locked her in, and she had never escaped. He had tied her hands together, and she had never gotten free. I looked down at my own hands, crossed at the wrists like hers and not even struggling.

"Didn't anyone come to help you?" I said.

"The pianoboard player," she said. "He beat the door down. He broke both his hands so he could not play anymore. He made my mother call the doctor. He told her he would kill her if she didn't. When he tried to help me, I ran away from him. I didn't want him to help me. I wanted to die. I ran and ran and ran, but I couldn't see to get away."

"Did he kill the tapper who blinded you?" I said.

"While he was trying to find me, my mother let the tapper out the back door. I ran and ran and then I fell down. The pianoboard player came and held me in his arms until the doctor came. I made him promise to kill the tapper. I made him promise to finish killing me," she said, so softly I could hardly hear her. "But he didn't."

The blowers kicked on again, and I looked into the mirror, but Taber wasn't there. Carnie had let him out the back way.

He did not come back for several shifts. When he did, it was to tell Jewell he was going to Solfatara. He told Pearl he would bring her a present and whispered to me, "What do you want for Christmas, Ruby? You've earned a present."

While he was gone Jack hit another tap, almost on top of the first one, and Jewell locked up the liquor. The men didn't want music. They wanted to talk about putting in a double, even a triple tap. I was grateful for that. I was not sure I could play with my hands tied.

Jewell told me to go meet Taber at the mooring, and then changed her mind. "I'm worried about those sotted fools out at Jick's sidon. Doubletapping. They kidd blow the whole star. You'd bitter stay here and hilp me."

Taber came before the shift. "I'll bring you your present tonight, Pearl," he said. "I know you'll like it. Ruby helped me pick it out." I watched the sudden twitching of Pearl's hands, but my own didn't even move.

Taber waited almost until the end of the shift, spending nearly half of it in the card room with Carnie leaning heavily over his shoulder. She had already gotten her present. Her eyes were bright from the sot-slice, and she stumbled once against him and nearly fell.

"Bring me a cigar, Ruby," he shouted to me. "And look in the inside jacket pocket. I brought a present back for everybody." Pearl was standing all alone in the middle of the music room, her hands in front of her. I didn't look at her. I went straight upstairs to my room, got what I needed, and then went back down into the anteroom to where Taber's tapper jacket was hanging, and got the cigar out of Taber's pocket. His sparker was there, too.

The present was a flat package wrapped in red and green paper, and I took it and the cigar to Taber. He had come into the music room and was sitting in Pearl's chair. Carnie was sitting on his lap with her arm around his neck.

"You didn't bring the sparker, Ruby," Taber said. I waited for him to tell me to go and get it. "Never mind," he said. "Do you know what day this is?"

"I do," Carnie said softly, and Taber slid his hand up to hold hers where it lay loosely on his shoulder.

"It's Chrissmiss Day," he said, pronouncing it with the Solfatara accent. He took his hand away from Carnie's so he could lean back and puff on his cigar, and Carnie took her red, bruised hand in her other one and held it up to her bosom, her sot-bright eyes full of pain. "I said to myself we should have some Chrissmiss songs. Do you know any Chrissmiss songs, Ruby?"

"No," I said.

"I didn't think you would," Taber said. "So I brought you a present." He waved the cigar at me. "Go ahead. Open it."

I pulled the red and green paper off and took out the hardcopies. There were a dozen Christmas songs. I knew them all.

"Pearl, you'll sing a Chrissmiss song for me, won't you?" Taber said.

"I don't know any," she said. She had not moved from where she stood.

"Of course you do," Taber said. "They played them every Chrissmiss time in the happy houses on Solfatara. Come on. Ruby'll play it for you."

I sat down at the pianoboard, and Pearl came and stood beside me with her hand on the end of the keyboard. I stood the hardcopies up against the music rack and put my hands on the keyboard.

"He knows," she said, so softly none of the men could have heard her. "You told him."

"No, it's a coincidence," I said. "Maybe it is really Christmas time on Solfatara. Nobody keeps track of the year on Paylay. Maybe it is Christmas."

"If you told him, if he knows how it happened, I am not safe anymore. He'll be able to get in. He'll be able to hurt me." She took a staggering step away from the pianoboard as if she were going to run. I took hold of her wrist.

"I didn't tell him," I said. "I would never let him hurt you. But if you don't sing the song, he'll know there's something wrong. I'll play the first song through for you." I let go of her wrist, and her hand went limp and relaxed on the end of the keyboard.

I played the song through and stopped. The version I knew didn't have an introduction, so I spread the fingers of my right hand across the octave and a half of the opening chord and touched her hand with my left.

She flinched. She did not move her hand away or even make any movement the men, gathered around us now, could have seen. But a tremor went through her hand. I waited a moment, and then I touched her again, with all my fingers, hard, and started the song. She sang the song all the way through, and my hands, which had not been able to come down on a single chord of warning, were light and sure on the keyboard. When it was over, the men called for another, and I put it on the music rack and then sat, as she stood silent and still, unflinching, waiting for what was to come.

Taber looked up inquiringly, casually, and Jewell frowned and half-turned toward the door. Scorch banged through the thick inner door and stopped, trying to get his breath. He still had his lantern strapped to his forehead, and when he bent over trying to catch his breath in gasping hiccoughs, the strip where the hair had been burned off was as red as his face and starting to blister.

"One of the sidons blew, didn't it?" Jewell said, and her scar slashed black as a fissure across her cheek. "Which one?"

Scorch still couldn't speak. He nodded with his whole body, bent over double again, and tried to straighten. "It's Jick," he said. "He tried to tripletap, and the whole thing wint up."

"Oh, my God," Sapphire said, and ran into the kitchen.

"How bad is it?" Jewell said.

"Jick's dead, and there are two burned bad—Paulsen and the tapper that came in with Taber last shift. I don't know his name. They were right on top of it when it went, putting the comprissor on."

The tappers had been in motion the whole time he spoke, putting on their jackets and going for their shoes. Taber heaved Carnie off his lap and stood up. Sapphire came back from the kitchen dressed in pants and carrying the remedy case. Garnet put her shawl around Scorch's shoulders and helped him into Pearl's chair.

Taber said calmly, "Are there any other sidons close?" He looked unconcerned, almost amused, with Carnie leaning limply against him, but his left hand was clenched, the thumb moving up and down as if he were clicking the sparker.

"Mine," Scorch said. "It didn't kitch, but the comprissor caught fire and Jick's clothes, and they're still burning." He looked up apologetically at Jewell. "I didn't have nithing to put the fire out with. I dragged the ither two up onto my comprissor platform so they widdn't cook."

Pearl and I had not moved from the pianoboard. I looked at Taber in the mirror, waiting for him to say, "I'll stay here, Jewell. I'll take care of things here," but he didn't. He disengaged himself from Carnie. "I'll go get the stretchers at the gaming house and meet you back here," he said.

"Let me get your jacket for you," I said, but he was already gone.

The tappers banged out the doors, Sapphire with them. Garnet ran upstairs. Jewell went into the anteroom to put her outside shoes on.

I stood up and went out into the anteroom. "Let me go with you," I said.

"I want you ti stay here and take care of Pearl," she said. She could not squeeze her bandaged foot into the shoe. She bent down and began unwinding the bandage.

"Garnet can stay. You'll need help carrying the men back."

She dropped the bandage onto the floor and jammed her foot into the shoe, wincing. "You din't know the way. You kidd git lost and fall into a sidon. You're safer here." She tried the other shoe, stood up and jammed her bandaged foot into it, and sat back down to fix the straps.

"I'm not safe anywhere," I said. "Please don't leave me here. I'm afraid of what might happen."

"Even if the sidons all go up, the fire won't git this far."

"It isn't those sidons I'm afraid of," I said harshly. "You let a sidon loose in the house once before and look what happened."

She straightened up and looked at me, the scar as black and hot as lava against her red face. "A sidon is an animal," she said. "It kin't help itself." She stood up gingerly, testing her unbandaged feet. "Taber's going with me," she said.

She was not as blind as I had feared, but she still didn't see. "Don't you understand?" I said gently. "Even if he goes with you, he'll still be here."

"Are you ready, Jewell?" Taber said. He had a lantern strapped to his forehead, and he was carrying a large red and green wrapped bundle.

"I've gitta git another lantern from upstairs," Jewell said.

"There's nithing left but town lanterns," she said, and went upstairs.

Taber held the package out to me. "You'll have to give Pearl her Chrissmiss present from me, Ruby," he said.

"I won't do it."

"How do you know?" he said.

I didn't answer him.

"You were so anxious to get me my jacket when I went next door. Why don't you get it for me now? Or do you think you won't do that either?"

I took the coat off the hook, waiting for Jewell to come back downstairs.

"Lit's go," Jewell said, hardly limping at all as she came down the steps. I took the jacket over to him. He handed the package to me again, and I took it, watching him put the jacket on, waiting for him to pat the sparker inside the pocket to make sure it was there. Jewell handed him an extra lantern and a bundle of bandages. "Lit's go," she said again. She opened the outside door and went down the wooden steps into the heat.

"Take care of Pearl, Ruby," Taber said, and shut the door.

I went back into the music room. Pearl had not moved. Garnet and Carnie were trying to help Scorch out of the chair and up the stairs, though Carnie could hardly stand. I took his weight from Garnet and picked him up.

"Sit down, Carnie," I said, and she collapsed into the chair, her knees apart and her mouth open, instantly asleep.

I carried Scorch up the stairs to Garnet's room and stood there holding him, bracing his weight against the door while Garnet strung a burn-hammock across her bed for me to lay him in. He had passed out in the chair, but while I was lowering him into the hammock, he came to. His red face was starting to blister, so that he had trouble speaking. "I shidda put the fire out," he said. "It'll catch the ither sidons. I told Jick it was too close."

"They'll put the fire out," I said. Garnet tested the hammock and nodded to me. I laid him gently in it, and we began the terrible process of peeling his clothes off his skin.

"It was thit new tapper thit came down with Taber this morning. He was sotted. And he had a sparker with him. A sparker. The whole star kidda gone up."

"Don't worry," I said. "It'll be all right." I turned him onto his side and began pulling his shirt free. He smelled like frying meat. He passed out again before we got his shirt off, and that made getting the rest of his clothes off easier. Garnet tied his wrist to the saline hookup and started the antibiotics. She told me to go back downstairs.

Pearl was still standing by the pianoboard. "Scorch is going to be fine," I said loudly to cover the sound of picking up Taber's package, and I started past her with it to the kitchen. The blowers had kicked on full-blast from the doors opening so much, but I said anyway, "Garnet wants me to get some water for him."

I made it nearly to the door of the cardroom. Then Carnie heaved herself up in the white chair and said sleepily, "Thit's Pearl's present, isn't it, Ruby?"

I stopped under the blowers, standing on the sidon.

She sat up straighter, licking her tongue across her lips. "Open it, Ruby. I want to see what it is."

Pearl's hands tightened to fists in front of her. "Yes," she said, looking straight at me. "Open it, Ruby."

"No," I said. I walked over to the pianoboard and put the package down on the stool.

"I'll open it then," Carnie said, and lurched out of the chair after it. "You're so mean, Ruby. Poor Pearl kin't open her own Chrissmiss presents, ivver since she got blind." Her voice was starting to slur. I could barely understand what she was saying, and she had to grab at the package twice before she picked it up and staggered back to Pearl's chair with it clutched to her breast. The sots were starting to really take hold now. In a few moments she would be unconscious. "Please," I said without making a sound, praying as Pearl must have prayed in that locked room, ten years old, her hands tied and him coming at her with a razor. "Hurry, hurry."

Carnie couldn't get the package open. She tugged feebly at the green ribbon, plucked at the paper without even tearing it, and subsided, closing her eyes. She began to breathe deeply, with her mouth open, slumped far down in the white chair with her arms flung out over the arms of the chair.

"I'll take you upstairs, Pearl," I said. "Garnet may need help with Scorch."

"All right," she said, but she didn't move. She stood with her head averted, as if she were listening for something.

"Oh, how pretty!" Carnie said, her voice clear and strong. She was sitting up straight in the chair, her hands on the unopened package. "It's a dress, Pearl. Isn't it beautiful, Ruby?"

"Yes, I said, looking at Carnie, limp again in the chair and snoring softly. "It's covered with lights, Pearl, green and red and gold, like a Christmas tree."

The package slipped out of Carnie's limp hands and onto the floor. The blowers kicked on, and Carnie turned in the chair, pulling her feet up under her and cradling her head against the chair's arm. She began snoring again, more loudly.

I said, "Would you like to try it on, Pearl?" and looked over at her, but she was already gone.

It took me nearly an hour to find her, because the town lantern I had strapped to my forehead was so dim I could not see very well. She was lying face down near the mooring.

I unstrapped the lantern and laid it beside her on the ground so I could see her better. The train of her skirt was smoldering. I stamped on it until it crumbled underfoot and then knelt beside her and turned her over.

"Ruby?" she said. Her voice was squeaky from the helium in the air and very hoarse. I could hardly recognize it. She would not be able to recognize mine either. If I told her I was Jewell or Carnie, or Taber, come to murder her, she would not know the difference. "Ruby?" she said. "Is Taber here?"

"No," I said. "Only the sidon."

"You're not a sidon," she said. Her lips were dry and parched.

"Then what am I?" I moved the town lantern closer. Her face looked flushed, almost as red as Jewell's.

"You are my good friend the pianoboard player who has come to help me."

"I didn't come to help you," I said, and my eyes filled with tears. "I came to finish killing you. I can't help it. I'm copying Taber."

"No," she said, but it was not a "no" of protest or horror or surprise, but a statement of fact. "You have never copied Taber."

"He killed Jack," I said. "He had some poor sotted tapper blow up the sidon so he could have an alibi for your murder. He left me to kill you for him."

Her hands lay at her sides, palms down on the ground. When I lifted them and laid them across her skirt as she had always held them, crossed at the wrists, she did not flinch, and I thought perhaps she was unconscious.

"Jewell's feet are much better," she said, and licked her lips. "You hardly limp at all. And I knew Carnie was on sots before she ever came into the room, by the way you walked. I have listened to you copy all of them, even poor dead Jack. You never copied Taber. Not once."

I crawled around beside her and got her head up on my knees. Her hair came loose and fell around her face as I lifted her up, the ends of it curling up in dark frizzies of ash. The narrow fretted soles of my shoes dug into the backs of my legs like hot irons. She swallowed and said, "He broke the door down and he sent for the doctor and then he went to kill the man, but he was too late. My mother had let him out the back way."

"I know," I said. My tears were falling on her neck and throat. I tried to brush them away, but they had already dried, and her skin felt hot and parched. Her lips were cracked, and she could hardly move them at all when she spoke.

"Then he came back and held me in his arms while we waited for the doctor. Like this. And I said, 'Why didn't you kill him?' and he said, 'I will,' and then I asked him to finish killing me, but he wouldn't. He didn't kill the tapper either, because his hands were broken and all cut up."

"My uncle killed him," I said. "That's why we're quarantined. He and Kovich killed him," I said, though Kovich had already been dead by then. "They tied him up and cut out his eyes with a sot-razor," I said. That was why Jewell had let me come to Paylay. She had owed it to my uncle to let me come because he had killed the tapper. And my uncle had sent me to do what? To copy whom?

The lamp was growing much dimmer and the twillpaper forehead strap on the lantern was smoldering now, but I didn't try to put it out. I knelt with Pearl's head in my lap on the hot ground, not moving.

"I knew you were copying me almost from the first," she said, "but I didn't tell you, because I thought you would kill Taber for me. Whenever you played for me, I sat and thought about Taber with a sidon tearing out his throat, hoping you would copy the hate I felt. I never saw Taber or a sidon either, but I thought about my mother's lover, and I called him Taber. I'm sorry I did that to you, Ruby."

I brushed her hair back from her forehead and her cheeks. My hand left a sooty mark, like a scar, down the side of her face. "I did kill Taber," I said.

"You reminded me so much of Kovich when you played," she said. "You sounded just like him. I thought I was thinking about killing Taber, but I wasn't. I didn't even know what a sidon looks like. I was only thinking about Kovich and waiting for him to come and finish killing me." She was breathing shallowly now and very fast, taking a breath between almost every word. "What do sidons look like, Ruby?"

I tried to remember what Kovich had looked like when he came to find my uncle, his broken hands infected, his face red from the fever that would consume him. "I want you to copy me," he had said to my uncle. "I want you to learn to play the pianoboard from me before I die." I want you to kill a man for me. I want you to cut out his eyes. I want you to do what I can't do.

I could not remember what he looked like, except that he had been very tall, almost as tall as my uncle, as me. It seemed to me that he had looked like my uncle, but surely it was the other way around. "I want you to copy me," he had said to my uncle. I want you to do what I can't do. Pearl had asked him to kill the tapper, and he had promised to. Then Pearl had asked him to finish killing her, and he had promised to do that, too, though he could no more have murdered her than he could have played the pianoboard with his ruined hands, though he had not even known how well a Mirror copies, or how blindly. So my uncle had killed the tapper, and I have finished killing Pearl, but it was Kovich, Kovich who did the murders.

"Sidons are very tall," I said, "and they play the pianoboard."

She didn't answer. The twillpaper strap on the lantern burst into flame. I watched it burn.

"It's all right that you didn't kill Taber," she said. "But you mustn't let him put the blame for killing me on you."

"I did kill Taber," I said. "I gave him the real sparker. I put it in his jacket before he left to go out to the sidons."

She tried to sit up. "Tell them you were copying him, that you couldn't help yourself," she said, as if she hadn't heard me.

"I will," I said, looking into the darkness.

Over the horizon somewhere is Taber. He is looking this way, wondering if I have killed her yet. Soon he will take out his cigar and put his thumb against the trigger of the sparker, and the sidons will go up one after the other, a string of lights. I wonder if he will have time to know he has been murdered, to wonder who killed him.

I wonder, too, kneeling here with Pearl's head on my knees. Perhaps I did copy Pearl. Or Jewell, or Kovich, or even Taber. Or all of them. The worst thing is not that things are done to you. It is not knowing who is doing them. Maybe I did not copy anyone, and I am the one who murdered Taber. I hope so.

"You should go back before you get burned," Pearl says, so softly I can hardly hear her.

"I will," I say, but I cannot. They have tied me up, they have locked me in, and now I am only waiting for them to come and finish killing me.

R.A. LAFFERTY

Golden Gate

R.A. Lafferty possesses a wickedly boisterous sense of humor, an enormous store of offbeat erudition, and one of the most outlandish imaginations in all of SF. Over the last 23 years he has drawn on these qualities to turn out a seemingly-endless string of mad and marvelous tall tales, including some of the freshest and funniest short stories ever published. In 1973 he won the Hugo Award for one of them, "Eurema's Dam." His books include *Past Master, The Devil Is Dead, The Reefs of Earth, Okla Hannali, The Fall of Rome, Arrive At Easterwine, The Flame Is Green,* and the collections *Nine Hundred Grandmothers, Strange Doings,* and *Does Anyone Else Have Something Further to Add?* His most recent books are the collections *Four Stories, Golden Gate and Other Stories,* and *Ringing Changes,* and the novel *Annals of Klepsis.*

In the funny and lyrical story that follows, a typically Laffertyesque tall tale, he takes us to the stylishly rowdy Golden Gate Bar and introduces us to a black-hatted Villain in an Old-Time Melodrama who is just a little *too* convincing . . .

GOLDEN GATE

R.A. Lafferty

When you have shot and killed a man you have in some measure clarified your attitude toward him. You have given a definite answer to a definite problem. For better or worse you have acted decisively.

In a way, the next move is up to him.

And it can be a satisfying experience; the more so here, as many would like to have killed him. And now it is done under the ghastly light, just as that old devil's tune comes to a climax and the voices have swelled to an animal roar.

And afterwards an overflowing satisfaction compounded of defiance and daring; and a wonderful clarity born of the roaring excitement. Not peace, but achievement. The shadows prowl in the corners like wolves, and one glows like a lantern.

But Barnaby did not shoot him till Thursday evening. And this was only Monday, and that state of clarity had not yet been attained.

It was clear to Barnaby that Blackie was really a villain. Not everybody knew this. A melodrama villain is only black behind the lights. Off stage he should have a heart of gold. Whether of wrestling match, or afternoon serial, or evening drama or film, or on the little stage here at the Golden Gate Bar, the villain should be—when his role is finished—kind and courteous, thoughtful and big-hearted, a prince of a fellow.

That is the myth. Here it was not entirely true.

"I have always suspected," said Barnaby, "that there is some bad in every villain. I would prove this if only I had proof. Why am I drinking cider?"

"We always give you cider when you have had enough beer."

"It is a dirty trick, and you are a dirty Irish trickster. Tell Jeannie to play 'Fire in the Cockleburs.' "

"There isn't any such song, dear."

"I know there isn't, Margaret, but once I asked her to play a song that wasn't, and she played it."

Barnaby was a confused young man. He was something of a rumdum as are many of the noble men of the world. And even with a broken nose he was better looking than most. He came to the Golden Gate because he was in love with three wonderful women there.

The Golden Gate Bar is not on the Pacific Ocean. It is on another ocean, at this point several thousand miles distant. But if the name of that ocean were known, people would go there, and range up and down that coast until they found this wonderful place. And they would come in every night, and take up room, and stay till closing time.

It is crowded here as it is. The most one can ever get is one wrist on the bar. All the tables are filled early, and no couple ever has one alone for long. The relentless and scantily dressed waitresses double them up. Then they double them up again as the crowd grows. Soon the girls and ladies have all the seats, and the men stand behind them at the tables. And later, as the drinking and singing continue, some of the men sit on the ladies' laps. They do things like that at the Golden Gate.

Clancy O'Clune, the singing bartender, began this custom. He sang ballads and love songs to the girls. He wandered as he sang, and picked out the plainest and shyest and most spinsterish creature he could find. He would sit on her lap and sing to her; and as soon as her embarrassment had faded a little, she would join in the fun and sing with the crowd.

Group singing was what brought the crowds to the Golden Gate. For people love to sing if they don't have to sing alone. Jeannie was marvelous at the piano, and with her, people would sing all the old ballads: "Tavern in a Town," "I Wonder Who's Kissing Her Now," "When You Were Sixteen," "Hot Time in the Old Town."

The Gate was a family place down on the old pier, and the only drinking spot along the beach where children were admitted. For them was cider in great steins. The motif was Gay Nineties. The bartenders wore moustaches and derby hats. The waitresses were scanty and seductive, and plumed and pretty in some old dance hall costume fashion. Even the customers liked to dress the part, and came in vintage gowns and old checkered vests from ancient trunks.

"I know the evil of him is largely compounded of soot and grease," said Barnaby who was still thinking of Blackie, the villain. "How do we know that the evil of the devil himself is not so compounded?"

On the floor was sawdust, and the lights were gas lights. The cuspidors were old brass, and stood up in their glory.

"Has Blackie a name, Margaret, like regular people?"

"Of course he has, dear, he is W.K. Wallingsforth."

Now that was interesting. The true name of the devil was sought by Faust, as to know it gives a power over him. And to learn it so casually was unheard-of luck. And if he had a name, then possibly he had also a habitation as though he were human.

The lamplighter turned out the lights in the barroom and fired the eerie gas torches at each end of the stage. For every evening was the melodrama. This was loud and wide, with pistols and boots and whips, and the bull-roarer voice of Blackie. Clancy O'Clune was the hero. Jenny, bustled and bosomed, was the thrilling heroine. And Blackie was the villain, that filthy old snake of a man.

The crowd would howl out "No! No! No!" to his monstrous demands, and hiss and catcall. And Jeannie at the piano ran a marvelous accompaniment as her sister Jenny fluted her outraged innocence and terror.

This was a Monday night that Barnaby first saw the villain. And an old passion came on him; for beyond the comic and burlesque he felt a struggle and a terror. The sandy hair raised on his neck, and he knew the villain for what he was.

Barnaby sat with a middle-aged couple and drank beer from a pitcher large beyond all believing.

"We love to come here," said Anne Keppel, "We have so much fun just watching the other people have fun. This is the only place this old bear will ever take me. I love to sing, but I wouldn't dare sing anywhere else. He makes jokes about the ghost of a dead cat coming back, and why does it have to suffer like that."

"The only place I ever sing," said Aurelius Keppel, "is here and in the bathtub. In the tub, I have to keep up a great splashing, or this shrew will beat on the door and announce that the doctor will be here in a minute, and to be brave. It isn't that I haven't a wonderful voice. It isn't that I haven't a wonderful wife. But my wonderful wife doesn't appreciate my wonderful voice."

If one is to hate the villain properly, he should love the heroine. Barnaby loved passionately, but knew only slightly, the heroine, Jenny. A little better he knew, a little more he loved her sister, Jeannie, the pretty piano player. But he knew Margaret, the mother of the two girls, quite well.

Margaret was more beautiful than her daughters. She was the tallest and best liked of those wonderful waitresses. And she was the owner of the Golden Gate.

And the girls were onto him. "It isn't us, it's mama you like. How does she do it?"

"I'll tell you. She's younger than her daughters. You're a couple of old maids. Young and pretty, but still old maids. You're not in your mother's class."

"Oh, we know it."

But they were no such thing. They were as exciting and heady a pair as were ever met. Jenny, the frail heroine, might toss a man over her shoulder like a sack and spin away with him. And there was never any telling what Jeannie would do.

The melodrama was over, and the little stage was dark. And it was then that Barnaby knew that he must kill the villain.

Clancy O'Clune, still in his hero's habiliments, picked a slightly gray and quietly amused pretty lady. He sat on her lap and sang to her softly a good-night lullaby. Afterwards, Jeanie brought the piano to a great volume, and everybody sang "We Won't Go Home Till Morning."

But they all went home at midnight when the Golden Gate closed.

And when Barnaby was home, he took out a little six-shot and fondled it as though it were a jewel.

2

Now it was Tuesday, the second day of the involvement. Barnaby was sitting in the company of four sophomores from City College. It is known by all, though not admitted by all, that sophomores are at the same time the most ingenuous, ingenious, and disingenuous people in the world. They are a wonder and a confrontation. Their hearts are ripe and their minds are on fire, and the door of the whole cosmos is open to them. Now, at the end of their second spring, they are imbued with clarity and charm.

"A survey reveals that eighty percent of the people believe in Heaven but only twenty percent in Hell," said Veronica. "That is like believing in up but not down, in a disc of only one side, a pole with a top but no bottom, *Making Love to Alice Bly*, in light but not in darkness."

That one line in the middle was not part of the argument. It was a line in the ballad that the crowd was singing, and Veronica sang it with them. And yet it too was part of the argument, for Miss Bly, who looked like an angel, had roots that went down to Hell.

It was odd that they would be talking of things like that. And only Barnaby knew the reason: that Blackie was so much a Devil that they were reminded of his homeland.

"If it weren't for the evil in it the world would be a fine place," said Simon. "But it is only the Evil who do not believe in evil, and only the

Hellish who do not believe in Hell. *There's Seven Men Going to the Graveyard.*"

"*And Only Six are Coming Back,*" sang Hazel. Then she said, "It is there like a cold wind, and curls in the corner like a dog. A whole room full of people can turn evil in a minute. The world grinds and shudders. It can come like a bolt and stand in the middle of you."

It did come like a bolt and stand in the middle of them, but perhaps only Barnaby knew what it was and shivered for it. And yet the rest shivered as with sudden cold. For the Villain had appeared costumed in his villainy, and the melodrama began.

Once more the short red hair rose on the nape of Barnaby, and the odd passion came over him. He breathed heavily, as did others in the room. There was a terror in the comic, and excitement danced like lightning over the burlesque stage.

And when the crowd howled "No! No! No!" in simulated fury, it was not entirely simulated. And there were some who crowed "Yes! Yes!" wickedly against the crowd; and one of these was Hazel, bright-eyed and panting, as she felt the evil, like a dog in the corner, rise within her.

So it thrashed to a climax. Did not Jeannie know that the accompaniment she played on the piano was diabolic? For the temptations of the dark villain were manifold. But for a word of his, the crippled brother of the heroine would go to prison; and he withheld the word. But for his testimony, the mine of the heroine's father would pass into the domain of the Fast Buck Mining Company, and he would not give the testimony. There was even evidence, clear to the more perspicacious, that he was himself the Fast Buck Mining Company. But for him, the dastardly lie about the heroine's mother would spread and spread; and perhaps he would be the one to spread it. There would be no bread in the cupboard, nor coal in the scuttle, nor milk for the small children. And against all this only the frail virtue of the thrilling heroine.

"She ought to go with him," said the girl at the next table. "He only wants her for the weekend. I'd go with him. Yes! Yes!" cried the girl at the next table.

And then Barnaby knew for sure that the old dark villain had to die.

Now the melodrama was over and the lamplighter lit the lights again. The suds rose in a hundred-headed fountain; everybody had a dozen more beers and sang the ballads of Jeannie. Clancy O'Clune put on his sheriff's badge that was eighteen inches across, and there was law and order, though a great deal of noise, in the Golden Gate Bar.

And when the midnight tide pounded under the pier, Clancy came and sat on the silken knees of a little houri named Maybelline, and sang to her "Good Night Little Sweetheart."

And after everybody sang "We Won't Go Home Till Morning," they all went home. Except those who went to the Buccaneer, and the Alamo, and the Town House, and places like that.

3

Wednesday morning Barnaby had a breakfast date with Jenny. It may not have been made clear that Jenny was really beautiful. Just how beautiful, it is impossible to say. Not, perhaps, as beautiful as her sister Jeannie. Not, certainly, as beautiful as her mother, Margaret. But nevertheless breathtaking, fantastic, and clear out of the world.

But she asked the oddest questions.

"Why don't you work? You're not working today. You didn't work yesterday. I don't think you even worked Monday."

"Listen," said Barnaby. "You can believe it or not, but before that I worked for four weeks straight. Naturally I'm entitled to a vacation. How could I work this week when I've met you wonderful people and have you to think about? If it wouldn't make you conceited, I'd tell you how wonderful you really are."

"No. It won't make me conceited. Please tell me. I know, of course, but I like to have people tell me."

"You are just a dream. You are that little heroine all the time. All of you are wonderful except that villain. I would like to strangle him with my hands."

"Why, he's the most wonderful of us all. He's a real flesh-crawler. I know what's the matter. You're jealous because it's really mama you're in love with. I guess all villains are really marvelous."

"I know a devil when I see one. I'll bring a gun some night and kill him."

"He says sometimes people do. Not kill him, but shoot at him. Then he knows he's getting across. But it'd be terrible if something happened to him."

"It would be grand."

"Don't talk like that. I have to go. I'm glad you asked me, but I'm mad that you asked Jeannie first. If I'm a dream, why did you ask her first? Now I have to leave because I'm always so busy. Wait till the waitress goes by, and then kiss me. Be in tonight and see how pretty I look."

Now it was Wednesday night, the third of the epic. Barnaby was at a table with three seamen. These were not unknown. Long John in particular was known all over town. He was not merely lantern-jawed, he was jawed like an eighteenth-century ship's lantern, copper bound and brass bottomed, and the nose on him as livid and red as an old beacon at night. His clothing was beyond description, and the hat on his head older than any man now living in the world.

And most know Benny Bigty and Limey Lynd, the other two. To know them, however, was not to like them. Benny had a muzzle like a fox and was always looking over his shoulder. Limey was a cockney dude. They were loud and obscene. If they hadn't been friends of Barnaby, he wouldn't have liked them either.

Already, through the early crowd there was running a tide of resentment toward the seamen; and this only for their insistence that all the songs that night should be sea songs. Now there is nothing wrong with "As I Was A-walking Down Paradise Street—with a Ho Ho Blow the Man Down," but it has seventeen choruses, and when it is sung seventeen times, that makes either two hundred and eighty-nine or two hundred and ninety-nine. That is too much.

And when another ballad slipped in sideways:

"I only ask you, Jack, to do your duty, that is all;
You know you promised that we should be wed,"
they sat in towering silence and would not sing.

"It isn't as though they were high-sea seamen," Blackie, the villain, said to Clancy O'Clune. "One of them works on a garbage scow, and one on a pile-driving barge, and one on a ferryboat."

But Barnaby was loyal to his friends, and he considered only the evil source of the remark. So he also howled for sea songs.

Now the crowd came like snow and filled the room.

"I have been in every Hell Hole of the world," said Long John. "Zanzibar, Devil's Island, Port Royal (that was before the earthquake), Oklahoma City, Cote der Pirates, Newport News, Mobile, Alabama; but I have never seen a more evil-looking man. Who is he?"

Barnaby was pleased. He had found a friend. Someone else who hated Blackie. "That is Blackie, the Villain."

"Ah, *Le Noire*, I should have known. I heard of him once in Marseille."

And yet that was hardly possible, for neither of them had ever been there.

The thing about Blackie, is that he was very easy to be afraid of. He had arms like a python. And if one cannot conceive of a python with arms, no more can he of Blackie. Barnaby was a handy young man. Though he fought less than he once did, yet he always won more fights than he lost. He measured Blackie with his gray eyes, and he knew that he was afraid of him.

"I wonder how it will be when he is dead," said Barnaby. "When the soul leaves the body, they speak of the Wings of the Dove. With him it will be the pinions of the vulture."

The little houri named Maybelline came over and made herself acquainted with Barnaby, and he was entranced with her. And however it happened, she was soon sitting on his knee, and they were drinking beer from the same mug.

It wasn't as though he weren't still in love with Jeannie, who now smiled and frowned at him together from her piano.

It wasn't as though he weren't still in love with Jenny who winked at him as she went by. And it was a wicked wink.

It wasn't as though he weren't still in love with Margaret who now wagged a finger at him from across the room. But an houri is different from other girls, and when you are entranced, what can you do?

Everybody sang:
"In a cottage down in Sussex
Live her parents old and lame,
And they drink the wine she sends them,
But they never speak her name."

And they sang:
"Shoot me like an Irish soldier,
Do not hang me like a dog."

Everybody sang together to the music of Jeannie, and the only lights in the place were those old gas lights. Something went out of the world with them. These new lights, they have no smell to them, they have no flicker or real glow. You can't reach up and light a cigar or dramatically burn a letter. It's almost as though they weren't alive.

And after a while, Jeannie began to play devil's music, and Evil uncoiled like a snake and slid into the room. The lights in the world went out, and the torches were lit in Hell; and the melodrama began on the little stage. The world shuddered on its axis, and the villain was prince of the world. Once more the odd passion came on Barnaby. An animal surge went through the crowd as the noble hero and the trilling heroine and the dark villain acted out the oldest epic in the world.

"No! No! No!" But tonight virtue would not triumph. The more he was hissed, the more powerful the villain became. For he also had his supporters, and now they rose like a ground swell. Virtue was howled down in a crescendo of devil's music played by Jeannie at the piano.

"O.K." said Jenny, the heroine, "let's go and get it over." So Jenny went with the evil villain, and everybody laughed as the lights were lit again with a taper.

Now they all had a dozen more beers and sang:

"Just break the news to Mother,
She knows how dear I love her,
And tell her not to wait for me,
For I'm not coming home."
And the words had a double meaning for Barnaby.
They sang:
"The cook she was a kind old soul.
She had a ragged dress.
We hoisted her upon a pole
As a signal of distress."
And this seemed inexpressibly sad to Barnaby, and not even the houri on his knees could cheer him up.

For over in the corner was Jenny, and she was sitting with Blackie, the villain, in a condition of extreme friendliness; and for all he knew they were drinking their beer from the same pitcher.

Then, as the night ran on, Clancy O'Clune picked out an eleven-year-old girl who was drinking cider with her father, who was a barber, and he came and sat on her lap and sang to her "Believe Me If All Those Endearing Young Charms" for a good-night song.

Afterwards everybody sang "We Won't Go Home Till Morning."

And they all went home at midnight.

4

Thursday morning Barnaby had a breakfast date with Jeannie, the outrageously beautiful piano player.

"Did Jenny turn you down? Why did you ask me first today?"

"I always ask you first."

"Jenny says you're mad at her because she's friendly with Blackie. But he's so nice. Don't you know that? He's one of the nicest men we ever met."

"He is a devil. He makes my flesh crawl."

"He is supposed to. But only on the stage. He's a consummate actor. I think that's the word that mama says he is. And mama says for us to keep an eye on you because you're acting so peculiar. We tell her you only act peculiar over her. Don't you think we'd make nice daughters-in-law?"

"You would be nice anything, Jeannie."

"And don't you wish you were a sultan and could have us all at once?"

"Yes I do. I never thought of it, but that's just what I wish."

"And the houri too?"

"How did you know she was an houri? I thought I was the only one who knew."

"I'm never sure you're serious. I do have to go, dear. Isn't it too bad that everyone always has to go all the time? You eat the rest of my jelly and egg. Kiss me. Good-bye."

And it was morning and evening, the fourth day.

And in the evening Barnaby sat with a table full of refinery workers. He had brought with him tonight his little six-shot loaded. And five were blanks and one was not.

The refinery workers were named Croesus Kahlmeyer, Midas Morressey, and Money-Bags Muldoon. These are the names that the waitresses gave to them, for refinery workers are the biggest tippers in the world. They tip lavishly. The reason they can do this is that all refinery workers get a hundred hours a week overtime, and the money they make is fantastic.

Gaiety Garrett was waiting their table. The boys all called her Gaiety Unrestrained. And in a larger sense gaiety unrestrained reigned through the whole of the Golden Gate.

Now the surf pounded loudly under the pier. It always seemed noisiest when the melodrama was about to start. For after the hours had passed, the lamplighter turned out the lights in the barroom and flared the torches on the stage. The smell of them came over the room like a weird fog.

Then Barnaby took the little six-shot from his pocket and fondled it. For the reign of the prince of evil was about to be ended in the world.

And when the melodrama was at its loudest, and the pistols barked, and the crowd roared like an animal, Barnaby raised his six-shot trembling.

And fired it six times.

It is such a little thing to kill a man and brings so much satisfaction, you wonder everybody does not do it. It is like walking through green meadows after an oppressing darkness.

Barnaby relaxed and the short hairs subsided on his nape; for the passion had left him. Peace came down on him like white snow.

"I have killed the villain," he said. And he had. The pinions of the vulture had sounded and the soul of the villain had gone.

But the act was for himself alone. Only he and the victim knew that it had happened.

For Blackie did not act as though he were killed. He strutted through the drama to its close while the crowd howled and everyone was happy.

Yet there was no doubt that the villain was dead, for a great clarity had descended on Barnaby. And Blackie was now more like an odd old friend who needed a shave, and no more a python or a devil.

*   *   *

Margaret came to the table and she was white-faced.

"Don't you ever do a thing like that again. Give me that. How could you do that to us? We all love you and thought you loved us."

And she looked at him queerly. He liked the way she looked at him: a sort of wild worry beneath the kindness.

Everybody drank an ocean of beer and sang thousands upon thousands of songs. And when it was late, Clancy O'Clune went over to Gladys, who wore glasses, and sat on her lap and sang "Just a Song at Twilight" for a good-night song.

And as always they sang "We Won't Go Home Till Morning." And as always they went home at midnight.

5

Friday morning Barnaby went to work; but there was only a half day's work for him. It often happens that a boy will find only a half day's work after he has laid off for a week and needs it.

And in the afternoon he went to the Golden Gate, which was closed in the daytime. He went in the back where deliveries were made.

The sour ghost of last night's beer permeated the place. And there was another ghost there, loud and wailing.

It was a terrible noise, a discordant clanging and chording that was the saddest thing he had ever heard: the woeful wailing of a soul that has been in purgatory a long century, and has just been told that it is not purgatory it is in. It was a hopeless crash filled with a deep abiding sorrow that had once been hope.

Blackie was playing the piano, and there was torture in his eyes. Yet he talked happily.

"Hello, Barnaby. I love the instrument. I play it every chance I get. Yet I am told that I do not play well. Do I play well, Barnaby?"

"No, no, you play quite badly."

Blackie, that old python who needed a shave, seemed discouraged.

"I was afraid you would think so. Yet to myself it is beautiful. Do you think it sounds beautiful to anyone?"

"No. I don't think it would sound beautiful to anyone in the world, Blackie."

"I wish it weren't so."

"I shot at you last night, Blackie."

"I know it. Six shots. I knew you would."

"One of them was not a blank."

"The third. I knew it would be the third. I dug it out of the plaster this morning."

"Does anyone else know?"

"No. How would anyone else know? I am going away, Barnaby."

"Where?"

"Kate's Klondike Bar. They need a villain there. Here they are changing the format. They will call this the Speakeasy. It will be a gin mill with flapper waitresses like John Held, Jr. pictures. They will have a lost generation motif and sing lost twenties songs. Clancy is practicing 'Star Dust' all the time. I could stay on as a gangster, but I am better as an old time villain. The gay days are about over. The twenties will be the new era of nostalgia."

"I will not like that."

He went to find Margaret where she was counting her money in a little room.

"Blackie says you are going to change this to a sad twenties place."

"Yes, dear, the twenties will be all the rage now."

"I don't remember them like I do the older times. I wasn't even born yet in the twenties. Do you remember them, Margaret?"

"Of course I do. It'll be sweet to have them back. We have some wonderful ideas. The girls play old scratchy records all day long to learn them."

"Will you still have the melodrama?"

"Well, no. But we'll have skits. Well, not skits really; we'll have ukelele players and things like that. You'll like it."

"There's only one thing bothers me."

"What, dear?"

"In the twenties, how did they know who was the villain?"

"I don't know, dear. Here are the men with the scenery. I have to show them where to put it."

But that Friday night it wasn't the same. The girls were all dressed in potato sacks with the belts only three inches from the bottom. Their stockings were rolled and their knees were rouged; and on their heads were sheathlike helmets that made them look like interplanetary creatures with the ears sheared off them. Jenny and Jeannie looked like two peeled onions with not enough hair on their heads to cover them. Oh, that those breathtaking creatures should come to this!

They sang "Yes sir, she's my baby." They sang "Oh you have no idea." They sang:

"You play the Uke,
You're from Dubuque,
I go for that."

The Speakeasy spoke, but Barnaby could not hear its message. To him it was dismal and deep. And then the long evening was over and the gin glasses were empty.

Clancy O'Clune was singing a good-night song to a bony flapper.

"Picture me
Upon your knee,
And tea for two,
And two for tea."

But he didn't sit on her lap. All at once none of the ladies were built like that anymore.

Barnaby went to Blackie's room. Blackie was packing.

"What town is Kate's Klondike Bar in?"

Blackie told him the town. But it shall be told to no one else. If it were known, people would go there, and come in every night, and take up room; and it's going to be crowded enough there as it is.

"That isn't very far," said Barnaby. "That's only a couple of hundred miles. I'll go there and get a job. Then at night I can come in and listen to them sing, and watch the melodrama."

JACK DANN

Blind Shemmy

One of the most respected writer/editors of his generation, Jack Dann began writing in 1970 and first established his reputation with the critically acclaimed novella "Junction," which was a Nebula finalist in 1973; he has been a Nebula finalist six more times since then and a finalist for the World Fantasy Award. His short fiction has appeared in *Omni, Orbit, Playboy, Penthouse, New Dimensions, The Magazine of Fantasy & Science Fiction, Shadows, Isaac Asimov's Science Fiction Magazine, New Worlds Quarterly, The Berkley Showcase,* and elsewhere. His books include the novels *Starhiker* and *Junction,* and *Timetipping,* a collection of his short fiction. As an anthologist, he edited one of the most famous anthologies of the '70s, *Wandering Stars,* a collection of fantasy and SF on Jewish themes; his other anthologies include *More Wandering Stars, Immortal, Faster Than Light,* (co-edited with George Zebrowski), and several anthologies co-edited with Gardner Dozois: *Future Power, Aliens!,* and *Unicorns!* Upcoming are a new novel (of which "Blind Shemmy," in somewhat different form, is a part) called *The Man Who Melted,* for Bluejay Books and another anthology co-edited with Gardner Dozois, *Magic Cats,* from Ace.

In "Blind Shemmy," he takes us to a lushly-decadent future world where jaded sophisticates play a bizarre high-tech game that redefines the outer limits of just how much a gambler is *really* willing to lose . . .

BLIND SHEMMY

Jack Dann

After covering the burning and sacking of the Via Roma in Naples, Carl Pfeiffer, a famous newsfax reporter, could not resist his compulsion to gamble. He telephoned Joan Otur, one of his few friends, and insisted that she accompany him to Paris.

Organ-gambling was legal in France.

They dropped from the sky in a transparent Plasticine egg, and Paris opened up below them, Paris and the glittering chip of diamond that was the Casino Bellecour.

Except for the dymaxion dome of the Right Bank, Joan would not have been able to distinguish Paris from the suburbs beyond. A city had grown over the city: The grid of the ever-expanding slung city had its own constellations of light and hid Haussmann's ruler-straight boulevards, the ancient architectural wonders, even the black, sour-stenched Seine, which was an hourglass curve dividing the old city.

Their transpod settled to the ground like a dirty snowflake and split silently open, letting in the chill night air with its acrid smells of mudflats and cinders and clogged drains. Joan and Pfeiffer hurried across the transpad toward the high oaken doors of the casino. All around them stretched the bleak, brick-and-concrete wastelands of the city's ruined districts, the fetid warrens on the dome's peripheries, which were inhabited by skinheads and Screamers who existed outside the tightly controlled structure of Uptown life. Now, as Pfeiffer touched his hand to a palm-plate sensor, the door opened and admitted them into the casino itself. The precarious outside world was closed out and left behind.

A young man, who reminded Joan of an upright (if possible) Bedlington terrier, led them through the courtyard. He spoke with a clipped English accent and had tufts of woolly, bluish-white hair inplanted all over his head, face, and body. Only his hands and genitals were hairless.

"He *has* to be working off an indenture," Pfeiffer said sharply as he repressed a sexual urge.

"Shush," Joan said, as the boy gave Pfeiffer a brief, contemptuous look—in Parisian culture, you paid for the service, not for the smile.

They were led into a simple, but formal, entry lounge, which was crowded, but not uncomfortable. The floor was marbled; a few pornographic icons were discreetly situated around the carefully laid-out comfort niches. The room reminded Joan of a chapel with arcades, figures, and stone courts. Above was a dome, from which radiated a reddish, suffusing light, lending the room an expansiveness of height rather than breadth.

But it was mostly holographic illusion.

They were directed to wait a moment and then presented to the purser, an overweight, balding man who sat behind a small desk. He was dressed in a blue camise shirt and matching caftan, which was buttoned across his wide chest and closed with a red scarf. He was obviously, and uncomfortably, dressed in the colors of the establishment.

"And good evening, Monsieur Pfeiffer and Mademoiselle Otur. We are honored to have such an important guest, or guests, I should say." The purser slipped two cards into a small console. "Your identification cards will be returned to you when you leave." After a pause he asked, "Ah, does Monsieur Pfeiffer wish the lady to be credited on his card?" The purser lowered his eyes, indicating embarrassment. Quite simply, Joan did not have enough credit to be received into the more sophisticated games.

"Yes, of course," Pfeiffer said absently. He felt guilty and anxious about feeling a thrill of desire for that grotesque boy.

"Well, then," said the purser, folding his hands on the desk, "we are at your disposal for as long as you wish to stay with us." He gestured toward the terrier and said, "Johnny will give you the tour," but Pfeiffer politely declined. Johnny ushered them into a central room, which was anything but quiet, and—after a wink at Pfeiffer—discreetly disappeared.

The room was as crowded as the city ways. It was filled with what looked to be the ragtag, the bums and the street people, the captains of the ways. Here was a perfect replica of a street casino, but perfectly safe. This *was* a street casino, at least to Pfeiffer, who was swept up in the noise and bustle, as he whetted his appetite for the dangerous pleasures of the top level.

Ancient iron bandits whispered "chinka-chinka" and rolled their picture-frame eyes in promise of a jackpot, which was immediately transferred to the winner's account by magnetic sleight of hand. The amplified, high-pitched voices of pinball computers on the walls called out winning hands of poker and blackjack. A simulated stabbing drew nothing more than a few glances. Tombstone booths were filled with figures working through their own Stations of the Cross. Hooked-in winners were rewarded with bursts of electrically induced ecstasy; losers writhed in pain and suffered through the brain-crushing aftershock of week-long migraines.

And, of course, battered robots clattered around with the traditional complement of drugs, drink, and food. The only incongruity was a perfectly dressed geisha, who quickly disappeared into one of the iris doors on the far wall.

"Do you want to play the one-armed bandits?" Joan asked, fighting her growing claustrophobia, wishing only to escape into quiet; but she was determined to try to keep Pfeiffer from going upstairs. Yet ironically—all her emotions seemed to be simultaneously yin and yang—she also wanted him to gamble away his organs. She knew that she would feel a guilty thrill if he lost his heart. Then she pulled down the lever of the one-armed bandit; it would read her finger- and odor-prints and transfer or deduct the proper amount to or from Pfeiffer's account. The eyes rolled and clicked and one hundred international credit dollars was lost. "Easy come, easy go. At least, this is a safe way to go. But you didn't come here to be safe, right?" Joan said mockingly.

"You can remain down here, if you like," Pfeiffer said, looking about the room for an exit, noticing that iris doors were spaced every few meters on the nearest wall to his left. *The casino must take up the whole bloody block*, he thought. "How the hell do I get out of here?"

Before Joan could respond, Johnny appeared, as if out of nowhere, and said, "Monsieur Pfeiffer may take any one of the ascenseurs, or, if he would care for the view of our palace, he could take the staircase to heaven." He smiled, baring even teeth, and curtsied to Pfeiffer, who was blushing. The boy certainly knows his man, Joan thought sourly.

Am I jealous? she asked herself. She cared for Pfeiffer, but didn't *love* him—at least she didn't think she did.

"Shall I attend you?" Johnny asked Pfeiffer, ignoring Joan.

"No," said Pfeiffer. "Now please leave us alone."

"Well, which is it?" asked Joan. "The elevator would be quickest, zoom you right to the organ room."

"We can take the stairs," Pfeiffer said, a touch of blush still in his cheeks. But he would say nothing about the furry boy. "Jesus, it seems that every time I blink my eye, the stairway disappears."

"I'll show you the way," Joan said, taking his arm.

"Just what I need," Pfeiffer said, smiling, eliminating one small barrier between them.

"I think your rush is over, isn't it? You don't really want to gamble out your guts."

"I came to do something, and I'll follow it through."

The stairwell was empty and, like an object conceived in Alice's Wonderland, it appeared to disappear behind them. "Cheap tricks," Pfeiffer said.

"Why are you so intent on this?" Joan asked. "If you lose, which you most probably will, you'll never have a day's peace. They can call in your heart, or liver, or—"

"I can buy out, if that should happen." Pfeiffer reddened, but it had nothing to do with his conversation with Joan, to which he was hardly paying attention; he was still thinking about the furry boy.

"You wouldn't gamble them, if you thought you could buy out. That's bunk."

"Then I'd get artificials."

"You'd be taking another chance, with the quotas—thanks to your right-wing friends in power."

Pfeiffer didn't take the bait. "I admit defeat," he said. Again he thought of the furry boy's naked, hairless genitals. And with that came the thought of death.

The next level was less crowded and more subdued. There were few electronic games to be seen on the floor. A man passed dressed in medical white, which indicated that deformation games were being played. On each floor the stakes became increasingly higher; fortunes were lost, people were disfigured or ruined but—with the exception of the top floor, which had dangerous games other than organ-gambling—at least no one died. They might need a face and body job after too many deformations, but those were easily obtained, although one had to have very good credit to ensure a proper job.

On each ascending level, the house whores, both male and female, became more exotic, erotic, grotesque, and abundant. There were birdmen with feathers like peacocks and flamingos, children with dyed skin and overly large, implanted male and female genitalia, machines that spoke the language of love and exposed soft, fleshy organs, amputees and cripples, various drag queens and kings, natural androgynes and mutants, cyborgs, and an interesting, titillating array of genetically engineered mooncalves.

But none disturbed Pfeiffer as had that silly furry boy. He wondered if, indeed, the boy was still following him.

"Come on, Joan" Pfeiffer said impatiently. "I really don't want to waste any more time down here."

"I thought it was the expectation that's so exciting to seasoned gamblers," Joan said.

"Not to me," Pfeiffer said, ignoring the sarcasm. "I want to get it over with." With that, he left the room.

Then why bother at all? Joan asked herself, wondering why she had let Pfeiffer talk her into coming here. *He doesn't need me. Damn him,* she thought, ignoring a skinny, white-haired man and a piebald, doggie mooncalf coupling beside her in an upright position.

She took a lift to the top level to be with Pfeiffer.

It was like walking into the foyer of a well-appointed home. The high walls were stucco and the floor was inlaid parquet. A small Dehaj rug was placed neatly before a desk, behind which beamed a man of about fifty dressed in camise and caftan.

He had a flat face, a large nose that was wide, but had narrow nostrils, and close-set eyes roofed with bushy, brown eyebrows, the color his hair would have been, had he had any.

Actually, the room was quite small, which made the rug look larger and gave the man a commanding position.

"Do you wish to watch or participate, Monsieur Pfeiffer?" he asked, seeming to rise an inch from the chair as he spoke.

"I wish to play," Pfeiffer said, standing upon the rug as if he had to be positioned just right to make it fly.

"And does your friend wish to watch?" the man asked, as Joan crossed the room to stand beside Pfeiffer. "Or will you give your permission for Miz Otur to become telepathically connected to you." His voice didn't rise as he asked the question.

"I beg your pardon?"

"A psyconnection, sir. With a psyconductor"—a note of condescension crept into his voice.

"I *know* what it is, and I don't want it," Pfeiffer snapped and then moved away from Joan. But a cerebral hook-in was, in fact, just what Joan had hoped for.

"Oh, come on," Joan said. "Let me in."

"Are you serious?" he asked, turning toward her. Caught by the intensity of his stare, she could only nod. "Then I'm sorry. I'm not a window for you to stare through."

That stung her, and she retorted, "Have you ever done it with your wife?" She immediately regretted her words.

The man at the desk cleared his throat politely. "Excuse me, monsieur, but are you aware that *only* games *organe* are played in these rooms?"

"Yes, that's why I've come to your house."

"Then, you are perhaps not aware that all our games are conducted with psyconductors on this floor."

Pfeiffer, looking perplexed, said, "Perhaps you had better explain it to me."

"Of course, of course," the man said, beaming, as if he had just won the battle and a fortune. "There are, of course, many ways to play, and, if you like, I can give you the address of a very nice house nearby where you can play a fair, safe game without hook-ins. Shall I make a reservation for you there?"

"Not just yet," Pfeiffer said, resting his hands, knuckles down, upon the flat-top Louis XVI desk.

His feet seemed to be swallowed by the floral patterns of the rug, and Joan thought it an optical illusion, this effect of being caught before the desk of the casino captain. She felt the urge to grab Pfeiffer and take him out of this suffocating place.

Instead, she walked over to him. Perhaps he would relent just a little and let her slide into his mind.

"It is one of our house rules, however," said the man at the desk, "that you and your opponent, or opponents, must be physically in the same room."

"Why is that?" Joan asked, feeling Pfeiffer scowling at her for intruding.

"Well," he said, "it has never happened to us, of course, but cheating has occurred on a few long-distance transactions. Organs have been wrongly lost. So we don't take any chances. None at all." He looked at Pfeiffer as he spoke, obviously sizing him up, watching for reactions. But Pfeiffer had composed himself, and Joan knew that he had made up his mind.

"Why must the game be played with psyconductors?" Pfeiffer asked.

"That is the way we do it," said the captain. Then, after an embarrassing pause, he said, "We have our own games and rules. And our games, we think, are the *most* interesting. And we make the games as safe as we can for all parties involved."

"What do you mean?"

"We—the house—will be observing you. Our gamesmaster will be telepathically hooked in, but, I assure you, you will not sense his presence in the least. If anything should go wrong, or look as if it might go wrong, then *pfft*, we intercede. Of course, we make no promises, and there have been cases where—"

"But anything that could go wrong would be because of the cerebral hook-in."

"Perhaps this *isn't* the game for you, sir."

"You must have enough privileged information on everyone who has ever played here to make book," Pfeiffer said.

"The hook-in doesn't work that way at all. And besides, we are contract-bound to protect our clients."

"And yourselves."

"Most certainly." The casino captain looked impatient.

"If both players can read each other's mind," Pfeiffer said to the captain, "then there can be no blind cards."

"Aha, now you have it, monsieur." At that, the tension between Pfeiffer and the desk captain seemed to dissolve. "And, indeed," the captain continued, "we have a modified version of chemin de fer, which we call blind shemmy. All the cards are played facedown. It is a game of control (and, of course, chance), for you must block out certain thoughts from your mind, while, at the same time, tricking your opponent into revealing his cards. And that is why it would be advantageous for you to let your friend here connect with you."

Pfeiffer glanced toward Joan and said, "Please clarify that."

"Quite simply, while you are playing, your friend could help block your thoughts from your opponent with her own," said the captain. "But it does take some practice. Perhaps, it would be better if you tried a hook-in in one of our other rooms, where the stakes are not quite so high." Then the captain lowered his eyes, as if in deference, but in actuality he was looking at the CeeR screen of the terminal set into the antique desk.

Joan could see Pfeiffer's nostrils flare slightly. *The poor sonofabitch is caught,* she thought. "Come on, Carl, let's get out of here now."

"Perhaps you should listen to Miss Otur," the captain said, but the man must have known that he had Pfeiffer.

"I wish to play blind shemmy," Pfeiffer said, turning toward Joan, glaring at her. She caught her breath: If he lost, then she knew he would make certain that Joan lost something, too.

"I have a game of nine in progress," the captain said. "There are nine people playing and nine others playing interference. But you'll have to wait for a space. It will be quite expensive, as the players are tired and will demand some of your points for themselves above the casino charge for the play."

"How long will I have to wait?"

The captain shrugged, then said, "I have another man waiting, who is ahead of you. He would be willing to play a game of doubles. I would recommend you play him rather than wait. Like you, he is an amateur, but his wife, who will be connected with him, is not. Of course, if you wish to wait for the other . . ."

Pfeiffer accepted, and while he and Joan gave their prints to the various forms, the captain explained that there was no statute of limitations on the contract signed by all parties, and that it would be honored even by those governments that disapprove of this particular form of gambling.

Then the furry boy appeared like an apparition to take them to their room where they would be given time to practice and become acquainted.

The boy's member was slightly engorged, and Pfeiffer now became frightened. He suddenly thought of his mother and the obligatory hook-in service at her funeral. His skin crawled as he remembered her last filthy thoughts. . . .

The furry boy led Joan and Pfeiffer into the game room, which smelled of oiled wood, spices, traditional tobacco, and perfume. There were no holos or decoration on the walls. Everything, with the exception of the felt top of the gaming table, cards, thick natural carpet, computer consoles, and cowls, was made of precious woods: oak, elm, cedar, teak, walnut, mahogany, redwood, ebony. The long, half-oval gaming table, which met the sliding partition wall, was made of satinwood, as were the two delicate, but uncomfortable, high-backed chairs placed side by side. On the table before each chair was a psyconductor cowl, each one sheathed in a light, silvery mask.

"We call them poker-faces," the boy said to Pfeiffer, as he placed the cowl over Joan's head. He explained how the psyconductor mechanism worked, then asked Pfeiffer if he wished him to stay.

"Why should I want you to stay?" Pfeiffer asked, but the sexual tension between them was unmistakable.

"I'm adept at games of chance. I can redirect your thoughts—without a psyconductor." He looked at Joan and smiled.

"Put the mechanism on my head and then please leave us," Pfeiffer said.

"Do you wish me to return when you're finished?"

"If you wish," Pfeiffer replied stiffly, and Joan watched his discomfort. Without saying a word, she had won a small victory.

The boy lowered the cowl over Pfeiffer's head, made some unnecessary adjustments, and left reluctantly.

"I'm not at all sure that I want to do this," Pfeiffer mumbled, faltering.

"Well," Joan said, "we can easily call off the game. Our first connection is just practice—"

"I don't mean the game. I mean the psyconnection."

Joan remained silent. Dammit, she told herself. I should have looked away when Pfeiffer's furry pet made a pass at him.

"I was crazy to agree to such a thing in the first place."

"Shall I leave?" Joan asked. "It was *you* who insisted that I come along, remember?" She stood up, but did not judge the distance of the cowl/console connections accurately, and the cowl was pulled forward, bending the silvery mask.

"I think you're as nervous as I am," Pfeiffer said appeasingly.

"Make the connection, right now. Or let's get out of here." Joan was suddenly angry and frustrated. *Do it*, she thought to herself, and for once she was not passive. Certainly not passive. *Damn him and his furry boy!* She snapped the wooden toggle switch, activating both psyconductors, and was thrust into vertiginous light. It surrounded her, as if she could see in all directions at once. But she was simply seeing through Pfeiffer's eyes. Seeing herself, small, even in his eyes, small.

After the initial shock, she realized that the light was not brilliant; on the contrary, it was soft and diffused.

But this was no connection at all: Pfeiffer was trying to close his mind to her. He appeared before her as a smooth, perfect, huge, sphere. It slowly rotated, a grim, gray planet, closed to her, forever closed. . . .

"*Are you happy now?*" asked Pfeiffer, as if from somewhere deep inside the sphere. It was so smooth, seamless. *He really doesn't need me*, she thought, and she felt as if she were flying above the surface of his closed mind, a winged thing looking for any discontinuity, any fault in his defenses. "*So you see*," Pfeiffer said, exulting in imagined victory, "*I don't need you.*" The words came wreathed in an image of a storm rolling angrily over the planet.

She flew, in sudden panic, around his thoughts, like an insect circling a source of light. She was looking for any blister or crack, any anomaly in the smooth surface. He would gamble his body away without her, that she knew, unless she could break through his defenses, prove to him how vulnerable he really was.

"*So you couldn't resist the furry boy, could you?*" Joan asked, her thoughts like smooth sharks swimming through icy water. "*Does he, then, remind you of yourself, or do I remind you of your mother?*"

His anger and exposed misery were like flares on the surface of the sun. In their place remained an eruption on Pfeiffer's smooth protective surface. A crack in the cerebral egg.

Joan dove toward the fissure, and then she was inside Pfeiffer—not the outside of his senses where he could verbalize a thought, see a face, but in the dark, prehistoric places where he dreamed, conceptualized, where he floated in and out of memory, where the eyeless creatures of his soul dwelled.

It was a sliding, a slipping in, as if one had turned over inside oneself; and Joan was sliding, slipping on ice. She found herself in a dark world of grotesque and geometric shapes, an arctic world of huge icebergs floating on a fathomless sea.

And for an instant, Joan sensed Pfeiffer's terrible fear of the world.

"*Mindfucker!*" Pfeiffer screamed, projecting the word in a hundred filthy, sickening images; and then he smashed through Joan's defenses and rushed into the deep recesses of her mind. He found her soft places and took what he could.

All that before the psyconnection was broken. Before the real game began. As if nothing had happened.

A man and woman, wearing identical cowled masks, sat across from Joan and Pfeiffer. The partition wall had been slid back, revealing the oval shape of the gaming table and doubling the size of the woodpaneled room. The dealer and the gamesmaster sat on each side of the long table between the opponents. The dealer was a young man with an intense, roundish face and straight black hair cut at the shoulders; he was most likely in training to become a gamesmaster.

The gamesmaster's face was hidden by a black cowl; he would be hooked in to the game. He explained the rules, activated the psyconductors, and the game began. Joan and Pfeiffer were once again hooked in, but there was no contact, as yet, with the man and woman across the table.

Pfeiffer cleared his mind, just as if he were before lasers or giving an interview. He had learned to cover his thoughts, for, somehow, he had always felt they could be seen, especially by those who wanted to hurt him politically and on the job.

White thought, he called it, because it was similar to white noise.

Pfeiffer could feel Joan circling around him like the wind. Although he couldn't conceal everything, he could hide from her. He could use her, just as she could use him . . . had used him. They had reached an accord via mutual blackmail. Somehow, during their practice hook-in, Joan had forced herself into Pfeiffer's mind; shocked, he attacked her.

So now they knew each other better.

They built a simple symbol structure: He was in the world, a perfect sphere without blemish, made by God's own hands, a world as strong and divine as thought; and she was his atmosphere. She contained all the elements that could not exist on his featureless surface. She was the protective cloak of his world.

They built a mnemonic in which to hide, yet they were still vulnerable to each other. But Pfeiffer guessed that Joan would remain passive—after all, she always had. She also had the well-developed conscience of a mystical liberal, and she was in love with him. He had seen that—or thought he had.

She would not expose him to danger.

Pfeiffer congratulated himself for being calm, which reinforced his calmness. Perhaps it was Joan's presence. Perhaps it was the mnemonic. But perhaps not. He had the willpower; this was just another test. He had managed to survive all the others, he told himself.

Joan rained on him, indicating her presence, and they practiced talking within geometric shapes as a protective device—it was literally raining geodesic cats and dogs.

When the gamesmaster opened the psyconductor to all involved, Joan and Pfeiffer were ready.

But they were not ready to find exact duplicates of themselves facing them across the table. The doppelgängers, of course, were not wearing cowls.

"First, mesdames and messieurs, we draw the wager," said the dealer, who was not hooked in. The gamesmaster's thoughts were a neutral presence. "For each organ pledged, there will be three games consisting of three hands to a game," continued the dealer. "In the event that a player wins twice in succession, the third hand or game will not be played." His voice was an intrusion; it was harsh and cold and came from the outside where everything was hard and intractable.

"*How do they know what we look like?*" Pfeiffer asked, shaken by the hallucination induced by his opponents.

But before Joan could reply, he answered his own question. "*They must be picking up subliminal stuff.*"

"*The way we perceive ourselves,*" Joan said. The doppelgängers became hard and ugly, as if they were being eroded by time. And Joan's double was becoming smaller, insignificant.

"*If we can't cover up, we won't have a chance.*"

"*You can't cover everything, but neither can they.*" Joan said. "*It cuts both ways.*" She noticed a fissure in the otherwise perfect sphere below, and she became black fog, miasma, protective covering. Pfeiffer was afraid and vulnerable. But she had to give him credit: He was not hiding it from her, at least. That was a beginning. . . .

"*Did you pick up anything from them, an image, anything?*" Pfeiffer asked.

"*We've been to busy with ourselves. We'll just wait and be ready when they let something slip out.*"

"*Which they will,*" Pfeiffer said, suddenly confident again.

From deep inside their interior, symbolized world, Joan and Pfeiffer could look into the external world of croupier, felt-top table, cards, wood-covered walls, and masked creatures. This room was simply a stage for the play of thought and image.

Pfeiffer was well acquainted with this sensation of perceiving two worlds, two levels: inside and outside. He often awakened from a nightmare and found himself in his living room or library. He knew that he was wide awake, and yet he could still see the dream unfurl before him, watch the creatures of his nightmare stalk about the room—the interior beasts let loose into the familiar, comforting confines of his waking world. Those were always moments of terror, for surely he was near the edge then . . . and could fall.

The dealer combined two decks of cards and placed them in a shoe, a box from which the cards could be slid out one by one. He discarded three cards: the traditional burning of the deck.

Then he dealt a card to Pfeiffer and one to his opponent. Both cards landed faceup. A queen of hearts for Pfeiffer. A nine of hearts for his opponent.

So Pfeiffer lost the right to call the wager.

Just as the object of blackjack was to draw cards that add up to twenty-one, or as near to that figure as possible, the object of blind shemmy was to draw cards that add up to nine. Thus, face cards, which would normally be counted as ten, were counted as zero. Aces, normally counted as eleven, became one; and all other cards had their normal pip (or face) value, with the exception of tens, which, like aces, were counted as one.

"Monsieur Deux wins, nine over zero," said the dealer, looking now at Pfeiffer's opponent. Pfeiffer was Monsieur Un and his opponent Monsieur Deux only because of their positions at the table.

"*A hell of a way to start,*" Pfeiffer said.

"*Keep yourself closed,*" Joan said, turning into mist, then dark rain, pure sunlight and rainbows, a perceptual kaleidoscope to conceal Pfeiffer from his enemies. "*Look now, he'll be more vulnerable when he speaks. I'll cover you.*"

"*Your choice,*" said the gamesmaster. The thought was directed to Pfeiffer's opponent, who was staring intently at Pfeiffer.

"*Look now,*" Joan said to Pfeiffer.

"Since we both turned up hearts, perhaps that is where we should begin." Pfeiffer's opponent said, speaking for the benefit of the dealer. His words felt like shards of glass to Pfeiffer. "They're the seats of our emotions: so we'd best dispose of them quickly." Pfeiffer felt the man smile. "Do you assent?"

"It's your choice." Pfeiffer said to the dealer tonelessly.

"Don't let anything out," Joan said.

Pfeiffer couldn't pick up anything from his opponent and the woman with him; they were both empty doppelgängers of himself and Joan, *"Pretend that nothing matters,"* she said. *"If you expect to see his cards and look inside of him for weakness, you must be removed."*

She's right. Pfeiffer thought. He tried to relax, smooth himself down: he thought innocuous white thoughts and ignored the knot of anxiety that seemed to be pulling at his groin.

"Cartes," said the dealer, dealing two cards from the shoe, facedown, one for Pfeiffer, the other for his opponent. Another two cards, and then a palpable silence; not even thoughts seemed to cut the air. It was an unnatural waiting. . . .

Pfeiffer had a natural nine, a winning hand (a queen and a nine of diamonds), and he looked up, about to turn over his cards, when he saw the furry boy sitting across the table from him.

"What the hell—"

"Call your hand," Joan said, feeling his glands open up, a warm waterfall of fear. But before Pfeiffer could speak, his opponent said, "My friend across the table has a natural nine. A queen and a nine, both diamonds. Since I called his hand—and I believe I am correct, then . . ."

The dealer turned Pfeiffer's cards over and said. "Monsieur Deux is correct, and wins by call." If Pfeiffer's opponent had been mistaken about the hand, Pfeiffer would have won automatically, even if his opponent had better cards.

The dealer then dealt two more cards from the shoe.

"You're supposed to be covering my thoughts," Pfeiffer said, but he was composed, thinking white thoughts again.

"I'm trying," Joan said. *"But you won't trust me: you're trying to cover yourself from me as well as your opponent. What the hell am I supposed to do?"*

"I'm sorry," Pfeiffer thought.

"Are you really so afraid that I'll see your true feelings?"

"This is neither the time nor the place." His rhythm of white thought was broken; Joan became a snowstorm, aiding him, lulling him back to white blindness. *"I think the gamesmaster is making me nervous, having him hooked in, privy to all our thoughts. . . ."*

"Forget the gamesmaster . . . and for God's sake, stop worrying about what I'll see. I'm on your side."

"Monsieur Un, will you *please* claim your cards," said the dealer. The gamesmaster nodded at Pfeiffer and thought neutral, papery thoughts.

Pfeiffer turned up the edges of his cards. He had a jack of diamonds—which counted as zero—and a two of spades. He would need another card.

"*Don't think about your cards,*" Joan exclaimed. "*Are you picking up anything from the other side of the table?*"

Pfeiffer listened, as if to his own thoughts. He didn't raise his head to look at his opponent, for seeing his own face—or that of the furry boy's—staring back at him from across the table was disconcerting, and fascinating. An image of an empty, hollow woman without any organs formed in his mind. He imagined her as a bag somehow formed into human shape.

"*Keep that,*" Joan said. "*It might be usable.*"

"*But I can't see his cards.*"

"*Just wait awhile. Keep calm.*"

"Does Monsieur wish another card?" the dealer asked Pfeiffer. Pfeiffer took another card and so did his opponent.

Pfeiffer had no idea what cards his opponent was holding; it promised to be a blind play. When the cards were turned over, the dealer announced, "Monsieur Deux wins, six over five." Pfeiffer had lost again.

"*I'm playing blind,*" Pfeiffer said anxiously to Joan.

"*He couldn't see your cards, either,*" she replied.

But that gave him little satisfaction, for by losing the first two hands, he had lost the first game.

And if he lost the next game, he would lose his heart, which, white thought or not, seemed to Pfeiffer to be beating in his throat.

"*Try to calm yourself,*" Joan said, "*or you'll let everything out. If you trust me, and stop throwing up your defenses, maybe I can help you. But you've got to let me in; as it is, you're giving our friends quite the edge. Let's make a merger . . . a marriage.*" But Pfeiffer was in no mood for irony. His fear was building, steadily, slowly.

"*You can fold the game,*" Joan said. "*That is an alternative.*"

"*And give up organs I haven't yet played for!*" The smooth surface of Pfeiffer's sphere cracked, and Joan let herself be swallowed into it. The surface of the sphere changed, grew mountain chains, lush vegetation, flowers, deserts, all the mingled moods of Joan and Pfeiffer.

Pfeiffer was no longer isolated; he was protected, yet dangerously exposed. Inside him, in the human, moist dark, Joan promised not to take advantage of him. She caught a fleeting thought of Pfeiffer's dead mother, who had been a fleshy, big-boned, flat-faced woman. She also saw that Pfeiffer hated his mother, as much now as when she was alive.

In the next hand—the opening hand of the second game—Pfeiffer held a five of clubs and a two of spades, a total of seven points. He would not take another card unless he could see his opponent's. But when he looked up, Pfeiffer saw the furry boy, who blew him a kiss.

"*You're exposed again,*" Joan said, and they thought themselves inside their world, thought protective darkness around themselves, except for one tiny opening through which to see into their enemies.

"*Concentrate on that image of the empty woman,*" Joan said to Pfeiffer. "*She has to be Monsieur Deux's wife or woman. I can't quite visualize it as you did.*" But Pfeiffer was trying to smooth down his emotions and the dark, dangerous demon that was his memory. The image of the furry boy sparked memories, fears, guilts. Pfeiffer remembered his father, who had been a doctor. There was always enough money, but his father extracted emotional dues for every dollar he gave his son. And, as a result, the young Pfeiffer had recurrent nightmares that he was sucking off his father. Those nightmares began again after his mother died: She had seen that homosexual fantasy when Pfeiffer hooked in to her on her deathbed.

Pfeiffer still had those nightmares.

And now, against his will, the image of him sucking off the furry boy passed through his mind, drawing its train of guilt and revulsion. The boy and his father, somehow one and the same.

"*You're leaking,*" Joan said, her thoughts an icestorm. She could see her way into Pfeiffer now, into those rooms of buried memories. Rather than rooms, she thought of them as subterranean caverns; everything inside them was intact, perfect, hidden from the harmful light and atmosphere of consciousness. Now she knew him. . . .

Pfeiffer collected himself and peered into his opponent's mind. He thrust the image of the organless woman at the man.

It was like tearing a spiderweb.

Pfeiffer felt the man's pain as a feather touching flesh: The organless woman was Monsieur Deux's permanent wife. Pfeiffer had broken through and into his thoughts; he could feel his opponent's name, something like Gayah, Gahai, Gayet, that was it, and his wife was used up. Gayet saw her, in the darkness of his unconscious, as an empty bag. She was a compulsive gambler, who had spent her organs; and Gayet hated gambling, but she possessed him, and he hated her and loved her, and was just beginning his self-destructive slide.

Now she was using him up. She was gambling his organs.

"*She's used up.*" Pfeiffer thought at Gayet. But Pfeiffer could only glimpse Gayet's thoughts. His wife was not exposed.

Nor was she defenseless.

She thrust the image of the furry boy at Pfeiffer, and Pfeiffer felt his head being forced down upon the furry boy's lap. But it suddenly wasn't the furry boy anymore. It was Pfeiffer's father!

There was no distance now. Pfeiffer was caught, tiny and vulnerable. Gayet and his wife were swallowing him, thoughts and all.

It was Joan who saved him. She pulled him away, and he became the world again, wrapped in snow, in whiteness. He was safe again, as if inside Joan's cold womb.

"*Look now,*" Joan said an instant later, and like a revelation, Pfeiffer saw Gayet's cards, saw them buried in Gayet's eyes with the image of his aging wife. In that instant, Pfeiffer saw into Gayet and forgot himself. Gayet's wife was named Grace, and she had been eroded from too many surgeries, too many deformation games. She was his Blue Angel (yes, he had seen the ancient film) and Gayet the fool.

The fool held an ace of hearts and a five of diamonds.

Now Pfeiffer felt that the odds were with him; it was a familiar sensation for gamblers, a sense of harmony, of being a benevolent extension of the cards. No anger, no fear, no hate, just victory. Pfeiffer called Gayet's hand, thereby preventing Gayet from drawing another card, such as a lucky three, which would have given him a count of nine.

Pfeiffer won the hand, and he thanked Joan. His thoughts were of love, but his repertoire of images was limited. Joan was now part of his rhythm and harmony, a constant presence; and she dreamed of the victorious cats that padded so gracefully through the lush vegetation of Pfeiffer's sphere.

The cats that rutted, then devoured one another.

Pfeiffer won the next hand to take the second game. Pfeiffer and his opponent were now even. The next game would determine the outcome. Pfeiffer felt that calm, cold certainty that he would take Gayet's heart. The obsession to expose and ruin his opponent became more important than winning or losing organs; it was bright and fast flowing, refreshing as water.

He was in a better world now, a more complete, fulfilling plane of reality. All gamblers dreamed of this: losing or winning everything, but being inside the game. Even Joan was carried away by the game. She, too, wanted to rend—to whittle away at the couple across the table, take their privacies, turn over their humiliations like worry beads. They were Pfeiffers enemies . . . and his enemies were her own.

Everyone was exposed now, batttleweary, mentally and physically exhausted, yet lost in play, lost in perfect, concentrated time. Pfeiffer could see Gayet's face, both as Gayet saw himself and as Grace saw him. A wide nose, dark complexion, low forehead, large ears; yet it was a strong face, and handsome in a feral, almost frightening way—or so Grace thought. Gayet saw himself as weak; the flesh on his face was too loose.

Gayet was a failure, although he had made his career and fortune in the Exchange. He had wanted to be a mathematician, but he was lazy and lost the "knack" by twenty-five.

Gayet would have made a brilliant mathmatician, and he knew it.

And Grace was a whore, using herself and everyone else. Here was a woman with great religious yearnings, who had wanted to join a religious order, but was blackballed by the cults because of her obsession for gambling and psyconductors. But Pfeiffer could see into her only a little. She was a cold bitch and, more than any of the others, had reserves of strength.

This last game would be psychological surgery. Tearing with the knife, pulping with the bludgeon. Pfeiffer won the first hand. This was joy; so many organs to win or lose, so little time.

Pfeiffer lost the next hand, Gayet exposed Joan, who revealed Pfeiffer's cards without realizing it. Gayet had opened her up, penetrated all that efficiency and order to expose anger and lust and uncontrolled oceanic pity. Joan's emotions writhed and crawled over her like beautifully colored, slippery snakes.

Pfeiffer had been too preoccupied to protect her.

Joan's first uncontrolled thought was to revenge herself on Pfeiffer, expose him; but he opened up to her, buried her in white thought, which was as cold and numbing as ice, and apologized without words, but with the soft, rounded, comforting thoughts he equated with love. She couldn't trust him, nor could she expose him. Right now, she could only accept him.

The dealer gave Pfeiffer a three of diamonds and an ace of clubs. That gave him only four points; he would have to draw again. He kept his thoughts from Joan, for she was covering him. She could attack Gayet and his whore, expose them for their cards. Gayet's heart was not simply his organ—not now, not to Pfeiffer. It was his whole life, life itself. To rip it away from him would be to conquer life, if only for a moment. It was life affirming. It was being alive. Suddenly he thought of his father.

"Close yourself up," Joan said. *"You're bleeding."* She did not try to penetrate his thoughts; that would have exposed Pfeiffer even more dangerously.

"Help me," Pfeiffer asked Joan. This hand would determine whether he would win or lose the game . . . and his heart.

Once again she became his cloak, his atmosphere, and she weaved her icy threads of white thought into his.

This was love, she thought.

Pfeiffer couldn't see Gayet's cards and nervously asked Joan to do something. Gayet was playing calmly, well covered by Grace, who simply hid him. No extravagance there.

Joan emptied her mind, became neutral; yet she was a needle of cold, coherent thought. She prodded, probed, touched her opponents' thoughts. It was like swimming through an ever-changing world of dots and bars, tangible as iron, fluid as water. It was as if Gayet's and Grace's thoughts were luminous points on a fluorescent screen.

And still she went unnoticed.

Gayet was like Pfeiffer, Joan thought. Seemingly placid, controlled, but that was all gingerbread to hide a weak house. He was so much weaker than Grace, who was supporting and cloaking him. But Grace was concentrating on her energies on Gayet; and she had the fever, as if she were gambling her own organs once again.

Undoubtedly, Grace expected Joan and Pfeiffer to go straight for Gayet, who had read the cards.

So Joan went for Grace, who was in the gambler's frenzy as the hand was being played. Joan slipped past Grace's thoughts, worked her way into the woman's mind, through the dark labyrinths and channels of her memory, and into the dangerous country of the unconscious. Invisible as air, she listened to Grace, read her, discovered: A sexual miasma. Being brutally raped as a child. After a riot in Manosque. Raped in a closet, for God's sake. The man tore her open with a rifle barrel, then inserted himself. Taking her, piece by bloody piece, just as she was taking Gayet. Just as others had taken her in rooms like this, in this casino, in this closet.

And Gayet, now Joan could see him through Grace, unperturbable Gayet, who had so much money and so little life, who was so afraid of his wife's past, of her lovers and liberations he called perversions. But he called *everything* a perversion.

How she hated him beneath what she called love.

But he looked just like the man who had raped her in that closet so long ago. She could not remember the man's face—so effectively had she blocked it out of her mind—yet she was stunned when she first met Gayet. She felt attracted to him, but also repelled; she was in love.

                    *   *   *

Through Joan, Pfeiffer saw Gayet's cards; a deuce and a six of clubs. He could call his hand, but he wasn't sure of the deuce. It looked like a heart, but it could just as easily be a diamond. If he called it wrong, he would lose the hand, and his heart.

"*I can't be sure,*" Pfeiffer said to Joan, expecting help.

But Joan was in trouble. Grace had discovered her, and she was stronger than Joan had ever imagined. Joan was trapped inside Grace's mind; and Grace, who could not face what Joan had found, denied it.

And snapped.

In that instant, Joan felt that *she* was Grace. She felt all of Grace's pain and the choking weight of memory, as souls and selves incandescently merged. But before Joan and Grace could fuse inescapably, Joan recoiled, realizing that she was fighting for her life. She screamed for the gamesmaster to deactivate the game. But her screams were lost as Grace instantly slipped into the gamesmaster's mind and caught him, too. She had the psychotic's strength of desperation, and Joan realized that Grace would kill them all rather than face the truth about herself and Gayet.

Furiously Grace went after Pfeiffer. To kill him. She blamed him for Joan's presence, and Joan felt crushing pain, as if she were being buried alive in the dirt of Grace's mind. She tried to wrench herself away from Grace's thoughts, lest they intertwine with and become her own.

She felt Grace's bloodlust . . . her need to kill Pfeiffer.

Grace grasped Pfeiffer with a thought, wound dark filaments around him that could not be turned away by white thought or anything else.

And like a spider, she wrapped her prey in darkness and looked for physiological weakness, any flaw, perhaps a blood vessel that might rupture in his head. . . .

Joan tried to pull herself away from the pain, from the concrete weight crushing her. Ironically, she wondered if thought had mass. What a stupid thought to die with, she told herself, and she suddenly remembered a story her father had told her about a dying rabbi who was annoyed at the minyan praying around him because he was trying to listen to two washerwomen gossiping outside. Many years later, her father confessed to her that it wasn't really a Jewish story at all; it was Buddhist.

She held on to that thought, remembered how her father had laughed after his confession. The pain eased as she followed her thoughts.

. . . If thought had mass.

She was thinking herself free, escaping Grace by finding the proper angle, as if thought and emotion and pain were purely mathematical.

That done in an instant.

But if she were to save Pfeiffer's life, and her own, she would have to do something immediately. She showed Grace her past. Showed her that she had married Gayet because he had the face of the man who had raped her as a child.

Gayet, seeing this too, screamed. How he loathed Grace, but not nearly as much as she loathed herself. He had tried to stop Grace, but he was too weak. He, too, had been caught.

As if cornered, as if she were back in the closet with her rapist, she attacked Gayet. Only now she had a weapon. She thought him dead, trapped him in a scream, and, as if he were being squeezed from the insides, his blood pressure rose. She had found a weakened blood vessel in his head, and it ruptured.

The effort weakened Grace, and a few seconds later the gamesmaster was able to regain control and disconnect everyone. Gayet was immediately hooked in to a life-support unit which applied CPR techniques to keep his heart beating.

But he was dead. . . .

There would be some rather sticky legal complications, but by surviving, Pfeiffer had won the game, had indeed beaten Grace and won all of Gayet's organs.

As Pfeiffer gazed through the transparent walls of the transpod that whisked him and Joan out of Paris, away from its dangers and sordid delights, he felt something new and delicate toward Joan.

It was newfound intimacy and gratitude . . . and love.

Joan, however, still carried the echoes of Grace's thoughts, as if a part of her had irreversibly fused with Grace. She too felt something new for Pfeiffer. Perhaps it was renewal, an evolution of her love.

They were in love . . . yet even now Joan felt the compulsion to gamble again.

PAT MURPHY

In The Islands

Halfbreeds are often outcasts, misfits, unable to feel comfortable in either of their parent's worlds, not quite one thing, not quite the other. Here's a quietly moving story about a boy who is literally caught between two worlds and an older man who must face a difficult decision about where his own loyalties ultimately lie . . .

Pat Murphy lives in San Francisco where she works for a science museum, the Exploratorium, and edits their quarterly magazine. Her elegant and incisive stories have been turning up for the past few years in *Isaac Asimov's Science Fiction Magazine, Elsewhere, Amazing, Universe, Shadows, Galaxy, Chrysalis,* and other places. Her first novel, *The Shadow Hunter,* was published in 1982. She is currently at work on a new novel, set in Yucatan, tentatively entitled *Ancient Voices*.

IN THE ISLANDS

Pat Murphy

Though the sun was nearly set, Morris wore dark glasses when he met Nick at the tiny dirt runway that served as the Bay Islands' only airport. Nick was flying in from Los Angeles by way of San Pedro Sula in Honduras. He peered through the cracked window of the old DC-3 as the plane bumped to a stop.

Morris stood with adolescent awkwardness by the one-room wooden building that housed Customs for the Islands. Morris: dark, curly hair, red baseball cap pulled low over mirrored sunglasses, long-sleeved shirt with torn-out elbows, jeans with ragged cuffs.

A laughing horde of young boys ran out to the plane and grabbed dive bags and suitcases to carry to Customs. With the exception of Nick, the passengers were scuba divers, bound for Anthony's Cay resort on the far side of Roatan, the main island in the group.

Nick met Morris halfway to the Customs building, handed him a magazine, and said only, "Take a look at page fifty."

The article was titled "The Physiology and Ecology of a New Species of Flashlight Fish," by Nicholas C. Rand and Morris Morgan.

Morris studied the article for a moment, flipping through the pages and ignoring the young boys who swarmed past, carrying suitcases almost too large for them to handle. Morris looked up at Nick and grinned—a flash of white teeth in a thin, tanned face. "Looks good," he said. His voice was a little hoarser than Nick had remembered.

"For your first publication, it's remarkable." Nick patted Morris's shoulder awkwardly. Nick looked and acted older than his thirty-five years. At the University, he treated his colleagues with distant courtesy and had no real friends. He was more comfortable with Morris than with anyone else he knew.

"Come on," Morris said. "We got to get your gear and go." He tried to sound matter-of-fact, but he betrayed his excitement by slipping into the dialect of the Islands—an archaic English spoken with a strange lilt and governed by rules all its own.

Nick tipped the youngster who had hauled his bags to Customs and waited behind the crowd of divers. The inspector looked at Nick, stamped his passport, and said, "Go on. Have a good stay." Customs inspections on the Islands tended to be perfunctory. Though the Bay Islands were governed by Honduras, the Islanders tended to follow their own rules. The Bay Islands lay off the coast of Honduras in the area of the Caribbean that had once been called the Spanish Main. The population was an odd mix: native Indians, relocated slaves called Caribs, and descendants of the English pirates who had used the Islands as home base.

The airport's runway stretched along the shore and the narrow, sandy beach formed one of its edges. Morris had beached his skiff at one end of the landing strip.

"I got a new skiff, a better one," Morris said. "If the currents be with us, we'll be in East Harbor in two hours, I bet."

They loaded Nick's gear and pushed off. Morris piloted the small boat. He pulled his cap low over his eyes to keep the wind from catching it and leaned a little into the wind. Nick noticed Morris's hand on the tiller; webbing stretched between the fingers. It seemed to Nick that the webbing extended further up each finger than it had when Nick had left the Islands four months before.

Dolphins came from nowhere to follow the boat, riding the bow wave and leaping and splashing alongside. Nick sat in the bow and watched Morris. The boy was intent on piloting the skiff. Behind him, dolphins played and the wake traced a white line through the silvery water. The dolphins darted away, back to the open sea, as the skiff approached East Harbor.

The town stretched along the shore for about a mile: a collection of brightly painted houses on stilts, a grocery store, a few shops. The house that Nick had rented was on the edge of town.

Morris docked neatly at the pier near the house, and helped Nick carry his dive bag and luggage to the house. "There's beer in the icebox," Morris said. "Cold."

Nick got two beers. He returned to the front porch. Morris was sitting on the railing, staring out into the street. Though the sun was down and twilight was fading fast, Morris wore his sunglasses still. Nick sat on the rail beside the teenager. "So what have you been doing since I left?"

Morris grinned. He took off his sunglasses and tipped back his cap. Nick could see his eyes—wide and dark and filled with repressed excitement. "I'm going," Morris said. "I'm going to sea."

Nick took a long drink from his beer and wiped his mouth. He had known this was coming, known it for a long time.

"My dad, he came to the harbor; and we swam together. I'll be going with him soon. Look." Morris held up one hand. The webbing between his fingers stretched from the base almost to the tip of each finger. The light from the overhead bulb shone through the thin skin. "I'm changing, Nick. It's almost time."

"What does your mother say of this?"

"My mum? Nothing." His excitement was spilling over. He laid a hand on Nick's arm, and his touch was cold. "I'm going, Nick."

Ten years ago, Nick had been diving at night off Middle Cay, a small coral island not far from East Harbor. He had been diving alone at night to study the nighttime ecology of the reef. Even at age twenty-five, Nick had possessed a curiosity stronger than his sense of self-preservation.

The reef changed with the dying of the light. Different fishes came out of hiding; different invertebrates prowled the surface of the coral. Nick was particularly interested in the flashlight fish, a small fish that glowed in the dark. Beneath each eye, the flashlight fish had an organ filled with bioluminescent bacteria, which gave off a cold green light. They were elusive fish, living in deep waters and rising up to the reef only when the moon was new and the night was dark.

At night, sharks came in from the open sea to prowl the reef. Nick did not care to study them, but sometimes they came to study him. He carried a flashlight in one hand, a shark billy in the other. Usually, the sharks were only curious. Usually, they circled once, then swam away.

On that night ten years before, the gray reef shark that circled him twice did not seem to understand this. Nick could see the flat black eye, dispassionately watching him. The shark turned to circle again, turning with a grace that made its movement seem leisurely. It came closer; and Nick thought, even as he swam for the surface, about what an elegant machine it was. He had dissected sharks and admired the way their muscles worked so tirelessly and their teeth were arranged so efficiently.

He met the shark with a blow of the billy, a solid blow, but the explosive charge in the tip of the club failed. The charges did fail, as often as not. But worse: the shark twisted back. As he struck at it again, the billy slipped from his hand, caught in an eddy of water. He snatched at it and watched it tumble away, with the maddening slowness of objects underwater.

The shark circled wide, then came in again: elegant, efficient, deadly.

The shadow that intercepted the shark was neither elegant nor efficient. In the beam of the flashlight, Nick could see him clearly: a small boy dressed in ragged shorts and armed with a shark billy. This one exploded when he struck the shark, and the animal turned with grace and speed to cruise away, heading for the far side of the reef. The boy grinned at Nick and glided away into the darkness. Nick saw five lines on each side of the boy's body—five gills slits that opened and closed and opened and closed.

Nick hauled himself into the boat. He lay on his back and looked at the stars. At night, the world underwater often seemed unreal. He looked at the stars and told himself that over and over.

When Nick was in the Islands, Morris usually slept on the porch of whatever house Nick had rented. Nick slept on a bed inside.

Nick was tired from a long day of travel. He slept and he came upon the forbidden dreams with startling urgency and a kind of relief. It was only a dream, he told himself. Darkness covered his sins.

He dreamed that Morris lay on a dissecting table, asleep, his webbed hands quiet at his sides. Morris's eyes had no lashes; his nose was flat and broad; his face was thin and triangular—too small for his eyes. He's not human, Nick thought, not human at all.

Nick took the scalpel in his hand and drew it through the top layers of skin and muscle alongside the five gill slits on Morris's right side. There was little blood. Later, he would use the bone shears to cut through the ribs to examine the internal organs. Now, he just laid back the skin and muscle to expose the intricate structure of the gills.

Morris did not move. Nick looked at the teenager's face and realized suddenly that Morris was not asleep. He was dead. For a moment, Nick felt a tremendous sense of loss; but he pushed the feeling away. He felt hollow, but he fingered the feathery tissue of the gills and planned the rest of the dissection.

He woke to the palm fronds rattling outside his window and the warm morning breeze drying the sweat on his face. The light of dawn—already bright and strong—shone in the window.

Morris was not on the porch. His baseball cap hung from a nail beside the hammock.

Nick made breakfast from the provisions that Morris had left him: fried eggs, bread, milk. In midmorning, he strolled to town.

Morris's mother, Margarite, ran a small shop in the living room of her home, selling black-coral jewelry to tourists. The black coral came from deep waters; Morris brought it to her.

Two women—off one of the sailing yachts anchored in the harbor—were bargaining with Margarite for black-coral earrings. Nick waited for them to settle on a price and leave. They paid for the jewelry and stepped back out into the street, glancing curiously at Nick.

"Where's Morris?" he said to Margarite. He leaned on the counter and looked into her dark eyes. She was a stocky woman with skin the color of coffee with a little cream. She wore a flowered dress, hemmed modestly just below her knees.

He had wondered at times what this dark-eyed woman thought of her son. She did not speak much, and he had sometimes suspected that she was slow-witted. He wondered how it had happened that this stocky woman had found an alien lover on a beach, had made love with such a stranger, had given birth to a son who fit nowhere at all.

"Morris—he has gone to sea," she said. "He goes to sea these days." She began rearranging the jewelry that had been jumbled by the tourists.

"When will he be back?" Nick asked.

She shrugged. "Maybe never."

"Why do you say that?" His voice was sharp, sharper than he intended. She did not look up from the tray. He reached across the counter and took her hand in a savage grip. "Look at me. Why do you say that?"

"He will be going to sea," she said softly. "He must. He belongs there."

"He will come to say good-bye," Nick said.

She twisted her hand in his grip, but he held her tightly. "His dad never said good-bye," she said softly.

Nick let her hand go. He rarely lost his temper and he knew he was not really angry with this woman, but with himself. He turned away without saying good-bye.

He strolled down the dirt lane that served as East Harbor's main street. He nodded to an old man who sat on his front porch, greeted a woman who was hanging clothes on a line. The day was hot and still.

He was a stranger here; he would always be a stranger here. He did not know what the Islanders thought of him, what they thought of Morris and Margarite. Morris had told him that they knew of the water-dwellers and kept their secret. "They live by the sea," Morris had said. "If they talk too much, their nets will rip and their boats sink. They don't tell."

Nick stopped by the grocery store on the far edge of town. A ramshackle pier jutted into the sea right beside the store.

Ten years before, the pier had been in better repair. Nick had been in town to pick up supplies. For a month, he was renting a skiff and a house on Middle Cay and studying the reef.

The sun had reached the horizon, and its light made a silver path on the water. Somewhere, far off, he could hear the laughter and shouting of small boys. At the end of the pier, a kid in a red baseball cap was staring out to sea.

Nick bought two Cokes from the grocery—cold from the icebox behind the counter. He carried them out to the pier. The old boards creaked beneath his feet, but the boy did not look up.

"Have a Coke," Nick said.

The boy's face was dirty. His dark eyes were too large for his face. He wore a red kerchief around his neck, ragged shorts, and a shirt that gaped open where the second button should have been. He accepted the Coke and took his first swig without saying anything.

Nick studied his face for a moment, comparing this face to the one that he remembered. A strange kind of calmness took hold of him. "You shouldn't go diving at night," he said. "You're too young to risk your life with sharks."

The boy grinned and took another swig of Coke.

"That was you, wasn't it?" Nick asked. He sat beside the kid on the dock, his legs dangling over the water. "That was you." His voice was steady.

"Aye." The boy looked at Nick with dark, grave eyes. "That was me."

The part of Nick's mind that examined information and accepted or rejected it took this in and accepted it. That part of him had never believed that the kid was a dream, never believed that the shark was imaginary.

"What's your name?"

"Morris."

"I'm Nick." They shook hands and Nick noticed the webbing between the boy's fingers—from the base of the finger to the first joint.

"You're a marine biologist?" asked the kid. His voice was a little too deep for him, a little rough, as if he found speaking difficult.

"Yes."

"What was you doing, diving out there at night?"

"I was watching the fish. I want to know what happens on the reef at night." He shrugged. "Sometimes I am too curious for my own good."

The boy watched him with dark, brooding eyes. "My dad, he says I should have let the shark have you. He says you will tell others."

"I haven't said anything to anyone," Nick protested.

The boy took another swig of Coke, draining the bottle. He set the bottle carefully on the dock, one hand still gripping it. He studied Nick's face. "You must promise you will never tell." He tilted back his baseball cap and continued to study Nick's face. "I will show you things you has got no chance of finding without me." The boy spoke with quiet confidence and Nick found himself nodding. "You know those little fish you want to find—the ones that glow?" He grinned when Nick looked surprised and said, "The Customs man said you were looking for them. I has been to a place where you can find them every new moon. And I has found a kind that aren't in the books."

"What do you know about what's in the books?"

Morris shrugged, a smooth, fluid motion. "I read the books. I has got to know about these things." He held out his hand for Nick to shake. "You promise?"

Nick hesitated, then put his hand in the kid's hand. "I promise." He would have promised more than that to learn about this kid.

"I has a skiff much better than that," Morris said, jerking his head contemptuously toward the skiff that Nick had been using. "I'll be at Middle Cay tomorrow."

Morris showed up at Middle Cay and took Nick to places that he never would have found. Morris read all Nick's reference books with great interest.

And the webbing between his fingers kept growing.

Nick bought a cold Coke in the grocery store and strolled back to his house. Morris was waiting on the porch, sitting on the rail and reading their article in the magazine.

"I brought lobsters for dinner," he said. Small scratching noises came from the covered wooden crate at his feet. He thumped on it with his heel, and the noises stopped for a moment, then began again.

"Where have you been?"

"Out to the Hog Islands. Fishing mostly. I spend most of the days underwater now." He looked at Nick but his eyes were concealed by the mirrored glasses. "When you left, I could only stay under for a few hours. Now, there doesn't seem to be a limit. And the sun burns me if I'm out too much."

Nick caught himself studying the way Morris was holding the magazine. The webbing between his fingers tucked neatly out of the way. It should not work, he thought. This being that is shaped like a man and swims like a fish. But bumblebees can't fly, by logical reasoning.

"What do you think of the article?" Nick asked

"Good, as far as it goes. Could say more. I've been watching them, and they seem to signal to each other. There's different patterns for the males and females. I've got notes on it all. I'll show you. The water temperature seems to affect them too."

Nick was thinking how painful this curiosity of his was. It had always been so. He wanted to know; he wanted to understand. He had taken Morris's temperature; he had listened to Morris's heartbeat and monitored its brachycardia when Morris submerged. He had monitored the oxygen levels in the blood, observed Morris's development. But there was so much more to learn. He had been hampered by his own lack of background—he was a biologist, not a doctor. There were tests he could not perform without harming Morris. And he had not wanted to hurt Morris. No, he did not want to hurt Morris.

"I'll leave all my notes on your desk," Morris was saying. "You should take a look before I go."

Nick frowned. "You'll be able to come back," he said. "Your father comes in to see you. You'll come back and tell me what you've seen, won't you?"

Morris set the magazine on the rail beside him and pushed his cap back. The glasses hid his eyes. "The ocean will change me," he said. "I may not remember the right things to tell you. My father thinks deep, wet thoughts; and I don't always understand him." Morris shrugged. "I will change."

"I thought you wanted to be a biologist. I thought you wanted to learn. And here you are, saying that you'll change and forget all this." Nick's voice was bitter.

"I has got no choice. It's time to go." Nick could not see his eyes or interpret his tone. "I don't belong on the land anymore. I don't belong here."

Nick found that he was gripping the rail as he leaned against it. He could learn so much from Morris. So much. "Why do you think you'll belong there. You won't fit there, with your memories of the islands. You won't belong."

Morris took off his glasses and looked at Nick with dark, wet eyes. "I'll belong. I has got to belong. I'm going."

The lobsters scratched inside their box. Morris replaced his sunglasses and thumped lightly on the lid again. "We should make dinner," he said. "They're getting restless."

During the summer on Middle Cay, Nick and Morris had become friends. Nick came to rely on Morris's knowledge of the reef. Morris lived on the island and seemed to find there a security he needed. His curiosity about the sea matched Nick's.

Early each evening, just after sunset, they would sit on the beach and talk—about the reef, about life at the University, about marine biology, and—more rarely—about Morris and his father.

Morris could say very little about his father. "My dad told me legends," Morris said to Nick, "but that's all. The legends say that the water people came down from the stars. They came a long time ago." Nick was watching Morris and the boy was digging his fingers in the sand, as if searching for something to grasp.

"What do you think?" Nick asked him.

Morris shrugged. "Doesn't really matter. I think they must be native to this world or they couldn't breed with humans." He sifted the beach sand with his webbed hands. "But it doesn't much matter. I'm here. And I'm not human." He looked at Nick with dark, lonely eyes.

Nick had wanted to reach across the sand and grasp the cold hand that kept sifting the sand, digging and sifting the sand. He wanted to say something comforting. But he had remained silent, giving the boy only the comfort of his company.

Nick lay on his cot, listening to the sounds of the evening. He could hear his neighbor's chickens, settling down to rest. He could hear the evening wind in the palms. He wanted to sleep, but he did not want to dream.

Once Morris was gone, he would not come back, Nick thought. If only Nick could keep him here.

Nick started to drift to sleep and caught himself on the brink of a dream. His hands had been closing on Morris's throat. Somehow, in that moment, his hands were not his own. They were his father's hands: cool, clean, brutally competent. His father, a high school biology teacher with a desire to be more, had taught him how to pith a frog, how to hold it tight and insert the long pin at the base of the skull. "It's just a frog," his father had said. His father's hands were closing on Morris's throat and Nick was thinking, I could break his neck—quickly and painlessly. After all, he's not human.

Nick snapped awake and clasped his hands as if that might stop them from doing harm. He was shivering in the warm night. He sat up on the edge of the bed, keeping his hands locked together. He stepped out onto the porch where Morris was sleeping.

Morris was gone; the hammock was empty. Nick looked out over the empty street and let his hands relax. He returned to his bed and dozed off, but his sleep was disturbed by voices that blended with the evening wind. He could hear his former wife's bitter voice speaking over the sound of the wind. She said, "I'm going. You don't love me, you just want to analyze me. I'm going." He could hear his father, droning on about how the animal felt no pain, how it was all in the interest of science. At last he sank into a deeper sleep, but in the morning he did not want to remember his dreams.

Morris was still gone when Nick finished breakfast. He read over Morris's notes. They were thorough and carefully taken. Nick made notes for another paper on the flashlight fish, a paper on which Morris would be senior author.

Morris returned late in the afternoon. Nick looked up from his notes, looked into Morris's mirrored eyes, and thought of death. And tried not to think of death.

"I thought we could go to Middle Cay for dinner," Morris said. "I has got conch and shrimp. We can take the camp stove and fix them there."

Nick tapped his pencil against the pad nervously. "Yes. Let's do that."

Morris piloted the skiff to Middle Cay. Through the water, Nick could see the reef that ringed the island—shades of blue and green beneath the water. The reef was broken by channels here and there; Morris followed the main channel nearly to the beach, then cut the engine and let the skiff drift in.

They set up the camp stove in a level spot, sheltered by the trunk of a fallen palm tree. Morris cracked the conch and pounded it and threw it in the pan with shrimp. They drank beer while the combination cooked. They ate from tin cups, leaning side by side against the fallen palm.

"You can keep the skiff for yourself," Morris said suddenly. "I think that you can use it."

Nick looked at him, startled.

"I left my notes on your desk," Morris said. "They be as clear as I can make them."

Nick was studying his face. "I will go tonight," Morris said. "My dad will come here to meet me." The sun had set and the evening breeze was kicking up waves in the smooth water. He drained his beer and set the bottle down beside the stove.

Morris stood and took off his shirt, slipped out of his pants. The gill slits made stripes that began just below his ribcage and ended near his hips. He was more muscular than Nick remembered. He stepped toward the water.

"Wait," Nick said. "Not yet."

"Got to." Morris turned to look at Nick. "There's a mask and fins in the skiff. Come with me for a ways."

Morris swam ahead, following the channel out. Nick followed in mask and fins. The twilight had faded. The water was dark and its surface shone silver. The night did not seem real. The darkness made it dreamlike. The sound of Nick's feet breaking the water's surface was too loud. The touch of the water against his skin was too warm. Morris swam just ahead, just out of reach.

Nick wore his dive knife at his belt. He always wore his dive knife at his belt. As he swam, he noticed that he was taking his knife out and holding it ready. It was a heavy knife, designed for prying rocks apart and cracking conch. It would work best as a club, he was thinking. A club to be used for a sudden sharp blow from behind. That might be enough. If he called to Morris, then Morris would stop and Nick could catch him.

But his voice was not cooperating. Not yet. His hands held the knife ready, but he could not call out. Not yet.

He felt the change in water temperature as they passed into deeper water. He felt something—a swirl of water against his legs—as if something large were swimming past.

Morris disappeared from the water ahead of him. The water was smooth, with no sign of Morris's bobbing head. "Morris," Nick called. "Morris."

He saw them then. Dim shapes beneath the water. Morris: slim, almost human. His father: man-shaped, but different. His arms were the wrong shape; his legs were too thick and muscular.

Morris was close enough to touch, but Nick did not strike. When Morris reached out and touched Nick's hand with a cold, gentle touch, Nick released the knife and let it fall, watched it tumble toward the bottom.

Morris's father turned in the water to look up at Nick and Nick read nothing in those inhuman eyes: cold, dark, dispassionate. Black and uncaring as the eyes of a shark. Nick saw Morris swim down and touch his father's shoulder, urging him away into the darkness.

"Morris!" Nick called, knowing Morris could not hear him. He kicked with frantic energy, not caring that his knife was gone. He did not want to stop Morris. He wanted to go with Morris and swim with the dolphins and explore the sea.

There was darkness below him—cool, deep water. He could feel the tug of the currents. He swam, not conserving his energy, not caring. His kicks grew weaker. He looked down into the world of darkness and mystery and he sank below the surface almost gladly.

He felt a cold arm around his shoulders. He coughed up water when the arm dragged him to the surface. He coughed, took a breath that was half water, half air, coughed again. Dark water surged against his mask each time the arm dragged him forward. He choked and struggled, but the arm dragged him on.

One flailing leg bumped against coral, then against sand. Sand scraped against his back as he was dragged up the beach. His mask was ripped away and he turned on his side to retch and cough up seawater.

Morris squatted beside him with one cold webbed hand still on his shoulder. Nick focused on Morris's face and on the black eyes that seemed as remote as mirrored lenses. "Good-bye, Nick," Morris said. His voice was a hoarse whisper. "Good-bye."

Morris's hand lingered on Nick's shoulder for an instant. Then the young man stood and walked back to the sea.

Nick lay on his back and looked up at the stars. After a time, he breathed more easily. He picked up Morris's cap from where it lay on the beach and turned it in his hands, in a senseless repetitive motion.

He crawled further from the water and lay his head against the fallen log. He gazed at the stars and the sea, and thought about how he could write down his observations of Morris's departure and Morris's father. No. He could not write it down, could not pin it down with words. He did not need to write it down.

He put on the red baseball cap and pulled it low over his eyes. When he slept, with his head propped against the log, he dreamed only of the deep night that lay beneath the silver surface of the sea.

TANITH LEE

Nunc Dimittis

Tanith Lee is one of the best known of modern fantasists, and one of the most prolific, with well over a dozen books to her credit, including (among many others) *The Birthgrave, Drinking Sapphire Wine, Night's Master, The Storm Lord, Sung In Shadow, Volkhavaar,* and most recently, the novel *Anackire* and the collection *Red as Blood.*

Lee has made her reputation as a novelist, but, for my money, she is even more adroit at shorter lengths, and 1983 saw a half-dozen or more first-rate short stories by Lee popping up in places such as *Isaac Asimov's Science Fiction Magazine, Amazing, The Dodd, Mead Gallery of Horror,* and *Whispers IV.* Several of these might well have been worthy of inclusion in a "Best of the Year" anthology, but here's my favorite of them all, the poignant and oddly gentle story of a servant devoted to the point of death . . . and beyond.

NUNC DIMITTIS

Tanith Lee

The vampire was old, and no longer beautiful. In common with all
living things, she had aged, though very slowly, like the tall trees in the
park. Slender and gaunt and leafless, they stood out there, beyond the
long windows, rain-dashed in the gray morning. While she sat in her
high-backed chair in that corner of the room where the curtains of thick
yellow lace and the wine-colored blinds kept every drop of daylight out.
In the glimmer of the ornate oil lamp, she had been reading. The lamp
came from a Russian palace. The book had once graced the library of a
corrupt pope named, in his temporal existence, Roderigo Borgia. Now
the Vampire's dry hands had fallen upon the page. She sat in her black
lace dress that was one hundred and eighty years of age, far younger
than she herself, and looked at the old man, streaked by the shine of
distant windows.

"You say you are tired, Vassu. I know how it is. To be so tired, and
unable to rest. It is a terrible thing."

"But, Princess," said the old man quietly, "it is more than this. I am
dying."

The Vampire stirred a little. The pale leaves of her hands rustled on
the page. She stared, with an almost childlike wonder.

"Dying? Can this be? You are sure?"

The old man, very clean and neat in his dark clothing, nodded
humbly.

"Yes, Princess."

"Oh, Vassu," she said, "are you glad?"

He seemed a little embarrassed. Finally he said:

"Forgive me, Princess, but I am very glad. Yes, very glad."

"I understand."

"Only," he said, "I am troubled for your sake."

"No, no," said the Vampire, with the fragile perfect courtesy of her class and kind. "No, it must not concern you. You have been a good servant. Far better than I might ever have hoped for. I am thankful, Vassu, for all your care of me. I shall miss you. But you have earned," she hesitated. She said, "You have more than earned your peace."

"But you," he said.

"I shall do very well. My requirements are small, now. The days when I was a huntress are gone, and the nights. Do you remember, Vassu?"

"I remember, Princess."

"When I was so hungry, and so relentless. And so lovely. My white face in a thousand ballroom mirrors. My silk slippers stained with dew. And my lovers waking in the cold morning, where I had left them. But now, I do not sleep, I am seldom hungry. I never lust. I never love. These are the comforts of old age. There is only one comfort that is denied to me. And who knows. One day, I too . . ." She smiled at him. Her teeth were beautiful, but almost even now, the exquisite points of the canines quite worn away. "Leave me when you must," she said. "I shall mourn you. I shall envy you. But I ask nothing more, my good and noble friend."

The old man bowed his head.

"I have," he said, "a few days, a handful of nights. There is something I wish to try to do in this time. I will try to find one who may take my place."

The Vampire stared at him again, now astonished. "But Vassu, my irreplaceable help—it is no longer possible."

"Yes. If I am swift."

"The world is not as it was," she said, with a grave and dreadful wisdom.

He lifted his head. More gravely, he answered:

"The world is as it has always been, Princess. Only our perceptions of it have grown more acute. Our knowledge less bearable."

She nodded.

"Yes, this must be so. How could the world have changed so terribly? It must be we who have changed."

He trimmed the lamp before he left her.

Outside, the rain dripped steadily from the trees.

The city, in the rain, was not unlike a forest. But the old man, who had been in many forests and many cities, had no special feeling for it. His feelings, his senses, were primed to other things.

Nevertheless, he was conscious of his bizarre and anachronistic effect, like that of a figure in some surrealist painting, walking the streets in clothes of a bygone era, aware he did not blend with his surroundings, nor render them homage of any kind. Yet even when, as sometimes happened, a gang of children or youths jeered and called after him the foul names he was familiar with in twenty languages, he neither cringed nor cared. He had no concern for such things. He had been so many places, seen so many sights; cities which burned or fell in ruin, the young who grew old, as he had, and who died, as now, at last, he too would die. This thought of death soothed him, comforted him, and brought with it a great sadness, a strange jealousy. He did not want to leave her. Of course he did not. The idea of her vulnerability in this harsh world, not new in its cruelty but ancient, though freshly recognized—it horrified him. This was the sadness. And the jealousy . . . that, because he must try to find another to take his place. And that other would come to be for her, as he had been.

The memories rose and sank in his brain like waking dreams all the time he moved about the streets. As he climbed the steps of museums and underpasses, he remembered other steps in other lands, of marble and fine stone. And looking out from high balconies, the city reduced to a map, he recollected the towers of cathedrals, the starswept points of mountains. And then at last, as if turning over the pages of a book backwards, he reached the beginning.

There she stood, between two tall white graves, the chateau grounds behind her, everything silvered in the dusk before the dawn. She wore a ball dress, and a long white cloak. And even then, her hair was dressed in the fashion of a century ago; dark hair, like black flowers.

He had known for a year before that he would serve her. The moment he had heard them talk of her in the town. They were not afraid of her, but in awe. She did not prey upon her own people, as some of her line had done.

When he could get up, he went to her. He had kneeled, and stammered something; he was only sixteen, and she not much older. But she had simply looked at him quietly and said: "I know. You are welcome." The words had been in a language they seldom spoke together now. Yet always, when he recalled that meeting, she said them in that tongue, and with the same gentle inflection.

All about, in the small café where he had paused to sit and drink coffee, vague shapes came and went. Of no interest to him, no use to her. Throughout the morning, there had been nothing to alert him. He would know. He would know, as he had known it of himself.

He rose, and left the café, and the waking dream walked with him. A lean black car slid by, and he recaptured a carriage carving through white snow—

A step brushed the pavement, perhaps twenty feet behind him. The old man did not hesitate. He stepped on, and into an alleyway that ran between the high buildings. The steps followed him; he could not hear them all, only one in seven, or eight. A little wire of tension began to draw taut within him, but he gave no sign. Water trickled along the brickwork beside him, and the noise of the city was lost.

Abruptly, a hand was on the back of his neck, a capable hand, warm and sure, not harming him yet, almost the touch of a lover.

"That's right, old man. Keep still. I'm not going to hurt you, not if you do what I say."

He stood, the warm and vital hand on his neck, and waited.

"All right," said the voice, which was masculine and young and with some other elusive quality to it. "Now let me have your wallet."

The old man spoke in a faltering tone, very foreign, very fearful. "I have—no wallet."

The hand changed its nature, gripped him, bit.

"Don't lie. I can hurt you. I don't want to, but I can. Give me whatever money you have."

"Yes," he faltered, "yes—yes—"

And slipped from the sure and merciless grip like water, spinning, gripping in turn, flinging away—there was a whirl of movement.

The old man's attacker slammed against the wet gray wall and rolled down it. He lay on the rainy debris of the alley floor, and stared up, too surprised to look surprised.

This had happened many times before. Several had supposed the old man an easy mark, but he had all the steely power of what he was. Even now, even dying, he was terrible in his strength. And yet, though it had happened often, now it was different. The tension had not gone away.

Swiftly, deliberately, the old man studied the young one.

Something struck home instantly. Even sprawled, the adversary was peculiarly graceful, the grace of enormous physical coordination. The touch of the hand, also, impervious and certain—there was strength here, too. And now the eyes. Yes, the eyes were steady, intelligent, and with a curious lambency, an innocence—

"Get up," the old man said. He had waited upon an aristocrat. He had become one himself, and sounded it. "Up. I will not hit you again."

The young man grinned, aware of the irony. The humor flitted through his eyes. In the dull light of the alley, they were the color of leopards—not the eyes of leopards, but their *pelts*.

"Yes, and you could, couldn't you, granddad."

"My name," said the old man, "is Vasyelu Gorin. I am the father to none, and my nonexistent sons and daughters have no children. And you?"

"My name," said the young man, "is Snake."

The old man nodded. He did not really care about names, either.

"Get up, Snake. You attempted to rob me, because you are poor, having no work and no wish for work. I will buy you food, now."

The young man continued to lie, as if at ease, on the ground.

"Why?"

"Because I want something from you."

"What? You're right. I'll do almost anything, if you pay me enough. So you can tell me."

The old man looked at the young man called Snake, and knew that all he said was a fact. Knew that here was one who had stolen and whored, and stolen again when the slack bodies slept, both male and female, exhausted by the sexual vampirism he had practiced on them, drawing their misguided souls out through their pores as later he would draw the notes from purse and pocket. Yes, a vampire. Maybe a murderer, too. Very probably a murderer.

"If you will do anything," said the old man, "I need not tell you beforehand. You will do it anyway."

"Almost anything, is what I said."

"Advise me then," said Vasyelu Gorin, the servant of the Vampire, "what you will not do. I shall then refrain from asking it of you."

The young man laughed. In one fluid movement he came to his feet. When the old man walked on, he followed.

Testing him, the old man took Snake to an expensive restaurant, far up on the white hills of the city, where the glass geography nearly scratched the sky. Ignoring the mud on his dilapidated leather jacket, Snake became a flawless image of decorum, became what is always ultimately respected, one who does not care. The old man, who also did not care, appreciated this act, but knew it was nothing more. Snake had learned how to be a prince. But he was a gigolo with a closet full of skins to put on. Now and then the speckled leopard eyes, searching, wary, would give him away.

After the good food and the excellent wine, the cognac, the cigarettes taken from the silver box—Snake had stolen three, but, stylishly overt, had left them sticking like porcupine quills from his breast pocket—they went out again into the rain.

The dark was gathering, and Snake solicitously took the old man's arm. Vasyelu Gorin dislodged him, offended by the cheapness of the gesture after the acceptable one with the cigarettes.

"Don't you like me anymore?" said Snake. "I can go now, if you want. But you might pay for my wasted time."

"Stop that," said Vasyelu Gorin. "Come along."

Smiling, Snake came with him. They walked, between the glowing pyramids of stores, through shadowy tunnels, over the wet paving. When the thoroughfares folded away and the meadows of the great gardens began, Snake grew tense. The landscape was less familiar to him, obviously. This part of the forest was unknown.

Trees hung down from the air to the sides of the road.

"I could kill you here," said Snake. "Take your money, and run."

"You could try," said the old man, but he was becoming weary. He was no longer certain, and yet, he was sufficiently certain that his jealousy had assumed a tinge of hatred. If the young man were stupid enough to set on him, how simple it would be to break the columnar neck, like pale amber, between his fleshless hands. But then, she would know. She would know he had found for her, and destroyed the finding. And she would be generous, and he would leave her, aware he had failed her, too.

When the huge gates appeared, Snake made no comment. He seemed, by then, to anticipate them. The old man went into the park, moving quickly now, in order to outdistance his own feelings. Snake loped at his side.

Three windows were alight, high in the house. Her windows. And as they came to the stair that led up, under its skeins of ivy, into the porch, her pencil-thin shadow passed over the lights above, like smoke, or a ghost.

"I thought you lived alone," said Snake. "I thought you were lonely."

The old man did not answer anymore. He went up the stair and opened the door. Snake came in behind him, and stood quite still, until Vasyelu Gorin had found the lamp in the niche by the door, and lit it. Unnatural stained glass flared in the door panels, and the window-niches either side, owls and lotuses and far-off temples, scrolled and luminous, oddly aloof.

Vasyelu began to walk toward the inner stair.

"Just a minute," said Snake. Vasyelu halted, saying nothing. "I'd just like to know," said Snake, "how many of your friends are here, and just what your friends are figuring to do, and how I fit into their plans."

The old man sighed.

"There is one woman in the room above. I am taking you to see her. She is a Princess. Her name is Darejan Draculas." He began to ascend the stair.

Left in the dark, the visitor said softly:

"What?"

"You think you have heard the name. You are correct. But it is another branch."

He heard only the first step as it touched the carpeted stair. With a bound the creature was upon him, the lamp was lifted from his hand. Snake danced behind it, glittering and unreal.

"Dracula," he said.

"Draculas. Another branch."

"A vampire."

"Do you believe in such things?" said the old man. "You should, living as you do, preying as you do."

"I never," said Snake, "pray."

"Prey," said the old man. "Prey upon. You cannot even speak your own langauge. Give me the lamp, or shall I take it? The stair is steep. You may be damaged, this time. Which will not be good for any of your trades."

Snake made a little bow, and returned the lamp.

They continued up the carpeted hill of stair, and reached a landing and so a passage, and so her door.

The appurtenances of the house, even glimpsed in the erratic fleeting of the lamp, were very gracious. The old man was used to them, but Snake, perhaps, took note. Then again, like the size and importance of the park gates, the young thief might well have anticipated such elegance.

And there was no neglect, no dust, no air of decay, or, more tritely, of the grave. Women arrived regularly from the city to clean, under Vasyelu Gorin's stern command; flowers were even arranged in the salon for those occasions when the Princess came downstairs. Which was rarely, now. How tired she had grown. Not aged, but bored by life. The old man sighed again, and knocked upon her door.

Her response was given softly. Vasyelu Gorin saw, from the tail of his eye, the young man's reaction, his ears almost pricked, like a cat's.

"Wait here," Vasyelu said, and went into the room, shutting the door, leaving the other outside it in the dark.

The windows that had shone bright outside were black within. The candles burned, red and white as carnations.

The Vampire was seated before her little harpsichord. She had probably been playing it, its song so quiet it was seldom audible beyond her door. Long ago, nonetheless, he would have heard it. Long ago—

"Princess," he said, "I have brought someone with me."

He had not been sure what she would do, or say, confronted by the actuality. She might even remonstrate, grow angry, though he had not often seen her angry. But he saw now she had guessed, in some tangible way, that he would not return alone, and she had been preparing herself. As she rose to her feet, he beheld the red satin dress, the jewelled silver crucifix at her throat, the trickle of silver from her ears. On the thin hands, the great rings throbbed their sable colors. Her hair, which had never lost its blackness, abbreviated at her shoulders and waved in a fashion of only twenty years before, framed the starved bones of her face with a savage luxuriance. She was magnificent. Gaunt, elderly, her beauty lost, her heart dulled, yet—magnificent, wondrous.

He stared at her humbly, ready to weep because, for the half of one half moment, he had doubted.

"Yes," she said. She gave him the briefest smile, like a swift caress. "Then I will see him, Vassu."

Snake was seated cross-legged a short distance along the passage. He had discovered, in the dark, a slender Chinese vase of the *yang ts'ai* palette, and held it between his hands, his chin resting on the brim.

"Shall I break this?" he asked.

Vasyelu ignored the remark. He indicated the opened door.

"You may go in now."

"May I? How excited you're making me."

Snake flowed upright. Still holding the vase, he went through into the Vampire's apartment. The old man came into the room after him, placing his black-garbed body, like a shadow, by the door, which he left now standing wide. The old man watched Snake.

Circling slightly, perhaps unconsciously, he had approached a third of the chamber's length toward the woman. Seeing him from the back, Vasyelu Gorin was able to observe all the play of tautening muscles along the spine, like those of something readying itself to spring, or to escape. Yet, not seeing the face, the eyes, was unsatisfactory. The old man shifted his position, edged shadowlike along the room's perimeter, until he had gained a better vantage.

"Good evening," the Vampire said to Snake. "Would you care to put down the vase? Or, if you prefer, smash it. Indecision can be distressing."

"Perhaps I'd prefer to keep the vase."

"Oh, then do so, by all means. But I suggest you allow Vasyelu to wrap it up for you, before you go. Or someone may rob you on the street."

Snake pivotted, lightly, like a dancer, and put the vase on a sidetable. Turning again, he smiled at her.

"There are so many valuable things here. What shall I take? What about the silver cross you're wearing?"

The Vampire also smiled.

"An heirloom. I am rather fond of it. I do not recommend you should try to take that."

Snake's eyes enlarged. He was naive, amazed.

"But I thought, if I did what you wanted, if I made you happy—I could have whatever I liked. Wasn't that the bargain?"

"And how would you propose to make me happy?"

Snake went close to her; he prowled about her, very slowly. Disgusted, fascinated, the old man watched him. Snake stood behind her, leaning against her, his breath stirring the filaments of her hair. He slipped his left hand along her shoulder, sliding from the red satin to the dry uncolored skin of her throat. Vasyelu remembered the touch of the hand, electric, and so sensitive, the fingers of an artist or a surgeon.

The Vampire never changed. She said:

"No. You will not make me happy, my child."

"Oh," Snake said into her ear. "You can't be certain. If you like, if you really like, I'll let you drink my blood."

The Vampire laughed. It was frightening. Something dormant yet intensely powerful seemed to come alive in her as she did so, like flame from a finished coal. The sound, the appalling life, shook the young man away from her. And for an instant, the old man saw fear in the leopard-yellow eyes, a fear as intrinsic to the being of Snake as to cause fear was intrinsic to the being of the Vampire.

And, still blazing with her power, she turned on him.

"What do you think I am?" she said, "some senile hag greedy to rub her scaly flesh against your smoothness; some hag you can, being yourself without sanity or fastidiousness, corrupt with the phantoms, the leftovers of pleasure, and then murder, tearing the gems from her fingers with your teeth? Or I am a perverted hag, wanting to lick up your youth with your juices. Am I that? Come now," she said, her fire lowering itself, crackling with its amusement, with everything she held in check, her voice a long, long pin, skewering what she spoke to against the farther wall. "Come now. How can I be such a fiend, and wear the crucifix on my breast? My ancient, withered, fallen, empty breast. Come now. What's in a name?"

As the pin of her voice came out of him, the young man pushed himself away from the wall. For an instant there was an air of panic about him. He was accustomed to the characteristics of the world. Old men creeping through rainy alleys could not strike mighty blows with their iron hands. Women were moths that burnt, but did not burn, tones of tinsel and pleading, not razor blades.

Snake shuddered all over. And then his panic went away. Instinctively, he told something from the aura of the room itself. Living as he did, generally he had come to trust his instincts.

He slunk back to the woman, not close, this time, no nearer than two yards.

"Your man over there," he said, "he took me to a fancy restaurant. He got me drunk. I say things when I'm drunk I shouldn't say. You see? I'm a lout. I shouldn't be here in your nice house. I don't know how to talk to people like you. To a lady. You see? But I haven't any money. None. Ask him. I explained it all. I'll do anything for money. And the way I talk. Some of them like it. You see? It makes me sound dangerous. They like that. But it's just an act." Fawning on her, bending on her the groundless glory of his eyes, he had also retreated, was almost at the door.

The Vampire made no move. Like a marvelous waxwork she dominated the room, red and white and black, and the old man was only a shadow in a corner.

Snake darted about and bolted. In the blind lightlessness, he skimmed the passage, leaped out in space upon the stairs, touched, leaped, touched, reached the open area beyond. Some glint of starshine revealed the stained glass panes in the door. As it crashed open, he knew quite well that he had been let go. Then it slammed behind him and he pelted through ivy and down the outer steps, and across the hollow plain of tall wet trees.

So much, infallibly, his instincts had told him. Strangely, even as he came out of the gates upon the vacant road, and raced toward the heart of the city, they did not tell him he was free.

"Do you recollect," said the Vampire, "you asked me, at the very beginning, about the crucifix."

"I do recollect, Princess. It seemed odd to me, then. I did not understand, of course."

"And you," she said. "How would you have it, after—" She waited. She said, "After you leave me."

He rejoiced that his death would cause her a momentary pain. He could not help that, now. He had seen the fire wake in her, flash and scald in her, as it had not done for half a century, ignited by the presence of the thief, the gigolo, the parasite.

"He," said the old man, "is young and strong, and can dig some pit for me."

"And no ceremony?" She had overlooked his petulance, of course, and her tact made him ashamed.

"Just to lie quiet will be enough," he said, "but thank you, Princess, for your care. I do not suppose it will matter. Either there is nothing, or there is something so different I shall be astonished by it."

"Ah, my friend. Then you do not imagine yourself damned?"

"No," he said. "No, no." And all at once there was passion in his voice, one last fire of his own to offer her. "In the life you gave me, I was blessed."

She closed her eyes, and Vasyelu Gorin perceived he had wounded her with his love. And, no longer peevishly, but in the way of a lover, he was glad.

Next day, a little before three in the afternoon, Snake returned.

A wind was blowing, and seemed to have blown him to the door in a scurry of old brown leaves. His hair was also blown, and bright, his face wind-slapped to a ridiculous freshness. His eyes, however, were heavy, encircled, dulled. The eyes showed, as did nothing else about him, that he had spent the night, the forenoon, engaged in his second line of commerce. They might have drawn thick curtains and blown out the lights, but that would not have helped him. The senses of Snake were doubly acute in the dark, and he could see in the dark, like a lynx.

"Yes?" said the old man, looking at him blankly, as if at a tradesman.

"Yes," said Snake, and came by him into the house.

Vasyelu did not stop him. Of course not. He allowed the young man, and all his blown gleamingness and his wretched roué eyes to stroll across to the doors of the salon, and walk through. Vasyelu followed.

The blinds, a somber ivory color, were down, and the lamps had been lit; on a polished table hothouse flowers foamed from a jade bowl. A second door stood open on the small library, the soft glow of the lamps trembling over gold-worked spines, up and up, a torrent of static, priceless books.

Snake went into and around the library, and came out.

"I didn't take anything."

"Can you even read?" snapped Vasyelu Gorin, remmbering when he could not, a woodcutter's fifth son, an oaf and a sot, drinking his way or sleeping his way through a life without windows or vistas, a mere blackness of error and unrecognized boredom. Long ago. In that little town cobbled together under the forest. And the chateau with its starry lights, the carriages on the road, shining, the dark trees either side. And bowing in answer to a question, lifting a silver comfit box from a pocket as easily as he had lifted a coin the day before. . . .

Snake sat down, leaning back relaxedly in the chair. He was not relaxed, the old man knew. What was he telling himself? That there was money here, eccentricity to be battened upon. That he could take her, the old woman, one way or another. There were always excuses that one could make to oneself.

When the Vampire entered the room, Snake, practiced, a gigolo, came to his feet. And the Vampire was amused by him, gently now. She wore a bone-white frock that had been sent from Paris last year. She had never worn it before. Pinned at the neck was a black velvet rose with a single drop of dew shivering on a single petal: a pearl that had come from the crown jewels of a czar. Her tact, her peerless tact. *Naturally*, the pearl was saying, *this is why you have come back. Naturally. There is nothing to fear.*

Vasyelu Gorin left them. He returned later with the decanters and glasses. The cold supper had been laid out by people from the city who handled such things, paté and lobster and chicken, lemon slices cut like flowers, orange slices like suns, tomatoes that were anemones, and oceans of green lettuce, and cold, glittering ice. He decanted the wines. He arranged the silver coffee service, the boxes of different cigarettes. The winter night had settled by then against the house, and, roused by the brilliantly lighted rooms, a moth was dashing itself between the candles and the colored fruits. The old man caught it in a crystal goblet, took it away, let it go into the darkness. For a hundred years and more, he had never killed anything.

Sometimes, he heard them laugh. The young man's laughter was at first too eloquent, too beautiful, too unreal. But then, it became ragged, boisterous; it became genuine.

The wind blew stonily. Vasyelu Gorin imagined the frail moth beathing its wings against the huge wings of the wind, falling spent to the ground. It would be good to rest.

In the last half hour before dawn, she came quietly from the salon, and up the stair. The old man knew she had seen him as he waited in the shadows. That she did not look at him or call to him was her attempt to spare him this sudden sheen that was upon her, its direct and pitiless glare. So he glimpsed it obliquely, no more. Her straight pale figure ascending, slim and limpid as a girl's. Her eyes were young, full of a primal refinding, full of utter newness.

In the salon, Snake slept under his jacket on the long white couch, its brocaded cushions beneath his cheek. Would he, on waking, carefully examine his throat in a mirror?

The old man watched the young man sleeping. She had taught Vasyelu Gorin how to speak five languages, and how to read three others. She had allowed him to discover music, and art, history and the stars; profundity, mercy. He had found the closed tomb of life opened out on every side into unbelievable, inexpressible landscapes. And yet, and yet. The journey must have its end. Worn out with ecstasy and experience, too tired any more to laugh with joy. To rest was everything. To be still. Only she could continue, for only she could be eternally reborn. For Vasyelu, once had been enough.

He left the young man sleeping. Five hours later, Snake was noiselessly gone. He had taken all the cigarettes, but nothing else.

Snake sold the cigarettes quickly. At one of the cafés he sometimes frequented, he met with those who, sensing some change in his fortunes, urged him to boast. Snake did not, remaining irritatingly reticent, vague. It was another patron. An old man who liked to give him things. Where did the old man live? Oh, a fine apartment, the north side of the city.

Some of the day, he walked.

A hunter, he distrusted the open veldt of daylight. There was too little cover, and equally too great cover for the things he stalked. In the afternoon, he sat in the gardens of a museum. Students came and went, seriously alone, or in groups riotously. Snake observed them. They were scarcely younger than he himself, yet to him, another species. Now and then a girl, catching his eye, might smile, or make an attempt to linger, to interest him. Snake did not respond. With the economic contempt of what he had become, he dismissed all such sexual encounters. Their allure, their youth, these were commodities valueless in others. They would not pay him.

The old woman, however, he did not dismiss. How old was she? Sixty, perhaps—no, much older. Ninety was more likely. And yet, her face, her neck, her hands were curiously smooth, unlined. At times, she might only have been fifty. And the dyed hair, which should have made her seem raddled, somehow enhanced the illusion of a young woman.

Yes, she fascinated him. Probably she had been an actress. Foreign, theatrical—rich. If she was prepared to keep him, thinking him mistakenly her pet cat, then he was willing, for a while. He could steal from her when she began to cloy and he decided to leave.

Yet, something in the uncomplexity of these thoughts disturbed him. The first time he had run away, he was unsure now from what. Not the vampire name, certainly, a stage name—*Draculas*—what else? But from something—some awareness of fate for which idea his vocabulary had no word, and no explanation. Driven once away, driven thereafter to return, since it was foolish not to. And she had known how to treat him. Gracefully, graciously. She would be honorable, for her kind always were. Used to spending money for what they wanted, they did not balk at buying people, too. They had never forgotten flesh, also, had a price, since their roots were firmly locked in an era when there had been slaves.

But. But he would not, he told himself, go there tonight. No. It would be good she should not be able to rely on him. He might go tomorrow, or the next day, but not tonight.

The turning world lifted away from the sun, through a winter sunset, into darkness. Snake was glad to see the ending of the light, and false light instead spring up from the apartment blocks, the cafés.

He moved out on to the wide pavement of a street, and a man came and took his arm on the right side, another starting to walk by him on the left.

"Yes, this is the one, the one who calls himself Snake."

"Are you?" the man who walked beside him asked.

"Of course it is," said the first man, squeezing his arm. "Didn't we have an exact description? Isn't he just the way he was described?"

"And the right place, too," agreed the other man, who did not hold him. "The right area."

The men wore neat nondescript clothing. Their faces were sallow and smiling, and fixed. This was a routine with which both were familiar. Snake did not know them, but he knew the touch, the accent, the smiling fixture of their masks. He had tensed. Now he let the tension melt away, so they should see and feel it had gone.

"What do you want?"

The man who held his arm only smiled.

The other man said, "Just to earn our living."

"Doing what?"

On either side the lighted street went by. Ahead, at the street's corner, a vacant lot opened where a broken wall lunged away into the shadows.

"It seems you upset someone," said the man who only walked. "Upset them badly."

"I upset a lot of people," Snake said.

"I'm sure you do. But some of them won't stand for it."

"Who was this? Perhaps I should see them."

"No. They don't want that. They don't want you to see anybody."

The black turn was a few feet away.

"Perhaps I can put it right."

"No. That's what we've been paid to do."

"But if I don't know—" said Snake, and lurched against the man who held his arm, ramming his fist into the soft belly. The man let go of him and fell. Snake ran. He ran past the lot, into the brilliant glare of

another street beyond, and was almost laughing when the thrown knife
caught him in the back.

The lights turned over. Something hard and cold struck his chest, his
face. Snake realized it was the pavement. There was a dim blurred
noise, coming and going, perhaps a crowd gathering. Someone stood on
his ribs and pulled the knife out of him and the pain began.

"Is that it?" a choked voice asked some way above him: the man he
had punched in the stomach.

"It'll do nicely."

A new voice shouted. A car swam to the curb and pulled up raucously.
The car door slammed, and footsteps went over the cement. Behind
him, Snake heard the two men walking briskly away.

Snake began to get up, and was surprised to find he was unable to.

"What happened?" someone asked, high, high above.

"I don't know."

A woman said softly, "Look, there's blood—"

Snake took no notice. After a moment he tried again to get up, and
succeeded in getting to his knees. He had been hurt, that was all. He
could feel the pain, no longer sharp, blurred, like the noise he could
hear, coming and going. He opened his eyes. The light had faded, then
came back in a long wave, then faded again. There seemed to be only
five or six people standing around him. As he rose, the nearer shapes
backed away.

"He shouldn't move," someone said urgently.

A hand touched his shoulder, fluttered off, like an insect.

The light faded into black, and the noise swept in like a tide, filling
his ears, dazing him. Something supported him, and he shook it from
him—a wall—

"Come back, son," a man called. The lights burned up again,
reminiscent of a cinema. He would be all right in a moment. He
walked away from the small crowd, not looking at them. Respectfully,
in awe, they let him go, and noted his blood trailing behind him along
the pavement.

The French clock chimed sweetly in the salon; it was seven. Beyond
the window, the park was black. It had begun to rain again.

The old man had been watching from the downstairs window for
rather more than an hour. Sometimes, he would step restlessly away,
circle the room, straighten a picture, pick up a petal discarded by the
dying flowers. Then go back to the window, looking out at the trees, the
rain and the night.

Less than a minute after the chiming of the clock, a piece of the static darkness came away and began to move, very slowly, toward the house.

Vasyelu Gorin went out into the hall. As he did so, he glanced toward the stairway. The lamp at the stairhead was alight, and she stood there in its rays, her hands lying loosely at her sides, elegant as if weightless, her head raised.

"Princess?"

"Yes, I know. Please hurry, Vassu. I think there is scarcely any margin left."

The old man opened the door quickly. He sprang down the steps as lightly as a boy of eighteen. The black rain swept against his face, redolent of a thousand memories, and he ran through an orchard in Burgundy, across a hillside in Tuscany, along the path of a wild garden near St. Petersburg that was St. Petersburg no more, until he reached the body of a young man lying over the roots of a tree.

The old man bent down, and an eye opened palely in the dark and looked at him.

"Knifed me," said Snake. "Crawled all this way."

Vasyelu Gorin leaned in the rain to the grass of France, Italy and Russia, and lifted Snake in his arms. The body lolled, heavy, not helping him. But it did not matter. How strong he was, he might marvel at it, as he stood, holding the young man across his breast, and turning, ran back toward the house.

"I don't know," Snake muttered, "don't know who sent them. Plenty would like to—How bad is it? I didn't think it was so bad."

The ivy drifted across Snake's face and he closed his eyes.

As Vasyelu entered the hall, the Vampire was already on the lowest stair. Vasyelu carried the dying man across to her, and laid him at her feet. Then Vasyelu turned to leave.

"Wait," she said.

"No, Princess. This is a private thing. Between the two of you, as once it was between us. I do not want to see it, Princess. I do not want to see it with another."

She looked at him, for a moment like a child, sorry to have distressed him, unwilling to give in. Then she nodded. "Go then, my dear."

He went away at once. So he did not witness it as she left the stair, and knelt beside Snake on the Turkish carpet newly colored with blood. Yet, it seemed to him he heard the rustle her dress made, like thin crisp paper, and the whisper of the tiny dagger parting her flesh, and then the long still sigh.

He walked down through the house, into the clean and frigid modern kitchen full of electricity. There he sat, and remembered the forest above the town, the torches as the yelling aristocrats hunted him for his theft of the comfit box, the blows when they caught up with him. He remembered, with a painless unoppressed refinding, what it was like to begin to die in such a way, the confused anger, the coming and going of tangible things, long pulses of being alternating with deep valleys of non-being. And then the agonized impossible crawl, fingers in the earth itself, pulling him forward, legs sometimes able to assist, sometimes failing, passengers which must be dragged with the rest. In the graveyard at the edge of the estate, he ceased to move. He could go no farther. The soil was cold, and the white tombs, curious petrified vegetation over his head, seemed to suck the black sky into themselves, so they darkened, and the sky grew pale.

But as the sky was drained of its blood, the foretaste of day began to possess it. In less than an hour, the sun would rise.

He had heard her name, and known he would eventually come to serve her. The way in which he had known, both for himself and for the young man called Snake, had been in a presage of violent death.

All the while, searching through the city, there had been no one with that stigma upon them, that mark. Until, in the alley, the warm hand gripped his neck, until he looked into the leopard-colored eyes. Then Vasyelu saw the mark, smelled the scent of it like singed bone.

How Snake, crippled by a mortal wound, bleeding and semi-aware, had brought himself such a distance, through the long streets hard as nails, through the mossy garden-land of the rich, through the colossal gates, over the watery, night-tuned plain, so far, dying, the old man did not require to ask, or to be puzzled by. He, too, had done such a thing, more than two centuries ago. And there she had found him, between the tall white graves. When he could focus his vision again, he had looked and seen her, the most beautiful thing he ever set eyes upon. She had given him her blood. He had drunk the blood of Darejan Draculas, a princess, a vampire. Unique elixir, it had saved him. All wounds had healed. Death had dropped from him like a torn skin, and everything he had been—scavenger, thief, brawler, drunkard, and, for a certain number of coins, *whore*—each of these things had crumbled away. Standing up, he had trodden on them, left them behind. He had gone to her, and kneeled down as, a short while before, she had kneeled by him, cradling him, giving him the life of her silver veins.

And this, all this, was now for the other. Even her blood, it seemed, did not bestow immortality, only longevity, at last coming to a stop for Vasyelu Gorin. And so, many many decades from this night the other, too, would come to the same hiatus. Snake, too, would remember the waking moment, conscious another now endured the stupefied thrill of it, and all that would begin thereafter.

Finally, with a sort of guiltiness, the old man left the hygienic kitchen and went back toward the glow of the upper floor, stealing out into the shadow at the light's edge.

He understood that she would sense him there, untroubled by his presence—had she not been prepared to let him remain?

It was done.

Her dress was spread like an open rose, the young man lying against her, his eyes wide, gazing up at her. And she would be the most beautiful thing that he had ever seen. All about, invisible, the shed skins of his life, husks he would presently scuff uncaringly underfoot. And she?

The Vampire's head inclined toward Snake. The dark hair fell softly. Her face, powdered by the lampshine, was young, was full of vitality, serene vivacity, loveliness. Everything had come back to her. She was reborn.

Perhaps it was only an illusion.

The old man bowed his head, there in the shadows. The jealousy, the regret were gone. In the end, his life with her had become only another skin that he must cast. He would have the peace that she might never have, and be glad of it. The young man would serve her, and she would be huntress once more, and dancer, a bright phantom gliding over the ballroom of the city, this city and others, and all the worlds of land and soul between.

Vasyelu Gorin stirred on the platform of his existence. He would depart now, or very soon; already he heard the murmur of the approaching train. It would be simple, this time, not like the other time at all. To go willingly, everything achieved, in order. Knowing she was safe.

There was even a faint color in her cheeks, a blooming. Or maybe, that was just a trick of the lamp.

The old man waited until they had risen to their feet, and walked together quietly into the salon, before he came from the shadows and began to climb the stairs, hearing the silence, their silence, like that of new lovers.

At the head of the stair, beyond the lamp, the dark was gentle, soft as the Vampire's hair. Vasyelu walked forward into the dark without misgiving, tenderly.

How he had loved her.

GREG BEAR

Blood Music

Here's another brilliant story by Greg Bear, whose "Hardfought" appears earlier in this book. In that story, Bear took us across vast expanses of space to the far reaches of the universe; here, instead, he looks within the human body to find worlds and creatures just as strange—or maybe even stranger.

BLOOD MUSIC

Greg Bear

There is a principle in nature I don't think anyone has pointed out before. Each hour, a myriad of trillions of little live things—bacteria, microbes, "animalcules"—are born and die, not counting for much except in the bulk of their existence and the accumulation of their tiny effects. They do not perceive deeply. They don't suffer much. A hundred billion, dying, would not begin to have the same importance as a single human death.

Within the ranks of magnitude of all creatures, small as microbes or great as humans, there is an equality of "elan," just as the branches of a tall tree, gathered together, equal the bulk of the limbs below, and all the limbs equal the bulk of the trunk.

That, at least, is the principle. I believe Vergil Ulam was the first to violate it.

It had been two years since I'd last seen Vergil. My memory of him hardly matched the tan, smiling, well-dressed gentleman standing before me. We had made a lunch appointment over the phone the day before, and now faced each other in the wide double doors of the employee's cafeteria at the Mount Freedom Medical Center.

"Vergil?" I asked. "My God, Vergil!"

"Good to see you, Edward." He shook my hand firmly. He had lost ten or twelve kilos and what remained seemed tighter, better proportioned. At university, Vergil had been the pudgy, shock-haired, snaggle-toothed whiz kid who hot-wired doorknobs, gave us punch that turned our piss blue, and never got a date except with Eileen Termagent, who shared many of his physical characteristics.

"You look fantastic," I said. "Spend a summer in Cabo San Lucas?"

We stood in line at the counter and chose our food. "The tan," he said, picking out a carton of chocolate milk, "is from spending three months under a sunlamp. My teeth were straightened just after I last saw you. I'll explain the rest, but we need a place to talk where no one will listen close."

I steered him to the smoker's corner, where three die-hard puffers were scattered among six tables.

"Listen, I mean it," I said as we unloaded our trays. "You've changed. You're looking good."

"I've changed more than you know." His tone was motion-picture ominous, and he delivered the line with a theatrical lift of his brows. "How's Gail?"

Gail was doing well, I told him, teaching nursery school. We'd married the year before. His gaze shifted down to his food—pineapple slice and cottage cheese, piece of banana cream pie—and he said, his voice almost cracking, "Notice something else?"

I squinted in concentration. "Uh."

"Look closer."

"I'm not sure. Well, yes, you're not wearing glasses. Contacts?"

"No. I don't need them anymore."

"And you're a snappy dresser. Who's dressing you now? I hope she's as sexy as she is tasteful."

"Candice isn't—wasn't—responsible for the improvement in my clothes," he said. "I just got a better job, more money to throw around. My taste in clothes is better than my taste in food, as it happens." He grinned the old Vergil self-deprecating grin, but ended it with a peculiar leer. "At any rate, she's left me, I've been fired from my job, I'm living on savings."

"Hold it," I said. "That's a bit crowded. Why not do a linear breakdown? You got a job. Where?"

"Genetron Corp.," he said. "Sixteen months ago."

"I haven't heard of them."

"You will. They're putting out common stock in the next month. It'll shoot off the board. They've broken through with MABs. Medical—"

"I know what MABs are," I interrupted. "At least in theory. Medically Applicable Biochips."

"They have some that work."

"What?" It was my turn to lift my brows.

"Microscopic logic circuits. You inject them into the human body, they set up shop where they're told and troubleshoot. With Dr. Michael Bernard's approval."

That was quite impressive. Bernard's reputation was spotless. Not only was he associated with the genetic engineering biggies, but he had made news at least once a year in his practice as a neurosurgeon before retiring. Covers on *Time, Mega, Rolling Stone.*

"That's supposed to be secret—stock, breakthrough, Bernard, everything." He looked around and lowered his voice. "But you do whatever the hell you want. I'm through with the bastards."

I whistled. "Make me rich, huh?"

"If that's what you want. Or you can spend some time with me before rushing off to your broker."

"Of course." He hadn't touched the cottage cheese or pie. He had, however, eaten the pineapple slice and drunk the chocolate milk. "So tell me more."

"Well, in med school I was training for lab work. Biochemical research. I've always had a bent for computers, too. So I put myself through my last two years—"

"By selling software packages to Westinghouse," I said.

"It's good my friends remember. That's how I got involved with Genetron, just when they were starting out. They had big money backers, all the lab facilities I thought anyone would ever need. They hired me, and I advanced rapidly.

"Four months and I was doing my own work. I made some breakthroughs," he tossed his hand nonchalantly, "then I went off on tangents they thought were premature. I persisted and they took away my lab, handed it over to a certifiable flatworm. I managed to save part of the experiment before they fired me. But I haven't exactly been cautious . . . or judicious. So now it's going on outside the lab."

I'd always regarded Vergil as ambitious, a trifle cracked, and not terribly sensitive. His relations with authority figures had never been smooth. Science, for him, was like the woman you couldn't possibly have, who suddenly opens her arms to you, long before you're ready for mature love—leaving you afraid you'll forever blow the chance, lose the prize, screw up royally. Apparently, he had. "Outside the lab? I don't get you."

"Edward, I want you to examine me. Give me a thorough physical. Maybe a cancer diagnostic. Then I'll explain more."

"You want a five-thousand-dollar exam?"

"Whatever you can do. Ultrasound, NMR, thermogram, everything."

"I don't know if I can get access to all that equipment. NMR full-scan has only been here a month or two. Hell, you couldn't pick a more expensive way—"

"Then ultrasound. That's all you'll need."

"Vergil, I'm an obstetrician, not a glamor-boy lab-tech. OB-GYN, butt of all jokes. If you're turning into a woman, maybe I can help you."

He leaned forward, almost putting his elbow into the pie, but swinging wide at the last instant by scant millimeters. The old Vergil would have hit it square.

"Examine me closely and you'll . . ." He narrowed his eyes and shook his head. "Just examine me."

"So I make an appointment for ultrasound. Who's going to pay?"

"I'm on Blue Shield." He smiled and held up a medical credit card. "I messed with the personnel files at Genetron. Anything up to a hundred thousand dollars' medical, they'll never check, never suspect."

He wanted secrecy, so I made arrangements. I filled out his forms myself. As long as everything was billed properly, most of the examination could take place without official notice. I didn't charge for my services. After all, Vergil had turned my piss blue. We were friends.

He came in late at night. I wasn't normally on duty then, but I stayed late, waiting for him on the third floor of what the nurses called the Frankenstein wing. I sat on an orange plastic chair. He arrived, looking olive-colored under the fluorescent lights.

He stripped, and I arranged him on the table. I noticed, first off, that his ankles looked swollen. But they weren't puffy. I felt them several times. They seemed healthy, but looked odd. "Hm," I said.

I ran the paddles over him, picking up areas difficult for the big unit to hit, and programed the data into the imaging system. Then I swung the table around and inserted it into the enameled orifice of the ultrasound diagnostic unit, the hum-hole, so-called by the nurses.

I integrated the data from the hum-hole with that from the paddle sweeps and rolled Vergil out, then set up a video frame. The image took a second to integrate, then flowed into a pattern showing Vergil's skeleton.

Three seconds of that—my jaw gaping—and it switched to his thoracic organs, then his musculature, and finally, vascular system and skin.

"How long since the accident?" I asked, trying to take the quiver out of my voice.

"I haven't been in an accident," he said. "It was deliberate."

"Jesus, they beat you, to keep secrets?"

"You don't understand me, Edward. Look at the images again. I'm not damaged."

"Look, there's thickening here," I indicated the ankles, "and your ribs—that crazy zigzag pattern of interlocks. Broken sometime, obviously. And—"

"Look at my spine," he said. I rotated the image in the video frame.

Buckminster Fuller, I thought. It was fantastic. A cage of triangular projections, all interlocking in ways I couldn't begin to follow, much less understand. I reached around and tried to feel his spine with my fingers. He lifted his arms and looked off at the ceiling.

"I can't find it," I said. "It's all smooth back there." I let go of him and looked at his chest, then prodded his ribs. They were sheathed in something rough and flexible. The harder I pressed, the tougher it became. Then I noticed another change.

"Hey," I said. "You don't have any nipples." There were tiny pigment patches, but no nipple formations at all.

"See?" Vergil asked, shrugging on the white robe. "I'm being rebuilt from the inside out."

In my reconstruction of those hours, I fancy myself saying, "So tell me about it." Perhaps mercifully, I don't remember what I actually said.

He explained with his characteristic circumlocutions. Listening was like trying to get to the meat of a newspaper article through a forest of sidebars and graphic embellishments.

I simplify and condense.

Genetron had assigned him to manufacturing prototype biochips, tiny circuits made out of protein molecules. Some were hooked up to silicon chips little more than a micrometer in size, then sent through rat arteries to chemically keyed locations, to make connections with the rat tissue and attempt to monitor and even control lab-induced pathologies.

"*That* was something," he said. "We recovered the most complex microchip by sacrificing the rat, then debriefed it—hooked the silicon portion up to an imaging system. The computer gave us bar graphs, then a diagram of the chemical characteristics of about eleven centimeters of blood vessel . . . then put it all together to make a picture. We zoomed down eleven centimeters of rat artery. You never saw so many scientists jumping up and down, hugging each other, drinking buckets of bug juice." Bug juice was lab ethanol mixed with Dr. Pepper.

Eventually, the silicon elements were eliminated completely in favor of nucleoproteins. He seemed reluctant to explain in detail, but I gathered they found ways to make huge molecules—as large as DNA, and even more complex—into electrochemical computers, using ribosomelike structures as "encoders" and "readers," and RNA as "tape." Vergil was able to mimic reproductive separation and reassembly in his nucleoproteins, incorporating program changes at key points by switching nucleotide pairs. "Genetron wanted me to switch over to supergene engineering, since that was the coming thing everywhere else. Make all kinds of critters, some out of our imagination. But I had different ideas." He twiddled his finger around his ear and made theremin sounds. "Mad scientist time, right?" He laughed, then sobered. "I injected my best nucleoproteins into bacteria to make duplication and compounding easier. Then I started to leave them inside, so the circuits could interact with the cells. They were heuristically programed; they taught themselves more than I programed them. The cells fed chemically coded information to the computers, the computers processed it and made decisions, the cells became smart. I mean, smart as planaria, for starters. Imagine an *E. coli* as smart as a planarian worm!"

I nodded. "I'm imagining."

"Then I really went off on my own. We had the equipment, the techniques; and I knew the molecular language. I could make really dense, really complicated biochips by compounding the nucleoproteins, making them into little brains. I did some research into how far I could go, theoretically. Sticking with bacteria, I could make a biochip with the computing capacity of a sparrow's brain. Imagine how jazzed I was! Then I saw a way to increase the complexity a thousandfold, by using something we regarded as a nuisance—quantum chit-chat between the fixed elements of the circuits. Down that small, even the slightest change could bomb a biochip. But I developed a program that actually predicted and took advantage of electron tunneling. Emphasized the heuristic aspects of the computer, used the chit-chat as a method of increasing complexity."

"You're losing me," I said.

"I took advantage of randomness. The circuits could repair themselves, compare memories and correct faulty elements. The whole schmeer. I gave them basic instructions: Go forth and multiply. Improve. By God, you should have seen some of the cultures a week later! It was amazing. They were evolving all on their own, like little cities. I destroyed them all. I think one of the petri dishes would have grown legs and walked out of the incubator if I'd kept feeding it."

"You're kidding." I looked at him. "You're not kidding."

"Man, they *knew* what it was like to improve! They knew where they had to go, but they were just so limited, being in bacteria bodies, with so few resources."

"How smart were they?"

"I couldn't be sure. They were associating in clusters of a hundred to two hundred cells, each cluster behaving like an autonomous unit. Each cluster might have been as smart as a rhesus monkey. They exchanged information through their pili, passed on bits of memory and compared notes. Their organization was obviously different from a group of monkeys. Their world was so much simpler, for one thing.

With their abilities, they were masters of the petri dishes. I put phages in with them; the phages didn't have a chance. They used every option available to change and grow."

"How is that possible?"

"What?" He seemed surprised I wasn't accepting everything at face value.

"Cramming so much into so little. A rhesus monkey is not your simple little calculator, Vergil."

"I haven't made myself clear," he said, obviously irritated. "I was using nucleoprotein computers. They're like DNA, but all the information can interact. Do you know how many nucleotide pairs there are in the DNA of a single bacteria?"

It had been a long time since my last biochemistry lesson. I shook my head.

"About two million. Add in the modified ribosome structures—fifteen thousand of them, each with a molecular weight of about three million— and consider the combinations and permutations. The RNA is arranged like a continuous loop paper tape, surrounded by ribosomes ticking off instructions and manufacturing protein chains . . ." His eyes were bright and slightly moist. "Besides, I'm not saying every cell was a distinct entity. They cooperated."

"How many bacteria in the dishes you destroyed?"

"Billions. I don't know." He smirked. "You got it, Edward. Whole planetsful of *E. coli*."

"But they didn't fire you then?"

"No. They didn't know what was going on, for one thing. I kept compounding the molecules, increasing their size and complexity. When bacteria were too limited, I took blood from myself, separated out white cells, and injected them with the new biochips. I watched them, put them through mazes and little chemical problems. They were whizzes. Time is a lot faster at that level—so little distance for the messages to cross, and the environment is much simpler. Then I forgot to store a file under my secret code in the lab computers. Some managers found it and guessed what I was up to. Everybody panicked. They thought we'd have every social watchdog in the country on our backs because of what I'd done. They started to destroy my work and wipe my programs. Ordered me to sterilize my white cells. Christ." He pulled the white robe off and started to get dressed. "I only had a day or two. I separated out the most complex cells—"

"How complex?"

"They were clustering in hundred-cell groups, like the bacteria. Each group as smart as a ten-year-old kid, maybe." He studied my face for a moment. "Still doubting? Want me to run through how many nucleotide pairs there are in a mammalian cell? I tailored my computers to take advantage of the white cells' capacity. Ten billion nucleotide pairs, Edward. Ten E-fucking ten. And they don't have a huge body to worry about, taking up most of their thinking time."

"Okay," I said. "I'm convinced. What did you do?"

"I mixed the cells back into a cylinder of whole blood and injected myself with it." He buttoned the top of his shirt and smiled thinly at me. "I'd programmed them with every drive I could, talked as high a level as I could using just enzymes and such. After that, they were on their own."

"You programed them to go forth and multiply, improve?" I repeated.

"I think they developed some characteristics picked up by the biochips in their *E. coli* phases. The white cells could talk to each other with extruded memories. They almost certainly found ways to ingest other types of cells and alter them without killing them."

"You're crazy."

"You can see the screen! Edward, I haven't been sick since. I used to get colds all the time. I've never felt better."

"They're inside you, finding things, changing them."

"And by now, each cluster is as smart as you or I."

"You're absolutely nuts."

He shrugged. "They fired me. They thought I was going to get revenge for what they did to my work. They ordered me out of the labs, and I haven't had a real chance to see what's been going on inside me until now. Three months."

"So . . ." My mind was racing. "You lost weight because they improved your fat metabolism. Your bones are stronger, your spine has been completely rebuilt—"

"No more backaches even if I sleep on my old mattress."

"Your heart looks different."

"I didn't know about the heart," he said, examining the frame image from a few inches. "About the fat—I was thinking about that. They could increase my brown cells, fix up the metabolism. I haven't been as hungry lately. I haven't changed my eating habits that much—I still want the same old junk—but somehow I get around to eating only what I need. I don't think they know what my brain is yet. Sure, they've got all the glandular stuff—but they don't have the *big* picture, if you see what I mean. They don't know *I'm* in there. But boy, they sure did figure out what my reproductive organs are."

I glanced at the image and shifted my eyes away.

"Oh, they look pretty normal," he said, hefting his scrotum obscenely.

He snickered. "But how else do you think I'd land a real looker like Candice? She was just after a one-night stand with a techie. I looked okay then, no tan but trim, with good clothes. She'd never screwed a techie before. Joke time, right? But my little geniuses kept us up half the night. I think they made improvements each time. I felt like I had a goddamned fever."

His smile vanished. "But then one night my skin started to crawl. It really scared me. I thought things were getting out of hand. I wondered what they'd do when they crossed the blood-brain barrier and found out about *me*—about the brain's real function. So I began a campaign to keep them under control. I figured, the reason they wanted to get into the skin was the simplicity of running circuits across a surface. Much easier than trying to maintain chains of communication in and around muscles, organs, vessels. The skin was much more direct. So I bought a quartz lamp." He caught my puzzled expression. "In the lab, we'd break down the protein in biochip cells by exposing them to ultraviolet light. I alternated sunlamp with quartz treatments. Keeps them out of my skin, so far as I can tell, and gives me a nice tan."

"Give you skin cancer, too," I commented.

"They'll probably take care of that. Like police."

"Okay, I've examined you, you've told me a story I still find hard to believe . . . what do you want me to do?"

"I'm not as nonchalant as I act, Edward. I'm worried. I'd like to find some way to control them before they find out about my brain. I mean, think of it, they're in the trillions by now, each one smart. They're cooperating to some extent. I'm probably the smartest thing on the planet, and they haven't even begun to get their act together yet. I don't really want them to take over." He laughed very unpleasantly. "Steal my soul, you know? So think of some treatment to block them. Maybe we can starve the little buggers. Just think on it." He buttoned his shirt. "Give me a call." He handed me a slip of paper with his address and phone number. Then he went to the keyboard and erased the image on the frame, dumping the memory of the examination. "Just you," he said. "Nobody else for now. And please . . . hurry."

It was three o'clock in the morning when Vergil walked out of the examination room. He'd allowed me to take blood samples, then shaken my hand—his palm damp, nervous—and cautioned me against ingesting anything from the specimens.

Before I went home, I put the blood through a series of tests. The results were ready the next day.

I picked them up during my lunch break in the afternoon, then destroyed all the samples. I did it like a robot. It took me five days and nearly sleepless nights to accept what I'd seen. His blood was normal enough, though the machines diagnosed the patient as having an infection. High levels of leucocytes—white blood cells—and histamines. On the fifty day, I believed.

Gail was home before I, but it was my turn to fix dinner. She slipped one of the school's disks into the home system and showed me video art her nursery kids had been creating. I watched quietly, ate with her in silence.

I had two dreams, part of my final acceptance. The first that evening—which had me up thrashing in my sheets—I witnessed the destruction of the planet Krypton, Superman's home world. Billions of superhuman geniuses went screaming off in walls of fire. I related the destruction to my sterilizing the samples of Vergil's blood.

The second dream was worse. I dreamed that New York City was raping a woman. By the end of the dream, she was giving birth to little embryo cities, all wrapped up in translucent sacs, soaked with blood from the difficult labor.

I called him on the morning of the sixth day. He answered on the fourth ring. "I have some results," I said. "Nothing conclusive. But I want to talk with you. In person."

"Sure," he said. "I'm staying inside for the time being." His voice was strained; he sounded tired.

Vergil's apartment was in a fancy high-rise near the lake shore. I took the elevator up, listening to little advertising jingles and watching dancing holograms display products, empty apartments for rent, the building's hostess discussing social activities for the week.

Vergil opened the door and motioned me in. He wore a checked robe with long sleeves and carpet slippers. He clutched an unlit pipe in one hand, his fingers twisting it back and forth as he walked away from me and sat down, saying nothing.

"You have an infection," I said.

"Oh?"

"That's all the blood analyses tell me. I don't have access to the electron microscopes."

"I don't think it's really an infection," he said. "After all, they're my own cells. Probably something else . . . some sign of their presence, of the change. We can't expect to understand everything that's happening."

I removed my coat. "Listen," I said, "you have me worried now." The expression on his face stopped me: a kind of frantic beatitude. He squinted at the ceiling and pursed his lips.

"Are you stoned?" I asked.

He shook his head, then nodded once, very slowly. "Listening," he said.

"To what?"

"I don't know. Not sounds . . . exactly. Like music. The heart, all the blood vessels, friction of blood along the arteries, veins. Activity. Music in the blood." He looked at me plaintively. "Why aren't you at work?"

"My day off. Gail's working."

"Can you stay?"

I shrugged. "I suppose." I sounded suspicious. I was glancing around the apartment, looking for ashtrays, packs of papers.

"I'm not stoned, Edward," he said. "I may be wrong, but I think something big is happening. I think they're finding out who I am."

I sat down across from Vergil, staring at him intently. He didn't seem to notice. Some inner process was involving him. When I asked for a cup of coffee, he motioned to the kitchen. I boiled a pot of water and took a jar of instant from the cabinet. With cup in hand, I returned to my seat. He was twisting his head back and forth, eyes open. "You always knew what you wanted to be, didn't you?" he asked me.

"More or less."

"A gynecologist. Smart moves. Never false moves. I was different. I had goals, but no direction. Like a map without roads, just places to be. I didn't give a shit for anything, anyone but myself. Even science. Just a means. I'm surprised I got so far. I even hated my folks."

He gripped his chair arms.

"Something wrong?" I asked.

"They're talking to me," he said. He shut his eyes.

For an hour he seemed to be asleep. I checked his pulse, which was strong and steady, felt his forehead—slightly cool—and made myself more coffee. I was looking through a magazine, at a loss what to do, when he opened his eyes again. "Hard to figure exactly what time is like for them," he said. "It's taken them maybe three, four days to figure out language, key human concepts. Now they're on to it. On to me. Right now."

"How's that?"

He claimed there were thousands of researchers hooked up to his neurons. He couldn't give details. "They're damned efficient, you know," he said. "They haven't screwed me up yet."

"We should get you into the hospital now."

"What in hell could they do? Did you figure out any way to control them? I mean, they're my own cells."

"I've been thinking. We could starve them. Find out what metabolic differences—"

"I'm not sure I want to be rid of them," Vergil said. "They're not doing any harm."

"How do you know?"

He shook his head and held up one finger. "Wait. They're trying to figure out what space is. That's tough for them. They break distances down into concentrations of chemicals. For them, space is like intensity of taste."

"Vergil—"

"Listen! Think, Edward!" His tone was excited but even. "Observe! Something big is happening inside me. They talk to each other across the fluid, through membranes. They tailor something—viruses?—to carry data stored in nucleic acid chains. I think they're saying 'RNA.' That makes sense. That's one way I programed them. But plasmiclike structures, too. Maybe that's what your machines think is a sign of infection—all their chattering in my blood, packets of data. Tastes of other individuals. Peers. Superiors. Subordinates."

"Vergil, I'm listening, but I still think you should be in a hospital."

"This is my show, Edward," he said. "I'm their universe. They're amazed by the new scale." He was quiet again for a time. I squatted by his chair and pulled up the sleeve to his robe. His arm was crisscrossed with white lines. I was about to go to the phone and call for an ambulance when he stood and stretched. "Do you realize," he said, "how many body cells we kill each time we move?"

"I'm going to call for an ambulance," I said.

"No, you aren't." His tone stopped me. "I told you, I'm not sick; this is my show. Do you know what they'd do to me in a hospital? They'd be like cavemen trying to fix a computer the same way they fix a stone axe. It would be a farce."

"Then what the hell am I doing here?" I asked, getting angry. "I can't do anything. I'm one of those cavemen."

"You're a friend," Vergil said, fixing his eyes on me. I had the impression I was being watched by more than just Vergil. "I want you here to keep me company." He laughed. "But I'm not exactly alone."

He walked around the apartment for two hours, fingering things, looking out windows, making himself lunch slowly and methodically. "You know, they can actually feel their own thoughts," he said about noon. "I mean, the cytoplasm seems to have a will of its own, a kind of subconscious life counter to the rationality they've only recently acquired. They hear the chemical 'noise' or whatever of the molecules fitting and unfitting inside."

At two o'clock, I called Gail to tell her I would be late. I was almost sick with tension but I tried to keep my voice level. "Remember Vergil Ulam? I'm talking with him right now."

"Everything okay?" she asked.

Was it? Decidedly not. "Fine," I said.

"Culture!" Vergil said, peering around the kitchen wall at me. I said good-bye and hung up the phone. "They're always swimming in that bath of information. Contributing to it. It's a kind of gestalt thing, whatever. The hierarchy is absolute. They send tailored phages after cells that don't interact properly. Viruses specified to individuals or groups. No escape. One gets pierced by the virus, the cell blebs outward, it explodes and dissolves. But it's not just a dictatorship. I think they effectively have more freedom than in a democracy. I mean, they vary so differently from individual to individual. Does that make sense? They vary in different ways than we do."

"Hold it," I said, gripping his shoulders. "Vergil, you're pushing me close to the edge. I can't take this much longer. I don't understand, I'm not sure I believe—"

"Not even now?"

"Okay, let's say you're giving me the, the right interpretation. Giving it to me straight. The whole thing's true. Have you bothered to figure out all the consequences yet? What all this means, where it might lead?"

He walked into the kitchen and drew a glass of water from the tap, then returned and stood next to me. His expression had changed from childish absorption to sober concern. "I've never been very good at that."

"Aren't you afraid?"

"I was. Now I'm not sure." He fingered the tie of his robe. "Look, I don't want you to think I went around you, over your head or something. But I met with Michael Bernard yesterday. He put me through his private clinic, took specimens. Told me to quit the lamp treatments. He called this morning, just before you did. He says it all checks out. And he asked me not to tell anybody." He paused and his expression became dreamy again. "Cities of cells," he continued. "Edward, they push pili-like tubes through the tissues, spread information—"

"Stop it!" I shouted. "Checks out? What checks out?"

"As Bernard puts it, I have 'severely enlarged macrophages' throughout my system. And he concurs on the anatomical changes. So it's not just our common delusion."

"What does he plan to do?"

"I don't know. I think he'll probably convince Genetron to reopen the lab."

"Is that what you want?"

"It's not just having the lab again. I want to show you. Since I stopped the lamp treatments. I'm still changing." He undid his robe and let it slide to the floor. All over his body, his skin was crisscrossed with white lines. Along his back, the lines were starting to form ridges.

"My God," I said

"I'm not going to be much good anywhere else but the lab soon. I won't be able to go out in public. Hospitals wouldn't know what to do, as I said."

"You're . . . you can talk to them, tell them to slow down," I said, aware how ridiculous that sounded.

"Yes, indeed I can, but they don't necessarily listen."

"I thought you were their god or something."

"The ones hooked up to my neurons aren't the big wheels. They're researchers, or at least serve the same function. They know I'm here, what I am, but that doesn't mean they've convinced the upper levels of the hierarchy."

"They're disputing?"

"Something like that. It's not all that bad, anyway. If the lab is reopened, I have a home, a place to work." He glanced out the window, as if looking for someone. "I don't have anything left but them. They aren't afraid, Edward. I've never felt so close to anything before." The beatific smile again. "I'm responsible for them. Mother to them all."

"You have no way of knowing what they're going to do."

He shook his head.

"No, I mean it. You say they're like a civilization—"

"Like a thousand civilizations."

"Yes, and civilizations have been known to screw up. Warfare, the environment—"

I was grasping at straws, trying to restrain a growing panic. I wasn't competent to handle the enormity of what was happening. Neither was Vergil. He was the last person I would have called insightful and wise about large issues.

"But I'm the only one at risk."

"You don't know that. Jesus, Vergil, look what they're *doing* to you!"

"To me, all to me!" he said. "Nobody else."

I shook my head and held up my hands in a gesture of defeat. "Okay, so Bernard gets them to reopen the lab, you move in, become a guinea pig. What then?"

"They treat me right. I'm more than just good old Vergil Ulam now. I'm a goddamned galaxy, a supermother."

"Super-host, you mean." He conceded the point with a shrug.

I couldn't take any more. I made my exit with a few flimsy excuses, then sat in the lobby of the apartment building, trying to calm down.

Somebody had to talk some sense into him. Who would he listen to? He had gone to Bernard . . .

And it sounded as if Bernard were not only convinced, but very interested. People of Bernard's stature didn't coax the Vergil Ulams of the world along, not unless they felt it was to their advantage.

I had a hunch, and I decided to play it. I went to a pay phone, slipped in my credit card, and called Genetron.

"I'd like you to page Dr. Michael Bernard," I told the receptionist.

"Who's calling, please?"

"This is his answering service. We have an emergency call and his beeper doesn't seem to be working."

A few anxious minutes later, Bernard came on the line. "Who the hell is this?" he asked quietly. "I don't have an answering service."

"My name is Edward Milligan. I'm a friend of Vergil Ulam's. I think we have some problems to discuss."

We made an appointment to talk the next morning.

I went home and tried to think of excuses to keep me off the next day's hospital shift. I couldn't concentrate on medicine, couldn't give my patients anywhere near the attention they deserved.

Guilty, anxious, angry, afraid.

That was how Gail found me. I slipped on a mask of calm and we fixed dinner together. After eating, we watched the city lights come on in late twilight through the bayside window, holding on to each other. Odd winter starlings pecked at the yellow lawn in the last few minutes of light, then flew away with a rising wind which made the windows rattle.

"Something's wrong," Gail said softly. "Are you going to tell me, or just act like everything's normal?"

"It's just me," I said. "Nervous. Work at the hospital."

"Oh, lord," she said, sitting up. "You're going to divorce me for that Baker woman." Mrs. Baker weighed three hundred and sixty pounds and hadn't known she was pregnant until her fifth month.

"No," I said, listless.

"Rapturous relief," Gail said, touching my forehead lightly. "You know this kind of introspection drives me crazy."

"Well, it's nothing I can talk about yet, so . . . ." I patted her hand.

"That's disgustingly patronizing," she said, getting up. "I'm going to make some tea. Want some?" Now she was miffed, and I was tense with not telling.

Why not just reveal all? I asked myself. An old friend of mine was turning himself into a galaxy.

I cleared away the table instead. That night, unable to sleep, I looked down on Gail in bed from my sitting position, pillow against the wall, and tried to determine what I knew was real, and what wasn't.

I'm a doctor, I told myself. A technical, scientific profession. I'm supposed to be immune to things like future shock.

Vergil Ulam was turning into a galaxy.

How would it feel to be topped off with a trillion Chinese? I grinned in the dark, and almost cried at the same time. What Vergil had inside him was unimaginably stranger than Chinese. Stranger than anything I—or Vergil—could easily understand. Perhaps ever understand.

But I knew what was real. The bedroom, the city lights faint through gauze curtains. Gail sleeping. Very important. Gail, in bed, sleeping.

The dream came again. This time the city came in through the window and attacked Gail. It was a great, spiky lighted-up prowler and it growled in a language I couldn't understand, made up of auto horns, crowd noises, construction bedlam. I tried to fight it off, but it got to her—and turned into a drift of stars, sprinkling all over the bed, all over everything. I jerked awake and stayed up until dawn, dressed with Gail, kissed her, savored the reality of her human, unviolated lips.

And went to meet with Bernard. He had been loaned a suite in a big downtown hospital; I rode the elevator to the sixth floor, and saw what fame and fortune could mean.

The suite was tastefully furnished, fine serigraphs on wood-paneled walls, chrome and glass furniture, cream-colored carpet, Chinese brass, and wormwood-grain cabinets and tables.

He offered me a cup of coffee, and I accepted. He took a seat in the breakfast nook, and I sat across from him, cradling my cup in moist palms. He was dapper, wearing a gray suit; had graying hair and a sharp profile. He was in his midsixties and he looked quite a bit like Leonard Bernstein.

"About our mutual acquaintance," he said. "Mr. Ulam. Brilliant. And, I won't hesitate to say, courageous."

"He's my friend. I'm worried about him."

Bernard held up one finger. "Courageous—and a bloody damned fool. What's happening to him should never have been allowed. He may have done it under duress, but that's no excuse. Still, what's done is done. He's talked to you, I take it."

I nodded. "He wants to return to Genetron."

"Of course. That's where all his equipment is. Where his home probably will be while we sort this out."

"Sort it out—how? What use is it?" I wasn't thinking too clearly. I had a slight headache.

"I can think of a large number of uses for small, super-dense computer elements with a biological base. Can't you? Genetron has already made breakthroughs, but this is something else again."

"What do you envision?"

Bernard smiled. "I'm not really at liberty to say. It'll be revolutionary. We'll have to get him in lab conditions. Animal experiments have to be conducted. We'll have to start from scratch, of course. Vergil's . . . um . . . colonies can't be transferred. They're based on his white blood cells. So we have to develop colonies that won't trigger immune reactions in other animals."

"Like an infection?" I asked.

"I suppose there are comparisons. But Vergil is not infected."

"My tests indicate he is."

"That's probably the bits of data floating around in his blood, don't you think?"

"I don't know."

"Listen, I'd like you to come down to the lab after Vergil is settled in. Your expertise might be useful to us."

Us. He was working with Genetron hand-in-glove. Could he be objective? "How will you benefit from all this?"

"Edward, I have always been at the forefront of my profession. I see no reason why I shouldn't be helping here. With my knowledge of brain and nerve functions, and the research I've been conducting in neurophysiology—"

"You could help Genetron hold off an investigation by the government," I said.

"That's being very blunt. Too blunt, and unfair."

"Perhaps. Anyway, yes: I'd like to visit the lab when Vergil's settled in. If I am still welcome, bluntness and all." He looked at me sharply. I wouldn't be playing on *his* team; for a moment, his thoughts were almost nakedly apparent.

"Of course," Bernard said, rising with me. He reached out to shake my hand. His palm was damp. He was as nervous as I was, even if he didn't look it.

I returned to my apartment and stayed there until noon, reading, trying to sort things out. Reach a decision. What was real, what I needed to protect.

There is only so much change anyone can stand. Innovation, yes, but slow application. Don't force. Everyone has the right to stay the same until they decide otherwise.

The greatest thing in science since . . .

And Bernard would force it. Genetron would force it. I couldn't handle the thought. "Neo-Luddite," I said to myself. A filthy accusation.

When I pressed Vergil's number on the building security panel, Vergil answered almost immediatly. "Yeah," he said. He sounded exhilarated now. "Come on up. I'll be in the bathroom. Door's unlocked."

I entered his apartment and walked through the hallway to the bathroom. Vergil was in the tub, up to his neck in pinkish water. He smiled vaguely at me and splashed his hands. "Looks like I slit my wrists, doesn't it?" he said softly. "Don't worry. Everything's fine now. Genetron's going to take me back. Bernard just called." He pointed to the bathroom phone and intercom.

I sat down on the toilet and noticed the sunlamp fixture standing unplugged next to the linen cabinets. The bulbs sat in a row on the edge of the sink counter. "You're sure that's what you want," I said, my shoulders slumping.

"Yeah, I think so," he said. "They can take better care of me. I'm getting cleaned up, go over there this evening. Bernard's picking me up in his limo. Style. From here on in, everything's style."

The pinkish color in the water didn't look like soap. "Is that bubble bath?" I asked. Some of it came to me in a rush then and I felt a little weaker: what had occured to me was just one more obvious and necessary insanity.

"No," Vergil said. I knew that already.

"No," he repeated, "it's coming from my skin. They're not telling me everything, but I think they're sending out scouts. Astronauts." He looked at me with an expression that didn't quite equal concern; more like curiosity as to how I'd take it.

The confirmation made my stomach muscles tighten as if waiting for a punch. I had never even considered the possibility until now, perhaps because I had been concentrating on other aspects. "Is this the first time?" I asked.

"Yeah," he said. He laughed. "I've half a mind to let the little buggers down the drain. Let them find out what the world's really about."

"They'd go everywhere," I said.

"Sure enough."

"How . . . how are you feeling?"

"I'm feeling pretty good now. Must be billions of them." More splashing with his hands. "What do you think? Should I let the buggers out?"

Quickly, hardly thinking, I knelt down beside the tub. My fingers went for the cord on the sunlamp and I plugged it in. He had hot-wired doorknobs, turned my piss blue, played a thousand dumb practical jokes and never grown up, never grown mature enough to understand that he was just brilliant enough to really affect the world; he would never learn caution.

He reached for the drain knob. "You know, Edward, I—"

He never finished. I picked up the fixture and dropped it into the tub, jumping back at the flash of steam and sparks. Vergil screamed and thrashed and jerked and then everything was still, except for the low, steady sizzle and the smoke wafting from his hair.

I lifted the toilet lid and vomited. Then I clenched my nose and went into the living room. My legs went out from under me and I sat abruptly on the couch.

After an hour, I searched through Vergil's kitchen and found bleach, ammonia, and a bottle of Jack Daniel's. I returned to the bathroom, keeping the center of my gaze away from Vergil. I poured first the booze, then the bleach, then the ammonia into the water. Chlorine started bubbling up and I left, closing the door behind me.

The phone was ringing when I got home. I didn't answer. It could have been the hospital. It could have been Bernard. Or the police. I could envision having to explain everything to the police. Genetron would stonewall; Bernard would be unavailable.

I was exhausted, all my muscles knotted with tension and whatever name one can give to the feelings one has after—

Committing genocide?

That certainly didn't seem real. I could not believe I had just murdered a hundred trillion intelligent beings. Snuffed a galaxy. It was laughable. But I didn't laugh.

It was not at all hard to believe I had just killed one human being, a friend. The smoke, the melted lamp rods, the drooping electrical outlet and smoking cord.

Vergil.

I had dunked the lamp into the tub with Vergil.

I felt sick. Dreams, cities raping Gail (and what about his girl friend, Candice?). Letting the water filled with them out. Galaxies sprinkling over us all. What horror. Then again, what potential beauty—a new kind of life, symbiosis and transformation.

Had I been through enough to kill them all? I had a moment of panic. Tomorrow, I thought, I will sterilize his apartment. Somehow. I didn't even think of Bernard.

When Gail came in the door, I was alseep on the couch. I came to, groggy, and she looked down at me.

"You feeling okay?" she asked, perching on the edge of the couch. I nodded.

"What are you planning for dinner?" My mouth wasn't working properly. The words were mushy. She felt my forehead.

"Edward, you have a fever," she said. "A very high fever."

I stumbled into the bathroom and looked in the mirror. Gai was close behind me. "What is it?" she asked.

There were lines under my collar, around my neck. White lines, like freeways. They had already been in me a long time, days.

"Damp palms," I said. So obvious.

I think we nearly died. I struggled at first, but within minutes I was too weak to move. Gail was just as sick within an hour.

I lay on the carpet in the living room, drenched in sweat. Gail lay on the couch, her face the color of talcum, eyes closed, like a corpse in an embalming parlor. For a time I thought she was dead. Sick as I was, I raged—hated, felt tremendous guilt at my weakness, my slowness to understand all the possibilities. Then I no longer cared. I was too weak to blink, so I closed my eyes and waited.

There was a rhythm in my arms, my legs. With each pulse of blood, a kind of sound welled up within me. A sound like an orchestra thousands strong, but not playing in unison; playing whole seasons of symphonies at once. Music in the blood. The sound or whatever became harsher, but more coordinated, wave-trains finally canceling into silence, then separating into harmonic beats.

The beats seemed to melt into me, into the sound of my own heart.

First, they subdued our immune responses. The war—and it was a war, on a scale never before known on Earth, with trillions of combatants—lasted perhaps two days.

By the time I regained enough strength to get to the kitchen faucet, I could feel them working on my brain, trying to crack the code and find the god within the protoplasm. I drank until I was sick, then drank more moderately and took a glass to Gail. She sipped at it. Her lips were cracked, her eyes bloodshot and ringed with yellowish crumbs. There was some color in her skin. Minutes later, we were eating feebly in the kitchen.

"What in hell was *that?*" was the first thing she asked. I didn't have the strength to explain, so I shook my head. I peeled an orange and shared it with her. "We should call a doctor," she said. But I knew we wouldn't. I was already receiving messages; it was becoming apparent that any sensation of freedom we had was illusory.

The messages were simple at first. Memories of commands, rather than the commands themselves, manifested themselves in my thoughts. We were not to leave the apartment—a concept which seemed quite abstract to those in control, even if undesirable—and we were not to have contact with others. We would be allowed to eat certain foods, and drink tap water, for the time being.

With the subsidence of the fevers, the transformations were quick and drastic. Almost simultaneously, Gail and I were immobilized. She was sitting at the table, I was kneeling on the floor. I was able barely to see her in the corner of my eye.

Her arm was developing pronounced ridges.

They had learned inside Vergil; their tactics within the two of us were very different. I itched all over for about two hours—two hours in hell—before they made the breakthrough and found me. The effort of ages on their timescale paid off and they communicated smoothly and directly with this great, clumsy intelligence which had once controlled their universe.

They were not cruel. When the concept of discomfort and its undesirability was made clear, they worked to alleviate it. They worked too effectively. For another hour, I was in a sea of bliss, out of all contact with them.

With dawn the next day, we were allowed freedom to move again; specifically, to go to the bathroom. There were certain waste products they could not deal with. I voided those—my urine was purple—and Gail followed suit. We looked at each other vacantly in the bathroom. Then she managed a slight smile. "Are they talking to you?" she asked. I nodded. "Then I'm not crazy."

For the next twelve hours, control seemed to loosen on some levels. During that time, I managed to pencil the majority of this manuscript. I suspect there was another kind of war going on in me. Gail was capable of our previous limited motion, but no more.

When full control resumed; we were instructed to hold each other. We did not hesitate.

"Eddie . . ." she whispered. My name was the last sound I ever heard from the outside.

Standing, we grew together. In hours, our legs expanded and spread out. Then extensions grew to the windows to take in sunlight, and to the kitchen to take water from the sink. Filaments soon reached to all corners of the room, stripping paint and plaster from the walls, fabric and stuffing from the furniture.

By the next dawn, the transformation was complete.

I no longer have any clear view of what we look like. I suspect we resemble cells—large, flat and filamented cells, draped purposefully across most of the apartment. The great shall mimic the small.

I have been asked to carry on recording, but soon that will not be possible. Our intelligence fluctuates daily as we are absorbed into the minds within. Each day, our individuality declines. We are, indeed, great clumsy dinosaurs. Our memories have been taken over by billions of them, and our personalities have been spread through the transformed blood.

Soon there will be no need for centralization.

I am informed that already the plumbing has been invaded. People throughout the building are undergoing transformation.

Within the old time-frame of weeks, we will reach the lakes, rivers, and seas in force.

I can barely begin to guess the results. Every square inch of the planet will teem with thought. Years from now, perhaps much sooner, they will subdue their own individuality—what there is of it.

New creatures will come, then. The immensity of their capacity for thought will be inconceivable.

All my hatred and fear is gone now.

I leave them—us—with only one question.

How many times has this happened elsewhere? Travellers never came through space to visit the Earth. They had no need.

They had found universes in grains of sand.

LEIGH KENNEDY

Her Furry Face

Born in Denver, Colorado, Leigh Kennedy moved to Austin in 1980 and is now widely accepted as an honorary Texan. She sold her first story in 1978, and in the last couple of years has become a frequent contributor to *Isaac Asimov's Science Fiction Magazine*; she has also sold to *Omni, Universe, Analog,* and *Shadows*. Last year, her story "Helen, Whose Face Launched Twenty-Eight Conestoga Hovercraft" attracted a good deal of attention and acclaim. This year, she published three other strong stories ("The Silent Cradle," "Belling Martha," and "Greek"), any one of which might well have been worthy of inclusion in a "Best" anthology in another year. They were pushed aside, however, by the piece that follows, one of 1983's most powerful and poignant stories, about a time when the line between animal and human has become even more blurred than it is now—with some unforseen and melancholy consequences.

Leigh Kennedy works at the University of Austin and is currently working on a novel.

HER FURRY FACE

Leigh Kennedy

Douglas was embarrassed when he saw Annie and Vernon mating.

He'd seen hours of sex between orangutans, but this time was different. He'd never seen *Annie* doing it. He stood in the shade of the pecan tree for a moment, shocked, iced tea glasses sweating in his hand, then he backed around the corner of the brick building. He was confused. The cicadas seemed louder than usual, the sun hotter, and the squeals of pleasure from the apes strange.

He walked back to the front porch and sat down. His mind still saw the two giant mounds of red-orange fur moving together like one being.

When the two orangs came back around, Douglas thought he saw smugness in Vernon's face. Why not, he thought? I guess I would be smug, too.

Annie flopped down on the grassy front yard and crossed one leg over the other, her abdomen bulging high; she gazed upward into the heavy white sky.

Vernon bounded toward Douglas. He was young and red-chocolate colored. His face was still slim, without the older orangutan jowls yet.

"Be polite," Douglas warned him.

"Drink tea, please?" Vernon signed rapidly, the fringe on his elbows waving. "Dry as bone."

Douglas handed Vernon one of the glasses of tea, though he'd brought it out for Annie. The handsome nine year old downed it in a gulp. "Thank you," he signed. He touched the edge of the porch and withdrew his long fingers. "Could fry egg," he signed, and instead of sitting, swung out hand-over-hand on the ropes between the roof of the schoolhouse and the trees. It was a sparse and dry substitute for the orang's native rain forest.

He's too young and crude for Annie, Douglas thought.

"Annie," Douglas called. "Your tea."

Annie rolled onto one side and lay propped on an elbow, staring at him. She was lovely. Fifteen years old, her fur was glossy and coppery, her small yellow eyes in the fleshy face expressive and intelligent. She started to raise up toward him, but turned toward the road.

The mail jeep was coming down the highway.

In a blurred movement, she set off at a four-point gallop down the half-mile drive toward the mailbox. Vernon swung down from his tree and followed, making a small groan.

Reluctant to go out in the sun, Douglas put down the tea and followed the apes down the drive. By the time he got near them, Annie was sitting with mail sorted between her toes, holding an opened letter in her hands. She looked up with an expression on her face that he'd never seen—it could have been fear, but it wasn't.

She handed the letter to Vernon, who pestered her for it. "Douglas," she signed, "they want to buy my story."

Therese lay in the bathwater, her knees sticking up high, her hair floating beside her face. Douglas sat on the edge of the tub; as he talked to her he was conscious that he spoke a double language—the one with his lips and the other with his hands.

"As soon as I called Ms. Young, the magazine editor, and told her who Annie was, she got really excited. She asked me why we didn't send a letter explaining it with the story, so I told her that Annie didn't want anyone to know first."

"Did Annie decide that?" Therese sounded skeptical, as she always seemed to when Douglas talked about Annie.

"We talked about it and she wanted it that way." Douglas felt that resistance from Therese. Why she never understood, he didn't know, unless she did it to provoke him. She acted as if she thought an ape was still just an ape, no matter what he or she could do. "Anyway," he said, "she talked about doing a whole publicity thing to the hilt—talk shows, autograph parties. You know. But Dr. Morris thinks it would be better to keep things quiet."

"Why?" Therese sat up; her legs went underwater and she soaped her arms.

"Because she'd be too nervous. Annie, I mean. It might disrupt her education to become a celebrity. Too bad. Even Dr. Morris knows that it would be great for fund-raising. But I guess we'll let the press in some."

Therese began to shampoo her hair. "I brought home that essay that Sandy wrote yesterday. The one I told you about. If she were an orangutan instead of just a deaf kid, she could probably get it published in *Fortune.*" Therese smiled.

Douglas stood. He didn't like the way Therese headed for the old argument—no matter what one of Therese's deaf students did, if Annie could do it one-one-hundredth as well, it was more spectacular. Douglas knew it was true, but why Therese was so bitter about it, he didn't understand.

"That's great," he said, trying to sound enthusiastic.

"Will you wash my back?" she asked.

He crouched and absently washed her. "I'll never forget Annie's face when she read that letter."

"Thank you," Therese said. She rinsed. "Do you have any plans for this evening?"

"I've got work to do," he said, leaving the bathroom. "Would you like me to work in the bedroom so you can watch television?"

After a long pause, she said, "No, I'll read."

He hesitated in the doorway. "Why don't you go to sleep early? You look tired."

She shrugged. "Maybe I am."

In the playroom at the school, Douglas watched Annie closely. It was still morning, though late. In the recliner across the room from him, she seemed a little sleepy. Staring out the window, blinking, she marked her place in Pinkwater's *Fat Men from Space* with a long brown finger.

He had been thinking about Therese, who'd been silent and morose that morning. Annie was never morose, though often quiet. He wondered if Annie was quiet today because she sensed that Douglas was not happy. When he'd come to work, she'd given him an extra hug.

He wondered if Annie could have a crush on him, like many schoolgirls have on their teachers. Remembering her mating with Vernon days before, he idly wandered into a fantasy of touching her and gently, gently moving inside her.

The physical reaction to his fantasy embarrassed him. *God, what am I thinking?* He shook himself out of the reverie, averting his gaze for a few moments, until he'd gotten control of himself again.

"Douglas," Annie signed. She walked erect, towering, to him and sat down on the floor at his feet. Her flesh folded onto her lap like dough.

"What?" he asked, wondering suddenly if orangutans were telepathic.

"Why you say my story children's?"

He looked blankly at her.

"Why not send *Harper's*?" she asked, having to spell out the name of the magazine.

He repressed a laugh, knowing it would upset her. "It's . . . it's the kind of story children would like."

"Why?"

He sighed. "The level of writing is . . . *young*. Like you, sweetie." He stroked her head, looking into the small intense eyes. "You'll get more sophisticated as you grow."

"I smart as you," she signed. "You understand me always because I talk smart."

Douglas was dumbfounded by her logic.

She tilted her head and waited. When Douglas shrugged, she seemed to assume victory and returned to her recliner.

Dr. Morris came in. "Here we go," she said, handing him the paper and leaving again.

Douglas skimmed the page until he came to an article about the "ape author." He scanned it. It contained one of her flashpoints; this and the fact that she was irritable from being in estrus, made him consider hiding it. But that wouldn't be right.

"Annie," he said softly.

She looked up.

"There's an article about you."

"Me read," she signed, putting her book on the floor. She came and crawled up on the sofa next to him. He watched her eyes as they jerked across every word. He grew edgy. She read on.

Suddenly she took off as if from a diving board. He ran after her as she bolted out the door. The stuffed dog which had always been a favorite toy was being shredded in those powerful hands even before he knew she had it. Annie screamed as she pulled the toy apart, running into the yard.

Terrified by her own aggression, she ran up the tree with stuffing falling like snow behind her.

Douglas watched as the shade filled with foam rubber and fake fur. The tree branches trembled. After a long while, she stopped pummeling the tree and sat quietly.

Douglas suddenly realized that Therese was afraid of the apes.

She watched Annie warily as the four of them strolled along the edge of the school acreage. Douglas knew that Therese didn't appreciate the grace of Annie's muscular gait as he did; the sign language that passed between them was as similar to the Amslan that Therese used for her deaf children as British to Jamaican. Therese couldn't appreciate Annie in creative conversation.

It wasn't good to be afraid of the apes, no matter how educated they were.

He had invited her out, hoping it would please her to be included in his world here. She had only visited briefly twice before.

Vernon lagged behind them, snapping pictures now and then with the expensive but hardy camera modified for his hands. Vernon took several pictures of Annie and one of Douglas, but only when Therese had separated from him to peer between the rushes at the edge of the creek.

"Annie," Douglas called, pointing ahead. "A cardinal. The red bird."

Annie lumbered forward. She glanced back to see where Douglas pointed, then stood still, squatting. Douglas walked beside her and they watched the bird.

It flew.

"Gone," Annie signed.

"Wasn't it pretty, though?" Douglas asked.

They ambled on. Annie stopped often to investigate shiny bits of trash or large bugs. They didn't come this far from the school much. Vernon whizzed past them, a dark auburn streak of youthful energy.

Remembering Therese, Douglas turned. She sat on a stump far behind. He was annoyed. He'd told her to wear her jeans and a straw hat because there would be grass burrs and hot sun. But there she sat, bareheaded, wearing shorts, miserably rubbing at her ankles.

He grunted impatiently. Annie looked up at him. "Not you," he said, stroking her fur. She patted his butt.

"Go on," Douglas said, turning back. When he came to Therese, he said, "What's the problem?"

"No problem." She stood, and started forward without looking at him. "I was just resting."

Annie had paused to poke at something on the ground with a stick. Douglas quickened his step. Even though his students were smart, they had orangutan appetites. He always worried that they would eat something that would sicken them. "What is it?" he called.

"Dead cat," Vernon signed back. He took a picture as Annie flipped the carcass with her stick.

Therese hurried forward. "Oh, poor kitty . . ." she said, kneeling.

Annie had seemed too absorbed in poking the cat to notice Therese approach; only a quick eye could follow her leap. Douglas was stunned.

Both screamed. It was over.

Annie clung to Douglas's legs, whimpering.

"Shit!" Therese said. She lay on the ground, rolling from side to side, holding her left arm. Blood dripped from between her fingers.

Douglas pushed Annie back. "That was bad, *very bad*," he said. "Do you hear me?"

Annie sank down on her rump and covered her head. She hadn't gotten a child-scolding for a long time. Vernon stood beside her, shaking his head, signing, "Not wise, baboon-face."

"Stand up," Douglas said to Therese. "I can't help you right now."

Therese was pale, but dry-eyed. Clumsily, she stood and grew even paler. A hunk of flesh hung loosely from above her elbow, meaty and bleeding. "Look."

"Go on. Walk back to the house. We'll come right behind you." He tried to keep his voice calm, holding a warning hand on Annie's shoulder.

Therese moaned, catching her breath. "It hurts," she said, but stumbled on.

"We're coming," Douglas said sternly. "Just walk and—Annie, don't you dare step out of line."

They walked silently, Therese ahead, leaving drops of blood in the dirt. The drops got larger and closer together. Once, Annie dipped her finger into a bloody spot and sniffed her fingertip.

Why can't things just be easy and peaceful, he wondered. Something always happens. *Always.* He should have known better than to bring Therese around Annie. Apes didn't understand that vulnerable quality that Therese was made of. He himself didn't understand it, though at one time he'd probably been attracted to it. No—maybe he'd never really seen it until it was too late. He'd only thought of Therese as "sweet" until their lives were too tangled up to keep clear of it.

Why couldn't she be as tough as Annie? Why did she always take everything so seriously?

They reached the building. Douglas sent Annie and Vernon to their rooms and guided Therese to the infirmary. He watched as Jim, their all-purpose nurse and veterinary assistant, examined her arm. "I think you should probably have stitches."

He left the room to make arrangements.

Therese looked at Douglas, holding the gauze over her still-bleeding arm. "Why did she bite me?" she asked.

Douglas didn't answer. He couldn't think of how to say it.

"Do you have any idea?" she asked.

"You asked for it, all your wimping around."

"I . . ."

Douglas saw the anger rising in her. He didn't want to argue now. He wished he'd never brought her. He'd done it for her, and she ruined it. All ruined.

"Don't start," he said simply, giving her a warning look.

"But, Douglas, I didn't do anything."

"Don't start," he repeated.

"I see now," she said coldly. "Somehow it's my fault again."

Jim returned with his supplies.

"Do you want me to stay?" Douglas asked. He suddenly felt a pang of guilt, realizing that she was actually hurt enough for all this attention.

"No," she said softly.

And her eyes looked far, far from him as he left her.

On the same day that the largest donation ever came to the school, a television news team came out to tape.

Douglas could tell that everyone was excited. Even the chimps that lived on the north half of the school hung on the fence and watched the TV van being unloaded. The reporter decided upon the playroom as the best location for the taping, though she didn't seem to relish sitting on the floor with the giant apes. People went over scripts, strung cords, microphones, set up hot lights, and discussed angles and sound while pointing at the high ceiling's jungle-gym design. All this to talk to a few people and an orangutan.

They brought Anne's desk into the playroom, contrary to Annie's wishes. Douglas explained that it was temporary, that these people would go away after they talked a little. Douglas and Annie stayed outside as long as possible and played Tarzan around the big tree. He tickled her. She grabbed him as he swung from a limb. "Kagoda?" she signed, squeezing him with one arm.

"Kagoda!" he shouted, laughing.

They relaxed on the grass. Douglas was hot. He felt flushed all over. "Douglas," Annie signed, "they read story?"

"Not yet. It isn't published yet."

"Why come talk?" she asked.

"Because you wrote it and sold it and people like to interview famous authors." He groomed her shoulder. "Time to go in," he said, seeing a wave from inside.

Annie picked him up in a big hug and carried him in.

"Here it is!" Douglas called to Therese, and turned on the video-recorder.

First, a long shot of the school from the dusty drive, looking only functional and square, without personality. The reporter's voice said, "Here, just southeast of town, is a special school with unusual young students. The students here have little prospect for employment when they graduate, but millions of dollars each year fund this institution."

A shot of Annie at her typewriter, picking at the keyboard with her long fingers; a sheet of paper is slowly covered with large block letters.

"This is Annie, a fifteen-year-old orangutan, who has been a student with the school for five years. She graduated with honors from another "ape school" in Georgia before coming here. And now Annie has become a writer. Recently, she sold a story to a children's magazine. The editor who bought the story didn't know that Annie was an orangutan until after she had selected the story for publication."

Annie looked at the camera uncertainly.

"Annie can read and write, and understand spoken English, but she cannot speak. She uses a sign language similar to the one hearing-impaired use." Change in tone from narrative to interrogative. "Annie, how did you start writing?"

Douglas watched himself on the small screen watching Annie sign, "Teacher told me write." He saw himself grin, eyes shift slightly toward the camera, but generally watching Annie. His name and "Orangutan Teacher" appeared on the screen. The scene made him uneasy.

"What made you send in Annie's story for publication?" the reporter asked.

Douglas signed to Annie, she came to him for a hug, and turned a winsome face to the camera. "Our administrator, Dr. Morris, and I both read it. I commented that I thought it was as good as any kid's story, so Dr. Morris said, 'Send it in.' The editor liked it." Annie made a "pee" sign to Douglas.

Then, a shot of Dr. Morris in her office, a chimp on her lap, clapping her brown hands.

"Dr. Morris, your school was established five years ago by grants and government funding. What is your purpose here?"

"Well, in the last few decades, apes—mostly chimpanzees like Rose here—have been taught sign language experimentally. Mainly to prove that apes could indeed use language." Rosie put the tip of her finger through the gold hoop in Dr. Morris's ear. Dr. Morris took her hand away gently. "We were established with the idea of *educating* apes, a comparable education to the primary grades." She looked at the chimp. "Or however far they will advance."

"Your school has two orangutans and six chimpanzees. Are there differences in their learning?" the reporter asked.

Dr. Morris nodded emphatically. "Chimpanzees are very clever, but the orang has a different brain structure which allows for more abstract reasoning. Chimps learn many things quickly, orangs are slower. But the orangutan has the ability to learn in greater depth."

Shot of Vernon swinging in the ropes in front of the school.

Assuming that Vernon is Annie, the reporter said, "Her teacher felt from the start that Annie was an especially promising student. The basic sentences that she types out on her typewriter are simple but original entertainment."

Another shot of Annie at the typewriter.

"If you think this is just monkey business, you'd better think again. Tolstoy, watch out!"

Depressed by the lightness, brevity, and the stupid "monkey-business" remark, Douglas turned off the television.

He sat for a long time. Whenever Therese had gone to bed, she had left him silently. After half an hour of staring at the blank screen, he rewound his video-recorder and ran it soundlessly until Annie's face appeared.

And then froze it. He could almost feel again the softness of her halo of red hair against his chin.

He couldn't sleep.

Therese had rumpled her way out of the sheet and lay on her side, her back to him. He looked at the shape of her shoulder and back, downward to the dip of the waist, up the curve of her hip. Her buttocks were round ovals, one atop the other. Her skin was sleek and shiny in the filtered streetlight coming through the window. She smelled slightly of shampoo and even more slightly of female.

What he felt for her anyone would call "love," when he thought of her generally. And yet, he found himself helplessly angry with her most of the time. When he thought he could amuse her, it would end with her feelings being hurt for some obscure reason. He heard cruel words come barging out of an otherwise gentle mouth. She took everything seriously; mishaps and misunderstandings occurred beyond his control, beyond his repair.

Under this satiny skin, she was troubled and tense. A lot of sensitivity and fear. He had stopped trying to gain access to what had been the happier parts of her person, not understanding where they had gone. He had stopped wanting to love her, but he didn't *not* want to love her, either. It just didn't seem to matter.

Sometimes, he thought, it would be easier to have someone like Annie for a wife.

Annie.

He loved her furry face. He loved the unconditional joy in her face when she saw him. It was always there. She was bright and warm and unafraid. She didn't read things into what he said, but listened and talked with him. They were so natural together. Annie was so filled with vitality.

Douglas withdrew his hand from Therese, whose skin seemed a bare blister of dissatisfaction.

*   *   *

He lay on the floor of the apes' playroom with the fan blowing across his chest. He held Annie's report on Lawrence's *Sons and Lovers* by diagonal corners to keep it from flapping.

Annie lazily swung from bars criss-crossing the ceiling.

"Paul wasn't happy at work because the boss looked over his shoulder at his handwriting," she had written. "But he was happy again later. His brother died and his mother was sad. Paul got sick. He was better and visited his friends again. His mother died and his friends didn't tickle him anymore."

Douglas looked over the top of the paper at Annie. True, it was the first time she'd read an "adult" novel, but he'd expected something better than this. He considered asking her if Vernon had written the report for her, but thought better of it.

"Annie," he said, sitting up. "What do you think this book is really about?"

She swung down and landed on the sofa. "About man," she said.

Douglas waited. There was no more. "But what about it? Why this man instead of another? What was special about him?"

Annie rubbed her hands together, answerless.

"What about his mother?"

"She help him," Annie answered in a flurry of dark fingers. "Especially when he paint."

Douglas frowned. He looked at the page again, disappointed.

"What do I do?" Annie asked, worried.

He tried to brighten up. "You did just fine. It was a hard book."

"Annie smart," the orang signed. "Annie smart."

Douglas nodded. "I know."

Annie rose, then stood on her legs, looking like a two-story fuzzy building, teetering from side to side. "Annie smart. Writer. Smart," she signed. "Write book. Bestseller."

Douglas made a mistake. He laughed. Not as simple as a human laughing at another, this was an act of aggression. His bared teeth and uncontrolled guff-guff struck out at Annie. He tried to stop.

She made a gulping sound and galloped out of the room.

"Wait, Annie!" He chased after her.

By the time he got outside she was far ahead. He stopped running when his chest hurt and trotted slowly though the weeds toward her. She sat forlornly far away and watched him come.

When he was near, she signed, "hug," three times.

Douglas collapsed, panting, his throat raw. "Annie, I'm sorry," he said. "I didn't mean it." He put his arms around her.

She held onto him.

"I love you, Annie. I love you so much I don't want ever to hurt you. Ever, ever, ever. I want to be with you all the time. Yes, you're smart and talented and good." He kissed her tough face.

Whether forgotten or forgiven, the hurt of his laughter was gone from her eyes. She held him tighter, making a soft sound in her throat, a sound for him.

They lay together in the crackling yellow weeds, clinging. Douglas felt his love physically growing for her. More passionately than ever before in his life, he wanted to make love to her. He touched her. He felt that she understood what she wanted, that her breath on his neck was anticipation. A consummation as he'd never imagined, the joining of their species in language and body. Not dumb animal-banging but mutual love . . . He climbed over her and hugged her back.

Annie went rigid when he entered her.

Slowly, she rolled away from him, but he held onto her. "No." A horrible grimace came across her face that raised the hairs on the back of Douglas's neck. "Not you," she said.

She's going to kill me, he thought.

His passion declined; Annie disentangled herself and walked away.

He sat for a moment, stunned at what he'd done, stunned at what had happened, wondering what he would do the rest of his life with the memory of it. Then he zipped up his pants.

Staring at his dinner plate, he thought, it's just the same as if I had been rejected by a woman. I'm not the kind that goes for bestiality. I'm not some farm boy who can't find someplace to put it.

His hands could still remember the matted feel of her fur; tucked in his groin was the memory of being in an alien place. It had made him throw up out in the field that afternoon, and after that he'd come straight home. He hadn't even said good-night to the orangs.

"What's the matter?" Therese asked.

He shrugged.

She half-rose out of her chair to kiss him on the temple. "You don't have a fever, do you?"

"No."

"Can I do something to make you feel better?" Her hand slid along his thigh.

He stood up. "Stop it."

She sat still. "Are you in love with another woman?"

Why can't she just leave me alone? "No. I have a lot on my mind. There's a lot going on."

"It never was like this, even when you were working on your thesis."

"Therese," he said, with what he felt was undeserved patience, "just leave me alone. It doesn't help with you at me all the time."

"But I'm scared, I don't know what to do. You act like you don't want me around."

"All you do is criticize me." He stood and took his dishes to the sink.

Slowly, she trailed after him, carrying her plate. "I'm just trying to understand. It's my life, too."

He said nothing and she walked away as if someone had told her not to leave footsteps.

In the bathroom, he stripped and stood under the shower a long time. He imagined that Annie's smell clung to him. He felt that Therese could smell it on him.

What have I done, what have I done . . .

And when he came out of the shower, Therese was gone.

He had considered calling in sick, but he knew that it would be just as miserable to stay around the house and think about Annie, think about Therese, and worse, to think about himself.

He dressed for work, but couldn't eat breakfast. Realizing that his pain showed, he straightened his shoulders, but found them drooping again as he got out of the car at work.

With some fear, he came through the office. The secretary greeted him with rolled eyes. "Someone's given out our number again," she said as the phone buzzed. Another line was on hold. "This morning there was a man standing at the window watching me until Gramps kicked him off the property."

Douglas shook his head in sympathy with her and approached the orang's door. He felt nauseated again.

Vernon sat at the typewriter, most likely composing captions for his photo album. He didn't get up to greet Douglas, but gave him an evaluative stare.

Douglas patted his shoulder. "Working?" he asked.

"Like dog," Vernon said, and resumed typing.

Annie sat outside on the back porch. Douglas opened the door and stood beside her. She looked up at him, but—like Vernon—made no move toward the customary hug. The morning was still cool, the shadow of the building still long in front of them. Douglas sat down.

"Annie," he said softly. "I'm sorry. I'll never do it again. You see, I felt . . ." He stopped. It wasn't any easier than it had been to talk to Oona, or Wendy, or Shelley, or Therese. . . . He realized that he didn't understand her any more than he'd understood them. Why had she rejected him? What was she thinking? What would happen from now on? Would they be friends again?

"Oh, hell," he said. He stood. "It won't happen again."

Annie gazed away into the trees.

He felt strained all over, especially in his throat. He stood by her for a long time.

"I don't want write stories," she signed.

Douglas stared at her. "Why?"

"Don't want." She seemed to shrug.

Douglas wondered what had happened to the confident ape who'd planned to write a bestseller the day before. "Is that because of me?"

She didn't answer.

"I don't understand," he said. "Do you want to write it down for me? Could you explain it that way?"

"No," she signed, "can't explain. Don't want."

He signed. "What *do* you want?"

"Sit tree. Eat bananas, chocolate. Drink brandy." She looked at him seriously. "Sit tree. Day, day, day, week, month, year."

Christ almighty, he thought, she's having a goddamned existential crisis. All the years of education. All the accomplishments. All the hopes of an entire field of primatology. All shot to hell because of a moody ape. It can't just be me. This would have happened sooner or later, but maybe . . . He thought of all the effort he would have to make to repair their relationship. It made him tired.

"Annie, why don't we just ease up a little on your work. You can rest. Today. You can go sit in the tree all of today and I'll bring you a glass of wine."

She shrugged again.

Oh, I've botched it, he thought. What an idiot. He felt a pain coming back, a pain like poison, without a focal point but shooting through his heart and hands, making him dizzy and short of breath.

At least she doesn't hate me, he thought, squatting to touch her hand.

She bared her teeth.

Douglas froze. She slid away from him and headed for the trees.

He sat alone at home and watched the newscast. In a small midwestern town they burned the issues of the magazine with Annie's story in it.

A heavy woman in a windbreaker was interviewed with the bonfire in the background. "I don't want my children reading things that weren't even written by humans. I have human children and this godless ape is not going to tell its stories to them."

A quick interview with Dr. Morris, who looked even more tired and introverted than usual. "The story is a very innocent tale, told by an innocent personality. Annie is not a beast. I really don't think she has any ability for, or intention of, corruption . . ."

He turned the television off. He picked up the phone and dialed one of Therese's friends. "Jan, have you heard from Therese yet?"

"No, sure haven't."

"Well, let me know, okay?"

"Sure."

He thought vaguely about trying to catch her at work, but he left earlier in the morning and came home later in the evening than she did.

Looking at her picture on the wall, he thought of when they had first met, first lived together. There had been a time when he'd loved her so much he'd been bursting with it. Now he felt empty, but curious about where she was. He didn't want her to hate him, but he still didn't know if he could talk to her about what had happened. The idea that she would sit and listen to him didn't seem realistic.

Even Annie wouldn't listen to him anymore.

He was alone. He'd done a big, dumb, terrible thing and wished he hadn't. It would have been different if Annie had reciprocated, if somehow they could have become lovers. Then it would have been them against the world, a new kind of relationship. The first intelligent interspecial love affair . . .

But Annie didn't seem any different than Therese, after all. Annie was no child. She'd given him all those signals, flirting, then not carrying through. Acting like he'd raped her or something. She didn't really have any more interest in him than Dr. Morris would in Vernon. I couldn't have misunderstood, could I? he wondered.

He was alone. And without Annie's consent, he was just a jerk who'd screwed an ape.

"I made a mistake," he said aloud to Therese's picture. "So let's forget it."

But even he couldn't forget.

"Dr. Morris wants to see you," the secretary said as he came in.

"Okay." He changed course for the administrative office. He whistled In the past few days, Annie had been cool, but he felt that everything would settle down eventually. He felt better. Wondering what horrors or marvels Dr. Morris had to share with him, he knocked at her door and peered through the glass window. Probably another magazine burning, he thought.

She signaled him to come in. "Hello, Douglas."

Annie, he thought, *something's happened.*

He stood until she motioned him to sit down. She looked at his face several seconds. "This is difficult for me," she said.

She's discovered me, he thought. But he put that aside, figuring it was a paranoia that made him worry. There's no way. No way. I have to calm down or I'll show it.

She held up a photograph.

There it was—a dispassionate and cold document of that one moment in his life. She held it up to him like an accusation. It shocked him as if it hadn't been himself.

Defiance forced him to stare at the picture instead of looking for compassion in Dr. Morris's eyes. He knew exactly where the picture had come from.

Vernon and his new telephoto lens.

He imagined the image of his act rising up in a tray of chemicals. Slowly, he looked away from it. Dr. Morris could not know how he had changed since that moment. He could make no protest or denial.

"I have no choice," Dr. Morris said flatly. "I'd always thought that even if you weren't good with people, at least you worked well with the apes. Thank God Henry, who does Vernon's darkroom work, has promised not to say anything."

Douglas was rising from the chair. He wanted to tear the picture out of her hands because she still held it up to him. He didn't want to see it. He wanted her to ask him if he had changed, that it would never happen again, that he understood he'd been wrong.

But her eyes were flat and shuttered against him. "We'll send your things," she said.

He paused at his car and saw two big red shapes—one coppery orange, one chocolate red—sitting in the trees. Vernon bellowed out a groan that ended with an alien burbling. It was a wild sound full of the jungle and steaming rain.

Douglas watched Annie scratch herself and look toward chimps walking the land beyond their boundary fence. As she started to turn her gaze his direction, he ducked into his car.

Angrily driving away, Douglas thought, why should an ape understand me any better than a human?

RAND B. LEE

Knight of Shallows

The alternate-worlds story—taking place in a universe where events have been skewed to a greater or lesser degree from the familiar history we know, an alternate present where the Nazis won World War II or Drake lost to the Spanish Armada or Columbus never discovered America—goes back at least as far as Murray Leinster's 1934's "Sidewise in Time." It includes some of the best work ever produced in the genre, classic stuff like L. Sprague De Camp's *Lest Darkness Fall* and "The Wheels of If," Ward Moore's *Bring the Jubilee*, Philip K. Dick's *The Man In The High Castle*, C.M. Kornbluth's "Two Dooms," and Keith Roberts' *Pavane*. The story that follows, by new writer Rand B. Lee, is a worthy addition to that distinguished list, a taut and exciting tale of a man who chases through the endless worlds of alternate possibility to find—himself.

Rand B. Lee, the son of mystery writer Manfred Lee (who was half of the collaborative team who published as "Ellery Queen"), has sold several stories to *Amazing* and to *Isaac Asimov's Science Fiction Magazine*. He lives in Key West, Florida, where much of the action of this story takes place.

KNIGHT OF SHALLOWS

Rand B. Lee

They were not at all gentle. "You are a murderer!" they told him, whereupon he told them what they could stuff where; whereupon they said, "We can prove it." So they dragged him from his senior secretary's desk down in the bowels of Lifetimes, Inc., and dragged him up many elevators and through many security clearances to a place he had not dreamed existed. It was a room, empty except for a beanbag chair and a wall-sized screen. "We're hooking you up," they informed him, although he neither felt any hooks nor saw to what he was being hooked up. "Now look," they said. So he looked in the screen, and saw, as they say in the Bible.

Afterwards, someone kindly cleaned him up; and they sat him down in a different room and talked it all over. "What do you know about probability mechanics, Roger Carl Shapiro?" they asked.

"Nothing," he said. "My God."

"Tell us what we showed you."

"You showed me some murders."

"Twenty-three, in fact. Did you see the murderer?"

"Yes." Dully.

"And whom did he resemble?"

"He was fat and he didn't have a beard."

"And whom did he resemble?"

"Abraham Ribicoff. Jesus, guys, what is this, some sort of psych—"

"And whom did he resemble?"

Silence. "Me. He looked like me." Pause. "Only overweight, and clean-shaven."

"Anything else?"

"And sad. He looked sad." Shapiro wept for some time.

When was he through weeping, they said, "What about his victims?"

"I don't know."

"Roger, this is important." [A consultation: "He's rejecting it. He's rejecting it." "Goddamn it, he's *got* to accept it." "Try the back door."] "Roger, where did the murders take place?"

This was easier. "A bar. It looked like a bar I knew—a long time ago. Beejay's. On Duval Street, in Key West."

"That's good. You lived in Key West for five years, didn't you?"

"Yes." Pause. "After I got out of college. I was a bartender for a little while. I didn't like it, so I left." Another pause. "But it wasn't Beejay's. Bill would never have let them put in that linoleum."

"Do you remember the bartender?"

A long silence. "Yeah."

"Yes, who, mister?" ["General, for Christ's sake." "General, please."]

"Yes, sir."

"What can you tell us about the bartender, Roger?"

"He had dark hair."

"Anything else?"

"And dark eyes. He was different in some of the pictures. In some of them he had a beard; in others he didn't."

"What about his clothes?"

"He had a tanktop, once."

"And whom did he resemble, Roger?"

"Nobody." Very quickly.

"And whom did he resemble, Roger?"

"Somebody—maybe—I don't—"

"And whom did he resemble, Roger?"

"The murderer. The guy who shot him over the counter." Shapiro put his hands over his face. "They both looked like me."

Much later they took him back into the featureless room and showed him other things in the screen. This time it was not murders he saw. "Probabilities, Roger," they said to him. "Probability mechanics is a phenomenon unfathomable to anyone wedded to the old physics. Consciousness as a basic force in the universe. Or rather, multiverse. You're looking at logical spin-offs from the eventualities of your life."

They showed him a farm somewhere, with fields growing many kinds of vegetables. It was a commune. He saw himself, digging sweet potatoes. He was more muscular in the picture, although in real life he was not too bad, either. "This *is* real life," they said to him.

"I thought about joining a commune once," he admitted. "East Wind, in Tecumseh. But I didn't."

They showed him his uncle's synagogue, in Bridgeport. He was sitting in the front row with a woman he did not recognize until he noticed the necklace she was wearing. His mouth went dry. "Shirley

Greenblatt," he moaned. "What in hell did I want to go and marry her for?" But the man on the screen looked happy.

["We're getting there. He's starting to accept it."]

They showed him alone in a darkened room, masturbating. "Hey," he said. One side of his face was badly scarred; he was sitting up in a chair with his legs bent queerly. The door opened; the man in the chair covered up. A woman came in with a face drained of life, bearing a tray. "That's Mom. What in hell?"

"We were going to ask you. Were you in a car accident?"

"Jesus. No, never."

"This 'you' was."

They showed him walking down a street somewhere in a shiny suit, looking prosperous. They showed him standing in front of a group of old people with a black yarmulke on his head. "The last time I wore one of those was when Dad died." The people on the screen were smiling. They showed him swinging a blond child in the air. They showed him running from a pack of dogs in a bombed-out city. They showed him swinging from a rope, one end of which was knotted around his neck. "Charming," he said.

"But it happened, somewhere."

"Somewhere where?"

"In another sequence of probabilities. All these men are you as you might have been—as you might be—if you had made or do make a certain series of choices."

"No way would I choose to hang myself."

"Haven't you ever considered suicide?"

"I'd take pills. I'm a coward."

"If you had no pills? And were driven to desperation?"

He remembered certain August nights in Key West. "Yeah."

They showed him a woman with dark hair working at a computer console. "Now *that* I like to see," he said. "Do I get to marry her?"

"Hardly. She's you."

"You guys are nuts."

"Not all probability sequences arise from human choice. Some of them arise from natural events: an extra chromosome, for instance, introduced to your biological makeup because one sperm made it to your mother's ovum first."

"That's me as I could have been if I'd been born a woman?"

"Yes. Now most sequences, like the Armageddon scenario—the dog-pack picture—are a combination of your choices, the choices of others, and natural event. You came to work here at Lifetimes, Inc., because the economy is bad and you couldn't get enough of your articles published to support yourself on your writing. God knows why we hired you; you're hardly efficient secretary material. A situation arising from many different factors, some of them dependent upon your choices."

"Bull. It was the only thing I could do. I needed work."

"You could have made it as a writer. You still can." Roger Shapiro stood up. They waited. He sat down again. "We've seen a sequence where you did stick it out and did very well. We've seen another sequence where you stuck it out, then quit, became a janitor at a grammar school, went back to writing, and won the Pulitzer Prize."

"These aren't actors, then."

"No. They live and breathe at this moment. The ones who aren't dead, of course."

"Where? Not here."

"No. In other universes."

After a very long time he said, "What about the murders?"

"What do you think?"

He thought. "If what you've been handing me is straight shit, they could be me. Could have been me. The bartenders I saw get shot. Because I did work at Beejay's for a while, and I guess I might have stayed on."

"The bartenders were you, all right."

"Then I don't get the murderer. He looks like me, too, if I'd let myself go, or gotten real depressed over a long time. Assuming these alternate universes exist, there's no way I could exist twice in the same one. Much less kill my other self. I mean, why would I want to?"

[A silent chorus of cheers from the observers behind the briefing room wall.]

"Twenty years ago, when we started this company, we would have agreed with you."

"But now?"

"We know it is possible. Not only to view our probabilities, from this screen here; but to enter them."

He laughed and laughed, and they decided it was enough for one day.

They did not let him go back to his sec desk, but they did not keep him a prisoner, either. He was given a considerable raise in salary, many security passes, and freedom to come and go between 5 P.M. and 8 A.M. The first night he did not go home at all, but sat watching dirty movies in a twenty-four hour theater. The next day they showed him more pictures, without commentary. He saw himself buried as a child in the corner of the family plot in Roxbury, Connecticut. In real life—in his base sequence, as they insisted upon calling it—he had recovered from the pneumonia. He saw himself giving blood in an

Army hospital. He had never been in the service. He saw himself working bar in a Beejay's identical to the one he remembered, until he looked more carefully and saw that the napkins had BIG RED'S printed on them and that his other self had a mermaid leering from his right arm.

He discovered that his apartment had been cleaned in his absence and the refrigerator-freezer freshly stocked. In his bedroom he found a folder. He opened it and drew out some photographs. One was of a diploma with his name on it, issued by a university from which he had not graduated. He had transferred following his sophomore year. The second was of him with a man in a large oval bed. The third was a photograph of a page of manuscript. It was somewhat blurred, as if it had been blown up from a detail. He sat on the edge of his bed and read it; then he read it again.

The next day they said, "Well?"

"I believe you."

Suspicion. "What convinced you?"

"None of your business."

"What con—"

"I said it's none of your goddamn business." He stood. "Now you want something from me. What is it?"

"Please calm yourself, Roger."

"Jesus." He sat, fighting back tears. "Okay. Shoot."

Carefully. "We're prepared to show you other proofs: retinal scans, handwriting comparisons, other documents we've photographed through the viewers. However, to answer your question in a nutshell: we want you to help stop this murderer."

"Why me, if you'll excuse the cliché?"

"Because you're the only person in this universe who can enter your chain of probability-sequences. And that's what it'll take to stop him."

"Wait, wait, wait." He viewed them through narrowed lids. "You people can look into my—probabilities—but you can't go into them?"

Discomfort. "I'm afraid so."

"How come?"

"We don't have the time and you don't have the background for us to explain that satisfactorily. You must accept that we are telling you the truth. We would far rather entrust this task to a trained operative if it were at all possible. That we are asking you to take it on should be evidence enough of our sincerity."

"Asking me to take it on?"

"Urging you."

"Ordering me. Coercing me. Shaming me."

"If you like."

"Jesus." He pondered. "I'm not a cop. I can't fight, and I don't know how to shoot a gun. And I've never killed anyone."

"We're not asking you to kill him."

"You've lost me. I thought you said you wanted me to stop this guy from murdering people. Shit—from murdering me."

"To answer that, we have to answer a question you haven't asked yet: how can this alternate 'you' travel from probability-sequence to probability sequence? In fifteen years of alternate monitoring, he is the first such interfacer we've encountered."

" 'Interfacer'?"

"Dimension-shifter. We've assumed that our probability-sequence was the only one in which probability mechanics has been developed. This may sound harsh to you, but the mere fact that you are murdered in sequence after sequence would not be enough to impel us to interfere. It is that an alternate persona is murdering your other selves—that is the crisis. So: how can he shift from sequence to sequence? We assume it's by the use of equipment similar to that which we have developed. Why do we not want you to storm into a sequence and gun him down? Because we need to know more about him. We need to know whether he is working alone or as the agent of someone else, some other-sequential person or persons. Imagine the possible danger to our universe if there exists an organization or culture of malevolent interfacers?"

"Come on," said Shapiro. "Come on, guys. Be realistic." Smothered laughter from behind the wall. "Look who's being murdered, will ya? Every murder you've shown me so far has me tending bar in goddam Key West. What organization of malevolent 'interfacers' would waste their time bumping off nobodies?" His interrogators exchanged embarrassed looks. "I mean, I'm important to me and maybe to God, for God's sake, but who the hell else?"

"We think it might be a test run."

"Swell."

"We don't know. That's just it, Roger. This is new to us. We don't know a thing. He could just be a nut. He's apparently been connected with probability mechanics work in his own sequence; he might even be someone important."

"Thanks for admitting the remote possibility," said Shapiro.

"It's his base sequence that we want to get to. Now we could search among your probabilities-line for eternity and not hit on the right sequence. Or we could send you to follow him home."

"Follow him home to his universe of malevolent interfacers?"

"That's it in a nutshell."

He sat quietly. "I have a lot of other questions."

"We'll do our best to answer them in the time we have."

"How much time do we have?"

"We don't know. That's why we'd like to get going on this project pronto."

"Who's going to pay my rent while I'm gone?"

"It may not take long enough for that to be a problem, but we'll support your obligations."

"My insurance payments, too?"

"Yes. Although why you need life insurance as well as major medical eludes us. You have no dependents or close relatives to benefit from your demise."

"There's my uncle, Sheldon."

"You hate your Uncle Sheldon."

"How convenient I'm turning out to be for all of you."

"Does that mean you'll do it?"

Silence. [Much tension behind the wall.] A grin. "Oy. And I thought I was working for a career-planning service."

[Pandemonium.]

It all had to do with brainwaves and energy fields, none of which Shapiro attempted to understand; to him it was just magic. They implanted things in his head and put a button under the skin of his left hand, which told them when he wanted to talk with them. He was given a weapon and made to practice firing it. They called it a burner; he called it his raygun. To everyone's astonishment, he was not a bad shot. They tried to give him lessons in self-defense but gave it up when he objected. "I'm not a fighter," he said. "I buckle under stress." This statement made them nervous, which was his intent. He watched his probabilities in the scanner by the hour. Most of them varied little from the lives he had glimpsed already; in none did a Lifetimes, Inc., appear. This intrigued him—the company had begun to figure so hugely in his existence that he could not understand why his other lines were not dominated by it also.

"The more improbable the involvement, the less likely it is that you'll see it in the screen," they told him.

He glimpsed the Pulitzer Prize sequence they had told him about and several more in which he was female. "Are my probabilities infinite?" he asked them. They said they didn't know. "May I see into somebody else's probabilities?" he asked.

Much apology. "We don't want to risk losing our focus on your sequences. It took a lot of time and effort to lock onto them."

To which he replied: "You lied to me."

"What makes you think that, Roger?"

"Maybe 'lied' is the wrong word. Omitted some information. To whit: which came first, looking into Roger's lifelines or stumbling onto Roger-the-Murderer?"

"Uh—"

"Allow me. If you say, 'Stumbling onto Roger-the-Murderer,' I will say, 'How? Were you looking through a catalog of random probabilities and chanced on little Roger's?' If you say, 'Looking into Roger's lifelines,' I will say, 'Why little Roger's? And who gave you the goddamn right, you warped bunch of voyeurs?' "

Very pale indeed, they told him the truth: they had selected him and a number of other employees of Lifetimes, Inc., without their knowledge, to be part of their experiments in probability-viewing. They had been doing that sort of thing for many years. Each had been chosen for their single, socially unencumbered status and tagged electronically to transmit their brainwave patterns to the viewer complex. "We lock onto those patterns," they told him, "and they access the probability-lines for us."

"Do the others know what I know?"

"No."

"Why not?"

"This is a top secret facility."

"These are very private lives."

"We're explorers, not voyeurs. We don't control what images come to us, or how long they stay on-screen."

"Liars."

"We don't—"

"Liars. You must have image-holding capacity. How else could you have been following my murdering career so closely?" They admitted it all. They admitted also that they had chosen the unencumbered against the chance that they might come across a sequence demanding personal investigation. This Shapiro heard calmly. He did not walk out. He knew that they would not let him go at this juncture. Instead he said, "I want to talk to someone who's done this before."

"Done what?"

" 'Interfaced.' "

They brought her to him. She was a woman of about sixty, iron-haired, sharp-nosed, and gruff. She had the look of someone who had been important once and had given it all up because it had bored her. She lived, she said, in Monaco, which impressed him. "What do you want to know?" she asked.

"Why you went."

She was taken aback, and showed it in the flicker of her gray eyes. "For science, of course."

"Not you the professional," Shapiro said. "You alone with yourself."

She did not do him the discourtesy of evading him. "All right. There was a young man, many, many years ago. We were lovers for a while; we planned to marry. There were career conflicts. It didn't happen. I found a probability in which it did." She shrugged. "I wanted to see him again."

He stared at her. "You're not bullshitting me?"

"I don't bullshit."

He examined his nails. "I had dreams," he said. "They showed me a photo of a page from a story I wrote. They saw me writing it in the screen and shot it from image." He looked at her. "I never wrote that story, really. But you know something? I remember planning it. Taking the notes."

"Why didn't you write it?"

"I was afraid it would be lousy. Because so much of my stuff was."

"Was it?"

"No. It was really good." He wiped his eyes. "I don't know who you are," he said, "but I want you to tell them some things from me. Tell them I'm not a kid, and I'm not a fool, and I resent like Hell how they've tried to intimidate me into this. I know they don't give a shit about me, or any of my 'me's; I'm convenient, a handle. I'm going to do this thing they want me to do because I don't think anybody has the right to put an end to somebody's choices."

"Fair enough." She rose to go.

"That includes them," he said. "Tell them that."

What she told them was, "You've got him."

And:

They flew him to Key West at night in a plane that did not have to change at Miami. He found himself staring at the clouds outside under the moon as though he might never see clouds or moon again. The gruff woman had sent a small package along to him, which when opened proved to contain a pocket notebook and a pen with a special ink supply. Inside the notebook, on the first page, she had written:

There is a tide in the affairs of men,
Which, taken at the flood, leads on to fortune;
Omitted, all the voyage of their life
Is bound in shallows and in miseries.
On such a full sea are we now afloat,

And we must take the current when it serves,
Or lose our ventures.

It has rained three days in succession, but the air lies so thick on Duval Street that even the mosquitoes are sluggish, even the fragrance of the frangipani dampered. The tourists are few and irritable. "Worst goddam weather I ever saw," says a man from Ohio to a man from Michigan.

"It's a blanket bearing down," agrees a woman from New Jersey.

"Stay drunk; that's what I do," suggests a resident retiree. "Bartender? More of the same." The bartender comes over. His furry chest is bared and gleaming with sweat, despite the laboring of the big ceiling fans. To the woman the retiree says, "You want a pineapple colada? Roj makes the best pineapple colada in the Keys."

"Make it a gin and tonic," says the woman. "How long have you been sweating down here, Roj?"

The bartender grins. "Would you believe ten years?"

"The man's insane," says the Michiganian.

Roj's hands move deftly among the bottles. "It's not so bad. I used to live in Connecticut. That was a place to get away from."

"My sister lives in East Hartford," says the man from Ohio.

There are people playing pool in the adjoining game room, and a few youths vying for a turn at Pac-Man; otherwise, the bar is empty. A stuffed flamingo stands in one corner. Above the bartender's station, Lucille Ball looks down from an autographed publicity still, as if presiding over this Friday night. "Ten o'clock," announces Roj. "Anyone want to hear the news?" No one does. Outside on Duval Street, the sign yells, *B.J.'S DEN*.

"I played Connecticut once," the woman is saying. "The old Wembley Theater in New Haven. I got the Mexicali trots from some lousy chop suey I gulped between acts. Talk about uncomfortable! It gave me eyestrain just to walk."

"Were you anybody important?" asks the Michiganian. She shrugs, then smiles.

"Nah," she replies. "But I could of been."

Roger Carl Shapiro walks out of the men's lavatory. He is wearing jeans and a loose cotton shirt, standard Key West costume. He halts near the cigarette machine and surveys the bar. At first he thinks, *It didn't work.* The same three tourists are sitting at the bar: the loud woman and the old man in the hibiscus shirt. The same flamingo stands in the corner. But the sign says *B.J.'S DEN*, not *BEEJAY'S*; and the floor has been painted ship-deck green; and the man behind the counter is himself.

ROGER-PRIME, says the wink-blink in his head. **HAVE YOU ESTABLISHED VISUAL CONTACT?**

He is like him, but unlike. His skin is darker; he looks almost Latino. There is a cigarette pack in the pocket of his shirt; Roger does not smoke. The greatest difference is the hardest for Roger to define: the man moves with a confidence that Roger cannot imagine possessing. *He's accepted things,* he thinks. *He's stopped running.*

All of a sudden he wants to go home. **ROGER-PRIME. WE ARE HAVING DIFFICULTY WITH THE VISUALS.**

He realizes that he has forgotten to engage the scanner circuit, which had to be turned off during transfer; he presses his left palm and receives, **ENGAGED,** in reply. He looks around, he needs a seat near the bar but not too near. In Beejay's there are booths; in B.J.'s Den there are none. He gathers his resolve and saunters up to the counter.

"Ever been to Montreal?" the man from Michigan is asking the woman from New Jersey. Roger selects a stool opposite the little group. At his back, the game-room door spills soft cures. The bartender comes over.

"What do ya need, friend?" Roj asks him. His eyes are very brown. **RETINAL SCAN CONFIRMED,** says the wink-blink. **THIS IS YOUR PERSONA FOR THIS SEQUENCE, ROGER-PRIME.**

"I know," says Roger.

"Pardon?"

"Sorry. I'll have a Perrier with lime, if you don't mind."

"Right." The man moves off. *He didn't notice,* wonders Roger. *He didn't see a thing.* He is conscious of the tourists looking him over, but his skin is light, his beard full, and the man behind the bar is clean-shaven. *Still,* he thinks *I would have known.* Roj brings him the drink and asks for seventy-five cents, which Roger pays in coin. He does not have much money with him. He does not expect to remain for very long in each sequence. The watchers have noticed that in each probability in which the rogue interfacer appears, not only does he appear in this Key West bar, but he appears about the same time, always between 10 and 10:20 P.M. on this sultry Friday evening in June. The murder is always committed at 10:33 P.M., whereupon the rogue drops out of interface. Roger has asked them why; they have admitted ignorance. "Perhaps it's some conservation law," they have suggested. "Perhaps some limitation in his equipment." *Or maybe,* Roger has thought, *it's God saying there are limits.*

He has thought a good deal about God in recent days. **ALL TRANSMISSIONS FUNCTIONING NORMALLY,** reports the light in his head. It does not sound very excited, but Roger realizes that his hand is shaking where it grips the Perrier. *Another universe*, he thinks. He watches himself fiddle with the cash register. *Me. That's me.* The days spent by the viewers have not prepared him for the tangibility of an interface. There are no sounds receivable through the viewers; no textures sensible. He smooths the wood of the bartop. It is scored beneath the polish. It has a history; it was once a tree growing somewhere. *Was there a Hitler here?* he wonders. *A Vietnam? Was FDR a polio victim? Are there Key Wests where Hemingway never wrote, where gay people never learned to flock, where women still don't have the right to vote? Is there a best of all possible worlds?*

His mind feels three times too big for his skull, and the exhilaration that grips him is savagely intense.

The place begins to fill up. Roj calls out greetings ("Hey, Rita!" "Howzit, Mr. Foley?"); Roger stares, trying to feel a kinship with these acquaintances of his self. Beer foams; glasses tinkle. It is a neighborhood crowd: everyone seems to know everyone else, the tourists included. *They must be regulars*, he thinks. *Back every year.* He finds himself assessing these people in an unaccustomed way. It is as if his realization that there exists a multiplicity of each one of them has enhanced his appreciation of each one's individuality. He wants to let them know how important they are.

ROGER-PRIME, says the wink-blink. **ROGER-PRIME, WE HAVE A NEW INTERFACE. REPEAT; A NEW INTERFACE.** He starts, looks toward the street entrance, then the men's room door. It is opening hesitantly. **GOING TO TELESCOPIC,** mutters the base. Roger's vision does not change, but he knows that back home, the viewers are zooming in. The rogue is wearing a light nylon jacket, too hot for this island; a conservative sports shirt; and rumpled dark trousers. He is baby-faced, overweight. He stands as if on eggs, unsure of himself, although Roger cannot think why he should be, having already killed as many as he has. He does not look like a murderer. **RETINALS CONFIRMED,** says the light in Roger's head. **THAT'S YOUR MAN, ROGER-PRIME. KEEP A LOW PROFILE.**

He's here, thinks Roger. *He's actually here.* They have told him not to interfere; they do not want the rogue knowing that he is under observation. The man moves slowly toward the drinks counter. He is looking at the bartender. Roger hunches over his Perrier and watches covertly. The resemblance between killer and victim is obscenely fraternal. Roger closes his eyes. **MAINTAIN VISUALS,** snaps the monitor primly. He opens his eyes and panics. The rogue is gone. Then he sees him a few yards away, making for the game room. *Is he that cold-blooded?* he thinks. The watch they have given him adjusts to the local time in each sequence; it says 10:22. *Eleven minutes*, he thinks, and is afraid.

He is not sure what he is afraid of. It is not of being hurt; it is not of seeing the violence: he has seen it so often in the screens, often dim, it is true, but unchoreographed, uncleanly. He looks at the rogue. *You're afraid of finding out there's really no difference between him and you.*

The rogue goes into the game room and hovers near the pool tables. Shortly thereafter he returns to the bar. He sits on a stool four customers down from Roger. Roj goes over. "Help you?" Roger hears him say. It is 10:27.

"Perrier with lime, please," says the rogue. His voice is the voice of a shy adolescent: Roj's voice, completely drained of confidence. Roj moves to fetch the drink. Roger wants to shout, *You idiot, can't you see? Can't you feel what's coming?* He watches money exchange hands. He is struck by a sudden fancy: *Fingerprinting by and large is useless in cases of intersequential homicides. —Multiversal Policeperson's Manual.* The woman named Rita catches Roj's sleeve as he whisks by her. He bends forward, so that she can whisper in his ear. Whatever she says makes him laugh softly, showing strong throat and white teeth. Suddenly Roger remembers her. He had met her shortly before he had left Key West; she had been one of his boss Bill's significant others. She had given him a very long kiss at his going-away party. *And here she is*, he thinks. She is wearing a white peasant blouse, which will show the blood.

The rogue's face bears no expression; but he is watching her, too. Roger's nerves shriek.

More people come into the bar. At 10:30, the rogue slips his right hand into his right-hand jacket pocket. The woman from New Jersey is announcing to all and sundry that she really, really could have been somebody in Hollywood if she hadn't given it all up for love. At 10:31, Roj is lighting a cigarette under the appreciative eye of Rita. At 10:32, the telephone next to the cash register rings; the bartender puts the receiver to his ear. The rogue gets to his feet. So does Roger. **PRIME**, says the wink-blink. **NO INTERFERENCE. WE'VE LOCKED ONTO THE SUBJECT: REMEMBER OUR OBJECTIVE.**

"But," says Roger. The woman to his right gives him a curious look. Roj is grinning into the phone. The end of his cigarette flips up and down as he talks. The rogue takes his hand out of his pocket. Roger recognizes the weapon he is holding; he has seen it in the screen so many times before. It ejects a quiet red zip of needle light. Roj is facing Rita; the beam passes through him from back to front, taking most of his heart with it and spreading it over Rita's chemise. He does not even have time to look surprised.

And the rogue simply is not there.

INTERFACE, says the base in his head. **WE ARE TRACKING.
PREPARE FOR TRANSFER, ROGER-PRIME.**

My God. Rita opens her mouth.

ROGER-PRIME, PREPARE FOR TRANSFER.

"My God." A tiny voice squawks from the dangling phone, just like in the movies. Roger gets off his stool. There are too many people around the screaming woman, and Roj's body has slipped down behind the counter. He stumbles toward the lavatory. He wonders how such a narrow beam can make a mess this size. His own raygun is much less dramatic. The lavatory swims toward him in the weak bar light. The door flies open and the retiree in the hibiscus shirt rushes out and past him. The bathroom is empty. He finds the rightmost stall, goes inside, and bolts the door. He sits down on the toilet seat, then remembers, and stands up. He presses his left palm. "Transfer," he says. "For God's sake."

TRANSFERRING, says the unemotional voice of the base.

His watch says 10:33.

Everything changes. There is no men's room, no bar, no uproar. He is standing hip-deep among weeds in a vacant field. Under a cloudless, moon-heavy sky, jasmine runs rampant where coral vine has not choked it out. He can smell the sea. Hidden frogs, with exquisite unconcern for probabilities, sound their territories in concert. He is shaking again. *Base,* he thinks. *Base, is this right?*

WE'RE SORRY, ROGER-PRIME, comes the reply. **WE'RE EXPE-RIENCING SOME DRIFT OF YOUR SIGNAL. WE'RE CORRECT-ING NOW. YOU'RE DOING WELL. DO NOT CHANGE POSI-TION; REPEAT, DO NOT CHANGE POSITION.**

He does not. The moonlight gleams off blades of palmetto scrub. He hears the stir of the huge dark roaches, the "palmetto bugs" of the keys, restless beneath the mangroves. He wonders why there are no big trees and no signs of buildings. *Maybe people have never come to this island,* he thinks. *No syphilis, no Cuban refugee "problem" no queer-bashing.* He wonders why he is not weeping. *He killed him,* he thinks. *He killed me. I killed me.* The chorus of the frogs touches his heart. All at once, he longs to remain here. *I'll welcome the Seminoles when they arrive,* he decides.

TRANSFERRING, says the base.

He is back in the toilet stall. The wall, which was green, is white where it is not scarred with graffiti. He is about to push open the stall door when it is opened for him. "Jesus, I'm sorry," says a man in a hibiscus shirt.

"No problem," says Roger-Prime. He walks past the man and washes his hands at a sink. In the mirror he observes Mr. Hibiscus go into the stall and close the door. It is the older man he has seen in the earlier sequence, but a more sober, more fit version of the older man. He looks at his watch. It says 10:04. He has half an hour before the next murder. He dries his hands and walks out into the bar.

The stuffed flamingo has become a stuffed pelican. The photograph of Lucille Ball now hangs over the cigarette machine. The floor is not painted green; it is wood left natural with sawdust sprinkled all over it. The television mutters a talk show; the picture quality is superb. No loud woman holds forth at the bar, no man from Michigan. The tourist from Ohio is there, however, and well on his way to intoxication. Of Roger's alter-egos there is no sign. The bartender is blond and very young. "What'll it be, bud?" he asks.

"Perrier with lime," Roger replies. The game-room door is shut; a sign on it declares it is closed for repairs. "When's your partner come on duty?"

"Carl? He's late now."

"Pardon me, sir," say the Ohioan, "but you're sitting in my friend's seat."

"Where do you know Carl from?" she asks the young man.

"Around," says Roger-Prime. *Carl*, he thinks. His parents had struggled for three months over whether to name him Carl Roger or Roger Carl. "He might not even remember me; it's been so long."

"Sir," says the Ohioan. Roger squelches an urge to turn around and shoot the man through the throat. He gets up and moves around to the other side of the bar, taking his Perrier with him. Mr. Hibiscus comes out of the lavatory and sits down next to the Ohioan. Roger-Prime squeezes the lime into the mineral water and wonders how he can possibly sit through the experience again. He sips; bubbles feather his palate. He wants a real drink, but he does not know what it will do to the things they have put in his head. He does not like the base's silent voice; it makes him feel exposed, as if he were walking around with his fly open. He looks up, and the young man is leaning against the cash register.

"Been in town long?" the boy asks.

Wrong move, buddy, Roger thinks. *A good barkeep should be able to tell when his customers want to be left alone.* "Not long. But frequently."

"You look kinda familiar. I been workin' here six months; you see a hell of a lot of faces in six months."

"Six months is a long time to work in one place down here," says Roger.

"No shit. Bill, the owner? He says the turnover at the Casa Marina's one person out of three every six months. What do ya expect? Key West is a dead-end town."

"We must take the current when it serves," murmurs Roger-Prime, "or lose our ventures."

"Hey, Phil." A hand comes down on the blond's shoulder. It is the murdered man, now moustachioed, and somewhat disheveled. "Sorry I'm late. Some faggot took my parking spot."

"No problem," says Phil. "It's been slow." He leaves, glancing at the two of them so as to catch some spark of recognition jump between them; but Carl is busying himself about the bar and Roger is busying himself with his drink. *Did I talk like that?* he thinks. *"Some faggot?"* He studies his new self. Like Roj, Carl is deeply tanned, competently muscular, confident in his movements. Nevertheless, he has a disturbing arrogance that Roj did not have. Carl glances Roger's way and smiles professionally. Roger smiles back. *What are you made of, my man?* he wonders.

CONFIRMED, reports the base. **THIS IS YOUR PERSONA, ROGER.**

No kidding, returns Roger. *I thought I'd been cloned in the crapper.*

On the TV, a film critic whom Roger-Prime does not recognize is discussing a new Paramount offering. The star's picture is flashed; it is the woman from New Jersey. The clock on the wall says 10:15. A couple of French sailors come in with women hanging to them. They are followed by some young men in T-shirts; the shirts bear the legend: *EAT IT RAW—KEY WEST OYSTER BAR.* They are shaved almost bald, American Marines on leave from Trumbo Point. They giggle at the red pompoms of the sailors. The bar fills slowly at first, then rapidly. He sees a great many military persons. Carl is kept busy, and by the time he has a moment free, it is nearly 10:28. "That was sudden," says Roger-Prime, because he must say something, do something.

"No fooling." Carl lights a cigarette, head cocked like the man in the Marlboro ads. "It's the base. The duty rosters are all screwy these days. Guys get off at weird hours."

No murderer yet. "Something up at Trumbo?"

"Falklands shit."

Roger hazards it: "I thought Thatcher had things pretty much under control."

"Thatcher? Where've you been, buddy? Maggie has gone home to that great brassiere factory in the sky."

"What?"

"Last week. Argentinian terrorists blew up her car. There've been rumors of British retaliation ever since. With Fidel backing Argentina and Uncle Sam backing England, a lot of kinds of shit could hit the fan. Excuse me."

The bartender wades away into dimness. *Ten-thirty*, observes Roger. The military people are drinking hard, as though they have things they want to forget. He is feeling very detached. He does not like Carl. *Where's our rogue?* he asks the base.

SCANNING, ROGER, they reply.

There are two minutes to go before Carl will be dead. He is shocked by his own thought: *No great loss, this one.* The wedge of lime lies belly-up at the bottom of his glass. The napkin says *BIG RED'S* on it. *Where is he?* he thinks.

EMERGENCY, PRIME. EMERGENCY. IMMEDIATE TRANS-FER NECESSARY.

What's happened?

IT SEEMS TO BE OUR DAY FOR MISCALCULATIONS. HURRY, PRIME.

He forgets Carl. He slips from his stool and pushes his way through the crowd toward the men's room. There are some people by the urinals. All the stalls are filled. He waits, fretting. A man comes out of the middle stall. He rushes into it and locks the door. There is a window high up; through it he can see the branches of the royal poinciana swaying, showing off their vermilion under the street lamps. *Ready*, he says. *Ready, base.*

The building shudders. The lights in the bathroom go out. Men curse, and in the next room, glass shatters. People are screaming, but he knows that this time they are not screaming because of Carl. *Hurry up, base*, he thinks. He presses his palm repeatedly. "Hurry up, base, goddam it, it's something bad." He remembers the screen image of the ruined city. *British retaliation?* he thinks. *Cuba's only eighty miles away.* "Base, what in Hell have you gotten me into?" He looks out the window. The sky is full of sea.

TRANSFERRING, says the wink-blink cheerfully. It is 10:33.

The wall is back to spotless green. The lights are back, and the building is quiet. *What happened?* he manages to ask. On the floor of the stall, a tract that was not there a moment previously says, *CHRIST IS THE ANSWER.* "What happened?"

SORRY, PRIME: WE PROJECTED YOU INTO A CATACLYSM LINE.

He sits down on the toilet and laughs weakly. *Taken at the flood*, he thinks. No wonder our rogue never showed up. Little Carl gets zapped by the commies. He has drunk too much Perrier and he finds he must urinate. The wall, he notices, is the only fixture of the stall that is spotless. There is no paper in the toilet roll, and the floor around the tract is littered with cigarette butts. *Where am I now?*

ON TARGET, UH, A LITTLE LATE. It is already 10:20. WE SCAN YOUR PERSONA NOT FAR. ALSO THE ROGUE.

I don't want to see another killing. Can't I wait out this one?

WE'RE HAVING TOO MUCH TROUBLE TRACKING HIM. YOU'RE GOING TO HAVE TO SLAP A TRACER ON HIM.

Swell. How?

WE'VE BEEN THROUGH THAT.

I do get murdered in this one, don't I? Not swallowed up in an earthquake, or kidnapped by aliens?

YOU KNOW WE CAN'T VIEW A PROBABILITY WHEN YOU'RE IN IT, SAVE THROUGH YOUR TELEMETRY. THE ROGUE IS, HOWEVER, AT INTERFACE.

Where's your sense of humor, folks? says Roger-Prime. He exits the stall. A man stands in front of him, combing his dark hair in the mirror. Roger moves past him; for an instant their reflections hang side by side. The man lowers his comb. It is the bartender. "Jesus Christ," he says. They are identical. There can be no mistake. Down to their beards, they are identical. The bartender faces Roger-Prime. He is high on something, and his skin is not deeply tanned. "Jesus, do you see that?"

"Sorry?"

"We could be twins." Roger-Prime does not know how to react. He affects mild interest.

"Huh. I guess. Didn't think anybody could match my mug for ugly." He starts to leave. The man will not let it go this easily.

"Wait." The bartender sticks out his hand. "This is like what they used to call a cosmic experience. You know, back in the sixties, when we all believed in that stuff? I'm Shep."

"Uh, Shifter. Charlie Shifter." They shake hands. Shep's grip is firm. *Shep from Shapiro*, thinks Roger. All of a sudden he longs to know this man. "It is pretty amazing, isn't it?"

"So it's not just me. I mean, it was good Colombian, but it wasn't *that* good." He laughs. "I can't get over it. They say everyone's got a double somewhere. Doppelgänger. When you meet him, you die." He raises his eyebrows in mock terror. *My God, the rogue*, thinks Roger. *I can't let him see us together.* "Wait till Bill sees this. You want a drink?"

"I was just leaving, actually."

"Damn. I mean, I am definitely up there, but this. Even our beards. You in town long?"

"Not long." says Roger Carl Shapiro. He goes to the sink and turns on the water. His heart is pounding. *Doppelgänger, shit!*"

"I'll bet you're a writer, aren't you? Shep?"

"Jesus. Yeah. Trying, trying." Delight. "How'd you know?"

"You have the look. And you talk like one. I hear Key West is good for writers."

"I used to live here right after I got out of college." The words pour out. "I worked bar here, right in this place, and I tried to write, you know, in my spare time. Couldn't hack it. Woman troubles and shit. I hadn't set foot in the Keys till last October. Thought I'd give it another try." He is combing his hair again, unnecessarily.

"And how's it going?" Roger washes and washes.

"Well." His twin grins at him. Roger can just make out the tiny scar below Shep's left eye, where a dog bit both of them when they were four. "I just sold a story."

Envy. Excitement. "No shit?"

"Just sold one. God damn, brother; it's better than orgasm! I've been trying for years. Giving up. Maybe it'll never happen again, but it happened once. Shit." Shep peers at him. "Come on in and have a drink. Business is shit."

"Uh." He imagines the people at the base, chewing their nails. It is 10:26. "Uh, Shep, actually, there's somebody in the bar I'm trying to avoid."

"Yeah?" Shep says, with sympathy.

"Uh, money matters. I'll tell you what. When do you get off?"

"Not till three, man."

"I'd, uh, really like to sit down with you some time. Do you have a number where I can get a hold of you?"

"Hey, yeah." The bartender searches his apron. Roger-Prime remembers the pad and pen that the grim woman has given him, and digs them out of his back pocket. Shep takes them and opens the book. Roger watches his eye strike the first page. "Fantastic. *Richard the Third.*"

"I wondered which one it was from."

Shep writes down his address and phone number. "Higgs Lane. It's right off Elizabeth between Eaton and Caroline. I work nights, but if I'm out when you call, my old lady'll take a message."

"Old lady, huh?"

He grins again. "Either feast or famine, isn't it? I knew her before; her name's Rita. You'll like her" They shake hands. "You can get out without going through the bar; just make a right just outside here. There's a phone by the storeroom and the back exit's marked."

"Just like a spy movie."

"Hey, man. This is Key West. Anything can happen in Key West." Shep leaves. "Give me a call," he tosses over his shoulder. The lavatory door swings shut. Alone in front of the mirror, Roger-Prime takes out his burner. It is light in his palm, toy-like; the very very latest thing from Dow, of all places. **PRIME,** says the wink-blink. **YOU MUST NOT INTERFERE.**

"The Hell I mustn't."

WE MUST TRACK THE ROGUE TO HIS BASE SEQUENCE. MORE THAN A FEW LIVES ARE AT STAKE.

"We don't know that."

YOU HAVE FOUR MINUTES TO ATTACH THE TRACER. ROGER-PRIME?

"*All right!*" he yells, mind and voice together.

He hurls himself through the door. The bar has been remodeled and it takes him a moment to recognize the old lines beneath the ugly new. The cleanliness of the bathroom is echoed in the bar. The game room is a disco, at the moment silent. The Pac-Man and the pool tables line the Duval Street wall. Lucille Ball is nowhere in evidence. The drinks counter has been moved against the far wall, which means that anyone sitting there has their back to the lavatory. He spots the rogue almost immediately. The fat man has not changed clothing. He is sitting pensive in the row of vacant stools. The Michiganian tourist is shooting pool with the retiree, who has exchanged his hibiscuses for palm trees.

Base, says Roger. *There's no way I'm going to be able to tag this pig without his seeing me. And once he sees me, he'll know what's what.* Shep wipes the bartop, moving around his killer so as not to disturb him.

WE MUST HAVE A TAG.

Not by me. Or do you want a universe of malevolent interfacers crawling up your asses?

There is silence for some time, for which Roger is grateful. He has put his gun back in his pocket, but as he watches Shep work, that foolish smile on his hairy face, he struggles once more with the temptation to kill the rogue. The fat man stirs in his seat; Roger ducks right, through an open door that has always been closed before, to the telephone and the EXIT sign. It is 10:30. He thinks, *If the rogue has a base backing him, why haven't they picked up on my presence yet?* He looks at the phone. A notion strikes him: a way he can interfere without giving away the game. *Our voices are the same,* he thinks. *If I call the cops and say it's him, they'll never know it isn't.* He picks up the receiver.

"There's no time," says a voice. "Besides, cops don't intimidate him. He can shoot in a second and interface as quickly." So Roger turns. She has come out of the men's room; she lets the door swing shut and approaches him quickly. She wears a gray jumpsuit; her dark hair is thickly looped about her head. *Uh, base,* he thinks. "They can't read you," she tells him. "Your telemetry is somewhat limited; a convergence of four personas is a little much for it."

"You're the woman I saw in the screen. Sitting at a console."

"Quite possibly. I've been following you, I'm afraid."

"You're me, then, too." His palms sweat.

"My name is Catherine. My mother's name. Catherine Shapiro." It is his mother's name, too. "I'm here to help. Our base has been monitoring him for a long time. I'm supposed to impress upon you the historicity of this occasion: the first meeting of representatives from the two benign, interfacing cultures."

"Is that what we are? Benign?"

There is concern in her face, but it is controlled.

He feels instinctively that he is in the presence of power. "We have to stop him. He's going to kill one of us in two minutes. And this one of us is a particularly nice guy. We have to stop him."

"That will be difficult. I've tried."

He starts.

"Oh, yes. I've tracked him through eleven sequences, personally."

"Does he work alone?"

"Yes. We're in contact with his base sequence. He's a genius, Roger. He's responsible for most of their breakthroughs in probability research. What he's got is an experimental, portable interface-unit, something we've never even begun to develop. He stole it on its test-run. His people want him back."

No rogue base. A weight lifts from him, and he is freed. He takes out the burner. "What are you doing?" she whispers.

"I won't let him kill Shep."

"I won't let you kill him." Her weapon is pointed at his chest. "Be reasonable, Roger. His people want him back alive. They're prepared to exchange technical data for him."

"I thought you said you'd never met anyone from an interfacing culture before."

"We haven't. You can't enter a probability that your persona has vacated. But we've learned to communicate with them. As we're communicating with your base, now."

"There has to be a way to save Shep. There has to be a way." *He has to finish,* he thinks. *He's going somewhere. He's off the shoals.*

"There is. Put your weapon away."

He believes her. He pockets the burner. *One minute.* A few new customers have entered. They hear the woman from New Jersey and Shep's delighted greeting.

"Does he know you're after him?"

She nods. "He's seen me several times. But he has no monitoring capability. All he can do is shift. Now listen." She lowers her gun, but does not put it down. "This is the first good chance I've had to get at him when the bar wasn't crowded. I'm going to shoot for his weapon-arm. I think I'm a better shot than you are, from what I've seen. When I hit him, he's going to interface. Don't let him see you. Follow him."

"How? On foot?"

"Your base will regain control when he interfaces. They'll want you going after him whether or not they believe my people."

"What about you?"

"I'll meet you. Between us, we may be able to trap him."

It is 10:32½.

It has all happened too quickly, and what happens next he is not prepared for. She races into the bar. He cannot keep himself from pursuing. She falls into a crouch and fires, all at once. The rogue is on his feet, raising his burner. Shep is out from behind the counter, facing the woman from New Jersey, his left side exposed. He is grinning from ear to ear. His shoulder is three feet from the rogue's muzzle. Catherine's beam strikes the fat man's wrists; he vanishes with a scream, like a sentient balloon when pricked. His burner clatters on the filthy wood floor. Instantly, Roger's head is full of chatter. Catherine starts forward, toward the gun. Something warns her; she flings herself backwards, ripples, and fades out.

"What in hell?" says Shep. He bends down to the spot where the rogue's weapon lies glowing. It blows up in his face.

TRANSFERRING, says the wink-blink happily.

He wails in darkness. He is in a box of a room with dust and skeletons. **TRANSFERRING.** He is in an open meadow, and people are flying kites. **TRANSFERRING.** He is buried, earth pressing. **TRANSFERRING, TRANSFERRING!** He is up to his ears in mud, surrounded by curious, long-necked animals with eyes like dinner plates. **TRANSFERRING, GODDAMIT!** He is in a bar with blue walls, a bar with gray walls, a bar full of naked men gyrating to music, a bar thick with sweet pot smoke, a bar of slime and ancient rot. He wails for Shep, whom he loves. **TRANSFERRING,** they say.

The shadow settles and stays. He is kneeling in a deserted room. There is no furniture, not even a drinks counter. The street windows have been boarded up. A few cracks admit anemic moonlight: no electric Duval glow. Wind whines outside. The only other creature in the room is a pregnant cat. With no place to hide, she stands with feet rigid and back arched in the center of the room, bristling with every night-fear. His watch has stopped.

The smell of the pot still clings to his clothing. He wonders who he is. *Roger Carl Shapiro*, comes the reply, but he seems to remember other names as well. He sits down, and a discomfort at his buttocks makes him rise. He draws the pen and notebook from the back of his jeans. *There is a tide*, he reads.

"Roger?"

She has materialized in the gloom. Her features are ashen, like her clothing. "Hello, Catherine," he says. "It took off his—it took—" He stops. On the second page, the name is written, in Roger's own sprawling loops, *R. C. Shapiro*, and the rest: *#8 Higgs Lane Key West Fla 33040 (Shep) Call me buddy!!! 66403*. He puts the book away. "What now?" he asks.

"I don't know." She stands peering out between some slats. "I'm not sure where we are. Rather, I know where we're not. This isn't a murder sequence. It's another cataclysm zone."

"You heard?"

"I'm afraid I was partly responsible. My following you is what's been causing the drift in your signal. My people have corrected for it now, but—"

"Where is he?"

"The rogue? Nowhere."

"Dead?"

"No. Unconnected as it is to an external power souce, his shifting equipment must carry its own energy supply. He needs to recharge after every shift. He does this between probabilities."

He does not even ask her what this means. "Then why are *we* here?"

"This is where he was heading when he dropped out of interface."

"You said I could help you trap him. How?"

She takes something from a pocket. "See these? They're like the tracer chips you're carrying. We've been able to do some scans of his unit, and we think that if we can manage to get these into him, we can remove the unit from his neural control and take over his shifting-capability."

"You think."

"We think."

"At least he doesn't have a burner any longer."

"At least we managed to do that much. He won't be killing any more Shapiros." She squats beside him. "Roger, I'm sorry."

"For me?" She cannot answer his tone. The cat has crouched, still suspicious, but no longer afraid. "You say this is a cataclysm zone?"

"See for yourself." He looks out at devastation. Under the Moon, the town is dead. The stucco looks scoured. Duval Street is strangled with rubble: rusted cars; masonry; blackened, leafless trees.

"What did it?"

"We don't know. My people have never monitored this probability before. They report no radiation or plague."

"Somehow, knowing that doesn't really comfort me." He looks at her. "You've sold out to them, haven't you? To your version of Lifetimes. You're their woman. You're sad because your lousy shot killed Shep, but not undone."

"Give me a break, you sanctimonious creep," she answers.

ROGER PRIME, says base. **WE HAVE RECEIVED A COM-MUNICATION FROM AN ORG—**

I know all about it. Be ready to transfer me out of here if the Crawling Eye shows up.

COOPERATE WITH THEM, ROGER.

"Roger," she says urgently. "My people say he's interfacing. Here in the building."

The rogue is there. He has a weapon in his hand. Catherine yells and grab's Roger's arm. The world flares. His head fills with a low hum. He opens his eyes. Catherine has kept a hold of him. A cocoon of opalescent light has woven itself around them; through it they can see the rogue, cowering against a wall. His mouth is open. Roger-Prime fumbles for his burner. "Don't be stupid. You'd fry us both."

The rogue vanishes. Their shield dissipates with a little sigh. The cat has managed to work its head between two slats in an effort to escape the room. Numb, he watches it wriggle, but cannot summon the interest to help it. "Who works your shield, you or your people?" he asks. *So much for our little gain.*

"There's no time for this. He's on the run now. We have to catch him. Come with me." She heads for the lavatory. It is shut tight. Roger realizes that he has not seen a women's room in any of the probabilities. This strikes him as funny, and he giggles. She gives him a sharp look and takes her gun to the locked door. It flames and sags. A stench envelopes them. "Oh, Christ," she says. "Don't look." He looks. The lavatory is packed with skeletons. Roger-Prime leaps backward with a cry. She fires the weapon a second time. Bones blacken, fall to charcoal. Heat hits their faces. The stench does not lessen. She clears a space for them and leads him into the bathroom. "Are you all right?" she asks.

"I don't like death." *They were running,* he thinks. *From what?*

"Nobody likes it. Not even our rogue."

"You could have fooled me."

She takes him by the shoulders. "Some people deal with death by ignoring it. My mother was one. For three years after Daddy died she kept his dressing-table exactly as it had been on the day of the accident. She'd talk to him when she thought I wasn't listening. Other people deal

with death by embracing it. The 'my life is over' bit. And some people
accept it as part of living and get past it. Which sort of person do you
think we're dealing with in our alter ego?"

"Let's talk about this someplace else," Roger says. She sighs and
consults her palm. **READY FOR TRANSFER,** his wink-blink announces.
TRANSFERRING. She vanishes. He is alone among the stinking
bones. *"What in Hell happened?"* he screams.

ROGER-PRIME, YOU'RE NOT TRANSFERRING. Something
thumps the eaves of the building. "A seagull," suggests Roger to a skull.
He knows it is not a seagull. He runs to the lavatory door. A dull green
light is leaking through the slats of the boarded windows. For the first
time he notices that the windows are boarded up on the inside. The
pregnant cat is still stuck, and her wriggling has become fevered. *"Get
me out of here, base,"* There is an unhealthy look to the light that makes
his skin crawl. *"Base!"*

"Roger." He jumps and yells. She is back. "Your signal is being
jammed. It might be the rogue, or whatever's out there."

" 'Whatever'?" he says. "I love horror movies. Can I link with you?"
One of the boards springs loose and clatters on the floor. He takes his
gun and fires at the frantic cat. She flames briefly, then hangs still.
"Can I link with you?" he asks again.

"Yes. We've never done this before, though; it might cut you off from
your own people."

"I'd rather be stuck in your probability than here. Hurry up, Catherine;
Jesus." Light slops from the space the board has vacated and leaks into
the room. They retreat to the lavatory. Masonry groans somewhere;
wood splinters and collapses. The doorway is filled with the sickly light.
The stench increases. Roger cannot stop giggling; it is so much like a
Lord Dunsany story he once read. The woman grips his left palm and
presses her left palm to it. Base squawks in his head, then goes silent. A
strange voice resonates within him: **TRANSFERRING, CATHERINE-
PRIME.**

It does not happen. The wall to the men's room dissolves into a
writhe of worms. Something rears up, not at all pleasant. *More power,
base,* thinks someone. *You have five seconds.*

READY, says her base.

Then do it! they cry together. The light sucks at them. Roger does not
notice the transfer; he is too busy screaming. It is 10:33.

They are falling, the three of them. It is a strange fall, more like a
dance than a fall: at junctures they seem to orbit one another, and
interweave, and very nearly coincide. Roger-Rogue fires his reserve

weapon repeatedly. The beams exit the nozzle and spread into rainbows, and ribbons. *Catherine!* cries Roger-Prime. *Between,* she replies. He reaches for her, and finds her moving away from him. Roger-Rogue fires a spray of silver, edged with blue. *You bastard!* cries Roger-Prime. *You filthy Nazi!* His words become pillows, which strike the rogue about the ears and send him tumbling in a great cartwheel.

Catherine-Prime is at Roger-Prime's elbow. *Let it take you,* she says to him. *Don't fight.*

I've never fought, he thinks. The words string themselves out against a milk-white sky, black as beads. *Give me the chips.*

Wait till it ends, she cries. *We're between interfaces.*

I know where we are, he says. *The chips.* She gives him two of the four. He dives for the tumbling rogue.

The first thing he notices is the sound of a fountain. He is lying under a curve of concrete. He pulls himself up to sitting position; he has materialized in a messy garden. It is surrounded by a high brick wall matted with jasmine. An arbor of glory-bower spills its blood-red, white-bracted blooms into the nights, but the trusses need trimming, and several of the slat supports are broken. In the fountain bowl, a bird floats gently. He does not put his hand into the water. The sky is clear. On the other side of the wall, a royal poinciana displays its plumage. He recognizes it as the one that has grown outside the bar in most of the sequences. *Base,* he calls. His mind is empty.

Another dead zone, he thinks. He gets to his feet. He feels fatigued but not exhausted. Catherine is nowhere to be seen.

The house at the back of which he stands is something from a Key West guidebook: a two-storied, New-England-style structure with peeling white paint and gingerbread railing on its balconies. He finds a door and opens it. There is a wood-burning stove, copper pans on hooks; copper sinks with ornamented fittings that look as though they are made of brass. Noting the disrepair of the garden, he is not surprised that the metals are tarnished and dull. Things tarnish quickly in the salt air of the island. He notices no plastics or paper toweling. He roams the house rapidly, searching for the rogue. There is much wickerwork, mostly white. There are no electric outlets. One room is a Victorian fantasy of lace, velvet, and polished wood. The wood has been polished recently, and smells of honey.

Throughout the house he finds many photographs of poor quality in gilt frames. They are all of stern bearded men and unsmiling dour women, dressed in clothing similar to that which was worn in the century before his own. One he picks up and studies. The man stands behind the woman. She is seated on a white chaise. They are dressed in black. Their expressions are restrained, but not miserable. The woman could be Catherine; the man, the rogue. He finds them in another portrait, too: she is aswirl with lace and satin and he wears a top hat. The formality of the moment cannot hide their happiness. Her hand is clasped in his.

The photograph is faded, and a bit smudged, as if it has been handled many times.

In one of the upstairs bedrooms he finds a chair, and he sits in it. It is a man's room, darkened by many mauves; but there is lace at the windows. He looks out of one of them. Duval Street has been stripped of its tarmac down to hard-packed earth. The trees far outnumber the houses. There are no streetlamps, no traffic lights. Men in queer costumes stalk up and down, some in groups of three and four, most alone. The moon touches sails on the harbor. A saloon spills noise far down the street; occasionally a horse trots by. Once he sees a black woman, burdened and solitary; some sailors catch at her, and she flees from their laughter. Mosquitoes dance about his neck.

Not a dead zone, he thinks. *Just a quiet house owned by an indifferent housekeeper. Maybe he's too poor to keep servants, or too fearful to.* He begins a methodical search of the room. At the base of the big oak wardrobe he feels something give; a hidden spring uncoils, and a drawer slides open. In it lies a raygun.

The creature must have screwed up our signals. I shifted sideways, and he shifted backwards and sideways. No other explanation occurs to him. He wonders if the bride is she. There is another bedroom; he walks into it. It is a woman's room, full of bric-a-brac. The bed is turned down, the mosquito netting lovingly arranged. About the dressing table hangs a scent of rose. He traces the perfume to a small porcelain jar filled with leathery petals, topped with a perforated cover. There are more photographs. The rogue is in some of them, but most of them are of her: perched on a horse looking uncomfortable; in an ugly travelling-costume, standing with an old woman against the backdrop of Big Ben; very young, with her hair down, at a piano.

Young, and with her hair down. He looks more closely. The girl is perhaps fifteen.

There is another wardrobe. Inside it he finds a row of gowns. Most of them are silken, many faded. Some are so rotted that they fray under his fingers. *Things rot fast here,* he thinks, *but none of these have been worn in years.* He looks around again, and for the first time notices the stain on the ceiling, high up near one corner. He rushes back to the photograph of the girl. "Damn," he murmurs. "Goddam, it isn't her!" Catherine has never had a childhood here. He goes back downstairs. In the photograph in the parlor, the woman is in her forties, the man in his fifties.

She never made it here, he tells himself. *But he did. At some point, sometime. His wife must have been our persona in this probability.* He does not understand the time inconsistency, and he does not care. *She died, and he left her dressing-table as it was.* It is all part of the same pattern: the ignoring of death. It is finally clear to him why the rogue has killed. *Probability sequences are choices made manifest,* he thinks. *Before shifting was brought home to us as a reality, we could dream of ourselves as we might have been, and somewhere deep down hold out to ourselves the illusion that there's still time to do that one great thing. To recoup our losses. Probability mechanics put an end to that indulgence. It told us, "Too late; you could have been this if you'd done this then, but not any more."*

The rogue has not been able to accept the reminders of his could-have-beens. Roger thinks of Catherine. *We're lucky,* he thinks. *I might be able to accept your sequence, and you might be able to accept mine. But would either of us be willing to change places with him?*

"So there you are," says Roger-Rogue. "I expected you years ago. You don't know our Amazon friend never made it here. Perhaps she did, and I killed her." He is no longer fat. There is a strange scar on his forehead, and he is whiskered. "I see you found my burner."

"You've done well for yourself," Roger says. The man laughs. There is much of Carl in him; a little of Roj. "You've been stranded, haven't you?"

"Beached," says the rogue, and jumps him.

He is strong, and he knows how to fight. He gets on top of Roger and pummels him. His face is full of glee. The burner bumps and skitters. Roger-Prime reaches up through the blood and slaps two chips against the man's neck. Then he puts the heel of his right hand under the rogue's chin and pushes hard. The gray head snaps back. They grapple, Roger biting and screaming Shep's name. He has never hit anyone as hard as he could; he does this now. The rogue sags. Roger scrambles to his feet and dives atop the burner. It is somewhat larger than his own, with a battery compartment. He points the muzzle.

The man has his face. "So get it over with, already," Roger-Rogue says.

"Where are we?"

"Somewhere to right angles of your 1982," his persona answers. "A retarded time, and quite racist. Kill me, will you?" The rogue keeps his tone light.

Roger grins, knowing better.

"You find this situation amusing?"

"Those telemetry-chips are glowing," Roger says. He grins and grins. They have not lost him. "You're about to enjoy a belated visit home." The man touches his neck. The chips have sunk into the flesh, shedding pearly light. "Beached, huh? That scar have something to do with it?"

"You're perceptive," Roger-Rogue says. "I knew you were both after me; I'd killed enough of us to feel reasonably avenged. I shifted at random. It was foolish. I shifted to—not a cataclysm zone, precisely, but a disaster sequence—an improbability. It was—" He laughs and rolls his bleeding head. "Oh, Jesus. I still dream about it. They weren't human at all. Not at all. We'd evolved into something quite different; I can't imagine what ancestry. I rather horrified them, I imagine. They attacked me."

"Sounds human enough."

"Yes. I was struck," he taps his forehead, "here. You may know that I designed the shifter to be a plate of microcircuitry, a glorified Fresnel disc, actually. I had them implant it against my skull. I had good reasons at the time: it made for a more efficient tie-in to the volitional centers. When our cousins struck me, they disrupted the circuitry. I made one more shift. I landed here."

"Was that before or after the rainbows?" demands Roger-Prime.

"What rainbows?"

"The ones in the between-place. You shot them out of your raygun."

"I'm not going home," says Roger-Rogue. He claws at his throat. "Goddam you, this is my home!"

"Calm down or I'll burn this house to the ground." It works. The man drops his hands. "Get up." He does. "Now tell me what was so goddam terrible that you had to kill twenty-five nebbish bartenders to avenge it."

The man looks astonished. "Don't joke with me."

"I'm asking. One of them could have been a very dear friend of mine."

"Why, to avenge this." He spreads his hands. "This. Look." There is a mirror hanging on the parlor wall. He stands before it, his lean face full of loathing. "Can't you see? It's indelible. I'll never lose their mark on me. It was always, 'Work, work,' and I was always alone. My private life? I didn't have one. They were surprised that I should even want one. I didn't look like something out of an ad campaign, you see. I was Roger the Researcher. I hope you're finding this entertaining."

"Illuminating."

"Confession is good for the soul. When people weren't there, food was. It was my only comfort for some years, that and masturbation. I

tried to shed the weight; I never could. Eventually I tried to quit that goddam research position. They wouldn't let me do that, either. Do you know what it's like to breathe air like sterile gauze day in and day out?"

"You could have left."

"Don't tell me what I could have done." The skin around his nostrils has turned pale. His fists are knotted. "*You've* made it. You got out. You've never had to wrestle night in, night out with the weight of your goddam flesh. Don't tell me what I could have done. Her family found me when I showed up here: the Sappers. It's unwise to be Jewish in this sequence. I convinced them I was their cousin, somehow; who knows? And she," he says, the tears streaming, "she loved me. Now old man Sapper is dead; now Kathy's dead; T.B., it's still deadly here. And I'm back where I started. Alone." Suddenly he laughs. "God, what a penchant I have for melodrama. I should have written plays. At least I ended up in Key West. You know? When I was in college I wanted to be a bartender? It seemed—so sexual. And free." He holds out his hands. "Please shoot me."

"I'm sorry," says Roger-Prime. "I understand what you're saying. But it's not enough." The rogue's eyes widen; Roger hears a sound behind him. He glances over his shoulder. It is Catherine, dressed in a blue jumpsuit, looking no older than he remembers her. "Well, hello," he says. "We've got to stop meeting like this."

"Good work, Roger." Her left hand smooths an antimacassar, and her right keeps her gun trained on the rogue's chest. "You can lower your weapon. Doctor Shapiro, if your present circumstances are as melancholy as you indicate, you're lucky we caught up with you when we did."

"It would be so simple if you'd just shoot me," says the rogue.

"What are you going to do?" Roger asks her.

"Shift him back to his home sequence. My base and his have linked equipment: our sensors isolate and amplify his signal, and they do the actual recalling. When he gets home, he'll have some minor surgery."

"I assumed that. I meant, what are you going to do with him after they've removed his portable shifter? What happens then?" She looks blank. "Catherine, he's a murderer. He has to be tried."

"Of course," she says. She is thumbing her left palm. The chips embedded in the rogue's neck have begun to glow a deeper color, an almost-peach.

"Wait," pleads Roger-Rogue. He points. Slowly Roger-Prime picks up the photograph of the happy newlyweds and hands it to the scientist. "Thank you," says the older man. He looks at the picture as if he has never seen it before. The blood trickling down his neck turns orange-red

in the glow from the chips. The rogue looks at his dead wife, then at Catherine. "You're nothing alike," he pronounces. "You looked exactly alike, and you're nothing alike." Puzzled, she frowns. Roger looks again at his older persona, and sees his face begin to crumble from the forehead down, wrinkle and crumble and twist with anguish. All at once, Roger-Prime feels the way he felt facing the skeletons in the cataclysm sequence. He backs off, awash with dread. *It's me*, he thinks, knowing it with a certainty with which he has known nothing else. *It's me, dear Christ, it really is me. Everything squandered. All the richness.*

He hears Catherine say, "They're transferring him—now." The peach light spreads suddenly over the rogue and swallows him. An instant later, he is gone. "Are you all right?" the woman asks him. "I drifted; they had to recall me and send me out again after you. You're all bloody; did you know that?"

"My head's empty," he says.

"Your base lost you when I transferred you out of the cataclysm sequence. I'm afraid you're going to have to shift home with me; it'll be easier to project you to your own sequence from our base. Is that all right?"

"Sure, Company Lady." He sticks the rogue's burner into his pocket. Her eyes are narrowed, trying to fathom him. "Bravo for us, huh?" He grins. "We caught him. No more bartender-Shapiros biting the dust. He married us in this sequence, you know."

"That's sick." **READY FOR TRANSFER,** her base says in his head.

"I think I understand it. I think he and I are a lot more alike than you and I."

But she surprises him. "We've all been beached and set adrift, Roger," she says. "That, and hugged the coastline waiting for the perfect wind to blow. And he's by no means the worst of us. I've sat at our scanners longer than you have, I think." She pauses, then smiles back at him. "There are no safe harbors."

They both laugh. "Then we'd better get a move on," he says. "New tide's in. And I'm sick to death of the shallows." He feels the pad in his back pocket. *I'll do it for you, Shep*, he thinks. *For you and Roj and Dodger and all of us. Who knows? Now that our three bases have started to work together, maybe we'll find one of us who's a publisher. The possibilities are endless.*

When the transfer comes, he is ready.

GENE WOLFE

The Cat

Gene Wolfe is perceived by many critics to be one of the best—perhaps
the best—SF and fantasy writers working today. His tetralogy *The Book
of the New Sun*—consisting of *The Shadow of the Torturer, The Claw of
the Conciliator, The Sword of the Lictor*, and *The Citadel of the Autarch*—is
being hailed as a masterpiece, quite probably the standard against which
all subsequent science-fantasy books of the '80s will be judged; ultimately,
it may prove to be as influential as J.R.R. Tolkien's *Lord of the Rings* or
T.H. White's *The Once and Future King. The Shadow of the Torturer*
won the World Fantasy Award. *The Claw of the Conciliator* won the
Nebula Award. Wolfe also won a Nebula Award for his story "The
Death of Doctor Island." His other books include *Peace, The Fifth Head
of Cerberus*, and *The Devil in a Forest*. His short fiction—including
many of the best stories of the seventies—has been collected in *The
Island of Doctor Death and Other Stories and Other Stories* and *Gene
Wolfe's Book of Days*. His most recent book is *The Castle of the Otter*, a
book about the writing of *The Book of the New Sun*. Wolfe lives in
Barrington, Illinois, with his wife and family, where he is the editor of
the trade publication *Plant Engineering*.

Here—in the first and (so far) only short story set in the universe of
Wolfe's *The Book of the New Sun*—he takes us to the mysterious House
Absolute, home of the Autarch Severian and of the sinister and enigmatic Father Inire, for a strange tale of stalking impalpable creatures
and a revenge that reaches from beyond the stars . . .

THE CAT

Gene Wolfe

I am Odilo the Steward, the son of Odilo the Steward. I am he who is charged by our Autarch Severian the Great—whose desires are the dreams of his subjects—with the well-being of the Hypogeum Apotropaic. It is now the fifth year of his reign.

As all who know the ways of our House Absolute (and I may say here that I neither hope nor wish for other readers) are aware, our Hypogeum Apotropaic is that part devoted to the needs and comforts of Father Inire; and in the twenty years in which I have given satisfaction (as I hope) at my post, and in the years before them when I assisted my father, also Odilo the Steward, I have seen and heard many a strange thing. My father likewise.

This evening, when I had reached a respite in the unending tasks entailed by such a position as mine, I took myself, as my custom is, to the culina magna of our hypogeum to obtain some slight refreshment. The cooks' labors too were ended or nearly; and half or more, with a kitchen boy or three and a gaggle of scullery maids, sat about the dying fire, seeking, as such people will, to amuse one another by diverse boasts and recitals.

Having little better to do and being eager to rest, I bid the chief cook surrender his chair to me and heard them as I ate. It is now Hallowmas Eve (which is to say, the full of the Spading Moon) and their talk had turned to all manner of ghosts and bogeys. In the brief time required for me to chew my bread and beef and sluice them down with hot spiced ale, I heard such recountings of larva, lemures, and the like as would terrify every child in the Commonwealth—and make every man in it laugh most heartily.

So I myself laughed when I returned here to my study, where I will scrutinize and doubtless approve the bills of fare for Hallowmas; and yet I find I am bemused by these tales and lost amid many wondering speculations. As every thinking man acknowledges, mighty powers move through this dark universe of Briah, though for the most part hidden from us by its infinite night. Is it not every man's duty to record what little he has glimpsed that may give light to it? And do not such idle tales as I heard by the fire but serve to paint yet blacker that gloom through which we grope? I am therefore determined to set down here, for the enlightenment (as it may be) of my successors and whoever else may read, the history, whole and in entire in so far as I know it, of a series of incidents that culminated (as I believe) this night ten years gone. For the earlier events, I give the testimony of my father, Odilo the Steward also, a contemporary of the Chatelaine Sancha.

She was (so my father said) an extraordinarily charming child, with the face of a peri and eyes that were always laughing, darker than most exulted children but so tall that she might have been supposed, at the age of seven or eight, to be a young woman of sixteen.

That such a child should have attracted the attention of Father Inire is scarcely to be wondered at. He has always been fond of children (and particularly of girls), as the oldest records of our hypogeum shows; and I sometimes think that he has chosen to remain on Urth as a tutor to our race because he finds even the wisest of us to be children in his sight. Permit me to say at once that these children have often benefited from his attention. It is true, perhaps, that they have sometimes suffered for it, but that has been seldom and I think by no means by his wish.

It has ever been the custom of the exultants resident in our House Absolute to keep their children closely confined to their own apartments and to permit them to travel the ten thousand corridors that wind such distances beneath the surface of the land (even so far as the Old Citadel of Nessus, some say) only under the watchful eyes of some trustworthy upper servant. And it has ever been the custom of those children to escape the upper servants charged with their supervision whenever they can, to join in the games of the children of the staff, so much more numerous, and to wander at will through the numberless leagues of the ten thousand corridors, by which frolic many have been lost at one time or another, and some forever.

Whenever Father Inire encounters such a child not already known to him, he speaks to her, and if her face and her answers please him, he may pause in the conduct of great affairs to tell her some tale of the worlds beyond Dis. (No person grown has heard these tales, for the children do not recall them well enough to recount them afterward, though they are often quite charmed by them; and before they are grown themselves they have forgotten them, as indeed I have forgotten all but a few scraps of the tale Father Inire once told me.) If he cannot take the time for that, he often confers upon the child some many-hued toy of the kind that wise men and humble men such as I, and all women and children, call magical.

Should he encounter that child a second time, as often happens, he asks her what has become of the toy, or whether she wishes to hear some other story from his store. Should he find that the toy remains unbroken and that it is still in the possession of the child, he may give another, and should the child ask politely (for Father Inire values courtesy above all knowledge) he may tell another. But if, as only very rarely happens, the child has received a toy and exhibits it still whole, but asks on this occasion for a tale of the worlds beyond Dis instead of a second toy, then Father Inire takes that child as a particular friend and pupil for so long as she—or more rarely he—may live. (I boast no scholarship of words, as you that have read this account do already well know; but once I heard a man who was such a scholar say that this word *pupil* in its most ancient and purest state denominates the image of oneself one sees in another's eyes.)

Such a pupil Sancha became, one winter morning when she was of seven years or thereabout and my father much the same. All her replies must have pleased Father Inire; and he was doubtless returning to his apartments in our Hypogeum Apotropaic from some night-long deliberation with the Autarch. He took her with him; and so my father met them, as he often told me, in that white corridor we call the Luminary Way. Even then, when my father was only a child himself, he was struck by the sight of them walking and chatting together, Father Inire bent nearly double, like a gnome in a nursery book, with no more nose than an alouatte; Sancha already towering over him, straight as a sapling, sable of hair and bright of eye, with her cat in her arms.

Of what passed between them in Father Inire's apartments, I can only relay what Sancha herself told a maid called Aude, many years later. Father Inire showed the girl many wonderful and magical appurtenances, and at last that marvelous circle of specula by whose power a living being may be coalesced from the ethereal waves, or, should such a being boldly enter them, circumfused to the borders of Briah. Then Sancha, doubtless thinking it but a toy, cast her cat into the circle. It was a gray cat, so my father told me, with many stripes of a darker gray.

Knowing Father Inire as I have been privileged to know him these many years, I feel certain he must have promised poor Sancha that he would do all that lay in his power to retrieve her pet, and that he must have kept faithfully to that promise. As for Sancha, Aude said she believed the cat the only creature Sancha was ever to love, beyond herself; but that, I think, was spite; and Aude was but a giddypate, who knew the Chatelaine only when she was old.

As I have often observed, rumor in our House Absolute is a self-willed wind. Ten thousand corridors there well may be (though I, with so many more immediate concerns, have forborne to count them), and a million chambers or more; and in truth no report reaches them all. And yet in a day or less, the least gossip comes to a thousand ears. So it became known, and quickly, that the girl Sancha was attended by some fey thing. When she and some friend sat alone at play, a pochette was knocked from a table and broken, or so it was said. On another occasion, a young man who sat conversing with Sancha (who must, I should think, have been somewhat older then) observed the ruffled body of a sparrow lying on the carpet at her feet, though she could scarcely have sat where she did without stepping upon it, had it been present when they began their talk.

Of the scandal concerning the Sancha and a certain Lomer, then seneschal to the Chatelaine Nympha, I shall say nothing—or at least very little, although the matter was only too well known at the time. She was still but a child, being then fourteen years of age, or as some alleged, fifteen. He was a man of nearly thirty. They were discovered together in that state which is too easily imagined. Sancha's rank and age equally exempted her from formal punishment; her age and her rank equally ensured that the the disrepute would cling to her for life. Lomer was sentenced to die; he appealed to the Autarch, and as the Chatelaine Nympha exerted herself on his behalf, his appeal was accepted. He was sent to the antechamber to await a hearing; but if his case was ever disposed of, I do not recall it. The Chatelaine Leocadia, who was said to have concocted the affair to injure Nympha, suffered nothing.

When Sancha came of age, she received a villa in the south by her father's will, so becoming the Chatelaine Sancha. The Autarch Appian permitted her to leave our House Absolute at once; and no one was surprised, my father said, to hear soon after that she had wed the heir of Fors—it was a country family not liable to know much of the gossip of the court, nor apt to care greatly for what it heard, while the Chatelaine was a young woman of some fortune, excellent family, and extraordinary beauty. Insofar as we interested ourselves in her doings, she then vanished for the space of fifty years.

During the third year in which I performed the consequential charge that had once been my father's, she returned and requested a suite in this hypogeum, which Father Inire granted in observance of their old friendship. At that time, I conversed with her at length, it being necessary to arrange a thousand details to her satisfaction.

Of the celebrated beauty that had been hers, only the eyes remained. Her back was as bent as Father Inire's, her teeth had been made for her by a provincial ivory-turner, and her nose had become the hooked beak of a carrion bird. For whatever reason, her person now carried a disagreeable odor; she must have been aware of it, for she had ordered fires of sandalwood to counter it.

Although she never mentioned her unfortunate adventure in our hypogeum, she described to me, in much greater detail than I shall give here, her career at Fors. Suffice it to say that she had borne several children, that her husband was dead, and that her elder son now directed the family estate. The Chatelaine did not get along well with his wife and had many disagreeable ancedotes to relate of her, of which the worst was that she had once denounced the Chatelaine as a *gligua*, such being the name the autochthons of the south employ for one who has traffic with diakka, casts spells, and the like.

Till that time, no thought of the impalpable cat said to accompany this old woman had crossed my mind; but the odd word suggested the odd story, and from that moment I kept the most careful watch, though I neither saw nor heard the least sign of the phantom. Several times I sought to lead our talk to her former relations with Father Inire or to the subject of felines per se—remarking, for example, that such an animal might be a source of comfort to one now separated by some many leagues from her family. The first evoked only general praises of Father Inire's goodness and learning, and the latter talk of birds, marmosets, and similar favorites.

As I was about to go, Aude (whom I had assigned to the Chatelaine Sancha's service already, for the Chatelaine had brought but little staff with her from Fors) entered to complain that she had not been told the Chatelaine had a pet, and that it would be necessary to arrange for its food and the delivery of clean sand. The Chatelaine quite calmly denied she possessed such an animal and demanded that the one Aude reported be expelled from the suite.

As the years passed, the Chatelaine Sancha had little need of birds or marmosets. The scandal was revived by doddering women who recollected it from childhood, and she attracted to herself a host of protégée, the daughters of armigers and exultants, eager to exhibit their tolerance and bathe in a notoriety that was without hazard. Rumors of a spectral cat persisted—it being said to walk upon the keyboard of the choralcelo—but there are many rumors in our hypogeum, and they were not the strangest.

It is one of my duties to pay my respects, as the prolocutor of all Father Inire's servants, to those who endure their mortal illness here.

Thus I called upon the Chatelaine Sancha as she lay dying, and thus I came to be in her bedchamber when, after having spoken with me only a moment before, she cried out with her final breath.

Having now carried my account to its conclusion, I scarcely know how to end it, save by an unembellished recitation of the facts.

At the dying Chatelaine's cry, all turned to look at her. And all saw, as did I, that upon the snowy counterpane covering her withered body there had appeared the dark pawprint of some animal, and beside it a thing not unlike a doll. This was no longer than my hand, and yet it seemed in each detail a lovely child just become a woman. Nor was it of painted wood, or any other substance of which such toys are made; for when the physician pricked it with his lancet, a ruby drop shone forth.

By the strict instructions of Father Inire, this little figure was interred with the Chatelaine Sancha. Our laundresses having proved incapable of removing the stain left by the creature's paw, I ordered the counterpane sent to the Chatelaine Leocadia, who being of the most advanced age was even then but dim of sight.

She has since gone blind, and yet her maids report that she sees the cat, which stalks her in her dreams. It is not well for those of high station to involve the servants of their enemies in their quarrels.

GEORGE R.R. MARTIN

The Monkey Treatment

Americans are a people obsessed with dieting, with the magic goal of Losing Weight, and there are almost as many diets as there are gurus to propose them, or fat people eager to try them out: the drinking man's diet, the high-protein diet, the grapefruit diet, the brown-rice diet, the monkey treatment . . .

Wait a minute. The *monkey* treatment?

If you don't know about *that* one, perhaps it's just as well. For as the very funny story that follows amply demonstrates, the cure can sometimes be worse than the disease . . .

Born in Bayonne, New Jersey, George R.R. Martin made his first sale in 1971, and soon established himself as one of the most popular SF writers of the seventies, winning his first Hugo Award in 1975 for his novella "A Song For Lya." In 1980 he went on to take three more major awards: his novelette "Sandkings" won both the Nebula and the Hugo, and his short story "The Way of Cross and Dragon" won a Hugo as well, making Martin the first author ever to receive two Hugo Awards for fiction in the same year. Martin's books include the novels *Fevre Dream*, *The Dying of the Light*, and (in collaboration with Lisa Tuttle) *Windhaven*, three collections, *Sandkings*, *A Song For Lya*, and *Songs of Stars and Shadows*, and, as editor, the *New Voices* series of anthologies (the latest volume of which, now retitled *The John W. Campbell Awards*, is from Bluejay Books). His most recent books are the collection *Songs The Dead Men Sing*, from Dark Harvest, and his big new novel of "blood, terror & rock 'n' roll," *The Armageddon Rag*, from Poseidon Press.

THE MONKEY TREATMENT

George R. R. Martin

Kenny Dorchester was a fat man.

He had not always been a fat man, of course. He had come into the world a perfectly normal infant of modest weight, but the normalcy was short-lived in Kenny's case, and before very long he had become a chubby-cheeked toddler well swaddled in baby fat. From then on it was all downhill and upscale so far as Kenny was concerned. He became a pudgy child, a corpulent adolescent, and a positively porcine college student, all in good turn, and by adulthood he had left all those intermediate steps behind and graduated into full obesity.

People become obese for a variety of complex reasons, some of them physiological. Kenny's reason was relatively simple: food. Kenny Dorchester loved to eat. Often he would paraphrase Will Rogers, winking broadly, and tell his friends that he had never met a food he didn't like. This was not precisely true, since Kenny loathed both liver and prune juice. Perhaps, if his mother had served them more often during his childhood, he would never have attained the girth and gravity that so haunted him at maturity. Unfortunately, Gina Dorchester was more inclined to lasagne and roast turkey with stuffing and sweet potatoes and chocolate pudding and veal cordon bleu and buttered corn-on-the-cob and stacks of blueberry pancakes (although not all in one meal) than she was to liver and prune juice, and once Kenny had expressed his preference in the matter by retching his liver back onto his plate, she obligingly never served liver and prune juice again.

Thus, all unknowing, she set her son on the soft, suety road to the monkey treatment. But that was long ago, and the poor woman really cannot be blamed, since it was Kenny himself who ate his way there.

Kenny loved pepperoni pizza, or plain pizza, or garbage pizza with everything on it, including anchovies. Kenny could eat an entire slab of barbecued ribs, either beef or pork, and the spicier the sauce was, the more he approved. He was fond of rare prime rib and roast chicken and Rock Cornish game hens stuffed with rice, and he was hardly the sort to object to a nice sirloin or a platter of fried shrimp or a hunk of kielbasa. He liked his burgers with everything on them, and fries and onion rings on the side, please. There was nothing you could do to his friend the potato that would possibly turn him against it, but he was also partial to pasta and rice, to yams candied and un-, and even to mashed rutabagas.

"Desserts are my downfall," he would sometimes say, for he liked sweets of all varieties, especially devil's food cake and cannoli and hot apple pie with cheese (Cheddar, please), or maybe cold strawberry pie with whipped cream. "Bread is my downfall," he would say at other times, when it seemed likely that no dessert was forthcoming, and so saying he would rip off another chunk of sourdough or butter up another crescent roll or reach for another slice of garlic bread, which was a particular vice.

Kenny had a lot of particular vices. He thought himself an authority on both fine restaurants and fast-food franchises, and could discourse endlessly and knowledgeably about either. He relished Greek food and Chinese food and Japanese food and Korean food and German food and Italian food and French food and Indian food, and was always on the lookout for new ethnic groups so he might "expand my cultural horizons." When Saigon fell, Kenny speculated about how many of the Vietnamese refugees would be likely to open restaurants. When Kenny traveled, he always made it a point to gorge himself on the area's specialty, and he could tell you the best places to eat in any of twenty-four major American cities, while reminiscing fondly about the meals he had enjoyed in each of them. His favorite writers were James Beard and Calvin Trillin.

"I live a tasty life!" Kenny Dorchester would proclaim, beaming. And so he did. But Kenny also had a secret. He did not often think of it and never spoke it, but it was there nonetheless, down at the heart of him beneath all those great rolls of flesh, and not all his sauces could drown it, nor could his trusty fork keep it at bay.

Kenny Dorchester did not *like* being fat.

Kenny was like a man torn between two lovers, for while he loved his food with an abiding passion, he also dreamed of other loves, of women, and he knew that in order to secure the one he would have to give up the other, and that knowledge was his secret pain. Often he wrestled with the dilemmas posed by his situation. It seemed to Kenny that while it might be preferable to be slender and have a woman than to be fat and have only a crawfish bisque, nonetheless the latter was not entirely to be spurned. Both were sources of happiness, after all, and the real misery fell to those who gave up the one and failed to obtain the other. Nothing depressed or saddened Kenny so much as the sight of a fat person eating cottage cheese. Such pathetic human beings never seemed to get appreciably skinnier, Kenny thought, and were doomed to go through life bereft of both women and crawfish, a fate too grim to contemplate.

Yet despite all his misgivings, at times the secret pain inside Kenny Dorchester would flare up mightily, and fill him with a sense of resolve that made him feel as if anything might be possible. The sight of a particularly beautiful woman or the word of some new, painless, and wonderfully effective diet were particularly prone to trigger what Kenny thought of as "aberrations." When such moods came, Kenny would be driven to diet.

Over the years he tried every diet there was, briefly and secretly. He tried Dr. Atkins's diet and Dr. Stillman's diet, the grapefruit diet and the brown rice diet. He tried the liquid protein diet, which was truly disgusting. He lived for a week on nothing but Slender and Sego, until he had run through all of the flavors and gotten bored. He joined a Pounds-Off club and attended a few meetings, until he discovered that the company of fellow dieters did him no good whatsoever, since all they talked about was food. He went on a hunger strike that lasted until he got hungry. He tried the fruit juice diet, and the drinking man's diet (even though he was not a drinking man), and the martinis-and-whipped-cream diet (he omitted the martinis).

A hypnotist told him that his favorite foods tasted bad and he wasn't hungry anyway, but it was a damned lie, and that was that for hypnosis. He had his behavior modified so he put down his fork between bites, used small plates that looked full even with tiny portions, and wrote down every thing he ate in a notebook. That left him with stacks of notebooks, a great many small dishes to wash, and unusual manual dexterity in putting down and picking up his fork. His favorite diet was the one that said you could eat all you wanted of your favorite food, so long as you ate nothing *but* that. The only problem was that Kenny couldn't decide what was really his one true favorite, so he wound up eating ribs for a week, and pizza for a week, and Peking duck for a week (that was an expensive week), and losing no weight whatsoever, although he did have a great time.

Most of Kenny Dorchester's aberrations lasted for a week or two. Then, like a man coming out of a fog, he would look around and realize that he was absolutely miserable, losing relatively little weight, and in imminent danger of turning into one of those cottage-cheese fatties he so pitied. At that point he would chuck the diet, go out for a good meal, and be restored to his normal self for another six months, until his secret pain surfaced again.

Then, one Friday night, he spied Henry Moroney at the Slab.

The Slab was Kenny's favorite barbecue joint. It specialized in ribs, charred and meaty and served dripping with a sauce that Kenny approved of mightily. And on Fridays the Slab offered all the ribs you could eat for only fifteen dollars, which was prohibitively high for most people but a bargain for Kenny, who could eat a great many ribs. On that particular Friday, Kenny had just finished his first slab and was waiting for the second, sipping beer and eating bread, when he chanced to look up and realized, with a start, that the slim, haggard fellow in the next booth was, in fact, Henry Moroney.

Kenny Dorchester was nonplussed. The last time he had seen Henry Moroney, they had both been unhappy Pounds-Off members, and Moroney had been the only one in the club who weighed more than Kenny did. A great fat whale of a man, Moroney had carried about the cruel nickname of "Boney," as he confessed to his fellow members. Only now the nickname seemed to fit. Not only was Moroney skinny enough to hint at a rib cage under his skin, but the table in front of him was absolutely littered with bones. That was the detail that intrigued Kenny Dorchester. All those bones. He began to count, and he lost track before very long, because all the bones were disordered, strewn about on empty plates in little puddles of drying sauce. But from the sheer mass of them it was clear that Moroney had put away at least four slabs of ribs, maybe five.

It seemed to Kenny Dorchester that Henry "Boney" Moroney knew the secret. If there were a way to lose hundreds of pounds and still be able to consume five slabs of ribs at a sitting, that was something Kenny desperately needed to know. So he rose and walked over to Moroney's booth and squeezed in opposite him. "It *is* you," he said.

Moroney looked up as if he hadn't noticed Kenny until that very second. "Oh," he said in a thin, tired voice. "You." He seemed very weary, but Kenny thought that was probably natural for someone who had lost so much weight. Moroney's eyes were sunk in deep gray hollows, his flesh sagged in pale, empty folds, and he was slouching forward with his elbows on the table as if he were too exhausted to sit up straight. He looked terrible, but he had lost so much *weight*. . . .

"You look wonderful!" Kenny blurted. "How did you do it? How? You must tell me, Henry, really you must."

"No," Moroney whispered. "No, Kenny. Go away."

Kenny was taken aback. "Really!" he declared. "That's not very friendly. I'm not leaving until I know your secret, Henry. You owe it to me. Think of all the times we've broken bread together."

"Oh, Kenny," Moroney said, in his faint and terrible voice. "Go, please, go, you don't want to know, it's too . . . too. . . ." He stopped in midsentence, and a spasm passed across his face. He moaned. His head twisted wildly to the side, as if he were having some kind of fit, and his hands beat on the table. "Oooooo," he said.

"Henry, what's wrong?" Kenny said, alarmed. He was certain now that Boney Moroney had overdone this diet.

"Ohhhh," Moroney sighed in sudden relief. "Nothing, nothing. I'm fine." His voice had none of the enthusiasm of his words. "I'm wonderful, in fact. Wonderful, Kenny. I haven't been so slim since . . . since . . . why, never. It's a miracle." He smiled faintly. "I'll be at my goal, soon, and then it will be over. I think. Think I'll be at my goal. Don't know my weight, really." He put a hand to his brow. "I am slender, though, truly I am. Don't you think I look good?"

"Yes, yes," Kenny agreed impatiently. "But how? You must tell me. Surely not those Pounds-Off phonies. . . ."

"No," said Moroney weakly. "No, it was the monkey treatment. Here, I'll write it down for you." He took out a pencil and scrawled an address on a napkin.

Kenny stuffed the napkin into a pocket. "The monkey treatment? I've never heard of that. What is it?"

Henry Moroney licked his lips. "They . . ." he started, and then another fit hit him, and his head twitched around grotesquely. "Go," he said to Kenny, "just go. It works, Kenny, yes, oh. The monkey treatment, yes. I can't say more. You have the address. Excuse me." He placed his hands flat on the table and pushed himself to his feet, then walked over to the cashier, shuffling like a man twice his age. Kenny Dorchester watched him go, and decided that Moroney had *definitely* overdone this monkey treatment, whatever it was. He had never had tics or spasms before, or whatever that had been.

"You have to have a sense of proportion about these things," Kenny said stoutly to himself. He patted his pocket to make sure the napkin was still there, resolved that he would handle things more sensibly than Boney Moroney, and returned to his own booth and his second slab of ribs. He ate four that night, figuring that if he was going to start a diet tomorrow he had better get in some eating while the eating was good.

The next day being Saturday, Kenny was free to pursue the monkey treatment and dream of a new, slender him. He rose early, and immediately rushed to the bathroom to weigh himself on his digital scale, which he loved dearly because you didn't have to squint down at the numbers, since they lit up nice and bright and precise in red. This morning they lit up as 367. He had gained a few pounds, but had hardly minded. The monkey treatment would strip them off again soon enough.

Kenny tried to phone ahead, to make sure this place was open on Saturday, but that proved to be impossible. Moroney had written nothing but an address, and there was no diet center at that listing in the Yellow Pages, nor a health club, nor a doctor. Kenny looked in the white pages under "Monkey," but that yielded nothing. So there was nothing to do but go down there in person.

Even that was troublesome. The address was way down by the docks in a singularly unsavory neighborhood, and Kenny had a hard time getting a cab to take him there. He finally got his way by threatening to report the cabbie to the commissioner. Kenny Dorchester knew his rights.

Before long, though, he began to have his doubts. The narrow little streets they wound through were filthy and decaying, altogether unappetizing, and it occurred to Kenny that any diet center located down here might offer only dangerous quackery. The block in question was an old commercial strip gone to seed, and it put his hackles up even more. Half the stores were boarded closed, and the rest lurked behind filthy dark windows and iron gates. The cab pulled up in front of an absolutely miserable old brick storefront, flanked by two vacant lots full of rubble, its plate glass windows grimed over impenetrably. A faded Coca-Cola sign swung back and forth, groaning, above the door. But the number was the number that Boney Moroney had written down.

"Here you are," the cabbie said impatiently, as Kenny peered out the taxi window, aghast.

"This does not look correct," Kenny said. "I will investigate. Kindly wait here until I am certain this is the place."

The cabbie nodded, and Kenny slid over and levered himself out of the taxi. He had taken two steps when he heard the cab shift gears and pull away from the curb, screeching. He turned and watched in astonishment. "Here, you can't . . ." he began. But it did. He would most definitely report that man to the commissioner, he decided.

But meanwhile he was stranded down here, and it seemed foolish not to proceed when he had come this far. Whether he took the monkey treatment or not, no doubt they would let him use a phone to summon another cab. Kenny screwed up his resolution, and went on into the grimy, unmarked storefront. A bell tinkled as he opened the door.

It was dark inside. The dust and dirt on the windows kept out nearly all the sunlight, and it took a moment for Kenny's eyes to adjust. When they did, he saw to his horror that he had walked into someone's living room. One of those gypsy families that moved into abandoned stores, he thought. He was standing on a threadbare carpet, and around and about him was a scatter of old furniture, no doubt the best the Salvation Army had to offer. An ancient black-and-white TV set crouched in one corner, staring at him blindly. The room stank of urine. "Sorry," Kenny muttered feebly, terrified that some dark gypsy youth would come out of the shadows to knife him. "Sorry." He had stepped backward, groping behind him for the doorknob, when the man came out of the back room.

"Ah!" the man said, spying Kenny at once from tiny bright eyes. "Ah, the monkey treatment!" He rubbed his hands together and grinned. Kenny was terrified. The man was the fattest, grossest human being that Kenny had ever laid eyes on. He had squeezed through the door sideways. He was fatter than Kenny, fatter than Boney Moroney. He literally dripped with fat. And he was repulsive in other ways as well. He had the complexion of a mushroom, and minuscule little eyes almost invisible amid rolls of pale flesh. His corpulence seemed to have overwhelmed even his hair, of which he had very little. Barechested, he displayed vast areas of folded, bulging skin, and his huge breasts flopped as he came forward quickly and seized Kenny by the arm. "The monkey treatment!" he repeated eagerly, pulling Kenny forward. Kenny looked at him, in shock, and was struck dumb by his grin. When the man grinned, his mouth seemed to become half of his face, a grotesque semicircle full of shining white teeth.

"No," Kenny said at last, "no, I have changed my mind." Boney Moroney or no, he didn't think he cared to try this monkey treatment if it was administered by such as this. In the first place, it clearly could not be very effective, or else the man would not be so monstrously obese. Besides, it was probably dangerous, some quack potion of monkey hormones or something like that. "NO!" Kenny repeated more forcefully, trying to wrest his arm free from the grasp of the grotesquerie who held it.

But it was useless. The man was distinctly larger and infinitely stronger than Kenny, and he propelled him across the room with ease, oblivious to Kenny's protests, grinning like a maniac all the while. "Fat man," he burbled, as if to prove his point he reached out and seized one of Kenny's bulges and twisted painfully. "Fat, fat, fat, no good. Monkey treatment make you thin."

"Yes, but . . ."

"Monkey treatment," the man repeated, and somehow he had gotten behind Kenny. He put his weight against Kenny's back and pushed, and

Kenny staggered through a curtained doorway into the back room. The smell of urine was much stronger in there, strong enough to make him want to retch. It was pitch black, and from all sides Kenny heard rustlings and scurryings in the darkness. *Rats*, he thought wildly. Kenny was deathly afraid of rats. He fumbled about and propelled himself toward the square dim light that marked the curtain he had come through.

Before he was quite there, a high-pitched chittering sounded suddenly from behind him, sharp and rapid as fire from a machine gun. Then another voice took it up, then a third, and suddenly the dark was alive with the terrible hammering noise. Kenny put his hands over his ears and staggered through the curtain, but just as he emerged he felt something brush the back of his neck, something warm and hairy. "Aieeee!" he screamed, dancing out into the front room where the tremendous bare-chested madman was waiting patiently. Kenny hopped from one foot to the other, screeching, "Aieeee, a rat, a rat on my back. Get it off, get it *off!* He was trying to grab for it with both hands, but the thing was very quick, and shifted around so cleverly that he couldn't get ahold of it. But he felt it there, alive, moving. "Help me, help me!" he called out. "A rat!"

The proprietor grinned at him and shook his head, so all his many chins went bobbing merrily. "No, no," he said. "No rat, fat man. Monkey. You get the monkey treatment." Then he stepped forward and seized Kenny by the elbow again, and drew him over to a full-length mirror mounted on the wall. It was so dim in the room that Kenny could scarcely make out anything in the mirror, except that it wasn't wide enough and chopped off both his arms. The man stepped back and yanked a pull-cord dangling from the ceiling, and a single bare lightbulb clicked on overhead. The bulb swung back and forth, back and forth, so the light shifted crazily. Kenny Dorchester trembled and stared at the mirror.

"Oh," he said.

There was a monkey on his back.

Actually it was on his shoulders, its legs wrapped around his thick neck and twined together beneath his triple chin. He could feel its monkey hair scratching the back of his neck, could feel its warm little monkey paws lightly grasping his ears. It was a very tiny monkey. As Kenny looked into the mirror, he saw it peek out from behind his head, grinning hugely. It had quick darting eyes, coarse brown hair, and altogether too many shiny white teeth for Kenny's liking. Its long prehensile tail swayed about restlessly, like some hairy snake that had grown out of the back of Kenny's skull.

Kenny's heart was pounding away like some great air hammer lodged in his chest, and he was altogether distressed by this place, this man, and this monkey, but he gathered all his reserves and forced himself to be calm. It wasn't a rat, after all. The little monkey couldn't harm him. It had to be a trained monkey, the way it had perched on his shoulders. Its owner must let it ride around like this, and when Kenny had come unwillingly through that curtain, it had probably mistaken him. All fat men look alike in the dark.

Kenny grabbed behind him and tried to pull the monkey loose, but somehow he couldn't seem to get a grip on it. The mirror, reversing everything, just made it worse. He jumped up and down ponderously, shaking the entire room and making the furniture leap around every time he landed, but the monkey held on tight to his ears and could not be dislodged.

Finally, with what Kenny thought was incredible aplomb under the circumstances, he turned to the gross proprietor and said, "Your monkey, sir. Kindly help me remove it."

"No, no," the man said. "Make you skinny. Monkey treatment. You no want to be skinny?"

"Of course I do," Kenny said unhappily, "but this is absurd." He was confused. This monkey on his back seemed to be part of the monkey treatment, but that certainly didn't make very much sense.

"Go," the man said. He reached up and snapped off the light with a sharp tug that sent the bulb careening wildly again. Then he started toward Kenny, who backpedaled nervously. "Go," the man repeated, as he grabbed Kenny's arm again. "Out, out. You get monkey treatment, you go now."

"See here!" Kenny said furiously. "Let go of me! Get this monkey off me, do you hear? I don't want your monkey! Do you hear me? Quit pushing, sir! I tell you, I have friends with the police department, you aren't going to get away with this. Here now . . ."

But all his protestations were useless. The man was a veritable tidal wave of sweating, smelling pale flesh, and he put his weight against Kenny and propelled him helplessly toward the door. The bell rang again as he pulled it open and shoved Kenny out into the garish bright sunlight.

"I'm not going to pay for this!" Kenny said stoutly, staggering. "Not a cent, do you hear?"

"No charge for monkey treatment," the man said, grinning.

"At least let me call a cab," Kenny began, but it was too late, the man had closed the door. Kenny stepped forward angrily and tried to yank it back open, but it did not budge. Locked. "Open up in there!"

Kenny demanded at the top of his lungs. There was no reply. He shouted again, and grew suddenly and uncomfortably aware that he was being stared at. Kenny turned around. Across the street three old winos were sitting on the stoop of a boarded-up store, passing a bottle in a brown paper bag and regarding him through wary eyes.

That was when Kenny Dorchester recalled that he was standing there in the street in broad daylight with a monkey on his back.

A flush crept up his neck and spread across his cheeks. He felt very silly. "A pet!" he shouted to the winos, forcing a smile. "Just my little pet!" They went on staring. Kenny gave a last angry look at the locked door, and set off down the street, his legs pumping furiously. He had to get to someplace private.

Rounding the corner, he came upon a dark, narrow alley behind two gray old tenement buildings, and ducked inside, wheezing for breath. He sat down heavily on a trash can, pulled out his handkerchief, and mopped his brow. The monkey shifted just a bit, and Kenny felt it move. "Off me!" he shouted, reaching up and back again to try to wrench it off by the scruff of its neck, only to have it elude him once more. He tucked away his handkerchief and groped behind his head with both hands, but he just couldn't get ahold of it. Finally, exhausted, he stopped, and tried to think.

The legs! he thought. The legs under his chins! That's the ticket! Very calmly and deliberately, he reached up, felt for the monkey's legs, and wrapped one big fleshy hand around each of them. He took a deep breath and then savagely tried to yank them apart, as if they were two ends of a giant wishbone.

The monkey attacked him.

One hand twisted his right ear painfully, until it felt like it was being pulled clean off his head. The other started hammering against his temple, beating a furious tattoo. Kenny Dorchester yelped in distress and let go of the monkey's legs—which he hadn't budged for all his efforts. The monkey quit beating on him and released his ear. Kenny sobbed, half with relief and half with frustration. He felt wretched.

He sat there in that filthy alley for ages, defeated in his efforts to remove the monkey and afraid to go back to the street where people would point at him and laugh, or make rude, insulting comments under their breath. It was difficult enough going through life as a fat man, Kenny thought. How much worse, then, to face the cruel world as a fat man with a monkey on his back. Kenny did not want to know. He resolved to sit there on that trash can in the dark alley until he died or the monkey died, rather than face shame and ridicule on the streets.

His resolve endured about an hour. Then Kenny Dorchester began to get hungry. Maybe people would laugh at him, but they had always laughed at him, so what what did it matter? Kenny rose and dusted himself off, while the monkey settled itself more comfortably on his neck. He ignored it, and decided to go in search of a pepperoni pizza.

He did not find one easily. The abysmal slum in which he had been stranded had a surfeit of winos, dangerous-looking teenagers, and burned-out or boarded-up buildings, but it had precious few pizza parlors. Nor did it have any taxis. Kenny walked down the main thoroughfare with brisk dignity, looking neither left nor right, heading for safer neighborhoods as fast as his plump little legs could carry him. Twice he came upon phone booths, and eagerly fetched out a coin to summon transportation, but both times the phones proved to be out of order. Vandals, thought Kenny Dorchester, were as bad as rats.

Finally, after what seemed like hours of walking, he stumbled upon a sleazy café. The lettering on the window said JOHN'S GRILL, and there was a neon sign above the door that said, simply, EAT. Kenny was very familiar with those three lovely letters, and he recognized the sign two blocks off. It called to him like a beacon. Even before he entered, he knew it was rather unlikely that such a place would include pepperoni pizza on its menu, but by that time Kenny had ceased to care.

As he pushed the door aside, Kenny experienced a brief moment of apprehension, partially because he felt very out of place in the café, where the rest of the diners all appeared to be muggers, and partially because he was afraid they would refuse to serve him because of the monkey on his back. Acutely uncomfortable in the doorway, he moved quickly to a small table in an obscure corner, where he hoped to escape the curious stares. A gaunt gray-haired waitress in a faded pink uniform moved purposefully toward him, and Kenny sat with his eyes downcast, playing nervously with the salt, pepper, ketchup, dreading the moment when she arrived and said, "Hey, you can't bring that thing in here!"

But when the waitress reached his table, she simply pulled a pad out of her apron pocket and stood poised, pencil in hand. "Well?" she demanded. "What'll it be?"

Kenny stared up in shock, and smiled. He stammered a bit, then recovered himself and ordered a cheese omelet with a double side of bacon, coffee and a large glass of milk, and cinnamon toast. "Do hash browns come with?" he asked hopefully, but the waitress shook her head and parted.

What a marvelous, kind woman, Kenny thought as he waited for his meal and shredded a paper napkin thoughtfully. What a wonderful place! Why, they hadn't even mentioned his monkey! How very polite of them.

The food arrived shortly. "Ahhhh," Kenny said as the waitress laid it out in front of him on the Formica tabletop. He was ravenous. He selected a slice of cinnamon toast, and brought it to his mouth.

And a little monkey darted out from behind his head and snatched it clean away.

Kenny Dorchester sat in numb surprise for an instant, his suddenly empty hand poised before his open mouth. He heard the monkey eating his toast, chomping noisily. Then, before Kenny had quite comprehended what was happening, the monkey's great long tail snaked in under his armpit, curled around his glass of milk, and spirited it up and away in the blink of an eye.

"*Hey!*" Kenny said, but he was much too slow. Behind his back he heard slurping, sucking sounds, and all of a sudden the glass came vaulting over his left shoulder. He caught it before it fell and smashed, and set it down unsteadily. The monkey's tail came stealthily around and headed for his bacon. Kenny grabbed up a fork and stabbed at it, but the monkey was faster than he was. The bacon vanished, and the tines of the fork bent against the hard Formica uselessly.

By then Kenny knew he was in a race. Dropping the bent fork, he used his spoon to cut off a chunk of the omelet, dripping cheese, and he bent forward as he lifted it, quick as he could. The monkey was quicker. A little hand flashed in from somewhere, and the spoon had only a tantalizing gob of half-melted cheese remaining on it when it reached Kenny's mouth. He lunged back toward his plate, and loaded up again, but it didn't matter how fast he tried to be. The monkey had two paws and a tail, and once it even used a little monkey foot to snatch something away from him. In hardly any time at all, Kenny Dorchester's meal was gone. He sat there staring down at the empty, greasy plate, and he felt tears gathering in his eyes.

The waitress reappeared without Kenny noticing. "My, you sure are a hungry one," she said to him, ripping off his check from her pad and putting it in front of him. "Polished that off quicker than anyone I ever saw."

Kenny looked up at her. "But I *didn't*," he protested. "The monkey ate it all!"

The waitress looked at him very oddly. "The monkey?" she said, uncertainly.

"The monkey," Kenny said. He did not care for the way she was staring at him, like he was crazy or something.

"What monkey?" she asked. "You didn't sneak no animals in here, did you? The board of health don't allow no animals in here, mister."

"What do you mean, *sneak?*" Kenny said in annoyance. "Why, the

monkey is right on my—" He never got a chance to finish. Just then the
monkey hit him, a tremendous hard blow on the left side of his face.
The force of it twisted his head half-around, and Kenny yelped in pain
and shock.

The waitress seemed concerned. "You OK, mister?" she asked. "You
ain't gonna have a fit, are you, twitching like that?"

"I *didn't twitch!*" Kenny all but shouted. "The goddamned monkey
hit me! Can't you see?"

"Oh," said the waitress, taking a step backward. "Oh, of course. Your
monkey hit you. Pesky little things, ain't they?"

Kenny pounded his fists on the table in frustration. "Never mind," he
said, "just never mind." He snatched up the check—the monkey did
not take that away from him, he noted—and rose. "Here," he said,
pulling out his wallet. "And you have a phone in this place, don't you?
Call me a cab, all right? You can do that, can't you?"

"Sure," the waitress said, moving to the register to ring up his meal.
Everyone in the café was staring at him. "Sure, mister," she muttered.
"A cab. We'll get you a cab right away."

Kenny waited, fuming. The cab driver made no comment on his
monkey. Instead of going home, he took the cab to his favorite pizza
place, three blocks from his apartment. Then he stormed right in and
ordered a large pepperoni. The monkey ate it all, even when Kenny tried
to confuse it by picking up one slice in each hand and moving them
simultaneously toward his mouth. Unfortunately, the monkey had two
hands as well, both of them faster than Kenny's.

When the pizza was completely gone, Kenny thought for a moment,
summoned over the waitress, and ordered a second. This time he got a
large anchovy. He thought that was very clever. Kenny Dorchester had
never met anyone else beside himself who liked anchovy pizza. Those
little salty fishes would be his salvation, he thought. To increase the
odds, when the pizza arrived Kenny picked up the hot pepper shaker
and covered it with enough hot peppers to ignite a major conflagration.
Then, feeling confident, he tried to eat a slice.

The monkey liked anchovy pizza with lots of hot peppers. Kenny
Dorchester almost wept.

He went from the pizza place to the Slab, from the Slab to a fine
Greek restaurant to a local McDonald's, from McDonald's to a bakery
that made the most marvelous chocolate éclairs. Sooner or later, Kenny
Dorchester thought, the monkey would be full. It was only a very little
monkey, after all. How much food could it eat? He would just keep on
ordering food, he resolved, and the monkey would either reach its limits
or rupture and die.

That day Kenny spent more than two hundred dollars on meals.

He got absolutely nothing to eat.

The monkey seemed to be a bottomless pit. If it had a capacity, that capacity was surely greater than the capacity of Kenny's wallet. Finally he was forced to admit defeat. The monkey could not be stuffed into submission.

Kenny cast about for another tactic, and finally hit on it. Monkeys were stupid, after all, even invisible monkeys with prodigious appetites. Smiling slyly, Kenny went to a neighborhood supermarket, and picked up a box of banana pudding (it seemed appropriate) and a box of rat poison. Humming a spry little tune, he walked on home, and set to work making the pudding, stirring in liberal amounts of the rat poison as it cooked. The poison was nicely odorless. The pudding smelled wonderful. Kenny poured it into some dessert cups to cool, and watched television for an hour or so. Finally he rose nonchalantly, went to the refrigerator, and got out a pudding and a nice big spoon. He sat back down in front of the set, spooned up a generous glob of pudding, and brought it to his open mouth. Where he paused. And paused. And waited.

The monkey did nothing.

Maybe it was full at last, Kenny thought. He put aside the poisoned pudding and rushed back to his kitchen, where he found a box of vanilla wafers hiding on a shelf, and a few forlorn Fig Newtons as well.

The monkey ate all of them.

A tear trickled down Kenny's cheek. The monkey would let him have all the poisoned pudding he wanted, it seemed, but nothing else. He reached back halfheartedly and tried to grab the monkey once again, thinking maybe all that eating would have slowed it down some, but it was a vain hope. The monkey evaded him, and when Kenny persisted the monkey hit his finger. Kenny yowled and snatched his hand back. His finger was bleeding. He sucked on it. That much, at least, the monkey permitted him.

When he had washed his finger and wrapped a Band-Aid around it, Kenny returned to his living room and seated himself heavily, weary and defeated, in front of his television set. An old rerun of "The Galloping Gourmet" was coming on. He couldn't stand it. He jabbed at his remote control to change the channel, and watched blindly for hours, sunk in despair, weeping at the Betty Crocker commercials. Finally, during the late late show, he stirred a little at one of the frequent public service announcements. That was it, he thought; he had to enlist others, he had to get help.

He picked up his phone and punched out the Crisis Line number.

The woman who answered sounded kind of sympathetic and very

beautiful, and Kenny began to pour out his heart to her, all about the monkey that wouldn't let him eat, about how nobody else seemed to notice the monkey, about . . . but he had barely gotten his heart-pouring going good when the monkey smashed him across the side of the head. Kenny moaned. "What's wrong?" the woman asked. The monkey yanked his ear. Kenny tried to ignore the pain and keep on talking, but the monkey kept hurting him until finally he shuddered and sobbed and hung up the phone.

This is a nightmare, Kenny thought, a terrible nightmare. And so thinking, he pushed himself to his feet and staggered off to bed, hoping that everything would be normal in the morning, that the monkey would have been nothing but part of some wretched dream, no doubt brought on by indigestion.

The merciless little monkey would not even allow him to sleep properly, Kenny discovered. He was accustomed to sleeping on his back, with his hands folded very primly on his stomach. But when he undressed and tried to assume that position, the monkey fists came raining down on his poor head like some furious hairy hail. The monkey was not about to be squashed between Kenny's bulk and the pillows, it seemed. Kenny squealed with pain and rolled over on his stomach. He was very uncomfortable this way and had difficulty falling asleep, but it was the only way the monkey would leave him alone.

The next morning Kenny Dorchester drifted slowly into wakefulness, his cheek mashed against the pillows and his right arm still asleep. He was afraid to move. It was all a dream, he told himself, there is no monkey—what a silly thing that would be, monkey indeed!—it was only that Boney Moroney had told him about this "monkey treatment," and he had slept on it and had a nightmare. He couldn't feel anything on his back, not a thing. This was just like any other morning. He opened a bleary eye. His bedroom looked perfectly normal. Still he was afraid to move. It was very peaceful lying here like this, monkeyless, and he wanted to savor this feeling. So Kenny lay very still for the longest time, watching the numbers on his digital clock change slowly.

Then his stomach growled at him. It was very upset. Kenny gathered up his courage. "There is no monkey!" he proclaimed loudly, and he sat up in bed.

He felt the monkey shift.

Kenny trembled and almost started to weep again, but he controlled himself with an effort. No monkey was going to get the best of Kenny Dorchester, he told himself. Grimacing, he donned his slippers and plodded into the bathroom.

The monkey peered out cautiously from behind his head while Kenny was shaving. He glared at it in the bathroom mirror. It seemed to have grown a bit, but that was hardly surprising, considering how much it had eaten yesterday. Kenny toyed with the idea of trying to cut the monkey's throat, but decided that his Norelco electric shaver was not terribly well suited to that end. And even if he used a knife, trying to stab behind his own back while looking in the mirror was a dangerously uncertain proposition.

Before leaving the bathroom, Kenny was struck by a whim. He stepped on his scale.

The numbers lit up at once: 367. The same as yesterday, he thought. The monkey weighed nothing. He frowned. No, that had to be wrong. No doubt the little monkey weighed a pound or two, but its weight was offset by whatever poundage Kenny had lost. He had to have lost *some* weight, he reasoned, since he hadn't been allowed to eat anything for ever so long. He stepped off the scale, then got back on quickly, just to double-check. It still read 367. Kenny was certain that he had lost weight. Perhaps some good would come of his travails after all. The thought made him feel oddly cheerful.

Kenny grew even more cheerful at breakfast. For the first time since he had gotten his monkey, he managed to get some food in his mouth.

When he arrived at the kitchen, he debated between French toast and bacon and eggs, but only briefly. Then he decided that he would never get to taste either. Instead, with a somber fatalism, Kenny fetched down a bowl and filled it with corn flakes and milk. The monkey would probably steal it all anyway, he thought, so there was no sense going to any trouble.

Quick as he could, he hurried the spoon into his mouth. The monkey grabbed it away. Kenny had expected it, had known it would happen, but when the monkey hand wrenched the spoon away he nonetheless felt a sudden and terrible grief. "No," he said uselessly. "No, no, no." He could hear the corn flakes crunching in that filthy monkey mouth, and he felt milk dripping down the back of his neck. Tears gathered in his eyes as he stared down at the bowl of corn flakes, so near and yet so far.

Then he had an idea.

Kenny Dorchester lunged forward and stuck his face right down in the bowl.

The monkey twisted his ear and shrieked and pounded on his temple, but Kenny didn't care. He was sucking in milk gleefully and gobbling up as many corn flakes as his mouth could hold. By the time the monkey's tail lashed around angrily and sent the bowl sailing from the table to shatter on the floor, Kenny had a huge wet mouthful. His cheeks bulged and milk dribbled down his chin, and somehow he'd gotten a corn flake up his right nostril, but Kenny was in heaven. He chewed and swallowed as fast as he could, almost choking on the food.

When it was all gone he licked his lips and rose triumphantly. "Ha, ha, ha." He walked back to his bedroom with great dignity and dressed, sneering at the monkey in the full-length bedroom mirror. He had beaten it.

In the days and weeks that followed, Kenny Dorchester settled into a new sort of daily routine and an uneasy accommodation with his monkey. It proved easier than Kenny might have imagined, except at mealtimes. When he was not attempting to get food into his mouth, it was almost possible to forget about the monkey entirely. At work it sat peacefully on his back while Kenny shuffled his papers and made his phone calls. His coworkers either failed to notice his monkey or were sufficiently polite so as not to comment on it. The only difficulty came one day at coffee break, when Kenny foolhardily approached the coffee vendor in an effort to secure a cheese Danish. The monkey ate nine of them before Kenny could stagger away, and the man insisted that Kenny had done it when his back was turned.

Simply by avoiding mirrors, a habit that Kenny Dorchester now began to cultivate as assiduously as any vampire, he was able to keep his mind off the monkey for most of the day. He had only one difficulty, though it occurred thrice daily: breakfast, lunch, and dinner. At those times the monkey asserted itself forcefully, and Kenny was forced to deal with it. As the weeks passed, he gradually fell into the habit of ordering food that could be served in bowls, so that he might practice what he termed his "Kellogg maneuver." By this strategem, Kenny usually managed to get at least a few mouthfuls to eat each and every day.

To be sure, there *were* problems. People would stare at him rather strangely when he used the Kellogg maneuver in public, and sometimes make rude comments on his table manners. At a chili emporium Kenny liked to frequent, the proprietor assumed he had suffered a heart attack when Kenny dove toward his chili, and was very angry with him afterward. On another occasion a bowl of soup left him with facial burns that made it look as though he were constantly blushing. And the last straw came when he was thrown bodily out of his favorite seafood restaurant in the world, simply because he plunged his face into a bowl of crawfish bisque and began sucking it up noisily. Kenny stood in the street and berated them loudly and forcefully, reminding them how much money he had spent there over the years. Thereafter he ate only at home.

Despite the limited success of his Kellogg maneuver, Kenny Dorchester still lost nine-tenths of every meal to the voracious monkey on his back. At first he was constantly hungry, frequently depressed, and full of schemes for ridding himself of his monkey. The only problem with these schemes was that none of them seemed to work. One Saturday, Kenny went to the monkey house at the zoo, hoping that his monkey might hop off to play with others of its kind, or perhaps go in pursuit of some attractive monkey of the opposite sex. Instead, no sooner had he entered the monkey house than all the monkeys imprisoned therein ran to the bars of their cages and began to chitter and scream and spit and leap up and down madly. His own monkey answered in kind, and when some of the caged monkeys began to throw peanut husks and other bits of garbage Kenny clapped his hands over his ears and fled.

On another occasion he allowed himself to visit a local saloon, and ordered a number of boilermakers, a drink he understood to be particularly devastating. His intent was to get his monkey so blind-drunk that it might be easily removed. This experiment, too, had rather unfortunate consequences. The monkey drank the boilermakers as fast as Kenny could order them, but after the third one it began to keep time to the disco music from the jukebox by beating on the top of Kenny's head. The next morning it was Kenny who woke with the pounding headache; the monkey seemed fine.

After a time, Kenny finally put all his scheming aside. Failure had discouraged him, and moreover the matter seemed somehow less urgent than it had originally. He was seldom hungry after the first week, in fact. Instead he went through a brief period of weakness, marked by frequent dizzy spells, and then a kind of euphoria settled over him. He felt just wonderful, and even better, he was losing weight!

To be sure, it did not show on his scale. Every morning he climbed up on it, and every morning it lit up as 367. But that was only because it was weighing the monkey as well as himself. Kenny knew he was losing; he could almost feel the pounds and inches just melting away, and some of his coworkers in the office remarked on it as well. Kenny owned up to it, beaming. When they asked him how he was doing it, he winked and replied, "The monkey treatment! The mysterious monkey treatment!" He said no more than that. The one time he tried to explain, the monkey fetched him such a wallop it almost took his head off, and Kenny's friends began to mutter about his strange spasms.

Finally the day came when Kenny had to tell his cleaner to take in all his pants a few inches. That was one of the most delightful tasks of his life, he thought.

All the pleasure went right out of the moment when he exited the store, however, and chanced to glance briefly to his side and see his reflection in the window. At home Kenny had long since removed all his mirrors, so he was shocked at the sight of his monkey. It had grown. It was a little thing no longer. Now it hunched on his back like some evil deformed chimpanzee, and its grinning face loomed above his head instead of peering out behind it. The monkey was grossly fat beneath its sparse brown hair, almost as wide as it was tall, and its great long tail drooped all the way to the ground. Kenny stared at it with horror, and it grinned back at him. No wonder he had been having backaches recently, he thought.

He walked home slowly, all the jauntiness gone out of his step, trying to think. A few neighborhood dogs followed him up the street, barking at his monkey. Kenny ignored them. He had long since learned that dogs could see his monkey, just like the monkeys at the zoo. He suspected that drunks could see it as well. One man had stared at him for a very long time that night he had visited the saloon. Of course, the fellow might just have been staring at those vanishing boilermakers.

Back in his apartment Kenny Dorchester stretched out on his couch on his stomach, stuck a pillow underneath his chin, and turned on his television set. He paid no attention to the screen, however. He was trying to figure things out. Even the Pizza Hut commercials were insufficiently distracting, although Kenny did absently mutter "Ah-h-h-h" like you were supposed to when the slice of pizza, dripping long strands of cheese, was first lifted from the pan.

When the show ended, Kenny got up and turned off the set and sat himself down at his dining room table. He found a piece of paper and a stubby little pencil. Very carefully, he block-printed a formula across the paper, and stared at it.

ME + MONKEY = 367 POUNDS

There were certain disturbing implications in that formula, Kenny thought. The more he considered them, the less he liked them. He was definitely losing weight, to be sure, and that was not to be sneered at— nonetheless, the grim inflexibility of the formula hinted that most of the gains traditionally attributed to weight loss would never be his to enjoy. No matter how much fat he shed, he would continue to carry around 367 pounds, and the strain on his body would be the same. As for becoming svelte and dashing and attractive to women, how could he even consider it so long as he had his monkey? Kenny thought of how a dinner date might go for him, and shuddered. "Where will it all end?" he said aloud.

The monkey shifted, and snickered a vile little snicker.

Kenny pursed his lips in firm disapproval. This could not go on, he resolved. He decided to go straight to the source on the morrow, and with that idea planted firmly in his mind, he took himself to bed.

The next day, after work, Kenny Dorchester returned by cab to the seedy neighborhood where he had been subjected to the monkey treatment.

The storefront was gone.

Kenny sat in the back seat of the taxi (this time he had the good sense not to get out, and moreover had tipped the driver handsomely in advance) and blinked in confusion. A tiny wet blubbery moan escaped his lips. The address was right, he knew it, he still had the slip of paper that had brought him there in the first place. But where he had found a grimy brick storefront adorned by a faded Coca-Cola sign and flanked by two vacants lots, now there was only one large vacant lot, choked with weeds and rubbish and broken bricks. "Oh, no," Kenny said. "Oh, no."

"You O.K.?" asked the lady driving the cab.

"Yes," Kenny muttered. "Just . . . just wait, please. I have to think." He held his head in his hands. He feared he was going to develop a splitting headache. Suddenly he felt weak and dizzy. And very hungry. The meter ticked. The cabbie whistled. Kenny thought. The street looked just as he remembered it, except for the missing storefront. It was just as dirty, the old winos were still on their stoop, the . . .

Kenny rolled down the window. "You, sir!" he called out to one of the winos. The man stared at him. "Come here, sir!" Kenny yelled.

Warily, the old man shuffled across the street.

Kenny fetched out a dollar bill from his wallet and pressed it into the man's hand. "Here, friend," he said, "Go and buy yourself some vintage Thunderbird, if you will."

"Why you givin' me this?" the wino said suspiciously.

"I wish you to answer me a question. What has become of the building that was standing there." Kenny pointed, "—a few weeks ago."

The man stuffed the dollar into his pocket quickly. "Ain't been no buildin' there fo' years," he said.

"I was afraid of that," Kenny said. "Are you certain? I was here in the not-so-distant past and I *distinctly* recall . . ."

"No buildin'," the wino said firmly. He turned and walked away, but after a few steps he paused and glanced back. "You're one of them fat guys," he said accusingly.

"What do you know about . . . ahem . . . overweight men?"

"See 'em wanderin' round over there, all the time. Crazy, too. Yellin' at thin air, playin' with some kind of animals. Yeah, I 'member you. You're one of them fat guys, all right." He scowled at Kenny, confused. "Looks like you lost some of that blubber, though. Real good. Thanks for the dollar."

Kenny Dorchester watched him return to his stoop and begin conversing animatedly with his colleagues. With a tremulous sigh, Kenny rolled up the window, glanced at the empty lot again, and bid his driver take him home. Him and his monkey, that is.

Weeks went dripping by and Kenny Dorchester lived as if in a trance. He went to work, shuffled his papers, mumbled pleasantries to his coworkers, struggled and schemed for his meager mouthfuls of food, avoided mirrors. The scale read 367. His flesh melted away from him at a precipitous rate. He developed slack, droopy jowls, and his skin sagged all about his middle, looking as flaccid and pitiful as a used condom. He began to have fainting spells, brought on by hunger. At times he staggered and lurched about the street, his thinning and weakened legs unable to support the weight of his growing monkey. His vision got blurry.

Once he even thought that his hair had started to fall out, but that at least was a false alarm; it was the monkey who was losing hair, thank goodness. It shed all over the place, ruining his furniture, and even daily vacuuming didn't seem to help much. Soon Kenny stopped trying to clean up. He lacked the energy. He lacked the energy for just about everything, in fact. Rising from a chair was a major undertaking. Cooking dinner was impossible torment—but he did *that* anyway, since the monkey beat him severely when it was not fed. Nothing seemed to matter very much to Kenny Dorchester. Nothing but the terrible tale of his scale each morning, and the formula that he had a scotchtaped to his bathroom wall.

ME + MONKEY = 367 POUNDS

He wondered how much was ME anymore, and how much was MONKEY, but he did not really want to find out. One day, following the dictates of a kind of feeble whim, Kenny made a sudden grab for the monkey's legs under his chin, hoping against hope that it had gotten slow and obese and that he would be able to yank it from his back. His hands closed on nothing. On his own pale flesh. The monkey's legs did not seem to be there, though Kenny could still feel its awful crushing weight. He patted his neck and breast in dim confusion, staring down at himself, and noting absently that he could see his feet. He wondered how long that had been true. They seemed to be perfectly nice feet, Kenny Dorchester thought, although the legs to which they were attached were alarmingly gaunt.

Slowly his mind wandered back to the quandary at hand—what had become of the monkey's hind legs? Kenny frowned and puzzled and tried to work it all out in his head, but nothing occurred to him. Finally he slid his newly discovered feet into a pair of bedroom slippers and shuffled to the closet were he had stored all of his mirrors. Closing his eyes, he reached in, fumbled about, and found the full-length mirror that had once hung on his bedroom wall. It was a large, wide mirror. Working entirely by touch, Kenny fetched it out, carried it a few feet, and painstakingly propped it up against a wall. Then he held his breath and opened his eyes.

There in the mirror stood a gaunt, gray, skeletal-looking fellow, hunched over and sickly. On his back, grinning, was a thing the size of a gorilla. A very obese gorilla. It had a long, pale, snakelike tail, and great long arms, and it was as white as a maggot and entirely hairless. It had no legs. It was . . . attached to him now, growing right out of his back. Its grin was terrible, and filled up half of its face. It looked very like the gross proprietor of the monkey treatment emporium, in fact. Why had he never noticed that before? Of course, of course.

Kenny Dorchester turned from the mirror, and cooked the monkey a big rich dinner before going to bed.

That night he dreamed of how it all started, back in the Slab when he had met Boney Moroney. In his nightmare a great evil white thing rode atop Moroney's shoulders, eating slab after slab of ribs, but Kenny politely pretended not to notice while he and Boney made bright, spritely conversation. Then the thing ran out of ribs, so it reached down and lifted one of Boney's arms and began to eat his hand. The bones crunched nicely, and Moroney kept right on talking. The creature had eaten its way up to the elbow when Kenny woke screaming, covered with a cold sweat. He had wet his bed, too.

Agonizingly, he pushed himself up and staggered to the toilet, where he dry-heaved for ten minutes. The monkey, angry at being wakened, gave him a desultory slap from time to time.

And then a furtive light came into Kenny Dorchester's eyes. "Boney," he whispered. Hurriedly, he scrambled back to his bedroom on hands and knees, rose, and threw on some clothes. It was three in the morning, but Kenny knew there was no time to waste. He looked up an address in his phone book, and called a cab.

Boney Moroney lived in a tall, modern high-rise by the river, with moonlight shining brightly off its silver-mirrored flanks. When Kenny staggered in, he found the night doorman asleep at his station, which was just as well. Kenny tiptoed past him to the elevators and rode up to the eighth floor. The monkey on his back had begun stirring now, and seemed uneasy and ill-tempered.

Kenny's finger trembled as he pushed the round black button set in the door to Moroney's apartment, just beneath the eyehole. Musical chimes sounded loudly within, startling in the morning stillness. Kenny leaned on the button. The music played on and on. Finally he heard footsteps, heavy and threatening. The peephole opened and closed again. Then the door swung open.

The apartment was black, though the far wall was made entirely of glass, so the moonlight illuminated the darkness softly. Outlined against the stars and the lights of the city stood the man who had opened the door. He was hugely, obscenely fat, and his skin was a pasty fungoid white, and he had little dark eyes set deep into crinkles in his broad suety face. He wore nothing but a vast pair of striped shorts. His breasts flopped about against his chest when he shifted his weight. And when he smiled, his teeth filled up half his face. A great crescent moon of teeth. He smiled when he saw Kenny, and Kenny's monkey. Kenny felt sick. The thing in the door weighed twice as much as the one on his back. Kenny trembled. "Where is he?" he whispered softly. "Where is Boney? What have you done to him?"

The creature laughed, and its pendulous breasts flounced about wildly as it shook with mirth. The monkey on Kenny's back began to laugh, too, a higher, thinner laughter as sharp as the edge of a knife. It reached down and twisted Kenny's ear cruelly. Suddenly a vast fear and a vast anger filled Kenny Dorchester. He summoned all the strength left in his wasted body and pushed forward, and somehow, somehow, he barged past the obese colossus who barred his way and staggered into the interior of the apartment. "Boney," he called, "where are you, Boney? It's me, Kenny."

There was no answer. Kenny went from room to room. The apartment was filthy, a shambles. There was no sign of Boney Moroney anywhere. When Kenny came panting back to the living room, the monkey shifted abruptly, and threw him off balance. He stumbled and fell hard. Pain went shooting up through his knees, and he cut open one outstretched hand on the edge of the chrome-and-glass coffee table. Kenny began to weep.

He heard the door close, and the thing that lived here moved slowly toward him. Kenny blinked back tears and stared at the approach of those two mammoth legs, pale in the moonlight, sagging all around with fat. He looked up and it was like gazing up the side of a mountain. Far, far above him grinned those terrible mocking teeth. "*Where is he?*" Kenny Dorchester whispered. "What have you done with poor Boney?"

The grin did not change. The thing reached down a meaty hand, fingers as thick as a length of kielbasa, and snagged the waistband of the baggy striped shorts. It pulled them down clumsily, and they settled to the ground like a parachute, bunching around its feet.

"Oh, no," said Kenny Dorchester.

The thing had no genitals. Hanging down between its legs, almost touching the carpet now that it had been freed from the confines of the soiled shorts, was a wrinkled droopy bag of skin, long and gaunt, growing from the creature's crotch. But as Kenny stared at it in horror, it thrashed feebly, and stirred, and the loose folds of flesh separated briefly into tiny arms and legs.

Then it opened its eyes.

Kenny Dorchester screamed and suddenly he was back on his feet, lurching away from the grinning obscenity in the center of the room. Between its legs, the thing that had been Boney Moroney raised its pitiful stick-thin arms in supplication. "Oh, nooooo," Kenny moaned, blubbering, and he danced about wildly, the vast weight of his monkey heavy on his back. Round and round he danced in the dimness, in the moonlight, searching for an escape from this madness.

Beyond the plate glass wall the lights of the city beckoned.

Kenny paused and panted and stared at them. Somehow the monkey must have known what he was thinking, for suddenly it began to beat on him wildly, to twist at his ears, to rain savage blows all around his head. But Kenny Dorchester paid no mind. With a smile that was almost beatific, he gathered the last of his strength and rushed pell-mell toward the moonlight.

The glass shattered into a million glittering shards, and Kenny smiled all the way down.

It was the smell that told him he was still alive, the smell of disinfectant, and the feel of starched sheets beneath him. A hospital, he thought amidst a haze of pain. He was in a hospital. Kenny wanted to cry. Why hadn't he died? Oh, why, oh, why? He opened his eyes, and tried to say something.

Suddenly a nurse was there, standing over him, feeling his brow and looking down with concern. Kenny wanted to beg her to kill him, but the words would not come. She went away, and when she came back she had others with her.

A chubby young man stood by his side and touched him and prodded him here and there. Kenny's mouth worked soundlessly. "Easy," the doctor said. "You'll be all right, Mr. Dorchester, but you have a long way to go. You're in a hospital. You're a very lucky man. You fell eight stories. You ought to be dead."

I want to be dead, Kenny thought, and he shaped the words very,

very carefully with his mouth, but no one seemed to hear them. Maybe the monkey has taken over, he thought. Maybe I can't even talk anymore.

"He wants to say something," the nurse said.

"I can see that," said the chubby young doctor. "Mr. Dorchester, please don't strain yourself. Really. If you are trying to ask about your friend, I'm afraid he wasn't as lucky as you. He was killed by the fall. You would have died as well, but fortunately you landed on top of him."

Kenny's fear and confusion must have been obvious, for the nurse put a gentle hand on his arm. "The other man," she said patiently. "The fat one. You can thank God he was so fat, too. He broke your fall like a giant pillow."

And finally Kenny Dorchester understood what they were saying, and he began to weep, but now he was weeping for joy, and trembling.

Three days later, he managed his first word. "Pizza," he said, and it came weak and hoarse from between his lips, but the sound elated him and he repeated it, louder, and then louder still, and before long he was pushing the nurse's call button and shouting and pushing and shouting. "Pizza, pizza, pizza, pizza," he chanted, and he would not be calm until they ordered one for him. Nothing had ever tasted so good.

PAT CADIGAN

Nearly Departed

Born in Schenectady, New York, Pat Cadigan is one of the best new writers in SF and is well on her way to becoming one of the Big Names of the '80s. For many years, Cadigan was primarily known as co-editor of *Shayol*, perhaps the best of the semiprozines (it was honored with a World Fantasy Award in the "Special Achievement, Non-Professional" category in 1981), but in 1980 she made her first professional sale, to *New Dimensions*, and soon became a frequent contributor to *Omni*, *The Magazine of Fantasy & Science Fiction*, *Isaac Asimov's Science Fiction Magazine*, and *Shadows*, among other markets. Cadigan has been making something of a mark of late as a writer of quiet but scary supernatural horror stories, but within SF she is perhaps best known so far for her sequence of "Pathosfinder" stories. Beginning with "The Pathosfinder" in *The Berkley Showcase* in 1981, this series details the adventures of "Deadpan Allie," a sort of high-tech psychoanalyst of the future who can hook directly into another person's mind to seek out the root causes of their psychological troubles. In the jazzy and multifaceted story that follows, one of the "Pathosfinder" sequence, she suggests that stock phrases like "the privacy of the grave," "quiet as a tomb" and "rest in peace" may soon be marked "obsolete" in the dictionary . . .

Cadigan lives in Overland Park, Kansas, where she works for Hall-mark Cards. She has served as a World Fantasy Award judge and as Chairwoman of the Nebula Award jury. She is currently at work on a novel, tentatively entitled *Captives*.

NEARLY DEPARTED

Pat Cadigan

"Three things," I said, and held up a matching set of three fingers.

Nelson Nelson looked tolerantly amused. "Run 'em."

"One—" I curled my index finger. "I don't do empaths. Two—" I bent my ring finger. "I don't get physical. Three—" I pointed the remaining finger at the old fox on the other side of the desk. "I don't rob graves."

The couch creaked as NN rolled over onto his back and folded one arm behind his head. "Is that all that's bothering you? Kitta Wren hasn't been buried."

"I don't do dead people. If God had meant me to pathosfind dead people, he wouldn't have invented the Brain Police."

A broad smile oozed over NN's saggy features as he reached for a cigarette. He was smoking those lavender things again. They smelled like young girls. "What's the matter, Allie? Are you scared of a dead person's brain?"

"I'm scarder of some live ones I know. Fear isn't the issue. I just have certain beliefs and this job you're asking me to take goes against every one of them."

"Such as?"

Sighing, I shifted position on my couch and scratched my forearm. The vulgar gold lamé upholstery NN was so enamored of was giving me a rash. You can dispute taste but you can't stop it. "Such as, death is the end. The end means there is no more. Dead people should be allowed to rest in peace instead of having their brains plundered and looted for any last bit of—of treasure, like Egyptian tombs."

"Eloquent. Really eloquent, Deadpan," NN said after a moment. "You're probably the most eloquent mindplayer this agency has ever employed. Someday you might talk yourself out of a job, but not this time." He winked at me. "Actually, I respect your feelings. Those are good feelings, especially for someone who trades on the name Deadpan Allie."

"Being deadpan doesn't mean you don't have feelings. You just don't show them."

"I personally don't share them. I feel there's a lot of validity in, say, going in and getting the last measures of unfinished music from a master composer who dropped dead at the harpsitron, or mining the brain of a gifted writer for the story that was unwritable in life. Postmortem art is highly regarded and a large number of artists, including Kitta Wren, signed postmortem art contracts. It's a sort of life after death— the only one we know about for sure."

I scratched my rash some more and didn't say anything.

"Kitta Wren *wanted* a postmortem. It's not grave robbing. If she hadn't signed the contract, it would be different."

"Kitta Wren was a five-star lunatic. She had a psychomimic's license and when she wasn't writing her poetry, she was bouncing off the walls."

"Ah, but she was brilliant," NN said dreamily. I blinked at him, astounded. I'd had no idea he liked poetry. "When it came to her work, she was totally in control. Somehow I always thought that control would bring her down. In a thousand years, I never would have guessed anyone would kill her."

I wanted to tear my hair and rend my garment. "NN," I said as calmly as I could, "I *hate* murder. I am *not* the Brain Police. If they want to find out who did her, let them send in one of their own to wander around in her mind."

"Oh, they will," Nelson Nelson said cheerfully. "Right after the postmortem." A cloud of lavender smoke dissipated over my head as NN flipped his cigarette into the suckhole in the center of his desk. "The Brain Police can't do anything until that's taken care of. Otherwise whatever poetry is left in there could be fragmented and irretrievably lost."

The rash had crept up past my elbow. I kept scratching. "There are mindplayers who postmortem for a living."

"I'll pardon the expression. Wren's manager hired you. Come along, now, it'll take you somewhere you've never traveled."

"I've never been to the heart of a white dwarf star and I don't see why I should go."

NN exhaled with a noise that was almost a growl. "Do you want to work for me?"

"I'm thinking."

He gave me that oozy smile again. "Deadpan, this is important. And you might learn something." He raised up on one elbow. "Just give it a chance. If you can't do it once you're in, fine. But try it."

I sat up, scrubbing my arm through my sleeve. "Don't make a habit of signing me up for postmortems."

My eyes popped out. I held them in my palms until I felt the connections to my optic nerves break and then lowered them gently into the bowl of solution. The agency's hypersystem would have removed them for me, but I've always preferred doing that little chore myself.

I lay down on the slab and felt it move me head first into the system. Even blind, I could sense the vastness of it around me as it swallowed me down to my neck. It was the size of a small canyon, big enough to spend the rest of your life in just wandering around. All I wanted at the moment was some basic reality affixing and reassurance. If I was going to run barefoot through a dead lunatic's mind, I needed all the reinforcement I could get. After an hour of letting the system eat my head, I almost felt ready.

I hadn't been gassing Nelson Nelson as to how I felt about postmortems just to cover a corpse phobia. To me, you ought to be able to take something with you—or at least make sure it goes the same time you do—and if it's your art, so be it. Hell, there were plenty of living artists with a lot to offer. Stripping a dead person's mind for the last odds and ends seemed close to unspeakable.

I supposed the appeal of postmortem art was partly what Nelson Nelson had said—life after death. But there seemed to be more than a little thanatophilia at work. Art after death made me think of sirens on rocks, and I wasn't the only one who heard them singing. Occasionally there'd be an item in the news-tube about some obscure holographer or composer—holographers and composers appeared to be particularly susceptible—found dead with a note instructing that an immediate postmortem be performed because the person had been convinced that the unreachable masterpiece he/she had been groping for successfully in life could be liberated only by the Big Bang of death.

So there'd be the requested postmortem and the mindplayer who hooked into the brain, which was all wired up and floating in stay-juice like a toy boat lost at sea, would come out not with a magnificent phoenix formed of the poor deader's ashes but with a few little squibs and scraps from half-completed thoughts that had turned in on themselves, swallowing their own tails for lack of substance, vortices that had gone nowhere and never would. Some people aren't happy just with being alive. They have to be dead, too.

At least Kitta Wren hadn't been one of those. The information

Nelson Nelson had dumped into the data center in my apartment was freckled with little details, but rather sketchy taken all together. I punched her picture up on my screen and sided it with her bio.

She'd been a very ordinary woman, squarish in the face with a high forehead and medium brown untreated hair. Her only physical affectation had been her eyes. Since the advent of biogems, everyone had at least a semi-precious stare. Jade and star sapphires had always been popular choices and moonstones proliferated among entertainers of the more mediocre stripe. I hadn't seen very many people with my own preference for the shifting brown of cat's-eye and it takes a certain coloring to carry off diamonds effectively, but Kitta Wren had gotten herself something I'd never seen before.

Her eyes seemed to be shattered blue glass, as if someone had deliberately smashed the gems before putting them in. Her pupils were spiderwebbed with white cracks. I enlarged them for detail and paused, staring at them. I was wrong. Her eyes weren't spiderwebbed with cracks— they were spiderwebbed with spiderwebs, thickened as if coated with dew or frost. "Come into my lunatic parlor," I muttered, wondering if the webs had been a manifestation of her psychosis, or some kink she'd always wanted to indulge, or if there was any way of separating her own ideas from her psychosis.

She'd gotten her psychomimic's license at nineteen and spent the five years after that almost continuously crazy, with a few months off here and there for extended periods of writing. Later she had begun limiting her psychotic times to summers while she worked on a cycle of poetry. The result, a long series called *Crazy Summer* had given Wren her first major recognition. From there, she'd gone to being crazy only at night, then only during the day, and once she'd spent six months orbiting the moon in high mania.

When she died, which had been—I punched for the date—just the day before, she'd been a week into a general schizophrenia no one seemed to know anything about. Cause of death—I blanched a little— disembowelment. There was a photograph of her office where she'd gotten it. She'd been strong all the way to the end, going clear across the room before collapsing. Dead just under an hour when her manager had found her. Not too bad—five hours was about the limit for an untreated brain. After that, it's not worth trying to hook in with it. No suspects and no murder weapon; the Brain Police were holding off their investigation of her brain until after the postmortem was performed. Standard procedure—their technique tended to wipe a mind clean.

Under Miscellaneous, I found a small picture of Wren's manager, a gold-skinned androgyne named Phylp with fan-shaped eyebrows. The request for a pathosfinder was entered as well. It seemed Phylp wanted someone who wouldn't treat her like just another deader. Sounded to me as if Phylp were hoping Wren hadn't left behind as little as he/she suspected.

A morgue is a morgue is a morgue. They can paint the walls with aggressively cheerful primary colors and splashy bold graphics, but it's still a holding place for the dead until they can be parted out to organ banks for burial in the living. Not that I would have cared normally, but my viewpoint was skewed. The relentless pleasance of the room I sat in seemed only grotesque.

The other two people in the room didn't see it that way. One had introduced himself as Matt Sabian, postmortem supervisor. The other was unmistakably Phylp. He/she overshadowed Sabian despite the latter's silver hair, garnet eyes, and polished skin. Phylp was the flashiest androgyne I'd ever seen—most of them preferred no higher an appearance profile than anyone else, but Phylp handled major talent. It was probably advantageous to have such a memorable manager. If anyone could remember the talent after seeing the manager, the talent must be pretty major. Show biz.

"I understand this is your first dead client," Sabian was saying. The absurdity of the statement made me want to laugh, but they don't call me Deadpan Allie and lie.

"Up till now, I've worked only with living minds, yes." I sneaked a glance at Phylp, who was more arranged in a chair than seated in it.

"You shouldn't have any trouble," Sabian said. His voice had an odd hint of disappointment. "Your own mind will have to provide a good deal of visualization, except for her memories and the like, so I hope you're not given to bizarre symbolism. Other than that, everything in a living mind is present in a dead one. Except life, of course. We leave this world as we come into it—without thoughts, personality, memories, talent. When life fades, it leaves these things behind, just like any other material item we have. You'll have to actively stimulate the mind to obtain any of them. It can't offer you anything voluntarily. It takes life to do that." He pulled his left ankle up onto his right knee and played with the elastic cuff of his pants. "It'll be very much like hooking into a computer program of Kitta Wren's identity, actually."

I sat up a little straighter. "But it's not really that simple, is it?"

Sabian opened his mouth to answer but Phylp spoke up for the first time. "That's why I wanted a pathosfinder for her."

"Pardon?" I asked.

"Someone who would understand that it's not just a matter of searching out data." The throatiness I had momentarily taken for emotion was Phylp's normal speaking voice. "I want whatever it is that comes out to come out sounding alive. Because she was alive when she created it."

Sabian pointedly did not look at Phylp, who returned the favor. It clicked for me then. Sabian, postmortem supervisor. If Phylp hadn't insisted on hiring a pathosfinder, Sabian would have been doing this job. A nice sweet plum of a job, too, doing a postmortem on someone of Kitta Wren's stature. I did a sight reading of his Emotional Index, but I couldn't tell who he was angrier at, me or Phylp. I supposed I could understand how he felt, but it was still extra stress I didn't need.

"How well did you know Kitta Wren?" I asked Phylp.

"Not at all. I managed her, but she was a stranger to me."

That was a lot of help. "What about family?"

"Only two brothers. One is at the South Pole. The other is under the Indian Ocean in a religious trance."

"Do you know anything about her early life?"

Phylp almost looked sheepish. "Only that her parents gave the children to the state and vanished." He/she spread his/her hands gracefully. "That's all anyone knows. In the five years I've handled her, she never showed the slightest inclination of opening up to me or anyone else. It was a major disclosure if she told me she liked her contracts."

"That sort of self-isolation isn't exactly normal behavior for a poet, is it?"

"Nothing about her behavior was *normal*." Phylp frowned at me. "She was crazy. All the time she was crazy, and when she wasn't, she wanted to be. God knows what she got out of it. I don't."

Her poetry, apparently. I turned my attention back to Sabian. "What about the psychotic dead mind? Is the psychosis still operable?"

"Very much, though in a strictly mechanical way. And it probably doesn't know it's dead."

I hesitated. "Which do you mean—the psychosis or the mind?"

"Both, I would think."

"How does a mind not know it's dead?"

Sabian's chin lifted defensively. "How does yours know it's alive?" I didn't answer. "It's the same question, really." Not the way I saw it, but I let him go on. "Minds contain information, but it takes the presence of life for it to *know* anything. What does a computer program *know*?" The polished skin stretched in a tight, triumphant smile, as if he'd given me a glimpse of Big Truth.

"And where is the brain?" I asked after a moment.

"Here." Sabian pointed his toe like a dancer and pressed a panel in the floor. A section of the far wall slid back and there it was. What had waited behind Kitta Wren's spiderwebs in life now hung in a tall, clear canister of stay-juice, trailing wires like the streamers on a Portuguese man-of-war. The wires went down through the bottom of the canister to the maintenance box, which kept a minimum number of neurons firing. Two more wires leading from the visual center were coiled on top of the canister.

"We're still within the optimum time to go in. In another day, the neurons will begin to cease firing efficiently and after that deterioration will be rapid. I hope you'll be able to get everything on the first try."

I hoped so, too.

They left me alone so I could set up my portable system. Assembling the three large components and five smaller ones was a kind of busy work. There are comparable systems that need no assembly, but there's a lot to be said for the ritual of preparation as relaxation therapy. I never needed it more than I did just then.

I worked in silence, rolling the system over to the brain and then fitting the pieces together until I had the familiar unbalanced-looking but actually quite stable quasi-cubist structure. Nothing showed in the way of circuits, wires, or guts of any kind. Good equipment, NN was fond of saying, doesn't have to show its guts.

Pulling out the drawer with the connections and thermal tank for my eyes, I paused. I would have hooked a living client into a relaxation exercise such as making colors, building landscapes, or running mazes, but what could I do with a dead one? It couldn't get much more relaxed. Or could it? I wouldn't have thought. On the other hand, I wanted it functioning a little more than minimally when I made contact.

In the end I decided on some abstract moving visuals since I would be connecting directly with the visual center anyway. I dragged over one of the chairs and made myself comfortable.

Despite the apprehension I'd felt about the job from the beginning, something like professional reflex took over. It didn't take any longer than usual to calm myself into a smooth, alert state of receptivity. I had positioned the thermal tank on the maintenance box next to the canister, where I could reach it easily. When I was absolutely sure of its location, I thumbed my eyes out and let them down into the solution. It never ceased to amaze me how well I could function blind, but most mindplayers had superior short-term eidetic memory.

I had only to hold the system connections under my eyelids; they crept in and found their way to my optic nerves by themselves. After a few moments, awareness of my body faded and I was through the system and in Kitta Wren's mind.

Every mind is different. Every mind is the same. Those are the first two laws of mindplay. Recognition in an unfamiliar land always came as a surprise to me no matter how often I met clients mind-to-mind. I was even more surprised to find that the initial impressions and sensations of contact with Kitta Wren's mind were not dissimilar to those I associated with living minds.

Normally I would have made my presence felt gradually so as not to startle my client by bursting in like an invader. But this client couldn't know that trauma and I was coming directly into the visual center instead of the less abrupt route through the optic nerve. After the usual slight disorientation of passing through the barriers of personality and identity, I found myself in the thick of random pictures and arbitrary memories. Around me, the mind seemed to tense as it felt the addition of something new and unpredictable. Then it ground on as before, accepting me as just another thought.

The abstract visuals program was still running and I was awash in lazy spiral rainbows and harlequin rivers. I set it for gradual fade-out. The program's wane uncovered more of the brain's own pictures, some of them mundane objects remembered for no reason, some of them vignettes from Kitta Wren's life. I let them swirl around while I decided on the best way to go about the postmortem. Hitch a ride on a memory? Follow a random thought? Get hold of some false starts or blind alleys and reconstruct them?

I had caught a false start when the mind tried to think me. There was almost no warning. The false start was in my grasp and I was receiving multiple over- and undertones accompanied by the memory of its creation and the frustration Kitta Wren had felt before finally giving up on it. A walk in the rain in the middle of the night during late summer. Taste of rain dissolving on lips and tongue and the first line. *Do I drink the rain or does the rain drink me . . . drink? think?* I was searching it for possible salvage when the mind clamped down on me and Kitta Wren's old, unfinished poem together.

It thought the poem piece by piece, starting with the memory. It remembered the night and then the season (why not the season and then the night, I wondered), and then moisture, pausing to associate it with varieties of wetness. I was overwhelmed by the smell of the ocean, followed by a brief image of a coffin covered with barnacles lying on the sea bottom. The taste of rain returned more strongly, eradicating the picture of the coffin (*my brother, that's all*) but not quite managing to suppress a fleeting thought of snow. *Do I drink the rain . . . I drink the rain and the rain drinks me . . . Drinking the rain I am drunk and am drunk by drunken rain . . .* The mind niggled and gnawed out each variation from the original line (what was it about rain that fascinated poets, anyway?). When it was through, I was next.

I made a mask of my face and then took it off. The mind reached down for me in its purely mechanical probing and I threw my face into its processes. Traveling at the speed of thought, my face was everywhere as the mind tried to find the correct association for it. Curiously, I saw it materialize on the smooth, blank surface of a writing slate before I slipped through a half-remembered dream—images of cold stone carvings on a cathedral wall and a quick impression of *I should write about a mad cathedral*—and found myself down in Kitta Wren's back burner.

There isn't a mind in the world that doesn't have a back burner and it was usually a lot more difficult to get a client to open it up. Sometimes the incomplete puzzlements and notions stewing there were capable of growing into full-fledged ideas; other times they changed into false starts or shrank away into un-existence. Kitta Wren's back burner was so full of images that some of them were teetering half-dissolved on the edge of forgotten, as if she had deliberately pushed every idea that occurred to her to the back of her mind and then tried to forget all of them. Not the most productive way to work. I propelled myself through them to see what I might be able to salvage, which, I thought, would yield more results than looking at material she'd given up on. I was learning.

It was like holo-collage, the self-indulgent beginner's exercise for holographers who aspired to feature-length work, with her inner voice fading in and out where she had found words to go with the pictures. In quick turn I was looking up from the bottom of a deep, narrow hole at a circle of innocent blue sky, staring across the surface of a bed at eye level, watching two people, their faces in shadow, touch hands and listening to the indistinct murmur of their low, womanly voices (each was Wren). I was caught in a storm in the desert with rare rain beating straight down (there was that rain again, she seemed to return to it over and over), observing a street scene populated only by machines with my cheek pressed against the pavement, tasting an empty cup and pretending there was something in it. I went back and reviewed that last one to see where she'd gotten it.

Something from nothing, Kitta Wren's intelligent inner voice said. *Something from nothing.* I saw a chrysanthemum in the bottom of the cup; it metamorphosed from live to painted on. The center of the flower was an eye. *Something from nothing. I fill me with something from nothing.*

I had almost focused on what she had meant to taste in the cup when I began to get the feeling I wasn't alone. Which was absurd—even *she* wasn't there anymore. I turned my attention from the cup and waited. Possibly what I had felt was the mind reaching out for me again. Lowering my energy level as much as possible, I moved in among the jumble of unfinished ideas and waited. Rain punched dents in the sand. The sideways view of the street shimmered in the soggy desert sky like a mirage.

The mind spasmed. I had given it a new combination of thoughts to think by the way I had juxtaposed her old fragments. It fixed on me just as the madness hit.

That was what I had felt approaching, her psychosis, and it struck like a concentrated, highly localized storm. I thought my perception of it had been colored by my exposure to the desert scene, but it remained stormlike even after the mind separated me from its own familiar concepts, and I realized the nature of what Kitta Wren had done to herself.

Had she still been alive, I would have been witnessing a localized psychotic episode, a variety of seizure meant to produce not a convulsion but an altered state of consciousness. Except there was no consciousness. The seizure tore into her ideas and images and they flew up, dropped, rose again and fell flat with no one to pick them up and use them. The rest of the mind seemed to come to a standstill while the storm raged on. She'd been hoping for a literal brainstorm, a creative madness that would tear through her mind, stirring her thoughts into new and better patterns, giving her the stimulation she had refused to seek outside of herself. The mind seemed to shimmer and its perception of me grew vague. I slipped away down to an area of learned reflexes and automatic behavior to wait things out. As soon as the seizure had passed, I would go back, collect her ideas, memorize them and get out. Phylp had been wrong. I would have to treat this strictly as a data retrieval operation, I couldn't deal with the mind as if it were living—

Reaching for a cigarette with only a dim awareness of the act I/she felt the first pain. I/she looked down at the slate on the desk and the stylus in my/her hand. It gleamed like a knife. (Memory run; it was a go; humans keep memories packrat style, who would have thought this one would be in Habits and Mannerisms?) But it couldn't cut away the blankness of the slate to reveal the words that should have been there. Stuck in my/her brain.

Then I was past the memory pocket and the mind had me again. Tropism. I should have known. Minds were meant to live and be conscious. Except there was no consciousness but mine. And if mine was there, then the mind must be alive.

Alive. It pulled at me and I passed through the psychosis like a kite in a high wind. The madness clutched at me, searching for a way in almost as if it were a separate, living intelligence as alien as I was. I tasted anger and spat it out; it came back to me distorted, a sea of strange faces registering disappointment, confusion, and hate. Kitta Wren's view of the world, vinegar laced with poison. The mind dragged me onward and I went, trailing the madness and the memory and the madness of the memory through the fireworks display of her emotional life.

Something from nothing. I looked to see who she was speaking to but there was no one. Just an affirmation. *Give me nothing, I take nothing. Offer me nothing; thank you. His eye may be on the sparrow but the Wren looks out for herself.* She had worked hard for her unhappiness and her mind showed her efforts to me as though they were trophies and prizes. A coffin under the Indian Ocean, something she'd never seen, an image invented and embellished for her own meditation. A silhouette in a blizzard at the bottom of the world. Empty pedestals labeled *Mother* and *Father* and an arena of thick, sweaty faces demanding a show, their greedy voices orchestrated by a golden-skinned androgyne. *Give them what they want. Something from nothing. Give me nothing. You take something.*

In her office, she faced the invisible, hungry multitude. Her mind tried to push me back into the memory but I clamped down and kept out of her perspective. The seizure had leaked into her visual center and the slate on the desk swelled to enormous size. She backed away from it, hallucinating patterns on the slate. Faces again. *Give them what they want.*

The pain doubled her over. She straightened up slowly, both hands on her belly. There was a dark stain on the stretchy material of the secondskins, just below navel level. *Something from nothing. Give them what they want.* Her fingers gripped the cloth. Psychotics frequently displayed extraordinary physical strength. And then there were those with a touch of telekinesis, unusable until a moment of crisis. It didn't matter if the crisis took the form of an hallucination brought on by an anxiety attack.

Her hands fell away. She didn't explode, or convulse, or even scream. She simply opened up and thirty years of misery poured out.

The memory went black, along with everything else. Then the mind stirred itself again and wrapped around me. Kitta Wren may have died, but her mind wanted life. Any life. Mine would do just fine.

Listen, she said. The memory was so worn only her words remained. *All they want is the show. Give them what they want, but never ask anything of them. Something from nothing. The Wren looks out for herself.*

I pulled back, preparing to withdraw. The mind flexed and the feel of it was almost plaintive now. Without warning I was face to face with the image of Kitta Wren as she had been, spiderwebs glistening. They still looked like shattered gems at first glance and they always would. I concentrated on that thought, sending it toward the image in steady waves. After some timeless interval, new lines appeared in the webs, running like fissures. The mind fought, trying to maintain solidity, but I was right. The cracks crept over her face slowly. I had to strain to keep them going, but they went, dividing her forehead into a myraid of little territories, fragmenting her cheeks, sundering her mouth. The image shuddered, almost held, and then just came apart, every piece sailing away from every other piece. When they were all gone, I withdrew without difficulty.

The first thing I saw after I put my eyes back in was the brain in the canister. The stay-juice looked milky now, a sign of imminent decay. Without really thinking about it, I leaned forward and shut the maintenance box off.

Nelson Nelson held up an official-looking chip-card. "This is a lawsuit."

I nodded. He put the card down on his desk and picked up another one.

"And *this* is a lawsuit."

I had my own card and I held it up. "And *this* is a countersuit. In case anyone actually has the nerve to go to court."

NN looked tired. "Everything's already being settled out of court. The agency took your side of course. No one can say I don't back my people, isn't it so?"

It was so. But I could tell by the way that puckered old mouth was twitching that he'd probably thought about filing against me himself for taking it upon myself to shut off the maintenance box. If the morgue laboratory had not come out and said that the composition of the stay-juice had indicated degeneration beyond the point where the mind could be re-entered, I would most likely have been signing my next thirty years of salary over to Nelson Nelson.

"Why'd you do it, Deadpan? What got into you?"

"She was dead. And nothing at all got into me."

"Sabian says the brain couldn't have deteriorated so quickly between the time you went in and the time you came out. Could it?"

I didn't attempt an answer right away. The brain had been a lot deader when I came out than it had been when I'd gone in. I kept thinking in the back of my mind that had something to do with it even though I couldn't have proved it one way or the other. Was there telekinesis after death as well as art? I didn't know and didn't want to know. "Maybe the solution was defective," I said after a bit. "Or hadn't been changed often enough." That was the argument in my countersuit anyway, that Sabian had allowed me to hook into an unstabilized brain which caused me to act in an irresponsible manner by shutting my client off instead of calling for him so he could do it. Sabian was just bitched because it meant he couldn't enter the mind after I was through to do his own little postmortem, figuring he could sell Phylp all the stuff I'd missed. He wasn't gassing me. Nobody filed a lawsuit over a protocol violation.

NN shrugged. "Phylp's charge is more serious."

"Seriouser and seriouser. It'll never hold up. He/she got all the postmortem fragments I could find. I had them all memorized. I did my job. It's not my fault he/she thinks none of them were worth the effort. And he/she can't sue me for the wrongful death of someone already dead."

"It's a little more complicated than that, Allie."

"But that's what it amounts to. He/she's charging that before I broke contact—"

"*Prematurely* broke contract."

"—I dissolved her Self and killed her a second time, compounding that by turning off the box."

"That's the way it looks in the transcript of your report."

"That's the way it was."

I thought Nelson Nelson was going to choke. I sat up, rubbing the small of my back with both hands.

"Just between you and me, NN, yes. That's exactly what I did."

He reached down and fiddled with something on the side of the desk facing him. Of course; he'd been recording. He was always recording. This one would have to be doctored.

"You know how a dead body will twitch when you send a current through it? A dead mind'll do the same. It takes more than current, but it's a good comparison. They had the neurons firing so well, it forgot it was supposed to be dead, and it tried to use me to come back."

"Could it have?"

"I don't know. It didn't work. I killed it."

"But what do you think?"

I sighed. "Possibly I might have ended up incorporating elements of her personality and some of her thoughts and memories. Then you'd have had to have me dry-cleaned to get rid of her."

NN raised his invisible eyebrows. "Now there's an interesting situation."

"Not for me. I wouldn't want any of that woman in me."

"I mean in terms of the legal definition of existence. If such a thing had happened and the agency did have you dry-cleaned, would we, in fact, have been killing her all over again?"

I glared at him. "No. She was already dead."

"But if she returned to life in you—well, never mind, Allie. It's just an intellectual exercise at this point." He waved the subject away. "All this aside, tell me. Did you learn something?"

From a bitter woman who had literally torn herself apart? "I learned she shouldn't have been buying psychoses. She was already fogged in."

"No, now really, Allie. Wasn't there anything in there at all—some insight, or a vision beyond—ah, any final knowledge of any kind?"

I lit a cigarette by way of stalling. How old was Nelson Nelson anyway? And how old was he expecting to get? I wanted to tell him that if there was an answer—or an Answer—it wouldn't have been in a dead mind because you couldn't ask the right questions in there. If you don't know now, you can't know then. Instead, I lay down on the couch again and blew smoke at the ceiling. "Life's a bitch. Then you die."

I could almost hear NN's mouth drop. There was a long, thick moment of silence and then he began to laugh. "That's a good one, Deadpan," he said finally, wiping his eyes. "You almost had me there."

I'd almost been there myself, but I just grinned as if he had caught me out. For his own sake, I hoped he always thought it was funny. Just to be on the safe side, I put myself in for dry-cleaning as soon as the lawsuits were settled. Just to be sure.

JOHN KESSEL

Hearts Do Not In Eyes Shine

To forget! To somehow wipe away the past and try again . . . How many countless thousands of men and women have longed for that throughout the ages? Wouldn't it be wonderful if we could press a magical button and somehow erase all the pain and trauma and sadness of our tangled and mismanaged lives, be given a clean slate, a fresh start? It *would* be wonderful—
Wouldn't it?
Alas, as the subtle and elegant story that follows suggests, it might not be quite that *simple* . . .
Born in Buffalo, New York, John Kessel now lives in Raleigh, North Carolina, where he is an assistant professor of American literature and creative writing at North Carolina State University. One of the most skilled and literate of the genre's new writers, Kessel made his first sale in 1975 and has since become a frequent contributor to *The Magazine of Fantasy & Science Fiction*; his stories have also appeared in *Isaac Asimov's Science Fiction Magazine*, *New Dimensions*, *Galileo*, *The Twilight Zone Magazine*, *The Berkley Showcase*, and other places. In 1983, Kessel won a Nebula Award for his brilliant novella "Another Orphan," which was also a Hugo finalist that year. Upcoming is a novel written in collaboration with James Patrick Kelly, tentatively entitled *Freedom Beach*.

HEARTS DO NOT IN EYES SHINE

John Kessel

Connie found Harry in the bar at Mario's. He saw her come in, finished his drink quickly and stood up.

"You came," he said, fumbling in his jacket pocket as if he'd lost something. "I have something for you."

He found a small envelope in an inside pocket and handed it to her; it felt like a card. "Don't open it now," he said. "Wait until later."

Connie felt strangely calm. "Okay. Let's eat."

She let him do most of the talking; he seemed to have marshalled his arguments. "I know this must seem like a crazy idea. I think I'm half crazy to suggest it, but people do it all the time and I couldn't let you go without trying something."

"You're not letting me go. You let me go a long time ago."

He pulled at his lower lip and sat silent. "You're right. I don't deny it . . ."

"You can't."

"Please . . . I know I've made mistakes; we've both made mistakes. But think about the way we felt about each other when we first met. The emotions then were real. You can't deny that. That's why I'm here asking this, even though I know I don't deserve to ask it. But in the last month or two, I've about gone crazy thinking about the good times we spent together."

Connie tried to stay calm, to think rationally. "Harry, why do we have to go through this? It's too hard. I remember other times. We wouldn't be separated otherwise."

"No. I think you're wrong there. We made mistakes and did things to hurt each other, but I've thought about it a lot—I've hardly thought about anything else—and I know, I *know* we are basically compatible. I knew that the first time I saw you. The things that have pushed us apart are only things that happened to us—they aren't who we are. Who we are doesn't change, and that's the whole point of getting erased. We stay the same people, but we get rid of the bad things that happened and get another chance to build our marriage up again. Please, Connie. You know this is the truth, don't you?"

She didn't know anything. She sipped her wine, sat back and watched him.

Harry seemed uncomfortable under her gaze. He closed his eyes, breathed deeply, opened them again. That was always the sign of his exasperation with her, when he couldn't get her to believe what he wanted, when the words failed him. The words had not failed him yet. He must have thought them up a long time before he had the nerve to call her. Perhaps the letter from her lawyer had jolted him. Perhaps the erasure clinic had given him the arguments he was using on her. That was something she would never have suspected of Harry in the early days; she would have taken him at his face value.

Connie must have smiled at her own cynicism: he looked at her angrily and said, "Don't laugh at me Connie."

"I'm sorry."

"That's okay. Just don't laugh."

There wasn't much trust left in her, and suddenly she realized that she did not like it. What had he done to her that she had come to be so suspicious, that the honesty of her emotions had been leached away until she responded to him as if he were a pitchman for a sex show? Maybe his exasperation—if it was exasperation, and not just fear or confusion—had a reason.

"I don't know, Harry. I'm afraid. You've hurt me too much, and I can never forget the things you've done."

He leaned forward. "That's right," he said quietly. "But they can make us forget. You don't have to give up anything. You just have to be willing to take a chance."

She played with the card he had given her, turned it over, ran her index finger along the edge of the smooth rectangle of cream-colored paper.

"I don't know," she said.

Harry looked hurt; the silence stretched. "Look, Connie, maybe this was a bad idea. Don't make me feel any more a fool than I am."

"I'm not making you a fool." God. The last thing she wanted was to feel sorry for him.

"I'm sorry I tried to make you do something you didn't want to do. Can you blame me for trying?" He looked at her levelly.

This was not going the way it ought to have. They ought not to let men like Harry live to reach twenty-one. They ought to test them when they hit puberty, and if the test showed a person wouldn't be able to tell if he was telling the truth or not, they could castrate him. While they were at it they could get rid of the ones with Harry's green eyes and Harry's voice.

She held up the card and stood to leave. "Can I open this now?"

He smiled a little sadly. "It doesn't say 'I love you.' "

Connie slid a fingernail under the flap and opened the envelope. The front of the card was blank, and inside, was written, "No matter what you decide, I will never lie to you again."

She put the card back in the envelope, put the envelope into her purse. At his station, the maitre d' had already cleared their table on his service screen and was watching them impatiently. Connie looked at him, looked at Harry, and sat down again.

She told Harry she would call him and returned to the office without having made up her mind. She spent that afternoon trading foreign currencies, with Fox, her computer trading model, hooked into her left ear and the newsline into her right. She stayed in front of the terminal without a break until the session ended, then retreated to her office to take client calls until most of the staff had left for the day.

The lowering clouds that threatened Connie and the other bicyclists riding home suggested that perhaps the streetcar would have been a better idea that morning. But the rain held off until after she reached her street. She lived in a large old house in a neighborhood that had declined to a near-slum in the third quarter of the century only to be refurbished in the eighties before its second genteel slide after the turn of the century. Harry and Connie had moved into the white frame monstrosity a year before they contracted; seven years later he had moved out, and it had taken her months to feel comfortable again there after a period of rattling around its twelve rooms like the drunkard in the random walk theorem.

That night a relapse threatened. In the mail printout she found a brochure for an erasure company, New Life Choices, Inc. She did not recognize the name. Harry had to have sent it; she threw it into the wastebasket without reading it. She skipped supper, fixed several stiff drinks and tried to forget about erasure. She walked through the house listening to the spring drizzle and breathing deep the humid air that blew through opened windows. She picked up her clothes from about the bedroom, did the laundry, had a couple more drinks, smoked a joint, tried to read a book. She sat by the phone for twenty minutes, then dialed Harry's number quickly to tell him to forget it. The face of a middle-aged woman came onto the screen and told her curtly she had the wrong number. She hesitated, then searched the wastebasket for the brochure.

FREEDOM IS A STATE OF MIND
The Immortal bard, William Shakespeare (1564-1616)
asked,

Can you cure a troubled mind,
Plunge a deep sorrow out of the memory
Erase the troubles written on a brain
And with a sweet potion
Clean all the pain and sadness
From a heavy heart?

—At New Life Choices, we can.

The next page told Connie:

We see the world through dark glass. By selective forgetting, we can take off the dark glasses that superimpose the fearful past upon the present, and begin to know that love is forever present. The Jacobovsky Process is used to selectively edit the memory. Forgiveness then becomes a process of letting go of whatever we thought others may have done to us, or whatever we may think we have done to others. Our safety and security are the simple words, "I don't remember."

Harry had been bright and moody and could make her laugh whenever he wanted. Connie remembered quite well.

She had loved to watch him fix things. He had beautiful hands, strong and skilled. His hands knew just how much force to give, could feel out the source of a problem without his having to think about it. Normally he was a talkative man who did not use words well, but when he was in the converted playroom in the attic he became a quiet one, concentrating on the task before him, devoted only to finding the solution to the problem; patient, intuitive. His eyes would sober, without the anger they would show during his depressions, and he would look at the machine as if somehow, if he waited in the right way, it might speak to him—and he would not be surprised when it did.

Harry had had that look for her, at first. She felt that when she spoke to him, he listened with all his substance. It made her want to say only true things—not to be silly or lie. He would laugh at her when she got so serious.

"You act like I might go away," he would say to her. "I won't go away."

Harry worked for Triangle Data Services. Connie had met him when he came in to replace their old computer trading link with the new

Triangle system. He seemed unaware of the class difference between a workman like himself and someone like Connie, with a couple of degrees in economics and a triple-A credit rating. He did not seem self-conscious hanging around their terminals watching, asking an occasional question. Strangely, the changeover was made without disrupting their work, and when on his way out of the building on his last day there Harry stopped to ask Connie out for dinner, she had surprised herself by saying yes.

The rain increased from a drizzle to a downpour, and Connie went through the house again, closing windows against the storm. She turned out all the lights and went to bed.

Harry had lied to her more than once. They'd lived together so naturally in that first year that it had amazed her she'd been able to live alone for so long. It was an open marriage, with disclosure, ten years and an option, with penalties for a breach on either side. Three years into it Connie realized that Harry saw other women without telling her. At first she said nothing, out of love, or perhaps fear that facing it would make the truth of his betrayal undeniable. Why should he keep his lovers a secret when she had agreed to accept anything he told her openly? She did not see herself as the jealous spouse, but keeping her knowledge to herself only made her anger and resentment grow. When at last she confronted him, Harry was unsurprised that she knew. He would have felt ashamed to tell her of those affairs even though it was okay to have them, he said. He still loved her, he said. It had nothing to do with her, he said.

Though it took her years more to realize it, it *had* nothing to do with her. It was not her fault, and whether or not it was Harry's was beyond her. She tried not to care. She just wanted to be done with trying to understand him when he did not understand her, done with his talk that never went anywhere and his silence that left her out, done with the fighting, his sudden joys and kindnesses, his silly jokes, his casual cruelty, his quiet eyes and calm hands, his lies, the pain of watching him and knowing that she loved and hated him. She might have done better, but it was not her fault.

Why did that sound too easy?

The rain was beating heavily on the roof now, punctuated by thunder and lightning whose flashes brought the darkened room into momentary sharp relief, like sudden memories. Connie realized that the windows in the playroom were probably open. She got her robe and went up the narrow stairs.

The lamp over Harry's workbench did not come on when she flipped the switch. The curtains of the west window snapped with the force of the strong, cold wind, and the rain blew well into the middle of the cluttered room. Like a person walking a tightrope, Connie stepped carefully between the broken machines with their spoor of dismantled parts. It was all that Harry had left when she'd kicked him out, and she had threatened more than once to throw all his toys away if he did not move them. Her feet were very cold. The window was stuck; the counterweights in the frame scraped and the pulleys squeaked as she leaned heavily on it. The window went down crookedly, one side fighting the other. She beat on the top with her fist, growing angrier and angrier as it inched its stubborn way down. The wind whistled as the gap closed, she became soaked with the rain, and the shadowed forms of Harry's machines watched impassively as she struggled. There was still a gap when she gave up, two inches at one end and one at the other, uneven, hopelessly jammed, the wind louder as it shot through the narrow slit, the curtains flapping fitfully. She sat on the floor crying. It was Harry's damned window, and Connie couldn't close it for him.

She found herself in the lobby of New Life Choices on a day she and Harry picked for the erasing. Connie would have been more comfortable with the dignified conservatism of Associated or Stratford: the walls of the New Life lobby were knotty pine hung with Miro prints; the receptionist had had his irises silvered in the latest nihilist style. Some people might have liked it.

She and Harry sat quietly together until one of the "counselors" came to greet them.

"Harry." He shook hands. "Good to see you again. I see you've persuaded her." He turned to Connie. "You've made the right decision, Constance. I'm John Holland. Call me John."

He insisted on shaking her hand as well, holding on a moment as if to reassure her of his sincerity. It was all she could do to keep him from putting his arm across her shoulder as he led them to his office.

Behind his desk he was more businesslike. "First of all, are you taking advantage of the special this week?"

Harry looked pained, glanced briefly at Connie, then took the coupon from his pocket. "No jokes about paying in advance, John. Let's get on with it."

"We have to do this by the book, Harry. It's not so unpleasant as all that, is it? You two are about to get a second chance, thanks to the service we're offering. People throughout history have longed for that chance. They've gone to their graves dreaming of it, they've killed each other and themselves because they couldn't get it. Now you can have it; think how blessed you are."

He drew two contracts from a desk drawer. "I myself have had numerous traumas erased," he continued. "So completely that the only way I know about them is that I kept records. My mother's death. The time I struck out with the bases loaded in the college world series. My baptism. I can talk frankly about these things now, without a trace of guilt or anger, because for me those events no longer exist. The people who hurt me no longer exist. Fifty years ago a psychiatrist might treat you for a decade trying to convince you that the past is over and can't hurt you. By this afternoon the past that hangs over both of you like a cloud—I can see it there now, and it's keeping you apart—will be gone. All that will be left will be the love you still feel for each other."

Connie wondered whether they would erase this meeting for no extra charge. Harry looked as if he wanted to die. Connie could almost believe Holland was taking some perverse pleasure in Harry's discomfort. Or perhaps this was part of the treatment: make the patient realize the significance of the step he was taking, magnify the pain of the events he wanted to have erased so that he would leap at the opportunity to have them expunged. If so, then Holland ought to be able to afford a better wardrobe.

Holland placed one contract before each of them and they talked for awhile about what memories they wanted to have erased, and longer about exactly what they wanted to remember of their time together. He assured Connie, as had the brochure, that she would lose no memories vital to her job. She would remember the difference between short covering and profit taking. If she had been a champion skiier, then she would remain one.

They signed the contracts. Harry took her hand and they were led to the preparation rooms for pre-testing of memory. His palm was sweaty. In another room they were greeted by attendants whom Holland briefed, though they had all the relevant facts in their computer. Harry embraced her and they were taken to separate rooms. Once alone she began to panic. The machine they hooked her up to smelled of the hundreds of others who had come before her to have their pasts negated. The headset that let them map her cortex was cold and hard. The technicians did not know her; they did not care who she was and it would not matter to them if by some mischance they wiped out her personality entirely. It was all the same. Harry had no right to do this to her. She couldn't remember anything about him that would make her want to go back. She started to speak, she started to sit up and take the headset off. Or did she just think that? Harry had no right to take away her memories. She felt sleepy; the room did not look so threatening. The clean smell of disinfectant reminded her of the hospital emergency room where she'd taken Harry after he'd cut his hand so badly carrying a video display across the playroom. That was a piece of junk. It was still up there. He simply had no right.

Connie got a call at work the next day. She asked Mary to keep an eye on forex trading and went to her office to use the view-phone.

"Constance, this is Harry," the man on the screen said, as if she could not see him. When she didn't answer immediately, he added, "Harry Gray."

Her pulse quickened. "Yes, I remember you."

He closed his eyes for a beat, opened them again. His hair was light brown, worn longer than the general style. He seemed to be trying to smile, but uncertain how she would take it. This was her husband, she thought. They stared at each other, uncomfortably.

"Long time no see," Harry said.

She laughed. He looked so timid, yet aware of the absurdity.

"I feel funny talking to you," he said. "You look vaguely familiar . . ." She repressed another laugh. ". . . but I feel like I'm imposing where I don't know what to say. Maybe we ought to wait awhile."

"No," she said suddenly, surprising herself. "I think we need to get to know each other. Why don't we meet for lunch? Do you know where Mario's is on 12th Street?"

He looked momentarily dazed, and then the smile came. "It's one of my favorites."

She liked his voice, his tentativeness. "Mine too," she said. She realized then that her memories of Mario's were in some particulars rather vague. She could remember the maitre d's name, and that the veal was the best thing on the menu, but she could not recall many specific visits to the restaurant.

The maitre d' knew them both: he gave them a secluded table. The conversation started tentatively. Connie hesitated to ask Harry if he remembered anything, while at the same time she was probing her own memory. She could recall no event that they had experienced together. The closest she came were curious half-memories of things she had done herself that did not seem complete, undoubtedly because Harry had been involved in some way. Holland had told her, in the post-testing, that she might lose memory or persons and things she strongly associated with Harry. Connie wasn't sure she wanted to speculate about their marriage. That was what they had gone to the clinic to forget. But listening to Harry Gray's self-deprecating little jokes, his warm voice, she could not help but realize that she had had some reason to have this man erased from her memory, and she wondered what that reason was.

Harry told her he worked for a communications firm; she recognized it as the company that leased the trading machines to her brokerage. She told him about commission trading in the foreign exchange markets. He seemed legitimately interested. He was not a good talker—he would lose the train of his thoughts in midsentence—but his attention to her seemed complete. He told her about his own family and upbringing. In the back of her mind she knew she had to have known all of this as recently as a day ago, but it was all new to her now. It was queer that they could say how they'd been employed for the last five years, who their friends were, discuss recent politics and films, discover they both had a passion for weightless vacations, and yet not know how long they had lived together.

They sat at the table long after the meal, ordered wine and talked. Harry's eyes were shy, and kind. He put his hand out to touch hers. They leaned forward in the light of the candle wrapped in plastic netting at the center of their table. He offered her some Lift; she declined, and he added a few drops to his own glass. Connie did not approve, but he did not seem to lose interest and his eyes remained bright and alert. She wondered how often they'd slept together.

When they were about to leave he offered to take her home. She thought that meant he had his own vehicle, but all he meant was that he'd ride the streetcar back with her. She wasn't sure she wanted to go that fast, knowing he would want to spend the night. Connie hesitated while the waiter took her credit matrix. Harry said nothing. Looking into her purse to avoid his expectant gaze, she found a small card tucked into one of the pockets. She pulled it out far enough to read, in handwriting not her own: "No matter what you decide, I will never lie to you again."

She slid it back into her purse.

"Okay," she said. "It's a cool evening. It'll be a nice ride."

Connie grew to know and like him. Soon he moved in with her; in the evenings he took to tinkering with his machines in the playroom. Connie found herself with new energy in her work. She had her mind right on the edge of trading, was able to get in and out of market positions before others in the electronic network even knew they had been established or were crumbling. She began trading for her own account in spare moments and made a killing when the Philippines exploded its first nuclear device and the yen dropped the limit. Harry and Connie talked about how to spend the windfall. They decided on an orbital vacation on Habitat Three.

In the weeks before they left, some things about Harry began to pluck

at the edges of Connie's contentment. At times he seemed too happy;
too desperately happy. He would take her hands in his and tell her how
much he loved her, and the next day would return late from work and
Lifted almost out of sight. He would never criticize her and he always
seemed more than contented, but sometimes she wondered if Harry was
actually seeing her, or only some projection of his own desire. When he
became aware of her moments of silence in the midst of their new
happiness, he begged her not to dwell on the past. How could she dwell
on a past she couldn't remember?

On a hot July day one of Harry's friends came by in a company
electric van and took them to the tube station where they boarded the
magnetic train for the Cape. They spent three days in the hotel on the
beach, swimming and sailing and eating seafood, a luxury they seldom
saw in the Midwest. After that they took the shuttle up to the resort.

They went to the free fall ballet and did some dancing of their own.
They spent hours in the transparent centrifugal pool, watching the
universe wheel in lazy circles below them as they swam low-G ara-
besques in the water. Beneath the observation dome Connie got a very
nice tan despite the ultraviolet screen that protected them from the hard
sunlight of the vacuum. They ate in the many restaurants and watched
the intricate exchange of partners, the formation and deformation of
couples and groups that took place in the bar every night. Few of the
guests were paired as strongly as Connie and Harry, and soon the
propositions ended. Making love in free fall was familiar to Connie, but
one of those experiences of which her memory would yield no details.
Somehow this comforted her. She knew the reason for this was the
forgotten knowledge that Harry had been her partner.

At the end of the first week, Connie met a woman in the lounge who
was vaguely familiar. She wore the uniform of one of the staff.

"Hello! I saw Harry this afternoon in the sauna. He told me you were
back again. I'm so glad to see you."

Connie could not place her. The woman had obviously spent considerable time with both of them on a previous trip. The name "Alićе"
presented itself to her, unbidden.

"Alice. How are you?" she said uncertainly.

Alice smiled. "Oh, I can see you must have been Lifted pretty high
last night. A little hung over?"

"Not really. It's been a long time since I've seen you."

Alice would not accept that and continued probing until Connie
admitted she'd been erased.

"Erased! How interesting! I wonder why Harry didn't tell me."

Given Alice's apparent nose for news it was not something Connie would have told her either. "Maybe it just didn't occur to him."

"But I asked him all about you. We rehashed old times. You look like you're doing better on the sunburn front now. Harry said you'd learned your lesson after that horrible burn you picked up last time when you fell asleep."

Connie remembered the sunburn. But as Alice rambled on, the thought nagged at her.

"Harry talked with you about my sunburn? From the last trip?"

"Just in passing. He said you'd vowed never to let anything like that put you in the hospital again."

"You talked about our last trip?"

Alice looked puzzled. "Dear heart, you must be a little strung out. You're sure you didn't do a little too much last night?"

Alice kept the puzzled expression as Connie made her excuses and quickly left. She found Harry in their suite, adjusting his jewelry in the mirror. "Hi," he said. "Am I late? I was just about to come down to the lounge."

She watched his eyes in the mirror. "I ran into Alice," she said.

His glance caught hers, then shifted away. He brushed his hair back from his earring. "I saw her today, too. I'm surprised we didn't run into her sooner; you know how nosey she is. She just lives to know what's going on among the guests."

"I didn't remember her."

"Oh." He turned from the mirror. "You must have associated her with me more than I connected her with you, so the erasing wiped her out of your memory. John told me this might happen."

"You and John are pretty friendly."

He came over to her, embraced her, ran his hand lightly down her spine.

"What's the matter?" he asked.

He sounded perfectly sincere. He did not seem to be afraid to look at her. She ought to just let it go at that. She remembered the card she still carried in her purse. "I will never lie to you again" meant that, although she could not remember, he had lied to her before.

"Alice said you talked about my sunburn."

"She brought it up, yes." Harry sounded as if he didn't understand what she was driving at.

"You remembered?"

A light seemed to dawn on him. "No. No, I didn't remember anything about it. When she brought that up it was all I could do to figure out what she was talking about."

"You acted as if you knew."

"I must be a better actor than I imagine, then." He laughed; he moved away. "Connie, I just didn't want to admit that I'd been erased. You must have felt the same way when she started talking to you. She's a gossip. She acted as it we were old friends, so I pretended to remember all the stuff she was talking about. I was embarrassed."

She watched him as he sat down on the edge of the bed and played with his wedding ring, turning it around and around his finger. "Why are you so suspicious?" Harry asked.

He had not been erased. Connie watched him sitting there and knew it was true. She shuddered with the enormity of it. She felt drugged, unable to grasp so huge a betrayal. She stared at him: how could he conceive of such an evil? She wanted to kill him. She rushed into the bathroom and closed the door. She sat on the edge of the tub and put her head in her hands, attempting to slow her breathing. Harry didn't come to the door, he didn't ask her what was wrong, he didn't plead. Stand and fight, her mind screamed, but as the minutes passed with still no response from him she began to have second thoughts. She couldn't know what he thought; she only had herself. The truth was that she *was* suspicious. The whole point of erasure was to give yourself a second chance. Maybe she had no reason to jump to such a drastic conclusion from such slim evidence.

The pastel tile of the floor gave no reassurance. The shock faded. Harry could not be such a monster. He could not have coldly tricked her into giving herself away so unawares; he was not so clever or heartless or selfish as to steal a second chance for himself without paying in equal coin. The card in her purse was—had to be—a voucher of his love for her, not a warning of his unreliability.

She opened the door. Still sitting on the bed, he looked up expectantly. "Are you all right?" he asked.

"Yes." She felt as if she were a ventriloquist speaking through a dummy.

"You have to believe me. I didn't know you'd take it this way. I lied to her; I didn't lie to you."

She sat beside him.

"Sometimes I wonder what made us get erased, too," he said.

She held him tightly and rested her head, eyes closed, on his shoulder.

"Go ahead," Harry said. "Sleep with Alice. I don't care."

A laugh forced itself to her lips. Tears were in her eyes. "Let's forget it," she said.

Constance told Harry she was concerned about being away from the markets for so long. He suggested she arrange a private comlink through the resort by which she could transact her business as well as she might at home. She told him she would not feel comfortable because such a link could easily be tapped, and moreover that her clients would have trouble reaching her.

At home they settled into a routine that left them less time with each other. Connie took on several new accounts that kept her busy in the office after the trading session ended each day, and she began working on a new economic model she wanted to merge into Fox. Harry had risen among the ranks of troubleshooters and was being sent out of town frequently to train people in other cities. When home, he spent more time in the playroom. On the surface everything was all right.

The one area of their lives that improved was sex. Harry seemed to want her more as the weeks went by, and for her part, Connie found herself trembling at his touch. She told herself she did not like being attacked with such energy; it was almost as if she were an object to him in those moments of frenzy, but his attention would be focused on her. He asked her continually what she wanted, he would be by turns rough and extraordinarily tender, as if she were as evanescent as snow in late spring, fallen way past its time, beautiful, transitory. She could ask him to do anything, and he would do it. His warm breath on her lips, her shoulder, was like the light, mysterious breath of a cat. She could no more read his thoughts than she could a cat's, yet she suspected something of the same feral blankness behind the eyes that gleamed in the darkness of their bedroom.

She responded with the same passion, surrendering thought in the night as she could less and less give it up during the day. The farther she drifted from him, the more pleasure she took in their lovemaking. *I'll never lie to you again.* She had thrown away the card the day they had returned to Earth, but it would not go away, and eventually she took an afternoon off and went to the office of New Life Choices.

Holland was busy and would be all afternoon, they told her, but she insisted on waiting. Ten minutes later he came out to the lobby and escorted her to his office.

"How can I help you, Constance?"

"I want to see your copies of the contracts."

He got them. She examined Harry's. Everything was in order. She compared the signature with one she had from their marriage license; it was the same. The terms of Harry's contract were identical to hers. Holland watched her silently.

"Something bothering you?" he asked when she put the papers down.

"Did you know Harry before we came here to be erased?"

"Not well. We met at a party a couple of months earlier. He had a few drinks. He was pretty broken up about your separation."

"You didn't talk business then?"

Holland seemed calm. "I suggested he get erased. It's my business, and he seemed a good prospect. It was a surprise to me later when he told me he was asking you to do it too."

Harry had asked *her* to get erased. For the first time Connie understood that it had not been her idea.

"That's all there was to it? And you erased him when you did me?"

Holland leaned back and frowned. "I know you don't like me," he said. "That's too bad. But you're not the first person to come in here accusing us of some fraud or other. They come in and tell me we didn't really erase them, that they can remember everything they paid to have wiped out. Or that we erased too much. Or that their personality's changed. Or that they can't do their jobs. You name it.

"You think I erased you and not Harry. How long do you think we could stay in business if that's true? There are laws. There are ethics of the business."

Connie almost laughed. "Ethics."

Holland did not get indignant. "Believe it or not. We did the job we were paid to do."

"That's an equivocal statement."

"We erased Harry Gray. You're married to him. Why don't you ask him?"

"Suppose he changed his mind on the couch, at the last minute?"

"I'm not lying to you."

"That's what Harry says."

"So you did ask him?"

Connie didn't say anything. Holland was not the lightweight she had taken him for, or maybe he had practiced this conversation. Some palm readers, they said, even believed the predictions they made.

"Look," Holland said. "You're smart. I'll tell you something I've found out that I don't like to admit. We can erase the memories— 'Pluck from the memory a rooted sorrow.' That's no problem. I used to think that we could 'minister to a mind diseased.' I'm not so sure anymore. The thing that makes a troubled memory is whatever happens to you. But people aren't as innocent as I used to think; they aren't just victims. Lots of the things that just 'happened to them' they worked long and hard to get themselves into."

Connie stood. "Don't preach to me."

"We can't change the person. If you don't trust Harry, it's likely you didn't trust him before you were erased. Erasure doesn't change who you are. No matter what we advertise."

"It didn't change Harry."

" 'Therein the patient must minister to himself.' I'd like to take you out for a drink, Constance, but if you're going to keep this up you might as well just talk to our lawyers."

"I'll bet they're good ones. Do they read Shakespeare?"

Holland gestured at the door. "Too bad," he said. "We might have had a nice time."

Harry had persuaded her to get erased. Connie could not put that thought away. It had been like a suicide pact. They had agreed to kill their memories together. But if Harry had not gone through with it, while Connie did—he had murdered her.

She had lunch with her lawyer, Barbara Curran. The weather had turned cold that morning and the first real autumn storm threatened, so they met at the seafood bar below Center City. Connie told Barbara about her suspicions and the visit to New Life. Barbara told her that no erasure company had ever been proved to have defaulted on a contract, a record of which the industry was so protective that the American Erasure Association had established a huge legal defense fund. Several suits were nonetheless pending. Then Barbara suggested that Connie perhaps ought to have gone through with the divorce she had planned, instead of deciding to get erased. Divorce. Connie felt as if someone had slapped her. Seeing how upset she was, after a little hesitation Barbara gave her a brief history of the marriage as Connie had told it to her a year earlier.

Harry was waiting in her office when Connie returned to the brokerage that afternoon. The other dealers were trying not to look curious.

"Harry. What brings you here?" She hung up her coat, trying to avoid his stare.

"I ran into John Holland today."

"Yes?"

"Why are you going around behind my back like this, Connie? If you've got some problem with the way things are going, why don't you tell me?"

She sat down behind her desk. "I don't have any problems."

He blew up. "Don't jerk me around, Connie! You think I'm stupid? What do you think Holland told me? You think I didn't go through with erasure, don't you? What kind of bastard do you take me for?"

Through the window that faced the trading room she could see the agents' faces turn toward the office.

"Don't shout. Draw the curtains."

"Screw the curtains! I want to know what's going on in that head of yours."

"That's a first. You never seemed to care much before. You wanted me to wipe out what's in my head. You want it now."

He paced back and forth before the window, hands knotted behind his back. "That's not fair," he said more quietly.

She felt vulnerable. "Maybe it's not. This has been a rough time for me. I can't help wondering about what things were like before I was erased."

"How would I know? Hasn't it been good since? Why rake up the past?"

"I can't change the past, Harry. It happened."

"What do you mean? Why would we get erased if not to change it?"

"So you did get erased?"

He stopped pacing and looked at her. The silence became uncomfortable. She wouldn't wilt under that stare anymore. He closed his eyes, opened them again.

"That question doesn't deserve an answer," he said. "I'm your husband."

Now she was mad. "I'm your wife. I deserve the truth."

He sat down in the chair meant for her clients. "You really hate me, don't you?"

"You lied to me before. I have to know that you're not lying again."

Harry seemed to relax. It was a comfortable chair—she always treated her clients well.

"I love you," he said. "I've always loved you."

"That's not enough. I have to know the truth."

Instead of rushing to reassure her, he sat in the chair as if he had come there to talk about investing in commodity options. His sudden withdrawal from her left Connie off balance, as if a door she had been pushing against had been suddenly opened.

"Say something, Harry. For God's sake."

"Would you believe me if I said yes, I was erased?"

She hesitated. "I think so."

"Yes, I was erased. I don't remember any lies. Now what happens the next time I don't do what you want? The next time I let you down?"

Connie felt dizzy. "I don't know. We'll have to see. It's not that simple . . ."

"You can explain it to me sometime." Harry shuddered visibly. He stood. "I've got to go. I'm tired. I feel like I'm losing everything."

You squandered it, she thought. "Harry . . ."

"I'm going to move out for awhile. I'll be gone by the time you get home."

Connie tried to say something, but he was gone. She could not say she wanted to see him there that evening or any other evening. She felt ill; she replayed the scene in her mind, shuddering herself as she thought of Harry sitting impassively in the chair like a stunned animal. The dealers were already back at their terminals; their curiosity evaporated when Harry left, or perhaps the gossip was put on hold until after hours.

Ten minutes later she went to her own terminal, read in the current market, hooked into Fox and the newsline. There were only forty minutes left in the trading session; the dollar was up against the major Eurocurrencies and off twenty against the yen. Activity was quiet: ninety-two traders in the pit curcuit and everyone waiting for the 1500 CST release of the latest U.S. Gross National Product report. Connie evened up several accounts and went long dollars for her own account in anticipation that the report would be positive, contrary to expectations. The GNP was up and she made $30,000 before the close of trading.

After work she went to one of the best restaurants in town, ate alone, had three drinks. She had no desire to get home early. The threatened storm was a reality when she left the restaurant; the lower level of the streetcar was crowded and it was after eleven when she reached home. She got soaked in the half-block from the stop to her door. Harry was not there. She undressed, towelled her hair and got into a robe. His closet was empty, the drawers of his dresser pulled open and bare, only his spare razor in the bathroom. By this time the wind had picked up and the rain rattled the windowpanes. She ran through the house, turning on lights, closing windows, shutting off the lights again.

The playroom was last. Harry must have been able to get a van on short notice; his computer was gone. The rest of his junk was still there. Maybe he still hoped to come back. The window beside his worktable was open two inches and the rain was blowing in. The light above the bench was dim. She ought to just leave it open, let Harry worry about his own machines, if he worried. She realized suddenly that despite all his concern for them, despite all the time he had for them, he might not care about the machines at all. Well, she couldn't leave them at that.

Connie struggled to close the window all the way but someone had jammed it downward crookedly so that it was caught at an angle in the frame and was fighting against itself. It could not be forced closed. She grabbed the handles at the bottom of the frame, bent her knees and pulled. Nothing. She jerked it to break it loose, and though she could feel the strain in her wrists and shoulders, it would not budge. When she let off, the muscles of her arms quivered with weakness. Already her slippers and the bottom of her robe were wet. The tree limbs outside the window raged back and forth in the wind; the rain was a constant drumming on the roof.

She found a large crescent wrench. Using a short length of pipe as a fulcrum, she levered the wrench under the lower side of the window and leaned all her weight on it. The rain made her hands slick, and her tight grip flushed the blood out of them. She put her shoulders into it and shoved the wrench downward. The window shot up an inch, the wrench slipped, the pipe fell off the sill and hit her foot, and she slipped and fell. A gash in the palm of her hand bled profusely. She got up and pulled the window open, jiggling it when it stuck. The storm was at its height, and the wind and water flew into her face as she crouched to draw the window down again. She gritted her teeth; it was almost a smile. The counterweights squeaked and thumped in the wall until the window was completely closed.

The rustle of the tree diminished, the drumming of rain on the roof increased. She sat on the floor in her wet robe and sucked the blood from her cut. It was not as bad as she thought.

DAN SIMMONS

Carrion Comfort

Few SF stories are actually *scary*, but here's one that is, an exceptionally taut and suspenseful tale by new writer Dan Simmons, about an elite circle of very old friends and the strange and deadly game they play with living pawns . . .

Born in Peoria, Illinois, Dan Simmons now lives in Longmont, Colorado, where he teaches sixth grade in the public school system. He has sold stories to *Omni, Isaac Asimov's Science Fiction Magazine, The Twilight Zone Magazine,* and *The Last Dangerous Visions,* and is currently at work on a novel.

CARRION COMFORT

Dan Simmons

Nina was going to take credit for the death of that Beatle, John. I thought that was in very bad taste. She had her scrapbook laid out on my mahogany coffee table, newspaper clippings neatly arranged in chronological order, the bald statements of death recording all of her Feedings. Nina Drayton's smile was radiant, but her pale-blue eyes showed no hint of warmth.

"We should wait for Willi," I said.

"Of course, Melanie. You're right, as always. How silly of me. I know the rules." Nina stood and began walking around the room, idly touching the furnishings or exclaiming softly over a ceramic statuette or piece of needlepoint. This part of the house had once been a conservatory, but now I used it as my sewing room. Green plants still caught the morning light. The light made it a warm, cozy place in the daytime, but now that winter had come the room was too chilly to use at night. Nor did I like the sense of darkness closing in against all those panes of glass.

"I love this house," said Nina.

She turned and smiled at me. "I can't tell you how much I look forward to coming back to Charleston. We should hold all of our reunions here."

I knew how much Nina loathed this city and this house.

"Willi would be hurt," I said. "You know how he likes to show off his place in Beverly Hills—and his new girl friends."

"And boyfriends," Nina said, laughing. Of all the changes and darkenings in Nina, her laugh has been least affected. It was still the husky but childish laugh that I had first heard so long ago. It had drawn me to her then—one lonely, adolescent girl responding to the warmth of another as a moth to a flame. Now it served only to chill me and put me even more on guard. Enough moths had been drawn to Nina's flame over the many decades.

"I'll send for tea," I said.

Mr. Thorne brought the tea in my best Wedgwood china. Nina and I sat in the slowly moving squares of sunlight and spoke softly of nothing important; mutually ignorant comments on the economy, references to books that the other had not gotten around to reading, and sympathetic murmurs about the low class of persons one meets while flying these days. Someone peering in from the garden might have thought he was seeing an aging but attractive niece visiting her favorite aunt. (I draw the line at suggesting that anyone would mistake us for mother and daughter.) People usually consider me a well-dressed if not stylish person. Heaven knows I have paid enough to have the wool skirts and silk blouses mailed from Scotland and France. But next to Nina I've always felt dowdy.

This day she wore an elegant, light-blue dress that must have cost several thousand dollars. The color made her complexion seem even more perfect than usual and brought out the blue of her eyes. Her hair had gone as gray as mine, but somehow she managed to get away with wearing it long and tied back with a single barrette. It looked youthful and chic on Nina and made me feel that my short, artificial curls were glowing with a blue rinse.

Few would suspect that I was four years younger than Nina. Time had been kind to her. And she had Fed more often.

She set down her cup and saucer and moved aimlessly around the room again. It was not like Nina to show such signs of nervousness. She stopped in front of the glass display case. Her gaze passed over the Hummels and the pewter pieces, and then stopped in surprise.

"Good heavens, Melanie. A pistol! What an odd place to put an old pistol."

"It's an heirloom," I said. "A Colt Peacemaker from right after the War Between the States. Quite expensive. And you're right, it *is* a silly place to keep it. But it's the only case I have in the house with a lock on it, and Mrs. Hodges often brings her grandchildren when she visits—"

"You mean it's *loaded?*"

"No, of course not," I lied. "But children should not play with such things . . ." I trailed off lamely. Nina nodded but did not bother to conceal the condescension in her smile. She went to look out the south window into the garden.

Damn her. It said volumes about Nina that she did not recognize that pistol.

On the day he was killed, Charles Edgar Larchmont had been my beau for precisely five months and two days. There had been no formal announcement, but we were to be married. Those five months had been a microcosm of the era itself—naive, flirtatious, formal to the point of preciosity, and romantic. Most of all, romantic. Romantic in the worst sense of the word: dedicated to saccharine or insipid ideals that only an adolescent—or an adolescent society—would strive to maintain. We were children playing with loaded weapons.

Nina, she was Nina Hawkins then, had her own beau—a tall, awkward, but well-meaning Englishman named Roger Harrison. Mr. Harrison had met Nina in London a year earlier, during the first stages of the Hawkinses' Grand Tour. Declaring himself smitten—another absurdity of those times—the tall Englishman had followed her from one European capital to another until, after being firmly reprimanded by Nina's father (an unimaginative little milliner who was constantly on the defensive about his doubtful social status), Harrison returned to London to "settle his affairs." Some months later he showed up in New York just as Nina was being packed off to her aunt's home in Charleston in order to terminate yet another flirtation. Still undaunted, the clumsy Englishman followed her south, ever mindful of the protocols and restrictions of the day.

We were a gay group. The day after I met Nina at Cousin Celia's June ball, the four of us were taking a hired boat up the Cooper River for a picnic on Daniel Island. Roger Harrison, serious and solemn on every topic, was a perfect foil for Charles's irreverent sense of humor. Nor did Roger seem to mind the good-natured jesting, since he was soon joining in the laughter with his peculiar *haw-haw-haw*.

Nina loved it all. Both gentlemen showered attention on her, and although Charles never failed to show the primacy of his affection for me, it was understood by all that Nina Hawkins was one of those young women who invariably becomes the center of male gallantry and attention in any gathering. Nor were the social strata of Charleston blind to the combined charm of our foursome. For two months of that now-distant summer, no party was complete, no excursion adequately planned, and no occasion considered a success unless we four were invited and had chosen to attend. Our happy dominance of the youthful social scene was so pronounced that Cousins Celia and Loraine wheedled their parents into leaving two weeks early for their annual August sojourn in Maine.

I am not sure when Nina and I came up with the idea of the duel. Perhaps it was during one of the long, hot nights when the other "slept over"—creeping into the other's bed, whispering and giggling, stifling our laughter when the rustling of starched uniforms betrayed the presence of our colored maids moving through the darkened halls. In any case, the idea was the natural outgrowth of the romantic pretensions of the time. The picture of Charles and Roger actually dueling over some abstract point of honor relating to *us* thrilled both of us in a physical way that I recognize now as a simple form of sexual titillation.

It would have been harmless except for the Ability. We had been so successful in our manipulation of male behavior—a manipulation that was both expected and encouraged in those days—that neither of us had yet suspected that there was anything beyond the ordinary in the way we could translate our whims into other people's actions. The field of parapsychology did not exist then; or rather, it existed only in the rappings and knockings of parlor-game séances. At any rate, we amused ourselves for several weeks with whispered fantasies, and then one of us—or perhaps both of us—used the Ability to translate the fantasy into reality.

In a sense, it was our first Feeding.

I do not remember the purported cause of the quarrel, perhaps some deliberate misinterpretation of one of Charles's jokes. I cannot recall who Charles and Roger arranged to have serve as seconds on that illegal outing. I do remember the hurt and confused expression on Roger Harrison's face during those few days. It was a caricature of ponderous dullness, the confusion of a man who finds himself in a situation not of his making and from which he cannot escape. I remember Charles and his mercurial swings of mood—the bouts of humor, periods of black anger, and the tears and kisses the night before the duel.

I remember with great clarity the beauty of that morning. Mists were floating up from the river and diffusing the rays of the rising sun as we rode out to the dueling field. I remember Nina reaching over and squeezing my hand with an impetuous excitement that was communicated through my body like an electric shock.

Much of the rest of that morning is missing. Perhaps in the intensity of that first, subconscious Feeding, I literally lost consciousness as I was engulfed in the waves of fear, excitement, pride—of *maleness*—emanating from our two beaus as they faced death on that lovely morning. I remember experiencing the shock of realizing, *this is really happening*, as I shared the tread of high boots through the grass. Someone was calling off the paces. I dimly recall the weight of the pistol in my hand—Charles's hand, I think; I will never know for sure—and a second of cold clarity before an explosion broke the connection, and the acrid smell of gunpowder brought me back to myself.

It was Charles who died. I have never been able to forget the incredible quantities of blood that poured from the small, round hole in his breast. His white shirt was crimson by the time I reached him.

There had been no blood in our fantasies. Nor had there been the sight of Charles with his head lolling, mouth dribbling saliva onto his bloodied chest while his eyes rolled back to show the whites like two eggs embedded in his skull.

Roger Harrison was sobbing as Charles breathed his final, shuddering gasps on that field of innocence.

I remember nothing at all about the confused hours that followed. The next morning I opened my cloth bag to find Charles's pistol lying with my things. Why would I have kept that revolver? If I had wished to take something from my fallen lover as a sign of remembrance, why that alien piece of metal? Why pry from his dead fingers the symbol of our thoughtless sin?

It said volumes about Nina that she did not recognize that pistol.

"Willi's here," announced Nina's amanuensis, the loathsome Miss Barrett Kramer. Kramer's appearance was as unisex as her name: short-cropped, black hair, powerful shoulders, and a blank, aggressive gaze that I associated with lesbians and criminals. She looked to be in her midthirties.

"Thank you, Barrett dear," said Nina.

Both of us went out to greet Willi, but Mr. Thorne had already let him in, and we met in the hallway.

"Melanie! You look marvelous! You grow younger each time I see you. Nina!" The change in Willi's voice was evident. Men continued to be overpowered by their first sight of Nina after an absence. There were hugs and kisses. Willi himself looked more dissolute than ever. His alpaca sport coat was exquisitely tailored, his turtleneck sweater successfully concealed the eroded lines of his wattled neck, but when he swept off his jaunty sports-car cap the long strands of white hair he had brushed forward to hide his encroaching baldness were knocked into disarray. Willi's face was flushed with excitement, but there was also the telltale capillary redness about the nose and cheeks that spoke of too much liquor, too many drugs.

"Ladies, I think you've met my associates, Tom Luhar and Jenson Reynolds?" The two men added to the crowd in my narrow hall. Mr. Luhar was thin and blond, smiling with perfectly capped teeth. Mr. Reynolds was a gigantic Negro, hulking forward with a sullen, bruised look on his coarse face. I was sure that neither Nina nor I had encountered these specific cat's-paws of Willi's before. It did not matter.

"Why don't we go into the parlor?" I suggested. It was an awkward procession ending with the three of us seated on the heavily upholstered chairs surrounding the Georgian tea table that had been my grandmother's.

"More tea, please, Mr. Thorne." Miss Kramer took that as her cue to leave, but Willi's two pawns stood uncertainly by the door, shifting from foot to foot and glancing at the crystal on display as if their mere proximity could break something. I would not have been surprised if that had proved to be the case.

"Jense!" Willi snapped his fingers. The Negro hesitated and then brought forward an expensive leather attaché case. Willi set it on the tea table and clicked the catches open with his short, broad fingers. "Why don't you two see Mrs. Fuller's man about getting something to drink?"

When they were gone Willi shook his head and smiled apologetically at Nina. "Sorry about that, Love."

Nina put her hand on Willi's sleeve. She leaned forward with an air of expectancy. "Melanie wouldn't let me begin the Game without you. Wasn't that *awful* of me to want to start without you, Willi dear?"

Willi frowned. After fifty years he still bridled at being called Willi. In Los Angeles he was Big Bill Borden. When he returned to his native Germany—which was not often because of the dangers involved—he was once again Wilhelm von Borchert, lord of dark manor, forest, and hunt. But Nina had called him Willi when they had first met, in 1931 in Vienna, and Willi he had remained.

"You begin, Willi dear," said Nina. "You go first."

I could remember the time when we would have spent the first few days of our reunion in conversation and catching up with one another's lives. Now there was not even time for small talk.

Willi showed his teeth and removed news clippings, notebooks, and a stack of cassettes from his briefcase. No sooner had he covered the small table with his material than Mr. Thorne arrived with the tea and Nina's scrapbook from the sewing room. Willi brusquely cleared a small space.

At first glance one might see certain similarities between Willi Borchert and Mr. Thorne. One would be mistaken. Both men tended to the florid, but Willi's complexion was the result of excess and emotion; Mr. Thorne had known neither of these for many years. Willi's balding was a patchy, self-consciously concealed thing—a weasel with mange; Mr. Thorne's bare head was smooth and unwrinkled. One could not imagine Mr. Thorne ever having *had* hair. Both men had gray eyes—what a novelist would call cold, gray eyes—but Mr. Thorne's eyes were cold with indifference, cold with a clarity coming from an absolute absence of troublesome emotion or thought. Willi's eyes were the cold of a blustery North Sea winter and were often clouded with shifting curtains of the emotions that controlled him—pride, hatred, love of pain, the pleasure of destruction.

Willi never referred to his use of the Ability as *Feedings*—I was evidently the only one who thought in those terms—but Willi sometimes talked of The Hunt. Perhaps it was the dark forests of his homeland that he thought of as he stalked his human quarry through the sterile streets of Los Angeles. Did Willi dream of the forest, I wondered. Did he look back to green wool hunting jackets, the applause of retainers, the gouts of blood from the dying boar? Or did Willi remember the slam of jackboots on cobblestones and the pounding of his lieutenants' fists on doors? Perhaps Willi still associated his Hunt with the dark European night of the ovens that he had helped to oversee.

I called it Feeding. Willi called it The Hunt. I had never heard Nina call it anything.

"Where is your VCR?" Willi asked. "I have put them all on tape."

"Oh, Willi," said Nina in an exasperated tone. "You know Melanie. She's *so* old fashioned. You know she wouldn't have a video player."

"I don't even have a television," I said. Nina laughed.

"Goddamn it," muttered Willi. "It doesn't matter. I have other records here." He snapped rubber bands from around the small, black notebooks. "It just would have been better on tape. The Los Angeles stations gave much coverage to the Hollywood Strangler, and I edited in the . . . *Ach!* Never mind."

He tossed the videocassettes into his briefcase and slammed the lid shut.

"Twenty-three," he said. "Twenty-three since we met twelve months ago. It doesn't seem that long, does it?"

"Show us," said Nina. She was leaning forward, and her blue eyes seemed very bright. "I've been wondering since I saw the Strangler interviewed on *Sixty Minutes*. He *was* yours, Willi? He seemed so—"

"*Ja, ja,* he was mine. A nobody. A timid little man. He was the gardener of a neighbor of mine. I left him alive so that the police could question him, erase any doubts. He will hang himself in his cell next month after the press loses interest. But this is more interesting. Look at this." Willi slid across several glossy black-and-white photographs. The NBC executive had murdered the five members of his family and drowned a visiting soap-opera actress in his pool. He had then stabbed himself repeatedly and written 50 SHARE in blood on the wall of the bathhouse.

"Reliving old glories, Willi?" asked Nina. "DEATH TO THE PIGS and all that?"

"No, goddamn it. I think it should receive points for irony. The girl had been scheduled to drown on the program. It was already in the script outline."

"Was he hard to Use?" It was my question. I was curious despite myself.

Willi lifted one eyebrow. "Not really. He was an alcoholic and heavily into cocaine. There was not much left. And he hated his family. Most people do."

"Most people in California, perhaps," said Nina primly. It was an odd comment from Nina. Years ago her father had committed suicide by throwing himself in front of a trolley car.

"Where did you make contact?" I asked.

"A party. The usual place. He bought the coke from a director who had ruined one of my—"

"Did you have to repeat the contact?"

Willi frowned at me. He kept his anger under control, but his face grew redder. "*Ja, ja.* I saw him twice more. Once I just watched from my car as he played tennis."

"Points for irony," said Nina. "But you lose points for repeated contact. If he were as empty as you say, you should have been able to Use him after only one touch. What else do you have?"

He had his usual assortment. Pathetic skid-row murders. Two domestic slayings. A highway collision that turned into a fatal shooting. "I was in the crowd," said Willi. "I made contact. He had a gun in the glove compartment."

"Two points," said Nina.

Willi had saved a good one for last. A once-famous child star had suffered a bizarre accident. He had left his Bel Air apartment while it filled with gas and then returned to light a match. Two others had died in the ensuing fire.

"You get credit only for him," said Nina.

"*Ja, ja.*"

"Are you absolutely sure about this one? It *could* have been an accident."

"Don't be ridiculous," snapped Willi. He turned toward me. "*This* one was very hard to Use. Very strong. I blocked his memory of turning on the gas. Had to hold it away for two hours. Then forced him into the room. He struggled not to strike the match."

"You should have had him use his lighter," said Nina.

"He didn't smoke," growled Willi. "He gave it up last year."

"Yes," smiled Nina. "I seem to remember him saying that to Johnny Carson." I could not tell whether Nina was jesting.

The three of us went through the ritual of assigning points. Nina did most of the talking. Willi went from being sullen to expansive to sullen again. At one point he reached over and patted my knee as he laughingly asked for my support. I said nothing. Finally he gave up, crossed the parlor to the liquor cabinet, and poured himself a tall glass of bourbon from father's decanter. The evening light was sending its final, horizontal rays through the stained-glass panels of the bay windows, and it cast a red hue on Willi as he stood next to the oak cupboard. His eyes were small, red embers in a bloody mask.

"Forty-one," said Nina at last.

She looked up brightly and showed the calculator as if it verified some objective fact. "I count forty-one points. What do you have, Melanie?"

"*Ja*," interrupted Willi. "That is fine. Now let us see your claims, Nina." His voice was flat and empty. Even Willi had lost some interest in the Game.

Before Nina could begin, Mr. Thorne entered and motioned that dinner was served. We adjourned to the dining room—Willi pouring himself another glass of bourbon and Nina fluttering her hands in mock frustration at the interruption of the Game. Once seated at the long, mahogany table, I worked at being a hostess. From decades of tradition, talk of the Game was banned from the dinner table. Over soup we discussed Willi's new movie and the purchase of another store for Nina's line of boutiques. It seemed that Nina's monthly column in *Vogue* was to be discontinued but that a newspaper syndicate was interested in picking it up.

Both of my guests exclaimed over the perfection of the baked ham, but I thought that Mr. Thorne had made the gravy a trifle too sweet. Darkness had filled the windows before we finished our chocolate mousse. The refracted light from the chandelier made Nina's hair dance with highlights while I feared that mine glowed more bluely than ever.

Suddenly there was a sound from the kitchen. The huge Negro's face appeared at the swinging door. His shoulder was hunched against white hands and his expression was that of a querulous child.

". . . the hell do you think we are sittin' here like goddamned—" The white hands pulled him out of sight.

"Excuse me, ladies," Willi dabbed linen at his lips and stood up. He still moved gracefully for all of his years.

Nina poked at her chocolate. There was one sharp, barked command from the kitchen and the sound of a slap. It was the slap of a man's hand—hard and flat as a small-caliber-rifle shot. I looked up and Mr. Thorne was at my elbow, clearing away the dessert dishes.

"Coffee, please, Mr. Thorne. For all of us." He nodded and his smile was gentle.

Franz Anton Mesmer had known of it even if he had not understood it. I suspect that Mesmer must have had some small touch of the

Ability. Modern pseudosciences have studied it and renamed it, removed most of its power, confused its uses and origins, but it remains the shadow of what Mesmer discovered. They have no idea of what it is like to Feed.

I despair at the rise of modern violence. I truly give in to despair at times, that deep, futureless pit of despair that poet Gerard Manley Hopkins called carrion comfort. I watch the American slaughterhouse, the casual attacks on popes, presidents, and uncounted others, and I wonder whether there are many more out there with the Ability or whether butchery has simply become the modern way of life.

All humans feed on violence, on the small exercises of power over another. But few have tasted—as we have—the ultimate power. And without the Ability, few know the unequaled pleasure of taking a human life. Without the Ability, even those who do feed on life cannot savor the flow of emotions in stalker and victim, the total exhilaration of the attacker who has moved beyond all rules and punishments, the strange, almost sexual submission of the victim in that final second of truth when all options are canceled, all futures denied, all possibilities erased in an exercise of absolute power over another.

I despair at modern violence. I despair at the impersonal nature of it and the casual quality that has made it accessible to so many. I had a television set until I sold it at the height of the Vietnam War. Those sanitized snippets of death—made distant by the camera's lens—meant nothing to me. But I believe it meant something to these cattle that surround me. When the war and the nightly televised body counts ended, they demanded more, *more*, and the movie screens and streets of this sweet and dying nation have provided it in mediocre, mob abundance. It is an addiction I know well.

They miss the point. Merely observed, violent death is a sad and sullied tapestry of confusion. But to those of us who have Fed, death can be a *sacrament*.

"My turn! My turn!" Nina's voice still resembled that of the visiting belle who had just filled her dance card at Cousin Celia's June ball.

We had returned to the parlor. Willi had finished his coffee and requested a brandy from Mr. Thorne. I was embarrassed for Willi. To have one's closest associates show any hint of unplanned behavior was certainly a sign of weakening Ability. Nina did not appear to have noticed.

"I have them all in order," said Nina. She opened the scrapbook on the now-empty tea table. Willi went through them carefully, sometimes asking a question, more often grunting assent. I murmured occasional agreement although I had heard of none of them. Except for the Beatle, of course. Nina saved that for near the end.

"Good God, Nina, that was you?" Willi seemed near anger. Nina's Feedings had always run to Park Avenue suicides and matrimonial disagreements ending in shots fired from expensive, small-caliber ladies' guns. This type of thing was more in Willi's crude style. Perhaps he felt that his territory was being invaded. "I mean . . . you were risking a lot, weren't you? It's so . . . damn it . . . so *public*."

Nina laughed and set down the calculator. "Willi *dear*, that's what the Game is *about*, is it not?"

Willi strode to the liquor cabinet and refilled his brandy snifter. The wind tossed bare branches against the leaded glass of the bay window. I do not like winter. Even in the South it takes its toll on the spirit.

"Didn't this guy . . . what's his name . . . buy the gun in Hawaii or someplace?" asked Willi from across the room. "That sounds like his initiative to me. I mean, if he was *already* stalking the fellow—"

"Willi dear," Nina's voice had gone as cold as the wind that raked the branches, "no one said he was *stable*. How many of yours are stable, Willi? But I made it *happen*, darling. I chose the place and the time. Don't you see the irony of the *place*, Willi? After that little prank on the director of that witchcraft movie a few years ago? It was straight from the script—"

"I don't know," said Willi. He sat heavily on the divan, spilling brandy on his expensive sport coat. He did not notice. The lamplight reflected from his balding skull. The mottles of age were more visible at night, and his neck, where it disappeared into his turtleneck, was all ropes and tendons. "I don't know." He looked up at me and smiled suddenly, as if we shared a conspiracy. "It could be like that writer fellow, eh, Melanie? It could be like that."

Nina looked down at the hands on her lap. They were clenched and the well-manicured fingers were white at the tips.

The Mind Vampires. That's what the writer was going to call his book.

I sometimes wonder if he really would have written anything. What was his name? Something Russian.

Willi and I received telegrams from Nina: COME QUICKLY YOU ARE NEEDED. That was enough. I was on the next morning's flight to New York. The plane was a noisy, propeller-driven Constellation, and I spent much of the flight assuring the overly solicitous stewardess that I needed nothing, that, indeed, I felt fine. She obviously had decided that I was someone's grandmother, who was flying for the first time.

Willi managed to arrive twenty minutes before I. Nina was distraught and as close to hysteria as I had ever seen her. She had been at a party in lower Manhattan two days before—she was not so distraught that she forgot to tell us what important names had been there—when she found herself sharing a corner, a fondue pot, and confidences with a young writer. Or rather, the writer was sharing confidences. Nina described him as a scruffy sort, with a wispy little beard, thick glasses, a corduroy sport coat worn over an old plaid shirt—one of the type invariably sprinkled around successful parties of that era, according to Nina. She knew enough not to call him a beatnik, for that term had just become passé, but no one had yet heard the term *hippie*, and it wouldn't have applied to him anyway. He was a writer of the sort that barely ekes out a living, these days at least, by selling blood and doing novelizations of television series. Alexander something.

His idea for a book—he told Nina that he had been working on it for some time—was that many of the murders then being committed were actually the result of a small group of psychic killers, he called them *mind vampires*, who used others to carry out their grisly deeds.

He said that a paperback publisher had already shown interest in his outline and would offer him a contract tomorrow if he would change the title to *The Zombie Factor* and put in more sex.

"So what?" Willi had said to Nina in disgust. "You have me fly across the continent for this? I might buy the idea myself."

That turned out to be the excuse we used to interrogate this Alexander somebody during an impromptu party given by Nina the next evening. I did not attend. The party was not overly successful, according to Nina, but it gave Willi the chance to have a long chat with the young, would-be novelist. In the writer's almost pitiable eagerness to do business with Bill Borden, producer of *Paris Memories, Three on a Swing*, and at least two other completely forgettable Technicolor features touring the drive-ins that summer, he revealed that the book consisted of a well-worn outline and a dozen pages of notes.

He was sure, however, that he could do a treatment for Mr. Borden in five weeks, perhaps even as fast as three weeks if he were flown out to Hollywood to get the proper creative stimulation.

Later that evening we discussed the possibility of Willi simply buying an option on the treatment, but Willi was short on cash at the time, and Nina was insistent. In the end the young writer opened his femoral artery with a Gillette blade and ran screaming into a narrow Greenwich Village side street to die. I don't believe that anyone ever bothered to sort through the clutter and debris of his remaining notes.

*   *   *

"It could be like that writer, *ja*, Melanie?" Willi patted my knee. I nodded. "He was mine," continued Willi, "and Nina tried to take credit. Remember?"

Again I nodded. Actually he had been neither Nina's nor Willi's. I had avoided the party so that I could make contact later without the young man noticing he was being followed. I did so easily. I remember sitting in an overheated little delicatessen across the street from the apartment building. It was over so quickly that there was almost no sense of Feeding. Then I was aware once again of the sputtering radiators and the smell of salami as people rushed to the door to see what the screaming was about. I remember finishing my tea slowly so that I did not have to leave before the ambulance was gone.

"Nonsense," said Nina. She busied herself with her little calculator. "How many points?" She looked at me. I looked at Willi.

"Six," he said with a shrug. Nina made a small show of totaling the numbers.

"Thirty-eight," she said and sighed theatrically. "You win again, Willi. Or rather, you beat *me* again. We must hear from Melanie. You've been so quiet. You must have some surprises for us."

"Yes," said Willi, "it is your turn to win. It has been several years."

"None," I said. I had expected an explosion of questions, but the silence was broken only by the ticking of the clock on the mantelpiece. Nina was looking away from me, at something hidden by the shadows in the corner.

"None?" echoed Willi.

"There was . . . one," I said at last. "But it was by accident. I came across them robbing an old man behind . . . but it was completely by accident."

Willi was agitated. He stood up, walked to the window, turned an old straight-back chair around and straddled it, arms folded. "What does this mean?"

"You're quitting the Game?" Nina asked as she turned to look at me. I let the question serve as the answer.

"Why?" snapped Willi. In his excitement it came out with a hard *v*.

If I had been raised in an era when young ladies were allowed to shrug, I would have done so. As it was, I contented myself with running my fingers along an imaginary seam on my skirt. Willi had asked the question, but I stared straight into Nina's eyes when I finally answered. "I'm tired. It's been too long. I guess I'm getting old."

"You'll get a lot *older* if you do not Hunt," said Willi. His body, his voice, the red mask of his face, everything signaled great anger just kept in check. "My God, Melanie, you *already* look older! You look terrible.

This is *why* we hunt, woman. Look at yourself in the mirror! Do you want to die an old woman just because you're tired of using *them?* Willi stood and turned his back.

"Nonsense!" Nina's voice was strong, confident, in command once more. "Melanie's *tired*, Willi. Be nice. We all have times like that. I remember how *you* were after the war. Like a whipped puppy. You wouldn't even go outside your miserable little flat in Baden. Even after we helped you get to New Jersey you just sulked around feeling sorry for yourself. Melanie *made up* the Game to help you feel better. So quiet! *Never* tell a lady who feels tired and depressed that she looks terrible. Honestly, Willi, you're such a *Schwachsinniger* sometimes. And a crashing boor to boot."

I had anticipated many reactions to my announcement, but this was the one I feared most. It meant that Nina had also tired of the Game. It meant that she was ready to move to another level of play.

It had to mean that.

"Thank you, Nina darling," I said. "I knew you would understand."

She reached across and touched my knee reassuringly. Even through my wool skirt, I could feel the cold of her fingers.

My guests would not stay the night. I implored. I remonstrated. I pointed out that their rooms were ready, that Mr. Thorne had already turned down the quilts.

"Next time," said Willi. "Next time, Melanie, my little love. We'll make a weekend of it as we used to. A week!" Willi was in a much better mood since he had been paid his thousand-dollar prize by each of us. He had sulked, but I had insisted. It soothed his ego when Mr. Thorne brought in a check already made out to WILLIAM D. BORDEN.

Again I asked him to stay, but he protested that he had a midnight flight to Chicago. He had to see a prizewinning author about a screenplay. Then he was hugging me good-bye, his companions were in the hall behind me, and I had a brief moment of terror.

But they left. The blond young man showed his white smile, and the Negro bobbed his head in what I took as a farewell. Then we were alone.

Nina and I were alone.

Not quite alone. Miss Kramer was standing next to Nina at the end of the hall. Mr. Thorne was out of sight behind the swinging door to the kitchen. I left him there.

Miss Kramer took three steps forward. I felt my breath stop for an instant. Mr. Thorne put his hand on the swinging door. Then the husky little brunette opened the door to the hall closet, removed Nina's coat, and stepped back to help her into it.

"Are you sure you won't stay?"

"No, thank you, darling. I've promised Barrett that we would drive to Hilton Head tonight."

"But it's late—"

"We have reservations. Thank you anyway, Melanie. I *will* be in touch."

"Yes."

"I mean it, dear. We must talk. I understand *exactly* how you feel, but you have to remember that the Game is still important to Willi. We'll have to find a way to end it without hurting his feelings. Perhaps we could visit him next spring in Karinhall or whatever he calls that gloomy old Bavarian place of his. A trip to the Continent would do wonders for you, dear."

"Yes."

"I *will* be in touch. After this deal with the new store is settled. We need to spend some time together, Melanie . . . just the two of us . . . like old times." Her lips kissed the air next to my cheek. She held my forearms tightly. "Good-bye, darling."

"Good-bye, Nina."

I carried the brandy glass to the kitchen. Mr. Thorne took it in silence.

"Make sure the house is secure," I said. He nodded and went to check the locks and alarm system. It was only nine forty-five, but I was very tired. *Age*, I thought. I went up the wide staircase, perhaps the finest feature of the house, and dressed for bed. It had begun to storm, and the sound of the cold raindrops on the window carried a sad rhythm to it.

Mr. Thorne looked in as I was brushing my hair and wishing it were longer. I turned to him. He reached into the pocket of his dark vest. When his hand emerged a slim blade flicked out. I nodded. He palmed the blade shut and closed the door behind him. I listened to his footsteps recede down the stairs to the chair in the front hall, where he would spend the night.

I believe I dreamed of vampires that night. Or perhaps I was thinking about them just prior to falling asleep, and a fragment had stayed with me until morning. Of all mankind's self-inflicted terrors, of all its pathetic little monsters, only the myth of the vampire had any vestige of dignity. Like the humans it feeds on, the vampire must respond to its own dark compulsions. But unlike its petty human prey, the vampire carries out its sordid means to the only possible ends that could justify such actions—the goal of literal immortality. There is a nobility there. And a sadness.

Before sleeping I thought of that summer long ago in Vienna. I saw Willi young again—blond, flushed with youth, and filled with pride at escorting two such independent American ladies.

I remembered Willi's high, stiff collars and the short dresses that Nina helped to bring into style that summer. I remembered the friendly sounds of crowded *Biergartens* and the shadowy dance of leaves in front of gas lamps.

I remembered the footsteps on wet cobblestones, the shouts, the distant whistles, and the silences.

Willi was right; I had aged. The past year had taken a greater toll than the preceding decade. But I had not Fed. Despite the hunger, despite the aging reflection in the mirror, *I had not Fed.*

I fell asleep trying to think of that writer's last name. I fell asleep hungry.

Morning. Bright sunlight through bare branches. It was one of those crystalline, warming winter days that make living in the South so much less depressing than merely surviving a Yankee winter. I had Mr. Thorne open the window a crack when he brought in my breakfast tray. As I sipped my coffee I could hear children playing in the courtyard. Once Mr. Thorne would have brought the morning paper with the tray, but I had long since learned that to read about the follies and scandals of the world was to desecrate the morning. I was growing less and less interested in the affairs of men. I had done without a newspaper, telephone, or television for twelve years and had suffered no ill effects unless one were to count a growing self-contentment as an ill thing. I smiled as I remembered Willi's disappointment at not being able to play his videocassettes. He was such a child.

"It is Saturday, is it not, Mr. Thorne?" At his nod I gestured for the tray to be taken away. "We will go out today," I said. "A walk. Perhaps a trip to the fort. Then dinner at Henry's and home. I have arrangements to make."

Mr. Thorne hesitated and half-stumbled as he was leaving the room. I paused in the act of belting my robe. It was not like Mr. Thorne to commit an ungraceful movement. I realized that he too was getting old. He straightened the tray and dishes, nodded his head, and left for the kitchen.

I would not let thoughts of aging disturb me on such a beautiful morning. I felt charged with a new energy and resolve. The reunion the night before had not gone well but neither had it gone as badly as it might have. I had been honest with Nina and Willi about my intention of quitting the Game. In the weeks and months to come, they—or at least Nina—would begin to brood over the ramifications of that, but by the time they chose to react, separately or together, I would be long gone. Already I had new (and old) identities waiting for me in Florida, Michigan, London, southern France, and even in New Delhi. Michigan was out for the time being. I had grown unused to the harsh climate. New Delhi was no longer the hospitable place for foreigners it had been when I resided there briefly before the war.

Nina had been right about one thing—a return to Europe would be good for me. Already I longed for the rich light and cordial *savoir vivre* of the villagers near my old summer house outside of Toulon.

The air outside was bracing. I wore a simple print dress and my spring coat. The trace of arthritis in my right leg had bothered me coming down the stairs, but I used my father's old walking stick as a cane. A young Negro servant had cut it for father the summer we moved from Greenville to Charleston. I smiled as we emerged into the warm air of the courtyard.

Mrs. Hodges came out of her doorway into the light. It was her grandchildren and their friends who were playing around the dry fountain. For two centuries the courtyard had been shared by the three brick buildings. Only my home had not been parceled into expensive townhouses or fancy apartments.

"Good morning, Miz Fuller."

"Good morning, Mrs. Hodges. A beautiful day, isn't it?"

"It is that. Are you off shopping?"

"Just for a walk, Mrs. Hodges. I'm surprised that Mr. Hodges isn't out today. He always seems to be working in the yard on Saturdays."

Mrs. Hodges frowned as one of the little girls ran between us. Her friend came squealing after her, sweater flying. "Oh, George is at the marina already."

"In the daytime?" I had often been amused by Mr. Hodges's departure for work in the evening: his security-guard uniform neatly pressed, gray hair jutting out from under his cap, black lunch pail gripped firmly under his arm.

Mr. Hodges was as leathery and bow-legged as an aged cowboy. He was one of those men who were always on the verge of retiring but who probably realized that to be suddenly inactive would be a form of death sentence.

"Oh, yes. One of those colored men on the day shift down at the storage building quit, and they asked George to fill in. I told him that he was too old to work four nights a week and then go back on the weekend, but you know George. He'll never retire."

"Well, give him my best," I said.

The girls running around the fountain made me nervous.

Mrs. Hodges followed me to the wrought-iron gate. "Will you be going away for the holidays, Miz Fuller?"

"Probably, Mrs. Hodges. Most probably." Then Mr. Thorne and I were out on the sidewalk and strolling toward the Battery. A few cars drove slowly down the narrow streets, some tourists stared at the houses of our Old Section, but the day was serene and quiet.

I saw the masts of the yachts and sailboats before we came in sight of the water as we emerged onto Broad Street.

"Please acquire tickets for us, Mr. Thorne," I said. "I believe I would like to see the fort."

As is typical of most people who live in close proximity to a popular tourist attraction, I had not taken notice of it for many years. It was an act of sentimentality to visit the fort now. An act brought on by my increasing acceptance of the fact that I would have to leave these parts forever. It is one thing to plan a move; it is something altogether different to be faced with the imperative reality of it.

There were few tourists. The ferry moved away from the marina and into the placid waters of the harbor. The combination of warm sunlight and the steady throb of the diesel caused me to doze briefly. I awoke as we were putting in at the dark hulk of the island fort.

For a while I moved with the tour group, enjoying the catacomb silences of the lower levels and the mindless singsong of the young woman from the Park Service. But as we came back to the museum, with its dusty dioramas and tawdry little trays of slides, I climbed the stairs back to the outer walls. I motioned for Mr. Thorne to stay at the top of the stairs and moved out onto the ramparts.

Only one other couple—a young pair with a cheap camera and a baby in an uncomfortable-looking papoose carrier—were in sight along the wall.

It was a pleasant moment. A midday storm was approaching from the west and it set a dark backdrop to the still-sunlit church spires, brick towers, and bare branches of the city.

Even from two miles away I could see the movement of people strolling along the Battery walkway. The wind was blowing in ahead of the dark clouds and tossing whitecaps against the rocking ferry and wooden dock. The air smelled of river and winter and rain by nightfall.

It was not hard to imagine that day long ago. The shells had dropped onto the fort until the upper layers were little more than protective piles of rubble. People had cheered from the rooftops behind the Battery. The bright colors of dresses and silk parasols must have been maddening to the Yankee gunners. Finally one had fired a shot above the crowded rooftops. The ensuing confusion must have been amusing from this vantage point.

A movement down below caught my attention. Something dark was sliding through the gray water—something dark and shark silent. I was jolted out of thoughts of the past as I recognized it as a Polaris submarine, old but obviously still operational, slipping through the dark water without a sound. Waves curled and rippled over the porpoise-smooth hull, sliding to either side in a white wake. There were several men on the tower. They were muffled in heavy coats, their hats pulled low. An improbably large pair of binoculars hung from the neck of one man, whom I assumed to be the captain. He pointed at something beyond Sullivan's Island. I stared. The periphery of my vision began to fade as I made contact. Sounds and sensations came to me as from a distance.

Tension. The pleasure of salt spray, breeze from the north, northwest. Anxiety of the sealed orders below. Awareness of the sandy shallows just coming into sight on the port side.

I was startled as someone came up behind me. The dots flickering at the edge of my vision fled as I turned.

Mr. Thorne was there. At my elbow. Unbidden. I had opened my mouth to command him back to the top of the stairs when I saw the cause of his approach. The youth who had been taking pictures of his pale wife was now walking toward me. Mr. Thorne moved to intercept him.

"Hey, excuse me, ma'am. Would you or your husband mind taking our picture?"

I nodded and Mr. Thorne took the proffered camera. It looked minuscule in his long-fingered hands. Two snaps and the couple were satisfied that their presence there was documented for posterity. The young man grinned idiotically and bobbed his head. Their baby began to cry as the cold wind blew in.

I looked back to the submarine, but already it had passed on, its gray tower a thin stripe connecting the sea and sky.

We were almost back to town, the ferry was swinging in toward the slip, when a stranger told me of Willi's death.

"It's awful, isn't it?" The garrulous old woman had followed me out onto the exposed section of deck. Even though the wind had grown chilly and I had moved twice to escape her mindless chatter, the woman had obviously chosen me as her conversational target for the final stages of the tour. Neither my reticence nor Mr. Thorne's glowering presence had discouraged her. "It must have been terrible," she continued. "In the dark and all."

"What was that?" A dark premonition prompted my question.

"Why, the airplane crash. Haven't you heard about it? It must have been awful, falling into the swamp and all. I told my daughter this morning—"

"What airplane crash? When?" The old woman cringed a bit at the sharpness of my tone, but the vacuous smile stayed on her face.

"Why, last night. This morning. I told my daughter—"

"*Where?* What aircraft are you talking about?" Mr. Thorne came closer as he heard the tone of my voice.

"The one last night," she quavered. "The one from Charleston. The paper in the lounge told all about it. Isn't it terrible? Eighty-five people. I told my daughter—"

I left her standing there by the railing. There was a crumpled newspaper near the snack bar and under the four-word headline were the sparse details of Willi's death. Flight 417, bound for Chicago, had left Charleston International Airport at twelve-eighteen A.M. Twenty minutes later the aircraft had exploded in midair not far from the city of Columbia. Fragments of fuselage and parts of bodies had fallen into Congaree Swamp, where fishermen had found them. There had been no survivors. The FAA and FBI were investigating.

There was a loud rushing in my ears, and I had to sit down or faint. My hands were clammy against the green-vinyl upholstery. People moved past me on their way to the exits.

Willi was dead. Murdered. Nina had killed him. For a few dizzy seconds I considered the possibility of a conspiracy—an elaborate ploy by Nina and Willi to confuse me into thinking that only one threat remained. But no. There would be no reason. If Nina had included Willi in her plans, there would be no need for such absurd machinations.

Willi was dead. His remains were spread over a smelly, obscure marshland. I could imagine his last moments. He would have been leaning back in first-class comfort, a drink in his hand, perhaps whispering to one of his loutish companions.

Then the explosion. Screams. Sudden darkness. A brutal tilting and the final fall to oblivion. I shuddered and gripped the metal arm of the chair.

How had Nina done it? Almost certainly not one of Willi's entourage. It was not beyond Nina's powers to Use Willi's own cat's-paws, especially in light of his failing Ability, but there would have been no reason to do so. She could have Used anyone on that flight. It *would* have been difficult. The elaborate step of preparing the bomb, the supreme effort of blocking all memory of it, and the almost unbelievable feat of Using someone even as we sat together drinking coffee and brandy.

But Nina could have done it. Yes, she *could* have. And the timing. The timing could mean only one thing.

The last of the tourists had filed out of the cabin. I felt the slight bump that meant we had tied up to the dock. Mr. Thorne stood by the door.

Nina's timing meant that she was attempting to deal with both of us at once. She obviously had planned it long before the reunion and my timorous announcement of withdrawal. How amused Nina must have been. No wonder she had reacted so generously! Yet, she had made one great mistake. By dealing with Willi first, Nina had banked everything on my not hearing the news before she could turn on me. She knew that I had no access to daily news and only rarely left the house anymore. Still, it was unlike Nina to leave anything to chance. Was it possible that she thought I had lost the Ability completely and that Willi was the greater threat?

I shook my head as we emerged from the cabin into the gray afternoon light. The wind sliced at me through my thin coat. The view of the gangplank was blurry and I realized that tears had filled my eyes. For Willi? He had been a pompous, weak old fool. For Nina's betrayal? Perhaps it was only the cold wind.

The streets of the Old Section were almost empty of pedestrians. Bare branches clicked together in front of the windows of fine homes. Mr. Thorne stayed by my side. The cold air sent needles of arthritic pain up my right leg to my hip. I leaned more heavily upon father's walking stick.

What would her next move be? I stopped. A fragment of newspaper, caught by the wind, wrapped itself around my ankle and then blew on.

How would she come at me? Not from a distance. She was somewhere in town. I knew that. While it is possible to Use someone from a great distance, it would involve great rapport, an almost intimate knowledge of that person. And if contact were lost, it would be difficult if not impossible to reestablish at a distance. None of us had known why this was so. It did not matter now. But the thought of Nina still here, nearby, made my heart begin to race.

Not from a distance. I would see my assailant. If I knew Nina at all, I knew that. Certainly Willi's death had been the least personal Feeding imaginable, but that had been a mere technical operation. Nina obviously had decided to settle old scores with *me*, and Willi had become an obstacle to her, a minor but measurable threat that had to be eliminated before she could proceed. I could easily imagine that in Nina's own mind her choice of death for Willi would be interpreted as an act of compassion, almost a sign of affection. Not so with me. I felt that Nina would want me to know, however briefly, that she was behind the attack. In a sense, her own vanity would be my warning. Or so I hoped.

I was tempted to leave immediately. I could have Mr. Thorne get the Audi out of storage, and we could be beyond Nina's influence in an hour—away to a new life within a few more hours. There were important items in the house, of course, but the funds that I had stored elsewhere would replace most of them. It would be almost welcome to leave everything behind with the discarded identity that had accumulated them.

No, I could not leave. Not yet.

From across the street the house looked dark and malevolent. Had *I* closed those blinds on the second floor? There was a shadowy movement in the courtyard, and I saw Mrs. Hodges's granddaughter and a friend scamper from one doorway to another. I stood irresolutely on the curb and tapped father's stick against the black-barked tree. It was foolish to dither so—I knew it was—but it had been a long time since I had been forced to make a decision under stress.

"Mr. Thorne, please check the house. Look in each room. Return quickly."

A cold wind came up as I watched Mr. Thorne's black coat blend into the gloom of the courtyard. I felt terribly exposed standing there alone. I found myself glancing up and down the street, looking for Miss Kramer's dark hair, but the only sign of movement was a young woman pushing a perambulator far down the street.

The blinds on the second floor shot up, and Mr. Thorne's face stared out whitely for a minute. Then he turned away, and I remained staring at the dark rectangle of window. A shout from the courtyard startled me, but it was only the little girl—what was her name?—calling to her friend. Kathleen, that was it. The two sat on the edge of the fountain and opened a box of animal crackers. I stared intently at them and then relaxed. I even managed to smile a little at the extent of my paranoia. For a second I considered Using Mr. Thorne directly, but the thought of being helpless on the street dissuaded me. When one is in complete contact, the senses still function but are a distant thing at best.

Hurry. The thought was sent almost without volition. Two bearded men were walking down the sidewalk on my side of the street. I crossed to stand in front of my own gate. The men were laughing and gesturing at each other. One looked over at me. *Hurry.*

Mr. Thorne came out of the house, locked the door behind him, and crossed the courtyard toward me. One of the girls said something to him and held out the box of crackers, but he ignored her. Across the street the two men continued walking. Mr. Thorne handed me the large front-door key. I dropped it in my coat pocket and looked sharply at him. He nodded. His placid smile unconsciously mocked my consternation.

"You're sure?" I asked. Again the nod. "You checked all of the rooms?" Nod. "The alarms?" Nod. "You looked in the basement?" Nod. "No sign of disturbance?" Mr. Thorne shook his head.

My hand went to the metal of the gate, but I hesitated. Anxiety filled my throat like bile. I was a silly old woman, tired and aching from the chill, but I could not bring myself to open that gate.

"Come." I crossed the street and walked briskly away from the house. "We will have dinner at Henry's and return later." Only I was not walking toward the old restaurant; I was heading away from the house in what I knew was a blind, directionless panic. It was not until we reached the waterfront and were walking along the Battery wall that I began to calm down.

No one else was in sight. A few cars moved along the street, but to approach us someone would have to cross a wide, empty space. The gray clouds were quite low and blended with the choppy, white-crested waves in the bay.

The open air and fading evening light served to revive me, and I began to think more clearly. Whatever Nina's plans had been, they certainly had been thrown into disarray by my day-long absence. I doubted that Nina would stay if there were the slightest risk to herself. No, she would be returning to New York by plane even as I stood shivering on the Battery walk. In the morning I would receive a telegram. I could see it. MELANIE. ISN'T IT TERRIBLE ABOUT WILLI? TERRIBLY SAD. CAN YOU TRAVEL WITH ME TO THE FUNERAL? LOVE, NINA.

I began to realize that my reluctance to leave immediately had come from a desire to return to the warmth and comfort of my home. I simply had been afraid to shuck off this old cocoon. I could do so now. I would wait in a safe place while Mr. Thorne returned to the house to pick up the one thing I could not leave behind. Then he would get the car out of storage, and by the time Nina's telegram arrived I would be far away. It would be *Nina* who would be starting at shadows in the months and years to come. I smiled and began to frame the necessary commands.

"Melanie."

My head snapped around. Mr. Thorne had not spoken in twenty-eight years. He spoke now.

"Melanie." His face was distorted in a rictus that showed his back teeth. The knife was in his right hand. The blade flicked out as I stared. I looked into his empty, gray eyes, and I knew.

"Melanie."

The long blade came around in a powerful arc. I could do nothing to stop it. It cut through the fabric of my coat sleeve and continued into my side. But in the act of turning, my purse had swung with me. The knife tore through the leather, ripped through the jumbled contents, pierced my coat, and drew blood above my lowest left rib. The purse had saved my life.

I raised father's heavy walking stick and struck Mr. Thorne squarely in his left eye. He reeled but did not make a sound. Again he swept the air with the knife, but I had taken two steps back and his vision was clouded. I took a two-handed grip on the cane and swung sideways again, bringing the stick around in an awkward chop. Incredibly, it again found the eye socket. I took three more steps back.

Blood streamed down the left side of Mr. Thorne's face, and the damaged eye protruded onto his cheek. The rictal grin remained. His head came up, he raised his left hand slowly, plucked out the eye with a soft snapping of a gray cord, and threw it into the water of the bay. He came toward me. I turned and ran.

I *tried* to run. The ache in my right leg slowed me to a walk after twenty paces. Fifteen more hurried steps and my lungs were out of air, my heart threatening to burst. I could feel a wetness seeping down my left side and there was a tingling—like an ice cube held against the skin—where the knife blade had touched me. One glance back showed me that Mr. Thorne was striding toward me faster than I was moving. Normally he could have overtaken me in four strides. But it is hard to make someone run when you are Using him. Especially when that person's body is reacting to shock and trauma. I glanced back again, almost slipping on the slick pavement. Mr. Thorne was grinning widely. Blood poured from the empty socket and stained his teeth. No one else was in sight.

Down the stairs, clutching at the rail so as not to fall. Down the twisting walk and up the asphalt path to the street. Pole lamps flickered and went on as I passed. Behind me Mr. Thorne took the steps in two jumps. As I hurried up the path, I thanked God that I had worn low-heel shoes for the boat ride. What would an observer think seeing this bizarre, slow-motion chase between two old people? There were no observers.

I turned onto a side street. Closed shops, empty warehouses. Going left would take me to Broad Street, but to the right, half a block away, a lone figure had emerged from a dark storefront. I moved that way, no longer able to run, close to fainting. The arthritic cramps in my leg hurt more than I could ever have imagined and threatened to collapse me on the sidewalk. Mr. Thorne was twenty paces behind me and quickly closing the distance.

The man I was approaching was a tall, thin Negro wearing a brown nylon jacket. He was carrying a box of what looked like framed sepia photographs.

He glanced at me as I approached and then looked over my shoulder at the apparition ten steps behind.

"Hey!" The man had time to shout the single syllable and then I reached out with my mind and *shoved*. He twitched like a poorly handled marionette. His jaw dropped, and his eyes glazed over, and he lurched past me just as Mr. Thorne reached for the back of my coat.

The box flew into the air, and glass shattered on the brick sidewalk. Long, brown fingers reached for a white throat. Mr. Thorne backhanded him away, but the Negro clung tenaciously, and the two swung around like awkward dance partners. I reached the opening to an alley and leaned my face against the cold brick to revive myself. The effort of concentration while Using this stranger did not afford me the luxury of resting even for a second.

I watched the clumsy stumblings of the two tall men for a while and resisted an absurd impulse to laugh.

Mr. Thorne plunged the knife into the other's stomach, withdrew it, plunged it in again. The Negro's fingernails were clawing at Mr. Thorne's good eye now. Strong teeth were snapping in search of the blade for a third time, but the heart was still beating, and he was still usable. The man jumped, scissoring his legs around Mr. Thorne's middle while his jaws closed on the muscular throat. Fingernails raked bloody streaks across white skin. The two went down in a tumble.

Kill him. Fingers groped for an eye, but Mr. Thorne reached up with his left hand and snapped the thin wrist. Limp fingers continued to flail. With a tremendous exertion, Mr. Thorne lodged his forearm against the other's chest and lifted him bodily as a reclining father tosses a child above him. Teeth tore away a piece of flesh, but there was no vital damage. Mr. Thorne brought the knife between them, up, left, then right. He severed half the Negro's throat with the second swing, and blood fountained over both of them. The smaller man's legs spasmed twice, Mr. Thorne threw him to one side, and I turned and walked quickly down the alley.

Out into the light again, the fading evening light, and I realized that I had run myself into a dead end. Backs of warehouses and the windowless, metal side of the Battery Marina pushed right up against the waters of the bay. A street wound away to the left, but it was dark, deserted, and far too long to try.

I looked back in time to see the black silhouette enter the alley behind me.

I tried to make contact, but there was nothing there. Nothing. Mr. Thorne might as well have been a hole in the air. I would worry later how Nina had done this thing.

The side door to the marina was locked. The main door was almost a hundred yards away and would also be locked. Mr. Thorne emerged from the alley and swung his head left and right in search of me. In the dim light his heavily streaked face looked almost black. He began lurching toward me.

I raised father's walking stick, broke the lower pane of the window, and reached in through the jagged shards. If there was a bottom or top bolt I was dead. There was a simple doorknob lock and crossbolt. My fingers slipped on the cold metal, but the bolt slid back as Mr. Thorne stepped up on the walk behind me. Then I was inside and throwing the bolt.

It was very dark. Cold seeped up from the concrete floor and there was a sound of many small boats rising and falling at their moorings. Fifty yards away light spilled out of the office windows. I had hoped there would be an alarm system, but the building was too old and the marina too cheap to have one. I walked toward the light as Mr. Thorne's forearm shattered the remaining glass in the door behind me. The arm withdrew. A great kick broke off the top hinge and splintered wood around the bolt. I glanced at the office, but only the sound of a radio talk show came out of the impossibly distant door. Another kick.

I turned to my right and stepped to the bow of a bobbing inboard cruiser. Five steps and I was in the small, covered space that passed for a forward cabin. I closed the flimsy access panel behind me and peered out through the Plexiglas.

Mr. Thorne's third kick sent the door flying inward, dangling from long strips of splintered wood. His dark form filled the doorway. Light from a distant streetlight glinted off the blade in his right hand.

Please. Please hear the noise. But there was no movement from the office, only the metallic voices from the radio. Mr. Thorne took four paces, paused, and stepped down onto the first boat in line. It was an open outboard, and he was back up on the concrete in six seconds. The second boat had a small cabin. There was a ripping sound as Mr. Thorne kicked open the tiny hatch door, and then he was back up on the walkway. My boat was the eighth in line. I wondered why he couldn't just hear the wild hammering of my heart.

I shifted position and looked through the starboard port. The murky Plexiglas threw the light into streaks and patterns. I caught a brief glimpse of white hair through the window, and the radio was switched to another station. Loud music echoed in the long room. I slid back to the other porthole. Mr. Thorne was stepping off the fourth boat.

I closed my eyes, forced my ragged breathing to slow, and tried to remember countless evenings watching a bow-legged old figure shuffle down the street. Mr. Thorne finished his inspection of the fifth boat, a longer cabin cruiser with several dark recesses, and pulled himself back onto the walkway.

Forget the coffee in the thermos. Forget the crossword puzzle. Go look!

The sixth boat was a small outboard. Mr. Thorne glanced at it but did not step onto it. The seventh was a low sailboat, mast folded down, canvas stretched across the cockpit. Mr. Thorne's knife slashed through the thick material. Blood-streaked hands pulled back the canvas like a shroud being torn away. He jumped back to the walkway.

Forget the coffee. Go look! Now!

Mr. Thorne stepped onto the bow of my boat. I felt it rock to his weight. There was nowhere to hide, only a tiny storage locker under the seat, much too small to squeeze into. I untied the canvas strips that held the seat cushion to the bench. The sound of my ragged breathing seemed to echo in the little space. I curled into a fetal position behind the cushion as Mr. Thorne's leg moved past the starboard port. *Now.* Suddenly his face filled the Plexiglas strip not a foot from my head. His impossibly wide grimace grew even wider. *Now.* He stepped into the cockpit.

Now. Now. Now.

Mr. Thorne crouched at the cabin door. I tried to brace the tiny louvered door with my legs, but my right leg would not obey. Mr. Thorne's fist slammed through the thin wooden strips and grabbed my ankle.

"Hey there!"

It was Mr. Hodges's shaky voice. His flashlight bobbed in our direction.

Mr. Thorne shoved against the door. My left leg folded painfully. Mr. Thorne's left hand firmly held my ankle through the shattered slats while the hand with the knife blade came through the opening hatch.

"Hey—" My mind shoved. Very hard. The old man stopped. He dropped the flashlight and unstrapped the buckle over the grip of his revolver.

Mr. Thorne slashed the knife back and forth. The cushion was almost knocked out of my hands as shreds of foam filled the cabin. The blade caught the tip of my little finger as the knife swung back again.

Do it. Now. Do it. Mr. Hodges gripped the revolver in both hands and fired. The shot went wide in the dark as the sound echoed off concrete and water. *Closer, you fool. Move!* Mr. Thorne shoved again, and his body squeezed into the open hatch. He released my ankle to free his left arm, but almost instantly his hand was back in the cabin, grasping for me. I reached up and turned on the overhead light. Darkness stared at me from his empty eye socket. Light through the broken shutters spilled yellow strips across his ruined face. I slid to the left, but Mr. Thorne's hand, which had my coat, was pulling me off the bench. He was on his knees, freeing his right hand for the knife thrust.

Now! Mr. Hodges's second shot caught Mr. Thorne in the right hip. He grunted as the impact shoved him backward into a sitting position. My coat ripped, and buttons rattled on the deck.

The knife slashed the bulkhead near my ear before it pulled away.

Mr. Hodges stepped shakily onto the bow, almost fell, and inched his way around the starboard side. I pushed the hatch against Mr. Thorne's arm, but he continued to grip my coat and drag me toward him. I fell to my knees. The blade swung back, ripped through foam, and slashed at my coat. What was left of the cushion flew out of my hands. I had Mr. Hodges stop four feet away and brace the gun on the roof of the cabin.

Mr. Thorne pulled the blade back and poised it like a matador's sword. I could sense the silent scream of triumph that poured out over the stained teeth like a noxious vapor. The light of Nina's madness burned behind the single, staring eye.

Mr. Hodges fired. The bullet severed Mr. Thorne's spine and continued on into the port scupper. Mr. Thorne arched backward, splayed out his arms, and flopped onto the deck like a great fish that had just been landed. The knife fell to the floor of the cabin, while stiff, white fingers continued to slap nervelessly against the deck. I had Mr. Hodges step forward, brace the muzzle against Mr. Thorne's temple just above the remaining eye, and fire again. The sound was muted and hollow.

There was a first-aid kit in the office bathroom. I had the old man stand by the door while I bandaged my little finger and took three aspirin.

My coat was ruined, and blood had stained my print dress. I had never cared very much for the dress—thought it made me look dowdy—but the coat had been a favorite of mine. My hair was a mess. Small, moist bits of gray matter flecked it. I splashed water on my face and brushed my hair as best I could. Incredibly, my tattered purse had stayed with me, although many of the contents had spilled out. I transferred keys, billfold, reading glasses, and Kleenex to my large coat pocket and dropped the purse behind the toilet. I no longer had father's walking stick, but I could not remember where I had dropped it.

Gingerly, I removed the heavy revolver from Mr. Hodges's grip. The old man's arm remained extended, fingers curled around air. After fumbling for a few seconds I managed to click open the cylinder. Two cartridges remained unfired. The old fool had been walking around with all six chambers loaded! *Always leave an empty chamber under the hammer.* That is what Charles had taught me that gay and distant summer so long ago, when such weapons were merely excuses for trips to the island for target practice punctuated by the shrill shrieks of our nervous laughter as Nina and I allowed ourselves to be held, arms supported, bodies shrinking back into the firm support of our so-serious tutors' arms. *One must always count the cartridges,* lectured Charles, as I half-swooned against him, smelling the sweet, maculine, shaving soap and tobacco smell rising from him on that warm, bright day.

Mr. Hodges stirred slightly as my attention wandered. His mouth gaped, and his dentures hung loosely. I glanced at the worn leather belt, but there were no extra bullets there, and I had no idea where he kept any. I probed, but there was little left in the old man's jumble of thoughts except for a swirling tape-loop replay of the muzzle being laid against Mr. Thorne's temple, the explosion, the—

"Come," I said. I adjusted the glasses on Mr. Hodges's vacant face, returned the revolver to the holster, and let him lead me out of the building.

It was very dark out. We had gone six blocks before the old man's violent shivering reminded me that I had forgotten to have him put on his coat. I tightened my mental vise, and he stopped shaking.

The house looked just as it had . . . my God . . . only forty-five minutes earlier. There were no lights. I let us into the courtyard and searched my overstuffed coat pocket for the key. My coat hung loose and the cold night air nipped at me. From behind lighted windows across the courtyard came the laughter of little girls, and I hurried so that Kathleen would not see her grandfather entering my house.

Mr. Hodges went in first, with the revolver extended. I had him switch on the light before I entered.

The parlor was empty, undisturbed. The light from the chandelier in the dining room reflected off polished surfaces. I sat down for a minute on the Williamsburg reproduction chair in the hall to let my heart rate return to normal. I did not have Mr. Hodges lower the hammer on the still-raised pistol. His arm began to shake from the strain of holding it. Finally I rose and we moved down the hall toward the conservatory.

Miss Kramer exploded out of the swinging door from the kitchen with the heavy iron poker coming down in an arc. The gun fired harmlessly into the polished floor as the old man's arm snapped from the impact. The gun fell from limp fingers as Miss Kramer raised the poker for a second blow.

I turned and ran back down the hallway. Behind me I heard the crushed-melon sound of the poker contacting Mr. Hodges's skull. Rather than run into the courtyard I went up the stairway. A mistake. Miss Kramer bounded up the stairs and reached the bedroom door only a few seconds after I. I caught one glimpse of her widened, maddened eyes and of the upraised poker before I slammed and locked the heavy door. The latch clicked just as the brunette on the other side began to throw herself against the wood. The thick oak did not budge. Then I heard the concussion of metal against the door and frame. Again.

Cursing my stupidity, I turned to the familiar room, but there was nothing there to help me. There was not so much as a closet to hide in, only the antique wardrobe. I moved quickly to the window and threw up the sash. My screams would attract attention but not before that monstrosity had gained access. She was prying at the edges of the door now. I looked out, saw the shadows in the window across the way, and did what I had to do.

Two minutes later I was barely conscious of the wood giving way around the latch. I heard the distant grating of the poker as it pried the recalcitrant metal plate. The door swung inward.

Miss Kramer was covered with sweat. Her mouth hung slack, and drool slid from her chin. Her eyes were not human. Neither she nor I heard the soft tread of sneakers on the stairs behind her.

Keep moving. Lift it, Pull it back—all the way back. Use both hands. Aim it.

Something warned Miss Kramer. Warned Nina, I should say, there was no more Miss Kramer. The brunette turned to see little Kathleen standing on the top stair, her grandfather's heavy weapon aimed and cocked. The other girl was in the courtyard shouting for her friend.

This time Nina knew she had to deal with the threat. Miss Kramer hefted the poker and turned into the hall just as the pistol fired. The recoil tumbled Kathleen backward down the stairs as a red corsage blossomed above Miss Kramer's left breast. She spun but grasped the railing with her left hand and lurched down the stairs after the child. I released the ten year old just as the poker fell, rose, fell again. I moved to the head of the stairway. I had to *see*.

Miss Kramer looked up from her grim work. Only the whites of her eyes were visible in her spattered face. Her masculine shirt was soaked with her own blood, but still she moved, functioned. She picked up the gun in her left hand. Her mouth opened wider, and a sound emerged like steam leaking from an old radiator.

"Melanie . . ." I closed my eyes as the thing started up the stairs for me.

Kathleen's friend came in through the open door, her small legs pumping. She took the stairs in six jumps and wrapped her thin, white arms around Miss Kramer's neck in a tight embrace.

The two went over backward, across Kathleen, all the way down the wide stairs to the polished wood below.

The girl appeared to be little more than bruised. I went down and moved her to one side. A blue stain was spreading along one cheekbone, and there were cuts on her arms and forehead. Her blue eyes blinked uncomprehendingly.

Miss Kramer's neck was broken. I picked up the pistol on the way to her and kicked the poker to one side. Her head was at an impossible angle, but she was still alive. Her body was paralyzed, urine already stained the wood, but her eyes still blinked and her teeth clicked together obscenely. I had to hurry. There were adult voices calling from the Hodgeses' townhouse. The door to the courtyard was wide open. I turned to the girl. "Get up." She blinked once and rose painfully to her feet.

I shut the door and lifted a tan raincoat from the coatrack.

It took only a minute to transfer the contents of my pockets to the raincoat and to discard my ruined spring coat. Voices were calling in the courtyard now.

I kneeled down next to Miss Kramer and seized her face in my hands, exerting pressure to keep the jaws still. Her eyes had rolled upward again, but I shook her head until the irises were visible. I leaned forward until our cheeks were touching. My whisper was louder than a shout.

"I'm coming for you, Nina."

I dropped her head onto the wood and walked quickly to the conservatory, my sewing room. I did not have time to get the key from upstairs; so I raised a Windsor side chair and smashed the glass of the cabinet. My coat pocket was barely large enough.

The girl remained standing in the hall. I handed her Mr. Hodges's pistol. Her left arm hung at a strange angle and I wondered if she had broken something after all. There was a knock at the door, and someone tried the knob.

"This way," I whispered, and led the girl into the dining room.

We stepped across Miss Kramer on the way, walked through the dark kitchen as the pounding grew louder, and then were out, into the alley, into the night.

*   *   *

There were three hotels in this part of the Old Section. One was a modern, expensive motor hotel some ten blocks away, comfortable but commercial. I rejected it immediately. The second was a small, homey lodging house only a block from my home. It was a pleasant but nonexclusive little place, exactly the type I would choose when visiting another town. I rejected it also. The third was two and a half blocks farther, an old Broad Street mansion done over into a small hotel, expensive antiques in every room, absurdly overpriced. I hurried there. The girl moved quickly at my side. The pistol was still in her hand, but I had her remove her sweater and carry it over the weapon. My leg ached, and I frequently leaned on the girl as we hurried down the street.

The manager of the Mansard House recognized me. His eyebrows went up a fraction of an inch as he noticed my disheveled appearance. The girl stood ten feet away in the foyer, half-hidden in the shadows.

"I'm looking for a friend of mine," I said brightly. "A Mrs. Drayton."

The manager started to speak, paused, frowned without being aware of it, and tried again. "I'm sorry. No one under that name is registered here."

"Perhaps she registered under her maiden name," I said. "Nina Hawkins. She's an older woman but very attractive. A few years younger than I. Long, gray hair. Her friend may have registered for her . . . an attractive, young, dark-haired lady named Barret Kramer—"

"No, I'm sorry," said the manager in a strangely flat tone. "No one under that name has registered. Would you like to leave a message in case your party arrives later?"

"No," I said. "No message."

I brought the girl into the lobby, and we turned down a corridor leading to the restrooms and side stairs. "Excuse me, please," I said to a passing porter. "Perhaps you can help me."

"Yes, ma'am." He stopped, annoyed, and brushed back his long hair. It would be tricky. If I was not to lose the girl, I would have to act quickly.

"I'm looking for a friend," I said. "She's an older lady but quite attractive. Blue eyes. Long, gray hair. She travels with a young woman who has dark, curly hair."

"No, ma'am. No one like that is registered here."

I reached out and grabbed hold of his forearm tightly. I released the girl and focused on the boy. "Are you sure?"

"Mrs. Harrison," he said. His eyes looked past me. "Room 207. North front."

I smiled. *Mrs. Harrison.* Good God, what a fool Nina was. Suddenly the girl let out a small whimper and slumped against the wall. I made a quick decision. I like to think that it was compassion, but I sometimes remember that her left arm was useless.

"What's your name?" I asked the child, gently stroking her bangs. Her eyes moved left and right in confusion. "Your *name!*"

"Alicia." It was only a whisper.

"All right, Alicia. I want you to go home now. Hurry, but don't run."

"My *arm* hurts," she said. Her lips began to quiver. I touched her forehead again and *pushed*.

"You're going home," I said. "Your arm does not hurt. You won't remember anything. This is like a dream that you will forget. Go home. Hurry, but do not run." I took the pistol from her but left it wrapped in the sweater. "Bye-bye, Alicia."

She blinked and crossed the lobby to the doors. I handed the gun to the bellhop. "Put it under your vest," I said.

"Who is it?" Nina's voice was light.

"Albert, ma'am. The porter. Your car's out front, and I'll take your bags down."

There was the sound of a lock clicking, and the door opened the width of a still-secured chain. Albert blinked in the glare, smiled shyly, and brushed his hair back. I pressed against the wall.

"Very well." She undid the chain and moved back. She had already turned and was latching her suitcase when I stepped into the room.

"Hello, Nina," I said softly. Her back straightened, but even that move was graceful. I could see the imprint on the bedspread where she had been lying. She turned slowly. She was wearing a pink dress I had never seen before.

"Hello, Melanie." She smiled. Her eyes were the softest, purest blue I had ever seen. I had the porter take Mr. Hodges's gun out and aim it. His arm was steady. He pulled back the hammer and held it with his thumb. Nina folded her hands in front of her. Her eyes never left mine.

"Why?" I asked.

Nina shrugged ever so slightly. For a second I thought she was going to laugh. I could not have borne it if she had laughed—that husky, childlike laugh that had touched me so many times. Instead she closed her eyes. Her smile remained.

"Why Mrs. Harrison?" I asked.

"Why, darling, I felt I owed him *something*. I mean, poor Roger. Did I ever tell you how he died? No, of course I didn't. And you never asked." Her eyes opened. I glanced at the porter, but his aim was steady. It only remained for him to exert a little more pressure on the trigger.

"He *drowned*, darling," said Nina. "Poor Roger threw himself from that steamship—what was its name?—the one that was taking him back to England. So strange. And he had just written me a letter promising marriage. Isn't that a *terribly* sad story, Melanie? Why do you think he did a thing like that? I guess we'll never know, will we?"

"I guess we never will," I said. I silently ordered the porter to pull the trigger.

Nothing.

I looked quickly to my right. The young man's head was turning toward me. *I had not made him do that.* The stiffly extended arm began to swing in my direction. The pistol moved smoothly like the tip of a weather vane swinging in the wind.

No! I strained until the cords in my neck stood out. The turning slowed but did not stop until the muzzle was pointing at my face. Nina laughed now. The sound was very loud in the little room.

"Good-bye, Melanie *dear*," Nina said, and laughed again. She laughed and nodded at the porter. I stared into the black hole as the hammer fell. On an empty chamber. And another. And another.

"Good-bye, Nina," I said as I pulled Charles's long pistol from the raincoat pocket. The explosion jarred my wrist and filled the room with blue smoke. A small hole, smaller than a dime but as perfectly round, appeared in the precise center of Nina's forehead. For the briefest second she remained standing as if nothing had happened. Then she fell backward, recoiled from the high bed, and dropped face forward onto the floor.

I turned to the porter and replaced his useless weapon with the ancient but well-maintained revolver. For the first time I noticed that the boy was not much younger than Charles had been. His hair was almost exactly the same color. I leaned forward and kissed him lightly on the lips.

"Albert," I whispered, "there are four cartridges left. One must always count the cartridges, mustn't one? Go to the lobby. Kill the manager. Shoot one other person, the nearest. Put the barrel in your mouth and pull the trigger. If it misfires, pull it again. Keep the gun concealed until you are in the lobby."

We emerged into general confusion in the hallway.

"Call for an ambulance!" I cried. "There's been an accident. Some- one call for an ambulance!" Several people rushed to comply. I swooned and leaned against a white-haired gentleman. People milled around, some peering into the room and exclaiming. Suddenly there was the sound of three gunshots from the lobby. In the renewed confusion I slipped down the back stairs, out the fire door, into the night.

Time has passed. I am very happy here. I live in southern France now, between Cannes and Toulon, but not, I am happy to say, too near St. Tropez.

I rarely go out. Henri and Claude do my shopping in the village. I never go to the beach. Occasionally I go to the townhouse in Paris or to my pensione in Italy, south of Pescara, on the Adriatic. But even those trips have become less and less frequent.

There is an abandoned abbey in the hills, and I often go there to sit and think among the stones and wild flowers. I think about isolation and abstinence and how each is so cruelly dependent upon the other.

I feel younger these days. I tell myself that this is because of the climate and my freedom and not as a result of that final Feeding. But sometimes I dream about the familiar streets of Charleston and the people there. They are dreams of hunger.

On some days I rise to the sound of singing as girls from the village cycle by our place on their way to the dairy. On those days the sun is marvelously warm as it shines on the small white flowers growing between the tumbled stones of the abbey, and I am content simply to be there and to share the sunlight and silence with them.

But on other days—cold, dark days when the clouds move in from the north—I remember the shark-silent shape of a submarine moving through the dark waters of the bay, and I wonder whether my self-imposed abstinence will be for nothing. I wonder whether those I dream of in my isolation will indulge in their own gigantic, final Feeding.

It is warm today. I am happy. But I am also alone. And I am very, very hungry.

VERNOR VINGE

Gemstone

Most stories about humanity's First Contact with aliens have as *dramatis personae* the Movers and Shakers of the world—politicians, generals, famous scientists, philosophers, crack reporters, millionaires, astronauts—and are usually set against similarly big and busy backgrounds: the Pentagon, the White House, the Kremlin, UN Headquarters, Buckingham Palace; at the very *least*, the alien space ships have always shown a strong tendency to land in some crowded urban locale like Times Square or Piccadilly Circus, preferably at rush hour.

Here, instead, the setting is an old wood-frame Victorian house in a quiet neighborhood in a sleepy northern California town, and at the crucial moment Earth is represented not by a general or a politician but by a stubborn old woman and a bright and inquisitive young girl . . .

Born in Waukesha, Wisconsin, Vernor Vinge now lives in San Diego, California, where he is an associate professor of math sciences at San Diego State University. He sold his first story, "Apartness," to *New Worlds* in 1965, and since has become a frequent contributor to *Analog*; he has also sold to *Orbit*, *If*, *Stellar*, and other markets. His novella "True Names" was a finalist for both the Nebula and Hugo awards in 1981, and has been optioned for a movie. Vinge's books include *Grimm's World* and *The Witling*. Upcoming are two more novels, *True Names* and *Peace War*, both from Bluejay Books. He is currently working on several sequels to *Peace War*, as yet untitled.

GEMSTONE

Vernor Vinge

The summer of 1957 should have been Sanda's most wonderful vacation. She had known about her parents' plans since March, and all through the La Jolla springtime, all through the tedious spring semester of her seventh grade, she had that summer to dream about.

Nothing ever seemed so fair at first, and turned out so vile:

Sanda sat on the bedroom balcony of her grandmother's house and looked out into the gloom and the rain. The pine trees along the street were great dark shadows, swaying and talking in the dusk. A hundred yards away, toward downtown Eureka, the light of a single street lamp found its way through pines to make tiny glittering reflections off the slick street. As every night these last four weeks, the wind seemed stronger when the daylight departed. She hunched down in her oversized jacket and let the driven mist wash at the tears that trickled down her face. Tonight had been the end, just the end. Daddy and Mom would be here in six days, and two or three days after that the three of them would drive back home. Six days. Sanda unclenched her jaws and tried to relax her face. How could she last? She would have to see Grandma at least for meals, at least to help around the house. And every time she saw Grandma she would feel the shame and know that she had ruined things.

And it isn't all my fault! Grandmother had her secrets, her smugness, her ignorance—flaws Sanda had never imagined during those short visits of years passed.

In the hallway beyond the bedroom, the Gemstone was at it again. Sanda felt a wave of cold wash over her. For a moment the dark around her and the balcony beneath her knees were not merely chill and wet, but glacially frozen, the center of a lifeless and friendless waste. It was funny that now that she *knew* the house was haunted and *knew* precisely the thing that caused these moods, it was not nearly as frightening as before. In fact, it was scarcely more than an inconvenience compared to the *people* problems she had.

It had not always been this way. Sanda thought back to the beginning of the summer, trying to imagine blue skies and warm sun. Those first few days had been like the other times she remembered in Eureka. Grandmother's house sat near the end of its street, surrounded by pines. The only other trees were a pair of small palms right before the front steps. (These needed constant attention. Grandma liked to say that she kept them here just so her visitors from San Diego would never feel homesick.) The house had two storeys, with turrets and dormers coming out of the attic. Against the blue, cloudless sky it looked like a fairy-tale castle. The Victorian gingerbread had been carefully maintained through the years, and in its present incarnation gleamed green and gold.

Her parents had left for San Francisco after a one-day stay. The summer conference at USF was starting that week, and they weren't yet sure they had an apartment. Sanda's first night alone with Grandma had been everything she imagined. Even though the evening beyond the porch was turning chill, the living room still held its warmth. Grandma set her old electric heater in the middle of the carpeted floor so that it shone on the sofa side of the room. Then she walked around the book-lined walls pretending to search for the thing she so liked to show her grandchild.

"Not here, not here. Oh my, I hardly ever look at it nowadays. I forget where . . ." Sanda tagged along, noticing titles where her earlier, younger self had been impressed only by color and size. Grandma had a complete collection of *National Geographics*. Where most families put such magazines in boxes and forget them, Grandmother had every issue there, as though they were some grand encyclopedia. And for Sanda, they were. On her last visit she had spent many an afternoon looking through the pictures. It was the only item she remembered for sure from this library. Now she saw dozens of books on polar exploration, meteorology, biology. Grandfather Beauchamp had been a great man, and Grandmother kept the library and its books, plaques, and certificates in honor of his memory.

"Ah, there it is!" She pulled the huge notebook down from its central position. She led Sanda back to the sofa. "Too big to sit in my lap, now, aren't you?" They grinned at each other and she opened the book across their laps, then put her arm across Sanda's shoulders.

The book was precisely organized. Every newspaper clipping, photo, article, was framed and had a short legend. Some of the pictures existed nowhere else in the world. Others could be found in articles in magazines like the *National Geographic* from the '20s and '30s. Rex Beauchamp had been on the "Terra Nova" expedition in 1910. If it hadn't been for a knee injury he would actually have been on Scott's tragic journey to the South Pole. Sanda sucked in her breath and asked the same question she had asked once before, "And so if his knee had been okay, why, he would have died with the others—and would never have met you, and you would never have had Dad, and—"

Grandma slapped the notebook. "No. I know Rex. He would have made the difference. If they had just waited for him to get well, they could have made it back to the coast."

It was an answer she had heard before, but one she wanted to hear again. Sanda sat back and waited for the rest of the story. After World War I, the Beauchamps had emigrated from Great Britain, and Grandfather participated in several American expeditions. There were dozens of pictures of him on shipboard and in the brave little camps the explorers had established along the Antarctic coast. Rex Beauchamp had been very handsome and boyish even in middle age, and it made Sanda proud to see him in those pictures—though he was rarely the center of attention. He always seemed to be in the background, or in the third row of the group portraits. Grandma said he was a doer and not a talker. He never had a college degree and so had to serve in technician and support jobs. But they depended on him nevertheless.

Not all the pictures were of ice and snow. Many of the expeditions had worked out of Christchurch, New Zealand. On one occasion, Grandmother had gone along that far. It had been a wonderful vacation for her. She had pictures of the city and its wide, circular harbor, and others of her visiting the North Island and Maori country with Grandfather.

Sanda raised her eyes from the picture collection as her grandmother spoke. There were things in this room that illustrated her story more spectacularly than any photographs. The area around the sofa was brightly lit by one of the beautiful stained-glass lamps that Grandma had in every room. But at the limits of its light, the room glowed in mysterious blue and red and yellow from the higher panes in the glass. Dark polished wood edged the carpet and the moldings of every doorway. Beyond the electric heater she could see the Maori statues the Beauchamps had brought back from their stay at Rotorua. In normal light those figures carved in wooden relief seemed faintly comical, their pointed tongues stuck out like weapons, their hands held clawlike. But in the colored dimness the mother-of-pearl in their eyes shone almost knowingly, and the extended tongues were no childish aggression. Sanda wriggled with a moment of delicious fright. The Maori were all civilized now, Grandmother said, but they had been more hideously ferocious than any savages on Earth.

"Do you still have the *meri*, Grandma?"

"Yes indeed." She reached into the embroidered sewing stand that sat next to her end of the sofa and withdrew a graceful, eight-inch piece of stone. One end fit the hand, while the other spread out in a smooth, blunt-edged oval. It was beautiful, and no one but someone like Grandma—or a Maori—could know its true purpose. "This is what they fought with, not like American Indians with spears and arrows." She handed it to Sanda, who ran her fingers over the smoothness. "It's so short you have to come right up to your enemy and *whack!* right across the forehead." Sanda tried to imagine but couldn't. Grandma had so many beautiful things. Sanda had once overheard her mother complain to Daddy that these were thefts from an ancient heritage. Sanda couldn't see why; she was sure that Grandpa had paid for these things. And if he hadn't brought them back to Eureka, so many fewer people could have admired them.

Grandma talked on, well past Sanda's La Jolla bedtime. The girl found herself half hypnotized by the multicolored shadows of the lamp and the pale red from the heater. That heater sat on newspapers.

Sanda felt herself come wide awake. "That heater, Grandma. Isn't it dangerous?"

The woman stopped in midreminiscence. "What? No, I've had it for years. And I'm careful not to set it on the carpet where it might stain."

"But those newspapers. They're brown, almost burned."

Grandma looked at the heater. "My, you're a big girl now, to worry about such things. I don't know. . . . Anyway, we can turn it off now. You should be going to bed, don't you think?"

Sanda was to sleep in the same room her father had used when he was little. It was on the second floor. As they walked down the hall to the bedroom, Grandma stopped by the heavy terrarium she kept there. Dad and Mother hadn't known quite what to make of it: the glass box was something new. Grandma had placed it so the wide skylight gave it sun through most of the day. Now moonlight washed over the glass and the stones. Pale reflections came off some of the smaller rocks. Grandma switched on the hall light and turned everything mundane. The terrarium was empty of life. There was nothing there but rocks of odd sizes mixed with river-washed gravel. It was like the box Sanda kept her pet lizards in. But there were not even lizards in this one. The only concessions to life were little plastic flowers, "planted" here and there in the landscape.

Grandma smiled wanly. "I think your Dad believes I'm crazy to put something like this here."

Sanda looked at the strange display for a moment and then suggested, "Maybe if you used real flowers?"

The old woman shook her head. "I like artificial ones. You don't have to water them. They never fade or die. They are always beautiful." She paused and Sanda remained diplomatically silent. "Anyway, it's the rocks that are the important thing here. I showed you pictures of those valleys your grandfather helped discover: the ones that don't have any snow in them, even though they're hundreds of miles inside Antarctica. These rocks are from one of those valleys. They must have been sitting there for thousands of years with nothing but the wind to upset them. Rex kept his collection in boxes down in the basement, but I think they are so much nicer up here. This is a little like what they had before."

Sanda looked into the cabinet with new interest. Some of the stones were strange. A couple looked like the meteorites she had seen in the Natural History Museum back home. And there was another, about the size of her head, that had a vaguely regular pattern in the gray and black minerals that were its substance.

Minutes later, Sanda was tucked into her father's old bed, the lights were out, and Grandmother was descending the stairs. Moonlight spread silver on the windowsills, and the pines beyond were soft, pale, bright. Sanda sighed and smiled. So far, things were just as she dreamed and just as she remembered.

The last she wondered as she drifted off to sleep was why Grandmother put flowers in the terrarium if she really wanted to imitate the bleak antarctic valleys.

That first day was really the last when everything went totally well. And looking back on it, Sanda could see symptoms of many of the things that were later to make the summer so unpleasant.

Physically everything was just as she remembered. The stair railings were a rich, deeply polished wood that she hardly ever saw in La Jolla. Everywhere was carpeting, even on the stairs. The basement was cool and damp and filled with all the mysterious things that Grandfather had worked with. But there were so many things that Grandma did and believed that were *wrong*. Some—like the flowers—were differences of opinion that Sanda could keep her mouth shut about. Others—like Grandma's use of the old electric heater—were really dangerous. When she spoke about those, Grandmother didn't seem to believe or understand her. The older woman would smile and tell her what a big girl she was getting to be, but it was clear she was a little hurt by the suggestions, no matter how diplomatically put. Finally Sanda had taken a plastic mat off the back porch and slipped it under the heater in place of the newspapers. But Grandma noticed, and furthermore pointed out that the dirty mat had stained the beautiful carpet—just the thing the nice clean newspapers had been there to prevent. Sanda had been crushed: she'd been harmful when she wanted to be helpful. Grandmother was very good about it; in the end—after she cleaned the carpet—she suggested putting the mat between the newspapers and the heater. So the incident ended happily, after all.

But this sort of thing seemed to happen all the time: Sanda trying to do something different, some hurt being caused property or Grandma, and then sincere apology and reconciliation. Sanda began to feel a little haggard, and to watch the calendar for a different reason than before. Just being with Grandma had been one of the big attractions of this summer. Both she and Grandma were *trying*, but it wasn't working. Sometimes Sanda thought that—no matter how often Grandma said Sanda was a young grown-up now—she still thought Sanda was five years old. She had seriously wanted Sanda to take afternoon naps. Only when the girl assured her that her parents no longer required naps did she relent. And Grandma never told her to do anything. She always asked Sanda "wouldn't you like to" do whatever she wanted. It was awfully hard to smile and say "oh yes, that would be fun" when in fact it was a chore she would rather pass up. At home it was so much easier: Sanda did as she was told, and did not have to claim to love it.

A week later the fair weather broke. It rained. And rained. And rained. And when it wasn't raining it was cloudy; not cloudy as in La Jolla, but a dripping, misty cloudiness that just promised more rain. Grandma said it was often this way; Sanda had just been lucky on the previous visits.

And it was about this time she began to be afraid of the upstairs. Grandmother slept downstairs, though she stayed up very late at night, reading or sewing. She would be easy to call if anything . . . bad happened. That did not help. At first it was like an ordinary fear of darkness. Some nights a person is just more fidgety than others. And after the weather turned bad it was easy to feel scared, lying in bed with the wind and the rattle of rain against the windows. But this was different. The feeling increased from night to night. It wasn't quite a feeling that something was sneaking up on her. More it was a sense of utter desolation and despair. Sometimes it seemed as if the room, the whole house, were gone and she was in just the antarctic wilderness that Grandfather had explored. She had no direct visions of this—just the feeling of cold and lifelessness extending forever. *Grandfather's ghost?*

Late one night Sanda had to go to the bathroom, which was down on the first floor next to Grandmother's bedroom. It was almost painful to move—so afraid was she of making a sound, of provoking whatever caused the mood that filled her room. When she passed the terrarium in the hallway, the feeling of cold grew stronger and her legs tensed for a sprint down the stairs. Instead she forced herself to stand still, then to walk slowly around the glass cage. Something in there was causing it.

The terror was insidious, growing as she stood there—almost as if what caused this now knew it had a "listener." Sanda slept at the foot of the stairs that night.

After that, when night came and Grandmother had tucked her in, Sanda would creep out of bed, unwrap her sleeping bag, and quietly carry it onto the balcony that opened off her room. The extra distance and the extra wall reduced the psychic cold to a tolerable level. Many nights it was rainy, and it was always chill and a bit windy, but she had bought a really good sleeping bag for the Scouts, and she had always liked to camp out. Nevertheless, it wore her down to sleep like that night after night, and made it harder to be diplomatic and cheerful during the days.

In the daytime there was far less feeling of dread upstairs. Sanda didn't know whether this was because the second floor was basically a sunny, cheerful place or whether the ghost "slept" during the day. Whenever she walked past the terrarium she looked carefully into it. After a while, she thought she had the effect narrowed down to one particular rock—the skull-sized one with the strangely regular patterns of gray and black. As the days passed, the position of some of the rocks changed. There had been five plastic flowers in the terrarium when Sanda first saw it; now there were three.

There was one other mystery—which under other circumstances would have been very sinister, but which seemed scarcely more than an intriguing puzzle now. Several times, usually on stormy nights, a car parked in the grass just off the other side of the street, about forty yards north of the house. That was all; Sanda had noticed it only by accident. It looked like a '54 Ford. Once a match flared within the cab, and she saw two occupants. She smiled smugly, wistfully to herself; she could imagine what they were up to. But she was wrong. One night, when the rain had stopped yet clouds kept out the stars, the driver got out and walked across the street toward the house. He moved silently, quickly. Sanda had to lean out from the balcony to see him crouch in the bushes next to the wall where the electric power meter was mounted. He spent only half a minute there. She saw a tiny point of light moving over the power meter and the utility cables that came down from the telephone pole at the street. Then the phantom meter reader stood and ran back across the street, quietly relatching the door of his Ford. The car sat for several more minutes—as if they were watching the house for some sign of alarm—and then drove away.

She should have told Grandma. But then, if she were being as open as a good girl should be with a grandmother, she would have also confessed her fear of the upstairs and the terrarium. Those fears were shameful, though. Even if *real*, they were the type of childish thing that could only make her situation with Grandma worse. Grandmother was a clever person. Sanda knew that if she told her about the mysterious car, the older woman would either dismiss the story—or question her in sufficient detail to discover that Sanda was sleeping on the balcony.

So she dithered—and in the end told someone else.

Finding that someone else had been a surprise; she hadn't really known she was looking. Whenever the weather dried a little, Sanda tried to get outdoors. The city library was about three miles away, an easy ride on her father's old bicycle. Of course Grandmother had been uneasy about Sanda carrying library books in the saddle baskets of the bike. There was always the risk of splashing water or a sudden rainstorm. It was just another of the polite little conflicts they had. One or the other of them could always see some objection to a given activity. In the end—as usual—they compromised, with Sanda taking grocery bags and a little waxed paper for the books.

Today wasn't wet, though. The big blocks of cloud left plenty of space for the blue. To the northwest, the plume from the paper mill was purest white across the sky. The sun was warm, and the gusty breeze dry. It was the sort of day she once thought was every day in Eureka.

Sanda took a detour, biking back along the street away from town. The asphalt ended about thirty yards past Grandmother's lot. There were supposed to be more houses up here, but Grandma didn't think much of them. She passed one. It looked like a trailer used as a permanent home. A couple old cars, one looking very dead, were in front. The trees came in close to the road here, blocking out the sun. It felt a little like those great forests they'd driven through to get to Eureka. Even after a half day of sun, there was still a slow dripping from the needles. Everything was so green it might as well be dipped in paint. Once she had liked that.

She went a lot farther south than she had before. The road stopped at a dead end. A one-storey, red-shingled house was the last thing on the street. It was a real house, but it reminded Sanda of the trailer. It was such a different thing from Grandmother's house. There were a lot of small houses in La Jolla, but the weather back home was so dry and mild that buildings didn't seemed to wear out. Here Sanda had the feeling that the damp, the cold, and the mildew were forever warring on the houses. This place had been losing the fight for some time.

She circled around the end of the road—and almost ran into a second bicyclist.

Sanda stopped abruptly and awkwardly. (The center bar on the bike was a little high for her.) "Where did you come from?" she asked a bit angrily.

The boy was taller than Sanda, and looked very strong. He must be at least fifteen years old. But his face was soft, almost stupid-looking. He waved at the red-shingled house. "We live here. Who are you?"

"Sanda Beauchamp."

"Oh, yeah. You're the girl staying with the old English lady."

"She is not an old lady. She's my grandmother."

He was silent for a moment, the babyface expressionless. "I'm Larry O'Malley. Your grandmother is okay. Last summer I did her lawn."

Sanda untangled herself from the bicycle and they walked their bikes back the way she had come. "She has regular gardeners now."

"I know. She's very rich. Even more than last year."

Grandma wasn't rich. It was on the tip of her tongue to contradict him, but his second statement made her pause, puzzled. *Even more than last year?*

They had walked all the way back to Grandmother's before Sanda knew it. Larry wasn't really sullen. She wasn't sure yet if he was smart or stupid; she knew he wasn't as old as he looked. His father was a real lumberjack, which was neat. Most of Sanda's parents' friends were geologists and things like that.

They parked their bikes at the steps, and Sanda took him in to see Grandmother. As she had expected, the elder Beauchamp was not thrilled with Sanda's plans for the afternoon.

She looked uncertainly at the boy. "But, Larry, isn't that a long ride?"

Sanda was not about to let Larry blow it. "Oh no, Grandma, it's not much farther than the library. Besides, I haven't been to a movie in so long," which was true, though Grandmother's television did a great job of dragging in old movies from the only available station.

"What's the film? It's such a nice day to waste in a theater."

"Oh, they're playing movies from the early fifties." That sounded safe. Grandma had complained more than once about the immorality of today's shows. Besides, if she heard the title, she would be sure to refuse.

Grandmother seemed almost distraught. Then she agreed, and walked out to the screened porch with them. "Come back before four."

"We will. We will." And they were off. She didn't know if it was the weather, or meeting Larry, or the prospect of the movie, but suddenly she felt wonderful.

The Thing from Outer Space. That's what it said on the marquee. She felt a little guilty deceiving Grandma about the title. It wasn't really the sort of show her parents would want her to see. But just seeing a movie was going to be fun. It was like home. The theater reminded her a lot of the Cove in La Jolla. After they got their tickets they drifted down the movie posters.

And Sanda began to feel a chill that was not in the air and that was not the vicarious thrill of watching a scary show. This *Thing* was supposed to be from outer space, yet the posters showed arctic wastes. . . .

She found herself walking more slowly, for the first time letting the boy do most of the talking. Then they were inside, and the movie had begun.

It was a terrible thing, almost as if God had created a personal warning, a personal explanation for Sanda Rachel Beauchamp. *The Thing* was what had been after her all these weeks. Oh, a lot of the details were different. The movie took place in the arctic; the alien monster—the Thing—was crudely man-shaped. Sanda sat, her face slack, all but hypnotized by these innocently filmed revelations. About halfway through the movie, Larry nudged her and asked if she were okay. Sanda just nodded.

The Thing had been stranded. In the polar wastes the temperature and lack of predators allowed it to survive a very long time. The dry antarctic valleys Grandpa discovered might be even better: Things from long, long ago would be right at the surface, not hidden beneath hundreds of feet of ice. The creature would be like a time bomb waiting to be discovered. When exposed to light and warmth—as Grandma had done by putting it in the sunny terrarium—it would come to life. The movie Thing looked for blood. Sanda's Thing seemed after something more subtle, more terrible.

Sanda was scarcely aware when the movie ended, so perfectly did its story merge with the greater terror she now felt. It was still middle afternoon, but the berglike clouds had melded together, thick and deep and dark. The wind was picking up, driving through her sweater and carrying occasional drops of wet. They recovered their bikes, Sanda dazed, Larry O'Malley silently observant.

It was uphill most of the way back, but now the wind was behind them. The forests beyond the town were blackish green, sometimes turned gray by passing mist. The scene didn't register with her. All she could think of was the cold and the ice and the thing waiting for her up ahead.

Larry reached out to grab her handlebars as the bike angled toward the ditch. "Really. What's the matter?"

And Sanda told him. About the strangely mottled antarctic rock and the terrarium. About its movement and the desolation it broadcast.

The boy didn't say anything when she finished. They worked laboriously up a hill past neat houses, some of them Victorian, none as beautiful as Grandmother's. As usual, traffic was light—nonexistent by the standards of home. They rode side by side with the entire road to themselves. Finally they reached the top and started down a gentle slope. Still Larry hadn't said anything. Sanda's haze of terror was broken by sudden anger. She pedaled just ahead of him and waved her hand in his face. "*Hey!* I was talking to you. Don't you believe me?"

Larry blinked, his wide face expresionless. He didn't seem to take offense. He spoke, but didn't directly answer her question. "I think your Grandma is a smart person. And I always thought she had some strange things in that house. She put the rock up there; she must know something about it. You should ask her straight out. Or do you think *she* wants to hurt you, too?"

Sanda lagged back even with Larry and felt a little bit ashamed. She should have brought this up with Grandma weeks ago. She knew why she had not. After all the little conflicts and misunderstandings, she had been afraid that a fearful story like this would have weakened her position even further, would have reinforced Grandma's view of her as a child. Saying these things out loud seemed to make them smaller. But having said them, she could also see that there was something *real* here, something to fear, or at least to be concerned about. She looked at Larry and smiled with some respect. Perhaps he wasn't very imaginative— after all, nothing seemed to disturb him—but being with him was like suddenly finding the ground in the surf, or waking up from a bad dream.

Blocks of mist chased back and forth around them, but they were still dry when they got home. They stood for a moment on the grassy shoulder of the road.

"If you want to go to the sand dunes tomorrow, we should start early. It's a long ride from here." She couldn't tell if he had already forgotten her story, or if he was trying to reassure her.

"I'll have to ask Grandmother," *about that and certain other things.* "I'll see you tomorrow, anyway."

Larry pedaled off toward his house, and Sanda walked the bike around to the tool shed. Grandma came out to the back porch, and worried over the damp on Sanda's sweater. She seemed nervous, and relieved to see Sanda back.

"My, you've been gone so long. I've got some sandwiches made up in the kitchen." As they walked into the house, Grandma asked her about the movie and about Larry. "You know, Sanda, I think the O'Malley boy is nice enough. But I'm not sure your Mum and Dad would want you spending so much time with him. Your interests are so different, don't you think?"

Sanda was not really listening. She took the other's hand. It was a childlike gesture that stopped the older woman short. "Grandma, there's something I've *got* to talk to you about. Please."

"Of course, Sanda."

They sat down, and the girl told her of the terror that soaked the upstairs every night so strongly that she must sleep on the balcony.

Grandma smiled tentatively and patted Sanda's hand. "I'll wager it's those Maori statues. They would scare anyone, especially in the dark. I shouldn't have told you all those stories about them. They're just wood and—"

"It's not them, Grandmother," Sanda tried to keep the frustration out of her voice. She looked out of the kitchen, down the hall into the living room. She could see one of the statues there, sticking its tongue at her. It was lovely, and frightening in a fun sort of way, but that was all. "It's the terrarium, and especially one rock there. When I'm near it, I can feel the cold get stronger."

"Oh dear." Grandmother looked down at her hands and avoided Sanda's eyes. For a moment she seemed to be talking only to herself. "You must be very sensitive."

Sanda's eyes widened. Even after all this time, she hadn't really expected anyone to believe. And now she saw that Grandma had known something about this all along.

"Oh, Sanda, I'm so sorry. If I thought you could sense it, I would never have put you up there." She reached out to touch Sanda, and smiled. "There really is nothing to fear. That's my, uh, Gemstone." She stumbled on the name, looked faintly worried. "It has always been a little secret of your grandfather's and mine. If I tell you about it, will you keep the secret, too?"

The girl nodded.

"Let's go up there, and I'll show you. You're right that the stone can make you feel things. . . ."

As Grandma had told her before, Rex Beauchamp had found the Gemstone on one of the first expeditions into the dry valleys. He probably should have turned his discovery over to the expedition's collection. But in those early days there was a more casual attitude about individual finds, and besides, Grandfather was continually shunted aside from the credit he deserved. He was simply the fellow who fixed all the little things that went wrong. After retirement he hoped to set up his own small lab here, to look into this and several other mysteries he had come across over the years.

Grandfather had kept the Gemstone in a special locker down in the lab/basement. He hoped to imitate its original environment. At first Grandpa thought the rock was some special crystal that stored and reflected back the emotions of those around it. When he held it in his hand, he could feel the winds and desolation of the antarctic. If he touched it an hour later, he felt vague reflections of his mood *at the time of the previous encounter.*

When he cut it with a lapidary saw, the mental shriek of pain showed both of them the Gemstone was not psychic mineral, but living thing.

"We never told anyone what we had discovered. Not even your father. Rex kept it in the basement, and as cold as possible. He was so afraid that it would die." They had reached the second floor and were walking down the short hallway toward the terrarium. The skylight was pale gray, and rain was beginning to splatter off it. The cold and loneliness were not quite as sharp as after dark, but it took an effort for Sanda to approach the rock.

"I looked at it differently. It seemed to me that if the Gemstone could survive all those centuries of no food, no water—well then, maybe it was tough. Maybe even it would like light and warmth. After your grandfather died, I took the stone and put it in this nice aquarium box up here where there is light. I know it is alive; I think it likes it up here."

Sanda looked down at the black and gray whorls that marked its rough exterior. The shape was not symmetrical, but it was regular. Even without the chill beating against her mind she should have known it was alive. "What . . . what does it eat?"

"Um." Grandma paused for just a second. "Some of the rocks. Even those flowers. I have to replace them now and again. But it's mindless. It's never done anything more than what Rex originally noticed. It's just that now—up here in the light—it does them a bit more often." She saw the pain on Sanda's face. "You can feel the stone even that far away?" she asked wonderingly.

Grandma reached down and touched the top of the Gemstone with the palm of her hand. She winced. "Ah, it is projecting that old cold-and-desolate pattern. I can see why that bothers you. But it's not intended to be hurtful. I think it's just the creature's memory of the cold. Now just wait. It takes a minute or so for it to change. In some ways it's more like a plant than an animal."

The psychic chill faded. What remained was not threatening, but— with her present sensitivity—was unsettling. Grandma motioned her closer. "Here. Now you put your hand on it, and you'll see what I mean."

Sanda advanced slowly, her eyes on her grandmother's face. Above them, the rain droned against the skylight. *What if it's all a lie?* thought Sanda. Could the creature take people over and make them go after others?

But now that the mental pressure was gone, it seemed just a little bit unbelievable. She touched the Gemstone first with her fingertips and then with the flat of her hand. Grandmother's hand was still on the rock, though not quite touching hers. Nothing happened. It was cold as any rock might be in this room. The surface was rough, though regular. The seconds passed and slowly she felt it: It was Grandma! Her smile, a wave of affection—and behind that, disappointment and an emptiness more muted than the stone usually broadcast. Still, there was a warmth where before there had been only cold.

"Oh, Grandmother!" The older woman put her arm across Sanda's shoulders, and for the first time in weeks, the girl thought there might be a lasting reconciliation. Sanda's hand strayed from the Gemstone and brushed through the pebbles that were its bed. They were ordinary. The Gemstone was the only strange thing in the terrarium. Wait. She picked up a smallish pebble and held it in the light, scarcely noticing the sudden tension in Grandma's arm. The tiny rock might have been glassy except for the milky haze on its surface. It felt almost greasy. "This isn't a real rock, is it, Grandma?"

"No. It's plastic. Like the flowers. I just think it's pretty."

"Oh." She dropped it back into the terrarium. Another time, she might have been more curious. For now, everything was swamped by her relief in discovering that what had terrorized her for so long was not a threat but something very wonderful. "Thank you. I was so afraid." She laughed a little ruefully. "I really made a fool of myself this afternoon, telling Larry I thought the Gemstone was some kind of monster."

Grandmother's arm slipped away from her shoulder. "Sanda, you mustn't—" she began sharply. "Really, Sanda, you mustn't be going out with the O'Malley boy. He's simply too old for you."

Sanda's reply was casually argumentative; she was still immersed in a rosy feeling of relief. "Oh, Gran. He's going into ninth grade this fall. He's just big for his age."

"No. I'm sure your mother and dad would be very upset with me if I let you be off alone with him."

The sharpness of her tone finally came through to Sanda. Grandma had on her determined look. And suddenly the girl felt just as determined. There was no valid reason for her not to see Larry O'Malley. Grandma had hinted around at this before: she thought her neighbors up the road were lower class, both in background and present accomplishment. If there was one thing really wrong with Grandmother it was that she looked down on some people. Sanda even suspected that she was racially prejudiced. For instance, she called Negroes "colored people."

The double injustice of Grandma's demand was too much. Sanda thrust out her quivering jaw. "Grandmother, I'll go out with him if I want. You just don't want me to see him because he's poor . . . because he's Irish."

"Sanda!" The older woman seemed to shrink in upon herself. Her voice was choked, hard to understand. "I had so looked forward to this summer with you. B-but you're not the nice little girl you once were." She stepped around Sanda and hurried down the stairs.

Sanda looked after her open-mouthed. Then she felt tears turning into sobs, and rushed into her bedroom.

She sat on the bedroom balcony and looked out into the gloom and the rain. The pine trees along the street were great dark shadows, swaying and talking in the dusk. From a hundred yards away, the light of a single street lamp found its way through the pines to make tiny glittering reflections off the slick street. She hunched down in her oversized jacket and let the driven mist wash at the tears that trickled down her face. Daddy and Mom would be here in six days. Six days. Sanda unclenched her jaws and tried to relax her face. How could she last?

She had sat here for hours, going around and around with these questions, never quite getting the pain rationalized, never quite finding a course of action that would not be still more painful. She wondered what Grandma was doing now. There had been no call to supper, or to help with supper. But there had been no sounds of cooking either. She was probably in her room, going through the same thing Sanda was. Grandma's last words . . . they almost described her own grief all these weeks.

Grandmother had looked so small, so frail. Sanda was almost as tall as she, but rarely thought about it. It must have been hard for Grandma to have a guest she thought of as a child, a guest to whom she must always show the most cheerful face, a guest with whom every disagreement was a tiny failure.

And even this vacation had not been all bad. There had been the evenings when the weather was nice and they had stayed out on the screened porch to play caroms or Scrabble. Those had been just as good as before—better in some ways, now that she could understand Grandma's little jokes and appreciate her impish grin when she made some clever countermove.

The girl sighed. She had been through these thoughts several times in the last hours. Each time she returned to them, they seemed to gain strength over the recriminations. She knew that in the end she would go downstairs, and try to make up. And maybe . . . maybe this time it could really work. This break had gone so deep and hurt so much that maybe they could start out in a new way.

She stood up and breathed the clean, cold, wet air. The keening of the Gemstone in the back of her mind was a prod now. There was more than cold in the Gemstone's call; there was a loneliness she knew came in part from those around it.

As Sanda turned to enter the bedroom, a flash of headlights made her look back. A car was driving slowly by. . . . It looked like a '54 Ford. She stayed very still until it was out of sight, then dropped to her knees so that just her head was above the balcony. If this were like the other visitations . . .

Sure enough, a couple minutes passed and the Ford was back—this time without its lights. It stopped on the other side of the road. The rain was heavy, and the wind came in gusts now. Sanda wasn't sure, but it looked like *two* people got out of the car. Yes. There were two. They ran toward the house, one for the power meter, the other heading out of sight to her left.

This was more than the mysterious intruders had ever done before. And somehow there was a purposefulness in it tonight. As if this were no rehearsal. Sanda leaned out from the balcony. Her curiosity was fast giving way to fear. Not the psychic, moody fear the Gemstone broadcast, but a sharp, call-to-action type of fear. *What is that guy doing?* The dark figure maneuvered a small light, and something else. There was a snapping noise that came faintly to her over the rain.

And then she knew. It wasn't just the power cable that came down to that side of the house; the phone line did, too.

Sanda whirled and dived back into her bedroom, shedding her jacket as she ran. She sprinted by the terrarium, barely conscious of the mood emerging from the Gemstone.

Grandmother stood at the bottom of the stairs, looking as if she were about to come up. She appeared tired, but there was a wan smile on her face. "Sanda, dear, I—"

"Grandma! Somebody's trying to break in. *Somebody's trying to break in!*" Sanda came down the stairs in two crashing leaps. There was a shadow on the porch where no shadow should have been. Sanda slammed the bolt to just as the doorknob began to turn. Behind her, Grandmother stared in shocked silence. Sanda spun and ran toward the kitchen. Once they had the intruders locked out, what could she and Gran do without a phone?

She nearly ran into him in the kitchen. Sanda sucked in a breath so hard she squeaked. He was big and hooded. He also had a knife. Strange to see such a man in the middle of the glistening white kitchen—the homey, comforting, *safe* kitchen.

From the living room came the sound of splintering wood, and Grandmother screamed. Running footsteps. Something metal being kicked over. Grandmother screamed again. "Shut your mouth, lady. I said, *shut it.*" The voice—though not the tone—was vaguely familiar. "Now where is that prissy little wimp?"

"I got her in here," called the man in the kitchen. He caught Sanda's upper arm in a grip as painful as any physical punishment she had ever received and marched her into the living room.

Grandma looked okay, just scared and very small next to the fellow holding her. Even with the hooded mask, Sanda thought she recognized him. It was the clerk from the little grocery store they shopped at. Behind them, the electric heater lay face down, its cherry coils buried in the carpet.

The clerk shook Grandma at every syllable he spoke. "All right, lady. There's just one thing we want. Show us where they are and we'll go." This was the sense of what he said, though not the precise words. Many of those words were ones Sanda knew but had previously heard only from the rougher girls in gym class, where there was much smirking and giggling over their meaning. Here, said in deadly anger, those words were themselves an assault.

"I've a couple rings—"

"Lady, you're rich and we know how you got it."

Grandma's voice was quaking. "No, just my husband's investments." That was true. Sanda had overheard Grandma telling Sanda's surprised father the size of Rex Beauchamp's estate.

The clerk slapped her. "Liar. Two or three times a year you bring a diamond into Arcata Gems. A rough diamond. Your husband was the big-time explorer." There was sarcasm in the words. "Somewhere he musta found quite a pile of 'em. Either that or you got a diamond machine in your basement." He laughed at his joke, and suddenly the girl saw through several mysteries. *Not in the basement—upstairs.*

"We know you got 'em. We want 'em. We want 'em. We want 'em. We—" As he spoke, he slapped her rhythmically across the face. Someone was screaming; it was Sanda. She barely knew what she did then. From the corner of her eye she saw Grandma's *meri* lying on the sewing table. She swept it up with her free hand and pivoted swiftly around her captor, swinging the flattened stone club into the clerk's chest just below the ribs.

The man went down, dragging Grandmother to her knees. He sat on the floor for several seconds, his mouth opening and closing soundlessly. Finally he could take great, gasping breaths. "I'll. Kill. Her." He came to his feet, one hand still on Grandma's shoulder, the other weaving a knife back and forth in front of Sanda.

The other fellow grabbed the *meri* from Sanda's hand and pulled the girl back from the clerk. "No. Remember."

The clerk pressed his knife hand gently against his chest, and winced. "Yeah." He pushed Grandmother down onto the sofa and approached Sanda.

"Lady, I'm gonna cut on your kid till you start talking." He barely touched the knife to Sanda's forearm. It was so sharp that a thin line of red oozed, yet the girl scarcely felt it.

Grandma came off the sofa. "Stop! Don't touch her!"

He looked around at her. "Why?"

"I-I'll show you where the diamonds are."

The clerk was genuinely disappointed. "Yeah?"

"You won't hurt us afterwards?"

The one holding Sanda touched his mask. "All we want are the diamonds, lady."

Pause. "Very well. They're in the kitchen."

Seconds later, Mrs. Beauchamp showed them where. She opened the cabinet where she kept flower and sugar and withdrew a half-empty bag of rock salt. The clerk grabbed it from her, then swept the salt and pepper and sugar bowl off the kitchen table. He carefully upended the bag of rock salt and spread it so that no piece sat on another. "Do you see anything?" he said.

The other man spent several minutes examining the table. "One," he said, and moved a tiny stone to the edge of the edge of Grandmother's china rack. It looked glassy except for a milky haze on its surface. "Two." He looked some more.

No one spoke. The only sounds were the clerk's harsh breathing and the steady throbbing of rain against the windows. The night beyond the windows was black. The nearest neighbors were hidden beyond trees.

"That's all. Just the two."

The clerk's obscenities would have been screamed if his chest had been up to it. In a way his quiet intensity was more frightening. "You sold ten of these the last three years. You claim you're down to *two?*"

Grandma nodded, her chin beginning to quiver.

"Do you believe her?"

"I don't know. But maybe it doesn't matter. We've got all night, and I want to cut on that girl. Either way, I'll get what's due me," He motioned with his knife. "C'mere you."

"Just as well. I think they recognize you." The vise on Sanda's upper arm tightened and she found herself pushed toward the point of the knife.

"Smell something burning?" her captor said abruptly.

The clerk's eyes widened, and he stepped out of the kitchen to look down the hall. "Jesus, yes! The carpet and some newspapers. It's that heater."

"Unplug the heater. Roll the carpet over it. This place burns, we got nothing to search!"

"I'm trying." There were awkward shuffling sounds. "Need help."

The man holding Sanda looked at the two women. She saw his hand tighten on his knife. "I know where the rest of them are," Grandma suddenly said.

He grabbed her, too, and hustled them to the basement door. Sanda was shoved roughly through. She crashed backwards against the rack of brooms and fell down the steps into the darkness. A second later Grandma's frail body fell on top of hers. The door slammed, and they heard the key turn in the lock.

The two of them lay dazed for a second. Next to her face, Sanda could smell the moldy damp of the stairs. Part of a mop seemed to be strung across her neck. "Are you okay, Grandmother?"

Her answer was immediate. "Yes. Are you?"

"Yes."

Grandma gave an almost girlish laugh. "You make rather a good pillow to land on, dear." She got up carefully and switched on the stairs light. There was that impish smile on her face. "I think they may have outsmarted themselves."

She led Sanda further down the steps and switched on another light. The girl looked around the small basement, made even smaller by the old sample crates and Grandma's laundry area. There was no way out of here, no windows set at ground level. What was Grandmother thinking of?

The older woman turned and slammed shut the interior hatch that Grandfather had mounted in the stairwell. Sanda began to see what she had in mind: The top of the stairs could be locked from the kitchen side, but this heavy door was now locked from their side!

Grandmother walked across the floor toward a stack of cases that sat under the living room. "Rex wanted this to be his laboratory. He was going to refrigerate—actually try to imitate polar conditions. That turned out to be much too expensive, but the heavy doors he installed can be useful. . . . Help me with these crates, please, Sanda."

They were heavy, but Grandma didn't care if they went crashing to the floor. In minutes Sanda saw that they were uncovering another stairway, one that must open onto the living room. "If they can put the fire out as easily as they should, then we'll simply wait them out. Even a small fire can be seen from the street, and I'll wager the Fire Department will be here straight away. But if the fire wins free and the whole house goes . . ." There were new tears streaking her face. She swayed slightly on her feet, and Sanda realized that the older woman had been limping.

Sanda put her arm about her grandmother's waist. "Are you sure you're okay?"

Grandma looked at her and smiled. Her face was little bit puffy, swelling from the blows to it. "Yes, dear." She bowed her head and touched her front teeth. "But my dentist will be overjoyed by all this, I fear."

Grandmother turned back to the door and wiped at a quartz port set in the metal. "I still don't know why Rex wanted this stair up to the living room. P'raps he just felt obliged to use both the surplus hatches he bought."

Sanda looked through the tiny window. It was a viewpoint on the living room she had never imagined. They were looking through the decorative drapes that covered the wall behind the sofa.

The robbers had pulled off their masks and were madly dragging furniture—including the sofa—away from the blaze. They had rolled the carpet over the fire, but it was still spreading, leaking out toward the TV and the Maori statues on the far wall.

The floor itself was starting to burn.

The men in the living room saw this, too. The clerk shouted something that came only faintly through the insulated walls. Then they ran out of view. The fire spread up the legs of the TV and onto a Maori statue. For a moment, the figure blazed in a halo of light. Flames played from the twisted hands, from the thrusting tongue.

The lights in the basement went out, but the red glow through the quartz window still lit Grandma's face. "They couldn't save it. They couldn't save it." Her voice was barely audible.

Heavy banging at the other hatch, the one to the kitchen. Sanda knew that was no rescue, but murder denied. The banging ceased almost immediately; these two witnesses would live to tell their story.

She looked back through the quartz. The fire was spreading along the far wall. Their side of the living room was untouched. Even the drapes seemed undamaged.

"I've got to go out there, Sanda."

"No! . . . I-I'm sorry, Gran. If they couldn't save it, we can't."

"Not the house, Sanda. I'm going to save the Gemstone." There was the strain of physical exertion in her voice, but the girl couldn't see what she was doing. Only Grandma's face was lit by the rose and yellow light. She was not pushing on the door; Sanda could see that much.

"You can't risk your life for diamonds, Grandma. Dad and Mom have money. You can stay—"

The older woman grunted as though pushing at something. "You don't understand. The diamonds have been wonderful. I could never have lived so free with just the money Rex left me. Poor Rex. The Gemstone was his greatest find. He knew that. But he kept it in a freezer down here, and never saw the miracle it really is.

"Sanda, the Gemstone is not just a thing that eats plastic flowers and passes diamonds. It is not just a thing that sends out feelings of cold and emptiness—those are simply its memories of Antarctica.

"Next to you and your dad—and your mum—I value the Gemstone more than anything. When I put my hand on it, it glows back at me—you felt that, too. It is friendly, though it scarce seems to know me. But when I touch it long enough, I feel Rex there, I feel the times he must have touched the stone . . . and almost I feel he is touching me."

She grunted; Sanda heard something spinning on oiled bearings. There was a popping noise from the hatch and Sanda guessed it could be pushed open now.

"The fire is along the outer wall. I have room to get to the stairs. I can pick up the Gemstone and get out down the back stairs—on the other side of the house from the fire. You'll be safe staying here. Rex was very thorough. The basement is an insulated hull, even over the ceiling. The house could burn right down and you'd not be harmed."

"No. I'm going with you."

Grandmother took a breath. There was the look on her face of someone who must do something very difficult. "Sanda. *If you ever loved me,* you will obey me now: stay here."

Sanda's arms hung numb at her sides. If you *ever* loved me . . . It was many years before she could live with her in-action of those next few seconds.

Grandma pushed the door back. The drapes parted and there was a wave of heat, like standing near a bonfire. The air was full of popping and cracking, but the drapes that swung into the opening were not yet singed. Gran pulled the cloth away and pushed the door shut. Through the quartz window Sanda saw her moving quickly toward the stairs. She started up them—was almost out of sight—when she looked down, puzzlement on her face.

Sanda saw the fire burning out of the wall beneath her an instant before the stairs collapsed and Grandmother disappeared. The house groaned and died above her.

"Grand*ma!*" Sanda crashed against the metal door, but it would not open now: ceiling timbers had fallen across it. The scene beyond the quartz was no longer recognizably a home. The fire must have burned behind the walls and up under the stairwell. Now much of the second floor had collapsed onto the first. Everything she could see was a glowing jumble. The heat on her face was like looking through a kiln window. Nothing out there could live.

And still the heat increased. The fallen center of the upstairs left a natural flue through the skylight. For a few moments the heat and rushing winds lived in equilibrium, and the flames steadied to uniform brilliance. Brief stillness in hell.

She would have felt it sooner if she had been waiting for it, or if its mood hadn't been so different from all that went on about her: a chime of happiness, clear and warm. The feeling of sudden freedom and escape from cold.

Then she saw it: Its surface was no longer black and gray. It glowed like the ends of the burning timbers but with overtones of violet that seemed to penetrate its body. And now that it moved, she could see the complete regularity of its shape. The Gemstone was a cross between a four-legged starfish and a very small pillow. It moved nimbly, gracefully through the red jumble beyond the quartz window, and Sanda could feel its exuberance.

Grandfather had been wrong. Grandmother had been wrong. The cold and desolation it had broadcast were not memories of antarctic centuries, but a wordless cry against what *still* was cold and dark to it. How could she have missed it before? Daddy's dog, Tyrann, did the same thing: locked out on a misty winter night he keened and keened his misery for hours.

Gemstone had been alone and cold much, much longer.

And now—like a dog—it frisked through the brightness, eager and curious. It stopped and Sanda felt its puzzlement. It pushed down into the chaos that had been the stairs. The puzzlement deepened, shaded into hurt. Gemstone climbed back out of the rubble.

It had no head, no eyes, but what she saw in its mind now was clear: it felt her and was trying to find where she was hiding. When it "saw" her it was like a searchlight suddenly fixing on a target; all its attention was on her.

Gemstone scuttled down from its perch and swiftly crossed the ruins. It climbed the wood that jammed shut the door and—from inches away—seemed to peer at her. It scampered back and forth along the timber, trying to find some way in to her. Its mood was a mix of abject friendliness, enthusiasm, and curiosity that shifted almost as fast as the glowing colors of its body. Before tonight it had taken minutes to change from one mood to another; before, it had been frozen to near unconsciousness. All those centuries before, it had been barely alive.

Sanda saw that it was scarcely more intelligent than she imagined dogs to be. It wanted to touch her and didn't realize the death that would bring. Gemstone climbed back to the little window and touched a paw to the quartz. The quartz grew cloudy, began to star. Sanda felt fear, and Gemstone immediately pulled back:

It didn't touch the quartz again, but rubbed back and forth across the surface of the door. Then it settled against the door and let Sanda "pet" it with her mind. This was a little like touching it had been before. But now the memories and emotions were deeper and changed quickly at her wish:

There was Grandmother, alive again. She felt Grandma's hand resting on her (its) back. Wistful sometimes, happy sometimes, lonely often. Before that there was another, a man. Grandpa. Bluff, inquisitive, stubborn. Before that . . . Colder than cold, not really conscious, Gemstone sensed light all around the horizon and then dark. Light and darkness. Light and darkness. Antarctic summer and antarctic winter. In its deadened state, the seasons were a flickering that went on for time the little mind in the starfish body could not comprehend.

And before that . . .

Wonderful warmth, even nicer than now. Being cuddled flesh against flesh. Being valued. There were many friends, personalities strange to Sanda but not unknowable. They all lived in a house that moved, that visited many places—some warm and pleasant, some not. It remembered the coldest. In its curiosity, Gemstone wandered away from the house, got so very cold that when the friends came out to search, they could not find. Gemstone was lost.

And so the long time of light-and-dark, light-and-dark had begun.

The pure, even hell of the fire lasted only a few minutes. Gemstone whimpered in her mind as the walls began to fall, and the wind-driven cycle of flame faltered. The hottest places were in the center of what had been the living room, but Gemstone remained propped against Sanda's door, either for her company or in hopes she could bring back the warm.

Rain was winning against fire. Steam and haze obscured the glowing ruins. There might have been sirens.

She felt Gemstone chill and slowly daze. Its tone was now the nearly mindless dirge of all the weeks before. Sanda slid to the floor. And cried.

KIM STANLEY ROBINSON

Black Air

When I was learning the anthologist's trade many years ago, sitting at the knees—metaphorically speaking, at least—of veteran anthologists like Damon Knight and Robert Silverberg, I was taught that you should always save your strongest and best story for last.

I've been true to this tradition here, because "Black Air"—a haunting and beautiful story about the mystic odyssey of a boy who is impressed into service aboard one of the doomed ships of the Spanish Armada—is my own personal favorite of 1983's stories, and one of the strongest stories to appear in the genre in years.

Kim Stanley Robinson, an alumnus of the Clarion Writers Workshop, sold his first story to Damon Knight's *Orbit 18* in 1976. He subsequently placed stories in *Orbit 19* and *Orbit 21*, and in the last few years has gone on to become a frequent contributor to *Universe* and *The Magazine of Fantasy & Science Fiction*. His quietly evocative story "Venice Drowned" was one of the best stories of 1981 and was a Nebula finalist; his novella "To Leave a Mark" was a finalist for the Hugo Award in 1982. His upcoming novel *The Wild Shore* has been selected to be the first title in the resurrected Ace Specials line; also upcoming are two more novels—*Icehenge*, also from Ace, and *The Memory of Whiteness*, from Arbor House—and a critical book, *The Novels of Philip K. Dick*, from University Microfilms Research Press. Robinson lives in Davis, California.

BLACK AIR

Kim Stanley Robinson

They sailed out of Lisbon harbor with the flags snapping and the brass culverins gleaming under a high white sun, priests proclaiming in sonorous Latin the blessing of the Pope, soldiers in armor jammed on the castles fore and aft, and sailors spiderlike in the rigging, waving at the citizens of the town who had left their work to come out on the hills and watch the ships crowd out the sunbeaten roads, for this was the Armada, the Most Fortunate Invincible Armada, off to subjugate the heretic English to the will of God. There would never be another departure like it.

Unfortunately, the wind blew out of the northeast for a month after they left without shifting even a point on the compass, and at the end of that month the Armada was no closer to England than Iberia itself. Not only that, but the hard-pressed coopers of Portugal had made many of the Armada's casks of green wood, and when the ship's cooks opened them the meat was rotten and the water stank. So they trailed into the port of Corunna, where several hundred soldiers and sailors swam to the shores of Spain and were never seen again. A few hundred more had already died of disease, so from his sickbed on the flagship Don Alonso Perez de Guzman el Bueno, seventh Duke of Medina Sidonia and Admiral of the Armada, interrupted the composition of his daily complaint to Philip the Second, and instructed his soldiers to go out into the countryside and collect peasants to help man the ships.

One squad of these soldiers stopped at a Franciscan monastery on the outskirts of Corunna, to impress all the boys who lived there and helped the monks, waiting to join the order themselves. Although they did not like it the monks could not object to the proposal, and off the boys went to join the fleet.

Among these boys, who were each taken to a different ship, was Manuel Carlos Agadir Tetuan. He was seventeen years old; he had been born in Morocco, the son of West Africans who had been captured and enslaved by Arabs. In his short life he had already lived in the Moroccan coastal town of Tetuan, in Gibraltar, the Balearics, Sicily, and Lisbon. He had worked in fields and cleaned stables, he had helped make rope and later cloth, and he had served food in inns. After his mother died of the pox and his father drowned, he had begged in the streets and alleys of Corunna, the last port his father had sailed out of, until in his fifteenth year a Franciscan had tripped over him sleeping in an alley, inquired after him, and taken him to the refuge of the monastery.

Manuel was still weeping when the soldiers took him aboard *La Lavia*, a Levantine galleon of nearly a thousand tons. The sailing master of the ship, one Laeghr, took him in charge and led him below decks. Laeghr was an Irishman, who had left his country principally to practice his trade, but also out of hatred of the English who ruled Ireland. He was a huge man with a torso like a boar's, and arms as thick as the yardarms of the ship. When he saw Manuel's distress he showed that he was not without kindness; clapping a callused hand to the back of Manuel's neck he said, in accented but fluent Spanish, "Stop your snivelling boy, we're off to conquer the damned English, and when we do your fathers at the monastery will make you their abbot. And before that happens a dozen English girls will fall at your feet and ask for the touch of those black hands, no doubt. Come on, stop it. I'll show you your berth first, and wait till we're at sea to show you your station. I'm going to put you in the main top, all our blacks are good topmen."

Laeghr slipped through a door half his height with the ease of a weasel ducking into one of its tiny holes in the earth. A hand half as wide as the doorway reemerged and pulled Manuel into the gloom. The terrified boy nearly fell down a broad-stepped ladder, but caught himself before falling onto Laeghr. Far below several soldiers laughed at him. Manuel had never been on anything larger than a Sicilian patches, and most of his fairly extensive seagoing experience was of coastal carracks, so the broad deck under him, cut by bands of yellow sunlight that flowed in at open ports big as church windows, crowded with barrels and bales of hay and tubs of rope, and a hundred busy men, was a marvel. "Saint Anna save me," he said, scarcely able to believe he was on a ship. Why, the monastery itself had no room as large as the one he descended into now. "Get down here," Laeghr said in an encouraging way.

Once on the deck of that giant room they descended again, to a stuffy chamber a quarter the size, illuminated by narrow fans of sunlight that were let in by ports that were mere slits in the hull. "Here's where you sleep," Laeghr said, pointing at a dark corner of the deck, against one massive oak wall of the ship. Forms there shifted, eyes appeared as lids lifted, a dull voice said "Another one you'll never find again in this dark, eh master?"

"Shut up, Juan. See boy, there are beams dividing your berth from the rest, that will keep you from rolling around when we get to sea."

"Just like a coffin, with the lid up there."

"Shut up, Juan."

After the sailing master had made clear which slot in particular was Manuel's, Manuel collapsed in it and began to cry again. The slot was shorter than he was, and the dividing boards set in the deck were cracked and splintered. The men around him slept, or talked among themselves, ignoring Manuel's presence. His medallion cord choked him, and he shifted it on his neck and remembered to pray.

His guardian saint, the monks had decided, was Anne, mother of the Virgin Mary and grandmother of Jesus. He owned a small wooden medallion with her face painted on it, which Abbot Alonso had given to him. Now he took the medallion between his fingers, and looked in the tiny brown dots that were the face's eyes. "Please, Mother Anna," he prayed silently, "take me from this ship to my home. Take me home." He clenched the tag in his fist so tightly that the back of it, carved so that a cross of wood stood out from its surface, left an imprinted red cross in his palm. Many hours passed before he fell asleep.

Two days later the Most Fortunate Invincible Armada left Corunna, this time without the flags, or the crowds of spectators, or the clouds of priestly incense trailing downwind. This time God favored them with a westerly wind, and they sailed north at good speed. The ships were arranged in a formation devised by the soldiers, orderly phalanxes rising and falling on the swells: the galleases in front, the supply hulks in the center, and the big galleons on either flank. The thousands of sails stacked on hundreds of masts made a grand and startling sight, like a copse of white trees on a broad blue plain.

Manuel was as impressed by the sight as the rest of the men. There were four hundred men on *La Lavia*, and only thirty were needed at any one time to sail the ship, so all of the three hundred soldiers stood on the sterncastle observing the fleet, and the sailors who were not on duty or sleeping did the same on the slightly lower forecastle.

Manuel's duties as a sailor were simple. He was stationed at the port midships taffrail, to which were tied the sheets for the port side of the mainmast's sails, and the sheets for the big lateen-rigged sail of the foremast. Manuel helped five other men pull these ropes in or let them out, following Laeghr's instructions; the other men took care of the belaying knots, so Manuel's job came down to pulling on a rope when told to. It could have been more difficult, but Laeghr's plan to make him a topman like the other Africans aboard had come to grief. Not that Laeghr hadn't tried. "God made you Africans with a better head for heights, so you can climb trees to keep from being eaten by lions, isn't that right?" But when Manuel had followed a Moroccan named Habedeen up the halyard ladder to the main top, he found himself plunging about space, nearly scraping low foggy clouds, and the sea, embroidered with the wakes of the ships ahead, was more often than not *directly below him.* He had clamped, arms and legs, around a stanchion of the main top, and it had taken five men, laughing and cursing, to pry him loose and pull him down. With rich disgust, but no real physical force, Laeghr had pounded him with his cane and shoved him to the port taffrail. "You must be a Sicilian with a sunburn." And so he had been assigned his station.

Despite this incident he got on well with the rest of the crew. Not with the soldiers; they were rude and arrogant to the sailors, who stayed out of their way to avoid a curse or a blow. So three-quarters of the men aboard were of a different class, and remained strangers. The sailors therefore hung together. They were a mongrel lot, drawn from all over the Mediterranean, and Manuel was not unusual because of his recent arrival. They were united only in their dislike and resentment of the soldiers. "Those heroes wouldn't be able to conquer the Isle of Wight if we didn't sail them there," Juan said.

Manuel became acquainted first with the men at his post, and then with the men in his berth. As he spoke Spanish and Portugese, and fair amounts of Arabic, Sicilian, Latin, and a Moroccan dialect, he could converse with everyone in his corner of the lower foredeck. Occasionally he was asked to translate for the Moroccans; more than once this meant he was the arbiter of a dispute, and he thought fast and mistranslated whenever it would help make peace. Juan, the one who had made the bitter comments to Laeghr on Manuel's arrival, was the only pure Spaniard in the berth. He loved to talk, and complained to Manuel and the others continuously. "I've fought *El Draco* before, in the Indies," he boasted. "We'll be lucky to get past that devil. You mark my words, we'll never do it."

Manuel's mates at the main taffrail were more cheerful, and he enjoyed his watches with them and the drills under Laeghr's demanding instruction. These men called him Topman or Climber, and made jokes about his knots around the belaying pins, which defied quick untying. This inability earned Manuel quite a few swats from Laeghr's cane, but there were worse sailors aboard, and the sailing master seemed to bear him no ill will.

A life of perpetual change had made Manuel adaptable, and ship-board routine became for him the natural course of existence. Laeghr or Pietro, the leader at Manuel's station, would wake him with a shout. Up to the gundeck, which was the domain of the soldiers, and from there up the big ladder that led to fresh air. Only then could Manuel be sure of the time of day. For the first few weeks it was an inexpressible delight to get out of the gloom of the lower decks and under the sky, in the wind and clean salt air; but as they proceeded north, it began to get too cold for comfort. After their watches were over, Manuel and his mates would retire to the galley and be given their biscuits, water and wine. Sometimes the cooks killed some of the goats and chickens and made soup. Usually, though, it was just biscuits, biscuits that had not yet hardened in their barrels. The men complained grievously about this.

"The biscuits are best when they're hard as wood, and bored through by worms," Habedeen told Manuel.

"How do you eat it then?" Manuel asked.

"You bang pieces of biscuit against the table until the worms fall out. You can eat the worms if you want." The men laughed, and Manuel assumed Habedeen was joking, but he wasn't certain.

"I despise this doughy shit," Pietro said in Portugese. Manuel trans-lated into Moroccan Arabic for the two silent Africans, and agreed in Spanish that it was hard to stomach. "The worst part," he offered, "is that some parts are stale while others are still fresh."

"The fresh part was never cooked."

"No, that's the worms."

As the voyage progressed, Manuel's berthmates became more intimate. Farther north the Moroccans suffered terribly from the cold. They came belowdecks after a watch with their dark skins completely goosepimpled, like little fields of stubble after a harvest. Their lips and fingernails were blue, and they shivered an hour before falling asleep, teeth chattering like the castanets in a fiesta band. Not only that, but the swells of the Atlantic were getting bigger, and the men, since they were forced to wear every scrap of clothing they owned, rolled in their wooden berths unpadded and unprotected. So the Moroccans, and then everyone in the lower foredeck, slept three to a berth, taking turns in the middle, huddling together like spoons. Crowded together like that the pitching of the ship could press them against the beams, but it couldn't roll them around. Manuel's willingness to join these bundlings, and to lie against the beams, made him well-liked. Everyone agreed he made a good cushion.

*   *   *

Perhaps it was because of his hands that he fell ill. Though his spirit had been reconciled to the crusade north, his flesh was slower. Hauling on the coarse hemp ropes every day had ripped the skin from his palms, and salt, splinters, belaying pins and the odd boot had all left their marks as well, so that after the first week he had wrapped his hands in strips of cloth torn from the bottom of his shirt. When he became feverish, his hands pulsed painfully at every nudge from his heart, and he assumed that the fever had entered him through the wounds in his palms.

Then his stomach rebelled, and he could keep nothing down. The sight of biscuits or soup revolted him; his fever worsened, and he became parched and weak; he spent a lot of time in the head, wracked by dysentery. "You've been poisoned by the biscuits," Juan told him. "Just like I was in the Indies. That's what comes of boxing fresh biscuits. They might as well have put fresh dough in those barrels."

Manuel's berthmates told Laeghr of his condition, and Laeghr had him moved to the hospital, which was at the stern of the ship on a lower deck, in a wide room that the sick shared with the rudder post, a large smoothed tree trunk thrusting through floor and ceiling. All of the other men were gravely ill. Manuel was miserable as they laid him down on his pallet, wretched with nausea and in great fear of the hospital, which smelled of putrefaction. The man on the pallet next to his was insensible, and rolled with the sway of the ship. Three candle-lanterns lit the low chamber and filled it with shadows. One of the Dominican friars, a Friar Lucien, gave him hot water and wiped his face. They talked for a while, and the friar heard Manuel's confession, which only a proper priest should have done. Neither of them cared. The priests on board avoided the hospital, and tended to serve only the officers and the soldiers. Friar Lucien was known to be willing to minister to the sailors, and he was popular among them.

Manuel's fever got worse, and he could not eat. Days passed, and when he woke up the men around him were not the same men who had been there when he fell asleep. He became convinced he was going to die, and once again he felt despair that he had been made a member of the Most Fortunate Invincible Armada. "Why are we here?" he demanded of the friar in a cracked voice. "Why shouldn't we let the English go to hell if they please?"

"The purpose of the Armada is not only to smite the heretic English," said Lucien. He held a candle closer to his book, which was not a Bible, but a slender little thing which he kept hidden in his robes. Shadows leaped on the blackened beams and planks over them, and the rudder post squeaked as it turned against the leather collar in the floor. "God also sent us as a test. Listen:

" 'I assume the appearance of a refiner's fire, purging the dross of forms outworn. This is mine aspect of severity; I am as one who testeth gold in a furnace. Yet when thou hast been tried as by fire, the gold of thy soul shall be cleansed, and visible as fire: then the vision of thy Lord shall be granted unto thee, and seeing Him shall thou behold the shining one, who is thine own true self.'

"Remember that, and be strong. Drink this water here—come on, do you want to fail your God? This is part of the test."

Manuel drank, threw up. His body was no more that a tongue of flame contained by his skin, except where it burst out of his palms. He lost track of the days, and forgot the existence of anyone beyond himself and Friar Lucien. "I never wanted to leave the monastery," he told the friar, "yet I never thought I would stay there long. I've never stayed long any place yet. It was my home but I knew it wasn't. I haven't found my home yet. They say there is ice in England—I saw the snow in the Catalonian mountains, once, Father, will we go home? I only want to return to the monastery and be a father like you."

"We will go home. What you will become, only God knows. He has a place for you. Sleep now. Sleep, now."

By the time his fever broke his ribs stood out from his chest as clearly as the fingers of a fist. He could barely walk. Lucien's narrow face appeared out of the gloom clear as a memory. "Try this soup. Apparently God has seen fit to keep you here."

"Thank you Saint Anne for your intercession," Manuel croaked. He drank the soup eagerly. "I want to return to my berth."

"Soon."

They took him up to the deck. Walking was like floating, as long as he held on to railings and stanchions. Laeghr greeted him with pleasure, as did his stationmates. The world was a riot of blues; waves hissed past, low clouds jostled together in their rush east, tumbling between them shafts of sunlight that spilled onto the water. He was excused from active duty, but he spent as many hours as he could at his station. He found it hard to believe that he had survived his illness. Of course, he was not entirely recovered; he could not yet eat any solids, particularly biscuit, so that his diet consisted of soup and wine. He felt weak, and perpetually light-headed. But when he was on deck in the wind he was sure that he was getting better, so he stayed there as much as possible. He was on deck, in fact, when they first caught sight of England. The soldiers pointed and shouted in great excitement, as the point Laeghr called The Lizard bounced over the horizon. Manuel had grown so used to the sea that the low headland rising off their port bow seemed unnatural, an intrusion into a marine world, as if the deluge was just now receding and these drowned hillsides were just now shouldering up out of the waves, soaking wet and covered by green seaweed that had not yet died. And that was England.

A few days after that they met the first English ships—faster than the Spanish galleons, but much smaller. They could no more impede the progress of the Armada than flies could slow a herd of cows. The swells became steeper and followed each other more closely, and the changed pitching of *La Lavia* made it difficult for Manuel to stand. He banged his head once, and another time ripped away a palmful of scabs, trying to keep his balance in the violent yawing caused by the chop. Unable to stand one morning, he lay in the dark of his berth, and his mates brought him cups of soup. That went on for a long time. Again he worried that he was going to die. Finally Laeghr and Lucien came below together.

"You must get up now," Laeghr declared. "We fight within the hour, and you're needed. We've arranged easy work for you."

"You have only to provide the gunners with slow match," said Friar Lucien as he helped Manuel to his feet. "God will help you."

"God will have to help me," Manuel said. He could see the two men's souls flickering above their heads: little triple knots of transparent flame, that flew up out of their hair and lit the features of their faces. "The gold of thy soul shall be cleansed, and visible as fire," Manuel recalled. "Hush," said Lucien with a frown, and Manuel realized that what Lucien had read to him was a secret.

Amidships Manuel noticed that now he was also able to see the air, which was tinged red. They were on the bottom of an ocean of red air, just as they were on top of an ocean of blue water. When they breathed they turned the air a darker red; men expelled plumes of air like horses breathing out clouds of steam on a frosty morning, only the steam was red. Manuel stared and stared, marveling at the new abilities God had given his sight.

"Here," Laeghr said, roughly directing him across the deck. "This tub of punk is yours. This is slow match, understand?" Against the bulkhead was a tub full of coils of closely braided cord. One end of the cord was hanging over the edge of the tub burning, fizzing the air around it to deep crimson. Manuel nodded: "Slow match."

"Here's your knife. Cut sections about this long, and light them with a piece of it that you keep beside you. Then give sections of it to the gunners who come by, or take it to them if they call for it. But don't give away all your lit pieces. Understand?"

Manuel nodded that he understood and sat down dizzily beside the tub. One of the largest cannon poked through a port in the bulkhead just a few feet from him. Its crew greeted him. Across the deck his stationmates stood at their taffrail. The soldiers were ranked on the fore- and sterncastles, shouting with excitement, gleaming like shellfish in the sun. Through the port Manuel could see some of the English coast.

Laeghr came over to see how he was doing. "Hey, don't you lop your fingers off there, boy. See out there? That's the Isle of Wight. We're going to circle and conquer it, I've no doubt, and use it as our base for our attack on the mainland. With these soldiers and ships they'll *never* get us off that island. It's a good plan."

But things did not progress according to Laeghr's plan. The Armada swung around the east shore of the Isle of Wight, in a large crescent made of five distinct phalanxes of ships. Rounding the island, however, the forward galleases encountered the stiffest English resistance they had met so far. White puffs of smoke appeared out of the ships and were quickly stained red, and the noise was tremendous.

Then the ships of *El Draco* swept around the southern point of the island onto their flank, and suddenly *La Lavia* was in the action. The soldiers roared and shot off their arquebuses, and the big cannon beside Manuel leaped back in its truck with a bang that knocked him into the bulkhead. After that he could barely hear. His slow match was suddenly in demand; he cut the cord and held the lit tip to unlit tips, igniting them with his red breath. Cannonballs passing overhead left rippling wakes in the blood air. Grimy men snatched the slow match and dashed to their guns, dodging tackle blocks that thumped to the deck. Manuel could see the cannonballs, big as grapefruit, flying at them from the English ships and passing with a whistle. And he could see the transparent knots of flame, swirling higher than ever about the men's heads.

Then a cannonball burst through the porthole and knocked the cannon off its truck, the men to the deck. Manuel rose to his feet and noticed with horror that the knots of flame on the scattered gunners were gone; he could see their heads clearly now, and they were just men, just broken flesh draped over the plowed surface of the deck. He tried, sobbing, to lift a gunner who was bleeding only from the ears. Laeghr's cane lashed across his shoulders: "Keep cutting match! There's others to attend to these men!" So Manuel cut lengths of cord and lit them with desperate puffs and shaking hands, while the guns roared, and the exposed soldiers on the castles shrieked under a hail of iron, and the red air was ripped by passing shot.

*   *   *

The next few days saw several battles like that, as the Armada was forced past the Isle of Wight and up the Channel. His fever kept him from sleeping, and at night Manuel helped the wounded on his deck, holding them down and wiping the sweat from their faces, nearly as delirious as they were. At dawn he ate biscuits and drank his cup of wine, and went to his tub of slow match to await the next engagement. *La Lavia*, being the largest ship on the left flank, always took the brunt of the English attack. It was on the third day that *La Lavia*'s mainmast topgallant yard fell on his old taffrail crew, crushing Hanan and Pietro. Manuel rushed across the deck to help them, shouting his anguish. He got a dazed Juan down to their berth and returned amidships. Around him men were being dashed to the deck, but he didn't care. He hopped through the red mist that nearly obscured his sight, carrying lengths of match to the gun crews, who were now so depleted that they couldn't afford to send men to him. He helped the wounded below to the hospital, which had truly become an antechamber of hell; he helped toss the dead over the side, croaking a short prayer in every case; he ministered to the soldiers hiding behind the bulwarks of the bulkheads, waiting vainly for the English to get within range of their arquebuses. Now the cry amidships was "Manuel, match here! Manuel, some water! Help, Manuel!" In a dry fever of energy Manuel hurried to their aid.

He was in such perpetual haste that in the middle of a furious engagement he nearly ran into his patroness, Saint Anne, who was suddenly standing there in the corner of his tub. He was startled to see her.

"Grandmother!" he cried. "You shouldn't be here, it's dangerous."

"As you have helped others, I am here to help you," she replied. She pointed across the purplish chop to one of the English ships. Manuel saw a puff of smoke appear from its side, and out of the puff came a cannonball, floating in an arc over the water. He could see it as clearly as he could have seen an olive tossed at him from across a room: a round black ball, spinning lazily, growing bigger as it got closer. Now Manuel could tell that it was coming at him, *directly* at him, so that its trajectory would intersect his heart. "Um, blessed Anna," he said, hoping to bring this to his saint's attention. But she had already seen it, and with a brief touch to his forehead she floated up into the maintop, among the unseeing soldiers. Manuel watched her, eyeing the approaching cannonball at the same time. At the touch of her hand a rigging block fell away from the end of the main yard; it intercepted the cannonball's flight, knocking the ball downward into the hull where it stuck, half embedded in the thick wood. Manuel stared at the black

half-sphere, mouth open. He waved up at Saint Anna, who waved back
and flew up into the red clouds toward heaven. Manuel kneeled and
said a prayer of thanks to her and to Jesus for sending her and went back
to cutting match.

A night or two later—Manuel himself was not sure, as the passage of
time had become for him something plastic and elusive and, more than
anything else, meaningless—the Armada anchored at Calais Roads, just
off the Flemish coast. For the first time since they had left Corunna *La
Lavia* lay still, and listening at night Manuel realized how much the
constant chorus of wooden squeaks and groans was the voice of the
crew, and not of the ship. He drank his ration of wine and water
quickly, and walked the length of the lower deck, talking with the
wounded and helping when he could to remove splinters. Many of the
men wanted him to touch them, for his safe passage through some of
the worst scenes of carnage had not gone unnoticed. He touched them,
and when they wanted, said a prayer. Afterwards he went up on deck.
There was a fair breeze from the southwest, and the ship rocked ever so
gently on the tide. For the first time in a week the air was not suffused
red: Manuel could see stars, and distant bonfires on the Flemish shore,
like stars that had fallen and now burnt out their life on the land.
   Laeghr was limping up and down amidships, detouring from his
usual path to avoid a bit of shattered decking.
   "Are you hurt, Laeghr?" Manuel inquired.
   For answer Laeghr growled. Manuel walked beside him. After a bit
Laeghr stopped and said, "They're saying you're a holy man now
because you were running all over the deck these last few days, acting
like the shot we were taking was hail and never getting hit for it. But I
say you're just too foolish to know any better. Fools dance where angels
would hide. It's part of the curse laid on us. Those who learn the rules
and play things right end up getting hurt—sometimes from doing just
the things that will protect them the most. While the blind fools who
wander right into the thick of things are never touched."
   Manuel watched Laeghr's stride. "Your foot?"
   Laeghr shrugged. "I don't know what will happen to it."
   Under a lantern Manuel stopped and looked Laeghr in the eye.
"Saint Anne appeared and plucked a cannonball that was heading for
me right out of the sky. She saved my life for a purpose."
   "No." Laeghr thumped his cane on the deck. "Your fever has made
you mad, boy."
   "I can show you the shot!" Manuel said. "It stuck in the hull!"
Laeghr stumped away.

Manuel looked across the water at Flanders, distressed by Laeghr's words, and by his hobbled walk. He saw something he didn't comprehend.

"Laeghr?"

"What?" came Laeghr's voice from across midships.

"Something bright . . . the souls of all the English at once, maybe. . . ." his voice shook.

"*What?*"

"Something coming at us. Come here, master."

Thump, thump, thump. Manuel heard the hiss of Laeghr's indrawn breath, the muttered curse.

"*Fireships,*" Laeghr bellowed at the top of his lungs. "Fireships! Awake!"

In a minute the ship was bedlam, soldiers running everywhere. "Come with me," Laeghr told Manuel, who followed the sailing master to the forecastle, where the anchor hawser descended into the water. Somewhere along the way Laeghr had gotten a halberd, and he gave it to Manuel. "Cut the line."

"But master, we'll lose the anchor."

"Those fireships are too big to stop, and if they're hellburners they'll explode and kill us all. Cut it."

Manuel began chopping at the thick hawser, which was very like the trunk of a small tree. He chopped and chopped, but only one strand of the huge rope was cut when Laeghr seized the halberd and began chopping himself, awkwardly to avoid putting his weight on his bad foot. They heard the voice of the ship's captain—"Cut the anchor cable!" And Laeghr laughed.

The rope snapped, and they were floating free. But the fireships were right behind them. In the hellish light Manuel could see English sailors walking about on their burning decks, passing through the flames like salamanders or demons. No doubt they were devils. The fires towering above the eight fireships shared the demonic life of the English; each tongue of yellow flame contained an English demon eye looking for the Armada, and some of these leaped free of the blaze that twisted above the fireships, in vain attempts to float onto *La Lavia* and incinerate it. Manuel held off these embers with his wooden medallion, and the gesture that in his boyhood in Sicily had warded off the evil eye. Meanwhile, the ships of the fleet were cut loose and drifting on the tide, colliding in the rush to avoid the fireships. Captains and officers screamed furiously at their colleagues on other ships, but to no avail. In the dark and without anchors the ships could not be regathered, and as the night progressed most were blown out into the North Sea. For the first time the neat phalanxes of the Armada were broken, and they were never to be reformed again.

When it was all over *La Lavia* held its position in the North Sea by sail, while the officers attempted to identify the ships around them, and find out what Medina Sidonia's orders were. Manuel and Juan stood amidships with the rest of their berthmates. Juan shook his head. "I used to make corks in Portugal. We were like a cork back there in the Channel, being pushed into the neck of a bottle. As long as we were stuck in the neck we were all right—the neck got narrower and narrower, and they might never have gotten us out. Now the English have pushed us right down into the bottle itself. We're floating about in our own dregs. And we'll never get out of the bottle again."

"Not through the neck, anyway," one of the others agreed.

"Not any way."

"God will see us home," Manuel said.

Juan shook his head.

Rather than try to force the Channel, Admiral Medina Sidonia decided that the Armada should sail around Scotland, and then home. Laeghr was taken to the flagship for a day to help chart a course, for he was familiar with the north as none of the Spanish pilots were.

The battered fleet headed away from the sun, ever higher into the cold North Sea. After the night of the fireships Medina Sidonia had restored discipline with a vengeance. One day the survivors of the many Channel battles were witness to the hanging from the yardarm of a captain who had let his ship get ahead of the Admiral's flagship, a position which was now forbidden. A carrack sailed through the fleet again and again so every crew could see the corpse of the disobedient captain, swinging freely from its spar.

Manuel observed the sight with distaste. Once dead, a man was only a bag of bones; nowhere in the clouds overhead could he spot the captain's soul. Perhaps it had plummetted into the sea, on its way to hell. It was an odd transition, death. Curious that God did not make more explicit the aftermath.

So *La Lavia* faithfully trailed the Admiral's flagship, as did the rest of the fleet. They were led farther and farther north, into the domain of cold. Some mornings when they came on deck in the raw yellow of dawn the riggings would be rimmed with icicles, so that they seemed strings of diamonds. Some days it seemed they sailed across a sea of milk, under a silver sky. Other days the ocean was the color of a bruise, and the sky a fresh pale blue so clear that Manuel gasped with the desire to survive this voyage and live. Yet he was as cold as death. He remembered the burning nights of his fever as fondly as if he were remembering his first home on the coast of North Africa.

All the men were suffering from the cold. The livestock was dead, so the galley closed down: no hot soup. The Admiral imposed rationing on everyone, including himself; the deprivation kept him in his bed for the rest of the voyage. For the sailors, who had to haul wet or frozen rope, it was worse. Manuel watched the grim faces, in line for their two biscuits and one large cup of wine and water—their daily ration—and concluded that they would continue sailing north until the sun was under the horizon and they were in the icy realm of death, the north pole where God's dominion was weak, and there they would give up and die all at once. Indeed, the winds drove them nearly to Norway, and it was with great difficulty that they brought the shot-peppered hulks around to a westerly heading.

When they did, they discovered a score of new leaks in *La Lavia's* hull, and the men, already exhausted by the effort of bring the ship about, were forced to man the pumps around the clock. A pint of wine and a pint of water a day were not enough. Men died. Dysentery, colds, the slightest injury; all were quickly fatal.

Once again Manuel could see the air. Now it was a thick blue, distinctly darker where men breathed it out, so that they all were shrouded in dark blue air that obscured the burning crowns of their souls. All of the wounded men in the hospital had died. Many of them had called for Manuel in their last moments; he had held their hands or touched their foreheads, and as their souls had flickered away from their heads like the last pops of flame out of the coals of a dying fire, he had prayed for them. Now other men too weak to leave their berths called for him, and he went and stood by them in their distress. Two of these men recovered from dysentery, so his presence was requested even more frequently. The captain himself asked for Manuel's touch when he fell sick; but he died anyway, like most of the rest.

One morning Manuel was standing with Laeghr at the midships bulkhead. It was chill and cloudy, the sea was the color of flint. The soldiers were bringing their horses up and forcing them over the side, to save water.

"That should have been done as soon as we were forced out of the Sleeve," Laeghr said. "Waste of water."

"I didn't even know we had horses aboard," Manuel said.

Laeghr laughed briefly. "Boy, you are a prize of a fool. One surprise after another."

They watched the horses' awkward falls, their rolling eyes, their flared nostrils expelling clouds of blue air. Their brief attempts to swim.

"On the other hand, we should probably be eating some of those," Laeghr said.

"Horse meat?"

"It can't be that bad."

The horses all disappeared, exchanging blue air for flint water. "It's cruel," Manuel said.

"In the horse latitudes they swim for an hour," Laeghr said. "This is better." He pointed to the west. "See those tall clouds?"

"Yes."

"They stand over the Orkneys. The Orkneys or the Shetlands, I can't be sure anymore. It will be interesting to see if these fools can get this wreck through the islands safely." Looking around, Manuel could only spot a dozen or so ships; presumably the rest of the Armada lay over the horizon ahead of them. He stopped to wonder about what Laeghr had just said, for it would naturally be Laeghr's task to navigate them through the northernmost of the British Isles; at that very moment Laeghr's eyes rolled like the horses' had, and he collapsed on the deck. Manuel and some other sailors carried him down to the hospital.

"It's his foot," said Friar Lucien. "His foot is crushed and his leg has putrefied. He should have let me amputate."

Around noon Laeghr regained consciousness. Manuel, who had not left his side, held his hand, but Laeghr frowned and pulled it away.

"Listen," Laeghr said with difficulty. His soul was no more than a blue cap covering his tangled salt-and-pepper hair. "I'm going to teach you some words that may be useful to you later." Slowly he said, *"Tor conaloc an dhia,"* and Manuel repeated it. "Say it again." Manuel repeated the syllables over and over, like a Latin prayer. Laeghr nodded. *"Tor conaloc an naom dhia.* Good. Remember the words always." After that he stared at the deckbeams above, and would answer none of Manuel's questions. Emotions played over his face like shadows, one after another. Finally he took his gaze from the infinite and looked at Manuel. "Touch me, boy."

Manuel touched his forehead, and with a sardonic smile Laeghr closed his eyes: his blue crown of flame flickered up through the deck above and disappeared.

They buried him that evening, in a smoky, hellish brown sunset. Friar Lucien said the shortened Mass, mumbling in a voice that no one could hear, and Manuel pressed the back of his medallion against the cold flesh of Laeghr's arm, until the impression of the cross remained. Then they tossed him overboard. Manuel watched with a serenity that surprised him. Just weeks ago he had shouted with rage and pain as his companions had been torn apart; now he watched with a peace he did not understand as the man who had taught him and protected him sank into the iron water and disappeared.

A couple of nights after that Manuel sat apart from his remaining berthmates, who slept in one pile like a litter of kittens. He watched the blue flames wandering over the exhausted flesh, watched without reason or feeling. He was tired.

Friar Lucien looked in the narrow doorway and hissed. "Manuel! Are you there?"

"I'm here."

"Come with me."

Manuel got up and followed him. "Where are we going?"

Friar Lucien shook his head. "It's time." Everything else he said was in Greek. He had a little candle lantern with three sides shuttered, and by its illumination they made their way to the hatch that led to the lower decks.

Manuel's berth, though it was below the gundeck, was not on the lowest deck of the ship. *La Lavia* was very much bigger than that. Below the berthdeck were three more decks that had no ports, as they were beneath the waterline. Here in perpetual gloom were stored the barrels of water and biscuit, the cannonballs and rope and other supplies. They passed by the powderroom, where the armorer wore felt slippers so that a spark from his boots might not blow up the ship. They found a hatchway that held a ladder leading to an even lower deck. At each level the passages became narrower, and they were forced to stoop. Manuel was astounded when they descended yet again, for he would have imagined them already on the keel, or in some strange chamber suspended beneath it; but Lucien knew better. Down they went, through a labyrinth of dank black wooden passageways. Manuel was long lost, and held Lucien's arm for fear of being separated from him, and becoming hopelessly trapped in the bowels of the ship. Finally they came to a door that made their narrow hallway a dead end. Lucien rapped on the door and hissed something, and the door opened, letting out enough light to dazzle Manuel.

After the passageways, the chamber they entered seemed very large. It was the cable tier, located in the bow of the ship just over the keel. Since the encounter with the fireships, *La Lavia* had little cable, and what was left lay in the corners of the room. Now it was lit by candles, set in small iron candelabra that had been nailed to the side beams. The floor was covered by an inch of water, which reflected each of the candle flames as a small spot of white light. The curving walls dripped and gleamed. In the center of the room a box had been set on end, and covered with a bit of cloth. Around the box stood several men: a soldier, one of the petty officers, and some sailors Manuel knew only by sight. The transparent knots of cobalt flame on their heads added a bluish cast to the light in the room.

"We're ready, Father," one of the men said to Lucien. The friar led Manuel to a spot near the upturned box, and the others arranged themselves in a circle around him. Against the aft wall, near gaps where floor met wall imperfectly, Manuel spotted two big rats with shiny brown fur, all ablink and twitch-whiskered at the unusual activity. Manuel frowned and one of the rats plopped into the water covering the floor and swam under the wall, its tail swishing back and forth like a small snake, revealing to Manuel its true nature. The other rat stood its ground and blinked its bright little round eyes as it brazenly returned Manuel's unwelcoming gaze.

From behind the box Lucien looked at each man in turn, and read in Latin. Manuel understood the first part: "I believe in God the Father Almighty, maker of heaven and earth, and of all things visible and invisible . . ." From there Lucien read on, in a voice powerful yet soothing, entreatful yet proud. After finishing the creed he took up another book, the little one he always carried with him, and read in Spanish:

" 'Know ye, O Israel, that what men call life and death are as beads of white and black strung upon a thread; and this thread of perpetual change is mine own changeless life, which bindeth together the unending string of little lives and little deaths.

" 'The wind turns a ship from its course upon the deep: the wandering winds of the senses cast man's mind adrift on the deep.

" 'But lo! That day shall come when the light that *is* shall still all winds, and bind every hideous liquid darkness; and all thy habitations shall be blest by the white brilliance which descendeth from the crown."

While Lucien read this, the soldier moved slowly about the chamber. First he set on the top of the box a plate of sliced biscuit; the bread was hard, as it became after months at sea, and someone had taken the trouble to cut slices, and then polish them into wafers so thin that they were translucent, and the color of honey. Occasional wormholes gave them the look of old coins, that had been beaten flat and holed for use as jewelry.

Next the soldier brought forth from behind the box an empty glass bottle, with its top cut off so that it was a sort of bowl. Taking a flask in his other hand, he filled the bowl to the midway point with *La Lavia's* awful wine. Putting the flask down, he circled the group while the friar finished reading. Every man there had cuts on his hands that more or less continuously leaked blood, and each man pulled a cut open over the bottle held to him, allowing a drop to splash in, until the wine was so dark that to Manuel, aware of the blue light, it was a deep violet.

The soldier replaced the bottle beside the plate of wafers on the box. Friar Lucien finished his reading, looked at the box, and recited one final sentence: "O, lamps of fire! Make bright the deep caverns of sense; with strange brightness give heat and light together to your beloved, that we may be one with you." Taking the plate in hand, he circled the chamber, putting a wafer in the mouths of the men. "The body of Christ, given for you. The body of Christ, given for you."

Manuel snapped the wafer of biscuit between his teeth and chewed it. At last he understood what they were doing. This was a communion for the dead: a service for Laeghr, a service for all of them, for they were all doomed. Beyond the damp curved wall of their chamber was the deep sea, pressing against the timbers, pressing in on them. Eventually they would all be swallowed, and would sink down to become food for the fishes, after which their bones would decorate the floor of the ocean, where God seldom visited. Manuel could scarcely get the chewed biscuit past the lump in his throat. When Friar Lucien lifted the half bottle and put it to his lips, saying first, "The blood of Christ, shed for you," Manuel stopped him. He took the bottle from the friar's hand. The soldier stepped forward, but Lucien waved him away. Then the friar kneeled before Manuel and crossed himself, but backwards as Greeks did, left to right rather than the proper way. Manuel said, "You are the blood of Christ," and held the half bottle to Lucien's lips, tilting it so he could drink.

He did the same for each of the men, the soldier included. "You are the Christ." This was the first time any of them had partaken of this part of the communion, and some of them could barely swallow. When they had all drunk, Manuel put the bottle to his lips and drained it to the dregs. "Friar Lucien's book says, all thy habitations shall be blest by the white brilliance that is the crown of fire, and we shall all be made the Christ. And so it is. We drank, and now we are the Christ. See—" he pointed at the remaining rat, which was now on its hind legs, washing its forepaws so that it appeared to pray, its bright round eyes fixed on Manuel—"even the beasts know it." He broke off a piece of biscuit wafer, and leaned down to offer it to the rat. The rat accepted the fragment in its paws, and ate it. It submitted to Manuel's touch. Standing back up, Manuel felt the blood rush to his head. The crowns of fire blazed on every head, reaching far above them to lick the beams of the ceiling, filling the room with light— "He is here!" Manuel cried, "He has touched us with light, see it!" He touched each of their foreheads in turn, and saw their eyes widen as they perceived the others' burning souls in wonder, pointing at each other's heads; then they were all embracing in the clear white light, hugging one another with the tears running down their cheeks and giant grins splitting their beards. Reflected candlelight danced in a thousand parts on the watery floor. The rat, startled, splashed under the gap in the wall, and they laughed and laughed and laughed.

Manuel put his arm around the friar, whose eyes shone with joy. "It is good," Manuel said when they were all quiet again. "God will see us home."

They made their way back to the upper decks like boys playing in a cave they know very well.

The Armada made it through the Orkneys without Laeghr, though it was a close thing for some ships. Then they were out in the north Atlantic, where the swells were broader, their troughs deeper, and their tops as high as the castles of La Lavia, and then higher than that.

Winds came out of the southwest, bitter gales that never ceased, and three weeks later they were no closer to Spain than they had been when they slipped through the Orkneys. The situation on La Lavia was desperate, as it was all through the fleet. Men on La Lavia died every day, and were thrown overboard with no ceremony except the impression of Manuel's medallion into their arms. The deaths made the food and water shortage less acute, but it was still serious. La Lavia was now manned by a ghost crew, composed mostly of soldiers. There weren't enough of them to properly man the pumps, and the Atlantic was springing new leaks every day in the already broken hull. The ship began taking on water in such quantities that the acting captain of the ship—who had started the voyage as third mate—decided that they must make straight for Spain, making no spare leeway for the imperfectly known west coast of Ireland. This decision was shared by the captains of several other damaged ships, and they conveyed their decision to the main body of the fleet, which was reaching farther west before turning south to Spain. From his sickbed Medina Sidonia gave his consent, and La Lavia sailed due south.

Unfortunately, a storm struck from just north of west soon after they had turned homeward. They were helpless before it. La Lavia wallowed in the troughs and was slammed by crest after crest, until the poor hulk lay just off the lee shore, Ireland.

It was the end, and everyone knew it. Manuel knew it because the air had turned black. The clouds were like thousands of black English cannonballs, rolling ten deep over a clear floor set just above the masts, and spitting lightning into the sea whenever two of them banged together hard enough. The air beneath them was black as well, just less thick: the wind as tangible as the waves, and swirling around the masts with smoky fury. Other men caught glimpses of the lee shore, but Manuel couldn't see it for the blackness. These men called out in fear; apparently the western coast of Ireland was sheer cliff. It was the end.

Manuel had nothing but admiration for the third-mate-now-captain, who took the helm and shouted to the lookout in the top to find a bay in the cliffs they were drifting toward. But Manuel, like many of the men, ignored the mate's commands to stay at post, as they were clearly pointless. Men embraced each other on the castles, saying their farewells; others cowered in fear against the bulkheads. Many of them approached Manuel and asked for a touch, and Manuel brushed their foreheads as he angrily marched about the forecastle. As soon as Manuel touched them, some of the men flew directly up toward heaven while others dove over the side of the ship and became porpoises the moment they struck the water, but Manuel scarcely noticed these occurrences, as he was busy praying, praying at the top of his lungs.

"*Why* this storm, Lord, *why?* First there were winds from the north holding us back, which is the only reason I'm here in the first place. So you wanted me here, but why why why? Juan is dead and Laeghr is dead and Pietro is dead and Habedeen is dead and soon we will all be dead, and why? It isn't just. You promised you would take us home." In a fury he took his slow match knife, climbed down to the swamped mid-ships, and went to the mainmast. He thrust the knife deep into the wood, stabbing with the grain. "There! I say *that* to your storm!"

"Now, that's blasphemy," Laeghr said as he pulled the knife from the mast and threw it over the side. "You know what stabbing the mast means. To do it in a storm like this—you'll offends gods a lot older than Jesus, and more powerful, too."

"Talk about blasphemy," Manuel replied. "And you wonder why you're still wandering the seas a ghost, when you say things like that. You should take more care." He looked up and saw Saint Anne, in the maintop giving directions to the third mate. "Did you hear what Laeghr said?" he shouted up to her. She didn't hear him.

"Do you remember the words I taught you?" Laeghr inquired.

"Of course. Don't bother me now, Laeghr, I'll be a ghost with you soon enough." Laeghr stepped back, but Manuel changed his mind, and said, "Laeghr, why are we being punished like this? We were on a crusade for God, weren't we? I don't understand."

Laeghr smiled and turned around, and Manuel saw then that he had wings, wings with feathers intensely white in the black murk of the air. He clasped Manuel's arm. "You know all that I know." With some hard flaps he was off, tumbling east swiftly in the black air, like a gull.

With the help of Saint Anne the third mate had actually found a break in the cliffs, a quite considerable bay. Other ships of the Armada had found it as well, and they were already breaking up on a wide beach as *La Lavia* limped nearer shore. The keel grounded and immediately things began breaking. Soupy waves crashed over the canted midships, and Manuel leaped up the ladder to the forecastle, which was now under a tangle of rigging from the broken foremast. The mainmast went over the side, and the lee flank of the ship splintered like a match tub and flooded, right before their eyes. Among the floating timbers Manuel saw one that held a black cannonball embedded in it, undoubtedly the very one that Saint Anne had deflected from its course toward him. Reminded that she had saved his life before, Manuel grew calmer and waited for her to appear. The beach was only a few shiplengths away, scarcely visible in the thick air; like most of the men, Manuel could not swim, and he was searching with some urgency for a sight of Saint Anne when Friar Lucien appeared at his side, in his black robes. Over the shriek of the dark wind Lucien shouted, "If we hold on to a plank we'll float ashore."

"You go ahead," Manuel shouted back. "I'm waiting for Saint Anne." The friar shrugged. The wind caught his robes and Manuel saw that Lucien was attempting to save the ship's liturgical gold, which was in the form of chains that were now wrapped around the friar's middle. Lucien made his way to the rail and jumped over it, onto a spar that a wave was carrying away from the ship. He missed his hold on the rounded spar, however, and sank instantly.

The forecastle was now awash, and soon the foaming breakers would tear it loose from the keel. Most of the men had already left the wreck, trusting to one bit of flotsam or other. But Manuel still waited. Just as he was beginning to worry he saw the blessed grandmother of God, standing among figures on the beach that he perceived but dimly, gesturing to him. She walked out onto the white water, and he understood. "We are the Christ, of course! I will walk to shore as He once did." He tested the surface with one shoe; it seemed a little, well, infirm, but surely it would serve—it would be like the floor of their now-demolished chapel, a sheet of water covering one of God's good solids. So Manuel walked out onto the next wave that passed at the level of the forecastle, and plunged deep into the brine.

"Hey!" he spluttered as he struggled back to the surface. "Hey!" No answer from Saint Anne this time; just cold salt water. He began the laborious process of drowning, remembering as he struggled a time when he was a child, and his father had taken him down to the beach in Morocco, to see the galley of the pilgrims to Mecca rowing away. Nothing could have been less like the Irish coast than that serene, hot, tawny beach, and he and his father had gone out into the shallows to splash around in the warm water, chasing lemons. His father would toss the lemons out into the deeper water, where they bobbed just under the surface, and then Manuel would paddle out to retrieve them, laughing and choking on water.

Manuel could picture those lemons perfectly, as he snorted and coughed and thrashed to get his head back above the freezing soup one more time. Lemons bobbing in the green sea, lemons oblong and bumpy, the color of the sun when the sun is its own width above the horizon at dawn . . . bobbing gently just under the surface, with a knob showing here or there. Manuel pretended he was a lemon, at the same time that he tried to remember the primitive dogpaddle that had gotten him around in the shallows. Arms, pushing downward. It wasn't working. Waves tumbled him, lemonlike, in toward the strand. He bumped on the bottom and stood up. The water was only waist deep. Another wave smashed him from behind and he couldn't find the bottom again. Not fair! he thought. His elbow ran into sand, and he twisted around and stood. Knee deep, this time. He kept an eye on the treacherous waves as they came out of the black, and trudged through them up to a beach made of coarse sand, covered by a mat of loose seaweed.

Down on the beach a distance were sailors, companions, survivors of the wrecks offshore. But there among them—soldiers on horses. English soldiers, on horses and on foot—Manuel groaned to see it—wielding swords and clubs on the exhausted men strewn across the seaweed. "No!" Manuel cried, "No!" But it was true. "Ah, God," he said, and sank till he was sitting. Down the strand soldiers clubbed his brothers, splitting their fragile eggshell skulls so that the yolk of their brains ran into the kelp. Manuel beat his insensible fists against the sand. Filled with horror at the sight, he watched horses rear in the murk, giant and shadowy. They were coming down the beach toward him. "I'll make myself invisible," he decided. "Saint Anne will make me invisible." But remembering his plan to walk on the water, he determined to help the miracle, by staggering up the beach and burrowing under a particularly tall pile of seaweed. He was invisible without it, of course, but the cover of kelp would help keep him warm. Thinking such thoughts, he shivered and shivered and on the still land fell insensible as his hands.

When he woke up, the soldiers were gone. His fellows lay up and down the beach like white driftwood; ravens and wolves already converged on them. He couldn't move very well. It took him half an hour to move his head to survey the beach, and another half hour to free himself from his pile of seaweed. And then he had to lie down again.

When he regained consciousness, he found himself behind a large log, an old piece of driftwood that had been polished silver by its years of rolling in sand. The air was clear again. He could feel it filling him and leaving him, but he could no longer see it. The sun was out; it was morning, and the storm was over. Each movement of Manuel's body was a complete effort, a complete experience. He could see quite deeply into his skin, which appeared pickled. He had lost all of his clothes, except for a tattered shred of trousers around his middle. With all his will he made his arm move his hand, and with his stiff forefinger he touched the driftwood. He could feel it. He was still alive.

His hand fell away in the sand. The wood touched by his finger was changing, becoming a bright green spot in the surrounding silver. A thin green sprig bulged from the spot, and grew up toward the sun; leaves unfolded from this sprout as it thickened, and beneath Manuel's fascinated gaze a bud appeared and burst open: a white rose, gleaming wetly in the white morning light.

He had managed to stand, and cover himself with kelp, and walk a full quarter of a mile inland, when he came upon people. Three of them to be exact, two men and a woman. Wilder looking people Manuel couldn't imagine: the men had beards that had never been cut, and arms like Laeghr's. The woman looked exactly like his miniature portrait of Saint Anne, until she got closer and he saw that she was dirty and her teeth were broken and her skin was brindled like a dog's belly. He had never seen such freckling before, and he stared at it, and her, every bit as much as she and her companions stared at him. He was afraid of them.

"Hide me from the English, please," he said. At the word *English* the men frowned and cocked their heads. They jabbered at him in a tongue he did not know. "Help me," he said. "I don't know what you're saying. Help me." He tried Spanish and Portugese and Sicilian and Arabic. The men were looking angry. He tried Latin, and they stepped back. "I believe in God the Father Almighty, Maker of Heaven and Earth, and in all things visible and invisible." He laughed, a bit hysterically.

"Especially invisible." He grabbed his medallion and showed them the cross. They studied him, clearly at a loss.

"*Tor conaloc an dhia*," he said without thinking. All four of them jumped. Then the two men moved to his sides to hold him steady. They chattered at him, waving their free arms. The woman smiled, and Manuel saw that she was young. He said the syllables again, and they chattered at him some more. "Thank you, Laeghr," he said. "Thank you, Anna. Anna," he said to the girl, and reached for her. She squealed and stepped back. He said the phrase again. The men lifted him, for he could no longer walk, and carried him across the heather. He smiled and kissed both men on the cheek, which made them laugh, and he said the magic phrase again and started to fall asleep and smiled and said the phrase. *Tor conaloc an dhia.* The girl brushed his wet hair out of his eyes; Manuel recognized the touch, and he could feel the flowering begin inside him.

—give mercy for God's sake—

HONORABLE MENTIONS—

1983

Brian Aldiss, "The Blue Background," *IASFM*, April
Lori Allen, "We Share," *Shadows 6*
Poul Anderson, "Deathwomb," *Analog*, November
——, "Ivory, and Apes, and Peacocks," *Time Patrolman*
——, "The Sorrow of Odin the Goth," *Time Patrolman*
——, and Gordon R. Dickson, "The Napoleon Crime," *Analog*, March
Isaac Asimov, "Potential," *IASFM*, February
Scott Baker, "The Lurking Duck," *Omni*, December
Barrington Bayley, "The Ur-Plant," *Interzone*, No. 4 Spring
Greg Benford, "The Touch," *Best of Omni #5*
Michael Bishop, "And the Marlin Spoke," *F&SF*, October
——, "The Gospel According to Gamaliel Crucis," *IASFM*, November
——, "Her Habiline Husband," *Universe 13*
——, "The Monkey's Bride," *Heroic Visions*
Paul Darcy Boyles, "She Sells Sea Shells," *Twilight Zone*, November/December
Ben Bova, "Sam Gunn," *F&SF*, October
David Brin, "Tank Farm Dynamo," *Analog*, November
Damien Broderick, "I Lost My Love to the Space Shuttle Columbia," *Amazing*, March
Warren Brown, "What We Did That Night in the Ruins," *F&SF*, August
Edward Bryant, "Bean Bag Cats," *Omni*, November
——, "The Overly Familiar," *Mile High Futures*, November
F. M. Busby, "Before The Seas Came," *Heroic Visions*
Octavia Butler, "Speech Sounds," *IASFM*, Mid-December
Pat Cadigan, "Eenie, Meenie, Ipsateenie," *Shadows 6*
——, "In the Shop," *Omni*, November
——, "The Pond," *Fears*
——, "Vengeance Is Yours," *Omni*, May

Grant D. Callin, "Deborah's Children," *Analog*, September
Susan Casper, "Spring-Fingered Jack," *Fears*
Michael Cassutt, "The Holy Father," *Best of Omni #6*
Hugh B. Cave, "What Say the Frogs Now, Jenny?" *Whispers IV*
Rob Chilson, "The Hand of Friendship," *Analog*, March
Michael G. Coney, "The Byrds," *Changes*
Mike Conner, "Below the Camel Barns," *F&SF*, September
Richard Cowper, "The Tithonian Factor," *Changes*
John Coyne, "The Crazy Chinaman," *The Dodd, Mead Gallery of Horror*
John Crowley, "Novelty," *Interzone*, No. 5, Autumn
Jack Dann, "A Cold Day in the Mesozoic," *Fears*
——, "Reunion," *Shadows 6*
——and Gardner Dozois, "Slow Dancing with Jesus," *Penthouse*, July
——and Gardner Dozois, "Time Bride," *IASFM*, December
Avram Davidson, "Buchanan's Head," *F&SF*, February
——, "Eszterhazy and the Autogondola-Invention," *Amazing*, November
——, and Grania Davis, "The Hills Outside Hollywood High," *F&SF*, April
Joseph H. Delaney, "In the Face of my Enemy," *Analog*, April
Thomas M. Disch, "Downtown," *F&SF*, October
Gardner Dozois, "A Traveller in an Antique Land," *Chrysalis 10*
——, "The Peacemaker," *IASFM*, August
Jeff Duntemann and Nancy Kress, "Borovsky's Hollow Woman," *Omni*, October
Malcolm Edwards, "After-Images," *Interzone*, No. 4 Spring
George Alec Effinger, "The World of Pez Pavilion," *F&SF*, July
Phyllis Eisenstein, "Subworld," *F&SF*, January
Harlan Ellison, "Chained to the Fast Lane in the Red Queen's Race," *Best of Omni #6*
Cynthia Felice, "Track of Legend," *Omni*, December
Gil Fitzgerald, "The Vengeance of Nora O'Donnell," *F&SF*, April
John M. Ford, "Boundary Echoes," *Omni*, September
Janet Fox, "Witches," *Tales By Moonlight*
Leanne Frahm, "A Way Back," *Universe 13*
——, "High Tide," *Fears*
George Florence-Guthridge, "Evolutions," *F&SF*, August

Greg Frost, "A Day in the Life of Justin Argento Morrel," *F&SF*, July

Stephen Gallagher, "Nightmare, with Angel," *F&SF*, November

William Gibson, "Hippie-Hat Brain Parasite," *Modern Stories*, No. 1

Mary R. Gentile, "The Harvest of Wolves," *IASFM*, December

Felix C. Gotschalk, "Conspicuous Consumption," *F&SF*, March

Charles L. Grant, "The Next Name You Hear," *F&SF*, January

——, "Recollections of Annie," *Twilight Zone*, January/February

Robert M. Green, Jr., "The Pallid Piper," *F&SF*, August

Eileen Gunn, "Spring Conditions," *Tales By Moonlight*

Jack C. Haldeman II, "My Crazy Father Who Scares All the Women Away," *IASFM*, Mid-December

Melissa Mia Hall, "Marianna," *Shadows 6*

Charles L. Harness, "Quarks at Appomattox," *Analog*, October

M. John Harrison, "Strange Great Sins," *Interzone*, No. 5 Autumn

Gary Jennings, "Rouge on an Empty Glass," *F&SF*, August

Richard Kearns, "The Power of the Press," *IASFM*, Mid-December

Gregg Keizer, "Edges," *Omni*, June

James Patrick Kelley, "The Cruelest Month," *F&SF*, June

Leigh Kennedy, "Belling Martha," *IASFM*, May

——, "Greek," *IASFM*, October

——, "The Silent Cradle," *Shadows 6*

John Kessel, "Below Zero," *Twilight Zone*, January/February

Stephen King, "Uncle Otto's Truck," *Yankee*, October

Stephen Kleinhen, "Tell Us about the Rats, Grandpa," *Whispers IV*

Damon Knight, "La Ronde," *F&SF*, October

Nancy Kress, "Night Win," *IASFM*, September

Michael P. Kube-McDowell, "Memory," *IASFM*, August

Michael Kurland, "A Brief Dance to the Music of the Spheres," *Best of Omni*, #6

R. A. Lafferty, "Bird-Master," *Four Stories*

——, "Marsilia V," *Golden Gate and Other Stories*

——, "Pine Castle," *Amazing*, September

——, "Tongues of the Matagorda," *Golden Gate and Other Stories*

Rand B. Lee, "Tales from the Net: A Family Matter," *IASFM*, May

Tanith Lee, "Black as Ink," *Red as Blood*

——, "Chand Veda," *IASFM*, October
——, "Elle Est Trois (La Mort)," *Whispers IV*
——, "The Golden Rope," *Red as Blood*
——, "Il Bacio (Il Chiave)," *Amazing*, September
Ursula K. LeGuin, "The Ascent of the North Face," *IASFM*, July
Fritz Leiber, "The Cat Hotel," *F&SF*, October
——, "The Curse of the Smalls and the Stars," *Heroic Visions*
Bob Leman, "Unlawful Possession," *F&SF*, September
Barry Malzberg, "Reparations," *F&SF*, August
——, "What We Do on Io," *F&SF*, February
Scott Elliot Marbach, "The Eternity Wave," *IASFM*, May
Lois Metzger, "The Best of Both Worlds," *Omni*, February
Jack McDevitt, "Crossing Over," *Twilight Zone*, January/February
——, "Melville on Iapetus," *IASFM*, November
Ian McDowell, "Son of the Morning," *IASFM*, December
Vonda McIntyre, "Transit," *IASFM*, October
M. E. McMullen, "Gandy Plays the Palace," *Amazing*, November
Thomas F. Monteleone, "The Mechanical Boy," *Chrysalis 10*
Cynthia Morgan, "Rememberance," *IASFM*, December
David Morrell, "But at My Back I Always Hear," *Shadows 6*
Richard Mueller, "A Song for Justin," *F&SF*, November
O. Niemand, "Afternoon Under Glass," *F&SF*, November
——, "The Man Outside," *F&SF*, April
Larry Niven, "A Teardrop Falls," *Omni*, June
Chad Oliver, "Ghost Town," *Analog*, Mid-September
Barbara Paul, "All the Dogs of Europe," *F&SF*, September
Peter Pautz, "Cold Heart," *Shadows 6*
Frederick Pohl, "Servant of the People," *Analog*, February
Michael Reaves, "The Tearing of Greymare House," *F&SF*, March
Rene Rebetez, "The New Prehistory," *F&SF*, June
Tony Richards, "Discards," *F&SF*, September
Kim Stanley Robinson, "Stone Egg," *Universe 13*
Joel Rosenberg, "Cincinnatus," *Amazing*, January
Rudy Rucker, "The Indian Rope Trick Explained," *The 57th Franz Kafka*
Joanna Russ, "Sword Blades and Poppy Seed," *Heroic Visions*
Jessica Amanda Salmonson, "The Impossible Cow," *The Last Wave*
Pamela Sargent, "Heavenly Flowers," *IASFM*, September
Michael Shea, "Creative Coverage, Inc.," *Whispers IV*
Hilbert Schenck, "Hurricane Claude," *F&SF*, April

Charles Sheffield, "Rogueworld," *F&SF*, May
Lucius Shepard, "Solitario's Eyes," *F&SF*, September
Lewis Shiner, "Mystery Train," *Omni*, April
——, "Nine Hard Questions about the Nature of the Universe," *F&SF*, December
John Shirley, ". . . and the Angel with Television Eyes," *IASFM*, May
Susan Schwartz, "Heritage of Flight," *Analog*, April
Robert Silverberg, "Basileus," *Best of Omni*, #5
——, "Homefaring," *Amazing*, November
——, "Needle in a Timestack," *Playboy*, June
——, "Dancers in the Time-Flux," *Heroic Visions*
Dan Simmons, "Remembering Siri," *IASFM*, December
John Skipp, "Go to Sleep," *Twilight Zone*, September/October
John Sladek, "The Next Dwarf," *The Last Wave*
——, "Scenes from the Country of the Blind," *IASFM*, August
Norman Spinrad, "Street Meat," *IASFM*, Mid-December
J. Michael Straczynski, "A Last Testament for Nick and the Trooper," *Shadows 6*
Bruce Sterling, "Spook," *F&SF*, April
——and William Gibson, "Red Star, Winter Orbit," *Omni*, July
Alex Stewart, "The Cauler Requiem," *Interzone*, No. 4 Spring
Stuart H. Stock, "In the Deserts of the Heart," *IASFM*, June
Theodore Sturgeon "Not an Affair," *F&SF*, October
Steve Rasnic Tem, "Derelicts," *The Dodd, Mead Gallery of Horror*
——, "The Enormous Lover," *The Last Wave*
——, "The Sky Came Down to Earth," *Tales By Moonlight*
Lisa Tuttle, "The Nest," *F&SF*, April
Karl Edward Wagner, "Into Whose Hands," *Whispers IV*
Ian Watson, "The Black Current," *F&SF*, November
——, "Cruising," *IASFM*, Mid-December
——, "The Width of the World," *Universe 13*
Chery Wilder, "Kaleidescope," *Omni*, July
Kate Wilhelm, "The Mind of Medea" *Omni*, January
——, "Sister Angel," *Omni*, November
Gene Wolfe, "A Solar Labyrinth," *F&SF*, April
——, "Four Wolves," *Amazing*, May
——, "On the Train," *The New Yorker*, May
Jane Yolen, "Names," *Tales of Wonder*
——, "Sister Light, Sister Dark," *Heroic Visions*
Timothy Zahn, "Cascade Point," *Analog*, December
Roger Zelazny, "Devil and the Dancer," *Chrysalis 10*